DRAGON
VESSEL

TRACY RENEE ROSS
AND
JAMES DANIEL ROSS

TRIMOON
ECLIPSE

Winter Wolf
PUBLICATIONS

| Cincinnati, Ohio

Copyright © 2019, Tracy Renée Ross & James Daniel Ross
Cover Design & Art © 2019, by Miriam Chowdhury
Edited by Tracy Renée Ross
Interior Design by Tracy Renée Ross

Published by TriMoon Eclipse,
An imprint of Winter Wolf Publications, LLC

ISBN: 978-1-945039-20-1 (paperback)

Other Work by Tracy Renee Ross (aka T. R. Chowdhury)

Shadow Over Shandahar
Dark Storm Rising
Echoes of Time
Whispers of Prophecy
Breaking Destiny
Embers at Dawn
Heroes' Fate
Dark Mists of Ansalar
Blood of Dragons
Shade of the Fallen
Forging the Bond
Tales from the Hapless Cenloryan
Cat Tales
The Dream Thief
The Time Swiper
The Deceit Master

Other Work by James Daniel Ross

The Radiation Angels
The Chimerium Gambit
The Key to Damocles
The Mission Files
The Legend of Fox Crow
I Know Not
The Opus Discordia
The Saga of Those Before
The Echoes of Those Before
The Secrets of Those Before
The Fate of Those Before
The Whispering of Dragons
The Last Dragoon
Song of Champions
Heart and Soul

Dedication

*I*n all things, *R*emember this: You are only *D*efeated if you give up. This is *T*rue for your *C*areer, your *T*alents, and your *L*ove. You are going to get *K*nocked down. But never stay *D*own. Thank you, *T*racy, for teaching me to *B*elieve in myself again.

–*James Daniel Ross*

To the *M*an whose *S*un rises and sets upon my *L*ife every day. *Y*ou have shown me what *L*ove is truly like. For that I *T*hank you with all my *H*eart. You say *I* saved you. *B*ut I think you just may have *S*aved me.

–*Tracy Renée Ross*

"You may encounter many defeats, but you must not be defeated. In fact, it may be necessary to encounter the defeats, so you can know who you are, what you can rise from, how you can still come out of it."

— Maya Angelou

"Darkness cannot drive out darkness: only light can do that. Hate cannot drive out hate: only love can do that."

— Martin Luther King Jr.

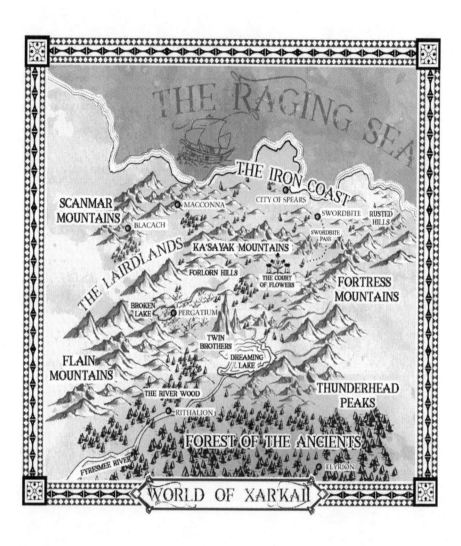

THE RAGING SEA

THE IRON COAST

SCANMAR MOUNTAINS

MACCONNA

CITY OF SPEARS

SWORDBITE

RUSTED HILLS

BLACACH

SWORDBITE PASS

THE LAIRDLANDS

KA'SAYAK MOUNTAINS

FORLORN HILLS

THE COURT OF FLOWERS

FORTRESS MOUNTAINS

BROKEN LAKE

PERGATIUM

TWIN BROTHERS

DREAMING LAKE

FLAIN MOUNTAINS

THE RIVER WOOD

THUNDERHEAD PEAKS

RITHALION

FOREST OF THE ANCIENTS

FYRESMEE RIVER

ELYRION

WORLD OF XAR'KAI

CHE CHAMBER WAS DARK: in color, in position, and in purpose.

Shelves, half filled with tomes, lined two walls before which were heavy tables and sturdy, unadorned chairs. One chair was never used anymore, for it bore the scars of fire and flame as a testament to when they had been less cautious. The surface was greasy with rendered fat, and had never lost the smell of burning meat. On the surface of the tables were slight divots used to set inkwells, and they bore the stains of their work proudly. Surrounded on two sides by the shelves, tables, and chairs, stood the Throne.

The Throne of Pain. It was never named such, but everyone who used the place knew what it was. It had no cushions, no decoration, nor comfort. It was a chair bearing thick, iron manacles and festooned with dull iron spikes set to worry at those seated in it. It stank of blood. The current occupant liked it no better than any other that had been forced into it and she visibly tried to fight the urge to shift. Movement just dug the spikes in deeper. If they drew blood, the wounds would fester. If they became rotten, they would stay there for the rest of the prisoner's life, however short it may be.

The elf woman was proud, defiant, even now. Her people had been routed on all sides, driven from all places of light and goodness, and she had been captured. She had suffered a wicked wound across her face that permanently opened her cheek and removed her nose completely, destroying her beauty forever. Her colorful robes were in tatters. Yet, still, she was defiant.

Fascinating. He smoothed out his own pearl white robes, starched to the point they looked carved of marble. He looked back to his junior partner and saw the young elf's face was strained. He had a blank book open, ready to take notes on the Inquiry. Next to it was the damning evidence of a dragon magic spellbook, also open and holding a spare writing implement off the table. The quill in his hand was shaking, but he still sat ready to do his duty. He was a good boy– well, no longer a boy. He was an adult by all measures and ready to take up the mantle as an Inquisitor himself. The Grand Inquisitor knew he was the last of his kind, and he needed his journeyman to become a master in his own right. As much as he needed to share this burden, he truly did not wish to curse another, with the war so close to being won. Perhaps if he delayed, the young man would be spared–

"Get on with it," the prisoner slurred.

The Grand Inquisitor faced her and nodded. It was time. He placed a palm gently on her forehead and one hand over her heart. She snapped at him with her sharply broken fangs and he snatched his hands away. He frowned. "I thought we were past such games, Ailis."

She growled at him, speaking as if her mouth was full around a swollen tongue, "Keep your indignation, mind rapist."

The Inquisitor slapped her, his hand left stinging with the blow. He could almost hear his junior partner wince. Many weeks with little water and less food, the prisoner's head lolled on the edge of consciousness. The Inquisitor stole the opportunity and strapped her head in place against the spikes on the back of the chair with thick leather restraints. Then he placed his hands over her head and heart and walked his mind into hers.

This was the art of the Inquisitors, and he plied it without hesitation. When first he had tested her, weeks ago, her will had been an unassailable fortress. Now her mind had been knocked into rubble that he flew into without pause. She was struggling, throwing scenes of torture and horror at him from every side as if he were exploring a haunted forest. He brushed past them all.

"Show me," he heard his body mumble. The images came faster and faster.

Her father banished her from his home. She almost starved one winter on march against Rithalion. Her lover ambushed by soldiers of Sharderia in the dead of night–Eating the dead to survive–Her stillborn child–Murdering an enemy's child in revenge as the mother watched–

Then he was through. He looked and saw the war council of the Liath. His body murmured, "Retreating... they are retreating to Pergatium." He looked more deeply. "The fragile peace is a sham. They are making pacts with larger dragons, stealing whatever they can to bribe them, whoever they can to feed and serve them to gain service..." In the utter silence of the room, he heard the junior's quill scratching furiously. "They will marshal at Pergatium and counterattack under the guise of peace to destroy Rithalion. We must send word. Rithalion can stop it if they attack now, drive out their forces and families–"

But there was another light within her, brighter and no longer hidden from him. He flew into it, hackles rising with suspicion. But what he saw...

"Dragons. Colossal, ancient dragons. They are summoning– She knows how–"

"Master!" The scribe screamed, snapping him back from his trance. He saw it all clearly, knew what had happened. The Liath were masters of the elemental forces of dragons. Her tongue had not been swollen in her mouth. It had been full of stone chips from her cell. He saw it all, knew what was to come, but it was too late.

She must have enchanted them slowly, with whatever trickle of power she could manage in this place cut off from magic. She had cast her spell subtly, with a mouth full of sharp rocks, but now she spat three stones at horrific speeds. One she spat at the Grand Inquisitor, he felt burning pain blossom in his neck under his ear. He slapped a hand against the warm stream of blood that already coated his neck as she launched the three others at the manacle on her wrist. The stones threw bright sparks where they hit, destroying the lock on the shackles and causing bloody cuts along her arm and legs from the shrapnel. One arm and her legs remained bound but it mattered little, she was free enough.

The scribe cried out in shock and surprise as the Liath smiled bloodily beneath a gaping nose hole and raised her hand, embers already gathering as she shrieked another spell. The Grand Inquisitor did not think, had no time, but simply stepped in front of his junior and raised his left, free, arm.

Flame erupted from her hand, drawn from some dragon soul in the aether. The Inquisitor let his sleeve fall, exposing rows of tied pendants, bracelets, bangles, and rings. The fire rushed at him like a hungry thing, but was turned aside like a charging horse happening upon a pack of wolves. The flames licked at him for what seemed an eternity, and he sweat from the deadly heat that wanted to turn his very bones to charcoal. One of his rings grew very bright, turned to ash, and fell from a finger. Then a bracelet, then a charm. Each one was ancient and priceless, and each had given their full measure of protection from the dragon magic for the Inquisitor and the young elf behind him. His kind had no access to the dragons, nor the fae. They had only the power of the mind. That, and the Throne of Pain.

Finally, the torrent ended, and the Grand Inquisitor lashed out with one foot. Though aged, his kick was true and struck Ailis in her sternum. It pushed her back, and the Grand Inquisitor knew the spikes of the chair had punctured her back.

The act left him drained, weak, and he fell straight down to the floor, only held upright by the table leg behind him.

Ailis was laughing, but it was a slurry of sound with infrequent modulation and haunting tones. The Junior Inquisitor came around the table with a book held in hand, looking at her warily.

The Inquisitor felt his limbs become leaden. He could barely keep his hand in place over his wound in his neck as she began to rant, the uncontrolled tones to her voice guaranteeing that her head had snapped back with the force of the kick and the spikes had also lodged into her brain, "You cannot stop it, mind rapists. The Vessel is coming. The Vessel will come, and she will destroy you all!"

The Junior looked at her with horror, but The Inquisitor knew he had run out of time, "Ignore her. Come here, come quickly." The junior turned and fell beside him, knees under his robes splashing in a pool of fresh blood. Ailis continued to laugh, but her mirth was beginning to drown in bloody froth and the junior turned to watch her. "No! Stay here. Delve quickly. I do not have long and you must write this down."

The junior paled. "Delve, sir?"

The Grand inquisitor snapped, sapping his remaining energy to dangerously low levels. "No questions! Delve into me. Now. I will show you."

His eyes were open as the junior opened the book, face anguished to see he had grabbed not the trial journal but the dragon mage's spellbook. The young man took up the quill that had been caught inside when it had been closed and the book flipped petulantly in his lap to the last pages. He had no free hand to fix it as he looked around fearfully for ink. He shook his head. "Please, let me get you help, Grand Inquisitor."

His strength was ebbing, flowing out of a neck wound he could no longer hold onto. "You… must… write…"

The junior put one hand to his head and cast the Delving. He again looked for ink, and with a pained expression, dipped the quill in his master's blood pooled on the floor. The Inquisitor felt him, there, in his mind, and gladly showed him what he had taken from Ailis.

In his mind, he looked upon the apprentice he had nurtured all through the war, into mastery, and through adolescence to adulthood. In his mind he spoke, *I am sorry but this is now your duty to your people. Be honest. Be proud. Be humble. Show mercy where you can. You are now the last Inquisitor of Isbandar, young man.* The younger's pen halted in its scratching. *I will not last, Orisar.* It began again, feverishly.

Orisar tried to write everything…

He managed only a single word. A name.

Before he finished, the Grand Inquisitor was gone.

Chapter One
Homecoming

α horn sounded in the distance, followed by another, and another. The army picked up its pace, knowing the end was finally near, and that by the end of the day everyone would be in the comfort of a bed, near the family and friends they had left behind many weeks ago. It was a beautiful summer morning, the leaves on the trees still damp with dew, sparkling in the rays of a sun that hung in a cerulean sky clear of clouds. The finches and sparrows twittered in the branches, and the beautiful song of the sunset tanager trilled in accompaniment. As the army neared the fortress that heralded the border of Rithalion, smiles abounded and the soldiers walked with a jaunty step. Talk was lighthearted, and they spoke of those who awaited them. And when the fortress finally came into view, they erupted into cheers.

Vivien's heart soared, caught up in a moment she would never forget. This was the true taste of victory, not just after the battle was won, but the homecoming. She felt a large, warm hand envelope hers and she turned to her companion. The Wolf, Ravn, smiled down at her, his storm-gray eyes alight with happiness. On impulse, she reached up and put her arms around his neck. He lifted her up and spun her around, making her laugh. They shared a heartfelt kiss before he set her down again.

The army stopped to prepare for their homecoming march. The carts of the dead, which had been bringing up the rear of the procession to save everyone from the smell, were brought to the front. The soldiers brought out the shrouds that had been saved for this auspicious moment, shrouds made of the finest material and packed away when the army left Rithalion several weeks ago. Approximately two hundred elves and one hundred tir-reath had fallen before the Iron Army, and now they would be given the honor they deserved.

The carts were covered in silks of gold, burgundy, crimson, and navy, then positioned at the forefront of the procession. They were pulled by tir-reath unscathed in the battle, ones that understood the responsibility being given to them. Next came more carts, these filled with the wounded still unable to carry themselves under their own propulsion, and after these, wounded soldiers able to sit the backs of their tir-reath. Then came the remaining soldiers, followed by the healers, mages, and generals. And bringing up the very end, were the commanders of the army, the Lord of Swords and Truth and the Grand Magister.

Vivien and Ravn stood behind the rest of the La'athai, between the healers and mages and the generals. They were given that place befitting their station and the necessary part they played in the battle. Vivien's heart beat in anticipation of the march, and she worried at the sunset tanager carving in her palm, the one that had given her so much luck throughout the past two months. The beautiful talisman had become a part of her, and she couldn't imagine taking it from around her wrist, even when she was safe at home.

ROSS & ROSS

Finally, they were walking once more. Horns blared again, this time closer. The tir-reath roared, knowing how close they were, and a tense expectancy filled the air. Vivien smiled at the thought of her own feline companion waiting for her back at the fortress. She couldn't wait to see her best friend, open her mind to what she had experienced so that Sherika could understand why Vivien had been forced to leave her behind. She couldn't wait to see her old friend, Lydia, and the Lady of Moonlight and Love.

The only person she dreaded to see was the Lord of Ice and Steel. Her husband had been one of the generals sent home to tell the city about their victory. He still thought her dead. She could only imagine his surprise when he heard of her and the Wolf in the Victory Homecoming March.

The horns sounded yet again, and this time, in the distance, they could hear the sounds of cheering. Everyone's eyes widened and a murmur went through the army. They were at least two hours from the border of Rithalion, but the people had come. *The people of Rithalion had come so far to see their army home.*

Vivien felt a swell in her chest one that threatened to take her breath away. She looked back down the line, past the generals to see her father. His face seemed to show the same emotion, and the esteemed Grand Magister gave her a smile that warmed her heart all the way down to the tips of her toes. A tear escaped one eye, trailing down her cheek...only to be caught by a big, warm finger.

She turned to see Ravn looking down at her, a smile spread across a face scarred by many battles, and hardened by the trials of his life, a face that she found handsome in so many ways. It was his eyes, colored like storm clouds in summer. It was the shape of his lips, full and sculpted to perfection. It was his nose, a noble-man's nose, long and straight. And finally, there was his hair, a mane that fell in thick, frosted chestnut curls down past his shoulders. She offered him a smile, one he returned, the corners of his expressive mouth pulling up into his beard, and his eyes glittered with merriment.

The sounds of people cheering became louder and louder. The army reached a bend in the road, and for a moment, the sound was deafening.

It started as a drizzle of people, the most dedicated or worried lining the road on every side. Their voices were joyous, welcoming the fallen warriors first, and then the living behind them. Soon there were hundreds of people: men, women, children. They waved banners of emerald green, silver, and black– the colors of the army of Rithalion. Family and lovers embraced, but the march did not stop. There were bards singing and playing their instruments, woman dancing to the music, children cavorting among the returning soldiers. In spite of the scent of death that filled the air, it was a celebration of the life those men, and even a few women, had given to the people of Rithalion with their sacrifice. The civilians walked alongside the road, meeting even more people along the way. Before long, there were thousands of people, all heading to the same place.

Dragon Vessel

It was a time Vivien would remember forever, one emblazoned into her mind. These were her people, and this was a show of their unity, of their caring for one another. This was a people she was proud to belong to, a people she wanted to serve as long as she was able. This was a people she could die for.

The procession walked past the towering walls of the Lady of Moonlight and Love's fortress, and to Mourning Hill, the cemetery near the entrance to the gorge. The tall, wide hill was a solemn place, covered by massive trees with boles twenty steps around. They vaulted into the sky, towering above the forest of stone markers below, spreading wide branches to shelter the graves from harsh sun and pounding rain. The graveyard of Rithalion would grow this day. The soldiers and generals, archers and footmen, gathered to gently unload the bodies to the soil where they would wait for families to come and say farewells. The carts were emptied sorrowfully, with tears and mourning for friends lost in heroic combat.

Vivien's heart ached to see so many shrouded corpses placed in neat, even rows. She bowed her head and dabbed at tears. Ravn placed an arm around her shoulders, pulling her close. She fought with herself for a moment, trying to stop the tears, to be brave, but when she looked to him, he was still focused on the unloading, fat droplets rolling unashamedly down his face. She wiped one away and he smiled sadly.

"They have protected their home. No soldier can ask for more," she said.

A solitary figure interrupted them. Her long cloak was colored a muted copper and black, but the second she lifted her hood, her blazing glamour touched all that saw her. She smiled like a benediction. Vivien sought to curtsey, but The Lady of Moonlight and Love embraced her warmly, voice rich and full. "None of that. You may have been sworn to my service, but today I am in your debt."

"You...you are too kind," she said. Vivien felt her cheeks fill with heat and she glanced at Ravn, still expecting him to be as smitten with the Lady as all others were, yet the mountain man only gazed at Vivien proudly.

Shaladrea took the warmage's face in her hands and kissed her forehead. "I am not. I am simply overjoyed that you are returned. These many years in my service you have become a daughter to me, my dear. And I have lost enough children for one lifetime. I would be broken without you."

Vivien shook her head, surprised at the sentiment. She looked to Ravn who only nodded. "Many of us would be without the sun in the sky if you were not there to feel it," he said.

"It is just so." Shaladrea regarded the barbarian with a twinkle in her eye. "And thank you, master warrior." Ravn bowed his head gravely. Vivien felt there was much left unsaid between the two, that they both understood far better than she, but the moment passed. Shaladrea nodded. "The cart with the La'athai is coming up."

Ravn echoed Vivien's thoughts. "We should be there."

Shaladrea moved past them to the group containing Xadrian, her ex-husband, and the Grand Magister. She engaged the men in conversation as the leaders of the La'athai went to tend their dead. The rest of the Wolf Pack was there already, pulling the broken bodies in their fabric cases from the carts and laying them gently into place.

Ravn moved one with the help of Gregor, both men subdued. Tyrell, second in command of the mages, and Vivien moved the next. She stopped for a moment when she saw a boot poking out from beneath the sheet. She knew it was Jernell, one of her mages. She was shocked at how heavy her earthbound form was. She lay it down, vowing to be there for every funeral, every burial. She touched Jernell's face through the sheet and murmured an apology as more La'athai came to carry their brothers in arms. Vivien moved up the slope and out of the way.

Tyrell followed. He shuffled for a moment, then whispered, "We lost twenty, only twenty. That is a miracle, and due because of the lessons you and the Wolf taught us."

She smiled, trying to let go of the guilt of their deaths, but as she hugged him, she looked over his shoulder to the hundreds of other bodies being set upon the ground. They parted and he did not linger, but rejoined his comrades. Vivien felt the loss of life settle in on her soul, and she followed the path amongst the beautifully carved headstones up the hill. She tried to heed Tyrell's wisdom, tried to find joy in what they gave their lives for and not the loss of life itself, but her strength faltered.

Then she stopped before a tiny grave marked with a simple marker adorned with the crest of her husband, The Lord of Ice and Steel. She felt more fingers of guilt slither into her heart and begin to squeeze.

Suddenly Ravn was there. He smelled of musk, spice and sweat, but had moved with no sound. He took her hand in his and squeezed gently. "This is your boy?"

Vivien closed her eyes and let her tears stream freely. "Gaelen was so tiny. He never had the chance to draw a single breath."

"I am so sorry you lost him. You would have been a wonderful mother." They stood silently for a moment then he continued, "You know it was not your fault?"

Vivien felt the words as a long-needed quenching inside her soul. She turned and hugged him fiercely. The last time she had been here, her husband had said exactly the opposite thing. She held him tight, worried that she was strangling him but unable to loosen her grip even a little. If he found any discomfort he did not say, but instead held her back, gently, with arms that could snap a man's back. Below, a bell rang three times. Only then did Vivien let go, looking into Ravn's stormy blue eyes.

"We are needed," he said.

She nodded, wiping her eyes. "We must live, for that is the gift they have given us."

Ravn's eyes widened in surprise. His face fell for a moment, then he nodded. "That is wise."

The last time, Vivien and her husband had left separately, heated words shared between them stinging like open wounds. This time she descended holding hands with a man who truly loved her. Below, Shaladrea was leaving the procession so they could continue. Xadrian, stoic in battle and unflappable under enemy assault, was flustered. She saw her white-haired father look for his daughter and finally see her on the hill holding hands with Ravn. His face was carved with worry and he frowned. She managed a sad wave as the two leaders of the La'athai stood at the back of their Pack, just before the generals of the army, and the procession continued on.

The numbers of people lining the street swelled, then again, and soon a tide of followers on every side engulfed the moving river of soldiers and became an ocean that surrounded them. The people cheered like crashing waves, welcoming the heroes home.

Chapter Two
The Dream Remembers the Truth

The lighting was dim, but it wasn't dark. *The floors and walls were blanketed in a layer of glowing fuzzy pink, and a blazing fire crackled nearby. She stood there before him like a goddess, her hair spilling down her shoulders in a river of fiery gold. Her breasts were round, easily the size of his palms, and the nipples pert and surrounded by a circle of bronze. Her hips flared from a trim waist, smoothing gracefully into the curve of her thighs. Nestled there was a thatch of crimson gold curls...*

Ravn wanted to touch her, to crush her against him and take her. He moved to do so, but a gentle staying hand on his chest kept him at bay.

Ravn felt a pulse of heat move through him, all the way from her hand, down his arms to his hands, down his legs to his feet, and through his core to the erection that stood at attention between them. Once he may have felt shame for it, but not now. It was a physical manifestation of how he felt about the woman standing before him, the desire that coursed through him at the sight of her, the love that had kept him alive day after day, year after year, decade after decade.

The goddess trailed her fingertips down his chest to his navel, then further to his manhood. When she wrapped her hand around his shaft, he had to swallow the groan that threatened to emerge. Her cool touch was like a shock, electrifying every part of him, all the way down to his toes and back up again. And when she slowly began to massage him, it took every erg of strength to keep from savagely grabbing her and throwing her to the ground.

He held on until he could no longer. He quelled his savagery, denying himself, for she was far too precious. He tempered his need with all the restraint he had within him, then enfolded her in his arms and gently pulled her down onto the mossy floor. Ravn felt her arms around his neck– embracing him, accepting him, wanting him. And he kissed her with a fierce abandon he'd never felt with anyone before, ever, in all his one hundred years. He slid his hand between her legs, and when he took her with his fingers, she arched against him. She whimpered against his lips and he groaned, pushing them deeper and faster, his want of her growing with every thrust into her warm, wet softness.

His goddess whimpered again. She shook her head as though trying to escape something and he withdrew his hand. He placed his knee between her legs and gently began to spread them apart. His manhood was throbbing, thick and full, aching to feel her the way his fingers had, the length of him enough so that the tip pressed against her belly. He released her mouth, took her hands in his, and raised them over her head. He then looked down at her. She was the epitome of beauty, her lips perfectly sculpted and swollen from the intensity of his kisses, her nose small and straight, her brows arched over eyes that opened to look at him from pools of hazel green, pools so deep he could become lost in them.

Most important, he saw the light inside her, the essence of her that made him love and desire her so very much.

He stopped breathing just long enough to speak a few simple words. "I want you, Vivien. Please tell me you want me too."

She looked up at him, her eyes fathomless. Time seemed to slow, and he could feel every beat of his heart, every beat of hers. Her voice was like that of an angel come to carry him away into the aether. "I want you, Ravn. I've always wanted you."

Ravn surged into wakefulness, the dream falling away to leave him trembling and shaken. The bed was drenched with his sweat, the sheet twisted around his hips to expose the full length of him jutting up towards the ceiling. He sat up and ran his hands over his face, then back through the wild mass of his hair. He huffed and grit his teeth in frustration. He dreamed of Vivien often, many of those dreams ending with him awake in the middle of the night with his hand on his penis, trying to quell an excitement that wasn't physically there.

He continued to sit there for a moment, trying to recall the dream. It was the one he had most often, but also the most difficult to remember. It was as though there was a block in his mind, keeping him from the intimate details. He thought about Vivien, what she might be doing at this hour. Even though he had no window or balcony, he knew it was still early, dawn barely cresting the summer horizon.

Vivien.

He missed her presence near him as they slept. It was when she was closest that the dreams weren't there, his body aware of her presence even in sleep. She was more than excitement, more than lust, she brought him peace in his deepest heart and he craved that. Craved her.

He rose from the bed, pulling on his Elvish-made trousers as he swept out of his room and up the dark stairs that led into the Lady of Moonlight's chamber suite. He then went out onto the small balcony and stood there, looking out to the one that belonged to Vivien. Sherika slept there, the black feline curled up in the center. He was surprised to see her, for she was customarily at the foot of Vivien's bed. But then he remembered how sultry it was, and chuckled to himself. Vivien had bidden the tir-reath sleep out on the balcony because the animal was too warm to keep beside her.

A madness crept upon him. He gauged the distance between the two balconies, wondering... wondering if he could make the leap. He looked down to the certainly fatal fall below and shook his head. What would he say?

I awoke like a child in the night and needed you there?

I had this dream where we made love and I need to know if you are really made for me?

Good evening, I love you with every part of my soul, but my cock needs you this very instant?

He smiled dryly at himself. She would cast him out and be right to do so. Yet he lingered, and judged the distance that could be jumped by a tir-reath in the throes of desperation and wondered if his strength would carry him as far. And when he finally decided it couldn't, he marveled at the cat who had once been able to manage it when her companion was in danger.

Ravn left the balcony back into the chamber. He barely hesitated as he walked out the door. Once into the fortress proper, he made his way down the corridor until he reached the stairway leading up to Vivien's tower and took it. Like a thief, he opened the unlocked door leading into her suite, closing it gently behind him. He was met there by Sherika. None of the tir-reath liked him for reasons he could not fathom, but this cat was different. She sniffed him curiously, and he reached out to scratch behind her ears. Having collected her toll, she padded away on silent paws.

Ravn walked towards the bed, and once there, he looked down at the vision before him. She looked just like she did in his dreams, so beautiful she took his breath away. Her hair was a halo around her head and shoulders, her lashes a smudge beneath her eyes, and her lips sculpted in perfect detail. A bed sheet was twisted about her legs and hips. Her skin was golden in the wan light coming through the small break in the balcony curtain, and her camisole was pulled up to reveal the flesh of her belly. He hesitated for a moment, but desire pushed him onward and he moved to her bedside.

He was careful as he lay down beside her, wrapping one arm around her waist and pulling her close. Immediately he realized his mistake as his body flared to life. He just lay there and tried to think of anything but her. Finding that futile, he focused on anything about her that was irritating. It was a lost cause, for even her quirks weren't off-putting, but sexy beyond belief.

Like the way she challenged the soldiers to a duel and it ended up being Ravn who fought as her opponent. She was so strong, so capable, never knowing how close she had come to winning that mock battle. She had moved gracefully, shapely legs moving like a dancer, arms swinging in powerful arcs, breasts heaving with effort.

Oh, gods yes...

He put his face close to her hair and just breathed in the scent of her. She smelled of bath oils, cinnamon and lavender to be precise, and he found he missed her natural aroma. Of course, she would never agree...

Vivien took a deep breath and he sensed her coming out of sleep. He remained still, just watching her, waiting for her to realize he was there.

Her breath hitched and she swiftly turned towards him, her eyes wide. "Ravn! What are you doing here?"

He smiled. "I just came… to watch you sleep."

It wasn't entirely the truth, but it was good enough.

She blinked at him for a moment, clearly nonplussed by the answer. Her brow clouded and she shook her head. "Sherika let you in?" He felt the fool for all of this, but shoved it down deep and regarded her with a half-smile and she grinned in return. "Of course she did." Vivien considered that for a heartbeat, then sunk into his embrace, allowing him this rare luxury. By the gods, he'd never lay in bed with her before, not in a real bed, and the way she curved against him...it was heaven and hell at the same time. He must have had a pained expression because suddenly she put a hand on his face and he snapped out of his reverie. "Are you alright?"

He widened his smile and pulled her closer. "Of course. I am here with you."

Vivien chuckled, but her eyes still reflected worry. "Ravn..."

He couldn't refrain any longer. He gently placed his lips over hers in the first intimate kiss they had shared alone since...since the one they had shared in the cavern before falling asleep to have a dream that would insinuate itself into so many waking moments. These joined forces with the sleeping ones to drive him mad with want of her.

And that want was abruptly there, pulsing between them like a living thing.

He deepened the kiss and she responded, her fingers threading into his hair to bring him closer. He pulled her body into him and she gasped when she felt the hardness of his manhood straining uncomfortably against the confines of the trousers. He took a moment to glance into her eyes, searching... He relaxed when all he saw was surprise. No shock, no fear.

It wasn't the first time he wished for a kilt, and he had the feeling it wouldn't be the last.

Ravn's desire twined about them, coiling around them like a serpent. It mounted, filling all the spaces between and around them. He ran his hands over her body, taking in the silky softness of her skin, the flare of her hips and the roundness of her naked bottom, the hard nubs of her nipples beneath the camisole. She ran her hands over his bare chest, over the scars that crisscrossed the hard planes, and back up to his neck. His arousal increased and he pulled down the straps of the camisole to expose her, taking one full breast in his mouth and suckling it.

"Ahhh!" Vivien gasped again and arched into him, her fingers pulling as she gripped his hair. He groaned against her breast, sucking harder, taking her hips into his hands and putting a knee between her legs. He lifted her for a moment and then pulled her down onto his thigh. Her hips bucked and she began to ride him, slowly, rhythmically, soft whimpers coming from deep in her throat...

The dream from the cavern abruptly came to the fore of his mind. It was the sounds she made as he pleasured her, the soft noises that told him that she wanted him the way he wanted her. It was the feel of her beneath him. It was the beating of her heart in tandem with his.

His breaths came faster and sweat trickled down the furrow at the center of his back. He moved to the other breast, took it in his mouth while his hand unbuckled the belt of the trousers, finally freeing him from imprisonment. Her smell surrounded him, filled him, made him feel alive and free. He remembered the taste of her in his dream– savory and light, delicate on the tongue, and he yearned to experience it again.

Her voice was a whisper, "Ravn."

He brought his mouth back to hers, kissed her lips the way he had her breasts, taking her lower lip and sucking it, gently roving his tongue over it. He murmured, "Vivien."

Her hips continued to move over his thigh, her hands gripping his backside, urging him to move with her, to press his erection against her belly. By the gods, he'd never wanted anyone the way he did this woman, to take her and spill into her everything that was in him– all his trust, love, and devotion. Suddenly he wanted to hear her speak it again. "Say it once more. Say my name."

Her lips curved into a smile. Her whisper this time was more facetious, "Ravn. Ravn, Laird of Blacach."

He gave a deep breath and expelled it. "My enchantress, my Elvish Jewel."

He kissed her again, a searing kiss that stuttered his senses and left him gasping for air. He lifted her hips again, spread her legs and placed himself between them. He then pulled back. The sight of her was stunning, a vee of crimson-gold curls leading downward to end at her slit, glistening with wetness. Between them his manhood rose, throbbing with desire.

"Ravn."

He heard the solemnity in her voice and his eyes rose to meet hers. She was stiff, trembling slightly, balanced on a precipice that, with only a little nudge, would travel downhill in all but a freefall. She hesitated then, swallowing convulsively.

He moved to lay beside her, cradling her in his arms. "What is it? You can tell me anything."

Her voice was leaden, with a hint of pleading for understanding, "We can't do this. I am still married to Torialvah."

Ravn stilled for a moment, then let out the breath his was holding in a gusty exhale.

Her voice cracked, "I'm sorry."

His passion cooled when he heard these words, and he looked into her eyes. "No, never be sorry. There is never anything to be sorry for, not with me." She cast her eyes away but he took her chin. "Vivien, look at me." She did as he bid, her eyes shimmering with unshed tears. "I mean it. There is nothing to be sorry about. I know you are still married. You have…a vow to uphold. I understand that more than you know."

Her lower lip trembled. "In Elvish society, a person is not supposed to take another sexual partner while he or she is in the middle of divorce proceedings. It goes against culture threaded into our society for centuries."

He nodded and tucked her head into the crook of his arm. He swallowed words, *To hell with culture and to hell with divorce proceedings*, and he did it because of his love and respect for her. She was too important, too wonderful, to feel badly that she was being honorable and true. "I understand."

Her voice cracked again. "I didn't intend to lead you on–"

"Shhhh." He stroked her hair. "You didn't. Circumstances are what they are. I love you, and I am willing to wait for you as long as it takes."

She simply nodded and sniffed. "We have to go in a while. The Council will be expecting us. We are to be honored and we must dress accordingly."

To hell with honor and dress up. But he pulled her closer, for she was all that mattered to him in this world. He would behave, and would dress in the clothes provided, because she deserved far more than this, and he had to be the kind of man who would give her what she deserved. *Or else, what good am I?* Yet...

"I know, but we have a few moments longer."

Vivien nestled against his side and he breathed deeply. There was nowhere else he'd rather be.

Chapter Three
Decorated Heroes

The guards still watched him warily after his last entrance to this place, and he ignored them. Ravn walked into the council chambers a free man, which was not how he had left them last time. His punishment had been short lived, magical manacles struck from his wrists by The Lord of Swords himself. He had sought to share in the punishment Vivien had been shackled with. She had broken some arcane law in defense of a child and his own life, and he never forgot that they had repaid that gift with judgment. He locked away these thoughts, for even as he looked to her, he saw she was happy and proud.

This time, at least, he had come dressed in proper clothes. They had been donated by a happy tailor, proud to clothe a man they had all feared only months before. Though Ravn chafed at wearing pants instead of a kilt like a proper man, the outfit was made of the best linen and soft, rock-rubbed doeskin, all of it in grays, blacks, and steel blues, with a hooded mantle pulled up. Vivien was a vision in her rich blue mage's robes and light hooded cloak. They were large garments, and billowing, but they hugged her just so at so many places, and gained perfection in line and curve simply by being near her body. Her green eyes glittered and their light calmed and cooled him. Their hands brushed and she took his. She squeezed it, and for that moment it was the part of him that felt most alive. Then she let it go and bowed her head like the others.

They had come in a group of commanders and generals, and all waited patiently. They did not speak once inside, not even Vivien, but all offered one another a nod. The Lord of Swords and Truth in freshly polished armor, and the Grand Magister in the rich blue of the mages, had joined them and both had nodded to Ravn. They too bowed their heads and stood without an iota of motion not made by breathing. They were all like that, meditating or praying. Every time Ravn shuffled, he felt he was making a horrible racket with his boots on the marble, and every time he swore, he would not fidget, his body did it to spite him. For some reason probably having to do with the inscrutable Elvish laws of formality, everyone still wore something to cover their heads. But finally, whatever archaic gathering was occurring on the chamber floor was concluded, and guards came to point to one leader of the army or another, who left without comment. The crowd around them dwindled until only four remained: The Grand Magister, Xadrian, and the two leaders of the La'athai.

They came for the Magister. The man looked to his daughter, then cast Ravn a strangely heavy glance. Vivien's head was bowed and did not see, but Ravn felt laid bare to the bone under that glance from a man who had always favored him. Ravn felt his stomach sink as the old elf's crystal blue eyes lingered on him, and long after he was gone, the projected suspicion remained. *Does he know I love his daughter? Does he disapprove? I am only a human, and she high born elf. Should that matter to him? Does it matter to her?*

He fidgeted more.

Xadrian, strong and unreadable was called next, and he spared them both a small smile from under his gray and brown hooded cloak. Vivien looked up this time and saw they were alone but for the honor guard along the walls. She stared at Ravn, who tried for a warm smile and she returned it, but this was obviously something unusual and it frightened her. He took her hand and she looked embarrassedly at the guards. Ravn almost spoke, to tell her it would be fine, to ask what was the matter, to say I love you and we can face anything together. Instead, he remained silent. She squeezed his hand again and kissed his knuckles quickly.

Finally, they were called to the floor. She let go of his hand and set the pace as slow and dignified. He followed, remembering the court functions of his youth. He had damned them as unneeded and overtly formal, but this was an order of magnitude worse.

They traveled down a short hall and into the open air of the council chamber proper. Only those highest in Elvish society were normally allowed here, and yet the rules had been relaxed for the celebration of the heroes of the war. The last time there had been many spectators for the trial, but now the gallery was packed. The council chambers were white, and this room opened up to a ceiling lost to the light far above, with balconies carved into the walls like the petals of a flower. Each low petal held the high-born elves of the city, and even more besides. The higher up on the wall, each nook became filled with citizens possessing thinner and thinner Elvish blood. They did not cheer, but looked upon him at least with some admiration, while they beamed at Vivien and her half-elvin bloodline.

Along the walls on the main floor were all those that had been honored before. Their head coverings had finally been removed. Some cried. Others beamed. A few still looked haunted and hunted by the fierce battle for which they were being honored. Those were the ones Ravn identified with the most. Xadrian watched solemnly, hood down. Where his cloak opened, his ceremonial armor gleamed. His head bore the wound on his shaved scalp, gained during the battle, prominent but healing. The Grand Magister looked upon his daughter with pride, but as he shifted to Ravn, the Laird could feel his fear. The two came to the tall council bench where the elders of the city sat. Behind Ravn was the ringed podium where Vivien had been put on trial. He had spent a century running in the forests, free. Here he felt trapped, and had to wrestle the apprehension to heel.

Up at the judge's bench, there were the four elders. Vivien bowed deeply to them. Ravn paused for only a fraction of a second before doing the same. It rankled to pay homage to these people who had ordered her hexed with an enchantment that had nearly cost her life, but while he could find it in himself to show lack of respect for them, this was Vivien's culture and he could not disrespect her. They both straightened.

The elders were white, drained of color by century after century of life. Male and female, they wore the brightest white robes and if their hair was not different Ravn could not tell them apart. Three of them stood, removed their hoods, and bowed in return, eliciting a gasp from the assembled multitude. Vivien snatched off her hood, and after only a second, did the same for Ravn.

Mistress Swansee, Lady of Principle and Grace spoke gravely. "You have been asked here last because it has been decided the greatest honor is to be bestowed upon you. It was the two of you who developed the integrated soldier and warmage units that formed up the La'athai." She smiled at the name, Wolf Pack. "It was these brave scouts that circled the Iron Army through the horrors of the Doomed City. It is you who decapitated their army and took their generals from the field."

Master Kilcahnn, Lord of Discipline and Morality frowned, but spoke with equal gravity, "Without your efforts to destroy the enemy supply train and kill the man called the Tactician, many more sons and daughters of Rithalion would have been lost."

Master Oilariann, Lord of Honor and Victory, smiled kindly at them. "All our people are in your debt. If there is anything you desire that we can provide, you have but to ask."

Ravn felt his heart leap. Here, then, finally he could make his proclamation to the world. He could free Vivien from her marriage and take her for his own. He summoned his noble voice from long ago and stood straight. "Elders, there is only one thing in this world I desire."

Master Orinoco, Lord of Ritual and Service, the only one not to stand, who now watched Ravn through sharp, disgusted eyes, spoke, "Name it, then."

Ravn set his jaw and felt his courage burn bright. "Elders, I ask..." He looked to Vivien.

She was looking back at him, eyes wide, and trembling slightly.

Orinoco 's mouth twisted as if he tasted something sour. "Name it, Barbarian."

Ravn could smell fear on Vivien, see her irises become pinpricks. She was flushed, and her breathing shallow. He had no doubt that she knew he wanted her marriage annulled, that he wanted her to be his. She had to know the truth of his heart. Yet still, she gave him an almost imperceptible shake of the head. It was like a dagger in the chest. He felt like he was falling.

"Barbarian?"

"I ask that you forgive my impertinence." His mouth became numb, his heart aching in his chest. The morning they had shared was so real, so honest, but now that they had an opportunity to be free to be together, she had asked him to cast it aside. He swallowed his emotions and lowered his head, hoping the Council took it to be contrition. Vivien began to breathe normally, tension leaking out of her.

Orinoco's face twisted in a nasty smile. "Done."

Vivien gasped, "Please Elders, he does not understand–"

Kilcahnn shook his head and sat. "It does not matter, Vivien Valdera. He has asked his boon, and it has been granted."

Mistress Swansee, Lady of Principle and Grace, kept her feet and narrowed her eye at Orinoco, but when she spoke, it was gentle. "The Wolf is pardoned of all transgressions from the past. He may not be held liable for them. And you, heroine of Rithalion? What would you ask?"

"Please, Elders. Rav– the Wolf has proven himself an honorable man. Set him free."

Kilcahnn nodded. "That is right and proper. You are a free man, Wolf. You may come and go as you please, and will be considered one of our people wherever you go, for however long as you breathe. You may take a home, and a wife from our people. You are one of us, and we bestow these upon you with our thanks."

Orinoco sniffed. "Freedom is all well and good, but where will he stay? We cannot have him hunting in the gorge, stirring up the animals and bathing in the river like his namesake."

The voice that answered was calm, clear, and trained to be heard over the pitch of battle. "I have accepted him into my house. I have no living children. He will reside there until he inherits it."

Xadrian, The Lord of Swords and Truth, commander of the armies of Rithalion, strode forward from his place against the wall. Every fiber of him spoke of a life of discipline, and up-close Ravn saw the new medal bouncing against his chest, glinting proudly. His boots clicked on the marble and his steel armor was a high shine. He walked boldly to stand before the two penitents. He hugged Vivien fiercely. "None of us would have survived without you." And he moved to the Wolf, who still watched the proceedings in a stunned haze. "Nor you."

Ravn looked at him, knowing his soul was hurt and bare before this elf, and still totally unable to do anything about it. The general, centuries older, saw into him, and understood. He pitched his voice again so all could hear. "It was I who struck the bonds levied upon you by this Council. It was I who asked if you would fight for us, and you did. Now I ask again: will you serve my people and my city of your own free will?"

Ravn paused but nodded.

Xadrian embraced him. "You are brother to me, human. And any that gives you disrespect, let them know you belong to a noble house of Rithalion. Accept no slight, and walk with honor for your actions are as mine."

Ravn felt mental walls tremble, and he hugged Xadrian back, tears beginning to flow as the volcano inside of him stilled from eruption.

Master Orinoco, Lord of Ritual and Service made a dismissive noise and snapped his fingers. Xadrian parted from him but took up position to the side and one step behind as young elvin girls came forward. They wore white slip dresses and padded barefoot on alabaster feet. One was of dark hair and eyes and stood before Ravn. The other was platinum blonde and gray eyed, and she stood before Vivien. Each held an identical box of rich stained wood with copper fittings.

Master Oilariann, Lord of Honor and Victory, cast Orinoco a withering glance, but faced the two heroes with pride. "You have rendered great service to us all, and the whole of the Elvish people will know of it." The girls opened the boxes.

Master Kilcahnn stood and intoned, "Wolf, you are hereby declared a guardian of this city. You are a Knight Protector, and shall be looked to as a source of safety and courage when all else is lost."

Ravn stared into the case. It was a circlet of blackened steel and silver, made with the images of the wild and cunningly wrought with a pack of wolves prowling around the circumference. Over the brow, two wolves sat and howled. The girl took the circlet from the box and looked to him expectantly, then blushed. Xadrian bumped him gently and he shook from his reverie, it finally dawning on him that the child could never reach his head. He bowed low.

Mistress Swansee smiled like a new mother. "And you, Vivien Valdera, have always shown the greatest of potential. We, the Elders, are proud to name you warmage no longer. You are Mage Protector, defender of the realm. Know you are held in our highest regard."

Ravn straightened as the girl placed the circlet on his head. It was heavy, cold, but somehow comforting. He looked to Vivien. Her own circlet was made of golden tir-reath pouncing and cavorting. She straightened and tears of joy streamed from her eyes. He made the smallest shift to go to her and envelop her in his arms, but Xadrian grabbed his elbow and held him like a statue of iron.

Master Orinoco, Lord of Ritual and Service finally stood. "Torialvah, your petition to end your marriage has been rescinded as you have asked." Ravn spun to the group along the wall, and picked out Vivien's husband, who was glaring at him. "It is happy when a couple can mend their hurts, especially in a kingdom that has so many. The Honoring is now completed. Go forth and bury the dead in the morning knowing the fullness of out debts to them, then we will celebrate life, so that we may show them we are thankful."

And the Book of Honor was lifted and struck upon the table.

Immediately the crowd of captains and leaders on the floor burst into a cloud of elves. Ravn saw the shock on Vivien's face and again made to go to her, but Xadrian still held him firmly by the elbow. Ravn glanced back at the commander, head buzzing with angry emotions and balled his fists. The Lord of Swords pulled the barbarian close. "If you must strike me, do so. I will forgive you. But if you strike the Lord of Ice and Steel, he will not forgive, and he will fight you, and perhaps he will lose, and she will never forgive you for murdering him," he hissed. "The hardest thing for a man of action to do is nothing. But you must do nothing, Wolf. *Nothing.*"

Ravn stared at his mentor in shock, then turned back to Vivien. She was surrounded by well-wishers, including her husband who doted upon her with a forced ferocity that turned Ravn's stomach. The Grand Magister, too was there.

ROSS ЄROSS

As Vivien looked around, Ravn was sure for him, the Magister turned her away from him and hugged her. His bright blue eyes were a hostile wall to the barbarian. They said, *This is her family. Do not hurt her family.*

Ravn felt all strength leave him. He carelessly took the circlet from his head and gave it to Xadrian, who let go and stepped back in shock. "Brother, your eyes..."

He needn't have said. Ravn could feel them. The color of his eyes was a deep red. The doors Ravn had shattered with his own body to join Vivien in her trial last year had been replaced, and now stood open. Ravn–

Wolf. I am the Wolf. Ravn is dead.

Wolf walked through them to the cheers of the multitude that could not fit inside the chamber. The city had been decorated with banners and flags, streamers strung impossible distances between towers and poles. Flowers were everywhere in bloom. But the riot of color was lost upon him. Elves came from all sides to congratulate him, to thank him, but he brushed passed without stopping. He paused before a clot of elves in the square and he bunched his shoulders as he paused to gather himself to push through. A delicate hand took his arm, stopping him as effectively as Xadrian had. The Wolf turned, and there was not Vivien, but the hunched fragile form of his aged teacher. Lydia was leaning heavily on a cane, and she shook slightly even when still.

"Oh, a big hero now. No time for the old woman who taught you Elvish?" she said in a dour voice from a mouth that smiled tiredly. She peered at his face, seeing more than he was comfortable with. "Bring this old woman around the corner so she might rest her bones on a bench, there."

Arm in arm, they went around the corner into the shade between the faces of a taproom and a clothier. There was, indeed, a bench. With gentle pressure, Lydia guided the Wolf to sit beside her. As they sat there, the Wolf could feel the hurt and rage swirling inside himself.

"Where are your manners, young man? Give this old woman a hug."

Lydia's waspish tone snapped him out of his dark thoughts, and he turned to embrace her warmly. Of all people in this city, she had believed in him most of all, but for Vivien.

"You are always so warm. Summer, winter, matters not. You are warm." Lydia slid from him but kept his arms in hers. "Now why don't you tell me what has your eyes like rubies today?"

On the street there was more cheering. Ravn looked up and saw Vivien and the rest of the leaders of the army walking in a loose group. She was arm in arm with her husband. Cold, aloof, he wore her like a badge of office. She was smiling, waving, but her eyes...

...her eyes were miserable.

Ravn's stomach fell away and took his hurt with it, down a bottomless hole. She loved him. she *loved* him whether he was Wolf or Ravn, or named anything else. She was his friend and she loved him. He had to look past himself, past his pain. He had to be there for her.

30

Lydia gasped, "Unseleighe dancing, Wolf! Your eyes! Now they're blue!"

Vivien passed out of sight and the barbarian turned back to his mentor. Her long hair was limp, her eyes had lost much of their luster, and she weight had fallen from her already spare frame. He closed his eyes and fat tears squeezed out. He felt like he was falling.

"Tell me, Wolf." Lydia caressed the big man's face. "Tell me."

He opened his eyes, and he knew from the pressure behind them, a pressure he had lived with for a hundred years, that they were red. She recoiled in shock.

"My name is Ravn Blacach."

Lydia's face, old and wrinkled, went ashen. "Laird Blacach?"

RavnWolf nodded.

Lydia stared at him as if he were a ghost. "I know your story. It is told all over the Lairdlands."

The Wolf turned away and held his head in his hands as Xadrian spied him from across the crowd in the shadowed nook and came over. He said nothing, but held out the wolf circlet to him, reminding him of his oath to defend the city. The Wolf nodded and stood, accepting the silver and steel trinket and placing it on his head. Xadrian nodded and turned to head off into the crowd. Before following, the Wolf turned to Lydia and said one, final thing. "The stories... they are true."

Chapter Four
Unexpected News

Vivien rushed through the halls of the fortress, her heart thundering in her chest. She'd somehow managed to escape the crowd that had followed her all the way there, and now she was free to let the tears come. They clouded her sight as she vaulted up the stairs to her tower, trickling down her cheeks to her neck where they dampened the neckline of her ceremonial mage robe.

Her breath hitched in her throat. When she escaped the crowd, she'd also escaped the Lord of Ice and Steel, the man who had so readily renounced her before a battle that almost took her life, the man who was still her husband.

Vivien swung open the door to her chamber suite. Once it was closed behind her, she flung herself down onto the bed and allowed the tears to come full force. *Oh gods, what has he done? What is he doing? I'm so confused, I don't know which way is up, or which way is down.* Feelings of hurt and betrayal suffused her heart and it quailed beneath the onslaught.

"Please, someone help me..."

The voice sounded so lonely and forlorn in the room, empty except for her. Not even Sherika was there to help ease her. The big cat had begged Vivien to be allowed out that morning, wishing to prowl the fortress. Of course, she had obliged her friend and, most likely, the feline was napping in some crevasse somewhere out of the way where no one would be bothered by her.

"Gods, please help me."

Vivien squeezed her eyes tightly shut, hot tears streaming down her cheeks. She sniffled and shucked her beautiful robes, tossing them onto the floor with a grunt of disgust. She took the shiny circlet off her brow and threw it down there as well. It landed on top of the robes and she kicked the entire pile away as far as she could. She wanted nothing to do with her society, including the accolades it had presented to her this day. For a brief moment she had been happy, standing there beside Ravn. He had frightened her for a moment, but that had been only a moment. She loved him, but her life was in such upheaval. She needed time, time to think. And then Torialvah had rescinded the divorce...

Vivien rose from the bed and padded over to the balcony. She stepped past the curtain and went up to the railing, putting her elbows on the smooth granite. It was a warm day, but the breeze cooled her heated body through the billowing trousers and sheer tunic she wore. She luxuriated in the feel of it, let the air dry her tears, let it whip the loose tunic around her breasts and waist. The view below her was one of magnificent beauty, the forest and the hills that characterized the land stretching as far as her eyes could see.

For several moments she just stood there, thinking about nothing, just being in the moment. She needed the break, deserved it, for life had been nonstop for so many weeks that she feared she might forget what it was like to just stop. The smells of cooking food wafted up to her in the breeze, and her stomach rumbled. She couldn't recall when she'd last eaten something. But still, she didn't move. It was something about the ambiance at that moment, something about the way she felt, that made her want to stay and just BE.

"There you are. I was wondering where you had gone."

Vivien's heart leapt in her chest as she spun around to find Torialvah standing there behind her, framed by the billowing curtain. He was handsome as always, his black hair pulled away from the sides of his face and braided down his back. Ice blue eyes regarded her intently, almost tenderly, as he reached out his hand. In it was a box.

Vivien looked at it, then back up at him, confused.

"It is for you. I meant to give it to you sooner, but circumstances did not allow that." Something lurked behind his eyes for a moment before he dispelled it. He stepped closer. "Please, take it. It is a gift to express my apologies, and... and my love."

Vivien simply stood there, aghast. Truly, this man was presenting her with a gift? And with words of love? It was simply not done.

"My Lord, I..."

Tor bridged the gap between her and moved close, his voice low. "Vivien, I am your husband. There is no 'Lord' between us."

"But–"

He reached out and cupped her face. "I never proceeded with the annulment. I was hurt and angry. I know it must have injured you and I'm sorry. Please forgive me." He held out the box again, this time slowly removing the lid. Inside, lying on a bed of navy satin, was a necklace. It was beautiful, obviously crafted from one of the master artisans of Rithalion. Thin ropes of white gold were woven about one another to make intricate designs that spoke to her. They shimmered in the rays of the late-day sun, beckoning her to touch them.

"I had it made especially for you." His voice lowered even more. "Can't you feel it calling out to you?"

Vivien frowned. As a matter of fact, she could, but somehow she resisted. "Torialvah, I can't..."

He took the necklace from the box and unfastened the clasp. "Turn around."

She closed her eyes and did as he instructed. It was just the way it was; she always did what he told her to do. Except...except maybe when he told her to drop her advanced mages classes. She didn't do that. She felt the weight of the necklace settle around her neck and it felt like it belonged there, like it was made just for her. Actually, didn't Tor just tell her it was?

She felt his hands on her shoulders and he turned her around. His eyes regarded her appreciatively as he took her in, and it was then she remembered what she was wearing– practically nothing on top but a sheer tunic. She was tempted to cover herself, really wanted to, but held herself still. He had seen her naked before, and really it didn't matter. Covering herself would only show him her weakness.

His voice was hushed, "Vivien, you are so beautiful." He dropped the box and cupped one breast in his hand, massaging the nipple with his thumb.

Her heart stuttered in her chest. *Oh no. No.*

Tor stepped closer. "I missed you more than I thought I ever would." He put his other hand in her hair. "You don't know how pleased I was to hear that my wife had returned to the army alive and well."

She closed her eyes, taking in his words, words she had dreamed he might one day say to her. Only...only now...

The Lord of Ice and Steel brought himself close, so close her nipples touched his chest. He brushed his lips across her cheek and ran his hand down her hip and across her backside. "You are mine. There is nothing holding you here now. I asked you this once before, and you refused. Come back home with me."

She blinked away tears. "Tor...Torialvah...I am..." She stuttered, trying to decide what she wanted to say. "We had a son. You blamed me for his death."

He nodded, placed his lips to her forehead, then her cheek, then her neck. "I know. I am sorry."

She relaxed slightly, wondering if this was for real instead of the dream it seemed to be. He was actually apologizing to her. It just wasn't done.

He took her mouth with his, and like always, she submitted. His kiss was deep, rough but not savage. He pressed his hand against her backside, pulling her into him, causing an ache to settle deep within her pelvis, an ache that hadn't subsided since this morning when Ravn...

Oh gods, is this really happening?

She spoke around his lips and put her hands against his chest. "Tor, please...what are you doing?"

His arms tightened around her; his voice was a husky whisper. "Vivien, we can have other children."

Tendrils of fear wriggled through her like a nest of hatchling snakes, twisting about in her belly and making her mute. *No, this can't be happening. Not again, not like last time.* She'd ached for two days after they had been together, and she'd bled a little. He'd taken her in every sense of those words, for none of her protests had been heard.

The Lord of Ice and Steel picked her up and swiftly carried her back into the chamber. Her heart was like a drum against her ribs, pounding faster and faster. *No, no, no.* She wanted to say the words aloud, but they had fallen on deaf ears before.

Gods, please help me.

His words were a low growl in her hear. "I want you so much." Torialvah lay her on the bed and followed her down, his weight crushing her into the pillows. A feeling of helplessness welled within her. *This is what they want. People want me to be with this man. He is important, has high standing in society. We are supposed to be right for one another.*

His hands were all over her at once, tearing away her tunic and pulling down her pants. She put her hands against his chest, pushing against him, pushing, pushing harder. His arms were like iron grips, burning into her sides and back, her waist and hips, immobilizing her. His lips were like a brand, claiming her as his, making sure that no one would want her after he was done with her.

"Tor, stop. Stop." Tears ran down her temples to wet the pillow beneath her head. She trembled as he spread her legs. And then, without preamble, he thrust himself inside.

Burning pain flared outward, aftershocks coursing through her pelvis and thighs. She cried out, but his lips covered her mouth, his tongue twining about hers in a cruel, macabre dance. His thrusts were powerful, and ravaged her in more ways than one. Her mind stuttered and then shut down, retreating to where she could be safe. Her body relaxed and the pain subsided, her tears ceased to flow. She just lay there, moving only with the force of his pounding.

Finally, it was done. Her husband lay over her, damp with sweat, his chest heaving with exertion. After a while he looked up at her. He kissed her tenderly on the forehead, then her cheek, and finally her lips. "I love you Vivien." He put a hand over one bare breast. "I am so happy you have come home to me. Your father is happy for us, and our friends too. I want things to be different... better. I believe we can make it that way."

She simply nodded.

Tor caressed the necklace laying at her throat. "This is a token of how I feel for you. I hope you keep it with you always."

He rose and pulled his trousers back up over his hips. "I am sure you are tired. I will see you tomorrow in council." He leaned over and kissed her brow before finally vacating the chamber.

Vivien just lay there, broken.

She awoke to pre-dawn darkness. A breeze wafted through the chamber, ruffling the balcony curtains, caressing the flesh of her naked body. She lay there, just as her husband had left her, one hand over her slightly distended belly. Every once in a while, she'd feel it, a fluttering deep inside. It was a strange sensation, one she'd been feeling more and more often as of recent, and she wondered what it was.

Finally, she rose. Sherika gave a mumble as she left the bed, the big cat wondering what she was doing up at such an early hour of the morning. Vivien vaguely wondered how the tir-reath had gotten back into the room as she donned a robe to cover her nudity, then padded towards the door. She heard a questioning trill from the bed and turned back. "No worries, my friend. I will return shortly."

Vivien walked down the tower stairs and into the fortress proper. It was a massive place, and it currently housed hundreds of soldiers in varying stages of healing. Master Healer Mikarvan was busy from the beginning until the end of every day, and that was the reason why she hadn't bothered him about her fears whilst they were out in the field. They had only been home a couple of days, but she couldn't wait any longer. Something was terribly wrong, and she needed to find out what it was and have him help her as best he could.

Vivien continued through the fortress, past halls filled with tables where people took their meals, past the kitchens already busy with staff preparing food for the morning meal, past corridors filled with chambers housing the healers that were helping with the wounded. It was down one of these that she went, and when she arrived at the appropriate door, she knocked. When she got no answer, she knocked again.

At last, it opened. A bleary-eyed Mikarvan stood there, but when he saw who it was, he came to full alertness. "Vivien! Come in, come in."

The Master Healer stood aside and she entered the dim chamber. He closed the door and brushed past her to take a few pillows off the nearest chair and bade her sit. She just stood there beside it and regarded him intently.

"Unseleighe dancing, what are you doing here at this hour?" His voice lowered. "Is something wrong?"

Seeing the concern reflected in his eyes, Vivien began to tremble, and overwhelmed with emotion, tears sprang to her eyes.

Mikarvan closed the distance between them and wrapped his arms around her. "Shhhh. It's going to be all right. I'm right here."

"I... I'm afraid, Mika."

His arms tightened and he shook his head. "No fears. Whatever it is, we will face it together. Now tell me what bothers you so."

Images of Torialvah came to her mind, but she thrust them aside as she focused on the pervading reason she was there to see him. "I've been sick."

He nodded. "I'm not surprised. Your body has endured much these past many weeks. It needs extra rest and nourishment now. Why didn't you tell me before?"

"I didn't want to take you away from the soldiers who needed you."

He gave a deep sigh. "You are also one of my soldiers. You should have come to me."

Vivien returned to her previous line of thought. "Until the Wolf gave me raspberry leaves, I would vomit every day."

Mikarvan pulled away and looked her in the eyes, a frown pulling at his brows. "Every day?"

She nodded. "Sometimes more than that. I felt sick *all* the time."

His gaze looked her up and down. "You are definitely much thinner than you were before you left."

"In many ways, yes."

His frown deepened. "What do you mean, 'in many ways'?"

She moved out of his embrace. "It's my belly." She put a hand over it. "It's bigger than it was before I left. And my pants no longer fit properly."

Mikarvan went to a lantern and opened the shutter. Light bathed the area in golden light. "Show me."

With trepidation, Vivien parted the robe. Once she was exposed, she just stood there and looked at his face. Mikarvan was good, very good. His expression didn't change as he looked up into her eyes.

"I need you to lay down on the bed."

It was then she hesitated. Wild thoughts swept through her mind and stripped her bare. Then, hardly a moment later, she was chastising herself. *No, Mika is my friend! He would never hurt me. Ever!* She nodded and did as he bid. In the meantime, he went to the washbasin and washed his hands with some soap and water. When he approached, he was drying his hands on a fresh towel. He joined her on the bed, sat next to her where she lay. She barely kept herself from flinching at his touch as he placed a hand over her belly and pressed gently down on it. He continued to press around the periphery, and then on top. Finally, he looked up at her. "Vivien, have you been experiencing your monthly cycle?"

She shook her head. "No. I haven't bled since I lost the baby. You told me it might take a while for it to return."

"Yes. Yes, I did. It usually takes four to six weeks."

Vivien was still as this information sank in. "Oh."

"It has been over three months."

She nodded.

"Have you noticed anything else besides being sick?"

She gave a heavy swallow and fear coursed through her. "Yes, it's like there's something inside." Her voice rose in pitch. "Could something have gone down my nose or mouth while I slept? The swamp was a terrible place. The denizens there were..."

Mikarvan took her hand and interrupted her in a firm tone. "No, Vivien. I don't believe you have a swamp worm in your belly."

Her eyes widened in shock. "There's a name for them? They actually exist?"

He shook his head. "No, there is no such thing. There is nothing you could have contracted in the swamp that would make itself felt from the inside."

She sat up. "Then what is it?"

He regarded her intently, hesitated to speak, almost as though he couldn't believe what he was about to say. "My dear, you are pregnant, probably several months along. It's hard to tell since you haven't been eating well and are so small."

She felt her face drain of blood. She stared at him, waited for him to tell her that he was joshing her. But his honey-brown eyes reflected only the utmost of solemnity. Again, tears sprang to her eyes. "No, I lost my baby." Her voice cracked under the force of her emotion. "I held him in my arms!"

Seeing her distress, Mikarvan once more took her in his arms. "Shhh, I know. I remember. I delivered him." He stroked her hair soothingly.

Her voice shook. "I don't understand. How can this be?"

"When were you last with your husband?"

Vivien flushed crimson. "Last night."

"And before that?"

"When I conceived Gaelen."

Mika nodded sagely. "Sometimes, in the rarest of circumstances, there are two children inside the mother. Most of the time, when one is lost, so is the other. But this time...this time the other one managed to keep holding on."

She sobbed in earnest, tears streaming down her face. Her husband hadn't seemed to notice the distention of her belly last night. At least, he hadn't said anything about it. Granted, he had been rather busy...

Vivien shuddered at the thought, and suddenly she felt lost. "I can't do this Mika. I can't do this alone."

His arms tightened around her. "Vivien, you are *never* alone! Ever. If the child needs a father, I will help fill that role, as will the Grand Magister. Don't you realize what this will mean to him?"

Finally she quieted. She lay back on the bed and placed a hand on her belly. Her tone was forlorn. "What if I damaged him somehow? Slogging through that nasty swamp, fighting a dead dragon, slinging spells left and right in the heat of battle, and falling down a waterfall."

Mikarvan shook his head and lay down beside her. "Vivien, you didn't damage the baby. If you did, he'd be gone like his brother. All that time, he was safe within the shelter of your body."

She nodded. Her voice lowered to almost a whisper. "I can feel him right now." She turned to him, her gaze intense. "You can't tell anyone about this."

He frowned. "About what?"

"The baby."

His frown deepened. "What? Why?"

"I have heard rumor that there are to be visits made to the other Elvish cities. The plan is for the Wolf and I to go together as a show of strength and solidarity in hopes to gain their support for the upcoming war that is certain to come. I don't want people telling me I can't go."

"Vivien! They would be right. You shouldn't go!"

She narrowed her eyes, and before he could move back, she had her hand at the back of his neck, pulling him towards her. "I mean it, Mika! Not a word to anyone. This is my prerogative, and you are bound to keep my secret by the oath you swore when you became a healer. My business is confidential and may not be shared unless I desire it."

He pursed his lips and his eyes flashed with anger and hurt. "Fine," he ground out between clenched teeth, "I'll keep your secret. But I don't have to like it." He grabbed her arm and pulled her hand from around the back of his neck. He then stood from the bed and looked down at her. "Dawn has arrived. I need to prepare for my day."

Vivien also rose, her body stiff beneath his scrutiny. She understood his hurt; she would feel the same way if their positions were reversed. A twinge of regret coursed through her, but she squelched it almost immediately. No, she couldn't change her mind now. There were things she needed to do, important things. And if what Mika said was true, the baby would not be harmed by those things. There was really no reason for her to not go as long as she had a safe place to give birth. The other Elvish cities certainly had their own healers; she would be fine.

And if she could escape her life in Rithalion for as long as possible, well, that was more the boon for her.

Sensing that she had been dismissed, Vivien turned away from her friend. Emotion welled up within her, and for a moment she was tempted to turn around and talk to him. But somehow, she felt she couldn't. She didn't know what had happened with Torialvah, couldn't dissect it enough to comprehend it. And if she couldn't understand it, how could she try to explain it to someone else? Her heart ached as she walked to the door, opened it, and strode out of the chamber. She supposed she deserved his ire, for she had forced his hand in spite of his better judgment. One day she would try and make it better. One day she would show him that she cared more about him than what she had shown him today.

Vivien walked down the hall, emotion building. A feeling of hopelessness overwhelmed her. *Oh gods, I have no choice; I never had a choice. What happened to me last night? I feel sick inside, despoiled, yet he treated me so much better than he ever has. He was so harsh with me, but yet so loving afterwards. I'm afraid of him, but I am going to bear his son.*

Vivien darted down a side passage and pressed her back against the wall. Her breaths were fast and shallow, ragged. The emotion within her built higher and higher, a pressure that could not be controlled. She clenched her hands into fists, her nails digging into her palms. *Oh gods, please no. This can't be happening to me. I don't want this. Please save me.*

For a few moments there was silence. She waited, waited, waited. *That's right, nothing can save me now.*

She finally hit capacity and the pressure found a way out. It poured forth like a geyser, taking with it her voice in an agonized cry. It echoed down the hallway, and people stopped in their duties. Vivien crumpled into a heap on the floor and darkness reigned.

Chapter Five
Secrets and Gifts

Vivien stepped into the chamber suite of the Lady of Moonlight and Love. The Lady had asked her to come, telling her she had a few things to discuss. Vivien took deep, easy breaths, still recovering from earlier this morning. She'd awakened in the hallway to a circle of faces hovering above her, all of them etched with concern. It had taken several moments for her to rid herself of the housekeeping staff, urging them to not tell anyone about her collapse. She'd then returned to her tower. Once walking inside, she'd found herself faced with the bed...

So, she'd gone out onto the balcony. She lay there on the pale granite, her head cushioned on Sherika's flank. The tir-reath had rumbled discontentedly, having felt the surge of strong emotion Vivien had experienced, not to mention what she had probably felt the evening before when Vivien was with Tor. Vivien rested for a while, rising only when she heard the knock on her door. She'd been a bundle of knots walking over to open it, relaxing only she saw it was just a messenger.

The chamber was quiet, and seemed empty. But she called out, "My Lady? Are you here?" Vivien waited patiently. "Shaladrea?"

Vivien frowned. she could have sworn that the message told her to be here at this time. She turned when she finally heard someone coming up the stairs leading down to the chambers that her old friend, Lydia, and Ravn occupied. Any other day, she might not have noticed the nearly silent footsteps. But today...

Ravn appeared at the entry and stopped. She just stared at him, saying nothing. She hadn't seen him since they had stood together before the Council the day before. Somehow, he had disappeared after the announcement that Torialvah had rescinded his grievance against her and dropped divorce proceedings. She could only imagine why, supposed she couldn't blame him. Indeed, why would Ravn stick around once discovering the woman he loved was still bound and possessed by her husband?

She closed her eyes tightly shut at that thought, and her heart ached. *I am coming undone. I can't come undone.*

"Vivien?" His voice was a breath near her ear.

Without opening her eyes, she could smell the spicy musk of him, feel the heat that emanated off him in waves, hear the beat of his mighty heart. She opened her mouth to get a deeper breath, her lips trembling. She promptly closed it, shaking her head slightly and sniffing away the tears. *No, I can't fall apart...*

Then there was a hand against her face, a large warm one. It was the one that had killed men, twice saving her life in the field of battle, the one that had cleaved a dragon in twain. It was the one that touched her with the utmost of gentleness, the one that had lifted her up to carry her when she lost her son, the one that held onto sheer rock to keep them from falling.

It was the one that touched her naked body like it was a temple to the gods. *No, no, no.*

His hand moved to cradle the back of her head and pull her against his chest and that was it. She couldn't help disintegrating, crying like a small child. Ravn just held her close, wrapping his arms protectively around her, keeping her warm and safe. For a moment she had nothing to fear, and she basked in his glow, taking it in, luxuriating in it. She returned his embrace, pressing herself against the length of him, remembering the feel of him against her fingertips.

She yearned to feel that again, ached for it. But now, now it felt so out of reach.

"Vivien."

There it was, that voice again at her ear, the one that she'd dreamed about for decades while she thought him dead and gone from this world. She looked up into storm-cloud blue eyes...eyes that could delve into her heart and make it settle into peace.

Her voice cracked despite all her efforts not to. "Ravn."

His lips enveloped hers in a soft embrace. Tears streamed down her cheeks to their joined mouths, and his tongue swept them away like they were never there. The kiss took nothing, expected nothing, sought nothing. Rather, it gave. Every breath, every caress, every stroke of his tongue against hers– was all for her.

Only when they heard footsteps coming up the stairs did they part, and when the Lady of Moonlight entered, followed by one of her wives, Ravn stood several feet away, and Vivien had wiped the tears from her eyes.

"Oh, my dear! Thank you for coming! I have something for you!" The Lady looked at the Wolf pointedly. "You may not wish to stay for this, for 'tis women's talk. That is, unless you wish to know..."

Ravn held up his hands in surrender, a smile pulling up the corners of his mouth. "Gods forbid I interrupt." He gave a deep bow. "Good day to you, Lady." He then bowed again. "Vivien."

The Lady's eyes were wide as she turned to her a moment later after he left. "Charming, if I may say so."

Vivien nodded. "He can be."

Shaladrea smiled widely. "We have a celebration to attend today. The entire city has taken a rest day and everyone will be participating. People have spent days preparing, and you and the Wolf are honored guests!"

Vivien's eyes widened. "W... what?"

The Lady nodded. "Yes, I know, it is exciting. You are to be celebrated, my dear, the Wolf and the rest of the La'athai too!"

Vivien reeled from the news, and feelings of inadequacy arose. She shook her head. "No, I can't do this. I..."

Shaladrea was suddenly standing there before her, hands on her shoulders. "Vivien! Of course you can come! It will be good for you, and people will get to see you. It will be good for them too. I even have something for you to wear."

"You have something for me to...what?" Vivien stared at her, confounded.

"Indeed, I had something made for you. It would have been something your mother would have done for you. "Her voice lowered then, and she spoke almost hesitantly, delicately. "But since she is not here, and I think of you as my own, I thought it would be all right if I took that honor."

Vivien stared at her through wide eyes, a bit of disbelief shadowing her thoughts. First of all, there was an occasion about to take place for which she needed formal attire. Second, that the Lady deemed it appropriate for her to acquire this attire for her. Vivien had money, a lot of money. So it wasn't like she couldn't have done it herself if she'd known.

Vivien's tone was low. "Why didn't anyone tell me there were to be formal festivities?"

The Lady had grown subdued. "We thought you would have asked about why everyone was in such a tizzy. Of course, you are too young to have ever seen one, but it is always so after a major battle. We didn't think you may have been so wrapped up in the council, and resting, and just being home, that you didn't notice."

Vivien's shoulders slumped. Formal festivities meant rubbing shoulders with some of the most highly ranked members of society. It meant there would be a dinner, and probably dancing. It meant Tor would be there. She put a hand to her belly as the baby inside moved. HIS baby.

"Vivien, I am sorry. Xadrian told me I should not have had the gown made without talking to you about it first. I'm so sorry I overstepped my bounds."

Vivien focused back onto her friend, saw the contrition in her eyes, the sorrow. In truth, she'd never seen Shaladrea look the way she did at that moment, both of those feelings overshadowed by rejection. "No, you didn't overstep any bounds. I truly appreciate the gown."

The Lady smiled as Vivien embraced her. Shaladrea returned it warmly, lovingly, the way she thought her mother may have if she were there with her. "Thank you for loving me so much, for wanting me. I couldn't ask for anything more."

"I shall always love you, Vivien. You are like my own. Your father knows this, and he has accepted it. All my wives know. Sherika knows." Shaladrea stepped away and held her shoulders. "Now I just need you to know."

Vivien just nodded, tears in her eyes. "I am trying."

Shaladrea smiled. "I know you are." Then her smile widened and she gestured to her wife, Kira, who held a bundle of cloth in her hands. Her other wives had also come, Betina and Naomi, and they watched with hopeful eyes. "Come, let us now try on this gown. I want to see it on you!"

As Vivien disrobed, all she could think was that she hoped Tor hadn't left any marks. Mika hadn't said anything, but that didn't mean...

The room was suddenly quiet. She looked up to see the four women looking at her. *Oh gods, there is a mark, one big enough to look...*

Shaladrea stepped towards her, gaze filled with awe. "Vivien, why didn't you tell me?"

Vivien frowned. "Tell you wh..." Suddenly she remembered and cursed herself for her stupidity. It was distended enough that the Lady noticed. She placed a hand over her belly, wishing it would just shrink back and go away. "I didn't realize it until today. I'd lost the other one, so..."

Shaladrea moved forward and placed a hand above hers over the swell. Her voice was hushed. "Unseleighe dancing! Twins! One was lost, but the other remains."

Vivien stiffened and said nothing. Her heart pounded in her ears. *It's over now. She will tell everyone. Tor will know and I will be his to keep, no matter what I want, no matter how I feel. He can do anything he wants with me...*

Shaladrea looked up, her eyes shining. "Do you know what this me..." She let her voice drift off, her eyes became shadowed, and she let her hand drop. She stood there, saying nothing, regarding Vivien with the utmost of patience and tenderness.

Vivien inwardly berated herself. *Dammit, I need to be better than this. I let people see too much!* She could only imagine the expression she'd had on her face for the Lady to react so grimly.

"Does Mikarvan know?"

Vivien nodded.

"Good, that is important."

Moments passed in silence. Then, "My dear, I cannot help my nature. This baby makes me feel happy in so many ways. Please don't begrudge me that."

Vivien looked at her friend. "I don't. But that means you cannot deny me my feelings as well."

Shaladrea's expression shifted to one of protective fierceness. "I love you. I shall deny you nothing."

Vivien swallowed past the lump in her throat, felt the emotion deep within burble its way forcefully out of her chest. The Lady was suddenly there, enveloping her within her embrace. Vivien wept, all of her fears and sorrows silently gushed out as the Lady caressed her hair and back. Then, when it was over, Shaladrea wiped away her tears and kissed her gently on the lips. "I am so sorry that you lost your mother so young, so no one may have ever told you this before. I need you to know that you can tell me anything. It doesn't matter what you say, I will love you all the same."

Vivien nodded and sniffed. She then looked at the bundle Kira carried and took the chance to leave her tears behind. "Let's see if we can get this gown to fit me."

Dragon Vessel

Shaladrea grinned and took the bundle, opening it to reveal something entirely different inside. She lifted it to reveal a gossamer green gown. "We will make it fit just fine. Betina is a seamstress. She can easily hide your condition."

Surprised, Vivien gave the Lady an intense look. *She understands.* She swallowed past another lump and nodded. She looked over at Betina. "I would love that."

Chapter Six
Wise Counsel

The elves debated. again.

They met in the Council Tower, but in the small chambers meant for private considerations, not the grand hall meant for trials. It contained only the leaders of the city: the Elders, The Grand Magister, The Lord of Swords, The Lady of Moonlight and Love, The Lord of Ice and Steel, Vivien, and Ravn. The Laird had been here before, too, when planning to repel the first onslaught from the Iron Coast. He had heard these words from them at that time as well. They debated, and contradicted, and prattled. He looked to his right where sat Xadrian. He, Ravn could respect, for the knowledge of what was to come was written plainly on his face. Beyond him, his wife was positively radiating sadness. The others had no idea what had happened just a few weeks ago, what the terrible battle had meant to their people and the Iron Coast.

"We have no eyes in the Iron Coast. Our best spy with any amount of Elvish blood suffered terribly after his capture. Now he has disappeared. He simply cannot be found." Master Kilcahnn, always before a voice of steely certainty shook his head slowly. Ravn looked into his pale eyes and knew the Elder had been terribly shaken by the torture of his servant. It had, in fact, broken him when that spy had escaped care and fled the elvin lands with his inner demons.

Orinoco frowned. "Then send some others. We must know how many of the Iron Army returned home to know the strength the humans have to call on."

Kilcahnn's mouth turned into a frown that trembled slightly. "The humans will be on the lookout for strangers. And if they caught my best, none of the others will survive."

Xadrian and Ravn exchanged looks, then the Elvish commander looked to his other side, where sat the Lady of Moonlight and Love. It struck Ravn again, for in that barest glance there was contained a world of caring and understanding between the two. In all the world, Xadrian was cloaked by his military prowess, and Shaladrea by her awesome beauty, but they had no secrets from one another. They could read each other as easily as an aged sailor knew the seas, as intimately as the farmer his fields. Ravn knew they suffered terrible losses together, half a dozen children dead in the war that tore this kingdom centuries ago, and it had caused a rift between them that still was not healed. He understood their hidden sadness, inches from the one person they loved most in the world, and forever apart.

"We have lost so much on the battlefield, and crushed the human army twenty times our size!" Torialvah, Lord of Ice and Steel, exclaimed. "Surely they will run home and lick their wounds and leave us be."

He gestured with his hands and then brought them down on the table, one covering Vivien's hand, as if to grab her by a leash and keep her there. It was not a sign of affection, but of ownership. Vivien was quiet, withdrawn. Her eyes were developing circles beneath, and every noise caused her to flinch. She was such a mighty woman, to see her so cowed turned his blood into molten iron made from the blades of a thousand bloody swords. He took a drink from the goblet of wine that had been set before him and wrestled his inner beast under control.

As he lowered the cup, he saw Vivien had met his gaze for the first time in the hours long war council session. Her sadness hit him like a blanket of icy nettles. It called to him, cried to him. He felt for sure she needed him, yearned for him to be near. Yet there she sat, as far from him as she could be and next to the husband that crushed her spirit. There were rumors that they argued fiercely during their marriage, and Ravn knew from experience the bastard had never treated her with an ounce of respect in public. Seeing her like this, so hurt after surviving armies, giants, and a dragon, Ravn knew something worse than yelling had to happen between them behind closed doors. Ravn set down the cup and lifted four fingers of his free hand from the table. Just four fingers, reaching for her across the impossible rift between them. She breathed faster, unable to look away from him, and her free hand did the same.

Then her husband turned languidly. Maybe he had noticed, maybe he had not. Regardless, her took her chin firmly in one hand and turned her face towards him and away from Ravn, then kissed her with strength but without an iota of tenderness. When he let go, Vivien looked down at the table and seemed to shrink a little more into her chair. The barbarian felt the pressure build behind his eyes and rubbed them as if fatigued, only to cover the red-hot glow that emanated from them until he could get himself under control. It was not the kiss, Vivien could kiss anyone she desired. She only had to desire it. Ravn felt his palms itch to grab Torialvah and slam him into the ground over and over until he came to pieces. He took a deep breath and the urge receded.

Mistress Swansee nodded hopefully. "Yes, that sounds reasonable. They certainly see the folly of their actions now. They will leave our forest no matter how much they need our trees." The Lady of Principle and Grace nodded again to herself, needing to be right.

The Lady of Moonlight and Love spoke up for the first time in the meeting. "They will not stop. They will not give up."

And those words sapped any false optimism from the room.

Torialvah made a dismissive wave. "Excuse my boldness, beautiful one, but I am not certain why you are even here. What does love have to do with battle? What experience in battle do you have other than losing to the small raiding party that started this war?"

Ravn felt Xadrian shift infinitesimally, and knew he wanted Tor's head right then as well. He caught Ravn's eye and nodded, admitting his feelings, then made a tiny head jerk toward his former wife as if to draw Ravn's attention to what was to happen next with a wry smile.

Shaladrea stood slowly, letting the room settle and unchaining her formidable presence upon the space. It filled every corner like light, first comforting, then glaring, then blinding. Only then did she fix Tor with her stare, and it was as if every rose's thorn was drawn across his skin by the power of her voice. "It was not a raiding party, but a scouting party. I had feared they were entering our wood from the reports I had from traders and scouts. Reports this Council dismissed." If possible, she stood taller, peering down at the raven-haired Lord of Ice and Steel. "And I am the one who had the foresight after the last war that shattered our people to build a fortress that could defend us if the time came. Not you, or your family." Tor's face flushed under the onslaught. "And for that matter, I understand you were not amongst the Wolf Pack when they fought for us against the Iron Army, nor even in the front lines. And when your wife, who led the La'athai, was lost, you were on your way back to the city and safety. Where was all your steel then?" She smiled, but there were only barbs in it. "I have met the Iron Men and faced them with my own blood ready to be spilled. I felt their iron packets stinging, and felt their rough hands on me. So, I would say I have seen far more of this war than you."

Ravn watched as the blood drained from Tor's face as Shaladrea spoke. He trembled with rage, and his grip on his wife's hand made her wince. She shrunk lower in her chair.

Oilariann stood. "This is not a place to question one another's motives, but to determine a course of action. We are even weaker now than when we began this war, and while we turned aside the first blow, we must know if another is coming."

"They are coming." As soon as she finished speaking the swirling blades in her soul stilled instantly. She smiled sweetly and sat. Ravn didn't know from where Shaladrea's venom came, but he no longer had any doubt of her inner strength. The two dozen Lords and Ladies looked at one another uncomfortably around the round table.

Torialvah glared at the Lady of Moonlight and Love and opened his mouth, but Xadrian stood, cutting him off. Oilariann nodded and relinquished the floor, sitting as the Commander spoke. "The spy, Simrudian," Ravn saw Kilcahnn wince at the name, "returned from the Iron Coast broken and beaten, likely mad, but he did confirm our worst fears. From the top of Swordbite Pass, as far as he could see, the land was nude of trees of any size. We have known that for two hundred years that the Iron Coast made an empire making the implements of war. They provide soldiers, weapons, armor, engineers, captured and trained beasts, and most importantly, warships. If they have destroyed their land, stripping it of trees, then they will soon be short of meat. They are importing all the beasts, and they cannot feed their men, build ships, or weapons." He paused, letting that sink in.

Orinoco shook his head. "But we defeated such a vast army that—"

Ravn shook his head. "It doesn't matter."

The whole room looked to him, and he shucked the pressure of it off of his shoulders. He was tired of being an outsider, a foreigner. He didn't know if he wanted to be a part of them, but he would be damned if he were damned for having round ears.

Orinoco huffed after a moment of silence. "Do you have any wisdom to impart?"

And Tor, still stinging from his exchange with Shaladrea, held Vivien's hand and sneered, "Yes, tell us what you think you know."

The Wolf looked around the table, took a long pull from his goblet, and stood slowly, making them wait. "Two hundred years is longer than most humans can even conceive. You see them as an upstart nation, but to themselves the Iron Coast is a mighty empire that has always been. They have grown rich and prosperous, selling weapons and waging war. It is the only life they know, and now it is ending. They will fight with everything they have to keep that from happening."

Tor huffed, "They tried."

Ravn nodded. "And if you have heard the stories of what they did to the spy we sent, you may begin to understand how much they hate you for having what they need and what they are willing to do in order to take it."

Tor waved a dismissive hand. "Let them try."

Ravn's jaw ground his teeth at the sheer arrogance. "They did. They sent twenty thousand men and beasts to destroy you, and only by the grace of the heavens, we prevailed."

Ignoring protocol, Torialvah stood, leaning forward on the table. "And we will do it again."

"You have no idea what you are saying." Despite himself, Ravn leaned against the table as well, hunching himself back at the Lord as they spat words at one another. "The Iron Army is not what you have seen. I have been there. I know what it is. It is endless barracks in the Iron City. It is a flotilla of ships, master engineers, pack-masters and their animals, smiths to make weapons and knights to wield them. And they are everywhere. In every major country along the Wounded Sea, and they have sold themselves to the highest bidder in every confrontation for two centuries."

"What possible motivation would they have to come back?"

"You still have the space, the wood, and the arable land they need. More than that, fear and revenge."

Tor chuckled darkly. "Revenge? For what?"

Ravn frowned. "Elves seem to put some greater weight of sin upon one of kind of killing over another. Humans do the same. We destroyed a fraction of their force, but we destroyed all the food for the rest. Those men trying to flee? They starved. We did that to them. I did that to them, if you cannot share the burden. I would do it again to save this city. But make no mistake; the men of the Iron Coast died slow, lingering deaths of city men trying to hunt with swords and long spears. Those that made it home will tell everyone and those that sail on their ships will know of it and want revenge."

Tor growled, "And what of it? Ships are no good here. And their men are in foreign lands."

Now they were the only two in the room, trembling like dogs pulling on chains to fight. "We destroyed one army. While we returned home, a few of their number must have reached the Iron Coast. Impossibly, we survived, which means those ships have already been dispatched from port. They are sailing to every city to gather their ships, their iron, and their men. They will take out loans, they will hire more men. For the first time, the Iron Coast will import soldiers and mass them in a force that will dwarf the first. In a few months' time they will return like locusts and burn their way across the land to come here, to attack a beautiful city without walls and strip Rithalion of every single person and every single thing they can carry to return it to the coast for sale as spoils or slaves. They will murder it, and settle down to live on the corpse."

Tor yelled, "We will stop them!"

Ravn roared, "You still only have a thousand men! You cannot breed fast enough! You cannot train hard enough! You will face a force as trained, as dedicated as the last, and steeped in tales of your evil and torture of the last invasion force!"

Tor's face clouded. "We did not torture–"

Ravn cut him off with eyes that glowed red and a voice that rattled the rafters. "IT WILL NOT MATTER!" Tor paled, as did every face in the room, and he sat down. The silence rang with tension. They looked to one another. Ravn looked to Vivien. He could feel her fear. Of him. Of his anger. He saw the Grand Magister, who considered him darkly. Ravn breathed, and felt his eyes stop glowing. "We have months, no more. Come spring they will march to enslave, and exterminate."

His words were answered only with silence for long heartbeats.

Oilariann, blinked back tears, but put on a brave face. "Why would they do this terrible thing?"

Ravn shrugged and sat heavily. "Because they cannot be seen as weak or their whole society will crumble. They can fathom sending men to die. They cannot abide losing their status, their power in the world, or their way of life. They will do anything, anything to stop these things from happening."

Shaladrea again stood. "We must call upon our cousins in the other Elvish cities. We must call for aid, and add their numbers to our own if we are to survive."

Kilcahnn shook his head. "They may come out of loyalty to blood, but they may not. The Dragon War stuck us hardest, but none forget that it was a battle between Rithalion and Pergatium that destroyed one and crippled the other. Many of their sons and daughters died as well."

Swansee shook her head. "None of them wants to see us succumb to a tide of iron wielding humans. We must convince them. I shall go. We shall tap our most eloquent speaker, and he shall be my voice."

The Grand Magister, quiet through the whole of the meeting, finally spoke quietly, "You are needed here, Elder."

Swansee shook her head, platinum hair rippling. "No. My presence will require an answer. My position can command an audience. We have months, only, and cannot wait."

Jor'aiden, Grand Magister of Rithalion, nodded. "Then I will attend as well."

Xadrian shook his head. "Foolish. You must train all the mages in the ways of battle magic. I will go."

"The Elder must be protected, and should not go. You are needed here to train the soldiers into fighting men, Commander," said Orinoco.

The Lady of Moonlight and Love drew herself up to her full height. She was an elf so beautiful none could remember the color of her eyes, or her hair, only that they were perfect in every detail. She stood tall and proclaimed bravely, "We all know our plight, but we will need to send those who have seen the army of the Iron Coast and met them with steel, to explain the La'athai and how they can train their own. We shall send our champions, Knight Protector Wolf and Mage Protector Vivien Valdera."

"No!" Tor spouted, "My wife—"

"Is a Mage Protector. Is in my service. Is sworn to defend this city, and is going, Lord of Ice and Steel. You must attend your forges. Xadrian must train the troops. I must prepare and stock my fortress. All of us wish to plead our case, and none wish it had to be done. Yet we will do our service to Rithalion. We will all be needed."

Tor seethed and glared daggers at the Lady, but said nothing more.

The votes were cast, Ravn having none, but the plan was decided. They would leave in two weeks' time.

The last words of the meeting were spoken by Oilariann, his heart heavy. "All of us should attend the celebration. We should all celebrate life now, and honor the dead."

The elves moved to leave. Tor lifted Vivien by the arm and marched her from the room, her blue mage robes fluttering passively. The Wolf tensed, but then Xadrian was between he and his retreating love.

"That is the most I have ever heard you speak. More than all other times combined."

Ravn chewed the words, looking past him at the retreating form of the best friend he had ever known. He saw the commander's stance, and knew the man had no intention of letting him by.

"Fitting then, that they are words of doom."

Xadrian ran a hand across his shaved head. "You did not bring this evil, only let them know the truth of it."

Ravn still followed the swatch of navy with his eyes as it disappeared into the halls. "Evil should not be tolerated."

Xadrian started to speak, then stiffened. Ravn knew the commander felt her before he saw her, standing from her place and laying a gentle, perfumed hand on his shoulder. "Some evil is for you to fight. Others need to face their own battles."

Her voice was music, her presence soothing, and it reached into Ravn even as he resisted it and felt his fires quench. He blinked back tears as frustration gave way to despair. The entire room was empty, leaders heading off to prepare and command. It was only the three of them. He shrugged in the void of those left behind. "Then what good am I?"

"Careful of that question, Wolf." Shaladrea came to stand with the two men. "I know an elf who asked the same question once, and it broke him." Ravn could feel Xadrian's ache as he closed his eyes. "But broken things, they can heal."

Xadrian nodded, almost imperceptibly.

"But what do I do?"

The Lord of Swords opened his eyes, determined, certain. "Whose needs matter, Wolf?"

There was no pause. "Hers."

Shaladrea nodded. "You will be there for her, in any way she needs. See to yourself, but never doubt she needs you." And she leaned in. Xadrian turned his head to look at her and their lips met. It was a long, light kiss, containing every moment of love ever expressed in a hundred lifetimes. The commander tensed, even trembled, but did not push her away. She backed away slowly, and Ravn saw Xadrian flushing. She smiled lightly, as if nothing had happened. "She will need you at the celebrations. She will need you to be a man, not a wolf. Can you do that for her?"

Ravn felt his stomach fall away. He knew no Elvish dances, few Elvish customs. He was conditioned to a life of silence in the wild. Yet, what was the value of facing a giant for her life if he could not face a festival for her love? He nodded solemnly.

Shaladrea looked surprised, then smiled sweetly. "Your eyes, Knight Protector, they are the most beautiful shade of blue. You should see to yourself for tonight." She turned to her former husband. "Please see that he does?"

And with that she was gone. Ravn had never been affected by the glamour she wore that struck all others so deeply, but he could feel its force.

Xadrian watched his former wife go, shaking his head. He motioned for Ravn and they started walking out of the chamber.

Ravn looked back as low elves began emerging from concealed doors in the walls and start clearing the meeting table. "What did she mean, 'see to myself'?"

Xadrian was still shaking off the kiss as he clapped the Wolf on the back wryly. "I'm sorry, friend." He raised his eyebrows and nodded. "She means you need a bath and some clothes."

Ravn stopped and looked down at himself. The clothes provided had always been simple, but of quality. "You mean I get a kilt?"

Xadrian pressed his lips together and reached back to grab Ravn's arm and pull him along. "No. Tonight you dress like an elf."

Ravn grimaced. "Lately, I am always dressed like an elf."

Chapter Seven
Celebration

It was a beautiful evening, sultry and filled with magic. Lanterns containing glow stones lit the pathways throughout the gorge, and fae danced and cavorted along the bridges spanning from one side to the other. The moon rose, filled only half-way with the stardust that kept it glowing night after night, and the stars littered the heaven with their brilliance.

True to Shaladrea's words, the entire city of Rithalion celebrated, everyone in his or her own way, with friends and family. The Lady had opened the gates to her fortress, and the most influential in Elvish society had come to share the night with one another, a rare occasion indeed. The castle was festooned with garlands. Torches set within filigreed wall sconces and massive floor braziers kept the place awash with light, the rare chandelier filled with baskets of ancient glowing rocks spaced between. Outside there were hanging lanterns and colorful light orbs, enough to make many places appear as though it were daylight. Vivien found herself walking amidst elders she'd met only in passing, pure elves that dominated the upper tiers of society. She walked among the high-elvin captains and generals of the army, master healers, artisans and smiths. There were even more people like herself, half-elves of high standing as a result of marriage or mastery of some profession or skill. Master bards played delightful melodies, the notes reaching even the farthest reaches of the celebratory grounds, the songs so touching they could make one's heart soar.

It was a celebration, and everyone was bare-headed. There was no formality, and it brought them closer as a people. Some part of her ached to be in the company of the rest of the La'athai, instead.

Vivien kept glancing around, seeing more and more faces as the evening slowly progressed. None of them were Tor, and none the Wolf. One absence she rejoiced, and the other she mourned. She supposed she didn't blame the latter, for he was not one for things such as this, no matter how many formalities he'd once undergone as a lord of his own manor. She remembered those occasions as rougher, but more honest, more open than these. She glanced over at the Lady, surrounded by men and women alike. They luxuriated in her presence, basked in her charisma. Nearby was her father. He wore his formal mages robes, but allowed himself the luxury of relaxation as he drank his third glass of wine. He smiled often and freely, and Vivien loved to see it. At his side was the Lord of Swords and Truth who, even while sitting, was standing at attention. The men had become close since the battle, and she wasn't surprised. They had more in common than they realized.

Vivien sipped at her own wine, enjoying the warm sparks of berry and hints of plum with a robust finish. It was enough just keeping out of the way and watching. After the war council, she had managed to escape her husband, taking herself to her tower and remaining there until she knew it was time to dress for the celebration. The Lady had helped her don the gown, and after, she had plaited Vivien's hair. Each braid was then placed into a whole and wound upon the back of her head. When Shaladrea was finished, they both stared solemnly at themselves in the mirror.

The Lady's voice was soft. "I am sorry I made you uncomfortable in the war council today."

Vivien shook her head. "Don't be. You were right to counter him."

There was no need to say whom. "You know, he doesn't own you."

Vivien simply nodded.

"I just want to warn you, it doesn't matter that Torialvah rescinded his grievances against you. There are some who will still make a play for you. The men may approach you tonight at the festivities."

Vivien inwardly shook a little at that thought and took a deep breath. "All right."

Shaladrea's blue eyes clouded. "Do something for me?"

"Anything."

"Don't send them all away. Allow yourself to be happy for once. Enjoy their company. Because I know they will more than enjoy yours."

Vivien stared into the Lady's eyes in the mirror, saw the sincerity there. She tried to smile a little and nodded.

Shaladrea smiled and once more there was light. She brushed the back of her hand against Vivien's face. "I love you more than you know..."

"Vivien?"

She startled out of her thoughts and turned around. Her breath hitched in her throat when she saw him, and her heart stuttered. He was dressed in tight-fitting black trousers, black boots, and a finely tailored sleeveless green doublet with gold embroidery. His beard had been closely trimmed, and his long, curling mane was gathered at the nape of his neck with a leather tie. "Ravn, what are you doing here?"

He spread his arms. "What, am I not supposed to be here? I thought the celebration was for everyone."

She shook her head. "No, no, no! You are supposed to be here. Only, I didn't think you would be."

A smile tugged at his lips. "Why not? This isn't a place for wolves, eh?"

She simply stared at him impassively until his smile faded. "No, no it's not."

He regarded her intently. She could tell there was a plethora of things he wanted to say, but he uttered none of them. Instead, he took her hand. "Let's walk for a few moments. I heard someone say that dinner will be served soon, but we have time."

Vivien looked around at the rest of the guests, who were beginning to make their way into the castle. "I'm not sure..."

He tugged on her hand. "Trust me."

She nodded and followed him away from the crowd and out into the night. Hand in hand, they left, and before long, it was dark as pitch but for the glow of the celebration behind them. They turned a corner and it was then Ravn stopped, pulling her close. Her senses flared to life and she could smell his spicy musk beneath the bath oils he'd used that afternoon, feel the heat of him where he gently gripped her upper arms, hear his heartbeat through the sound of his breathing. She felt a finger under her chin urging her to look up, and then she felt his warm breath against her lips.

The sensation made her start to tremble, and her legs felt weak. He put an arm around her waist, a loose one. His deep voice cracked, "Vivien, are you afraid of me?"

Taken aback, Vivien pulled back. His eyes glowed blue in the darkness, his brows furrowed with hurt. "No."

"Then why are you trembling when I hold you?"

She studied him for a moment, then opted with the truth even though she was nervous to say the words, making them so much more real. She looked down to make it easier. "It's because of the way you make me feel when you hold me."

Ravn relaxed and once more put his hand beneath her chin until she was looking up at him. His voice was husky. "And how is that?"

She gave a trembling breath. "That I could be everything in the world to you."

She smiled then, a genuine smile, one full of promise. "You already are."

He kissed her gently, lovingly, tenderly. His tongue swept over her lips and she let him in. It slid along hers, slowly and sensually. She loved the feel of it, so soft in spite of the hardness of his muscular body. He deepened the kiss, his lips pressing more tightly against hers, his breaths coming faster. She felt his emotion, usually free like a wild river, being kept in check...

She almost stopped when the revelation flitted through her mind. Somehow, he knew she'd been hurt. He didn't know details; no one did. But he knew something had happened. And he was holding back.

The mighty Wolf was holding back. For her. Because he loved her.

And somehow, this night, she loved him more than she ever had before.

She broke away, put her forehead against his chest. His heart was beating fast, faster than usual. Because of her.

"I love you RavnWolf. I love you."

His arms enveloped her, holding her as tight as he dared. She nestled close, the crown of her head in the crook of his arm. For several moments they just stayed that way, content to be in each other's presence.

And for those moments, she was happy.

Finally, they walked back to the celebration. No one was outside, everyone having retreated indoors for the promised feast Shaladrea was hosting. As they neared, they disengaged their hands. Vivien felt a brief moment of loss before looking up to see him watching her. He said something, his lips moving without sound. *I am here.* Then they walked through the entry.

"Vivien! Wolf! We have been waiting for you!" Shaladrea's voice chimed.

Though Ravn stood tall against the onslaught of eyes, Vivien's heart sank as she found most of the room looking in their direction. The Lady took note of this mistake on her part, but continued on and embraced both her and Ravn. Vivien looked out upon those gathered. Nearest her was the Grand Magister, regarding her with an inscrutable expression, and beside him the Lord of Swords, who glanced at Shaladrea with a look of incredulity. Swansee was there, with the rest of the Council, as well as members of the Mage Elite. Lydia sat at the nearest table, a knowing look in her blue eyes.

Then there was a gruff voice at her side. "Vivien, where have you been?" Torialvah took her hand and pulled her towards him, his gaze coldly taking in the Wolf. Ice swept through her veins at the feel of his touch, and when he kissed her, just like he did in council, she shuddered.

Shaladrea's musical voice shattered the encroaching darkness. "The meal is ready to be served. Come, please sit. Vivien, your father is over here with me, and Wolf, the Lord of Swords is right across." Vivien felt Tor's hand tighten around hers at the sound of the Wolf's name. *He knows we have something together. It's only a matter of time before he questions me. I've done nothing wrong, never taken him inside of me, but Tor will berate me for what little we have done even though society doesn't prohibit it.*

The meal went by without incident, only that Tor kept his hand on her the entire time, showing her, and anyone else, to whom she belonged. She knew the Wolf noticed, for his eyes were the color of strong red wine and flashed with bright sparks when Tor held on too hard. The food smelled and looked delicious, but she didn't bother eating. With her stomach in so many knots, she would just lose it all later, somewhere in the bushes for some poor grounds-keeper to find the next day. But she listened to the music being played, and to the surrounding conversations even if she didn't join them herself. She loved hearing her father's voice, and Xadrian's. She remembered them the most from her girlhood. Shaladrea glanced at her a time or two, a crease of worry furrowing her brow, but didn't say anything. To make her feel better, Vivien finally took a roll and slathered it with butter, biting at it every now and then.

Finally, the meal was over and many of the guests moved back outside. Torialvah was engulfed in a conversation with another Lord, and Vivien was left to herself. She reveled in the time away and escaped to where the dancing was beginning to take place. She moved among the crowd, smiling and nodding to all who greeted her. Members of the La'athai were there, many of them with their partners. Even Allain, though still bandaged from the battle, stood with his husband in the corner and waved bravely despite his injuries. The Elders had brought their families, and high-elvin men and women stood together, listening to the music play. Vivien stood there too, out of sight unless Tor went searching for her there. She felt the baby move inside and a wave of guilt suffused her. Tor hadn't hurt her, not really. What had happened this morning had just been rough, dominating sex. He'd wanted her, and she was his wife. It was their responsibility to give in to one another's needs, as long as they were physically able.

Vivien blinked away tears that threatened. *This is the way it is with everyone, yes? Then why does it seem somehow wrong? Why am I so...*

"Lady Valdera?"

She spun around at the masculine voice and found herself looking up into the handsome face of a man she'd never met before. His clothing was tightly bound to him, but flared at the edges. His blonde hair, too, was pulled tight to his head, but splayed into free strands from his ponytail. His eyes were an unrelieved brown, but sparkled to be almost amber deep inside, hinting at constant thoughts that worked in his mind. His long, thin ears marked him as not quite a pure, but a high-blood elf and of very lofty station. Even though his voice sounded very little like her husband's, a feeling of relief washed through her. "Yes?"

He smiled and his brown eyes lit with warmth. "I knew it was you even from across the room. My name is Marcán."

Taken in by his geniality, she couldn't help smiling and returning the banter. "And how did you know it to be me?"

His cheeks flushed and he lowered his eyes for a moment before bringing them back up to hers. "Because of how beautiful you are. They told me, but I didn't believe it until I saw it for myself."

Vivien just stood there, a wave of heat passing over her own cheeks. For a moment she wanted to believe him, but the next saw her in reality. This man was good, very good, to disarm her so swiftly. "Thank you, my Lord. That is kind of you," she said, taking a step back.

Seeing her reaction, the man closed his eyes tightly shut. "I'm sorry. That was the wrong thing to say. I didn't mean to..." He took a deep breath and averted his eyes. "I just ruined this." He then gave a short bow. "I am sorry to have made you uncomfortable." He gave a sad smile. "Enjoy the rest of your evening."

The man turned and began to walk away. Recognizing the sincerity of his words, she found herself calling out. "Wait. My Lord?"

He stopped and looked back. "Yes?"

"What is it you wanted to say? When you came over?"

He smiled and shook his head, looking abashed. "I was going to ask you to dance with me." He looked over at those who were already doing so, and she followed his gaze. The couples looked content, happy. She remembered a time, many years ago, when she was happy to dance too. "Lady Valdera?"

She looked back to see he was standing beside her again, his hand held out to her. "Would you care to share one with me? A dance?"

She hesitated, but then recalled the promise she had made to the Lady. She hated to go back on her oaths. Fighting the whispering voices of inadequacy, she accepted his hand. "Thank you, my Lord. I would love to."

Just as they moved to join the other couples, the song ended and another one began. It had been a while since the last time she'd danced, but the movements came easily. Marcán was good, and he had a flare for the dramatic. She easily indulged him, apparently having one of her own, and by the end of the song they were chuckling beneath their breaths and waiting for the next song. The world came to a stop, and as they stood there, hand in hand, so did reality. She forgot her burdens, left them behind as the next song started. Marcán led them into the next dance and she easily accompanied him, step for step, beat for beat. It was liberating to let go, to enjoy the moment. The fact that he was so good at helping her accomplish it was extraordinary.

However, when the music stopped this time, there was someone standing beside them. It was Gregor, one of the La'athai. Marcán graciously stepped aside as Gregor took his place. Vivien raised a brow, but allowed him to lead her in the next dance. He was good, better than she thought he might be, and it told her a bit more about who he was. They laughed together as they moved to the music, and happiness swelled within her.

The song ended and there was another man to take Gregor's place, and after that, another. And then, just as she started to get tired, the song ended, and she found the Wolf standing there. He bowed low and took her hand, his eyes looking up at her almost mischievously.

Drunk on happiness, Vivien chuckled. "You know how to dance?"

He raised a thick brow. "You doubt?"

She thought back to a similar conversation they had once had when they were in the cavern system after running from the fire. He'd caught a fish with his bare hands, and she'd told him she thought it was a lucky catch. "I think you might be running out of luck, my friend."

He cocked his head. "I guess we are about to find out."

The song was one of her favorites, not too fast and not too slow. It was a combination of the best of both worlds. Ravn started to move, and right away she could tell it would be different. In no way was this going to be an Elvish dance.

It was one from the Lairdlands.

Vivien called upon all the skill she possessed, a skill she'd perfected over the course of a century, and followed him in a dance she'd never moved to before. As they continued, she noticed that everyone in attendance began to stop and watch. His hands were light where they touched her, and she kept hers the same way. When their bodies touched, it was like they were one for a moment before pulling apart. She followed his steps, kept her eyes locked on his so that he could guide her to the next move. Her heart beat madly, and she could feel his do the same. His blue eyes never left her, flickers like fireflies inside proclaiming his love to her alone. It was beautiful, hauntingly intimate, and more than just a dance. It was like making love. By the time they were finished, all she wanted to do was fall into his arms.

Instead, Tor was there. His hand circled her wrist like a shackle and he pulled her towards him. His voice was low so that only the three of them could hear. "Vivien, I've been looking for you. Funny I would find you here, making yourself so readily available to every man in attendance."

Her heart skipped a beat and whatever joy she felt fell away like a distant dream. "No, I was only dancing. Everyone dances."

Tor's hand tightened around her wrist. "Obviously with everyone but me. I never got the word that you would be here."

She winced in pain. "I...I'm sorry. You are right, I should have told you. But I didn't wish to interrupt–"

"Let her go. You are hurting her."

Vivien looked up at the commanding tone in Ravn's voice. *Oh gods no. Please no.*

Tor's crystal blue eyes blazed white. "And who are you to tell me anything about my wife?"

The Wolf's eyes had become red, with enough light they shone like fresh blood on freshly fallen snow. "I am her friend. And I tell you that you are hurting her. You will let her go."

Vivien barely kept from wincing again as Tor's grip tightened even more, so tight she could feel the bones shift.

"Walk away barbarian." Tor's voice was a warning. "Just walk away."

Huge hands tightened into fists and the knuckles crackled. "No. Let her go, or I will make you."

Torialvah stepped closer to the Wolf, not intimidated in the least by the difference in height. "And you think you can really do that?"

The Wolf shrugged. "It doesn't matter what I think. But it might matter what they think." His eyes shifted to the crowd and there, standing at the periphery, was the Grand Magister. At his side was the Lord of Swords and Truth.

Vivien closed her eyes, wishing all this was just a dream and that she would simply wake up. She could only imagine the backlash she would suffer as a result of this night and regretted allowing the Lady to cajole her into coming. Tor's death grip loosened, and he wrapped an arm around her waist. He leaned forward towards the Wolf, and spoke in barely perceptible words. "You're right, it doesn't matter what you think. All that matters is what I have, and what you never will."

Chapter Eight
Letting Go

RAVN BREATHED. His eyes were closed, keeping him in darkness. He only breathed.

The silence of the place was broken by the sound of birds, but he let them go. Outside, Xadrian's tir-reath growled as she stalked some rodent, bird, or butterfly. He let that go. He heard his own lungs pull in powerful winds, and expel them slowly. The sound of his heart was everywhere, but as a vision of Vivien sprang to his eyes, he knew she was more a part of him than what pumped his blood.

Xadrian's frown was plain in his voice. "Let it go."

Ravn didn't ask how the commander knew. Did not protest. He tried to let it go.

She smiled. She was nude. He made love to her on the floor of a glowing cave.

That was a dream. It never happened.

She cried.

Tor was there, squeezing her so tightly her face was a mask of misery.

His heart beat faster. He could hear it. He could feel it.

Pressure built behind his eyes, hot and painful. The vision disintegrated into a field of red. His eyes were glowing, radiating the glow of rage from his deepest parts through his eyes.

"Let it go, Wolf."

But she was struggling. Tor was laughing.

You must do nothing, Wolf. Nothing.

You were never good enough.

He was falling.

The pressure built higher, and higher. His heart started to stutter, beat like his ribcage was being pummeled open by giant fists. His hands, far away in his body and placed on his knees, began to tremble. More real by far was something in his soul that struggled against him. It slithered and yanked at the chains of his will. It roared.

The Wolf jerked back as if burned, falling to his back and quivering there for a moment. Everything stung, everything hurt, and he struggled to pack all his tears in his mind into the little locked chests where he kept them from destroying his sanity. He gulped in air as if he had never been able to breathe in his whole life. He was soaked with sweat; it dripped down his face and into his beard, coated his back, and grabbed the simple shift to stick to his skin like clammy, dead flesh. Finally his heart slowed, the red haze left his eyes, and he turned over on the floor and looked to where Xadrian knelt as serene as a mountain pool.

The elvin commander frowned. "I wish you would go to one of the priests. They are better at teaching serenity than I am."

Already the visions were fading, like daggers held in cloaked hands, leaving only bleeding wounds behind. The Wolf frowned and shook his head, droplets of perspiration leaping from his hair. "You said you would teach me."

Xadrian's frown deepened. "I remember exactly the promise that was made on the practice field, brother." He took a deep breath, his next words not so edged. "I said you would teach the Elvish people aggression, and in exchange *we* would teach you peace. Not I. I am a commander, not a teacher. I can instruct you in weaponless combat, and you have done well. You will never excel until you can find stillness inside you. I am not the best for this, there are others who are far more skilled."

The Wolf began to pick himself up off the floor, stretching muscles that felt like he had run for days. "Maybe I am too damaged to repair."

Xadrian's expression became almost pitying. "You are alive. Living things can heal, Wolf."

Just for an instant, Ravn felt he was falling again, and he wavered on his feet. He thought of Vivien and snapped back to where he was. "Vivien needs to be healed. Why do not the priests help her?"

Xadrian stood. They were both wearing the simple shifts used in Elthari Sath'hara, Elvish hand-to-hand fighting, during both practice and meditation. His was pure white, with militarily clean lines, and devoid of wrinkles. He stood straight, as if the accusation had simply bounced off his armor of certainty. "For the same reason. Neither of you have *asked*." Ravn stood there, bitterly considering his friend. "Do not be a child, Wolf. You have no idea what kind of chains and expectations she has to live with, because you have never bothered to find out. Go, put on clothes and go see the priest if you want to be what she needs you to be."

The Wolf frowned and left the sparse, plain, hardwood floored room that served to practice Elvish hand-fighting. It was far different than the uneven dirt and grass of the castle courtyard where he had practiced combat in his youth. The empty walls and lack of any color or coverings seemed to mock the utter chaos inside his mind.

"Go," Xadrian repeated, "clear your head. You will need your wits about you."

The Wolf knew a dismissal when he heard it, and he stomped from the room into Xadrian's manor. He walked to his den, anger escaping in wisps of growls and grunts. He reached his room and threw off the white shift and pants, replacing them with rough-spun shirt, breeches, and boots. Lastly, he strapped on an Elvish steel dagger, thick-bladed and longer than his forearm. In minutes he left the manor. It was the one place in Rithalion that felt like home, carved as it was to look as much like nature inside as out, but it brought no comfort this day. He stood in the woods only a moment to align himself with the city heart, and began maneuvering his way through the tall trees to where he might get clearance to run. A small shock of white stopped him, and he looked down.

It was an animal skull, picked clean by the life of the forest. He saw it, and it gave him pause.

Last winter, Vivien had been very angry with him. She had cast him out of her life for a time. He had run, tried to escape the city and his pain, tried to return to the mindless life where the ghosts of the past could not harry his every waking moment, where love did not make him feel powerless and weak. He had stood here, in the dead of winter, and seen an old wolf. It had died in his arms, too tired to fight, too proud to give up, as age took its last breath.

Am I as strong as you, old man? Am I? I have walked so very far for her already, and she spurns me and burns me though I feel her want for my presence every moment we are together. You and I lost our homes, cast out when we were no longer of use. You chose the wild, a death honorable and stoic. Can I choose differently? Should I? How can I fight for her when she doesn't even remember her own strength?

Ravn's anger winked out as if doused by snow. His shoulders slumped, and even in the summer air, he was cold. He wiped tears from his burgundy eyes and sought wisdom from the old skull lying in the dirt. None came. *Go see the priest if you want to be what she needs you to be, Wolf.*

He frowned, then heard a voice. A sweet symphony of syllables that grew stronger, faster, fiercer. He cast his eyes about him. He turned and saw Jor'aiden, Vivien's father. He was chanting. The Wolf cast him a guarded look as he felt the hairs on the nape of his neck stand up. He held out his hands, empty of weapons. "Grand Magister?"

The supreme spellcaster of Rithalion completed his spell, and black fae launched from the depths of his robe. They hurtled forth like a cloud, tiny fae made of charred oak and the memories of forest fires. The little winged creatures screeched and linked arms as they surrounded the Wolf. They clasped him tightly, whipping around his wrists and lashing them to trees as thick as a man's thigh on either side. The Wolf growled and jerked, but was held firm. The fae pulled more tightly, shortening the chains and dragging his arms to either side. His heart raced, he felt the panicked need to attack, to run, to hide. Something deadly awoke and roared inside of him. He looked to the trees, looked to the fae. Instantly he wanted to crack them, crush them, pull the whole forest down upon the Magister. Then he saw the Magister, saw him past the pain, the surprise, and fear. He saw the parts of him that were Vivien. The elf, as powerful and knowledgeable as he was, smelled of fear.

Ravn closed his eyes and breathed. He tried, tried to let go. His heart slowed, the pressure behind his eyes faded. He accepted the moment, accepted the chains, and accepted the world as it was. He opened his stormy blue eyes. The Grand Magister was just out of reach.

"Hello Laird Ravn Blacach." He said in a menacing tone. "You should be dead a century ago."

The Wolf stood there, arms held high, and said nothing.

The silence needled the Magister and his lips parted to bare his teeth. "I know your secret."

The Wolf waited. He let go.

Forgetting even his own safety, the Magister lunged forward and balled up the Wolf's tunic in his hands, shaking him where he stood. The man's knuckles brushed his chin. "What do you want with my daughter, you monster?"

Monster. Ravn closed his eyes and took another steadying breath. "I am in love with your daughter. I have been for over a hundred years."

The Magister gaped, then struck Ravn with an open palm across his face. "Do not lie to me! You were human! You had to have died! What pact have you made? What unseleighe infest you? What kind of thing are you?"

Ravn felt the sting of his cheek and closed his eyes. He took in air, ignoring the slithering scales of waking anger in his breast. He let the strike go. He let it all go.

His voice was level, calm, but powerful and deep even in his own ears. "I am in love with your daughter."

"You came here as a wild thing, and finally, finally I recognized you! I know who you are and you do not deny it!" The Magister struck him again, and again. "Tell me the truth! Love will not keep you alive!"

Ravn breathed, feeling it circulate through him and carry his wrath away through his mouth. "It is the only thing that will keep one alive, Grand Magister."

Anger blasted from the wizard, and furious fae flitted out of the aether around him to answer his unconscious summons. They were sharp things, frigid things, fiery things. "Forget the damned city. Forget her vacuous husband. What kind of proof could you ever give me that you mean her no harm?"

Ravn stood up straight, the slack on the chains taken up by fae that had no intention of ever letting him go. "When your people placed a curse on her to punish her for saving me, when that curse was going to kill her, I tried to die to set her free." He turned his head to the side.

Jor'aiden glared at him for looking away, then peered closer. Ravn tilted his head more to the side, exposing the fine white scar on his throat that Vivien's husband had helped provide. Torialvah's blade had cleft an artery, but Ravn's blood had broken the curse. He had nearly died.

The Magister paled, stumbling back as the fae of his ire winked out. He fell over a root and flopped down onto the turf. All he could say was, "You..."

"I didn't die. But I thought I would. Everyone thought I would. Perhaps it would have been better for everyone if I had. I don't understand your justice. I don't understand your love. I don't understand your..." He looked to the chains that bound him and then to the Magister, "gratitude."

Though Ravn was still bound, Jor'aiden raised a hand as if to ward him off. "What. Are. You?"

Over the next several minutes, Ravn told him the sordid story. He told the other man everything he knew.

It was enough.

The Magister stood, smoothing dead leaves from his blue robes. He looked upon Ravn with an endless well of pity. "I can believe you are the same man, but you are not human. Not any longer. You can never be with her, and you will only bring her pain."

Ravn stared at him gravely, silent.

"Does she know *who* you are?"

Ravn just nodded.

"How long?"

"Since the battle, when we were in the cavern system. But she had suspicions before that."

The Magister's eyes became unfocused, staring into nothing as he looked at the larger whole. "If my people find out *what* you are, they will kill you."

Ravn shrugged. "Elves are a fickle people."

The Magister made a motion, and the Wolf's bonds flickered into dust, the fae released back to whatever place they went. "Hero or not, Knight Protector or not, they *will* kill you."

"Time has not done it. If your people have to, then let it be."

The magician hesitated. "Dammit, Ravn, you were a good man, like your father before you. You don't deserve this, but it is the reality we must deal with. I won't let you harm her."

A growl forced itself out. "You let her husband do that, already."

Jor'aiden flinched. "She has an oath, a duty…"

"I am not here to hurt her, Magister. I love her. I love her in a way even she does not understand. I have given her my heart, my blood, and if she needs my life, she has only but to ask."

"I see how she looks at you, Ravn!" The elf was nearly an elder, but instead of exuding certainty, he gulped in air like a fish. "Your death at the hand of the elves will destroy her."

Ravn looked down to the skull sitting forlorn in the wild. "Then I will not allow your people to kill me." Then, one foot in front of the other, he walked past the Magister and headed toward the city center.

The wizard called after. "You will only hurt her."

Ravn felt his temper surge, an echoing roar of battle in his breast. When he turned, he knew his eyes were alight enough to make the dark wine color into bright blood. "Then tell your people. Have them come for me. I denied everything I felt for years knowing she was an elf with a duty to marry for her people," he spat in disgust, "and I was a mortal with nothing to offer her but the truest love of my heart." Ravn closed his eyes, breathed, let go. His eyes darkened. "But, in the end, we robbed each other of the time we would have had together, the love we would have shared. I am told I cannot wed her, and I may not bed her. I accept these things. Yet, I prize her above owning her, or belonging to her. I treasure her more than any riches, or any honor you could imagine. I have proven it over and over. I have a chance to be near the woman I love and I am going to be there until she doesn't want me anymore. If death is the price, I will pay it gladly." Ravn paused. "Tell me Magister, your human wife, her mother, what would you ask in payment in order to never have known her? What could you be offered to never know her smell, or hear her voice? Or Vivien's?"

The words he spoke struck the old elf hard. His face became a mask of surprise, crumpling into pain and sorrow. He put a hand to his chest and grabbed a tree for support lest he fall. Jor'aiden shook his head. "Vivien has a duty... to the people."

Ravn frowned. "Well, the people have a duty back to her! And everyone in this city seems to have forgotten it." He started walking again. "She sacrifices for them. They owe her acceptance, if not support. I will do these things, even if they, and you, will not."

Jor'aiden gathered his wits and stood up straight. "What now?"

Ravn stopped, facing away. He gathered his rage into his mind and breathed deeply. As he exhaled, he let it go. A perfect image of Vivien came to the stillness beyond. She was dressed for war, one hand glowing with fae and the other her father's sword– since lost in battle. "You tell her to be someone other than she is. Her husband orders her to be someone other than she is. Society expects her to be someone other than she is." His eyes snapped open and he began to run.

"What will you do Ravn?"

He roared back, over his shoulder, "I will remind her of who she wants to be!"

His legs pumped tirelessly, carrying him away from the Magister, away from Rithalion, away from Vivien, toward what he hoped she truly needed.

Chapter Nine
War Trophy

with shaking hands, Vivien placed the bracelet around her wrist. The sunset tanager at the center stared up at her from an onyx eye, almost as though he could see into her quivering soul. She considered removing it, but then thought better and let him stay. He was her good luck, after all. And her best childhood friend had fashioned him for her. How could she leave the tanager behind?

The fact was, she wasn't sure she deserved him.

Vivien moved to pack the rest of the bags she would need for her journey. It would be a long one, but hopefully one that would reap the greatest of reward. Having the other Elvish cities on their side for the upcoming war would be a boon, and if she could help sway them to Rithalion's cause, they just might have a chance. If only... if only this trip wasn't a double-edged blade, and she wasn't using it as an excuse to escape.

Silent tears streaked down her face. She was a decorated warmage, best in her class, chosen by the Lady of Moonlight and Love to be in her service. Yet, she was a coward. What would that mean when she was once again in the midst of battle? Her soldiers and mages would not be able to depend on her. The Wolf, so fearsome and brave, would not be able to depend on her. And already he had abandoned her. He had judged her unworthy and fled the city. None knew where he was, not even the Lord of Swords. She was weak and he knew it. What had happened to her between that battle with the Iron Army and now?

Torialvah. You discovered you are carrying his child, and that there is really no escape from him.

Vivien shook her head smartly and wiped the tears from her eyes, speaking into the silence of the room. "I will find escape where I can, when I can. And then I will have this child. I will care for the boy as any mother would, but I will not love him."

The admission drained her, leaving her chest echoing with emptiness.

A knock on her door made her look up, and her heart galloped in her chest. Sherika growled and leapt off the bed, went to the door and sniffed. Only when the cat relaxed did Vivien do the same, wiping her eyes one last time. "Enter."

The door opened and Mikarvan sauntered into the room. She returned to shoving things into her pack, unwilling to face the censure he might have in store for her. Regardless, she far preferred him over the alternative. Tor had visited her almost nightly since the morning of the celebration. Quite truthfully, she was hurt and tired, and the thought of him made her cringe. Mika was merely an inconvenience.

Mikarvan stopped to stand a few feet away, simply watching her as she went from her bureau to her dresser, and then back again when she realized she'd forgotten something. She then shoved it all, unceremoniously, into her pack. He put his hands on his hips and lowered his head, saying nothing.

Finally, she looked up. She felt raw, beaten. Her voice was harsher than she meant it to be. "What do you want Mikarvan?"

He slowly approached her, his eyes taking her in. She couldn't help remembering the last time she had left on a mission. He had been there, and the suppressed emotions of youth had bubbled up between them. She could not be that vulnerable to him now. She went about adjusting things in the pack, hoping to bring her notebook. She wanted to document all the important people she met and their influence on society. It might be important for future endeavors. He reached out, and when he touched her, her flesh rippled like she'd been stung and she jumped back.

Mikarvan dropped his hand and embarrassment swept through her. She averted her eyes, pursing her lips to keep from showing her dismay. His words were a whisper, "By the gods, what has he done to you?"

Vivien swallowed the sudden, painful lump in her throat, furrowed her brows, and pushed past him to get some things from another bureau. She heard him curse beneath his breath, something about saying something stupid. It was then she realized he might not be there to lecture her, and maybe he had simply come to say goodbye since he wouldn't be seeing her for a long while.

She let the anger drain away, anger that had sustained her since the Wolf had left the fortress, since Torialvah had continued to take her even though she didn't want him to, since her father had shown that he wished for her to stay with a man who loved her only as a status symbol instead of a woman. She let it fall at her feet and she faced Mikarvan without it, hoping, praying he was still her friend.

Sensing the shift in her demeanor, he closed the distance between them and ardently embraced her. His voice was thick with emotion, muffled by her hair. "It doesn't matter. I am here for you Vivien. I may get angry with you, but I will never leave you. I will never forsake you. My love will never subside. Ever."

A rush of emotion swept through her, first and foremost, relief, quickly followed by love. She pulled back, placed her hands alongside his face, and pressed her lips to his. She could feel his surprise, his happiness, his love roaring in his soul. After a moment she made to pull back, but he hung onto her like he never wanted to let her go, his eyes squeezed tightly shut. So, she just stood there and let him hold her. Sherika rubbed against their sides, her purr a rumble that shook their entire bodies. Finally Mikarvan released her, pulling one of her hands to his chest and laying it there. He caressed the sunset tanager around her wrist and his lips curved into a smile.

"You still wear it."

She breathed past the ache in her chest as she replied. "Of course I do. He is my good luck."

He shook his head. "You really believe that?"

Surprised, she looked into his face. "Don't you?"

He shrugged. "I don't know. It's doesn't matter what I think. What matters is what you think, and that you believe in him."

She nodded. "I do."

He smiled, not just any smile, but the smile of a man who felt he'd made a difference in the world. "I made him. That means you believe in me."

She nodded again. "I do."

He suddenly wrapped his hand around the wrist with the bracelet and tightened it. "Then I am with you always."

She smiled and traced her fingers over his face. "I already knew that."

He just stood there and blinked. He then nodded to himself and lifted the full travel pack. He shook his head and grimaced. "This is heavy."

She smiled sweetly. "No heavier than the packs we traveled with to the Doomed City." She suppressed a shudder and took it from his hands, positioning it over her shoulders.

"But you aren't going to war, Vivien. Why are you carrying it?"

She laughed. "I'm not silly. It's what the pack moose are for."

Abashed, he lowered his head and bit at his lower lip, smiling and shaking his head. "You..." He let his voice trail off.

She had begun walking towards the door. "I what?" She raised a brow.

"You always make me think. You are my equal in everything."

She simply smiled. "Come, I have to go."

Something came to his mind. "Wait. I have something for you." He dug around in the pockets within his robes and withdrew a couple pouches. "The red one is filled with the raspberry leaves that help you so much. The blue one is..." He stopped and looked up at her, his expression one of fear.

She walked back to stand before him and wrapped her hand around the one holding the pouch. "What?"

"It's black fennelberry."

"What is it for?"

He gave a heavy swallow. "If you think you are in labor, and the baby seems too early, or if you need to make it back in time to me, drink it. Drink it every four hours to keep the labor from progressing."

She nodded and took the pouch.

"But you can only use it for three days! Beyond that, and you will be putting yourself and the baby at risk."

She nodded. "I will remember."

She turned away, and just as she made it to the door, his voice stopped her. "Vivien, I love you."

She spoke without turning back. "I know. I love you too, Mika."

She swept a hand over Sherika's back and walked out the door. She quickly headed down the stairs and into the fortress proper before making her way towards the gate. The last time she'd had the walk, there were people lining the corridor to see her out on a mission that no one thought she would return from. Now it was empty but for the household staff.

Vivien walked out into the bailey. The rest of the retinue was waiting. There were two moose being laden with travel packs and bedrolls. The two scouts were there with their tir-reath, as well as the men who would be acting as guards for the mission: Gregor, another one of the La'athai called Rohan, three men, and a woman she'd never met before. That left her and the Wolf. But she saw another man standing beside the moose, giving orders to have things placed in a certain fashion. He had his back to her, and he wore a red sleeveless vest trimmed in black.

"No, I need that space free so that she can access her packs without hindrance. Yes, there is good."

Vivien frowned as she approached and tapped him on the shoulder. Any biting words were stricken from her mind as she took in his face. "Lord Marcán, what are you doing here?"

He smiled, brown eyes glittering. "Lady Valdera, I am your ambassador. I thought they had told you I would be accompanying you on your mission."

Disappointment surged through her and she shook her head. "N... no..."

"Here, let me take that heavy pack from you." Marcán cringed with the weight, flipping the free end of his tightly restrained blond hair from his shoulder. "Yes, let's put that on the moose, shall we?" He nodded at the man who took it from him. "Yes, let's put it right here with the others."

Vivien put a hand on her hip and cocked her head to the side as she took in the distracted man. "Tell me again who said you should..."

She suddenly felt a hand on her shoulder. "Daughter! It is good to see you have finally arrived. The wagon is almost packed and everyone ready to see you off."

She twisted around to look at the Grand Magister. As always as of recent, his gaze was hooded. She responded in kind and slammed up her barriers. Her father had made his stance on some things very clear over the past several days, and it hurt to know that he would rather she remain with her husband than go the path less traveled and break away from societal norm. "Indeed, Magister, but who is this young lord in our midst?" She indicated towards Marcán.

The Magister seemed sad for a moment, but recovered before she could really determine if the emotion was really there. "He is the son of Elder Killian, Lord Marcán. He will be the one who speaks on behalf of Rithalion."

Vivien frowned. "Magister, excuse my ignorance, but I thought I was going to be doing the speaking. In truth, why am I even going on this mission? Why is the Wolf going?"

"Now Vivien, this was discussed..."

She shook her head. "If there was a discussion, I wasn't privy to it. Why am I going?"

The Magister pressed his lips into a thin line. "You and the Wolf won the war. People will be more likely to help us if we send our most highly decorated heroes to their cities."

Vivien stepped back as though she'd been slapped. She even pressed a hand to her face and kept it there as she turned in place so that her father couldn't see the war of emotions she was sure struggled for dominance over her features. *By the gods, I'm not a trophy just to Torialvah.*

A terrible ache arced through her and she almost doubled over with the agony of it, so much she could hardly breathe. But then she was wiping all that away on her forearm, taking a deep breath and standing tall. She turned back to Jor'aiden and gave him a solemn bow. "Of course, Magister. My life is pledged to Rithalion and her people, always."

Behind the Magister, another man finally arrived. The Wolf looked towards the scene with a frown and her gaze was momentarily drawn to him. He was disheveled, again, as if he had spent weeks on the road already. His chest plate, axe, and shield were immaculate, but every other item of clothing was spattered with ground-in dirt. His packs showed signs of being thrown together, the only neat item being a meticulously wrapped package that was obviously some kind of sword, probably purchased as a status symbol for this mission. She had thought him above such vanity. *A fine ambassador*, she thought grimly. It was good to know the party hadn't just been waiting on her. She flicked her gaze away from him and back to the man who'd shown her just what she meant to the city. The Magister's expression looked much the way she felt, but she didn't bother considering it as she turned to leave him standing there.

Vivien saw to the packing of the moose, then to the well-being of the reindeer as the rest of the entourage said their goodbyes. Lydia came to offer a frail embrace, and the Lady a kiss. "I wish for your safe return my dear," she said.

Vivien waited for a man she knew would not come. She and Tor had fought about her leaving the night before, and his anger had never known such bounds. In truth, she'd wondered if he would actually strike her this time instead of just making the motions like he might. He'd left her in a flurry of ice and steel, just like his namesake, and her dreams had been those borne from memories of the past two weeks since she'd been home, dreams that left her crying in her bed sheets, begging for him to stop. The Wolf hovered nearby, waiting to show her his new bundled sword, as if she cared since he had not stayed by her side in her darkest hours. Sherika was the only one who had been there to comfort her, and Vivien was leaving her behind...

She suddenly felt overwhelmed and it was difficult to breathe. She needed Sherika. She couldn't leave without her! She shot from beside the moose and into the fortress. No one stopped her. Vivien's mind called out for her friend as she ran through the main hall and then down the side corridors that led to her tower. She vaulted up the stairs, ignoring the pain in her sides as she took them two at a time. And then, as she opened the door...

Sherika was sitting there in the middle of the floor, waiting for her.

Vivien wrapped her arms around her companion and held her tight. The animal made a tiny squeak but didn't move. Then, when all was right again, she grabbed her riding gear and they walked down the stairs together.

By the time they reached the bailey, the small retinue was ready to move out. Vivien quickly harnessed Sherika and then mounted her. The animal seemed to relax once she was there, and Vivien felt the same. She startled when the Grand Magister was suddenly there. He grabbed onto the saddle with a steel grip and looked up at Vivien. "I would like to w..."

She interrupted in a low voice, her expression deadpan. "Don't worry Father. Your trophies will be home before you know it."

With a mental command that brooked no argument, Sherika broke free of the Magister's grip. At her approach, Gregor shouted, "All out!"

The scouts leapt forward and Rohan, the Wolf, and the other four guards urged their own mounts to follow. The entourage clattered out of the bailey and down the road. Vivien chanced one glance back.

The Magister stood there, shoulders slumped, a forlorn expression on his aging face.

Chapter Ten
Isolation

The fear fell away as they left Rithalion behind; the further they moved, the stronger she began to feel. The icy sensation of Torialvah's grip on her soul began to lessen, and a sense of freedom overcame her. Vivien took a deep breath of the early evening air, luxuriated in the feeling of being herself once again without the strictures society liked to impose.

Vivien lay over Sherika's back. The tir-reath's long legs ate up the miles, the muscles bunching and relaxing beneath her in a soothing rhythm that urged her body into a state of repose. Sherika was fast, much faster than the pack moose, so activity had come in spurts as they leapt ahead only so far before stopping to wait until the rest of the entourage caught up. During those times Vivien would dismount, and she and Sherika would laze around, catch some moments of sleep together before bounding ahead again. A couple of times it had not been the full retinue, but the Wolf on his lathered mount who arrived before the others. She'd jumped on Sherika's back and left him in the dust. He had swiftly gotten the point and now rode sedately with the group and did not try and catch up to her.

Evening strolled in on quiet feet and the retinue stopped to make camp. Vivien was more tired than she liked to admit and she wondered about it as she went to the moose to get her bedroll and other supplies. The other men were there, pulling their own things off the backs of the animals, and when hers were reached, Rohan handed them to her with a smile. Vivien returned the gesture. She turned to walk away and collided into a tall form standing in her way.

"Oooof." She bounced back off the bedroll as it caught the man in the midsection. She looked up to see it was the Wolf. She regarded him intently for a moment as her barriers shot up. He'd left for two weeks with nary a word telling anyone where he was going or for how long. She knew she wasn't his keeper, his wife, or even his mistress to question his whereabouts. So she didn't. She simply accepted that he had left. She'd felt so alone with his desertion. In spite of her friendships and knowing the people who cared most about her were near, she felt abandoned under the duress of Tor's nightly ministrations. To see Ravn standing there before her now only drove those feelings home, and all she wanted was to be away from him, to keep those feelings as far away as possible.

Ravn wrapped his arms around the bedroll. His voice was kind and soft, but she did not believe it was sincere. "You look tired. Let me take that for you."

She tightened her grip. "No, it's alright. I can carry it myself."

He pursed his lips, easily plucking it from her arms and proceeding to carry it across the camp to where Sherika rested. Her eyes burned into his back and she cursed under her breath as she followed. She stood there as he finished laying it out for her, irritation building as Sherika watched, giving a low, shrill growl at the big man. Ravn looked shocked at the reception, and his face fell as if deeply wounded. He finished and retreated without a word.

Meanwhile, Gregor was starting a fire and the scouts and their tir-reath were heading out to try and hunt something for the evening stewpot. Two of the guards were seeing to the reindeer, giving each animal his or her serving of grain before checking to be certain the feet were in good health. It was obvious by the way they spoke to the animals, and patted them, that they cared. It was beautiful to see and Vivien felt her ire melt away.

At that moment she felt peace. She was tired, but in a good way, and she felt blessed to be there sharing this time with these people. She sensed Ravn come to stand beside her and her spirits abruptly fell again. The hurt he had done to her was simply too new, too raw.

"Vivien?" His voice was soft.

She hesitated before answering, not sure she wanted to hear anything he had to say. "Yes?"

"I've missed you." He was carrying that damned bundled sword again, had been all day.

A surge of... something... swept through her. *Dragon's mercy, what is he thinking? What does he expect me to feel? What does he expect me to say?* She didn't look at him, just brushed past him to sit on her bedroll beside Sherika. He just stood there for a moment, saying nothing. His shoulders were slumped and his hands curved into fists. He finally turned and walked away, dropped his unwrapped toy onto his bedroll and left the encampment entirely to do whatever it was he did in the wilderness when no one was looking.

Vivien lay there and continued to watch the goings on of the camp. Her focus shifted in and out and she found herself blinking away sleep a few times. The scouts returned with a deer, easily felled by one of their tir-reath. Quick work was made of the gutted carcass, skinning it and cutting it into pieces to be cooked over the fire. She ran a discrete hand over her belly. The child within was quiet, and she remembered she hadn't eaten anything that day, even before leaving Rithalion. He was most energetic after a meal, and guilt suffused her. She might not love him, but it was her duty to take care of him. She made a mental note to be certain to partake of the evening meal.

"Lady Valdera?" She turned to see Marcán standing at the end of her bedroll. "May I sit?"

She hesitated a moment, not really sure she wanted him there, before she nodded. Marcán seated himself and regarded her intently. To all outward appearances, he seemed calm and self-assured. But she could see beneath his exterior, and uncertainty reigned.

She waited patiently. If nothing else, she could be patient.

"I want to apologize for this morning. I didn't realize you weren't aware that I would be joining you on this mission."

She gave a nod. "Is that why you approached me at the festivities?"

His gaze wavered. "In part, yes. I wanted to meet the woman with whom I would be spending so much of my time."

"Why couldn't you tell me who you were?"

He looked abashed. "I'm sorry. It took enough nerve simply to approach you and tell you my name."

She nodded and looked away. At least he was truthful. She didn't know why, but it hurt to know that the only reason he'd sought her company was because they were fated to be a part of the same diplomatic mission.

"It was unnerving to talk to the woman who had played such a pivotal role in the war, someone who had become a hero to our people."

She lowered her head and scoffed. "Believe me, I am no hero."

He frowned. "How can you say that? I've heard the stories. I know they are true."

She shrugged. "I did what any other warmage would have done in my position."

He leaned forward. "No, I don't agree. You went above and beyond."

She was quiet for a while. Finally she looked back up. "I accept your apology."

He nodded. "Thank you."

Silence rang between them. Then, "Is there anything else you need to say? Anything I can do for you?"

Marcán simply shook his head, his ponytail swishing against his shoulders, his eyes sad. "No, Lady. That is all."

Vivien nodded and watched him leave. She just sat there, looking over the group again, and this time, when her eyes closed, she didn't feel the need to open them again.

Vivien surged into wakefulness, vague dreams clinging to her like sticky spider webs. It was dark, and quiet, and for a moment she didn't know where she was. Her heart thundered in her chest, and she instinctively called on her magic.

For a moment, there was nothing.

She concentrated on it, and only then did the fae come to her beckoning. They danced along her hands and forearms, their light piercing the darkness. Vivien was surrounded by the walls of a tent. The men must have erected it around her as she slept. At her feet lay the dark, shadowy form of Sherika, exhausted and sleeping away the activity from the day.

It wasn't long before the fae began to wink out. Inexplicably, it was an effort to keep them there, so she allowed them to go. Once more plunged into darkness, Vivien ran her hands up and down her arms, remembering the tingling magic, the tiny feet dancing, the wings fluttering against her skin. There had been something different this time, almost forced...

Like the fae hadn't wanted to come.

Vivien lay back down on the bedroll. She idly ran her hands over the small mound of her belly, pondering the magic more deeply. Calling the fae had never required concentration before, not for something so simple, not since she was a young girl. Thinking back on it, she hadn't cast magic since being in the cavern system with Ravn after the battle. She frowned, for oftentimes, the magic just came to her, whether she called it or not, and to finally realize that it hadn't been, after so many weeks, was disturbing.

Disturbing not only that it hadn't been coming to her, but because she hadn't noticed its absence.

Vivien called the light fae again, grimacing at the effort it took, berating herself for not noticing it before, and wondering what had happened to her. Her power had been so great during the battle and the days leading up to it. She had never before managed to cast at that magnitude, to create life from nothing but the presence of nature fae, and to use it as a means of destruction...

Maybe that was it. Maybe the gods were punishing her for misusing her magic. Only, none of the Elders had berated her for it, not even her father, the Grand Magister, who ruled over all things arcane in the city of Rithalion.

Perhaps the fae had seen her cowardice and had judged her unworthy as well.

Tears gathered at the corners of her eyes and trickled down her temples to wet her hair. Once more the fae winked out. She felt so cold, so alone. Those feelings knocked against her mental reserve, battered against her sense of worth. But then she felt a movement deep inside, followed by another, and another. The presence of the small boy growing inside was suddenly there with her, a tiny beacon in her nest of darkness. She reached out and embraced it, pulled it close, and held it safe within her arms. Along her soul, she felt tiny hands reach back. They knew nothing of her pain, had no idea she could fail. But they touched her and held her with unconditional love that permeated her in ways she could never describe.

She was a fool. It didn't matter who had sired him. This child was hers. He would be raised and nurtured by her, learn from her, be guided by her. She was a fool, because indeed, he would be loved by her too. Because he was her boy, and no one would take him away.

Or they could die trying.

Chapter Eleven
A Sharp Reminder

The days melted into one another as they traveled. The heat was a constant companion, and in the night, Vivien slept without gown or blankets in the privacy of the tent the men never failed to erect for her. In the evenings everyone would sit around the fire, and a camaraderie had developed. There was one woman among them and she bantered right along with the rest. Vivien had caught her name, Katriona, and every once in a while, she noticed the woman glance at her a time or two. Despite that he was a lord, Marcán fit in rather well and told his stories along with the guards and scouts. The Wolf often remained separate, but sometimes he too would join in though his eyes often drifted to her. Vivien would listen to the talk, and sometimes the drone of their voices would lull her into sleep. Those nights were dream-free; it was the others during which she would awaken in a cold sweat, the feeling of helplessness binding her hands and arms. And the pain...

This night was much like the others. The tir-reath had felled another deer and the group ate well. The remaining meat cooked over the fire so that it could be eaten the following day, and everyone was settling in for rest. The air was sultry and still. Vivien lay on her bedroll, sweat damping her skin in spite of her nudity. She was taking a risk sleeping thusly, but a small one, she hoped. The men, even Ravn, never entered the tent, but in the case of some kind of emergency, they would have to, and her secret... well, it would not be a secret anymore.

Just like every night, she cried. They were silent tears, but Sherika always knew. The tir-reath gave a sweet trill at her feet, a sound meant to offer comfort, and Vivien sensed feelings of love trickle through the link they shared. Vivien clutched at it and held it tight. Her feline companion loved her more than she'd ever been loved before. Ever.

Her mind began to drift. She was so tired at the end of every day, it was enough that she rolled out her bedroll and ate some of her rations or took from the stewpot. She made a cup of raspberry tea every morning and it helped calm her belly as they traveled. The clothing she wore was light and billowy, easily hiding her thin frame and swollen abdomen. The clothes were a gift from the Lady, given with a beautiful letter written with words of love and devotion. She felt blessed to have her and Mikarvan, who seemed to always stand by her even when times were hard.

Vivien suddenly heard a shout, followed swiftly by another. She sat up in the damp darkness, felt Sherika's warning growl rumble from her feet to her chest. The feline then rose and darted to the tent flap. More shouting ensued, followed by cursing and the sound of swords being drawn from their sheaths. Strange jibbering noises she'd never heard before reached her ears, and she rose from the pallet. A sense of trepidation overwhelmed her, for her primary weapon was no longer at its best. *Oh gods...*

ROSS ÊROSS

Sherika's growl deepened before she leapt out of the tent, claws digging runnels in the ground. With wide eyes, Vivien just stood there for a moment. The animal had never been one to show much aggression before, or to go and attack something. But by the ensuing sounds outside the tent, that was precisely what was happening.

Vivien rushed to the flap and opened it. There, highlighted by the light of the fire, were multitudes of small, dark-skinned creatures hardly taller than her knees. Their legs were long, as were their arms, and their squat bodies had a sparse covering of coarse hair. Many ran amok throughout the encampment, while others were busy attacking the men. Sherika had one by the throat, but shrieked when another leapt onto her haunches and gouged her with thick, sharp claws at the end of three fingered hands. Vivien recoiled at the sight of its face: a mouth filled with razor-sharp teeth, slits for nostrils, and not only one, but four eerie sets of eyes that reflected the light from the fire. *By the gods, are these the dukovus I've heard about? They are creepier than I thought they would be!*

Vivien strode forward, and with her bare hands, she lifted the fell creature from Sherika's back. The thing jibbered menacingly, and without warning, sunk its teeth into the soft flesh of her forearm. She bit back the scream that threatened, but Sherika, instantly knowing what had happened, lunged for the beast. She ripped it away from Vivien with her teeth, savagely shaking it until it was limp in her maw.

Vivien clutched at her arm, felt the poison as it slowly began to work through the limb. *Oh, gods no, please no. The baby! The poison could reach my baby.* She sank to her knees, fear coursing through her like a wild river. *I can't lose him again! I can't lose him.* She placed her mouth on the bloody wound, sucked at the two largest puncture wounds, sucked as hard as she could. She tasted the foulness left by the dukovus, turned her head and spat it out onto the ground beside her.

Meanwhile, the rest of the company continued to fight. The guards used their swords, daggers, and whatever else at their disposal. The Wolf was growling mercilessly, eyes glowing red like coals as his axe spun and sheared dukovus after dukovus into pieces. Gregor took a branch from the fire and stabbed it into the side of the one nearest him; the shrill cry of the thing pierced the night over all other sounds. Sherika dropped the dead body and went back to Vivien. The feline licked at the wound on her arm with her rough tongue, and Vivien had to push her away, unwilling to have her best friend fall ill from the poison. Vivien sucked again, spat, and sucked again. But it was to no avail. The arm had become paralyzed and she could no longer hold it up. She could feel it creeping up to her shoulder, and from there it would go to her chest...

Anger.

Anger surged through her and the sounds of battle sank into the background. She concentrated on her magic, called the fae to her aid. It was a strong call, one borne of desperation. She remembered the rally from the fight against the Iron Army, but it was not to be. The fae that came were sluggish, their numbers paltry at best. Tears stung behind her eyes as she called again, and again.

And then her call shifted. It was a call filled with darkness, anger, and hate. It filled her up and spread out from her like a malevolent wave.

The fae answered. Only, it wasn't the fae of light and life.

Vivien rose to her feet. Sherika remained close to the ground, looking up at her lady from bright gold eyes that shone like beacons in the darkness. The warmage raised her good arm, and the dark fae gathered like flies to a lantern. The unseleighe circled her hand first, then her arm, then her torso, shimmering black with red and orange highlights. They were deadly sharp, their bodies sometimes flying too close and slicing into her naked flesh. Tiny rivulets of blood trickled from the wounds, mixing into the sweat coursing over her body.

There was a moment of quiet as everything living sensed the presence of something greater than themselves. The guards turned towards the source, and when they saw her, their eyes widened. She then cast the fae outward. With terrible glee, fae shaped like tiny, obsidian daggers swept towards their targets. They cut into the enemy, piercing their dark flesh without hesitation, without regret, without care. Screams filled the air– shrill, gibbering screams that made her toes curl and her spine tingle.

The metallic tang of freshly spilled blood permeated the area and within moments they began to fall. Dukovus from all around toppled to the ground. They looked like lumps of meat that had been placed through the butcher's grinder, their bodies shredded nearly beyond recognition. Vivien lowered her arm, ending her siren's call. It wasn't long before the terrifying fae were gone, and silence reigned.

The guards stared at her, varying expressions on their faces, faces covered with the blood of their opponents. Her gaze focused on Ravn, his broad, muscular chest heaving with exertion. The expression on his face registered fear, concern, and...

Her heart stuttered.

Vivien fell once more to her knees. It was suddenly hard to breathe. She felt the clawing numbness in her chest and the insidious grip of the poison wanted to take her down into the...

Her heart stuttered again. She didn't feel herself hit the ground.

She ran. Dark stone hallways looked like they stretched for miles. It hurt to breathe, but Vivien kept running, fear coursing through her in waves. He needed her. She should have been there, and now she wouldn't reach him in time.

The corridor stretched on and on, endlessly draped in shadows. She wanted to run faster, but somehow, she'd begun to slow. No matter what she did, her legs simply refused to move the way she knew they should. Her chest ached and it no longer just hurt to breathe, it was difficult. Panic surged through her. She needed to get to him!

Finally, she saw an end to the corridor. It was a chamber. Bright sunlight spilled out the half-opened door and lit the darkness of the hallway. She struggled to keep moving in spite of the pain, in spite of the heaviness, in spite of the breathlessness.

And then she was there. She collapsed at the door, pushing it open as she fell to her knees. She squinted her eyes against the light, a light that wasn't from the sun like she had thought, for there were no windows.

His small body lay on the floor in the center of the room. Chestnut hair framed a beautiful face devoid of the flush of life. If his eyes were open, she knew they would be green. She screamed but she didn't hear the sound of her cry. She was much, much too late; he was gone.

The agony of loss seared through her veins. She wanted to move towards him, but her body was no longer under her command. She tried to inhale, but she could no longer take a breath. The pain was excruciating, but all she could see was the boy that she loved so much lying so small and still...

But then there was the light. It moved towards her, becoming brighter and brighter. She tore her eyes away from the boy, and the sight that met her gaze made her heart stop in her chest.

It was a young girl. She was the most beautiful child she'd ever seen. Curly blonde hair tumbled around her shoulders and her eyes were the color of storm clouds before a rain. Light surrounded her like a halo, so bright that the edges of her hair looked like they were on fire.

The girl moved away from the boy and approached. Her expression was the epitome of solemnity, but in her eyes shone fierce determination. She moved closer, closer. Vivien's eyes watered from the intensity of the light, and she began to feel the heat of it.

The girl knelt beside her. She was like an angel borne of fire, so beautiful, so intense. She leaned forward, raising a hand towards Vivien. She just watched as it came closer, closer, closer... and when the girl finally lay her small palm over Vivien's chest, a pulse swept through her like an electric shock.

She screamed again...

Vivien swam in darkness. It was difficult to move, like she was in a quagmire, but it was warm, and she wasn't necessarily in any rush to get anywhere. Time was her companion and so she floated. Slowly, it became easier to move. She ascended, slowly, slowly...

Vivien felt a warm rumbling on her chest, a rumbling so deep it felt like it massaged her heart. Her HEART.

Her eyes flew open and she found herself lying on a padded pallet. Sherika's head and chest lay over hers. Sunlight filtered in through the break around the tent flap, bright and shining, and the sound of men talking floated in on the midday air. The tir-reath was heavy and she shifted. An answering trill could be heard, and black ears cocked back, listening for the sound of her voice. It was a whisper– all she could give. "Sherika, my dearest friend. Was it you who saved me?" She went to raise her uninjured hand. It was heavy, so heavy, but she managed to rest it on Sherika's soft face. She just lay there, caressing the fur, listening to the gentle purr. She thought of how she'd almost left the big cat behind in Rithalion and guilt suffused her. "I'll never leave you again. You are a part of me."

Vivien closed her eyes and drifted.

When next she awakened it was early evening; there were shadows in the tent. Sherika was still there, rumbling away, keeping her from drifting too far. There was someone else there as well. One of the guards took a poultice off her arm, replacing it with another. It smelled medicinal and the arm tingled and itched like she had slept on it for days on end. "How does a soldier know so much about remedies?"

The man startled but quickly composed himself. "I come from a family of healers."

Vivien narrowed her eyes. "What is your name again?"

"Quentin, my lady."

A small fire caught on a suspicion in her head and sizzled. "Did Mikarvan send you?"

The man's face fell. "Yes."

She reached up and grabbed the neckline of his tunic, the act weak and clumsy. "Why am I still alive?" she hissed.

His eyes widened. "Jashi, I don't know. Certainly, you were dying. It was easy for all of us to see. The Wolf– he was beside himself. He breathed for you. Then you grew cold and your cat..." His fingers shook as he pointed to Sherika. "...your cat lay right where she is now. Her purring could be heard outside the tent."

Vivien released the man, only then realizing the heaviness in her limbs was gone. She put a hand to her belly beneath the thin sheet covering her. His eyes followed the movement. "If Mika sent you, then you knew about this already."

He nodded. "Yes Jashi."

"She swallowed heavily. "Now everyone knows."

"Yes."

She just lay there for several moments, allowing this reality to sink in. *What would they say? What would they DO?* She wanted to ask Quentin what he had heard the guards talking about, but she dared not show him her insecurity.

"Lady Mage Protector, I don't know why you are alive. For all intents and purposes, you should be dead right now. I can only assume that the methods the Wolf used to save your life... worked."

"What did he do?"

"When you stopped breathing, he breathed for you. He blew air into you when you could not for yourself. For an hour or more. And when you heart stopped beating..." He glanced at Sherika. She stared at him through golden eyes. "Your tir-reath– she pushed past him and lay over you, put her head on your chest. Her growling... well, purring, became loud. It was like she was trying to keep you alive."

Vivien was pensive. "But you don't really believe any of those things saved me." It was a statement, not a question, and she regarded him solemnly.

He slowly shook his head. "No, not from a poison such as this."

She nodded and looked away, feeling strangely vulnerable.

Quentin reached out, hesitated before finally laying a gentle hand on her shoulder. He shook his head. "I wish I could help you more, but I am just as baffled as you are, maybe even more so. Right now, we should be planning your funeral."

She swallowed heavily and he rose from her side. "The guards are anxious to see you."

She nodded, shrugging away her fears for another time. "Go ahead and let them in."

Quentin helped her sit up, then aided her in donning a light robe. He looked down at her, his brows furrowed in thought. "I am going to think upon this my lady. I WILL find the answers we seek."

She nodded. "Thank you."

He turned and left the tent. It wasn't long before she received her first visitor. She wasn't surprised it was Ravn. He looked down at her, lying there in the bed, and knelt beside her. He took her hand and his eyes fell to the floor. He sat there, breathing deeply like a bellows. Several minutes passed with no words until the silence became too heavy even for him. "I thought I had lost you."

Vivien heard the pain in his voice. The agony. "I... I'm sorry."

His eyes narrowed as if facing a light far too bright. "Why?"

"Because I never want to hurt you."

He gave a bittersweet smile. "Why didn't you tell me about the pregnancy?"

Her breath hitched in her throat. She'd known it would come to this, and she didn't know what to say except, "I was afraid."

His pained expression returned. "Why?"

"Because I was afraid you would want to make me stay home."

He shook his head. "When have I ever tried to make you do something you don't want to do?"

She swallowed heavily. *He is right. When has he?*

Ravn leaned towards her, his breath washing over her face. "I do not own you, Vivien," he whispered.

"But... you are always so adamant about some things. Like when you wanted to save me from the punishment of the Council, and later when you insisted on carrying me back to my tower and I had to beg you not to."

He gazed at her solemnly, then nodded and lowered his eyes. "Yes, there are those things. When you are in danger, I seek to protect you. I always have and I always will. But there was also the time I backed you up when you wanted to go into battle with me. I stood by you when the enemy surged around us and we were both fairly certain we wouldn't survive."

She nodded in concession. "Yes, there was that."

"You don't know what that did to me, knowing that you would be lost to this world, when the thing I want most is for you to be in it."

"Wolf..." the name was plaintive, uncertain.

He winced as though pained. "Yes, Vivien?"

She regarded him intently, took in the planes of his face, handsome beneath the beard, the scars, and the lines of age. She looked at his hair, the crazy curled mass bound at the nape of his neck, and his eyes, colored storm grey and clouded with worry. She was going to tell him about what the healer said, but then thought better of it. He already knew how close she'd come to Death's Gate; he didn't need any more reminders. And he didn't need the added complication that the man didn't know why she was still alive.

She swallowed and ran with the first thing that entered her mind. It came out as an accusation. "You didn't seem to care as much when you left Rithalion for two weeks prior to our trip."

He silently nodded. "It was important."

She frowned, cursing the tears that gathered in her eyes. She trembled before him, and her mind shouted, *What was more important to you than me?*

He saw her pain and his eyes widened. His face became stoic and he nodded in understanding. "You don't understand. Please, I have something for you."

She watched as he rose and left the tent. It wasn't long before he returned. In his arms was that damned sword wrapped in cloth. He laid it down on the bed beside her.

"What is this?"

He nodded. "Open it."

She hesitated briefly before unwrapping the cloth. And when she was through, she was not surprised to see an Elvish sword. When she unsheathed it, she gasped.

The balance was unmistakable, the maker's mark barely visible. Lying there between them was her sword, the one her father had given her, the one she'd lost in battle against the Iron Army.

It had lay for weeks in the open weather, and been buried under soot and ash left by the burned grasses on the plains where they had fought the giant.

Ravn had traveled all that way to retrieve the sword she had discarded out of gravest necessity and brought it to her. Yet, there was more. Some master craftsman had cleaned the blade, scouring the rust and soot from the steel. Such an act may return it to brightness, but it would always bear the scars of abuse.

But Ravn had done more.

She lifted the bright steel and let the light coming in through the tent flap dance across it. The pitted wounds left by the teeth of fire and rain had been redone. Black lines arced across the surface creating birds in flight, the sun, fae, the moon and stars. The edge was as keen as it had ever been, and all the ugliness that war had forced upon it had been turned into beautiful art that went from the new crosspiece to the tip. She felt the secure wire-wrapped leather of the grip and was certain Ravn had done it himself. She had spent hour after hour drilling with the Lord of Swords using this very weapon. It had been a gift from her father when he had truly believed in her and supported her desire to become a shield for her people, a fist to strike their enemies. And now it had been returned to her... by Ravn.

She blinked back tears. "Why?"

He nodded solemnly. "You are my equal, brave and proud. You have told me you have your own battles, and the war you fight against your husband has been more wounding than against those from the Iron Coast. I have feared that you are losing yourself, for I see his cruelty and how much it injures you.

"I could not fight for you, could not even fight with you. My very presence caused him to increase your misery. The only course left to me was to find any way I could to remind you of who you are. You are brave. You are honorable. You are worthy. You are the woman I love. But even more than these things, you are my dearest friend.

"I am so sorry I left. Please believe me when I say I suffered every moment of my absence, and pushed myself to return with this reminder for you as fast as I could. But I thought this was best, and I will always do what I feel is best for you."

Again, she shifted the blade, seeing the birds more clearly as black lines on bright steel. They were sunset tanagers.

Vivien dropped the blade beside her and reached out. Ravn fell over her, wrapping her in large, strong arms that radiated heat like a campfire. She cursed herself, for she felt the sobs begin to rack her body and she felt small and weak. But then she felt him spasm and he was crying with her. Suddenly her sorrow was acceptable... because they shared it together. She spoke in a broken voice, "By the gods Ravn, I thought you had left me."

His arms tightened. "Silly woman, don't you know? Don't you know that you are my heartbeat? You are my driving force, my reason for being. Without you I am this aimless soul forever searching. You are my light in the darkness, my shining star." His voice cracked. "Don't you know?"

DRAGON VESSEL

Her heart soared and she twined her fingers in his thick hair. In all her life, she'd never heard a man speak the words that Ravn said to her. *He makes me feel like I'm a precious thing, a treasure he can't live without.*

It was a long time before she loosened her grip around his neck, and several breaths passed before he reluctantly backed away. She only let him retreat until she could look into his stormy blue eyes and she saw love and respect there. He looked down at the hand she'd put over her belly. He smiled innocently and she moved it so that he could place his much larger hand gently, tenderly, on her distended abdomen. Despite the tears, she laughed, and so did he. Then he kissed her. He kissed her like the world was ending, and unable to quell her thoughts, she realized it just might be. But as long as he was by her side, she dared to believe they might be able to stop it.

Chapter Twelve
A Gift of Understanding

Vivien entered the dark tent, carrying the lantern before her. The flame wavered and danced as she hung it on the peg just inside the flap, and then felt the press of a hard, warm body behind her. Ravn splayed his hands over her distended abdomen as he nuzzled her neck and she inhaled deeply, letting the emotions wash over her. She loved the feel of his hands on her, gentle despite their size, and the sensations they evoked. Sensations that awakened her body to the pleasures she imagined she could feel if she but allowed it.

It was almost painful to move away from him, walking towards her bedroll and the promise of rest. She'd been more tired of late, her brush with death having taken its toll: mind, body and spirit. Much to her dismay, Ravn followed her there and her tension flared anew, tension that stalked her every moment they spent alone together in the confines of her tent, away from the prying eyes of the men without.

She didn't have the heart to resist as Ravn gently pulled her down onto the pallet. He enfolded her in his embrace and his scent enveloped her, a scent that spoke to her of love and safety, strength and courage. She closed her eyes and just inhaled his spicy musk, reveled in the feel of his touch. She slipped her fingers through his thick hair, felt the tight curls spiral around them, and when his lips found the curve of her neck, she shivered with delight.

Oh Ravn, if only you knew how much I want you.

But she couldn't say that. Wouldn't.

Ravn's hands swept along her sides and to her backside, slipping beneath to raise her hips to meet his. The swell of her belly was very little impediment, and he was gentle. He made her feel beautiful and desired even though her waist grew rounder by the week. His lips trailed down her neck to her chest, and they plucked at the fabric covering her breasts. She allowed herself the luxury of his touch just a few moments longer. She knew she shouldn't; it was wrong of her to lead him on so. But she couldn't help wanting him, needing him to love her, to show her what true love was like. Not what Tor had done...

Thoughts of her husband stilled her in Ravn's arms, her eyes widening. *No, I can't do this.* "Ravn, stop," she said breathlessly.

His face rose from between her breasts, his eyes dark with suppressed passion. He traced her lips with his forefinger. "What is it?"

She hesitated. *Gods, how do I speak my fears without causing a rift?* She finally settled on an appropriate deferment. "It's getting late. We should get some rest."

He nodded thoughtfully. "I understand. You are undoubtedly tired."

Ravn shifted onto his back and pulled her close against his side. Vivien lay there for a moment before moving away. "I need to prepare for bed. You should do the same."

He regarded her intently before rising and beginning the process of removing his armor. She watched for a moment, struggling with her next words. After the attack, Ravn had stayed with her in her tent, not wanting to let her out of his sight. This was accepted by the rest of the party, they knowing how much she had come to mean to him and the rest of their people. But as the nights passed, and her strength returned, the guards became restless and uncertain. She'd caught the glances they cast her as they traveled, and she'd heard them talking. All of them but Gregor and Rohan, two veterans of the La'athai.

Vivien rose to stand before him, staying his hand before he could toss his breastplate onto the floor. "Ravn, I think it best if you return to your own tent."

His body stiffened and his eyes clouded. "Vivien, what's going on? Why can't I stay with you?"

Her hands shook, testament of the power of the emotion she suddenly felt in the small tent. She swallowed the dryness that suddenly permeated her throat. "It doesn't look right, us staying the night in the same tent."

His brows furrowed. "We've been sleeping in the same tent for several nights now."

She nodded. "Yes, and the guards have begun to talk at the impropriety."

His gaze became thunderous. "Who's talking? I will end..."

Vivien shook her head. "No! You will end nothing by making threats, only make it worse. The way to end it is to end the reason for it."

He obstinately pursed his lips into a thin line and his eyes had begun to glow red. "I will not be a slave to what others believe is right or wrong!" he growled.

She felt an answering flash in her eyes, and she stood straight before him. "But I will. These are the ways of my people and I will uphold them."

He stepped close, looming over her in all his majesty. Thick muscle bulged beneath the thin fabric of his tunic, tensed as though he were about to go into battle. Stray tendrils of curling hair hung beside his face as he glared down at her, his eyes narrowed. He regarded her intently for another moment, his chest rising and falling with his breaths.

But then he changed. His eyes lost their intensity, and the blue began to peek through. His hands rose, palms up from his sides in supplication. "Vivien, please. All I want to do is be near you, nothing more!"

Oh gods...

He went down to one knee and took her hands in his. "I want to feel you in my arms as we fall into that place we call sleep, hold you close to keep your nightmares at bay. I would champion you!"

Her heart beat a staccato rhythm against her ribs. *How can I tell him nay? Why would I want to?* "Ravn, please..."

His face was falling, pulling at her heart as he nearly begged. "Have me at your side. That is all I ask, nothing more."

Tears threatened and she struggled to blink them away. His eyes, they were twin doorways into his soul. The ache reached out to embrace her the way he did her hands, making her want to rescind her words.

But she simply could not.

"Ravn, I am married! And not only that, pregnant with my husband's child. I should be sharing no one's tent but his, taking succor from no one's body but his. It is simply the way of things." She took her hands from his grasp. "Please Ravn, stop making this so difficult for me!"

He lowered his head and his hands dropped to his sides, clenching into fists. She felt his anger rise again, flaring between them like a living thing, breathing the air from the tent and making it hard for her to inhale. Still kneeling, he looked up at her, his eyes blazing red hot.

"Difficult, for *you*. Thank you for finally telling me my place my Lady." His words were like a slap and she stepped back as though physically hit. Ravn rose, breastplate in hand. "It might have helped to know this earlier, since I have shown over and over again how besotted I am with you to the exclusion of much else. I am sure I appeared foolish. I will be sure to mend my ways as we move forward. Good eve to you."

The first tear fell as he turned abruptly on his heel. "Ravn, wait. I..." There was no time to finish as he swept the flap aside and walked out of the tent. The action caused the lantern to knock loose from the peg and it fell to the ground, plunging the area into darkness.

Vivien slumped down onto the bed pallet, the tears coursing freely down her face. "What have I done?" she whispered. "What have I done?"

She lay back on the bedding, and not bothering to remove her clothes. The tears continued, damping the pillow and causing her to sniffle. *I want to sleep with you too, Ravn. I cherish the feel of you beside me in the darkest hours of the night.*

At the beginning of her marriage to Torialvah, it had taken her weeks to get used to sleeping beside him in bed. It wasn't just the presence of someone there beside her, the sound of their breathing, and the warmth they exuded. Falling asleep in the presence of another showed the epitome of trust. At no other time was a person more vulnerable.

Vivien groaned into the pillow, squeezing her eyes tightly shut. Memories of sleepless nights came back to her, not the nights at the beginning of her marriage, but those just before she left Rithalion on their current mission. Many times, Tor would leave her bed once he'd finished with her, but on the nights he didn't, she would slip out of the bed and wander the hallways. Fatigue dogged her footsteps, but she would not return to her chambers, unwilling to sleep in the same room with a man who had so little care for her body, much less share the same bed with him. She rejoiced the times he left her alone, for in spite of the hurt he inflicted, at least she would get to sleep afterward. Maybe not in the bed, but the sofa was nice, and Sherika would join her there, curling up in front of it as though to protect her...

Her voice wavered. "Sherika?"

"Mrrrow?"

The answering trill was immediate, albeit mayhap a bit sad, and made her breathe a bit easier. When the big cat came to settle beside her, she swept her fingers through the thick, soft fur. Vivien hurriedly stripped off her clothes and when they were all in a heap beside the pallet, she curved an arm around her friend. The big cat purred in contentment and Vivien smiled as she closed her eyes. "I love you, Sherika."

Several moments passed as she began to slip into slumber. Barely a whisper floated on the air, "I love you, Ravn."

They always think themselves silent, but they do not realize that they smell like springtime all year 'round, Ravn thought sourly. *When there is the smell of springtime in summer, winter, or fall, there are elves.*

Yet, this was not the hushed step of a scout, but the tread of one born of the city. It did not quite miss the driest of leaves or the shifting of stones. It may have passed by the ears of many men, but Ravn had wandered the wildest of places for more than a century. He felt the wilderness in his blood, and only the oldest elder scouts were his equal.

Silently, he sunk beneath the churning waters of the stream that ran near the road. He lay at the bottom of the stream, the frothing surface hiding him from the world above. He saw a shadow fall across the waves as he held his breath and sat, unmoving. He had come to be alone. Alone in the only home that was honest about being uncaring of his life and his death. He watched the shadow and he waited, unmoving, conserving his breath. He wondered for an instant if it was guileless Gregor with some word, honest Rohan with some question, or Vivien, seeking...

He crushed all thoughts except one.

Go away!

Minutes passed, and he felt the pressure build. He closed his eyes and tried to let go, was marginally successful, and felt his anger riddled heart slow in his chest even as it became louder in his ears. He could feel the hands of the water's swift passage against him. He gripped the scoured rocks of the bottom of the stream to hold himself in place. The pleasant chill leached the heat from his body. He felt almost normal. Almost human. He opened his eyes.

The shadow was still there.

Go away!

He closed his lids again and wished it away, wished it all to disappear. He scrambled for peace inside his mind and found none. His heartbeat louder and his chest constricted. Bubbles dribbled from his mouth, racing to join the froth at the surface. Louder. Louder his heart beat. The last of his lungful of air escaped. Still he held on, but it was even louder. He remembered the last time his heartbeat was so deafening.

His eyes snapped open and the shadow was gone. There was nothing but the glittering golden light of the late day sun and the endless blue of the unmarred sky above the rippling surface. He immediately let go of the large rock that kept him submerged and flexed his legs, coming to the surface in a roar of water. He gasped in air, shaking his mane of hair and sending water in every direction in long clear fans. Immediately the water grasped at him and sought to push him, but he braced his feet against the rocky bottom and struggled against the current. He pushed locks of chestnut hair from his face and relished the silence, broken only by the flow of the stream– the flow of the stream and the words, "Hello, Knight Protector. I hope for a word."

The Wolf shifted, eyes glowing with the lowest of fires. It was the diplomat, Marcán. He had retreated from the edge of the fast stream and sat on a fallen log, removing his shadow from the surface and waiting with damnable Elvish patience. Ravn frowned and did nothing to hide it. The high elf pretended not to notice, perched delicately on the dead tree as if he had centuries at his disposal. Marcán nodded towards the pile of cloth and leather on the rocky beach. "I thought you might be back from wherever you went."

Ravn considered the tattletale pile, then focused on the diplomat in his tightly bound finery, all tassels and fringe at the edges. They jiggled as he spread his hands helplessly, as if to offer an apology of sorts. Ravn forewent the frown and began to glower.

He looked slightly surprised. "So, it is true. You only ever really speak to *her*."

Vivien. Ravn clenched his jaw and felt the pressure behind his eyes, a nagging pain that let him know his eyes were starting to glow.

Marcán raised his hands in surrender. "I have offended you and I offer my apologies. You are a friend to my people, and have rendered great service to us. For that, I thank you and would offer something in return."

The elf, like most of his kind, was thin and delicate, built like a willow. Ravn felt like a galloping clod just looking at him. His hair was arrow straight and refused to tangle. His skin was pale as ivory, and it shed dirt just by virtue of the wind's kiss. He was untouched by scar or imperfection.

So very elvin.

Ravn closed his eyes and breathed deeply, letting his consternation float away into cool water that swirled around his shoulders. The pressure faded and he leaned into the water, walking forward to the beach. His body, thick, muscled, and scarred, appeared moment by moment. Marcán gasped, "Your scar. I had heard of it, but I did not imagine…"

Ravn breathed, letting the words sluice over him even as the stream ran from his body in little channels. He had many scars, but it was the thick one in the center of his chest that Marcán referred to. It was red, and always looked fresh. Ravn bundled his hair, a bit longer since they had left Rithalion, and strung the water from it. He then began weaving it into a thick braid.

"Are you not curious about my gift?"

Ravn did not pause in his weaving, yet his eyes fixed flintily on the elf. *Yours was one of the voices that disapproved, wasn't it? You and yours are the reason I cannot even take comfort in her presence. The reason she cannot be there to quiet the nightmares. I save your people from rape and murder, and I am still not good enough for her.* Ravn turned away and finished the plaited rope at the nape of his neck. He bent to the pile of clothes drying on the wide rock. The sun and wind had done some work, but they were still damp if marginally cleaner. He pulled on the breeches anyway.

"I bring you understanding, Wolf."

Ravn paused, tunic in hand. His chest filled with a growl, primal and primordial. It was a dark urge as deep as any ocean and as hard as any mountain, as hot as the heart of a brushfire. His words were low and soft, but hit like arrows with the power to crack bone. "I understand that the whispered words of people who don't care that she was married to a monster for breeding are the same voices I bled for, voices *she* bled for. They are the same that make her ashamed to be around me, ashamed of my love and devotion." Ravn turned back to Marcán, the words giving a pinprick to the dam that held back his temper and forming cracks in his self-control. The pressure was back, and it was growing. "Do I have the measure of it, elf?"

Marcán no longer sat delicately, but instead looked very much like a rabbit caught in an open field under the shadow of a hawk. Ravn could hear his breathing increase. That was good, for as the agitated coils of rage built in him, Ravn hoped he would leave so the barbarian could tame it back into submission.

But Marcán did not flee. His nostrils were flared, his irises shrunk to pinpricks, but he sat perfectly still and spoke. "I know you love her. Anyone with eyes can see you love her, and I believe she truly loves you back. Yet, you do not grasp the world she lives in."

Ravn threw the tunic down with a wet smack onto the rock and began to stalk toward the diplomat, eyes glowing even in the daylight. "The world that uses her for her womb? The one that sacrifices her heart and soul for propriety?"

Marcán saw him come and raised his hands in surrender. "The question remains. You are brave enough to die for her, but do you have courage enough to listen?"

Ravn jerked to a stop, balled fists hungry to break bone. He was breathing like a bellows, heart pumping double time. His thoughts were a tangled jumble of spikes and blade. He teetered there on the edge of violence, caught up in the storm of fears.

He closed his eyes. He breathed. He heard Xadrian's voice in his mind. *"Let go."*

His eyes went dark, his fists unclenched.

"Speak."

Marcán watched Ravn for a few more moments, then visibly relaxed. His fingers played with the decorative fringe at one wrist. "I know something about their betrothal, and her place in Elvish society. What was done, was not done blindly. Vivien was a free spirit with awesome potential. She can give birth to high blood elves. Not pure blood, but still pure enough. If her talent breeds true, they will be the rarest of mixed-race births– mages. You saw how few casters there are, and you know how important they are to our lives. By mating her to a somewhat distant husband, it was believed that his absences and devotion to his work would give her the time she would need to complete her training, to train others in the ways of magic, and to bear young who would then be trained. She knows all this from the time she was old enough to know she was a summoner of the fae. She has embraced this her entire life, and whatever other duties she has undertaken, this was always her first and foremost duty to her people. None believed The Lord of Ice and Steel would be..."

"Then why does she not take me as another husband.? I know that is allowed."

Marcán shook his head. "Not without her husband's permission, and not until their first child is born."

Slithering thoughts and feelings burned again on the floor of his mind. Ravn sought to let go. "Have her marriage to Torialvah annulled."

After wincing to hear the true name spoken out loud, Marcán shook his head, his golden pony tail swinging free. "I can't."

Ravn growled, "The elders, then."

The diplomat spread his hands helplessly. "They can't."

"They can jail a human for delirium, but can't stop an elf from hurting his wife?"

Marcán pursed his lips. "She can. She is the only one who can."

Ravn stood, stunned, his insides hollowing out as if he bled from a mortal wound. "She can? All this time and she can end it herself?"

The elf came to his feet, hands held out as if to ward off a charge. "Wait. You do not grasp. We are close, Wolf. You are so close to the truth, but on the wrong road. Listen. Please."

Ravn looked down and his hands had become hard fists again. He closed his eyes and didn't need the ache to know he was glowing with rage again. He struggled, then let go.

"Go on."

Marcán nodded, licking his lips. "Elves live for a very long time. Marriages are hard enough for a human, but we have them that last many human lifetimes. We find it natural that elves may take many lovers, even husbands or wives. In ancient times, there were terrible feuds that began over broken hearts and crumbling homes. Intrigues were endemic, and nearly destroyed the elvin people. A Concordat between couples was drawn up, rules we dare not break, for every elf knows the power of a broken heart. That power is hate, and when it lasts centuries it can rattle a whole society and weaken us as a people. The Concordat is holy to us. It allows us freedom to love, and live, to be free and yet bind our lives together. You are a temptation to break that holy vow, Wolf. You are a grave temptation and I see her struggle with it every second you are near her."

"So, I should just depart? Leave her to her misery?"

Marcán's face fell. He approached Ravn slowly, carefully, like he was a wild animal. Gently, tenderly, he placed a hand on Ravn's cheek. "I think you are her strength. I think you have loved her in a way she has always yearned for. Your hearts are aligned in ways most people can only ever dream of."

Ravn's face crumbled, anger giving way to a hollow despair in his chest. "Then why does she not say that?"

The elf cupped the barbarian's face and brought him to look in the eye. "She has not?"

Ravn winced. *I think she has, but...* He pulled away from Marcán's touch. His heart wept, sheer terror enveloping his soul in icy waters. "What should I do?"

Marcán smiled sadly. "Be brave. Be strong."

Then, upright though slightly stiff, like a man coming away from a steep cliff, the elf backed away a few steps. Ravn's shoulders slumped. He stood, empty and alone.

You were never good enough.

Ravn let go, but the memory scrabbled with sharp talons to hold on.

"One last bit of advice, Wolf?" Ravn looked at him with forlorn eyes. "With a husband like the Lord of Ice, don't you think she has seen enough anger directed at her in her life, already?"

Ravn nodded and the diplomat finally gave him the solitude he had craved, only to find he no longer wanted it.

Chapter Thirteen
Island City

They crested the rise on noon of the next day. The lake valley spread before them in endless, green, rolling hills covered in farms and orchards. Like ripples in a pond the ground undulated to the edge of the massive lake at the center, spanning from one horizon to the other. Bridges, wider than most roads, reached into the lake, grounding its heart to the shore. Off in the distance, half a mile from shore, lay where the bridges ended at an island enveloped in white marble and beautiful red roofs. The sun was only now burning off the last wisps of fog amongst the elegant towers and stately buildings.

Gregor grinned at the Wolf, who sat on his reindeer with gaping mouth. The young man waved his hand to encompass the city, a mile long and half that wide, swallowing the island completely. "Elyrion."

The Wolf nodded dumbly. Rithalion was larger, but emptier, and could not be seen at once, packing the force of the massed number of elves at a single glance. The smoke of cooking fires rose from the homes, and banners unraveled from flagpoles and down buildings in streams of color. Alternating from emerald green and silver to crimson red and gold. Most of the flags were the crimson red of Elyrion, but those nearest the bridges were the emerald green of Rithalion.

Marcán laughed and clapped. "The flag for our city! The messenger hawks got through! They are expecting us!"

Rohan nodded, tapping one of the scouts' tir-reath on the side of the head when she glared at the Wolf and growled. "They keep a good watch. That may bode ill."

Gregor laughed. "Always looking for the storm attached to any rainbow, eh?"

The whole party, elves and mounts, began the trek along the octagonal paved road toward the city of their kin. The Wolf, thoughts leaden, paused to consider the magnificent city, wondering if Rohan was right. Then Vivien passed him, and his mind was torn asunder by doubts and hurt. The reindeer shifted, the dappled pelt shining in the noon day sun, but he did not urge it forward, so it waited. Ravn squeezed his eyes and felt tears roll out of them, hot and wet.

He took a deep breath, and when he opened them, Vivien was there, waiting as the rest of the party rode sedately away, watching Ravn with troubled eyes.

But she was waiting. For him. He saw her eyes glitter for a moment with hope. Ravn tried to muster words, but his mouth flapped uselessly. Then she turned, head low, and she urged Sherika forward to a slow walk. Ravn felt his heart gripped with panic. He looked down to the Elvish road where his mount stood– to the untamed wilds behind, to the gleaming bastion of civilization ahead. A single word bubbled up. It fought against the fears and pains, past the anger and useless pride. It was exhausted by the trip and exited his mouth as a mere whisper, "Wait."

She heard. She stopped, looking back at him.

Ravn despised his fear, his weakness. He vaulted from the mount and walked bravely to Vivien, who blinked fearfully as he strode with strength and purpose to her side. He watched her brace for some meanness, some recrimination, some violence as he reached up and pulled her gently from Sherika's saddle and into his arms. He felt her stiffness, her hurt. Then he felt her relax, sinking into him. It was if a hole inside him was filled with molten gold, and he felt at one with her.

She pulled back from his fiercely beating heart encased in Elvish steel and turned sad eyes up to his.

Finally, the ocean of his mind became calm. He breathed in, placed one of her hands over his heart, over his terrible scar, and his words came. "I will be waiting for you in this wild place, where I have always been, searching for your heart. And if you ever get lost, simply call my name. I will build such a fire in my soul that it will reflect off of the heavens and guide you to your home in my arms."

Tears glistened in her eyes, flowing over her cheeks. "How can you say such horrible things to me one night, and such beautiful things the next?"

His tears came as well, following many brothers to hide in the forest of his beard. "Because I am afraid. I have spent my life looking for you, yearning for you. Every time I think we are close, you disappear into one Elvish rule, or duty, or obligation that I do not understand." His voice hitched and he pressed on. "I have worked so hard to be the man you need me to be, but I am imperfect, and I am going to stumble. I am going to fail. And when I feel you slipping away, all the work I have done is like nothing to the winds of fate. I am afraid of never being in your arms and at peace."

She looked at him, stricken. She looked like she wanted to say so much more, but she swallowed all her thoughts and simply placed these five words before his feet. "So, what will you do?"

Ravn drew himself up to his full height, certain. "The only thing I can do, Jashi."

She nodded, resigned, sure of his answer. "And what is that?"

He knelt before her and drank her in with eyes drowning with tears. "Work harder, Jashi. I will work harder."

He watched the words hit her like a charging carriage. She shook her head and cupped his face in her hands. "I am broken, RavnWolf."

Ravn shot from the ground and swept her tenderly into his arms. He whispered fiercely into her ear. "You are never broken, for you fight for me. Even when all is lost, you fight for me."

"We fight..." she gasped, "for each other."

They held each other for several moments, and even if everything was not well between them, it would find a way to heal. Then there was a loud rumble beside them and a black face pushed its furry head between their chests, purring loud enough Ravn felt it to his core. They both laughed as Sherika continued to weave in and out between them, trailing her long tail behind.

Vivien wiped at her tears, smiling at Ravn with wonder. "She loves you. Of all tir-reath, she alone loves you."

"She does." Ravn scratched the beast between her ears. She responded by rubbing her huge head against his chest, pushing him back despite his size. The big cat plopped her haunches down directly between them and enjoyed being loved from both sides. Ravn watched the delight fade from Vivien's face and she nodded to herself, a decision made. "I need some time to think through some things. I am in love with you Ravn, but I have a lot at stake. The lives of so many hinge on the decisions I make in my life, and I need to examine what I can give up and what I can't."

Ravn nodded. "Whatever time you need, take."

As if remembering other people exist, Vivien looked back down the road to the retreating party. She turned back to Ravn and gave him a chaste kiss on his hairy cheek. Then she pulled away. "We should go."

He nodded. They mounted and continued to Elyrion in silence together, side by side. Wordlessly, the company pulled back as they approached, and Marcán motioned them to the front of their procession.

The welcome was warm and spectacular.

The messenger hawks had been sent before they ever left Rithalion, and Elyrion scouts had indeed spotted them as they approached the city. There was no big fanfare, but people lined the road, hoping to get a look at the barbarian and master mage that had helped save their sister city. The pennants and flags had been unrolled on cue, and the whole city knew they were crossing one of the long, wide bridges into town. Windows high up on shops and in homes were thrown open, and all who could crowded to every open portal to cheer to them and even throw some flowers if they had them at hand. There was clapping and cheering as the Wolf and Vivien passed, she on Sherika and he on the massive silver reindeer he'd been given, riding at the forefront of their small entourage.

The Wolf remembered parades and processions through small towns in his domain when he was a Laird, and waved back to the people with only a hint of awkwardness. He watched Vivien, however, and she almost shrank from the attention. He leaned over and plucked at her arm, smiling at her until she waved to the crowd, and the elves all around cheered even more loudly. She looked amazed and then sheepish. "Why do they cheer for me?"

Ravn smiled. "Because they more clearly judge your worth than you do."

"No, that's–" She blinked at him, stifling a shake of her head as a small boy ran up to Sherika, a red carnation in hand.

She reached down to pull him across her lap on Sherika's back and he planted a wet, chaste kiss on her cheek, handing her the flower and reciting what he obviously had been told to say. "My cousin fights for you, Mage Protector of the Realm. His letters say you are a fine commander and saved the city!"

Then he impishly slid from her lap and ran back to the side of the street where he buried his face, embarrassed, in his mother's skirts. Ravn watched Vivien sit stunned astride Sherika. She turned back to the Wolf, mouth empty but moving as her cheeks colored bright red.

"Must be true." The Wolf shrugged wryly. "I didn't get a flower... or a kiss."

Then a hand reached from the street on the side away from Vivien and snagged the top of his breastplate. It belonged to a beautiful elvin maid. She was dressed simply in green, with hair like a waterfall of straight brown locks and eyes like a churning river, passionate and proud. She had deftly planted a foot in the stirrup and heaved herself effortlessly up to stand on top of his boot. She pressed her mouth to his, and her tongue explored him deeply, if only for a moment. She tasted of strawberries and he felt his insides churn with the force of her want. She parted, smiling, and dismounted to disappear into the crowd. Ravn sat upright in his saddle, mind shocked into utter stillness.

Vivien's laugh was honest and brought him back to the procession. "Well, now we are even, Knight Protector."

Ravn shook his head, trying to clear it as if he had been struck. "Indeed."

The road ended at a wide fountain before a colossal building that was nearly a palace. Standing there was the city Council, three men and three women, all with long silver hair, elegant pointed ears, almond shaped eyes, and deep crimson robes. Timeless and exuding wisdom, they all bowed. Vivien and the Wolf pulled to either side, allowing Marcán to ride to the fore, and once before the elders, he dismounted his reindeer.

One lady stepped forward and spread her arms. "I am Autumn Fire and we are the Council of Elyrion. Welcome to our home. Please leave some of the peace that you bring, and take some of the happiness we have with you on your journey."

Marcán opened his arms, smiling wide. "We seek to bring joy, and hope to leave happy memories."

They embraced warmly. When they parted, she began giving introductions of the other council members, all pure blood elves and so all referred to by title instead of name. Ravn nodded to each in turn, and remained stoic as each of them assessed him clinically. Each of them smiled warmly at Vivien, and that was enough for him. Servants, less festive and far more functional than those from Lady Shaladrea's estate, came from the council building dressed in simple long tunics and shoes to collect the pack moose and his reindeer. Ravn dismounted easily, and rubbed the beast's silver muzzle in farewell. He was snatched from the moment however, by Marcán's next words. Words that made his blood run cold.

"The Liath are on the move, then?"

Autumn Fire was somber. "They have not attacked the city, but they are on the warpath. Caravans and outlaying farms have been attacked. Sections of the army are out riding them down, following their trails." She shook her head. "These appear to be scouts. The Liath have never been able to settle into large groups for long, but one of the larger tribes seems to have splintered into several factions, dragon priests and warlords vying for power."

Ravn felt the familiar pressure on his eyes, and a stirring in his breast as he thought about the deaths of his mother, his father, and many of his subjects over a century ago. The Liath brought wanton destruction wherever their shadows fell. He looked to Vivien, who glanced back at him, properly alarmed.

Autumn Fire shook her head, "They are probably looking for some ruin to inhabit. We are vigilant. Yet here we are, in the streets. Let us get you all into your rooms, nephew."

Ravn grunted in surprise, for the relation between Marcán and Autumn Fire, and then for the fact that none of them were disarmed as they were led into the council chambers. The chamber was similar to that in Rithalion, but different enough to be striking. Instead of the interior of a sea of flower petals, it was the interior of a massive tree, with leaves forming balconies and whorls of the wood grain carved into the walls with lifelike precision.

The envoy was moved from the main hall into the chambers beyond, and from there outside to another sprawling building. They walked through a lush garden and entered it, walking up the stairs and into a wide corridor. They were shown to suites, each of them given his or her own apartment during their stay. Those that rode tir-reath took them with into their new homes. Soon, one of the servants gestured to Ravn and opened the door to show him into his place. Ravn looked after Vivien, who bit her lip and watched him apprehensively. He nodded to her and entered, letting the door shut behind him. The rooms were richly appointed, and appeared to be the height of comfort. He unbuckled his belts and left his sword, axe, and heavy armor plates on the large table in the front room. He walked through the chambers, then out onto the balcony, feeling caged despite the luxury. No matter where he went, or where he looked, all he thought about was Vivien, close but separated by more than walls and doors. He came to the bed. Large, covered in woven blankets of the softest threads, it was more than big enough for him and anyone else. Yet he would sleep there alone.

But alone was always best, for it was in the dark of night when he could not center himself that the nightmares would come. It had been a century, and they always had. He had drowned them in drink, exhausted them with labor, ran from them in the deepest forest, and yet the nightmares of his life continued to hunt him down and eventually find him. Only one thing kept them away for any length of time, only one person. Her. And now she was hurt and would not be there to keep them at bay. He cursed himself for his anger and his sharp tongue and-

He closed his eyes and breathed. He let go.

When he opened them, the calm waters of Lake Emeron had been turned into a bright mirror by the shining of the sun. He smiled at it a little, and marveled at how much easier centering himself had become. He reconsidered Marcán's words and how he really only knew Vivien like the tops of trees and the thoughts she had like birds flying through them. There were darker thoughts, larger thoughts, deep in the shadows of her mind. He thought he knew her, but if he could not work to know these thoughts then how would he ever be a fit companion for her for however long he was going to live?

He nodded to no one.

I am awash in a sea and I do not know my course. I must know more.

He had battled against men, fought fearsome beasts, and wrestled with a dragon for her love and life. He could not fail in this, for she was his everlasting sky, and without her he was truly lost.

Chapter Fourteen
Haunted Past

Dearest Lady,

Great news! We have made it safely to Elyrion. I must say, the city is more beautiful than I remember it as a child. I am feeling well, and my belly tells the tale of a quickly growing baby. I feel much better about him now, just like you said I would, and I love him so much. I can't wait for him to come as I wish to see what he looks like and smile into his eyes to let him know I love him. The selfish part of me hopes he has many of my features.

I am beginning to wish that I hadn't been so stubborn and not allowed you to give us the use of your carriage. My growing belly presses a bit more on Sherika's back as we travel, and the past couple days I've kept her to a walk. I feel so guilty, because I know she wants to run but she seems to understand and always endeavors to move as fluidly as she possibly can. She is my truest companion.

The Wolf seems to be doing well, although he and I have had words as of late. I will share with you when I can. I have so much to tell you when I return home, so be sure to set aside an entire day for me. I love you and miss you.

Vivien

With the light of mid-morning streaming through the window, Vivien read through the letter to be sure it sounded right. There was so much more she wanted to say, but she didn't wish to worry her friend unnecessarily. The issue of her magic weighed heavily on her mind. What she had done the night of the attack was an abomination, and the very thing that she had been punished for no more than ten months ago. She wished she had someone, anyone, to talk to about it, and the only one who came to mind was Shaladrea. But how could she put such a thing in a letter? Best to leave something like that for a conversation upon returning home.

Vivien gave a deep sigh as she rolled up the letter. Truth be told, the men talked a lot about her when they thought she couldn't hear. Not just about her relationship with the Wolf, they whispered about the arcane atrocity of that attack. While she had certainly saved them all from certain injury, and possibly death if anyone else had been bitten, what she had done was terribly wrong. The men were afraid of her, and she supposed they had every right to be. A part of her wanted to move among them, be a part of them the way she had been with the La'athai. But she somehow couldn't find it in her to do it. Maybe she was just as afraid of them as they were of her, afraid of the rejection she imagined they might impart.

Vivien finished rolling the parchment. She poured a glob of hot wax at the seam and with the talisman she wore around her neck and stamped it with the seal of her new office, Mage Protector. She then wrote the Lady of Moonlight and Love's title on it. She looked up from the scroll as a knock sounded on the door. "Enter."

She rose as a young man opened the door, a scroll in his hand. He gave a slight bow. "A message for you, Lady Vivien."

She took the scroll and pressed her letter into his palm. "Please have the aerie keeper send this to Rithalion for me?"

He nodded. "Of course, Lady Vivien."

"Thank you." The man turned to leave but she held out a hand. "Wait!"

He turned back. "Yes, Lady?"

"What is your name? I'd like to address you properly when next you come to my chamber suite."

The man beamed, his smile filling his entire face. "It's Colm, my Lady."

The smile was infectious and she returned it. "May the rest of your day be a good one, Colm."

He bowed again. "Yes, Lady Vivien. Thank you!"

She watched him leave before breaking open the seal of the Council of Elyrion and reading the contents. It was convening this evening, and her attendance had been requested, along with that of the Wolf and Marcán. After there would be a dinner held in their honor, a gift from the people of Elyrion to the heroes of Rithalion. The Lady had warned her that such a thing might happen, so the beautiful gown that had made for her had been carefully packed in her bags, along with matching slippers.

Vivien's belly clenched. The last time she'd been at a formal dinner, her husband had embarrassed her in front of a room filled with her peers, then taken her back to her chambers and...

She started as another knock sounded at the door. She blinked away tears and schooled her expression into one of indifference. "Enter."

An older half-elvin woman entered at the prompt, a pile of towels and washcloths in hand, followed by two younger, lesser elves. "My Lady Vivien, we are here to help you with your bath." The woman must have seen something in her expression, for she looked down at her pile indecisively. "Would you care to have us?"

Vivien just stood there for a moment, staring down at the offending scroll, allowing her memories of Tor to fall away. *He is not here. He's back home, in Rithalion. He can't hurt me. He's not here...*

Finally she looked back up at the handmaid. "Yes, I will have you."

The woman gave her a hesitant smile. "I am glad, for it is an honor for me and my comrades." She gestured to the two others behind her, one a woman, and the other what appeared to be an effeminate man. My name is Cora, and these are Rahael and Sonora. "Let us have your bath called, shall we?"

Vivien luxuriated in the gentle ministrations of the elves. She half expected them to say something about her condition, but no words were uttered about it. She allowed her cares to melt and float away in the warm bath waters. Listening to the three prattle on as she bathed lifted her spirits. Once they finished bathing her, she was dressed in one of her flowing tunics with matching pants, her hair brushed simply so it could be styled later. Her evening gown would wait until closer to dinner.

Vivien nodded. "Thank you for scrubbing the road from me."

Cora smiled. "You are very welcome, my dear."

Once the bath had been taken away, and everything put in order, the three handmaids gave her a small bow. "Thank you for allowing us to serve you Lady Vivien."

Vivien blinked at the formality, but chose to go with it. "The honor was mine."

All three smiled as they vacated the chamber. Vivien was left alone, but with a feeling of wellbeing. *Maybe I can do for Ravn what these people did for me. That is, if he hasn't been given a bath yet already!*

Vivien rushed from her room and down the hall to where she knew Ravn's room was located. She was about to make a turn when a pair of voices pulled her up short.

"I'm not sure we should be here," said one voice.

"Hush! Master maid Cora said that would draw lots on this one. We won," said a second.

"Not fairly!" exclaimed a third.

"I am afraid to go in. He's terribly big. And hairy!" said the first.

"I find all that hair sexy! Do you think he might take us?" said the second with a tone of excitement.

"Of course, you would say that," muttered the third.

Vivien stood there, hand over her mouth, barely suppressing the mixture of feelings that bubbled forth. *Who the hell were these young fools and why were they given the task of serving one of the esteemed guests from their sister city? These girls are young, in the middle of adolescence. It seems so unlikely they would even be given the chance to serve someone such as the Wolf, much less cheat to win the honor.*

She straightened her shoulders and strode around the corner as the second girl was speaking again. "I think I could persuade him to see things my way. I've been told that I'm good at such things, and he is just a barbarian after all."

One of the girls, most likely the first one, the fearful one, saw her coming. Her mouth opened as though to say something, but nothing emerged. It opened and closed a couple times.

"I think that your sources are biased. I'm not so sure..." The third voice trailed off as she, too, saw Vivien striding towards them.

It was only then the owner of the second voice noticed anything amiss. "What are you two..." Her eyes widened and she stepped back as Vivien approached.

Vivien plastered a smile onto her face, one that never quite reached her eyes. She stopped before the three girls and raked them over with her gaze. Each one flinched beneath the onslaught. Surprisingly, it was the fearful one who spoke up. "G... good noon my Lady Vivien."

Vivien raised an arched brow, and her tone was chilly. "And what lofty task has you three girls standing here in the corridor outside the chamber of a *barbarian*?"

The first and third girls quailed. "We were sent to take care of his Lord's needs, of course," said the second girl, her voice tinged with haughtiness.

Inside Vivien, a surge of anger compressed into a mass of white hot. These girls sought to use the Wolf as nothing but a stallion, like a thing. He was a man. He was her friend, and no one's trophy. Vivien's hand quickly snaked out and grabbed the girl by the neckline of her tunic, pressing her back into the stone wall. "I will not be spoken down to, especially by the likes of you, little mouse," she hissed. "If I were you, I would be careful in the future."

The girl trembled beneath her hand. "Y... yes Lady Mage Protector. My apologies."

Vivien released the girl and addressed the other two. "I suggest you get back to your duties. I bet your services are being missed somewhere."

The three bowed slightly, the second with a hand at her throat as they vacated the corridor, disappearing around the corner as swiftly as their legs would carry them. Vivien turned towards the door, her mind once more set to her task. She shook her head as the anger left as fast as it had come. She took a deep breath. *First to order him a bath, and maybe...*

Her mind set to spinning and an idea was born.

Ravn stood before the small bookshelf, assessing his possibilities. All of the titles looked a bit on the dry side, but one caught his attention: A History of Elyrion. He took it from its companions and carried it outside to the balcony, settling down on a sturdy wooden chair. He looked out over Lake Emeron, the crystal-clear waters lapping lazily against the shoreline. Silver birds hovered overhead, searching for the fishes they knew swam beneath the surface, and huge turtles waited to claim an avian meal if they got too close.

Ravn opened the book and settled down to read. It felt peaceful, and it was easy to get immersed in the history. He was afraid his admittedly limited knowledge of Elvish would be a problem, but he could break down the words easily enough if he concentrated. It was using parts of his mind he had rarely exercised, and it was the good kind of labor one feels following strenuous work after a long time abed. It proved to be more interesting than he originally thought, and he began to flip the pages more and more rapidly as he continued.

Tiktiktik.

Ravn looked up from his book to see a tirinian sitting there, close to his left foot. He frowned. It was very obviously the same kind of creature found in the keep of the Lady of Moonlight and Love. The small, catlike animals loved to sit on him whenever he was still. He gave a deep sigh. This one was colored a pale blond and the plumed tail was nearly white, quite different from the deep auburn of those in Rithalion. He went back to his book.

Tiktiktik.

He raised his eyes again. This time there were two sitting there.

He determinedly returned to his reading.

Tiktiktik.

He slowly raised his gaze, his eyes widening when he saw three more had joined the first two. They all sat, respectfully, and waited. They were like children awaiting a special treat, and he smiled a little at their polite insistence. He gave a sigh of resignation and lowered his hand. The first tirinian happily approached. Ravn felt the tiny claws as it scampered up his arm and settled upon his shoulder, the others quickly following. He returned to his book. More tirinian came through the open doorway as he read about the trials and tribulations of a city surrounded by...

Suddenly he heard a swift intake of breath. "Ravn! What are you doing?"

He looked over to find Vivien standing there in a flowing blue tunic that set off her green eyes. His eyes roved over her coppery blonde hair lying unbound around her shoulders, her face radiant with beauty. He struggled to keep himself seated. *I have hurt her, and I must respect her distance.* So he quelled the urge to fly to her and crush her to him and satisfied himself with a small gesture to the book. "Reading."

Vivien covered her mouth and took a long breath. "All these tirinian! Do you know what this means?"

He glanced at the animals. "Lydia said something about them being lucky."

"I've never seen them..." she struggled for a word, "converge on a man quite like this before."

Ravn took a good look at himself. Small blond, squirrel-like felines had taken up almost every bit of usable space on his person, and all rested peacefully. He shook his head. "This has happened before, Jashi."

Ravn held her eyes, hoping, praying, she could feel how sorry he was for being angry the other night when they argued in her tent. She looked back to him with soft eyes, lowered her hands from her face and smiled gently. "Of course, it has."

She said it sagely, as if it meant so much, but had to be another finer point of Elvish society he just did not understand. She grinned and stepped closer, sweeping one from off his shoulder into her palm. It *tikked* as she held it close and contentment suffused her features. "Aren't they so soft?"

She had been so troubled lately, so worried and so devoid of joy. He always remembered her being so in tune with animals. He had seen her tame a devilish stallion to accept the touch of a young girl, and feed birds from her hand in the forests around his old home in the Lairdlands. He smiled at the expression on her face, glad to see her old self returning. "Yes, indeed they are soft."

Her expression abruptly shifted as she remembered her business and she let the tirinian leap from her hands to the floor, only to have it skitter back onto its perch upon Ravn. "Did you get the message from the Elyrion Council?"

He nodded.

Her eyes brightened. "Let me help you get ready."

He rubbed a hand through the unkempt beard adorning his jaws and chin. "What, you don't think I'm debonair just as I am?" He smiled at her playfully, hoping he had been forgiven.

She grinned. "You look like a beast from the wilds, and these people have had a healthy enough look at you as your namesake. My people need them to see you now as the commander of elves to entrust their lives to our defense." She began to move back into the chamber. "Come, let me help you prepare."

He raised a thick eyebrow and then glanced down at his person. "First tell me how I am supposed to get up."

She cocked her head. "Just simply stand up. They will be fine."

Blanketed in little sparks of life, he felt his own size and their fragility. He gave her a skeptical look.

Vivien came back over and began to take the tirinian from off of him. She'd managed to remove three before the first leapt back onto his lap and settled there. There was a steady pace for a few moments before she realized what was happening. She then looked at him with a beautiful scowl, tirinian making themselves comfortable once more. "Come now, Wolf. Certainly, you can manage to follow me into the other room. I am sure your furry friends will forgive you use of your legs and find your lap again later."

Guiltily he slowly stood. The creatures hung on as long as they could before leaping off of him and running into the chamber. He followed them inside just to see them settling themselves around the place. Vivien gave him an 'I told you so' look. He shrugged sheepishly as his cheeks burned. She made her way towards the front of the suite.

"I took the liberty of having a bath brought. It should be here any moment."

He looked at her in surprise. "Thank you. You didn't have to do that."

She shrugged. "I did, since I am going to be the one giving you that bath."

He suddenly felt his heart thumping like a brass drum in his chest, and there was a ringing in his ears. He could taste metal, and he was sure he did little but gawp at her, a hundred thoughts turning his mind into a crowded wreck as they crowded in at once. "You are?"

She looked into his eyes. There was no hint of seduction. "Is that alright?"

He breathed and let go, the thoughts draining away. "Well, yes. I have been bathed before, but isn't that what the household staff is for?"

She put a hand on his arm, not his chest. Whatever he had hoped for, this was not it. It was a different thing. An Elvish thing. She smiled. "It is. But I would like to help this time."

He nodded just as there was a knock on the door. "Enter," called Vivien.

The door opened and the staff entered the room with the tub. Within moments there was a line of people with buckets of steaming water. The tub was filled in no time and before long the room was quiet again. Ravn just stood there.

"You might want to consider taking off your clothes. I believe they have a tendency of getting in the way during the bathing ritual. Not only that, but clothes have their own bath that they get, much separate from the wearer."

He looked up at Vivien to see her mouth curved up in a smirk. He couldn't help but chuckle. "As you say, Lady."

Without further ado, Ravn removed his clothing letting it fall to a pile on the floor at his feet. A century of living in the wilds, sometimes wearing bloody, stinking furs and sometimes nothing at all, had stripped him of his modesty, but he suddenly felt very naked standing there before her, scars exposed and manhood hanging free. For a moment he was tempted to find some type of cover, but then she was beckoning him over to the tub.

He stepped into the water, mist rising all around. Vivien braided her hair as he sunk slowly into depths that embraced him in their heat. His muscles began to relax and for a while he just lay there, his knees rising like twin mountains because his legs were too long for the tub. She watched him and he watched her back. The smile on her face was not lusty, or condescending. He felt her acceptance of everything he was, and an ache settled in his chest, as good ache. One for her.

Vivien took a bar of soap and lathered up a scrub cloth. "Lean forward, Laird."

An electric shock ran down his spine and he glanced at her. He hadn't heard that word in a long time. She smiled and began to rub the cloth over his back and he let the word go. Her touch felt good, much better and firmer than he thought it would. Under her ministrations, he felt knots in his back and shoulders un-kink as the heat of the water suffused him and sapped the energy from him. She started with his shoulders, then down his back and over his sides. She asked him to lay back again and she scrubbed his arms and chest. The entire time she had a small smile, one that he knew was just for him, and her green eyes danced.

He'd always loved her eyes. Her laughing eyes.

She proceeded to his legs, which she asked him to stretch out of the waters, and she even ministered to his feet, scarred and calloused. In the end, after she had scrubbed every bit of him, she took his hair down and washed it too. And when it was clean, she took a wide-toothed comb and ran it through the unruly mass, picking through all the snarls and smoothing it out. He was no fool. He towered over most of the elves. His hands were like mattocks, his legs like tree trunks. Yet despite having seen him fight giants and been pierced by arrows, she held his hair to comb at the tips so it did not pull at his scalp. She treated him so... *gently*. He closed his eyes and just let his thoughts drift.

Memories came to the fore of his mind, memories of his mother. *She'd been the last one to bathe me. No, no wait. It was Neála. She'd done it the night before I left on my quest for the heart.* An arc of pain swept through him and he winced.

He instantly felt a cool hand on his face. "Ravn? Did I hurt you? I'm sorry, I'll be more careful."

He opened his eyes and put a hand over Vivien's. "No," he breathed. *Let go. Let go.* "You didn't hurt me." He forced a smile. "I'm fine."

She looked at him askance, but continued.

When he finally stepped out of the tub, she dried him off with a soft towel. She dried every inch of him, every nook and cranny. Even his man parts, and he knew he blushed again as they responded to her touch. He offered no resistance when she led him across the room, but all of a sudden, he had a moment of vertigo...

...falling...

He wavered and put a hand to his head.

Vivien clutched his arm, her brow furrowed. "Wolf, are you alright?"

He nodded. "It's just an old wound." *Ravn. I am Ravn.* He had spent so long with so many different names: Wolf, Beast, Wild Man, Hunter. None of them felt like him anymore. None but the ones she used at the moment they touched her lips.

Her eyes went wide. "You are injured? Truly?"

Ravn shook his head. "It is nothing."

She accepted that and smiled, leading him into the other room. "I have a surprise for you. Do you trust me?" Ravn sucked in air and nodded, wondering if she knew how much her very presence gave to him, shored up his mind, and healed his deepest wounds.

She led him to a simple wooden table and chair where a large cloth was spread beneath. The table had two flat boxes and some metal instruments on it.

A standing mirror was nearby, but had chastely been turned away. She motioned to the chair.

He chuckled. "What? No clothes for me?"

She folded her arms and grinned. "I found you half naked in the woods, just spent the last hour bathing you, but you are modest now?"

He shook his head and smiled, seating himself in the chair. He watched her walk around him, saw her wince at the trails of old wounds across his body, no longer hidden by dirt or by the suds from the tub bath. It was nothing new; she always did. Everyone always did. None were as horrible as the huge scar that sliced across his breast, as if he had been opened by some massive beast...

...agonized screams that ended in strangled gurgling...

Moray!

Ravn grabbed the dark image and shoved it back into a cave inside his head. The nightmares had been quiet for years, but ever since the battle, he...

Vivien brought her face down to his, smiling impishly. Her smell, like rosewater and spun sugar, honeysuckle and sandalwood, drove the dark thoughts away. She held up a short knife, straight as an arrow and gleaming. "So, you trust me?"

Ravn felt his feelings for her well up inside and threaten to overtake him. His heart was thumping like a galloping horse. He had once tried to give his last breath for her without hesitation, and he knew now if she wanted it, she had only to ask. "With my life."

"Good." She smiled, set down the knife and took a small pot from the table. She scooped out a dollop of thick grease and smeared it on his lower face and jaw.

Ravn felt he was being tested, and was still as a tombstone. She worked the grease into his thick beard, still damp from the bath. She brought forth the knife, again. As she came close, he tamped down the wild instincts that told him to growl, to fight, to flee. He had trusted once, and had lost so much for it. *Not her. Never her. She is worthy of your trust.* She tilted his face upwards and dragged the blade along his cheek. The oiled hair came away easily, and the grease caused the blade to slide effortlessly against his skin.

"This is far easier in the light, away from a cave, is it not?"

He gave a small smile, images of what he imagined her naked body looked like soaring through his mind's eye. The most prevalent was the dream he'd had of them together, making love in a sea of pink moss. He longed to talk to her about it but...

She had shaved him then, too, careful of the fresh wound he had received from their plunge into the waterfall, the plunge that had would have killed him if not for her. That was when she'd learned the truth of his identity. Ravn swallowed convulsively, his eyes drawn to the neckline of her tunic. He nearly shook his head, and barely quelled the urge to look within. He loved Vivien, as much as his heart would allow. She had been a stalwart friend, a wonderful champion, and a powerful ally. Yet she was female, and he was male, and as she leaned over to continue her work, he saw down the front of her blouse and was moved by the petite breasts and pink nipples there. He averted his eyes, for they were hers to show, not his to leer at. The image, however was burned into his mind. They were just as he had imagined them, if not slightly fuller. His body responded to the sight, but if she noticed, she said nothing.

The task didn't take long, and when she was done, he reached up to touch his face. "No! Not yet," she admonished. He dropped his hand and she nodded approvingly. "I am glad to see that wound on your face is just a thin line now."

Vivien picked up another metal object from the table and walked behind him. The shears made that distinctive sound through his hair. He jerked for a moment, and she put a firm hand on his head. He could have brushed her off like a tirinian, but let her control him, moving his head one way or the other to clip free whole locks of his curly chestnut mane. He sat quietly, his heart beating far too fast. Again, in minutes she was done, finishing by brushing his chest and shoulders with a soft tir-reath mane brush.

"Now you may rise, but keep your hands down and close your eyes."

He did as she asked. He heard a box open and moments later he felt cloth being pressed into his hands. "Put these on."

It was insane, but Ravn felt as if his head was far lighter. He took the clothes she offered. There was a loose-fitting shirt with billowed sleeves. The socks were made of wool and high. She had included a small fold of cloth for his groin and he slipped into it and tied it off easily, but something was missing.

He heard the second box open and could feel excitement radiating off of her in waves. A familiar weight settled around his waist and she fumbled at what sounded like a buckle in the front. She finally drew away, took his hands in hers, and brought them up before him as if praying.

"Keep your eyes closed." She patted his arm. "Stay there." She moved away and he heard the slight rumble of the mirror being moved. "Alright, open them now."

Ravn opened his eyes. A familiar stranger looked at him from the glass.

Vivien beamed. "Say hello to me, Ravn Lairdson, Laird and Master of Blacach."

It was him. All sun-bleached strands taken from his head, his hair was darker. It had been trimmed to just above his shoulders, pulled away from a face he hadn't seen in decades. His beard was tightly trimmed, showing his nose and cheekbones in stark relief. He had on a Lairdlands kilt, deep green like his family tartan, pleated cleanly and held in place with a wide black leather belt. His mother's eyes stared out of the face that had been respected, loved, and hated.

You were never good enough.

The image hit Ravn like a fist and he staggered away from the specter in the glass. Vivien's face became troubled, worried. Ravn could not hear her words because his heart was beating so loudly it blotted out the world. He could feel it in his chest, trying to escape. Everything was tinged in red. He looked at his doppelganger and the eyes were glowing like bloody jewels. He finally saw what she must have seen in the caves, a familiar face turned into a glowing nightmare. He shut his eyes. He breathed like Xadrian had commanded. He breathed. He breathed.

Ravn felt Vivien embrace him and her smell wafted over him. Only three words cut through his pain and found a place to calm his heart.

"I love you. Ravn, I love you."

He breathed deeply, pushing aside the curtain of panic and pain within. He looked to the floor, covered in his curling locks and thick beard hair. *I am not there. That was in the past. It will not happen again.* He spun and swept Vivien in his arms. He heard her gasp and he tried not to crush her with his powerful arms. *She loves me. She loves me. I must trust her. I must.*

How long he held her, he didn't know, but he backed away when she pushed him, wishing only to hold her more. Inside her hazel eyes was a riot of conflict. Her brow was furrowed, and her mouth turned down in a worried frown.

She took his hand and led him back into the other chamber with the bookshelf and a suede sofa. She sat him down and situated herself next to him. The tirinian did not come to him, but hid among the furnishings. Harsh light streamed in through the hand sized panes of glass set into a lattice of one window. She sat in the rays of sun, but he remained in the shadow outside of it. He lowered his head and she studied him for a while.

"Ravn?"

Got to breathe. Must let go. He nodded.

"Please tell me what is going on."

He felt the monster inside recede, leaving a gaping hole behind where it had crashed through his fortified walls of sanity. Silence reigned.

"Is it something about your past?"

He looked through the hole in his mind. He heard voices, long dead, beg for mercy. More silence.

"Please, don't I deserve something?" He heard the tears in her voice. "Don't I deserve to know at least something about you?"

His throat tightened and he stared resolutely at the floor. *Now was not the time for this. They had a council to attend...*

Her voice was filled with sorrow. "I've asked you time and time again to tell me some bits and parts about yourself. Something. Anything."

He breathed deeply, his nostrils flaring as the pain rose up from the depths of his soul. It scorched him with its intensity, setting his nerve endings on fire. *Gods please, no. Not today. I'm not ready.*

She persisted. "I went back to your castle a century ago. They said you were dead."

Ravn waited a moment, then nodded.

"Tell me."

He raised his eyes to the ceiling, his insides falling away.

...falling...

He shook his head, sniffing at the tears that threatened. He felt so small. So powerless.

She crossed her arms and spoke like a commander, like a soldier despite the cracking of her voice. "You said you trusted me with your life."

His voice was a harsh whisper. "I should have died. I should have died–"

"What?"

...the desperate cries of an infant... "–instead of them."

Her voice was pleading. "Ravn, please tell me what happened."

He squeezed his eyes shut, wanting–*needing* to blot out the world that was as much as the world that was. *Gods, please no.* "I can't."

Vivien rose abruptly from the sofa. He looked at her where she stood, her teary eyes filled with hurt. "You don't trust me. She swallowed convulsively, her words more a statement than a question. "You don't trust me with your life even though I trust you with mine."

He stared at her, feeling the walls begin to close in on him.

She snorted and gave him a smile that never reached her eyes. "Thank you, my Lord, for finally telling me my place. It might have been better to have known this earlier since I would have thought more carefully about sharing my entire world with you."

The words, echoes of the same ones uttered from his own lips not more than three days before were like a dagger to the heart. He reached towards her but she stepped out of his reach.

Her words were monotone. "I will endeavor to be much more selective of my words in the future."

He barely managed to croak, "Vivien..."

But it was too late. In a swirl of floral scented fabric she was gone, rushing out of the chamber as though being haunted.

And he was alone. Alone with himself. Alone as all the demons of hell crawled from hiding places in his mind and blotted out his personal sky. They set upon him with sharp teeth and all he saw was the long ago past. It had come to claim him, and this time mayhap it would consume him and keep him there forever.

Ravn opened his mouth to scream.

Deep inside him was a well, and it reached into the core of his being. It flexed talons and wings, it arced sinuously and powerfully. It was strength. It was war. It was rage. These were the only bastions available to him since *that day.*

Since Neála and...

What came out was not a scream. It was a roar, and the tirinian fled before it.

Chapter Fifteen
Fire Hunter

Vivien watched Ravn from across the room. She'd separated from him as soon as she could after leaving the council chamber, weary of the raw energy he emoted every moment she was in his proximity. The hour spent in council had only tuned his boiling rage into a simmering haze that anyone could feel. He had forgotten to wear the circlet denoting his rank, but no one mentioned it. No one dared.

His eyes were like rubies and he was unfailingly polite when he spoke, but this was not Ravn. He looked more like the handsome Laird than ever, but really this was the Wolf that she and the Lady of Moonlight and Love had brought back from the wild after he had saved them from the ambush. Her presence had always turned him from a wild beast into a tamed animal, but seeing him in his natural state, she understood now why her people had put him in prison. Just getting near the human, elves knew he was dangerous. She recoiled from him, and he made no move toward her. Yet he was a hero of Rithalion, and their hosts treated him with a distant cordiality. About the only good thing to come out of his savage petulance was none of their hosts now doubted he had fought giants in hand-to-hand combat. At this point they might even be surprised he had needed Vivien to keep away from death's door.

So she'd found this nice corner and had taken up residence there. She was hidden, but not. Separate, but still a part. Marcán stood at Ravn's side. The ambassador had spoken pretty words at the meeting, words that matched his frilly sleeves. He'd spoken much more eloquently than she could ever have, and was able to tell the tale about the La'athai in battle in a way that would have sounded like bragging from her own lips. She now knew why he was a part of this mission. Her father had been right to include him. The truth no longer bothered her, because she actually liked the ambassador, but the pain it had once evoked still had a place that ached in her chest.

Vivien stared at the two men, unseen in her corner. People came up to them, people introducing themselves and their families. They would ask questions and finally get to the one where both men had the same reaction: a glance at one another, furrowed brows, a quick look around the room, and raised hands that showed they didn't know something. She knew what it was they couldn't find, but at that moment, she couldn't move herself to care.

She took a deep breath to calm her racing heart. She should be ashamed, standing there in a corner, leaving her comrades to face the masses alone. She was a coward, not fit to be a commander in battle. What had happened to her since that time? That time when she commanded men to fight a battle from which they thought they would never return. *I should be dead, but here I stand, hiding in some corner in a majestic Elyric building. The Wolf doesn't have any faith in me, and I suppose I can't blame him. My magic is deserting me, and after being named Knight Mage, all I can cast is...*

Her rumination was interrupted by a woman. She walked up to the Wolf and Marcán. She was tall and her blonde hair was long, woven in thick plaits that wrapped around one another and clipped at the back of her head. Her body was that of a warrior, the parts of her uncovered by clothing muscular and toned. When she turned enough for Vivien to see her profile, she saw that it was Katriona, the one guard in her entourage that was a woman. Her smile was wide and sincere, and she was pretty, confident, and powerful.

She was everything that Vivien was not.

Vivien watched an elder approach and he and Marcán began talking animatedly. Meanwhile, Katriona deftly inserted her arm into Ravn's. The barbarian regarded her intently, face still stoic, but she showed no fear. She steered him from the conversation and away a few paces. She spoke softly, smiling subtly, but she alone in the room stood before his inarticulate rage and did not bow before the storm. Rather, she reveled in it. She was asking questions, and his usual curt answers were becoming longer. His body, tensed for battle, was relaxing. The aura of impending destruction was calming. Everyone felt the tide recede, and they were grateful for it. Ravn's eyes lit up as the conversation continued and Vivien couldn't help wondering what she was saying, knowing it must be something rather profound.

She watched the Wolf calm and iron bands across her chest that she hadn't known were there began to loosen. The baby within started to kick and it felt different than normal– ardent, dissatisfied. She placed a hand on her distended belly and looked again to the couple across the crowded room. She was so slender, so poised. She was graceful, with hidden power inside her like a forest cat. Vivien felt a moment of awkwardness, her belly having become big enough that she was uncomfortable riding Sherika. She must look so rotund compared to the beauty beside him now, so...

Tinkling laughter floated from across the room and Vivien watched as Katriona thumped Ravn playfully on one wide shoulder. His eyes flashed a bit from burgundy to ruby, but he said nothing. Vivien's jaw twitched. *He does not like to be hit.* But the barbarian made no complaint, and the warrior woman guided him out of the crowded room. The mountain Laird relaxed again and walked arm-in-arm from the chamber and away from the celebration.

Vivien blinked back tears and tried to breathe. *Maybe this is it. Maybe this is his chance to be happy. I am not for him. I am a half-breed mage and he a human. There is no future for us by the dictates of Elvish society. I am pregnant with another man's child. Why would he want to shackle himself with that kind of responsibility? I have been so selfish, leading him on with professions of love. What is wrong with me?*

Her chest ached. *Yes, what is wrong with me? Dear gods...*

"Jash'ari?"

She swiveled around at the use of the diminutive form of her childhood name, coming face to face with a woman she hadn't seen in many decades. She was a pure elf, young, with crimson hair and startling blue eyes. Her smile lit the entire room, and Vivien's heart soared. She nearly called her Evey, but instead her mouth remembered to use her shield-name, "Starling?"

She found herself enveloped in the woman's arms. Feelings of love and devotion swept through her, and in spite of her earlier ruminations, a sense of peace. She returned the embrace and held on for dear life, tears cascading down her face in a gentle waterfall.

"Jash'ari, words cannot say how happy I am to see you!"

Vivien stepped closer, wanting to be as close to her friend as possible, a friend that was more than a friend, but family. Starling stiffened in her grasp and abruptly pulled away. A feeling of loss swept over her, and she looked at the other woman questioningly. Starling was giving her a similar look, only, one hand was held over her mouth and the other was reaching out towards her midsection.

Vivien gave a slight nod, the epitome of solemnity.

Blue eyes widened with joy and once more Vivien felt herself swept up in unadulterated love. She basked in the warmth, took it all in and gave back what she could in return. "My Starling," she breathed. "My little Starling, you have grown."

A small hand was placed on her belly. "So have you, Jash'ari."

Vivien chuckled. The name meant 'little jewel'. Her father used to call her that as a child, and it was used by all in her acquaintance. "I'm not so little now though, am I?"

Starling pulled away and kissed her on the cheek. "No, I suppose I should call you Jashi instead."

Vivien put her hands on her beloved niece's face and kissed her on the forehead. "Whatever you wish."

Starling's eyes were bright. "When is the baby going to come?"

Vivien shook her head. "I'm not sure. Master Healer Mikarvan says I am already several months along, but because of my human heritage, gestation will vary. We will just have to see."

"I am so excited for you!" Starling's expression developed a seductive look. "So how is your Lord of Ice and Steel?"

Vivien suddenly became still. She'd been expecting this question, only, she didn't know how to answer it. Starling noticed the shift in her demeanor, and her blue eyes clouded with concern. She put a hand on her arm. "What is it?"

Vivien shook her head. "It's nothing. I can tell you..."

"There you are Starling. I should have known you would track down my little sister."

Vivien felt her heart plummet at the sound of his voice, one she hadn't heard in over a century. She looked at Starling before turning around, the young woman's eyes reflecting eons of sadness. She mouthed the words *I'm sorry* just as Anlon came into view.

Anlon, Fire Hunter– Master Cartographer for the far-off city of Isbandar, the Grand Magister's youngest son, and her pure elvin half-brother.

Vivien rose her gaze up to meet his eyes, eyes so much like hers, eyes that almost looked surprised before his features were schooled into the cold frown she remembered about him most. *Is it because I look so much like him now, no longer the child he remembers but a fully-grown woman with our father's features, features he passed on to both of us despite our disparate maternal heritages?* Their eyes were the same color, grey with propensity towards green, and their hair a coppery blonde kissed by the fiery rays of the sun. He was handsome despite his frown, and she wondered if he had always been so attractive. She wondered if she might be his feminine counterpart and that was why the Wolf found her so beautiful.

Vivien struggled to find some words and spoke the first suitable ones to come to her mind even though they bore falsehood. "Fire Hunter. It is good to see you after so many years."

Anlon arched an eyebrow and gave a smile that never reached his eyes. "It is interesting that you say so since I do not feel the same."

Despite knowing the hatred he felt for her, hearing it spoke aloud was like a hammer to her gut. The child within kicked again, almost as though in defense. A mixture of emotion rose within her as a battle waged inside her soul, a battle she could barely understand since one of the sides was so alien to her. It burned bright with fire and anger, blotting out the part of her that was so familiar, so gentle and docile.

Vivien stepped close to Anlon, pitching her voice low. "Then why are you here, Brother? Why are you here at a celebration being given in my honor?"

He stepped away, taken aback by her candor. His eyes searched her face, wondering just as much as she did where her boldness came from. "I assure you it wasn't my decision, Jashi." He spoke the last word almost as a pejorative as he narrowed his eyes and glanced at his daughter. Starling just stood there, her eyes wide at the altercation unfolding before her.

Vivien stepped towards him again, her tone deepening. "When I walked in, I saw a plethora of exits from this room. You can help yourself to any of them at any time. No one is keeping you here."

Anlon searched her face again and his expression became condescending. "I see that the stories just might be true. The *Elthari* mit'saori has become as barbaric as the human companion she fights for."

She recoiled, lurching back before she could stop herself. She knew some kind of reputation had preceded her, only it was much more negative than she would have imagined. In Rithalion she was a hero. Here in Elyrion, she was nothing more than...

The Wolf's *trophy.*

Her throat burned with the force of her emotion. Instead of shrinking away as she once would have done, she lashed out. Quicker than lightening her hand was at the neckline of his tunic and she was pressing him back, back, back into the wall behind him. She pressed her body close to his, much like a lover might, and placed her face alongside his, her fist pushing into his throat. She could feel the pulse there, beating erratically, and she realized he was afraid of her. "That's right, brother. I have become a force to be reckoned with." She pressed her hand harder against his jugular and she felt him struggle to breathe. "But you should know, I fight for no man. I fight for my people. You would be best to remember that."

Vivien stepped back, releasing Anlon. He slumped forward, a hand around his neck, his eyes wide with shock. Then, without even looking at Starling, she turned and stalked away.

She walked out of the celebration hall and into the wide corridor. She had no idea where she was going, so she just walked around until she got her bearings. She then left the building to make her way to the grand home where she and the rest of her party were being kept for the duration of their stay.

It was a beautiful place, home to one of the pureblood elites. Strewn with winding paths, plush gardens surrounded the sprawling structure. Vivien continued her walk there, finally letting the tears come. Long ago memories danced about in her mind, memories of some of the happiest days of her life. Eveleen and Emma were her dearest friends, and her closest family besides her brother and her father. The girls were close in age: Vivien had been eighteen, Evey only twenty, and Emma twenty-three. They had been in the prime of adolescence, and their potential in life shone like bright beacons in the fog that had descended upon the Elvish people.

Vivien finally stopped, her hands clenched in fists. Anlon had always hated her, even before Emma's death. Vivien was the daughter his father had sired upon the unsophisticated, undeserving, human woman who had captured his heart. Vivien was tarnished in his eyes, her human blood making her less than his sister, less a person, not fit to be a companion to his own pureblood daughters.

Only... Evey and Emma didn't care.

They loved me just as I am. They loved me like the sisters I always yearned for.

The tears came fast and hot. Great wracking sobs shook her body. She slumped down beside a bench and rested her arms and head on it. She let the deluge envelop her, let it suffuse her every fiber. Then she just sat there, exhausted. *I will never be worthy. My title is merely that, a title. I will never be worthy of Anlon, or my father, or the Wolf, or my people. I'm just a half-breed living in an Elvish world filled with people who wish to use me as a pawn, as a trophy. Torialvah, my father, and even Ravn. I am...I am nothing.*

It struck her then, like a bolt through the gut. She remembered those words coming from the mouth of a barbarian almost a year ago and understanding inundated her. *Oh gods...*

Vivien rose from the bench and ran. *I am nothing.* She darted through the beautiful garden and into the house, up the stairs and into the chamber suite she'd been provided. *I am nothing.* She threw herself onto the bed, grimacing when too much pressure was placed on her expanding belly. She then curled up around herself, cradling the child within. She felt sorrow, for a child deserved so much more than nothing.

The Wolf cast one look back at the hall, then he realized that he was looking for Vivien and hated himself a little for it. *She hates me. I should be able to tell her my story. I should be brave enough to share it. No! She would hate me more if she knew what happened. She would see it was my fault.* His heart ached, a great pit inside that yawned wide, threatening to envelop him in its darkness.

Katriona pulled slightly on his arm and turned him towards an exit. He'd spoken to her briefly a few times during their journey to Elyrion, but knew very little about her except what was visible. As they walked, the pure elvin warrior pulled the wooden nails from the leather clips in her hair and let the blonde braids fall about her shoulders. Ravn's eyes swept her involuntarily. She was lithe and muscled, in a simple dress of reds with a complex gold trim. She walked with measured assurance and without hesitation, like an acrobat.

Her blue eyes twinkled as she slipped the leather hair pieces onto her belt and smiled. "Angry again so soon?"

Ravn felt a lurch in his chest and looked at her with wide eyes as his cheeks colored. "I am sorry."

"The man who broke a dragon's spine apologizes to this poor, poor archer. How refreshing." Her smile was in her voice, taking the sting from her words.

Ravn glanced back once, to the doorway empty of Vivien. His heart sank again. "You are an archer?"

She nodded, tossing off this fact without pride or humility. "I am considered a master of it. I have bent the bow in many conflicts for over three centuries, fighting first men and animals, then hunting the Liath."

Ravn saw his mother laying on the ground, a lifeless doll. He blinked the image away and frowned. "You serve your people well then. The Liath are a scourge upon the world."

She arched a perfectly shaped brow. "You know the Liath?"

"The first thing I killed with a blade was a Liath leader."

She looked surprised, then impressed, and the next few steps were taken in silence.

"You know, that's how the Liath pass leadership, from the death of the old. How many summers were you?"

Ravn felt the memories churn inside him. He let them, they filled the hole left by the lack of green, laughing eyes. "Thirteen."

She blinked. At the age of thirteen, elves were still children, while humans were entering adolescence and on the cusp of adulthood. He had not felt on the cusp of anything but a bloody death. It was not a heroic tale. He had been lucky, and so many of his kinsman had died in the attack on his home it could hardly be considered a victory. He had lost both his mother and father that terrible day.

Katriona waited for an explanation that would never come. She stopped them as they circled the building and walked down a beautiful paved roadway lined with trees. At the end, the moonlight sparkled off water rippling like a sea of jewels. She tuned under the boughs of the trees reaching overhead from either side, placing a hand to his chest. "Stranger and stranger."

He looked to his companion and she stood there like a trained soldier, relaxed but ready without anticipation or anxiety. He took a deep breath, feeling his mental defenses drop slightly around her as he felt the kinship grow. "You are accomplished. Did you ever marry?"

She nodded sadly, guiding him down the lane. "I did. He was a brilliant swordsman and commander. He met his end by the Liath dragon magic and iron blades."

Ravn darkened. "I understand."

"You do, don't you? So many elves live lives so detached from that kind of horror, they can scarcely understand. It is refreshing to meet someone who does, someone who has seen the evil in the world and knows it needs a sharpened point in the eye instead of cowering fear." Her eyes swept over his face again and again, but they narrowed in spite of the speculative smile that curved her mouth. "Did you really wrestle a dragon in Pergatium?"

He nodded stoically.

She gave a girlish chuckle. "I almost believe you."

He only shrugged.

They exited the wide paved road almost to the edge of the lake. She guided him to a bench carved of one piece of wood to resemble kneeling tir-reath. She pulled gently and he sat next to her, the cool wind a blessing in the heat they had been experiencing as of late. "You really did it, didn't you? And the giants, too?"

Ravn met her eyes and then nodded silently. He thought about the part Vivien had played and knew he owed her his life many times over. It again caused a deep emptiness inside of him, and he looked away. Ravn cast his eyes out to other places along the shore where couples walked.

Katriona smiled slightly. "Sad again? But you have such a beautiful companion sitting beside you."

Ravn shook himself from his dark thoughts. "I am sorry–"

She shrugged. "When I first heard about you, I thought you would be a braggart, full of yourself and bedding any maiden within reach. Then I saw you after you and Vivien Valdera came back to the army after the battle and thought you were an attractive braggart…"

A low flying bird came in down at the edge of the water. A gigantic turtle snapped it off of a rock where it drank, making it disappear in a shower of feathers. Ravn sympathized with the bird. Despite himself, the Laird smiled. "And now?"

"I have never known a liar to ever be this sorry for imagining he has given offense, nor to walk into any Elvish council chamber like he was about to walk into war."

Ravn winced and sighed.

"I find you very attractive, Wolf Barbarian of the far-off mountains. More importantly, I find you puzzling. I like puzzles. I would know you better."

Her words reached into his chest. *If Vivien cannot know me, who can? If Vivien cannot love me, who ever would?* His heart began beating fast. He felt like he was falling.

"What is wrong, Knight Protector? You look like a commander who has lost his men in ambush." Her smile died by inches.

Ravn could only look away, death and misery and eternal loss drowning out his thoughts. If he looked at her, he was sure she would see. He was sure she would know.

"You are pale." She touched his forehead. "And hot."

Ravn tried to breathe, tried to let go. Katriona took his arm and stood. He followed meekly, fighting the horrible storm inside and ignoring everything outside of him. He felt his balance fail and he stumbled as he continuously felt himself falling.

Thrown. I was thrown. We were thrown.

Katriona walked him through the rest of the garden and to his room, avoiding all other people as she brought him there. She only stopped when they stood by his bed. She took him by the shoulders, leveling a warrior's stare at him. "Are you sick?"

Ravn saw the bed, and fear battered aside his pain and anger. The bed alone meant only one thing for him now. It was like a monster hulking in the dark room, waiting, always waiting for him...

Katriona sighed, frowning. She reached forward and began working at his belt.

Ravn grabbed her hands. "What are you doing?"

With strong hands, calloused though delicate, she slapped his away. She undid his belt and the kilt came free. "Getting you ready for bed."

Ravn blinked, ideas creeping in to the fog of his misery. "You know where I sleep?"

Katriona pursed her lips and reached to slip his shirt from his unresisting body. "You are a giant human, and you have been very angry. Of course, I found out where you sleep! Someone must protect my people."

Ravn looked into her eyes, and saw the truth of it. He nodded. She smiled at him, a small thanks for understanding, one soldier to another. Then she pulled the knots on his smallclothes loose and let them fall. Ravn covered himself. "Wait. What is happening here?"

By the end of his question her tunic was on the floor, her trousers a second later. Her naked body was toned, bronzed, and beautiful. She kicked off her slippers. "I have been fighting for over a century. I have seen this before." She moved to the bed, folded down the blankets, and slipped beneath them. "But you take care of your own boots. I don't do boots."

Numb, weakened, he complied. Then he got into bed stiffly, like an automaton.

He lay on his back and she watched him, head propped on one hand. The beautiful warrior just watched him and the silence stretched onward.

He took a deep breath. "What is happening here?"

She smiled impishly and looked at him beneath the covers. "Your body knows."

"But I'm not–"

She frowned, "Of course you are not. Now turn on your side." He began to turn towards her. "Other side, Wolf Barbarian."

Ravn turned away and lay there, looking out the window where a cool breeze snuck in. He repeated, "What is happening here?"

Then he felt her. She curved against him, naked skin soft and pliant. He felt her breasts first, but it was the crinkly hair between her legs pressed against his buttocks that made him stir a little. She relaxed against him and then she just simply held him. Tears slipped from his eyes. They lay there for only gods knew how long, deep into the night. Neither slept, but simply held one another, guarding against personal demons and undead memories.

Finally, slick with dampness, she pulled away. "Holding you is like sleeping inside a bonfire."

Ravn turned over to watch her. Her breasts were dewed with sweat, and she smiled to catch him looking at them. Then she became serious. "What troubles you so much?"

A simple question, without guile or judgment.

Ravn felt the personal guard on all his thoughts and feelings scream in protest, but he said, "A friend asked me to tell her about my past. I… I couldn't and now she is very angry with me."

Katriona nodded knowingly. "Do you trust her?"

His tone was vehement. "With my life."

She nodded again, then leaned down and lay her head on his chest. Her fingers traced the massive scar in the center, as if it had been cracked open and sewn shut. "Does she trust you?"

He paused a moment. Then he remembered Tor and his horrible anger, and how one kiss to her in front of him would drive him to insane jealousy and her disownment. How she had spent so much time with him, even letting him into her tent and her bed to simply be held, while some men would do despicable things while she slept. "I… I think she is trying."

Katriona nodded, silken braids sliding across his skin releasing the scents of musk, cedar, and lavender. "Then she is right to be angry. She wants to know about you. Trust her, Wolf. Believe in her."

He had a spike in panic that her presence smoothed into glass. Ravn lay there, her naked truth pressed against him. He felt her strength, her confidence.

He had to be honest. He was attracted to this woman, but there was something much more than that. Friendship, camaraderie, honesty and respect. "When do I tell her?"

Katriona looked up into his eyes. "As soon as possible, Wolf. Trust must be given and reinforced often. It is a horribly fragile thing."

Ravn heard her and nodded. He pulled her close, glad for her and unwilling to leave her for just a few moments yet.

Chapter Sixteen
All That Was Lost

vivien startled at the knock on her door. She looked around the chamber to see that darkness had fallen and that she must have dozed off. The knock sounded again and she jumped. "Who is there?"

Silence.

She moved to sit on the edge of the bed, her gown splayed all around, and stared at the door, heart pounding. Somehow, she knew who was on the other side.

His voice was deep and the sound of it made her tremble. "Vivien, please let me in."

She collected herself for a moment before standing and making for the door. She opened it and Ravn raised his head and let his hand drop. His hair was unbound, cascading down his shoulders in curled spirals, and his eyes roiled with the intensity of storm clouds. He still wore the kilt she'd dressed him in, and the crisp white shirt. The wide black belt looked better than she had imagined it would. He looked like the Laird she had seen over a century ago, only more filled out, bigger, more muscular. He looked beautiful.

Ravn entered the chamber, closing the door behind him. She instinctively stepped back and he stopped. He regarded her intently and she returned his stare with one of her own. She gathered the strength to break the heavy silence. "Why are you here?"

He swallowed convulsively. "You wanted to know, so I came to tell you."

"Tell me what, Ravn?"

"My story." He looked left, then right, then like a man jumping from a high cliff, he closed his eyes and began to speak. "I had finally come home after months of being on the road. It was a quest I'd chosen to undergo in order to prove myself to Ròs, one that I'd hoped would show her my worth as a husband, one that I'd hoped would protect the child I'd sired upon my mistress. I'd taken one after you left Blacach, having listened to your words on the balcony that night when you told me to pursue my happiness. I swore to return with a heart of a creature that had the strength of my oath to keep my child from the line of succession. I found such a creature at Pergatium. A dragon. I was the one who killed that dragon we battled, and I broke the sword called Arisil."

Vivien swallowed convulsively at the pain she heard in his voice. She wanted him to stop right there, was going to tell him so, but his eyes got a faraway look as he began his tale. He included every detail his mind's eye provided, and even those lying deep within his heart. It was as though he was taking her a century back though time, and it was as if she was there, living those moments with him...

ROSS ⊕ROSS

I scrubbed and scrubbed, drawing a silver knife across my face to hack away at months of wildlife. I cut my hair in Moray's quarters, then sent my most loyal retainer to fetch my best clothes. It was a white shirt with a dark blue doublet and green tartan. The old man had not thought to bring the honor blade of my family, but I had a broken Elvish sword in a loose scabbard. The dragon heart never left my side as I prepared. I had spent a year away from my home and people. I had the heart, the price for the lives and well-being of my lover and our child. I was hale and whole. Moray watched me dress and fretted in the corner. For the first time in a year, I had hope.

"Mi'laird, I do not like this ambassador from the Iron Coast. He spends long days in the company of your wife, and he is far too familiar."

The words the man-at-arms did not say hit me like a physical thing. Since we had met as children, I had known I was to marry Ròs. I'd spent my life trying to love her, only to have it crumble to burning ash in my hands again and again. She had sent me to find comfort in the arms of another, and so I had sired a child upon my beloved Neála. I had made a pact to save them and I had the heart I'd promised. If Ròs found comfort in another, what did that matter? The thought cut through me, for I had hoped that someday she would see me as a worthy husband. But the numbness of the horrors and suffering I had endured to get the dragon heart washed the wound in bitter spirits. If that was not to be, I could live with that. As long as I had Neála and our baby, all would be well.

I clamped down on my feelings and set my jaw. "It matters not."

"Laird, his men act as her personal guard, usurp your soldiers on your wife's orders."

I clenched the satchel containing the heart, long shrunk to something the size of two fists. "Not now, Moray. Please. I must—"

The elderly swordsman looked at his feet and frowned. "Of course, of course."

I pressed my lips together and clapped my retainer on the shoulder. "You trained me in the arts of war, trained me to be a man. I never would have survived without you." Moray rushed forward to embrace me, and I clasped him closely to my chest. "It is over. From this day forth, happiness reigns."

The old man's eyes were full of doubt as we parted, but I summoned my courage and pressed passed him.

"Mi'laird?"

I paused. "Yes, Moray?"

"A dragon?"

I smiled, holding the satchel closer. "The Warlock at the falls guided me to him."

The old man went pale but nodded. I started up the stairs towards my wife's chambers. It was done, the long journey finally over. But every step upwards into the sleeping castle, Moray's warning that my wife may have taken a lover poisoned my joy. Finally, my feet brought us to her door. I had to come to terms that my wife would never want me, never accept me, so I clenched the pack to my chest, knocked lightly, and opened her door.

Ròs was there. She had never been an enchanting beauty, but she was my wife, and she was nude. Her mouse brown hair lay over her shoulders, and her pale skin glowed like alabaster in the moonlight shining in through the part in the curtains hanging over the window. She lay on the bed, watching me with unsurprised eyes, her small breasts as pert and firm as ever, the triangle of hair at the juncture of her thighs brown and downy, her hips slim to the point of girlhood. It was as if the years had not moved her since our wedding day, her virgin body waiting for me. A year ago, her nudity would have caused me to avert my eyes. I would have known that I should avert my eyes. Instead, I drank in the sight of her as if she poured from a broken barrel into me. She smiled and opened her mouth to say something, but under the power of my desire she paused, her cheeks coloring, her breath coming faster.

I couldn't stop myself. I knew her rules, remembered her taunts and her refusals. I knew she would voice them again, but instead of heeding the small voice screaming for me to stop, I crossed the distance to the bed and dropped the satchel.

Then I was on the bed, and she was in my arms.

I crushed her to me, pressing my lips to hers with brazen desire. She struggled for a moment, but only a moment, before she sank into me. With one hand I unbuckled my belt and let my kilt fall where it may. I kissed her with fierce abandon, pausing only to get my shirt off.

She pulled away, her lips swollen, and she gasped, "My... husband returns."

In my head was a pounding thought, My wife... *I tossed my shirt to the side and fell upon her. I took her wrists and moved them above her head, pushing them into the pillows. She spread her legs as she had never done before, lifting them to produce a cradle for my passion. My erection thrummed in anticipation and her womanhood was wet and accommodating as I slipped in without guidance. The feel of her body cupping me tenderly reached into my soul and nearly brought tears to my eyes. I plunged into her and she gasped, her breasts jiggling and her nipples hardening. My manhood continued to swell, the tip becoming achingly full as it caressed the hard rock of her mound deep inside. She made a small noise of pain laced with surprised pleasure and I groaned with the intensity of my response.*

My wife... Always, always, I had been gentle. Always I had been soft and understanding. Always I had looked to be accepted as an equal. Now, I took her like a stallion does a mare, like a lord takes a chambermaid, like a wolf takes a deer. I consumed her, pumping into her with ferocious power, speed, and urgency. She moaned and writhed beneath me, her nectar dampening the bed beneath us. She bucked her hips, trying to match my time until finally giving up and lifting her legs and pointing her feet skyward. I pushed my tongue into her mouth, tasting her submission in every thrust. I transferred her* *wrists to one hand and used the other to press around one breast, tweaking the nipple to make it hard and tall.*

My Wife... My lips left hers and I took half her breast in my mouth. My tongue played with her nipple and I sucked so hard I heard another gasp of pleasure borne of pain. Her hips shifted and her tight passage rubbed my manhood along different walls of her body, touching new things. Her lips slid along my shaft, holding on as if trying to pull me in and hold me forever. I pumped harder, felt as her body clamped tightly upon me. A familiar tension built in the base of my shaft, rumbling with increasing pressure the harder and longer I thrust into her.

Ròs thrashed, unable to free her hands from my grip. Long, gossamer brown strands of hair fell across her face as she moaned, "You are an animal. An animal!"

A red rash instantly spread across her breasts and neck. She bucked and her womanhood clamped upon me again, pulsing over and over as if milking me.

My manhood let go.

I went blind, and it was as if parts of my very soul were spurting inside of her. I filled her, a sacrifice of myself to be one with my wife. Wave after wave shuddered through me as I climaxed again, and again. For a brief moment I gazed into her glazed eyes and thought about an heir. I climaxed again.

Vivien just stood there. His face had a sheen of sweat, an indicator of the strain he felt. Such intimate details revealed how much the event mattered to him, details he recalled even after a century. He saw nothing but the memory playing in his head. Ròs was gone, long gone, but yet he remembered her as though he'd seen her yesterday.

She was flushed, sweaty, and panting beneath me. I let go of her wrists and rolled off her so she could breathe. She just lay there, legs open, my seed leaking from her in thick ropes.

Ròs stared toward the ceiling, thoughts stuttering behind her eyes. She turned to me, mouth working, but no sound issuing. Her face betrayed shame, hurt, loss, and the fading burn of physical ecstasy. I felt my heart quail, and I gave her a small smile.

"Please, wife," I said, chill sweeping over me as sweat dried across my body, "I have walked in the darkest places in the world to fulfill my oath and have brought you the heart of the mightiest creature that walks. Please, tell me you love me."

She opened her mouth, but then the door opposite the bed was kicked open. What issued forth was not words, but armed men.

Ravn took another shuddering breath and he ran his hands through his hair.

ᴆʀᴀɢᴏɴ Vᴇꜱꜱᴇʟ

Still nude and unsteady from exertion, I sprang shakily from the bed. I crouched to hurl myself upon the intruders, when they pulled after them my mistress. Neála was naked and weak, weeping, with fresh bruises on her pale skin. I froze. A finely dressed man, dark of eye and hair, followed them in. His curly hair bobbed as he suppressed laughter, the smile on his face created by tears and screams for mercy.

His voice was languid, accented like those born on the Iron Coast. "The Lord of Blacach has returned. I see you have tasted my mountain flower. My men and I have tasted yours in return."

Ravn's eyes flashed to Neála. The anguish, the shame, the pain there trebled. The agent of the ironmongers said something else, but I was already moving. I could not hear, and I would not be stopped. The first soldier touching Neála looked up only in time to catch a kick to his sternum. He doubled over, and the I drew the soldier's dagger. The other tried to pull my mistress close, but I reached with the dagger and stabbed him in the eye, then reversed it and plunged it into the first man's skull. It was quick. It was efficient. It was completed while I spoke only in the language of an enraged beast. It was the first time I had felt such all-consuming rage. It was born that day. I have never been without it since.

Again, he paused. He squeezed his eyes shut and breathed. He breathed like a bellows, loud and powerful as if to blow away the thoughts inside him. His eyes were glowing red.

Neála fell to the floor, the two men holding her dying in succession. The coastman's smile had disintegrated into gaping shock. He cried out as the dagger swung towards him in a powerful arc. He flinched away, sparing his spine, but his cheeks were cleft open, the weapon shattering his upper teeth in a cloud of white and red fragments. But more men poured from the door, and I, still clutching the dagger in one hand, grabbed Neála's wrist and hauled her to her feet.

I spared only one glance at my traitor wife, who lay on the bed and gaped at the instant and total ferocity on display. Then I shouldered open the door to Rós' room and pulled Neála into the hall. From behind, a wordless bellow followed, and it seemed that the nighttime castle was coming alive. Men from the Iron Coast were coming from every door and up the stairs. One had a drawn sword and I pounced forward like an animal, riding the soldier to the ground and savaging him with a steel fang. Then we were running, running, down the hall and up the stairs, onto the marble floor even as my mind screamed in protest and we came to the balcony.

My rage cleared and left me weak and confused. There was no way up or out. Only the valley far below held any escape, at the bottom of a massive maw with stone teeth. Men were coming up the stairs, cautious of the me and my dagger, but they were coming and nothing would stop them.

I took Neála in my arms and pulled her close, both of us naked and cold. I could smell the fear in her, the hurt, the sweat of the men that had forced themselves upon her. She was weeping openly, and crumbling against the bulwark of my chest. I stroked her hair. "I am so sorry, Neála. I will always love you." Weapons drawn, the soldiers crept onto the balcony. I turned her away from them, so she would not have to see them coming. "I am so sorry. So very sorry."

"Ravn," she said, voice brittle between gasps, "our son..."

A tiny cry echoed up the staircase and I felt my blood run cold. Neála spun from my arms and took one step toward the barbican of men before her legs gave out and she fell, weeping, to her knees.

"My son. In my haste to protect my lover," Ravn covered his eyes with his hands, "I had forgotten my son."

The men of the Iron Coast hung back, and Ròs strode through them like a queen. Sweaty and disheveled, she was wrapped in a pristine white silk gown I had never seen before. My sword belt was tightened comically around her waist, the hilt of the broken blade protruding from the sheath, the tongue of the belt nearly reaching the ground. In her arms she carried two precious things. The first was the travel-battered satchel that contained the dragon's heart, and the second was the squalling form of my first-born child. She came to the edge of the men, bristling steel and ready for battle, and paused there.

Doom and fear swirled through me like a caustic liquor. I could feel my heart beating as if trying to escape, finding some means out as it panicked and died by inches in my chest. Ròs gazed upon me coolly, regally, as the I felt my world start to crumble. She looked pointedly at my lover collapsed on the floor, and then at my dagger. My numb fingers dropped it and it rang off the marble.

My voice was weak and plaintive, "Please, Ròs..."

She blinked, unemotional and unaffected.

I tried again, and my words were whining, dying on my lips, "Please, Ròs... that child is my son."

The Lady of Blacach looked at the crying babe, wrapped in a simple blanket, as if she had never seen him before. She walked forward as if in a trance. Neála reached up desperately for the infant and Ròs gave him to her gently, lifting the mother to her feet without ever putting her eyes upon her.

Then, satchel in hand, she took dainty steps toward me. I saw the cold nothingness in her eyes and shook my head. "I won the heart of a dragon. I came back to fulfill my oath." Ròs placed the bag in my arms, against my chest. I held it reflexively as my only shield against what may come. "Please, Ròs, I proved my word is strong. I proved I am worthy."

Ròs stared into my eyes, then drew the broken blade. For a brief moment, I saw a blaze of hatred as she plunged it through the bag and into my chest. Pain radiated from the wound throughout my body, but suddenly went silent. Only the ice-cold shard of Arisil in my heart felt of anything, and it was blinding agony. My strength left in an instant and was replaced with seeping, crawling death.

She whispered, "You were never good enough."

Then she pushed me over the railing into the open air.

Vivien shuddered. He still covered his eyes, and his muscular chest rose and fell. She looked at his shirt and remembered the scar beneath it, far bigger than what would be caused by the blade of a longsword. She wanted to reach out to him, but didn't, waited until he could continue. His next words were broken, much like that Elvish sword...

I tumbled as I fell. It felt like all night, but it had to have been but mere moments. I heard the crunch of my landing, but felt nothing. The blade protruded from my chest like a flag of surrender, keeping the bag in place as a macabre trophy. I couldn't twitch even a single finger, couldn't move or close my eyes. I had bested the giant. I had killed the dragon. But I had not been able to defeat Ròs or her hate for me.

There was a shadow above, a warbling cry like a broken bird, then a terrific impact of blood and muscle. My head slumped to the side and I saw her. Broken... dying. Neála's body shuddered as it took its last tortured breath and was still, robbed of every sweet smile or tender moment that could have been.

I could not reach for her, could not touch her. I was trapped there watching the blood trickle from rents in her skin caused by the impact. I was forced to watch, forced to take in her death, knowing full well my part in it.

Then there was another impact, much smaller, but no less agonizing, right beside me. Thump...

I knew who it was without seeing him, and within moments I felt the warmth of his blood pool around my left hand. In my mind's eye I could see my son's skull split open like a melon. I never even got the chance to hold him. He never had the chance to hear my voice tell him how much I loved him.

My heart stopped, but it would not stop hurting.

It has never stopped hurting.

His eyes winked out, as if the light had died with his story.

Vivien just stared at him for a few moments. Tears streamed down his face, down into the silver-streaked beard she'd trimmed just that morning. His shoulders were slumped, like the weight of a hundred years rested upon them. One hand was pressed against his chest as though he still felt the broken sword pushed into his soul.

Oh gods, what have I done? What have I done?

Vivien flung herself at him, felt him jerk as she wrapped her arms around his wide torso. She let the tears come and she sobbed onto the wall of his chest.

ROSS EROSS

She felt his arms wrap around her and hold her close. By the trembling of his body, she knew he was crying too, and for a while they just stood there, swaying in the dim light coming from the moonlight streaming through the window.

At last, they stepped apart, but she kept her head lowered. Guilt suffused her, and she was almost afraid to look up at him. *I've been wanting him to tell me these things from his past. But they are so terrible, he was right to want to keep them to himself. I feel so selfish. He must think I'm a terrible friend.* Anger surged in, taking away the guilt in a tidal wave of dark, churning waters. Damn Ròs for being the despicable creature that she was, a vile construct who had felt the lives of three people were hers to take.

Something slithered inside her then, and she could feel it, power just waiting to be tapped.

She abruptly looked up at Ravn, and she blinked in wonder. *By the gods, the colors! I've never seen him like I do now!* His hair was made up of individual stands, each with a different hue. Some were like spun gold, others chestnut brown, and then there were the ones that were like crimson flame. They spiraled along his face and down to his shoulders to a bright white. It was his shirt, and she could see every crease, every fold where it fit loosely over his broad shoulders. Her heart began to thunder in her chest as she looked back up at his beautiful hair, further up to his chin, his mouth, so expressive even now. She made it to his eyes and her heart stopped. They were the blue gray she had come to experience the most, but now she could see something more. It danced within those blue depths, wavering, waiting for that moment to leap forth. It was not alien, for she'd seen it many times before. It was the red of his anger. But it wasn't just any red. It was the dark red of drying blood mixed with the bright crimson of freshly spilled. They mingled together to make...

A wave of weakness swept over her and she swayed on her feet. She put a hand on Ravn's chest to steady herself and instantly his arms were around her, steadying her. "Vivien, are you alright?"

The flood suddenly sizzled away under the onslaught of what she felt now. Passion flared through her like a bolt, and every sense erupted into life. His hands around her were like searing brands, burning into her despite the gown she wore. The fabric beneath her hands was coarse and unrefined and she dropped her hands. She could smell the scent of the bath soap she'd used on him that morning, the oil she'd used to shave his beard, and something more. Something more... feminine. She stepped back, confused at this influx of sensations, and his arms dropped from her sides. She heard his breathing, and hers, but over that, she heard his heart like a drumbeat to the gods.

"Vivien?"

She looked up at him then, into his eyes, and she saw a forlorn expression before he flinched.

She blinked with the shock of that small motion and her breath came out in a great sigh. *What must he think of me?* She swayed again, but Ravn caught her

132

once more. She gripped his thick arms, hung onto him almost for dear life as her breath hitched making its way back into her lungs. Her voice was barely the breath she managed to inhale. "Ravn..."

The pupils of his eyes widened and his expression shifted.

He stepped into her and his lips crushed hers in a burning kiss, one that took away whatever breath she had. She returned it like her life depended on it, opening her mouth to give him access. His teeth ground against hers, his lips almost punishing in their fervor. She felt it again from deep inside her, that coiled power ready to strike. But she quelled it. *No, I don't need you. Not against this man.*

In an uncharacteristic, wanton display, Vivien stood on the tips of her toes and wrapped her arms around Ravn's neck. She pressed her body along the length of his, opening herself to him fully, letting him take what he chose. Something inside her roared to life and she bit down on his lower lip.

Ravn jerked, and for the briefest moment, she was appalled at what she'd done. Tor would have...

Ravn growled deep in his throat, easily lifting her in his arms and carrying her with purposeful strides over to the bed. She imagined that he would toss her down on it, but as it was, he lay her down gently, his hands roaming over her sides and distended belly. An ache settled low in her pelvis, one she'd only felt a handful of times in her life.

I want you.

The words were so loud in her mind she thought she'd spoken them aloud. She was about to say something, but then his lips were on hers again. The blood from her bite touched her tongue and a wild tanginess suffused her taste buds. She inhaled sharply and plunged her fingers into his thick hair. The curls captured them and so she just took the untamable hair in fistfuls and held it there.

His mouth was everywhere at once, his hands scooping up beneath her gown and around to her backside to cup her buttocks. His lips trailed along her jaw and down her neck to her chest. She splayed her palms over his shoulders, and irritated by the shirt, moved her hands to the laces at the front. Then for a moment he stilled. He brought his head up and looked deep into her eyes. Meanwhile she slowly removed the laces, captivated by the beauty she saw there, the play of color, the swirling emotions captured within.

He didn't say anything, and neither did she.

Ravn moved one hand beneath her gown, sliding it along the curve of her hips and to the juncture of her thighs. His gaze bore into hers, almost daring her to stop him, and the color of his eyes darkened. His hand cupped her womanhood, his fingers probing along her soft folds. She pulled the unlaced shirt over his shoulders and her gaze admired the taut muscle beneath. Dear gods he was beautiful. The scars were merely that... scars. She saw past them to the unmarred flesh beneath. But there were the times she didn't, and they simply were a part of him, a part of the whole man she had come to love so deeply.

Suddenly she gasped. His fingers plunged inside of her and her hips involuntarily arched up to meet him. She heard him moan at her response just before his lips once again claimed hers. She gripped his shoulders as he moved his hand along her pubis, his fingers moving in and out of her slick entry. His kiss deepened as she bucked against him, the familiar sensation just before climax arriving much too swiftly. She tried to resist, tried pushing him away as she fought against him.

It was to no avail.

She dug her fingernails into the tops of his shoulders as her world shattered into a million shining stars. She screamed. Or she would have if his lips hadn't still been over hers. She trembled and shook beneath him, his mouth absorbing her fevered cries. He took his hand away and she could feel the warm wetness of his fingers as they slid over her hips and up her back. Never had she had such a powerful response, and every muscle in her body quivered in the aftermath.

Ravn released her lips, kissed her on her chin, the tip of her nose, and then her forehead as she regained her breath. He brought his hands up to cup her face and she could smell her damp scent on his fingertips. His gaze was intent as he kissed her again, his lips soft and gentle. Then, smelling the same thing she did, he put his fingers into his mouth.

His eyes widened, the pupils suddenly dilating and the irises shifting to a brilliant blue. It was as though a flash of recognition swept over him. However, he said nothing, merely positioned himself at her side, wrapped his arms around her, and pulled her close against him. She gave a deep sigh and allowed herself to relax, allowed herself the luxury of lying against him.

She closed her eyes and floated in blissful peace. Within moments she was asleep.

Chapter Seventeen
Swirling Doubts

Vivien awakened that morning to find Ravn gone. She got up, wondering if the entire encounter after his revelation had been a dream. After all, the details were rather vague and strangely muzzy. She'd slept in her gown, but the fabric was of the light and airy variety, and it hadn't crinkled over the night. She tried putting on a pair of her trousers. They no longer buttoned at the front, and she had to take them off and find another pair. Those were tight. She wondered how much one little baby could grow overnight.

Once dressed, Vivien stepped out of the room and into the house proper. She thought about looking for Ravn, their vague tryst swirling about in her mind. But then she remembered what he'd told her, how guilty she'd felt about it, and the woman she'd seen him talking to at the gala. Maybe hers was the scent she'd perceived...

She stopped in the middle of the hallway and frowned. It was a detail that suddenly stood out among all the others. Somehow, she'd smelled the scent of another woman on him. Somehow, it hadn't mattered. She put a hand to her forehead, trying in vain to recall other details more clearly. She heard someone's approach and looked up. It was Starling.

Suddenly she remembered. She'd seen Anlon, her elitist older brother. He'd offended her. She'd pushed him against a wall. *Oh gods...*

Starling was suddenly at her side, a comforting arm around her back, her voice tinged with concern. "Jashi, are you alright?"

Vivien looked at her friend, the dearest one she had besides Mikarvan and the Wolf. She kept her voice low, and used the diminutive of Starling's given name. "Evey, I'm having a hard time remembering things. Did your father...?"

Evey nodded before she could finish. "Yes, he approached us at the gala. He said some things. You...you got upset."

Vivien lowered her head. "I'm sorry. I shouldn't have done that."

Evey pursed her lips. "Why not? He deserved it." Her friend urged her back down the hallway. "Come, let's get you back to your chamber suite. You look pale."

She shook her head. "I can't recall when last I ate something. And my clothes don't fit. And I should try to find..."

Sensing Vivien's rising distress, Evey put a calming hand up to her cheek and interjected. "Yes, we should do those things. Let me come with you."

Vivien hesitated before finally nodding.

Evey locked arms with hers and they walked in the direction Vivien chose to go. She looked up and down the hallways they passed, hoping to see Ravn. But he wasn't there. She hoped to see Cora, maybe thinking she might be able to help with the fit of her clothes, but she didn't see the handmaid either. Her belly growled. *Where are the damned kitchens?*

"So, I have heard tell that the Council is in favor of rendering aid to Rithalion in the event that she is once again beset by the Iron Coast."

Thoughts of food forgotten, Vivien turned to Evey, her eyes wide.

"Don't look so surprised, Vivien. Your ambassador speaks well." She smiled, her eyes shining with happiness. "He speaks more than well, and his words resonated with the people of Elyrion.

"Evey, why are you telling me this? Isn't it the duty of someone on the Council to..." She stopped and her niece lost her smile. "Anlon was supposed to come and tell me, wasn't he."

It was more a statement than the question it had been phrased as, yet Eveleen answered all the same. "He was. He chose me to come in his stead." A blush suffused her cheeks. "Actually, I insisted."

Vivien nodded, and she felt a weight lifted from off her soul, the weight of an entire city. Now only three rested there–Isbandar, Moirdem, and Sharderia– the ones left that Rithalion hoped might swear allegiance to their cause. She swept Starling into an embrace, pressing a cheek against hers. They stood there and held one another, tears mingling at the place where their faces met. "We will be leaving soon. I will miss you."

Evey pulled away and shook her head. "Not before you meet with the Council." She looked Vivien in the eyes. "And you won't have to miss me for a while yet. Father and I will be accompanying you to Isbandar."

Vivien nodded. "I've been wondering why you are here. You are far from home."

"Since Father is on the Isbandarian Council, he was asked to come here with some others to discuss the Liath threat and formulate a plan to counter them. I decided to accompany him, knowing I would get to see family we don't get to see very often. Not only that, I would get to see you that much sooner." Evey smiled.

Vivien looked into her niece's eyes. "I've missed you too."

"Come! Let's get you something to eat and clothes that fit. But then we must plan for our trip to Isbandar. We absolutely must have a carriage. You are too far along to be riding astride your tir-reath!"

Vivien nodded and allowed Evey to lead her through a couple corridors. Within moments, the smell of food reached her nose and her belly rumbled. It was about time...

Suddenly she slowed. She heard him before she saw him, his deep voice getting closer as they reached an intersecting hallway. She'd finally put the Wolf out of her mind, deciding that her memories upon waking were simply the result of an overactive imagination during sleep. But now, hearing his voice, her mind was awash with images filled with intimacy and her face flushed. The barbarian stepped into view, his body bare from the waist up, his mouth turned up into a smile as he looked at the woman walking beside him.

Katriona.

Vivien came to a halt. Her arm jerked when Evey was thrown off balance. Her heart stuttered in her chest as she was assaulted by a myriad of thoughts, all of them tearing her asunder.

He looked so... *happy.*

Evey turned back to look at her just as Ravn looked away from his companion and into her direction. His smile disintegrated and his brows furrowed as she reached out a hand to the closest wall for support. His shoulders... each of them bore faint traces of having been deeply scratched...

She felt a hand on her upper arm. "Vivien, are you alright? You look pale."

Vivien looked away from Ravn and leaned against the wall. "I'm fine. Just a little dizzy," she lied. She closed her eyes. *He deserves to be happy. He doesn't need me. I'll be just fine without him. I'll have this baby and I'll be fine.*

She felt another hand, this one on the side of her face, and the heat of it told her to whom it belonged. She opened her eyes to find the Wolf standing there, his eyes filled with worry. Still beside him was the woman Katriona. She breathed deeply, struggling to contain her emotions, when a scent hit her.

Another memory came to the fore of her mind, another one from the night before. It was the feminine scent she'd picked up from Ravn.

Vivien felt as though a boulder had crashed down on her, and her world spun. He'd been with Katriona before he'd come to see her in her chamber suite. But that wasn't the part that disturbed her. He'd proceeded to share an intimate moment with her even when he'd just shared his bed with another woman not long before.

Hurt enveloped her in a tight cocoon and her chest constricted. *I suppose I can't blame him, I have been so heinous after all. My lack of understanding pushed him away, but why did he bother to come back if he'd found that understanding in the arms of the beautiful master archer?* Certainly, the elves lived in a polyamorous society where people took lovers as they chose, but there were rules to that, and Ravn had claimed to care about her, to love her. He should have told Vivien about his intentions towards Katriona before bedding her, and if it had been an impromptu thing, at least told Vivien before proceeding with intimacy with her. Only, all of this was new to Ravn. How would he know the rules?

It didn't make the hurt less. Ravn didn't come from such a society. It was alien to him. Yet he took another lover without telling her.

But doesn't he deserve it? Doesn't he deserve happiness?

His voice was close, close enough that she could feel his breath on her face. "Vivien, you don't look well. Let me carry you back to your apartment."

She numbly pushed his hand away, cringing from his presence. "No, don't touch me. I'm fine."

She sensed his recoil more than felt it, saw his eyes darken under the onslaught of her rejection.

"Vivien..."

"Please, you've done enough. Just leave me."

His hand dropped and she turned to make her way back down the corridor to her apartment, a confused Evey following behind.

Astride her reindeer, Katriona moodily looked over the caravan. It was big, five times larger than the one they had ridden in with. Instead of just two scouts and their tir-reath, four guards and their mounts, the ambassador, a spellcaster, the Wolf, their mounts, and the pack moose, they now had much, much more. They had two carriages, twenty-four additional guards, six additional scouts, two handmaids, ten personal attendants, five recalcitrant councilmen and the daughter of one of those councilmen who happened to also be the niece of one very pregnant Mage Protector, Vivien Valdera. With them were all of their reindeer, tir-reath, and moose. She rolled her eyes and shifted her bow over her shoulder, grunted when her reindeer stumbled over something on the uneven path. She missed the more intimate group they had on their way to Elyrion, and hated they were stuck acting as part of the escort for the stuffy council members making it back to their home in Isbandar.

It wasn't long before they stopped for the night and began preparations for camp. Half of the scouts did a perimeter check while the rest went hunting. Sometimes she would accompany them, but tonight she had a shift at the watch and she didn't want to make herself overly tired. That was the only benefit to traveling with a larger group; there were more people to rotate sitting the night watch.

Katriona made herself busy with the cooking fires while keeping an eye on the immediate vicinity. They traveled through forest and it was impossible to view everyone, so she had to keep happy with what she could see. The carriages stopped nearby and the reindeer teams were promptly unharnessed and seen to by those who preferred the duty at the end of every day. The door of the closest one opened and Katriona watched as Vivien and Starling stepped out of it. Even though she had the luxury of sitting all day on the plush seats within, the Mage Protector looked tired. Her lips were pinched, her face pale. She held a hand over her burgeoning belly, almost as though in pain.

The camp was rife with talk. Rumors of the Mage Protector had preceded her, and not all of them good. Some of those rumors had probably been perpetuated even more by her comrades from Rithalion, the men who had escorted Vivien, the Wolf, and Ambassador Marcán to Elyrion. The rumors went for miles, some of them bordering on the ridiculous. It was moments like these, seeing the woman in obvious physical distress, that Katriona discounted all that craziness and went with what lay before her. Vivien was no warrior. She was no leader. The aggrandizing stories the La'athai painted were nothing more than that: stories. She had been nothing but a pretty piece in the fighting force sent to rout the Iron Coast, one that hid behind the loincloth of a human barbarian who was the most unlikely of heroes.

Since the moment of their departure from Rithalion, Vivien had kept to herself. She didn't bother speaking with the guards and scouts, and even more, never mixed with them in any capacity. She only spoke with the Wolf, and when the hushed talk from the others became too much, she cast him away as well. She never cast her magic, and when she did, it was the magic for which she had supposedly been punished for many months ago. Somehow, she was pregnant with a child that had died before their battle, one that she had lied about so that she could continue to do the things she wished to do. Either that, or she wasn't pregnant at all, simply engorged with the darkness she used when she cast the magic of the dark fae.

Katriona continued to watch Vivien from the corner of her eye. She didn't believe the last part about the pregnancy. That was part of the crazy talk from some of the others. But she did believe much of the rest. Vivien was definitely no leader. Hells, Katriona wouldn't be caught dead in a retinue with her as the figurehead. The La'athai talk of her circling the encampment every night before the soldiers went to bed was simply unbelievable to Katriona in light of what she had seen the past month. Vivien was simply a spellcaster who had ridden to fame atop the shoulders of a good soldier. It didn't make Katriona hate her, but she didn't necessarily like her either.

But the Wolf did. It was plain to see he loved her, no matter what everyone else thought. This irked Katriona, but it didn't stop her from giving him her best advice. She felt she owed it to a man whom she had come to respect and appreciate in spite of his own flotilla of rumors. It had been nearly a week since the convoy had departed Elyrion, and every day since that day, the tension around Vivien's part of the camp noticeably rose. Yet, Katriona remained close, wanting to be a friend to him whenever she could. If the other guards noticed, they said nothing of it to her, best since she could squash most of them in the sparring ring, even without her weapon of choice.

The Wolf arrived astride his massive white reindeer. He dismounted, his thick brows furrowed just like they were every evening. He handed the beast off to the one who came for him, then went in search of the pack moose, but not before he glanced in Vivien's direction. His shoulders slumped for a moment and a look of grief passed over his face before he squared up again and schooled his expression.

As Katriona watched him walk away, a niggling of unease swept over her, followed by a surge of anger. *Why does she persist in treating him this way? Can't she see he's stupid in love with her? Why does she keep what is bothering her to herself? Why not tell him so at least he's not hanging in limbo, wondering what he did that was so wrong?*

She turned back to the fire, stoking it with the dry tinder that had placed beside her by the one responsible for that task this evening. She pensively watched the flames grow, the unease remaining after the anger had died away. She tried to think what it was that made her feel thusly besides the obvious fact that it was in regards to the Mage Protector and her Wolf.

Her Wolf.

Katriona tensed at that thought, not liking the sound of it.

She busied herself with another fire, and then helped Gregor start preparing the evening meal for their side of the encampment. Soon other people started sitting around the fires, and before long, there were fifteen men sitting there, bowls in hand, patiently waiting. By then the sun had begun to set and the tents had been erected. Katriona scoffed. The tents were only for the privileged few among them, and that definitely did not include her. Not that she needed it to. She loved the stars in the open sky, beacons in the darkness of the night. When she was a girl her mother would write songs about them, and people from all over the city would come to hear her sing. Katriona missed her voice, rising like a living thing over the masses, reaching into every soul and setting it free.

At long last, the meal was served, and after, the men sat around and drank a nightcap of chamerian tea. There were no stories to be told, not this night, for the day had been unbearably hot and everyone was tired to the very bones that held them upright in the saddle. They lay down on their pallets, some with blankets, some without, some fully dressed, some with nothing on but the cloth between their thighs.

Katriona continued to sit there for quite some time. The men taking the first shift spread themselves throughout the camp, making sure that every spot was covered in the case of ambush. Sound drifted to her on the small breeze, the voices of men from other campfires. They were comforting to hear, and made her feel like she was a part of something larger than herself, much the way she felt when she was in war-camp leading up to the battle against the Iron Coast. No fool, she realized where her thoughts had gone and made a slight amendment to her dislike of the larger group with which they now journeyed, giving it another positive notch on her mental staff.

She finally lay down on her pallet, allowed herself to relax from the rigors of the day. Footsteps heralded someone's approach, and she looked up to see the Wolf sit down at the fires. *He looks more haggard than I have ever seen him, the lines on his face made more defined by the shadows provided by the dancing flames. He seems older somehow, more worldly, like he has seen things no other man has seen before. And for all I know, maybe he has.* She thought to rise from her bed to join him there, but hesitated.

Instead, she just watched him. She watched him as he sat there, the weight of what seemed like a hundred years etched upon his face.

Chapter Eighteen
Ambush

Marcán solved problems. It was his nature, and his calling. He was gifted, talented, and insightful. He had always been the one to make peace between childhood friends. Marcán had to remind himself there was only so much he could do. His eyes were drawn across the lake of men to the tall form of the Wolf and shook his head, sighing.

The barbarian was already stinging from being chastised by the council members' guards for wanting them to pull their tents into the main mass of the host. He was then berated for balking at stopping at the appointed time instead of at a more defensible place. Finally, he was rebuked for putting so many men on guard duty as if they were at war. The combination left the Wolf in rare form. Marcán had wanted to intercede, but had only found out about the altercation as it ended, the captain of the council members' private guard having delivered the lesson in no gentle terms. The Wolf had kept his tongue, but not his calm, and everyone could feel his indignation radiating outward. Then he had come upon Vivien. Whatever words they exchanged had been short and heated.

Across the settling men, the Wolf became a towering inferno of hurt and anger. Vivien walked away without further comment. He just stood there, his helplessness giving way to fear, hope and happiness crumbling into a pile in the center of his being. Marcán knew the only warmth that filled his soul would be from fury, and he watched that pile of debris begin to catch fire. The rest of the camp gave them both a wide berth but for Evey, who met with Vivien and steered her away from him and toward her tent, speaking low and soothingly.

In his youth, Marcán was the one to find sad souls wandering the gardens and walkways of Rithalion and gotten them to open up about their problems. It was only a matter of time before he entered the service of a Lord and learned the art of statecraft. He had brokered trade deals from distant cities, ended tensions between outlying human nations, and now gained support from another elvin city to fight a war. Yet, as he watched the Wolf school his face into a stoic mask, the diplomat knew there were some things that he just could not fix. He sighed, finished tensioning the lines for his tent, and let his brain gnaw at the problem anyway.

Elyrion had been gracious in supplying men to fight for Rithalion, but there was reason to believe that asking the other cities for troops would be far less straightforward. There were fewer family ties the further they travelled, and the danger to their cities much less even if the Iron Coast made good with the attack. The personal problems between the heroes tasked with showing themselves to be the best and brightest would cripple the negotiations. Vivien obviously did not want to be near the Wolf. That would be fine, but the council members that Elyrion had sent to help make their case in the next cities were beginning to notice the two acting like lovers in a spat. That would add complications.

Marcán tossed his pack into the tent and was about to take off his sword belt, thankful he was not forced to wear armor like the now multitude of bodies in the mission, when he saw the Wolf looking agitated and hemmed in. They were no longer a small party, but their twelve was now sixty with the four council members - two from Elyrion and two returning to Isbandar - their aides, and guards. The Wolf did not set up a tent, but simply unrolled his blankets and set his pack at the head. He made no move to undo his armor or put up his weapon, but instead scanned the road and the thick mass of trees on every side. Marcán thought he was looking for something to worry about rather than dwell on Vivien, but Marcán doubted he would find such a distraction. The choices were talk to him now, in the anonymous hubbub of the camp, or try to find him in the woods wherever he made off to. Dark was coming fast, and any traces would be hidden by the night. That made the decision easy.

Marcán tightened his belt and walked toward the Wolf. Either by accident or design, the huge barbarian picked up his shield, turned away and bounded off through the camp towards the wild. Marcán sighed. In general, he was fit, but nothing to match the muscled barbarian's pace and unflagging endurance. That left him with Vivien, who was chatting amicably with Evey just outside her tent as the original party lit up their communal fire. Her mount, Sherika, curled up beside the low blaze, greedy for any warmth she could steal after a long day going far too slowly.

Marcán strode over, noticing Fire Hunter near his own fire watching Vivien and Evey. The councilman frowned at the women. *Another problem. Well, that one will wait. Fire Hunter is Vivien's brother, but he is on the Council for Isbandar, and if he has a problem...* He filed it away and for later and forced a smile. "Good evening, Starling... Mage Protector."

Evey returned an innocent grin. "Evening Ambassador."

Vivien smiled at him wanly. Marcán took it as the invitation it wasn't and stepped closer, taking her by the elbow. "Might I have a word?"

Vivien blinked at him, suddenly a hare caught in the shadow of a hawk. Evey nodded graciously and withdrew, giving the two a dozen paces more than was probably necessary into the gathering night.

Marcán looked into Vivien's green eyes, and could see the turmoil there. Whatever was going on was eating at her, and his brows arched with worry. "Vivien, please, you have to talk to someone." Her eyes became wet with tears that glistened in the firelight. He did not remove his hand but moved it to a more supportive place on her elbow. "Things are going on and I am worried for this mission if they continue."

Vivien's face fell. "I should just go home, Marcán. I don't even know why I am here."

Marcán's mouth dropped open. He was flabbergasted, all his prepared thoughts blasted to bits. "Vivien, you are here because you are critical to convincing the elvin nations to come to war." Her eyes fixed on him and she shook her head, but he saw her doubt went deeper and he pressed on. "You and the Wolf risked Pergatium. You and the Wolf fought the dragon, the giants, and masterminded how to face the Iron Coast with the La'athai."

"But you are so much more..."

Marcán set his jaw. "Yes, I am a brilliant orator, and there is no way to make you one in a few weeks. Yet, you are a Mage Protector of Rithalion, and you are here because you stood against the hordes of stinking rabble that would have sacked and raped our city for a hundred years or more. I may dabble in a few magics, but you are a mage. I may carry a sword, but you are a swordswoman. It would take me a lifetime to become half of what you have made of yourself. You are here for you. You were only chosen here to be yourself, to show them that we are willing to fight for ourselves. We are in need of helping, not saving. You are the strength of our people."

Tears streamed freely down her face. "I am not just a trophy?"

"Vivien, you are respected and adored, not an ornament of vanity." Suddenly Marcán understood a lot of her behavior over the past weeks. "It was always known you and the Wolf would be in this mission to help Rithalion. I was not decided upon until much later."

"I thought... my father..." She covered her mouth, her eyes widening. "My father! I left him without word of love or farewell!"

Marcán folded her into his arms, pressing her to him as well as her distended belly allowed. "He is your father, my dear. He will understand and knows you love him."

She sobbed into his chest once, twice, then pulled away slightly and smiled at him, a true smile, and wiped at her eyes. "You are a good man, Marcán." Then she kissed him lightly on the lips.

Marcán felt his mind blank and his mouth tingle from the contact. He blinked and smiled awkwardly. It had been a sweet endearment, beautifully and perfectly her. Pure elves did not kiss as much as the lower castes but—

Marcán felt, more than saw, the burning flames that bathed him in murder.

He turned with Vivien to see the red eyes of the Wolf, glowing so bright they were like lanterns in the evening dusk. The entire camp had come to a standstill, every eye on the pair if, for no other reason, than the glowing eyes of the barbarian. He held his axe in one hand, shield strapped to one arm, his chest heaving with his hard breathing. Some of the elves of Elyrion were even looking for their weapons. Marcán's mouth went dry. A metallic taste flooded it and suddenly he had the urge to urinate.

Vivien looked into that bright red light and frowned. "What is it?"

Marcán quelled the urge to shush her. He had seen the Wolf in battle. He had seen him angry. He had never seen him like this. When he spoke, the Lairdland native's voice was deep, ominous, and forged of burning iron. "You move on quickly."

Marcán looked from one to the other. He could feel something between them, something far outside his realm of experience, but it was there. Rather than crumble and shrink, he felt the same kind of growl come soundlessly from Vivien as if a slumbering beast had been awakened.

"Uncivil accusations from a man who came to me bathed in the scent of another woman!"

Marcán took a double lungful of breath. *It is true. The rumors are true.* All the whispers he had discounted, the innocent explanations he had believed, yet here they were speaking as severed lovers for all the camp to see.

The bloody light from the Wolf's eyes became more focused, piercing. While he did not raise his voice one iota, his next words were a visible slap. "When I needed someone to talk to, she was there when the one who should have been was not."

She threw back. "I am happy you have found someone you can open up to so easily, and does not have to work and earn your trust as I did."

His next words were nearly a whisper but roared like a thunderclap, "I am happy you have found some prettier person you can show affection to so easily, and does not have to work and earn your love as I did."

"Earn my love? You were a much better man at twenty."

Marcán blinked, for he abruptly saw nothing, the near-blinding glow suddenly gone. Through the blue spot afterimages of his eyes, the ambassador saw the Wolf stiffly walking away. The camp relaxed slightly but none made a sound. The diplomat turned to Vivien who stood, pale as death, with her fingers over the mouth that had betrayed her.

Marcán reached out, but instead she grabbed the neckline of his tunic and pulled him close as if in an embrace. She whispered fiercely, "If you bear any love for me, go to him now, Marcán."

"But, Vivien, you–"

She stopped him with a look. It was despair, it was anger, it was hurt. But it was also undying love. "I have hurt him, Marcán. Please. Now."

Marcán nodded and loped into the camp. The Wolf acted as the brow of a ship, soldiers and servants parting before his smoldering, hunched shoulders, allowing Marcán to catch up past the tents and firepits. Seeing an opening, he dodged around the big man and stood in his way, holding up empty hands. The barbarian kept coming, and Marcán flinched slightly, but then the warrior stopped, only inches from touching him. It wasn't just the armor, the shield, or axe held in powerful hands. There was something otherworldly and enraged inside of him and he was only barely keeping it at bay. Marcán caught a strange, musky scent from the mountain man, and felt small and puny even as the heat coming off of him was easily a match for a noon day sun. His eyes glowed like iron ready for forging. In the silence around him, Marcán caught a dull, fast percussion and wondered if it was the Wolf's racing heart.

The voice, however, was low and feral. "What?"

Marcán tried for a smile, but was sure that it failed. He opened his mouth, but movement far behind the Wolf drew his eye. Past the tents of the soldiers, turning into shadows highlighted by cooking fires by the sinking sun, there were the pavilions of the council members, set coyly apart as if to remind that they were of higher station than the rest. The Wolf had argued against it, but been overruled. The councilmen did not want to sleep surrounded by soldiers, snoring, coughing, rustling, and walking to and from guard posts. All of that hit him again as a long, reptilian snout poked out from around a dense brush at shoulder height. It moved with utter serenity, a toothy maw the size of a man's chest. It floated like a ghost, and his whole body went rigid as it came closer and closer behind a servant by the council tents who was busy preparing a meal.

Marcán could not speak, though he shook his head in denial. *They are far north. We were told. They can't be here.*

The Wolf saw him and spun on his heel and he turned in time to see the fanged mouth open up impossibly wide and with a certainty few beings could match, snapped shut on the head and upper chest of the servant with fearsome power. The low elf made no sound, but jerked once, and then was dragged from sight.

The Wolf's voice was like an explosion, "To arms! To arms!"

The camp simply watched as he hefted his axe and bolted back toward the pavilions of the elite. Only a few seemed capable of movement at all as the barbarian's legs, as thick as adult trees, pounded at the ground to propel him forward. Guards in the camp of the councilors watched him come, and some even visibly braced to meet him as he called for them to prepare for battle. Thus, they were facing the wrong way when the dracoari burst from their hiding places into the middle of the councilors' camp.

They looked like massive swamp alligators on tall, powerful legs. They had sharp teeth, short horns, and eyes that radiated hungry evil. Strapped to their back were green clad elves, holding on for dear life as they reached into the dracoari's minds. The elite guard were scattered in seconds by four of the things, limbs broken by strokes of the powerful tails or snatched away into slavering jaws with steel protection crumbling like foil.

Marcán vomited out a single word, tinged in terror, "Liath!"

And that was all he got out before the sky dissolved into iron arrows.

Men caught in the middle of armoring and arming themselves screamed. The iron tips pierced deeply and would make the wounds tingle, and numb, and eventually fester if the soldier lived. The fires made excellent light to mark their targets, and the dragon elves launched wave after wave into their ranks.

Marcán saw an elf next to him take an arrow to the chest, and he dropped his shield from nerveless fingers. As the lifeless body fell, the diplomat dove for the steel rimmed wood and held it over him as he curled underneath. Arrow after arrow *thunked* into the treated wood as he tortoised beneath. It was like having some fell creature pounding on your door, knowing that the moment you opened it, you would be consumed. Marcán risked a look.

The scene was utter chaos. Fae were being summoned by the few wizards in attendance and sent to meet the incoming horde of dragon elves. All of them were met with gouts of fire from the mouths of robed men and women. Then arrows came again. Marcán ducked down and tried to breathe as they stuttered on his shield.

When he looked again, a dragon elf was running upon him with weapon raised. Marcán yelped, heart in his throat, and staggered to his feet. He raised the shield with its sparse forest of shafts embedded within it and took the first swing on the surface. Splintered arrows went flying, and Marcán managed to get his arming sword out of its sheath.

The diplomat continued to parry with the shield, shocked at his attacker. The dragon elves had been expelled from Pergatium centuries ago. This was the result. His clothes were dark, plain, and not well made. The blade was iron, wrapped in leather at the grip and crossguard so he did not burn himself. His face was painted fiercely with blue dye and piercings covered his ears, eyebrows, and nose. The pointed top of one ear had been clipped in some long-ago fight, and a scar traversed his cheek. But it was more than that. Marcán could feel, even as he reached for his own Elvishness to steady his heart, that his opponent had none. He had lost himself a long time ago, or had it beaten out of him. The Liath, though elves, were the very worst of human inside now. He saw how low they had sunk as a people, and it was truly terrifying.

Another wild swing came at him and he stepped forward to block it on the steel rim of the shield, then brought his own sword up in a classic disengage, catching his opponent as he leapt out of striking range and opening his inner thigh. The dragon elf screeched and grabbed the wound that poured blood, going to his knees. Marcán did as he had been taught, and lunged forward like a cat and put the tip of his sword into the neck of the Liath. The elf thing spit blood and gurgled, falling over, dead or dying.

A surge of warmth swelled within Marcán, and he trembled with excitement. His childhood lessons had worked. He had lived. The dragon elves were not invincible by any means.

Then he looked up to the rest of the battle raging on every side, and saw how very many of them there were. As his eyes went wide, he forgot to breathe, and the sound of metal and suffering descended upon him like a physical force.

Evey was still by her tent, screaming at the arrows in her arm and thigh. She was trying to pull them clear but the barbs had penetrated to exit the other side of her limbs, and held them in place. Vivien stood over her, sword in hand. She was not calling on the fae, but her sword moved as if it had a life of its own. She killed three men in as many strokes, and her face was somewhere lost in the rift between panic and exultation.

Behind her, two of the dracoari, the lesser dragons, lay in bloody heaps. Another was opening its mouth to snap, but the Wolf howled like a madman and dove to the side, making a powerful swing into the mouth with his axe, which severed the jaw muscles. The lower set of teeth hung loosely and the rider moved sluggishly, so both were too slow as the Wolf brought his axe down upon the rider, cutting him nearly in half across the shoulders. The dracoari immediately went feral and lurched from the fight, grievously injured as another set upon the Wolf, who shoved his shield vertically into the deadly maw.

Marcán felt the blade coming at him, and rolled to the side as it passed through the place where his head had been. His mouth was dry, and he tasted metal as he came to his feet. The next combatant was fast, and yet Marcán was lost in the details of the fresh blood spatter on the man's face and spittle flying from his mouth. Half of his teeth were rotted, and he showed them as he grimaced and attacked. Marcán blocked and parried, wary of the simple though vicious attacks that sought out his tender flesh. He was oddly detached, his emotions somewhere else as he saw his opponent fall into a pattern, and he brought his own sword in an easy parry and then flicked it forward to take half the thumb from his attacker's sword hand. The dragon elf howled in pain and brought his sword in a clumsy over-handed strike. Marcán batted it away, then struck it harder. His opponent's weakened thumb could not hold onto it and the weapon tumbled away into the dark. The opponent raised his shield, but Marcán simply drew a cut along his calf with his blade. The shield came down and Marcán put the tip of his sword into the dragon elf's eye. He watched it all happen as if his body belonged to someone else, and felt no remorse or pride. It simply was.

Marcán's head snapped around at the sound of a scream that clawed above the din of battle. He saw Vivien fall, pushed back by the attacks of five swordsmen. She raised her sword to block more strikes, but it was over. All the faces, triumphant and despondent, knew it.

Then, with a somehow civilized cry, Vivien's brother, Fire Hunter, rushed into the fray. He wasn't even half the swordsman Marcán was, flipping his sword about as if to make a wall of steel, but neither connecting with his opponents nor causing them to withdraw. Vivien lay, mouth open in shock, but started to stand on legs wobbly from carrying the weight of her pregnancy and fatigue. Marcán broke into a run to join the clot of fighting, but tripped and fell. His leg was humming, throbbing, and refused to bend. He rolled to his side and saw an iron tipped arrow blossoming from his bloody leg. It was then the pain hit him like a rabid animal. Tears streamed from his eyes and he breathed in short bursts to keep from screaming. The arrow was deep, but had not traversed the thigh. He could feel the razor point inside, burning against his skin and poisoning his blood. He looked up for help when one of the attackers intercepted Fire Hunter's blade with his own, then another dragon elf made a powerful over-handed slash that cut the councilman from shoulder to sternum. The elf's body hit the ground and was still.

Marcán tried to get to his feet as Vivien howled denial to the sky. She killed two dragon elves with newfound zeal. Vivien's tir-reath, the lady archer, and the last of her La'athai from the original group rallied to her side and she shouted a quick order. Gregor grabbed the arrow-riddled form of Evey and hauled her to the tir-reath. Katriona fired arrow after arrow from point blank range into the Liath, covering Vivien's flanks as she dove headlong into the fray. She lay about like a star made of blades, the tanager-engraved sword snipping lives short on every side. But while she had brought the attackers away from Evey, she was now surrounded. All around, knots of resistance were snuffed out and dragon elves were converging on her. Marcán struggled to his feet and limped on only one good leg toward the last resistance. He fell again, snapping the shaft on the arrow and ripping from him a scream of agony.

Then he heard her. Vivien called out, "Sherika, go now! Take them from here! Flee! Flee!"

He felt his hope finally die as Katriona grabbed Gregor by the nape of his neck and turn him around. Tir-reath carrying the limp form of Fire Hunter, Evey, Katriona, and Gregor took to their heels and disappeared into the woods. A good number of dragon elves gave chase, but a roar caused them to halt. From the direction the four had fled, there he came. Eyes blazing like an out-of-control forge, covered in blood from fists to shoulders, bearing a nicked and battered steel axe, the Wolf barreled past the escapees and toward Vivien. Liath turned to face the new threat, and Marcán saw Vivien glance at the big man and saw her hope soar to life.

It was that second, where she saw him in all his fury, that Marcán knew that no iron, no hurt, no adversity would take her love from him. Not even death.

It was during this window of distraction that a spearman thrust, piercing her just off center of the heart. She screamed and fell.

Marcán pushed aside everything but the need to stand. He lurched to his feet and hobbled forward, his leg cramping deep inside near the bone. He did not know what it meant, but it could not be good.

The Wolf was much faster, barreling into the Liath. The barbarian seemed to feel no fatigue, seemed to feel no pain. He was covered by dozens of cuts from swords and teeth, but he moved like an avalanche. He enveloped those he was near, axe hewing arms, legs, and heads with abandon. Strikes shattered swords and cleft skulls. He was a storm of blood and the whole body of them recoiled from the fury. Within seconds twenty were already dead, and more would have followed, but he was not looking for them. He was there for Her.

Marcán fell, leg throbbing and stealing away his strength. He looked down and saw blood was coming from the arrow wound like wine poured from a bottle. He felt cold, so very cold. Through the gap in the attackers, he could see it all, could not force himself to look away. The Wolf came to her right next to the half-trampled fire by her demolished tent. She was bleeding from the wound in her chest, no armor present to turn aside the strike had been made for her pregnant frame. His eyes winked out and his body looked like it collapsed around a hollow core. He was no longer a titan, no longer a force of nature, he was a man… empty and forlorn. His axe clattered from nerveless fingers and he took her in his arms, placing his forehead on her breasts. He sobbed like a child, each Liath looking at the others and wondering who would be the first to move in, who would be the first to strike. More were gathering around, but none wanted to get within reach. None dared.

The Wolf kissed her lips, eyes beginning to pulse with light. He lay her down gently as if into sweet rest with her unborn child and he looked to the dragon elves on every side. He clenched his eyes shut, shaking. Ghosts began to rise from his skin: sweat, blood, and tears being transformed into steam. Marcán watched without breathing as strange shadows played along his face. They gave him phantom creases, protrusions, attributes that were inhuman. The Wolf opened his mouth and made a sound that defied description.

It was not his voice. There was no mistaking it as anything but the roar of a dragon and it pushed back his attackers a step or two.

He stood, his eyes blazing a bloody red so brightly they turned his skull into a lamp. He picked up his axe and a discarded iron sword, then fell onto the mass of dragon elves like a writ of execution. Blood and limbs went flying. His voice was thunder. His rage unquenchable. He screamed his loss to the heavens in a voice as old as creation. Marcán finally knew. He was not human. He may have been, once. Not anymore.

More dragon elves were arriving, but these were dressed in brightly chaotic robes. One came forward and breathed out a line of fire to envelop the Wolf. The barbarian used a dragon elf as a shield. He carried the soldier with him before the mage and beat the spellcaster to death with the flaming body. The Wolf, beyond reason, roared at the others and sprang to attack. A mage made gestures, ghostly reptiles winging around his shoulders as rocks as large as anvils coalesced and flung from him as fast as an arrow. A dozen were launched but one, two, three, hit the Wolf, tumbling him in midair and stopping him dead. He fell to the ground unmoving, his eyes ceasing to glow. He had fallen into a puddle of blood, and it was steaming all around his skin. The field was clear of the fae elves of Rithalion, Isbandar, and Elyrion. Only dragon elves and Marcán remained.

The priests surrounded the Wolf, talking for a second, but one dressed in red and gold walked through the mass of remaining raiders to Vivien's body. The soldiers bowed their heads to him and made way as he passed.

Marcán began to shiver. Keeping his eyes open was a struggle.

Then he saw what the priest saw. Vivien shifted. She moved. She was alive.

The priest smiled like a dracoari ready to feast on a living elf.

ROSS CROSS

It was cold, so cold. Marcán tried to draw a breath, but somehow, the air wasn't there. Then the darkness, filled with flitting stars, enveloped him.

So beautiful...

Chapter Nineteen
The Ruins of Hope

it was an elvish city, a very old one, older than anyone she knew, and probably older than anyone her oldest friends or relatives knew. The stone buildings were pitted and eroded by the elements, overgrown by vines and tree roots that climbed overtop the buildings and down walls and into the hard-packed dirt streets. It was an eerie place, those roots looking like they had taken the form of some tentacled beast from lore and frozen in place. People lined the streets. Their clothes were simple, nothing like that found in Rithalion or Elyrion. Their skin was weather-worn bronze, and their hair short. The women were tattooed with vivid colors. The men were pierced: their ears, noses, eyebrows...anything that could be pierced, was.

Vivien was led through the streets, clothing in shambles. Whatever passed as healers for the savage Liath had bound her chest wound and smeared it with poultices. She had been examined several times on the weeks long travel to this place, and as soon as she had regained her strength, she had been shackled and forced to march. The robed priests had praised the witchdoctor, who had glowed at the accolades, but privately looked strangely at Vivien as the wound closed day by day. It still twinged, and she had hoped for a few more days to heal before they arrived so she could mount an escape.

The people simply watched, their faces devoid of expression. Even the children stood solemnly by, and not a word was uttered. She was flanked on either side by the huge reptilian creatures that had wreaked such havoc during the ambush, shackled, the chains held by the malcontents astride them. Just ahead of her was their leader, shoulders squared and scepter held high as he walked, his crimson and gold sleeveless long tunic swishing around his booted feet. He led them deep into the city to its center where a structure towered high over the others. It was there he stopped.

Vivien glanced to either side, her gaze raking over the men sitting astride the vicious beasts barely kept in check by whatever magic held them under their thrall. It was easy to see that this was a relationship of dominance, much different than the one of mutual respect and love she had with Sherika. She scoffed inwardly, knowing these animals would have their riders in their maws at the slightest provocation were circumstances different. Vivien glanced again, first left, then right. Then she pulled. Hard. The wound in her chest burned with the effort.

The man to her right grunted as he fell from his lofty position, and suddenly bereft of contact with its rider, the dracoari acted on instinct. It hissed, and quick as lightening, struck. The man screamed as the massive jaws closed on his arm. Blood sprayed in every direction as the limb was torn from his body, and the other men, shaken out of their momentary shock, leapt to his defense. Vivien felt herself savagely jerked to the side, the rider to her left reining her in as the offending croc was subdued. Pressed against the thick, scaled hide, she watched as the maimed man was carried into the structure.

Vivien felt a hand grab her wrist and she was jerked away from her scaled wall and pulled against the chest of the archpriest. His breath stank as it washed over her face his eyes alight with anger. "That, my dear, was very unwise," he growled. "I suggest in the future, that if you wish to stay alive, do not replicate it."

His expression abruptly shifted, and his gaze intensified. One of his hands settled at her waist. Her heart thundered against her ribs, and her breaths were fast and shallow as she tried to squirm out of his grip. *No, gods, please no...* His hand moved around to rest upon her distended belly...

"So, it appears the little minx is expecting." His eyes brightened again and his mouth curved into a cruel grin. She squirmed again, this time breaking free of his grip. She darted out of his reach, only to be brought up short by that damned chain still held by the remaining dracoari rider. The priest chuckled, the sound of it reaching into the very depths of her soul. "I smell none of the filthy fae upon you. So surprising since you were supposed to be this grandiose mage. Well, for whatever reason, you are bereft of your degenerate talent. You have nowhere to go little Vivien Valdera, and there is no one who knows where you are." He stepped close to her again, his fingertips tracing the racing pulse at the hollow of her neck. "And there is no one to hear you scream who shall care."

Vivien's heart plummeted. *Yes, there is no one. The entire convoy is dead. The Wolf is dead.*

"Yetin, get her to my personal chamber!"

Another man rushed forward to hold his mount while the rider hastily dismounted his croc. He disengaged the chain first from the shackle on her right arm, next that from her left. He then proceeded to pull her into the opening of the structure before them. He was stopped short by the priest. "You are not to touch her, you understand? She is mine!"

Yetin was taken aback by the priest's vehemence but nodded. "Yes, my lord."

The rider led her into the building. It had been a place of wonders, but no longer. Stone had been taken from the breast of the ground and carved into tight fitting patterns to jut into the sky as a structure that would never topple. Now time had eroded the seams to make them into wide cracks and gaming joints. Beautiful murals must once have covered the walls that were now just sullen, blackened breeding grounds for mold. Mosaics of ceramic lay in tiny fragments on the floor beside walls and beneath shafts where the sun fought feebly to enter past centuries of vegetation. Whatever laughter and joy had once been had long since died. Yetin's hand was tight around her arm, too tight. Vivien glared at him out of the corner of her eye, and when she felt it was a good moment, she pulled back unexpectedly. His grip was more tenacious than she thought it was, or mayhap he was expecting such a maneuver because of what she'd done to the other rider. All she managed was to take him off balance before the pain of her wound robbed her of strength. He quickly regained it, growled as he tightened his grip and roughly pulled her towards him.

Warm breath washed over her face, foul as a result of poor hygiene. "I don't care what Drakkon says, I will make you regret it if you do that again," he hissed.

The threat was not lost on her, and a part of her quailed inside. Her hands were bound, and with her magic gone, she had no defense. But the other part of her... all it felt was anger.

Yetin's hand a vice, he pulled her along through the torch-lit darkness, up a long staircase, until they reached a door. He paused for a moment as though preparing for something, then he opened it. He jerked her inside, and once she was through, the door slammed shut behind them.

Her eyes widened as he rushed her through the chamber. It was dark, lit by multitudes of candles situated all around, and within the shadows cast by that flickering light, there were...

...dragons.

No, not really dragons yet, although they looked like they would be. Their bodies were long and serpentine, about three to four feet in length, their small, immature wings pinned close to their backs. Their heads were wedge-shaped, and from the tops sprouted a pair of twisted horns. Each was a different color: crimson and burgundy, white and gold, emerald and navy, and their eyes had an amber glow. First one, then the others opened their mouths and hissed, each one filled with razor sharp teeth that could rend and tear.

The guard veered away from the brazen beasts, giving wide berth as he pulled her along. Some of the long wyrms looked like they would follow, their maws open wide, growling and hissing menacingly. He hurried through to the next room, this one darker than the last. A large bed dominated it, covered in rich red silks. Taking her roughly by the shoulders, he threw her down on it. Vivien twisted to the side so that she would not fall on her belly, and she looked up at him through hooded eyes.

Yetin just stood there, looking down at her. His eyes roved over her, glinting in the light cast by the nearest candle. She could see the desire reflected there, and that he battled against the orders he'd been given. He clenched his hands into fists, then turned and left the room.

For a while she just lay there, working on the bronze shackles around her wrists. They dug deeply, and the longer she kept at it, they got tighter and tighter as the flesh swelled and began to bleed. Tears streamed down her face for her lack; with her magic she would have been loose in moments, and the men left behind on the road would not be dead. And Ravn...

A moan burst from between her lips and her shoulders shook. *How will I do it again? How will I live my life and never feel his hand in mine, never feel his lips brush against my cheek, never hear his rich voice, never see the way the sun plays upon the highlights of his hair? How will I do it? How will I do it knowing he will never breathe the air, knowing his heart will never beat again?*

Despair enveloped her within its deep, suffocating embrace. *The last words we spoke were so hateful. Why in the world did I say such things? Who cares if he loves another? Who cares if he chooses to be with her over me? What matters is that he is still here, his feet walking beside mine in a journey I don't wish to complete without him. Gods, where is his body now? Is it rotting out in the heat with all the others I have failed?*

Her voice was a whisper, "Ravn, please! Please live again and come for me! Please..."

Snick.

She stiffened as she heard the door in the outside chamber open. Her heart galloped like one of the beautiful horses Ravn used to breed so long ago, hoping beyond hope that it was he who had come to save her. Silence reigned, but she kept her eyes riveted on the doorway. Could it be true? She had told him many times she didn't need saving but could he have truly risen and followed her here to this fell place to save her? A shadow emerged there just as the man stepped through the door.

Vivien's heart plummeted to the soles of her boots.

In a flourish of red and gold, Drath Drakkon entered the chamber. He took one look at her and his eyes gleamed. He stepped towards the bed, riveted upon her where she lay. "Ah, it seems your thoughts have taken you to those you have lost today, most importantly, the hulk of a man you so aptly call 'Wolf.'" She flinched when he said it and he leaned in, enjoying her obvious pain, "Such a shame he was lost. I would have loved to keep him in one of the cells I use for showcasing some of my most triumphant victories. One day you will have to tell me how you found him."

Vivien swallowed past the painful lump in her throat, more tears joining their brethren to damp the silk sheets. She'd be damned if she told this man anything about anyone in her life, in particular, Ravn of Blacach.

The man walked closer, unwinding the intricately embroidered sash from around his waist and removing his long tunic. He was lean, his muscle exhibiting that of a spellcaster who practiced weaponry often, but still just as it suited him. Much like the rest of him, his chest was bronzed, and like most elves, devoid of hair. Only those tainted with human blood had hair, and these men were instantly considered beneath anyone else. Now that she thought of it, that comprised most of the La'athai, the brave men she and the Wolf had led into battle. They were some of the finest people she knew, and sometimes she wondered if it was because of that chest hair, because of where it came from...

Vivien's breath started to come faster. He continued towards the bed and she prayed his trousers weren't destined to follow the long tunic. Disrobing meant one thing, and one thing only. It was a prospect that struck fear into the heart of her being, and the child within thrashed about at the sudden surge of emotion. Yet, she kept her face blank, hoped it showed nothing that would make him want to do any of the things that Tor liked to do.

Her breaths hitched. But Tor had not always been that way. She wondered what had changed him. Or really, had he always been that way but never told anyone, even her, for so many years, so many decades? What had made him hate her so much, that he would willingly cause her physical pain?

Drakkon reached the bed and stared down at her. His voice was quieter, deeper. "There is something about you Lady Valdera. Certainly, you are lovely, but it is more than just that. Your flame beckons and calls, drawing a man closer and closer."

Vivien remained where she was on the bed, not moving but trembling inside. She wanted to retreat, to scuttle far away from him, but she forced herself to stay in place. By the gods, she'd never been so afraid of a man in her entire life, and he hadn't even touched her yet. Somehow, she knew he would.

"The moment I saw you I knew there was something about you, something I had to discover, something I needed to have. I'm looking forward to seeing exactly what that is." His gaze became intense. "Come here, Vivien."

She recoiled from the command and shrank away, her back pressing into the pillows behind her. One side of Drakkon's mouth quirked up at the response, as though he enjoyed the effect he had on her. "What is wrong, my dear? Not feeling very obstinate now, are we?" His gaze hardened. "Come." He held out his hand, palm up.

She stared at it for a moment. A memory suddenly enveloped her, a warm, soothing one. It was one that made her feel safe. She continued to stare at the hand, remembered the words Ravn had asked her when he wanted to take her down the steep escarpment in order to escape the fire that had overtaken the battlefield during their battle with the Iron Army.

"Vivien, do you trust me?"

She felt the heat at her back, the flames reaching to devour her. By the gods, she did trust him. She believed in this man like she had none other her entire life...

She looked from the hand and back up into the face of the Liath leader, the memory falling away like a beautiful dream. She trembled, this time not just on the inside. She was afraid. She was afraid to go to him. She was afraid *not* to.

Chapter Twenty
Brath Drakkon

She didn't know the time. It was impossible to tell the time in a place with no way to see the outside. Her prison was dark, lit only by candles and the eerie light cast by floor braziers within which flames ate a strange substance she'd never seen before. They cast an odd bluish glow that permeated the room and made weird shadows. She wasn't permitted to leave the archpriest's chambers, kept there by the wyrms that he'd imprisoned as well. She'd stare at them when she thought he wasn't looking.

"They are beautiful are they not?" He came to stand beside her where she sat on the floor. It was the only place to sit besides the bed, and she refused to sit there as long as he was anywhere in the chambers. "I have spent my life in the study of dragons and the wondrous magic they hold." He regarded her intently, his eyes shining. "I can see you are curious about them." He took her hand and pulled her up. "Come, I'll give you a closer look."

Vivien recoiled, but he held fast to her hand and hauled her towards the monsters he kept at the entry to his chambers. She hated her fear, hated that he could see it, hated that it stank up the room enough that the wyrms could smell it even before they got close. The wyrms' heads rose from their paws as they drew near, eyes glowing with interest. Twin tendrils of smoke rose from each pair of nostrils set in slender snouts lined with sharp, protruding teeth. Wide bronze collars circled their slender necks, and when she stared close enough, the etched runic designs over each one seemed to shift and waver.

Magic. Dragon magic.

Drakkon stepped among the three wyrms, passing his hands over them as he dragged her after. They seemed to bow at his touch and made sounds deep in their throats like a cat might make as a purr of contentment. The beasts stared at Vivien, their eyes peering right through her as though into her soul, and she quailed. She pulled back on her hand, hoping to not proceed any further, but Drakkon jerked her to his side. The abrupt movement caused two of the wyrms to hiss, one burgundy-red, the other navy-green, their mouths opening wide to reveal another set of teeth within. They reminded her of the dragon she had faced in Pergatium, and the fear she had felt as she was swept towards the massive maw of that fell beast while the Wolf fought valiantly to save her. She struggled to keep from screaming, instead swallowing at the dryness in her throat and focusing on the sweat the rolled down the valley of her spine.

Drakkon chuckled at the wyrms' response. "You wonder how they came to be here." He raised his arms and held them wide. "With my power I summoned them here and they stay at my behest. They are mine to keep and control as long as I wish." He looked down at her. "Just as you are."

A stillness swept over her at the sound of these words and she looked up to meet his gaze.

Drakkon raised a dark brow. He reached up and grabbed a fistful of her hair. "I dare you to refute me, warmage."

Something deep within her stirred and she looked down. She remained silent, just as she always did in his presence. She had yet to speak to him even once.

He pulled savagely at her hair, jerking her head back until she was forced to stare up at him. "Go ahead, try and deny me," he growled.

Her scalp burned with pain and her eyes watered. Her nostrils flared as she breathed through them, her jaws clenched tight against any sound she might make. Somehow, she knew it would please him to hear it, and she didn't want to give him the satisfaction. He gave her a malicious grin and let up on her hair without letting it go. "Why don't you go ahead and caress one of my pets. They love to be touched."

Vivien felt her eyes widen at his command shrouded in the form of a request. *By the gods, he can't be serious? He means to maim me?* She looked at the vile creatures before her, the knobby growths along the sides of their heads and the twisted horns rising from the top. They were certainly ugly to behold. Once she may have found a beauty in them, but not now, after what Pergatium had done to her.

Drakkon pushed her towards the wyrms, his knuckles in the small of her back, his other hand releasing her hair. She fell to the floor, barely catching herself by her hands in time to keep from landing on her belly. Terrible shrieks filled the air and without looking up, she knew that the wyrms circled her where she lay.

Every muscle in her body tremored, her arms shaking so badly they could hardly hold her up. Behind her she heard the priest chuckling, waiting for the entertainment to unfold. The child within her was quiet, almost like, he too, could sense the danger of the moment. Then, with all the courage she could muster, with painstaking slowness, Vivien looked up...

...and the eyes of a terrible beast stared back at her.

She was back in Pergatium again. She was sliding into the wide maw of a huge dragon that was supposed to be dead, one that caused such hopelessness that she wanted to give up on everything, including her life and the lives of her people. Only the Wolf had been there. He'd been her beacon in the darkness. He'd fought for her, saved her from certain death. He'd done it time and time again, not just in Pergatium, but at home when she was dying from the effects of the terrible geas imposed upon her by the Council, during the fight with the giant during the battle with the Iron Coast, and then after when the fire threatened to consume her. And now he was gone, gone and left to rot in the summer sun.

Vivien looked into the eyes of the next thing that wished to kill her, eyes that glowed a deep amber. It was the largest wyrm of the three. Her gold and white scales shimmered in the light cast by the candles throughout the room, and somehow Vivien couldn't find it in her to believe she was ugly.

Dragon Vessel

She? How do I know it is a she?

The other two wyrms hissed and spat at one another, mayhap fighting to see who would get the first taste of her, their sinuous bodies coiling tightly. Their dance was a vicious one, their razor teeth rending one another in a ferocious display of savagery. Vivien settled onto one hip, slowly raised her hand from the floor. Her fingers wavered in the air as she struggled to maintain the bravery that was nothing more than a will to go down fighting in her own way, the only way she knew.

Another memory came to the fore of her mind, one of a large stallion contained within a stall that was a bit too small for him. He was all muscle and barely suppressed power just waiting to be unleashed. Cowering beside him was a girl, barely thirteen years old, and deathly afraid. Without hesitation, Vivien had entered the stall and gentled him with naught but the touch of her hand and the sound of her voice. She'd been afraid of the stallion as well, only, she didn't let him know that.

Vivien brought her hand closer, closer, closer. It was the arm on her wounded side and the closed hole ached terribly. The golden wyrm hissed, her forked tongue coming out to taste the flesh of her forearm, her teeth ever so close. Vivien's fingertips lightly brushed the scales along the side of the narrow face. And then...

...nothing.

The wyrm closed her mouth and just stayed there, allowing Vivien's hand to caress the contours of her face. Vivien released the breath she'd been holding, and her body relaxed. The scales were smooth, much smoother than she'd thought they would be, and this time, when smoke rose from the wyrm's nostrils, she didn't feel intimidated. *The priest is right. They* do *like to be touched...*

Vivien felt a hand close over her upper arm and she was hauled backward and onto her feet. Face to face with Drakkon, there was a maniacal gleam in his blue eyes that wasn't there before. "What did you do to it? Who are you?" he growled. She stumbled as he dragged her back away from the wyrms, taking her once more into the depths of the chamber. Confusion reigned, amplified by the pain shooting through her shoulder and down her arm. Once before the bed, he picked her up and threw her onto it. This time she was unable to shift quickly enough and she landed onto her belly. She cried out, stunned for a moment by the pain that reverberated throughout her abdomen.

Vivien gasped, curved protectively around herself, tears streaming down her face as she looked up at the archpriest, his features twisted into a hateful grimace. He looked like a madman standing there over the bed. *What does he want? What can he possibly want from me?* His breaths heaved in and out of his chest, like he'd run for miles, and his gaze intensified.

With a snarl Drakkon fell upon her. His hands were like claws, tearing at her clothes and into her flesh. She screamed at the pain and indignity of it, flipped onto her sore belly to try and escape. She made it to the edge of the bed before his hands closed around her waist and pulled her back. His razor-sharp nails raked over her again, through her clothing and down her sides. She could feel the flesh parting beneath them and it burned. A wind had picked up and it swept through the room. In the background, amidst the struggle against her captor, she heard things tumbling from their places on the shelves that lined the walls, falling to shatter upon the floor. In desperation she kicked and clawed her way to the edge of the bed, to the freedom she perceived lay there.

But Drakkon was still there to pull her back.

The priest picked her up and forced her onto her back. More vulnerable than ever, Vivien kicked and screamed. Her foot connected with his chest, his stomach, his legs. But he was strong, muscle rippling throughout his lean frame as he fought to restrain her. But he'd had enough. He screamed in anger, laying one hand on her belly, raising his face to the ceiling. She felt the power before it manifested, felt the raw heat as it spilled from his other hand and towards the far wall. Liquid fire crashed into the shelf there, engulfing it in lurid crimson flames that swallowed it within the blink of an eye. Drakkon's shock was palpable, but exhaustion from the fight kept her from taking advantage of it.

That and the reality that, with his power, she would never be able to escape this place.

Drakkon was still, his eyes wide. Only the sounds of their breathing could be heard in the ensuing silence. The liquid slowly spread across the floor, but cooled before it reached the bed, having thickened into a black sheet veined with red. He looked down at his hand, then at Vivien lying beneath him, his legs straddling her hips. Her gown had been shredded and it lay in tatters around them. Her breasts glistened with sweat, rising and falling with each breath she took, and her belly was a pale mound that rose between them, his hand still laying over it.

His gaze rested on that hand, or rather, the belly beneath it. She saw it then, the myriad of emotions playing over his face: stupefaction, incredulity, excitement, and maybe even a little fear. His hand lost its weight and splayed over her belly like it was something precious, much like Ravn had once done in a time that now seemed so long ago.

"Indeed, who are you? But more important, who is *this*?" His tone was one of reverence, and when he looked back up at her, his eyes were filled with wonderment.

Vivien's mind reeled a bit. *Who the hells is this man? He sounds completely and utterly insane.* Much to her chagrin, more fear swept through her. *What does he expect me to say, if anything?*

He rubbed his hand over her, across her belly and up to her breasts. "By the gods, what wonders have they discovered in Rithalion?" He glanced back towards the front of the chamber, towards the wyrms that guarded the entry. "This explains a few things." His eyes were piercing as he swung them back towards her and he chuckled. "No one is going to believe me. I'll have to prove it to them."

Drakkon slid off the bed. It was difficult to miss the bulge in his pants despite the confines of the leather. Then, without another word, he left and went into the fore-chamber. Despite her aches, she slunk off the bed and onto the floor, crawling along it until she could see what he was doing. He'd found some thick chain, and he'd threaded it through a ring at the top of each of the wyrms' bronze collars. He attached the chain to a mounted bracket on the wall. Then, with the last bit of chain, he strode towards her.

Vivien scuttled backward as Drakkon approached. He threw the chain onto the bed, then stooped to pick her up. Shock swept through her as he carried her to the bed and placed her there beside the chain. It was swiftly followed by terror as he took a pair of bracers from one of the shelves that had not been decimated by his liquid fire and brought before her. He proceeded to place one, then the other, over her wrists, then threaded the thick chain through them much as he did the wyrm's collars. He affixed the other end to a bracket above the bed, and she wondered how many other women he'd held in exactly the same way. The chain was long, long enough for her to use the waste pot and for her to walk along the side of the bed. But that was it.

Finally, he was finished. He stood back to look at her and again she was aware of his desire, not just straining his leathers, but shining in his eyes and displayed in every movement he made. He may have wanted her before, but it had been much outweighed by his cruelty and his desire to see her scream before he would take her. But now that had somehow changed. Now his want of her didn't hinge upon her fear and blood. It was her pregnancy.

Vivien watched as he took one last look at her before turning and leaving the chambers. With her toes she grasped the end of the blanket that was scrunched at the bottom of the bed and slowly brought close enough that she could manipulate it overtop her, hiding her nudity. She curled beneath it and tears leaked from her eyes. *He knew I was pregnant right from the start. What has changed?* She trembled with trepidation. *What will he do to me? Why am I being chained now? And those poor wyrms?* Listening closely, she could hear them in the fore-chamber. They made faint mewling sounds, sad sounds that made her heart ache.

Wolf, where are you? Please come for me. Please come.

The archpriests had come to see her, each dressed in the robes for the element they represented: sky blue and metallic lavender for the air, brown and emerald green for the earth, royal blue and silver for the water, and of course crimson and gold for fire. They were younger than she imagined they should be for those who ruled an entire city. They had touched her, touched her more than she'd ever been touched by a group of strangers, but of course she could do nothing but lay there, naked upon the bed. They spoke in excited whispers filled with awe: *I feel it! Me too! How is she still alive? To whom does it*

belong? One of Fire to be sure! And the most prevalent: *How can this be?* Drath Drakkon had stood there and taken it all in, a smile on his face. Vivien supposed it was because he had something they did not, whatever that was.

What made her the most nervous was that their excitement centered around her unborn son.

But now the priests had left. Vivien watched as Drakkon walked back and forth in front of the bed, hand at his chin, regarding her contemplatively. After what seemed an eternity, he stopped. "The moment I saw you on the battlefield I knew you were a treasure I had to have. There was something about you that beckoned to me, and now I know what it is. You certainly know how special your child is, yet you behave as though you have no idea."

Vivien said nothing, yet her mind raced. Of course, she knew her son was special. He was going to be a spellcaster, and a powerful one for her to be able to sense it. She'd heard stories of only one other magic user who had been sensed within the womb. It was her father, and he was the Grand Magister, the most powerful spellcaster in Rithalion, mayhap even in all the Elvish realms.

"How did you get pregnant?"

The question surprised her, so much that she drew back at the sheer stupidity of it. She just stared at him, not believing that the Liath were really this dumb. Everyone knew how children were made except for children.

Drakkon's eyes darkened. "Lady Valdera, you *will* provide an answer. I tire of your little game of silence."

She remained impassive, wondering what he would do to her if she didn't speak. She supposed he could do any manner of things, including throwing her to his wyrms. She supposed he could rape her, but wouldn't he have done so already?

He moved swiftly, and before she could react, his hand was around her throat, pinning her to the pillow behind her. "You may now be the first living Umesh in history, but it doesn't mean I can't make you wish your life wasn't worth living!"

She knew the word. Umesh... Vessel.

Vivien struggled to breathe, brought her hand up to his in an effort to dislodge it. Once seeing she'd been amply educated, he removed his hand and she finally spoke for the first time in days. "I slept with my husband," she croaked.

Drakkon stared at her as though she was sprouting horns. "You can't seriously believe that I will accept this as your answer."

She frowned. "Wh... what?"

He pursed his lips. Instead of persisting he moved on to another question. "How long have you been pregnant?"

"M... maybe about eight and a half months."

"How long has Rithalion been dabbling in dragon magic?"

She frowned again. "What?"

"You heard me."

"No one in Rithalion practices dragon magic. Only fae magic is allowed."

"Don't lie to me!" he shouted. "I'm not a fool!"

Her heart skipped a beat. This man was easily angered. She was trying to be compliant, but it didn't matter if he didn't believe her.

"Who was the dragon that impregnated you?"

By the gods, the man was more insane than she thought. How in the world would a woman lay with a dragon and live to tell about it? "I...I don't understand what you are asking. There are no dr..."

His hand found her throat again. "Stop lying to me! I've felt it, and so have the other priests!"

The chains jangled as Vivien wrapped her hands around his, once more struggling to breathe. She began to thrash, hoping to buck him off of her, but his knees were tight around her hips.

"Who is he? I know he's a fire element!"

Vivien's sight began to darken about the periphery. She ceased her struggle, focused only on trying to get air into her lungs. It hurt. *There are no dragons. No dragons.* Her hands fell away from his as darkness engulfed her.

Chapter Twenty-One
Dragon Jewel

vivien slowly awoke to the sounds of activity going on inside the chamber. She swallowed and grimaced with the soreness of her throat. Memories flashed through her mind and she opened her eyes wide, searching the chamber for Drakkon. All she saw were a handful of women pouring buckets of water into a tub that had been positioned at the foot of the bed. The mess left behind by Drakkon's spell had been cleaned up, all except for a charred mark on the wall.

Seeing that she'd awakened, one of the women made her way over. She wore a pair of low-riding silk trousers and a band of the same material crossed over her chest to cover her breasts and leave her torso bare. "Umesh, I am Mirkari. Let me get you out of these bracers."

Vivien grimaced at the name, hated the meaning behind it and what the Liath thought she was. She'd heard the stories. They were taught to all of Rithalion's youth, regardless of how frightening it might be. A few centuries ago, there were two schools of magic, one dedicated to the fae, and the other to dragons. The dragon mages became lofty in their goals and wanted to become as close to those from whom they got their power as possible. Their mission was to create a breed of dragon-elf hybrids, one that would share the best of both races to create the perfect being.

So they took volunteers, young women in the prime of their lives, to accept the seed of the dragons the mages brought into the realms of elves and men from their place in the formless chaos of the elements. Since these women obviously could not lie with their dragon partners, the seed was taken from the dragons by a method that remains undisclosed to any but the mages who performed it, and placed into the women. The pregnancy rate was high, and almost all of the women were soon carrying draconic offspring. They were called Vessels, and were revered by those who trucked with dragons.

But then something happened. It was terrible to behold, characterized by agonizing abdominal pain, seizures, and bleeding. Then the women would die, every single one. Countless women were sacrificed to the endeavor, and not a single one survived past the first several weeks of pregnancy.

It was one of the things that caused the rift between the two schools of magic, and ultimately the war.

Mirkari produced a key from the pouch secured by a cord around her waist, then opened the bronze shackles. Vivien lowered her arms and rubbed at the soreness in each one, looked up when she noticed the girl standing there and staring. She looked away, her cheeks coloring despite her golden complexion.

"What is it?"

The girl just shook her head. "Come, let's get you into this tub."

Vivien allowed Mirkari to take her hand and lead her to the steaming water. There were no clothes to remove; Drakkon had done that already during their encounter the day before. The girl held her arm as she stepped over the high side and was there as she lowered herself into the warm depths.

It felt so good.

Once her hair was wet, Mirkari and another girl, Risa, lathered it. The soap had a pleasant, albeit unfamiliar, smell but Vivien didn't speak up to inquire about it. Once she was finished, they toweled her off, then had her sit on the bed. Risa brought over a jar of black ink, a needle, and a small, wooden hammer. The two girls looked at one another nervously, then back at Vivien. "Umesh, you must lay down now, on your belly," said Mirkari.

Vivien frowned, a feeling of trepidation washing over her. "Why?"

"Drath Drakkon has commanded that you be marked, just like your forebears," said Risa.

"My forebears?"

"Yes, the other Umesh that came before you."

She swallowed convulsively. "But they are all dead."

Mirkari nodded. "Yes, you are the only one of your kind."

Vivien's lower lip began to tremble. Tattooing was a long, painful process, and she was more than afraid. "He's made a mistake. I'm not any vessel. I'm just a woman who's pregnant with her husband's child! Please, I beg you—"

Mirkari sadly shook her head. "We are not here to decide. We are slaves, and just do as the archpriest tells us to do."

She looked back and forth between the two girls. "Y...you are s...slaves?"

"Yes, Umesh," said Risa.

Vivien blinked and tears crawled down her cheeks. *By the gods, how did I end up here in this terrible place? Am I being punished because I didn't stay home like I should have?*

"Here, let me help you get comfortable." Risa moved to the bed and placed some pillows near Vivien. "Hold these as you lay down. Don't put all your weight on your belly. We will make due."

Vivien just nodded. Instead of running out of the room like she wanted to, she lay down and held the pillows close, exposing her back. She felt feather-light fingers trace the contours of it, and she was reminded of herself, smoothing her hands over the muscle over Ravn's chest. She'd loved the feel of him. More tears came and she closed her eyes.

"Umesh, this will hurt quite a bit."

She nodded and squeezed her eyelids together. She felt a prick on the right side of her back, followed by a sharp stabbing pain. She screamed.

Vivien was led through the city of Zormoth, the name these people called the ancient Elvish ruins in which they lived. She wore silk of crimson and gold, cut like the clothing of the rest of the slaves within the temple that easily displayed her pregnancy for all to see. This time she was not in chains, but that didn't matter. She was too tired to run, too tired from the pain she'd endured the day before. Her back was one big, raw wound from which she'd suffer for days and weeks to come, all because of Drakkon's overpowering need to mark her like the original Vessels. Obviously, he didn't care much for her well-being or that of the child within, no matter how much he claimed to his brethren that they were his highest priority.

He'd strangled her until she passed out from lack of breath. How much could she possibly mean to him? Oh yes, she was just the Vessel. *But he doesn't think that the child requires her beating heart in order to maintain his life? The fool.*

By his side, Drakkon led her through the city and back to where they began, at the temple where he and the other priests resided. The people gathered and followed, and at the end, they filled the streets leading up to the temple. Their faces were curiously expectant, knowing something big was about to happen. She heard their excited chatter, and they pointed to the ink that was now a part of her back, ink that had been patterned into the image of unfurled dragon's wings.

The archpriest took her up to the top of the building, and from there they could see the sprawling city and all who had followed them. He spoke in a loud voice for all to hear, and the streets were abruptly silent. "People of Zormoth! Hear my words! Today, before you I have an Umesh! The first in over a century!"

The people cheered. The sound as louder than she thought it would be, mayhap amplified by the surrounding stone. Their faces were filled with such joy like she'd never seen before, even when the Rithalion army returned from their battle against the Iron Coast. More than that, there was hope, a hope of which she could only guess the meaning.

And once again, she was a trophy. Vivien shook at the thought, and tried to force it from her mind. *I am a trophy, just like I am to my father, the Wolf, and all my people.* Then she remembered the words of Marcán. *"Vivien, you are respected and adored, not an ornament of vanity."* No, not wholly a trophy. Only a trophy to these people.

"Let me present to you Vivien Valdera of Rithalion, Umesh of Zormoth, Fyr'kaii!"

The people cheered again, her new name on their lips. "Fyr'kaii! Fyr'kaii!"

Fyr'kaii... fire heart.

Vivien followed Drakkon through the torch-lit hallways of the temple. She hated entering the ruins again, wanting so much to remain outside under the sun, the first light she'd seen in gods knew only how many days. His demeanor was different than it had been before his presentation, somewhat calm and subdued. He looked back at her every now and again, almost as though to be sure she was really there, and she couldn't help thinking that she sensed an air of anticipation.

Once back in his chambers, they walked past the wyrms that no longer hissed or screeched at her passing. They just stared at her through gleaming amber eyes. Drakkon turned when they stepped into the bedroom, appraising her solemnly. He removed the cloak of his station and flung it onto the bed, over the chains that still lay there attached to a pair of bronzed bracers.

"You did well today."

She remained in place, saying nothing. *What is there to say? There is no reasoning with the insane, is there?*

He nonchalantly walked over to where she stood, and once before her, lifted a hand to her face. His voice was low. "My Mirkari made you look more beautiful than I ever imagined."

Deep inside, Vivien began to tremble.

Drakkon traced the lines of her face down to her lips. His heated gaze settled there and her breath stopped. She sensed his intent, tried to step back. Too late. The kiss was harsh, his teeth bruising her lips, his tongue thrusting inside her mouth. One arm snaked around to grab her by the waist, his hand cupping her backside. His other hand swept into the thick tresses of her hair, which Risa had insisted she keep down over her shoulder as opposed to in the braid she preferred. Now it was a hindrance as Drakkon gripped a fistful of it and pulled her head back in a gesture of dominance.

His lips finally released hers, his breath coming fast. "In our little skirmish I heard your people call you Elthari Jashi. I've come up with my own name for you." He kissed her again, his lips a cruel caress that stole her breath away and made her want to heave. "Drakkaria Jashi. I like that much, much better."

Vivien made her voice soft, placating. "Please, you have made a mistake. I am not the Umesh you think I am. No dragon spawn lies within my belly. I've never even seen a dragon, not a live one anyway."

His eyes searched hers intently, as though scouring her very soul. His pupils widened as though he recognized that she told the truth, but right after, his lips pursed. "Do you take me for such a fool?"

She shook her head. "N...no..."

His grip tightened uncomfortably. "My senses don't lie, and neither do those of my peers. All of them felt it inside of you, felt it's power thrumming from deep inside."

"No, please. I promise you," she gasped.

He brought his lips close to her ear. "I can feel it even now," he whispered.

Vivien struggled. His grip was much too tight, and the pressure against her belly was becoming unbearable. He brought his face to the curve of her neck and chuckled. "I love the feel of your resistance, the scent of your fear, the look in your eyes when I tell you you're mine." He placed his teeth onto her flesh and bit down.

"Ahhh!" The shock rippled through her down to the tips of her toes. She splayed her hands over his chest, struggling in earnest as he pushed her backward and onto the bed. Panic surged through her as she found herself in the place she least wanted to be, scrambled away from him across the bed the way she had the day he'd thrown her to his wyrms.

And just like he did then, Drakkon pulled her back.

Vivien cried out as he roughly flipped her onto her back and straddled her, a knee on each side of her hips. The wound across her back from the tattooing burned as she pushed against him, but he pinned her wrists against the bed and lay over her, his lips once more over hers. He brought her hands over her head, tried securing her wrists with only one of his hands. She wrested one of hers free and clawed at his face, her fingernails raking across his cheek.

"Aaaggh! You little maggot!"

In one mighty swing, he slapped her across the face. Hard.

Her head swam after the impact. Dazed, she only vaguely felt him secure her hands with one of his over her head and tear away the silk trousers secured around her hips and beneath her belly. He easily pulled the cloth away from her breasts and she winced as he roughly squeezed one soft mound. A metallic taste had filled her mouth and she imagined her teeth had cut her lip. He positioned a knee between her thighs and a surge of alarm swept through her. *No, please no.*

She thrashed, freeing her hand yet again only to have it caught in his iron grip just before it reached his face. He savagely twisted her arm and she heard a pop. She cried out with the pain, and when he released it, he struck her again, this time a backhand against her temple.

Her world faded to gray and she floated, but abject fear kept her from completely slipping away into the darkness. He spread her legs and she kicked, struggled for all she was worth despite the repercussions. He struck her again and again. His arousal was manifest– at some point he'd removed his leather trousers. His thick member probed at her entrance and she clenched her muscles even though, deep in her mind, she knew it would only make it worse.

She screamed. His entry ripped through her, burned as he thrust past the muscles that strained to keep him out. The pain renewed her struggles, but her energy had waned. Her wrists were trapped beneath the strength of his grip, and by the heat emanating from him, she knew he was using his powers against her, his powers as a dragon mage.

Drakkon had easily subdued her, striking her because it was empowering and exciting. He liked hearing her cries for him to stop. She could see it in his eyes as he thrust again and again, more and more vigorously. He went deep, and the ache it caused made her wonder if he was harming the pregnancy. Her pelvis rocked with the force of his penetration and he smiled when he saw the tears and heard the pathetic whimpers that involuntarily escaped her lips. His grunts soon overshadowed her sobs, followed by shouts of ecstasy as he finally climaxed.

Afterward he just lay over her, spent, his heavy breathing punctuating the otherwise still air. She wanted to push him off. Every part of her trembled and ached so she just lay there and allowed silent tears to continue creeping down her temples and into her hairline. Drying blood seeped from one nostril and her lip was swollen. Her left ear rang, had continued to do so after he'd struck her so many times along the side of her head.

After a while, his breathing slowed and he shifted his weight. He put a hand over her distended belly, digging his nails, sharper than most other men's, into her flesh. "Finally, after so long, the dreams of my people are coming true. And I am alive to see it, to *feel* it! Never in my most far-flung fantasies did I ever imagine this. Never did I imagine that I could climax so strongly, so completely."

He looked up at her, his blue eyes shining with lust. He rose over her again, and when she felt his erection throbbing against her hip, her heart stuttered. *No. Dear gods, someone please help me. Please.*

But she knew there was no one. The only one there was Drath Drakkon.

Chapter Twenty-Two
Duty

The lord of swords and Truth watched over the parade grounds of the Castle of Moonlight and Love. The elves of Rithalion drilled endlessly, tirelessly, all knowing that the Iron Coast was coming. There were far too many of the very young and the elderly, and not enough of those young adults that made up the core of any army. Too many of those had been lost throughout the years, but too much was at stake to be picky. The La'athai trained harder than anyone under the leadership of Tyrell, showing up before dawn and leaving well after dinner had been called. The new troops were coming along, but none of the La'athai that had marched in last year's campaign would allow the new members to call themselves wolves. Xadrian had mentioned it to Tyrell in passing, usually the only thing he had to do in order to put an end to any practice he deemed inappropriate, but it continued. If anything, Tyrell had only pushed the whole unit harder. He seemed determined beyond reason to not let Vivien or the Wolf down while they were off being diplomats.

"General! General!"

Xadrian turned and saw a low elf in the brown and black robes of the messenger hawk scribes, quickly running towards him. The only time they did that was when...

Xadrian felt his cape snap out behind him like a flag in a tornado as he bolted to a full sprint. He covered the ground in just a few seconds and took the unrolled message. He scanned it and his heart fell away, leaving a gaping hole inside his chest. It ached with loss and dread, an uncomfortably familiar feeling that brought back the snap of dragon wings and the endless roar of water.

He nodded and found all his emotions scattered about his soul like lost toys. He shoved them into the closets of his mind as he let go a four-part whistle that startled the acolyte. Then he dismissed the Hawksman and watched the army's messengers run to him from different parts of the field. He gave three each a message, who it was for, then had them repeat it and sent them off. The fourth he sent to the supply master to requisition for a force of forty, moving fast. By the time he had finished, he saw Tyrell across the parade grounds get the first delivered message whispered in his ear. The man stiffened as if being struck, then finally turned to see Xadrian nod silently and walk into the Castle of Moonlight and Love.

Xadrian's boots clicked incessantly as he entered the palace. He paused at the side of the servant at the front door and declared, "I am going to the aerie," and then continued with purposeful strides that brooked no further questions or delay. He took the steps two at a time and blamed them for his pounding heartbeat, but the churning emotions in his gut were not from these and he knew it. He navigated the innards of the castle and saw no person that passed by, nor the beautiful adornments that spoke of the artistic mind of his former wife. He simply put one foot in front of the other until he opened the door onto the gigantic chamber made like a marble tree holding dozens of real hawk's nests all around in easy reach.

The acolyte who had delivered his message and his partner startled and made to come forward.

"Get out."

The two robed figures paused for just a moment before scuttling toward the door. The acolyte that had handed the paper over stopped, lowered his hood, and bowed to Xadrian sadly. The Lord of Swords and Truth nodded back stoically and then they were gone. They left him with nothing but the gentle wind and empty sky, several hawks preening quietly, and three tirinian scuttling through the realistic stone branches. Xadrian reached for the peace that could be found there, tried to drink of it as deeply as he could, for the next few weeks of his life were guaranteed to be chaos and blood. He was marginally successful. Then the door flew open, and he pulled on the mask of a warrior general to cover the grieving uncle from the world.

Tyrell entered at a half run and skidded to a stop, breaths coming in ragged gasps. His voice was tinged with panic, his whole person aflutter with emotion. "General?"

Xadrian met him with a calm gaze made of stone and steel. "Catch your breath, Captain."

"No, please sir, what does the message mean?"

He was not gaining control of himself, and likely would not. There was loyalty there, but something else as well. It would not be the first difficult talk he would have this day. Best to get it done quickly. "It means what it said. Isbandar has received two diplomats from Elyrion, one of our La'athai, and one of the guards sent with the mission. The rest of the diplomatic envoy was wiped out. The Wolf was likely killed, and Vivien perhaps dead, maybe taken by Liath. Neither body has been found."

Xadrian watched Tyrell struggle for a moment. He went from pale to beet red, then pale again as the icy calm of helplessness found a needle hole of hope. "I will gather the La'athai. We will march within the hour." With that proclamation he turned on his heel to go.

"Halt." The word was soft from Xadrian's lips, but it stopped him nonetheless. "You will stay here and continue to train your new wolf cubs. They will be direly needed to defeat the Iron Coast."

Xadrian watched Tyrell's irises shrink to pinpricks, all blood drain from his face except for two bright spots on his cheeks, and his fists tremble until they clenched into fists. "General you cannot expect me to..."

"Captain?"

But Tyrell had opened the barrel from the bottom of his emotion, and it had him now. "... stay here while she is in danger. The La'athai will revolt! They will mutiny and..."

"Captain!"

His voice became loud with rage and he hunched for a fight, his hand straying toward his sword, "...THEY WILL DROP THIER UNIFORMS IN THE DIRT AND DESERT TO GO FIND HER, AND I WILL BE FIRST AMONGST THEM!"

The Lord of Swords summoned his Elvishness and put it all behind a single word. Xadrian's voice rang off the walls, sending tirinian skittering and hawks flapping from nests into lazy circles at a safe distance. "CAPTAIN!"

The shock of it straightened Tyrell's spine and set him to shuddering as if dipped in icy waters. He looked left and right, as if seeing the aerie for the first time. "I... I... my apologies General. I..."

Tyrell began to weep.

Xadrian waited, steps away. He had feared but expected this. Expected this much of all the Wolf Pack. They loved their commanders, Vivien and the Wolf. Loved them too much maybe. "Captain, the Wolf has been dead a week, Vivien captured for as long. If they are suffering, they are suffering and there is nothing we can do about it right now."

Tyrell's eyes were glassy, cheeks still flushed. He had seen horrible combat against the Iron Coast but this, this could break him. In his grief, he was trying to let it break him. "General, I apologize. I wish to report myself for intention to desert and gross insubordination. I should be stripped of my rank and immediately discharged."

Xadrian looked at him, then left and right. "I see no witnesses to this insubordination or desertion." Tyrell blinked at him, not understanding. Xadrian sighed tiredly. "This is going to be heartbreaking news to your unit. Remember mercy, remember leniency. Words spoken in private may not mean actions in public. We all grieve the loss of An'drath. He fought for us when no other would have or should have. Vivien had a duty, but he did not." He felt his throat close and he cleared it, stabilizing himself with a deep breath. "Vivien had a duty to us and she fulfilled it better than anyone could have expected. Now she needs us and we are going to her aid. But, as I remember, they gave you a duty to fulfill- train wolves so that the La'athai can protect their home. Will you continue to do your duty to them and this city?"

Tyrell breathed in great gasps, eyes shamefully on the floor, and nodded.

Xadrian nodded back. "I do not envy you. You must break the news to the soldiers and get them to continue training. Then you must tell them that some of them have to stay."

Tyrell wiped his eyes, for a moment looking like a small child. "Some?"

"Split the La'athai. Veteran troops with tir-reath only will go, home mounts or war mounts, I do not care. I will lead them and search for the missing captain. I have seen the maneuvers, but you are intimately familiar with them. You can train them while the other officers train bowmen and swordsmen. I will go and find her and bring her back to safety."

Tyrell finally remembered he was a soldier of Rithalion and stood straight, snapping a salute. Xadrian returned it. "Dismissed, but... Tyrell?" He took a deep breath, "If you think someone will react badly to the news, take them somewhere private first. Then have them stand with you to deliver the news to the rest."

Tyrell nodded, then his face clouded. "Do you want me to stay while you tell...?"

"Don't be foolish. You have your own job to do. I am a General, and can deliver news on my own." Xadrian gave a cold smile. "Dismissed."

And Tyrell left. Again, Xadrian sought peace in the few minutes he had until the next person he had to tell arrived. He did not have to wait long, but when the first arrived, sadly, so did the second.

Jor'aiden came in, breathless and despondent, hood thrown back by his haste and steps unsure beneath his robes. "Xadrian, Xadrian please, tell me that my daughter is well."

Behind him, dark, cold, and unmoved, Torialvah slunk into the room like a snake looking to steal an egg. Xadrian ignored him. "You are the closest relation she has, Grand Magister. Tell me, can you feel your daughter?"

The Grand Magister closed his eyes as if having an attack, his whole body fraught with stress and strain. "No, not since the battle with the Iron Coast. Now please tell me..."

Xadrian told them.

Jor'aiden collapsed into Xadrian's arms as if he had been struck by an arrow. Torialvah looked incensed, but Xadrian could not tell if the Lord of Ice and Steel was angry at the Liath or Vivien. The Grand Magister abandoned all pride and decorum as he sobbed into The Lord of Sword's cloak. Torialvah looked disgusted. Xadrian stuffed his own venom at the Lord of Steel down deeply and pulled The Grand Magister away from him, holding him by his biceps.

"You must focus. If you could not feel her before now, you cannot know she is gone. I am divvying up the La'athai. Some will come with me and I will scour the forest for her. Isbandar and Elyrion have already sent out search parties, but it is a sizable group of Liath we will have to slay to retrieve her."

Jor'aiden continued to weep, but ceased to sob. "I am going, Xadrian."

The Lord of Swords nodded grimly. "I thought as much."

The Lord of Steel spoke up for the first time, voice oily. "I have many duties here to go chasing after–"

Xadrian spared him making a fool of himself, trying to spare Jor'aiden more than Torialvah. "Before you continue, there is one more piece of news." Jor'aiden ceased glaring at his son-in-law and both sets of eyes fixed on Xadrian, "Vivien is pregnant."

Jor'aiden gaped. Torialvah turned blood red, skin flushing everywhere Xadrian could see. A heavy silence descended upon the aerie. It built and built, but Xadrian left it there to grow into a monumental pressure upon Tor's pride.

His mouth moved like a man picking a maggot out of a bite of apple with his teeth. "I should go."

Jor'aiden drew himself up, tears still cascading from his eyes, "She will need a Master Healer, and I know the one that will brave the journey with us."

"Then make ready. We must move quickly. Everyone will be mounted. No carriages. And we must be always prepared for battle."

Tor looked like he would object, but Jor'aiden flipped up his hood to signal the conversation was over. He laid a weary hand on Xadrian's shoulder.

"Be brave." It was the only advice that the Lord of Swords could give. The other two then left the aerie without a word.

Then, again, there was silence. Solitude. Peace. At times these things were a solace to some elves, but now it gave license for his fears to break loose and gibber in his mind. He wrestled with them, struggling for hope both for Vivien and for the Wolf. Xadrian paced the aerie, wearing a path through the leaves and detritus that covered the floor. The three tirinian watched him move back and forth, every once in a while tensing as he sent a bit of debris skidding away, hoping whatever moved may be a juicy bug to eat. Several messenger hawks watched him dispassionately, unaware and uncaring of what missive they might bring. Xadrian, however, lifted the parchment to his eyes again, his stomach roiled in a way it hadn't in centuries. He read it again and again, still unbelieving.

"My love?"

It was Her. Of course, Her. She would know. She always did. Take her across the mountains, on the other side of the great seas, to the ends of all creation and she would still know and find a way to get to his side. He turned to face Shaladrea, The Lady of Moonlight and Love, and took her in his arms. She tensed for a moment, and then melted into him. She said nothing, and in the silence between them there was the most precious gift one person can bestow upon another. Acceptance.

Xadrian pulled away slightly and looked into her eyes. Every other person who saw her was mesmerized by her unearthly beauty. He watched as the glamour broke apart, stripping away the threads to leave behind simply the woman he loved. The only one he loved. The only one he would ever love. He leaned in and his lips met hers. She responded instantly, pressing herself into him. They kissed for what seemed like forever, and every second of yearning in the centuries since she had been his wife was captured in every moment.

They parted, and her eyes were dripping with grief. "You always kissed me like that when you were leaving for war."

He nodded.

"Is that happening?"

"It has already happened."

He gave her the, by this time, crinkled message. She gasped. He forestalled any grand gesture with an order. "Stay and guide the troops. Motivate them. Make them work to defend their homes. I must gather a rescue party and go after her, and with the blessings of the gods, him."

She blinked at him. "And the Council?"

He set his face and for just a moment he knew he was wearing the expression of the Wolf. "I am going. I'll inform them when I am ready to do so."

She nodded, looked thoughtful for a moment. He waited patiently for her to gather her thoughts. Then, "What is it?"

Still, she hesitated, but finally took a deep breath. "I already knew of the pregnancy."

He raised a questioning brow.

"I found out before she left. She asked me to keep it a secret."

Xadrian nodded. "So, the child is Tor's."

It was a statement more than a question, but one to which she still offered a response. "Yes. You thought differently?"

He gave her a solemn look. "I have seen her with my brother. They have great love for one another."

"Yes, but that does not mean that she broke her oath."

He nodded. It was his turn to be thoughtful. "A surviving twin. That is very rare."

She nodded. "Indeed."

He offered her his arm, and together they turned and walked from the aerie. It was the first time they had done so in centuries and could be the last time they ever did. They were aware of the rifts between them, of the wounds that were imperfectly healed, but these young people had supplanted their own children, long dead. They leaned upon one another in order to begin the plan to see them safely home.

Chapter Twenty-Three
Secrets and Dragon Magic

Vivien sat in the darkness, on the floor at the foot of Drakkon's bed. Nothing but a thin pallet, it was where he'd chosen to keep her during the night while he slept, not trusting her to sleep in the bed beside him. She didn't blame him, she wouldn't trust her either, but at least he could have provided her one of the many other chambers in the temple. One with a bed.

No. He needed her there with him, craved her so much that he had to keep her shackled at his feet to keep her in her place, even in the dank recesses of the night.

This night, blood trickled from between her legs. He liked to hurt her, but refused to hit her face like he'd done the first night he'd raped her. It had left her looking ugly, and the following morning she was bruised and swollen. Mirkari had found her lying there on the bed, and with the utmost tenderness, had helped clean her up. Drakkon had managed to come up with a story to the other priests, all of who knew he was lying to them, a story telling of her attempt at escape with a weapon that never existed. Their expressions of discontent made him more careful in the future, so he hurt her only where they could not see, and sometimes she bled just like she did now. Miraculously nothing ever came of it, and by the morning it stopped like it had never happened. The only indication was the blood that remained on the pallet, but it simply blended in with the dark stains that were there already, and he never cared, nor thought, to look at it.

Just like she had after the ambush, the injuries healed swiftly. So did the tattoo across her back. The wound in her chest no longer hurt, but she hardly noticed. Drakkon had noticed, but said nothing.

Thoughts filled her mind, the same thoughts she had every night. *How long have I been here? Did Sherika manage to carry Evey and my brother away? Did anyone else escape? Did they make it to Isbandar? Or maybe back to Elyrion? Is anyone searching for me? Anyone at all? What must the Lady be thinking? My father? Mika? Even if no one comes, certainly these people won't keep me here forever. My son will be born, and when they see he is a normal baby, mayhap I can bargain for our lives.*

She'd ceased thinking about the Wolf. It simply hurt too much.

Vivien pulled at the shackles around her wrists, and the chains that bound her to the bed rattled as she pulled at them too. It was a nightly ritual. She hoped, prayed she might find a weak link somewhere, anywhere. There was never any, but it didn't stop her from trying.

She didn't hear him until his hand was in her hair, jerking her head back to look into his eyes. He pulled up and she was forced to stand beside him in the darkness, his eyes glowing like twin sapphires. His voice was deep and raspy. My Drakkaria Jash'ari, what are you hoping to find?" He chuckled. "You will discover no weakness in those links. They are fashioned of the finest Elvish steel that can be found." Blood trickled down one leg, making a warm, tickling sensation, and her belly ached deep inside. "How many times do I have to tell you that you are mine? And when your son is born, he will be mine as well. He will grow up with the Liath and he will become the breeding stock for the first generation of dragon elves to ever exist. And you, dear Umesh? You will serve your purpose again and again. Knowing you have the ability to carry these offspring, that will be your duty. You will have daughters, daughters that may have that ability. They also will carry these offspring. And then, when you can no longer perform it, we will kill you."

A spark erupted into being inside her soul. It fizzed into existence by words alone and settled into her heart.

"Go to sleep, Jash'ari. There is no escape for you." He pushed her as he released her hair and she fell onto the crusty pallet on the floor. Drakkon climbed back into his bed, the one he raped her in every night, and made himself comfortable beneath the threadbare sheets. Vivien huddled there on the pallet, her legs streaked with blood, her belly aching painfully in little waves.

But the spark had become a tiny flame. She held it close, nurtured it, loved it. She pondered the priest's words, and it grew.

The acolyte came barging into the chamber, his brow beaded with sweat. Drakkon looked up from his book, startled by the intrusion. "My Lord, there is..." The young man's eyes darted to Vivien and then back to the priest. "There is an emergency that requires your immediate attention. You must come quickly."

Hearing the alarm in the young man's voice, Drakkon rose from his seat, his eyes troubled. "Certainly. I will be right there, Minos."

"With all respect my Lord, please..."

An ominous crashing sound emanated from the temple below them. Drakkon's eyes widened and he rushed from the bedroom and out the chamber suite, the acolyte behind him. Vivien followed, stopped in the middle of the antechamber when she heard a key hastily placed in the lock outside and turned.

She let out the breath she'd been holding. *Still trapped. Still unable to escape my prison.* She morosely walked back into the bedroom, stood there at the entry and stared at the scene before her: the pallet on the floor, the large, wooden, four-poster bed with a length of chain attached to a wide bracket around the left rear post and another length attached to another bracket around the right front, the disheveled blankets lying on top, partially covering the portion of chain that lay there. She glanced at her arms, her wrists encased within brushed bronze bracers. She stared at the thick metal. *I am not free of this chamber, but I am free of my chains.*

Her heart leapt and she did a small dance. She looked over at the priest's table, spied the book lying there. She tiptoed over to it and picked it up. It was a small volume with a faded brown cover that bore no title. She looked at the pages Drakkon had been studying before he left so precipitously. Her eyes widened. It was an incantation.

Vivien read over the words. It was some kind of fire spell, but like none she had ever seen before. She riffled through the pages, pages filled with spell after spell. She giggled to herself, overwhelmed by such a treasure. *No wonder he guards it so well. This is his spellbook. Only today, he hasn't taken it with him, and he hasn't chained me away from it.*

Vivien read through the pages, took in all the words. She consumed them, like during her decades of study. The words leapt off of the page and burned into her mind, lodging there like arrows shot from a powerful bow. Even more, she began to understand the patterns in the spells, accurately guessing how the flow of the magic progressed. It was so different, so alien, but in the end, it was a kind of magic and thus was something she always understood in her deepest parts of her heart. She glanced at the candle on the desk, noting how far the lonely thing had burned in Drakkon's absence. There must have been an emergency, indeed, to keep him way so long. She could not, however, count on the emergency giving her another, better chance. She had to read, had to know, and had to understand to free herself. There was a note scratched hastily in the margin:

Fire spells not enough. Fire element immune to fire. Air and Water useless tripe. Collect or steal more earth element spells.

One spell near the end bid her pause. The words were complex, and it took her a few moments to learn the enunciation. It was a heat spell. She looked at her bracers again, wondering. *No, I can't try it out on me. I have to find something else.*

She put the book just as she'd found it and wracked her mind, pacing the room. She looked around the chamber, then beyond into the fore-chamber. She saw the wyrms lying there, coiled in a beautiful pile...

...a beautiful pile of shimmering scales and bronze collars.

Fire is immune to fire.

Vivien slowly walked towards the wyrms. Her heart beat a staccato rhythm. She'd not been near them since the day Drakkon had thrown her to their mercy. Their wedge-shaped heads rose as she approached, their amber eyes watching her solemnly. Closer...closer...

Finally, she stood before them. They remained still, regarding her intently. There was no hissing, no screeching. They were calmer than she'd ever seen them. They could easily lurch towards her, take a bite out of any part of her. But for some reason, they did not. They had been chained to the wall because of her, yet they did not seem to bear her any ill will.

Vivien had always borne an attraction for the things that lived in the natural world. She was good with animals, and seemed to have a connection with them. She had faith in their inherent goodness. She understood them, and they seemed to sense that. Mayhap it was the same with dragons.

Put your faith in what you most believe in...

Vivien reached out a hand. It didn't tremble the way it did before, but it didn't mean the fear wasn't there. She couldn't show them that emotion. They needed to believe in her too, believe that there was nothing to be afraid of.

The wyrms didn't move, except for one. The white/gold rose from the pile, her scales gleaming. She was like the sun and the moon together in the same being, glowing softly in the torchlight. She was tall, much taller than Vivien realized, her body thick as her thighs, her tail becoming thinner and thinner as it reached the tip. The wyrm rose over her, but then lowered her head to Vivien's height, pressing her jaw against her hand.

Vivien held her breath, her fingers gently caressing the smooth scales. She stepped closer, trailing her hand down the long sinuous neck. Tendrils of wispy smoke rose from perfectly shaped nostrils, and she couldn't help smiling. *She likes the feel of my touch just as much as I like the feel of her skin beneath my fingertips.* The wyrm began to move, and before Vivien realized it, she was surrounded by the beautiful body. The serpentine form didn't press too close, yet it circled her within its protective embrace. The wyrm positioned her head over Vivien's shoulder and grunted, blowing out a stream of warmth that engulfed her.

And then the bronze collar was before her, a prison to this beast just as her bracers were a prison to her. Vivien placed her hands over the thick shackle and doubt suffused her. *Can I really do this?* The wyrm puffed again, placing her head beside Vivien's arm, watching her with curiosity. *Does she know what I'm doing?* She turned towards the head, saw the eyes studying her, trusting her...

Suddenly she could feel its power, and she knew, knew in her soul, it was a creature of fire. It was at that moment she decided.

Vivien placed a finger to her lips. "Shhhh."

The wyrm's amber eyes sparkled and the other two wyrms also rose from their coil, watching with avid interest as Vivien placed her hands back onto the bronze collar circling the gold's neck. Then she began the incantation.

She had no idea why she thought she could cast it; it was dragon magic after all. She shouldn't have been able to even remotely touch that kind of power, trained only in the use of fae magic for her entire life. But it was there. It answered her call, surged towards her like a herd of runaway antelope, closer, closer, closer. She trembled with the influx of power, a magic she'd never experienced before. It washed through her body, touched every part of her being, every fiber. Then it concentrated in her hands, building higher, higher, higher. The metal beneath her fingers began to glow, began to burn her fingertips. It was painful, yet she kept going, continued saying the words of the spell from Drakkon's spellbook.

And then it happened. The bronze began to warp, and within moments, it slipped from off the white/gold neck, the dragon as untroubled by the heat as a child was by a light drizzle.

Vivien slumped to the floor, suddenly exhausted. The other two wyrms investigated the twisted metal, then the place on their comrade where it used to be. Smoke rose from all their noses, and they slithered around her as much as their chains would allow. Vivien stared at her hands, unburned despite the pain she'd felt moments before.

Then, suddenly the wyrms became still and they looked towards the door. Fear swept through Vivien. Drakkon was returning. Despite her fatigue, Vivien struggled from the floor, her hands clutching at the white/gold who remained in place to act as a support. The key turned in the lock as she toddled across the room to the bedchamber, the white/gold curling by the wall, tail flipping the warped collar behind her and then crouching low to hide her naked neck. Vivien fell onto her crusty pallet as Drakkon entered. She calmed her breathing, closed her eyes and allowed her fatigue to wash over her once more.

She heard Drakkon's footsteps, heard them pause when he reached her pallet. She sensed his eyes on her, sensed the questions that ran through his mind, questions about how long she'd been laying there, and questions about why she hadn't tried to escape.

From the floor she could smell a host of things upon her rapist. He smelled of sweat, and blood. There was a spiciness to it that calmed her, making her mind wander tiredly... somewhere. But her head was full of new formulae, new ideas, new understanding, and it was leaden. She began to float, exhaustion overtaking her, and she felt a calmness she hadn't felt in a long time.

Shhhh. She need not fear. The dragons would keep her secret.

Chapter Twenty-Four
The Love of a Dragon

It was dark in the chamber, darker than it usually was. Vivien shifted on the pallet and her body ached. Her belly rumbled, and she recognized it as the thing that had ultimately awakened her. She was hungry. She sat up and looked towards the place where food was often left for her. A plate sat on the small table, and when she concentrated enough, she could smell the bread, fruits, and nuts that lay on it. She always hoped for some kind of meat; she craved meat, but it was rare for it to be offered. Regardless, she always ate what was provided on that plate, because it was all she had and never enough.

Vivien rose from the pallet, started towards the plate, and was jerked back. She looked down at the bracers on her arms, saw that the chains had been attached. Anger coursed through her. *Damn Drakkon! Damn the entire lot of them! He rapes me every night, but you let him, no matter what it might mean for me and the baby you value so highly. All of you are weak, unworthy of your positions of meager power, unworthy of the magic you cast from the essence of the dragons you keep chained to your infernal walls.*

Vivien pulled at her bonds, pulled with all her strength. The anger had become a swiftly flowing river, moving through her veins like rapids around sharp rocks. She pulled, and pulled, and pulled, each moment making her more determined to break free, fierce against those who might stop her. Sweat beaded her brow and ran down her bare back, bare but for the cloth that spanned the lower part, cloth that crossed over her chest to cover her breasts and tied behind her neck. The clothes of a slave in Zormoth.

Nothing happened. The chain links never gave, and the post with its steel bracket remained straight. Tears of frustration trailed down her cheeks, and her heart was filled with the sadness of tens of generations. *My son will be naught but a tool, a stud for breeding He will never become the wonderful man I envision he can be. He will never swim the Fyresmee River, never run through the fields outside of Lady Shaladrea's fortress, never learn the true ways of sword fighting from the Lord of Swords, never learn the intricacies of fae magic from the Grand Magister. He will never have a father to run home to after a difficult day at the lore house, or a mother to hold him tight when he's been hurt.*

He will never know what it is like to truly love.

An imagined dagger plunged deep into her breast. "No! No, no, no." Vivien strained against her bonds, pulled with all of the might within her, and then more. Her wrists and forearms, covered in scratches while sustaining attempts to pull away the bracers, dripped blood onto the floor. At last she ceased, hunkered down on the pallet and cried a sea of tears that was absorbed by the stained fabric over the old pallet, taken away like it was never there. She scrabbled at the bracers again, her nails sharp like the claws of some animal trying in desperation to be free.

Then she stopped. She looked up and into the antechamber, saw the wyrms staring at her from their place near the wall. Vivien's breath was harsh, even to her own ears, and she looked from the gold wyrm and then back to her own bracers. *Drakkon is not here. I can escape my bonds. I can be free.* Fear swept through her. *No, you can never be free. He will bring you back to this place and he will punish you. He will hurt you. He will hurt your son.*

A moment of clarity insinuated itself. *He will hurt you no matter if you escape. He will hurt your son. He will hurt all you hold dear, forever.*

He killed the Wolf.

Vivien concentrated on the spell. It came slowly at first, but then the power was there, at the doorway into her mind, just waiting to be tapped. She opened the doorway...

...and she let the fire in.

It was all consuming, stripping away all her barriers, all her fears. She spoke the words of the spell, agony playing up and down her arms and threatening to disrupt her spell. She could not block it out, but instead reveled in it, using the pain to feed her energy until she watched the bracers fall from her arms into smoking heaps onto the pallet. Her body burned with the inferno inside of her, so hot that her flimsy clothing fell away in ashes. She stood on the pallet, her feet making holes in it. She took deep gulping breaths, looked at her hands. Veins of gold streaked along the backs, and up her arms. Her palms glowed.

By the gods, what power is this?

She pushed against the fire, banked it enough so that she could pick up the pallet and flip it over onto its other side, hiding the holes and the twisted bracers. She then sat on the edge of Drakkon's bed. Her senses assailed her: the texture of the bed sheets rougher than she remembered, the moldy mildew scent of the old temple, the sight of the minute cracks in the stone walls surrounding her. The sound of...

Vivien lay back on the pillow behind her as Drakkon opened the door. Her heartbeat thrummed against her ribs, beating faster than it ever had before. She watched him from her place on the bed, watched him stop before the wyrms. They bowed as he reached out to touch them, but unlike before, when she thought that his touch contented them, she realized that they merely tolerated it.

It was then he looked towards the bedchamber. His brows pulled into a frown when he saw that she was no longer on the pallet. She hid her arms as he strode determinedly across the antechamber, and when he reached the bedroom, he saw her lying there on the bed. For a moment she watched him rationalize why she would be there instead of on the pallet, mayhap imagined that Mirkari or Risa had been there, much as they had been in the past, and reattached her there when they had work to do around the suite. He didn't see that her bracers were no longer affixed. His brows evened out and a smile curved up his cruelly expressive lips.

"Jash'ari, it is good to see you here waiting for me." His gaze raked over her naked form. "And in the way I like to see you most."

Vivien struggled to maintain her impassive expression. He was such a monster, the cruelest being she'd ever met. That included the dragon in Pergatium, who had fought so that he could once more experience life as he'd known it before, even if it meant that she lose her own. Drakkon was worse than that, taking her life and threatening all the lives she would bear for him in the future, innocent lives that had yet to draw their first breaths.

Drakkon began removing his clothes— first the cloak of his station, followed by his sleeveless longtunic. His chest was lean and muscular, attractive if not for the man it belonged to. He unfastened his trousers and his erection sprung free of its bonds. He approached her slowly, almost menacingly. She'd given up fighting him weeks ago; he liked it too much, and it caused more pain. He made up other things to try and intimidate her, but today...

The priest reached her side of the bed. He fell upon her, crushing her lips, his hands groping at her breasts and between her thighs. Her belly ached with the pressure of his weight, but she made no sounds. He liked it when she cried. Her arms she still kept hidden beneath her, fear warring with the predominant anger in her mind, creating a soup of negative emotion that swirled around in the recesses of her soul.

Let him rape me again. He will take his next piece of me and break me down. My people have never come for me, they have left me here to experience this hell firsthand. But I will persevere. Nothing in this hell hath fury greater than mine, for I have become fire.

Drakkon forced her legs apart, and without preamble, he took her. His thrust was forceful, as always, and her flesh cringed away from the intrusion. Vivien took that as her cue, and raising her hands above her head, she submitted. It was an action she'd never performed before, so he noticed. That, and the bareness of her wrists.

Drakkon hesitated, and as he raised himself over her, she lay one hand over his chest, right above his wildly beating heart, and began to mumble her incantation.

"By the everlasting gods! You cretin! How did you...aaaghhh!"

Her hand began to glow, and much like it had the other two times, it burned. Only, this time, she wasn't afraid she would be harmed. Drakkon tried to lurch back from her, but her legs snaked around his hips, holding him in place. Her hand continued to burn. She thought there would be more resistance, but none came.

Drakkon screamed.

It was a terrible sound, filling the chamber with a chilling song that reached into her very bones. Her hand sank through the flesh of his chest, deeper, deeper, deeper, until she reached the pulsing organ within. Vivien grabbed it and pulled. Hard. The scream came to an abrupt halt and blood spurted from the gaping hole, covering her in warm stickiness. In her hand, Vivien held Drakkon's heart. The muscle quivered even as it smoked, still trying to pump blood through the body, and for a moment she thought she might even drop it. Her legs relaxed and Drakkon slumped over onto his side, his eyes open wide, his mouth opening and closing like a fish as it struggles to breathe out of water.

And there, behind him, was the white/gold wyrm. She had pushed Drakkon down toward Vivien's hand, holding him still for his execution.

The young dragon slowly approached Vivien, slithering closer and closer. She could sense the beast's hesitancy, similar to the way she felt when she approached her the day before. The wyrm drew towards her, neck extending in a position of vulnerability. Vivien reached out with her other hand, laying her palm over the pale muzzle...

...and was bombarded with an influx of emotion.

Pleasure, pain, fear, love– it was all there in the wyrm's mind. A gate had been opened between them and, just like Sherika, Vivien could feel the dragon in her mind.

Dari'sii.

It was her name. The wyrm's name was Dari'sii.

Vivien began to tremble, and within the barest moment, Dari'sii enveloped her within her coils. The dragon was warm, warmer than she ever thought a reptilian creature could be, and it was then she realized that the beast was born of fire.

Just like me.

Vivien held up the heart of her enemy, a show of victory despite her momentary fatigue. Dari'sii hissed at it, but then bowed, waiting for what Vivien would do next. The warmage looked at the heart, warm from the body from which she'd stolen it, and brought it to her mouth.

It tasted wonderful, better than she would ever have imagined it might. Her teeth tore through the muscle, and she chewed, her appetite for meat finally satiated. She then offered the heart to the friend who had helped subdue the enemy from behind without her knowing. Such friends were difficult to come by.

Gratitude filled the link they shared as Dari'sii bit into the heart. Blood trickled down the wyrm's chin, staining the white scales. Vivien imagined she must look the same way. Consumed with hunger, she took another bite of the heart, and another, sharing with Dari'sii until the tastiest parts of the organ were completely gone.

Then she tossed the remains beside the body and rested. Wrapped within the protective coils of the beautiful wyrm, Vivien rested until she felt her energy had returned. Then, when she'd had enough of laying next to the dead body of Drath Drakkon, she rose from the bed and looked around the chamber. There was nothing for her to wear. Nothing. Unfortunate really, for she must look a sight covered in blood, pregnant, and naked. She made her way out of the chamber and up to the other two wyrms chained to the wall. They raised their heads, staring at her through eyes filled with hope and the desire for freedom.

Vivien looked at them, really looked at them. She saw deep into their essence, and saw that the one colored burgundy-red was an earth element, and the navy-green one was one of water. She could also see something else.

They were dying.

Their spirits, their young spirits, not given ample and appropriate sustenance for far too long, were snuffing out like the flames in a shuttered lantern. Ultimately, it would be as though those spirits had never been.

Anger warred with sorrow as she reached out towards the wyrms. Both slithered close and placed their heads over her shoulders. Her heart broke for them. Even if she set them free, there was no guarantee they would live. But a short life of freedom was better than a longer one in chains. Once more Vivien set her hands upon bronze, and again she called to the power that lay so close to her soul. It was already there, waiting like an earnest lover. It was only moments before the bronze collars fell away, and their happiness was indicated by the smoke swirling from their noses and the coiling around her body. They wanted to touch her, touch as much of her as they could, mayhap hoping to remember her in the future. And when they came close to her ears, they spoke to her.

Enk'mahris.

Sah'rubiek.

It was their names, so that, one day, she could call on them should she ever need them. It was powerful, the most powerful thing a dragon could give someone. It was a piece of themselves, a piece they could never get back. Once it was given, it was gone forever. Vivien promised to keep those pieces close to her heart. With her, those pieces would know peace.

The beautiful wyrms looked deep into her eyes, and when they were ready, they faded away back into the spirit plane from whence they'd come. Vivien lowered her head, suddenly feeling very alone. Only then did she realize how much they'd been a part of her over the past many days and weeks since she'd been there. *How did I not realize this? How did I not know they had become a part of me, fortifying me, feeling the things that I have felt?* Because she knew, deep in her heart, that's what it would have taken for them to have been the bastions of support they'd proven to be.

Vivien sensed movement to her left and jerked her head up. I was the white/gold wyrm. Her breath hitched in her throat, but she managed to speak anyways. "You should go. You have a chance at freedom."

The feelings in her mind expressed resistance. Vivien wondered at this, not understanding. "No, I will be alright. I will find my people. Thank you for helping me. I will never forget you."

Again, she felt the resistance. Dari'sii curved around her, coils gently encasing her in a secure embrace.

A loving embrace.

Vivien stopped her pondering and looked at her new friend, truly looked at her. She was a fire element, a fire that burned so bright, Vivien could scarcely see. And within that fire, she saw more than just a bright light. She saw commitment. No, more than commitment.

The wyrm pressed her face against Vivien's belly. Her breath trembled, knowing what that might mean. It was love. But the dragon didn't just love Vivien. She loved the child growing within her.

And Dari'sii would not leave the ones she'd come to love most.

Chapter Twenty-Five
Two Hearts on Fire

almost in a haze, Vivien burned down the door and strode down the corridor of the temple, clad only in her white/gold dragon. She knew not where she was going, for the few times she'd been out of Drakkon's chamber suite, he'd taken different routes to get her back there. Despite the heat radiating from her body, Dari'sii was wrapped around her: body twined around Vivien's torso, neck around her shoulders, tail around her hips and right leg. She could feel the energy within the wyrm, and realized why Drakkon had kept her and the others so close. He used them as energy wells, places upon which to draw strength when he was unsure his own would sustain him.

He was a fool to misuse them, and even more a fool to believe they would have borne him any good will.

Hatred burned within her. It was an inferno within her soul, urging her along the next corridor, and the next. It urged her down the staircase to the lower level where priests stared at her in shock. She had already spoken her incantation, another one she'd somehow managed to memorize from Drakkon's book of spells. All she had to do was put out her hands...

...and fire erupted from her fingertips.

The priests were incinerated within moments, their final cries barely making it past their lips. She continued past the charred corpses lying in the pathway, stepping over them with calm deliberation. Men began to run from her path, praying she would not visit hell's wrath upon them.

Those who thought to stop her, died.

Vivien continued, and finally reached a large chamber. A part of her had expected to see other priests there, even expected them to bring her down, but the only ones present were novices. She blasted them with the same fire, sweeping it across the chamber to encompass nearly everything in its wake.

The acolytes were caught in the inferno, their clothes burning off their bodies as they screamed. When they fell, they lay upon the floor in heaps of charred flesh, moaning in agony, barely moving. Through clouds of greasy black smoke, Vivien's gaze swept the chamber and took in the raised dais. Upon it was a massive table, and situated atop it was a complex device. Dark red liquid moved along the many tubes and valves, moving along to a destination at the end where it was deposited into a glass vial. With the death of the novices, the device had become backed up, and the next vial was not moved into place. The thick red liquid spilled over the table and trickled over the side to puddle on the floor. Behind the table was a shelf, and upon it rested at least a hundred of the glass vials. Dari'sii hissed.

Vivien took a moment to be astounded, but then turned away. She cared not for these things. All that mattered was... "Aghh."

She turned to the sound of the moan, and looking deep into the darker recesses of the chamber, she made out the shape of another table. Upon it was the large form of a man. She stepped closer to the table, curious in spite of her desire to continue to make her way out of the temple. Once the other priests were aware of what had happened, they would come for her. Dari'sii trilled into her ear and she was calmed.

Vivien approached the table. Curly chestnut hair hung off the side, as well as one thick arm that was connected to a tube. The tube ran down and was connected to something else on the other end, something that appeared to be a much larger version of the glass vials on the shelf.

She rushed the rest of the way over to the table. Lying there was Ravn. His face was pale, and blue circles rested beneath his closed eyes. His arm was bruised where the tube was connected, and his veins bulged. He was thin, much thinner than she'd ever seen him, and his pants barely covered his hips they were so loose.

By the gods, he is alive! For so long I thought him gone, but here is lying right here before me. Vivien reached out to touch his face, the flames within her cooled. She rested her fingertips on his cheek, but quickly pulled back. *He's so cold!* Anger washed over her again, stronger than ever before. *They are taking his blood, slowly draining away his life force. He is suffering...*

Vivien grabbed the tube connected to his arm and yanked. A long needle came out of his flesh, followed by a trail of blood. The tube warped in her grip and she dropped it to the floor. She put her hand over the wound, trying to staunch the flow, but afraid she would burn him. *Gods, what do I do?* She heard voices coming down the corridor, and footsteps. They were coming for her.

She shook him. When nothing happened, she shook harder. *Please, please wake up.* She shook him again.

RavnWolf suddenly lurched into awareness, his eyes the color of the fire that burned within her soul. His muscles bunched as he tried to move, and it was then she saw the shackles, each one chained to the table.

"Vivien?"

She startled at the sound of her name, recoiled from it. She hadn't heard it in so long, it sounded strange to her. She was Umesh. She was Drakkaria Jashi. She was Fyr'kaii. She blinked at RavnWolf, his hand reaching for her, his wide eyes pleading.

The voices down the corridor became louder. "Aagggghhh!" RavnWolf strained at the bonds holding him to the table and Vivien could hear the pounding of his heart over his groans. She grabbed the shackle on the wrist nearest her, again intoning the spell that lay on the tip of her tongue.

His eyes bulged as the shackle fell away in a twisted heap, and he remained silent as she quickly moved to the one around his other wrist. Unsteadily, he sat up on the table as she rushed over to his feet, and when he was free, the priests swept into the chamber.

Vivien was ready.

Dragon Vessel

Dari'sii spread her wings wide behind her as a swath of fire sprouted from Vivien's hands, almost reached the first of the five priests before it was diverted by a strong gust of wind cast by an air mage. The fire veered to the side, hitting a massive tapestry that hung on the wall. Curses whipped through the air for a moment before the winds came to an abrupt halt, and the dusty weave was enveloped in flame. Vivien took advantage of the diversion and cast another stream of fire. The ground beneath her feet began to rumble just as the flames struck the priests. Screams erupted and she ran forward towards the conflagration to keep from falling into the giant crack that suddenly appeared in the floor where she'd been standing. Debris rained down from the ceiling, pelting her head and shoulders, the work of an earth mage.

Vivien glanced frantically around through the thick billows of smoke rising from the burning tapestry, saw RavnWolf making his way towards the shelf full of glass vials. Her eyes stung and she began to cough. Sensing Vivien's distress, Dari'sii loosened from around her and dropped to the floor. Vivien crouched low alongside her and they crept along the floor, stopped only by her fits of coughing.

They existed the chamber via a door opposite from the entry they'd used on the way in. The hallway here was empty. Vivien hesitated before continuing, looking back into the smoke-filled chamber. She didn't want to leave without RavnWolf, but she knew her life, and the life of her child, depended on her escaping. She had to believe that he would find a way to get out.

Vivien turned away, once again consumed by rage. She hated what she had become, hated herself for the fear that dictated her footsteps, hated herself for being a whore to it just as she had been to Drakkon. She swept through the corridor, incinerating everything and anything in her path, living or no. A tempest rose within her, blotting out time until she no longer recognized its passage. The hot winds whipped about her, lifting her hair from around her shoulders, and blasting a hole through the walls of the temple. She strode over the rocky debris, her feet barely touching the ground as she moved, and when she stood out in the street, she set her sights to the sprawling Liath city.

Anger coiled like a deadly serpent within the depths of his gut as Ravn picked his way through the charred corridor. Heated winds from up ahead scoured over him and he could feel the intensity of the one causing them, could sense the wildness in her. He'd experienced something like it before, only, not from another person. All his experiences lay only with himself, and the control he'd learned to exercise with decades of practice and perseverance. That thing within him yearned to embrace that thing in the corridor ahead, no matter how strongly she might burn him.

Only, he wasn't easily burned.

A crash reverberated along the surrounding walls. Ravn hastened his pace as the winds ceased. He adjusted the strap of the pack he carried over his shoulders, a pack containing as many of the blood-filled vials as it could carry. He'd consumed half a dozen of them before exiting his prison chamber, giving himself the strength he needed to carry on and make it as swiftly as he'd managed after Vivien. The sight of her standing over him was burned into his mind.

Like a goddess she stood there, green eyes sparkling like emeralds, long hair lying in crimson waves down her shoulders to cover naked breasts. Her body was wrapped within the coils of a white and gold wyrm, its mouth open in a slow hiss. The very air around her seemed to shift and waver like a living thing, a manifestation of the power that surrounded her in a halo. She was beauty incarnate, the most gorgeous thing he'd ever seen in all his hundred years, and love poured out of him like an erupting geyser, enveloping him in its warmth.

But then she was moving, breaking the bonds that held him to the infernal table that would ultimately have claimed his life. Her movements were like that of a predatory animal, graceful yet lethal, and he was disconcerted to see that, indeed, all of her was nude, and that dried blood was on her face, neck, and chest. Memories of what they had done to him seared through his mind and his thoughts invariably went to her and what she must have endured at the cruel hands of the Liath priests.

And then the battle was ensued as the masters of that fell place swooped into the temple chamber to reclaim their prize. And he was beyond certain that prize was Vivien.

He barely had time to marvel as sheets of flame were cast from delicate fingertips, fingertips that could brush ever so lightly over his skin heated from passion, and when the ground beneath them was torn asunder, a large crevasse marring what had once been solid stone beneath their feet, Vivien was gone.

Ravn reached into the pouch at his side and removed another vial. He uncorked it and downed the contents, his blood mixed with whatever restorative potion the priests had devised. The effects were immediate, yet his stomach threatened to rebel and vomit the liquid at any moment. It would take several more of the vials to get regain his strength, but he had to drink slowly. After the battle that had resulted in his and Vivien's captivity, and the priests realized his ability to heal, they had kept Ravn immobilized for gods only knew how long, taking his blood and using it to develop the potion vials.

How ironic.

Another crash shook the walls as Ravn burst from the confines of the corridor and out into the open. To either side lay smoldering boulders the size of his head, the weight of their impact having made deep furrows in the stone street. Rubble from what had once been some kind of platform lay beneath the one to his right, and flames still danced over the one to his left. In front of him stood Vivien, her arms reaching up to the heavens as another flaming ball of rock plummeted towards the ground. Inked upon her back, from shoulder to shoulder, was a set of dragon's wings rendered in artful detail. Shock and confusion coursed through him, for the symbolism of such a tattoo was powerful indeed.

Ravn's eyes widened as he leapt out of the way, the ground shuddering with the impact of the third boulder right where he'd been standing a moment before. Then there was another, and another. He looked up to see the sky filling with more and more flaming spheres, all prepared to decimate the Liath city surrounding them.

Ravn took a deep breath, closed his eyes, and clenched his fists. Anger coursed through him, anger towards the priests who had tormented him and the woman whom he loved more than life itself. He let it wash over him, igniting every part of him the way Vivien's anger did her, lapping at her heart and soul in the hopes of finding some kind of justice for the wrongs that had been done.

Deep within the very essence of him, Ravn knew that this was not justice.

He took in a deep breath, unfurled his hands, and quieted the fire that burned within. He stoked the flames, easing them back down into the pit from whence they'd come, slowly easing the gate back into place. Every fiber of him wished to join Vivien, destroy every stone that made up the Liath city, and the people that resided there. But the voice of reason within him plead with him to reconsider. If they murdered all the people of Zormoth: the young, the elderly, the slaves, they would be no better than the priests who had captured them.

"Vivien." His voice was a croak emerging from a throat that had emitted only screams for so many days he couldn't remember the number. "Vivien?"

He knew she heard him only by the tensing of her posture. She did not lower her arms, nor did she turn, just continued to cast the spell that called forth balls of flaming destruction. It was only then he heard the terrified screams of the innocent, lives being taken from the world to pay for the crimes of the vile few who had visited atrocities upon the woman standing before him.

He took another vial from his pouch, drinking it even as he stepped closer to Vivien. Energy flowed through him, strengthening his resolve to end her madness even as his stomach roiled. She didn't acknowledge his presence as he stepped up to her side, and the thing he noticed first was the heat emanating from her in waves. His flesh responded in ways he couldn't fathom, and he reveled in it, goose-pimples rising over every inch of him. His nipples hardened, followed by his sex, his body responding to something more than the heat. And when he flared his nostrils and breathed deeply of her, he knew what it was.

He could smell her anger, deep and raw within her. He could smell the last vestiges of her fear, searing away with the fiery power at her behest. He could smell her sex, and desire coursed through him like the wildest of rivers, making him want to take her then and there on the ground beneath their feet. The briefest moment later that desire was quelled by another scent, one that made the monster within him raise his mighty head and snarl. It was the scent of another man, not just his sweat, but his seed.

Without thinking, Ravn reached out and clamped a hand down on Vivien's shoulder, and the world erupted around him.

Vivien spun, the anger radiating from Ravn making her act on instinct alone. She swung back her right hand, and with all the fury within her, she struck him.

He staggered back with the force of her blow, his eyes wide with shock. And then, before he could regroup, she cast her spell. Flame struck Ravn in the chest, washing around and over him, encapsulating him within a cocoon of fire. He howled in agony. Regret surged through her, followed by fear, a small voice within her protesting, *You love this man, and now you have killed him?*

She stood there, watching, as the fire died away. But instead of a withered husk of charred flesh, the whole man continued to stand there without a single mark on his naked body. His trousers had burned away, as well as the pouch he'd carried over his shoulder, pieces of shattered glass littering the ground around his feet. Eyes rose to meet hers, blazing like rubies within a face etched with betrayal. A part of her shrank away from that glare, the small part of her that was puny and weak. But the other part, the greater part, continued to stand there, unmoving, unyielding.

Her voice shook as she spoke. "Don't... don't touch me."

Ruby eyes blinked, began to shift to storm grey, and betrayal gave way to an expression of pain. Vivien turned away from the man, unwilling to look at him anymore, wanting only to return to the task that battered at her soul waiting to be completed. She was tired, and would rest only when the Liath city of Zormoth was nothing but a pile of smoldering rubble. After, she would release all the dragon wyrms from their infernal prisons.

She raised her arms skyward, the spell at the tip of her tongue...

"Vivien."

His voice was deep as the ocean, a voice that had haunted her dreams almost every night since the battle she'd thought had taken his life. It was a voice she'd longed to hear in reality every moment of every day, one she'd thought was lost to her forever. It tugged at her heart, urging her to turn back, but she resisted, continuing the incantation that longed to be spoken. "Encaris icarathhys dromanais. Sherwovin moranith volcanis..."

"Vivien, this isn't the path you want. Vengeance is not a good bedmate. Please, come home with me. Let me lead you out of this place."

She ignored him, finishing the incantation without pause. *What does he know? What could he possibly know about how it feels to be violated again and again, not just here in this place, but in Rithalion in the sanctuary of my own home? Why would he truly care? These people, they are a scourge upon the land, a pestilence. They are the vilest of any people, even more so than the humans of the Iron Coast. They deserve what they get, and what they deserve is death. I can be merciful and make it swift.*

She felt the power sweep through her, fleet and seemingly without end. The winds picked up, buffeting her hair around her face. The feel of the strands against her cheeks was something out of normal life, something mundane that she welcomed, yet she refused to let it distract her from her task. "Rains, come to me. Come to me." She reached to the heavens, a supplication to whatever gods heard her call.

A rain began to fall, not cool and wet, but fiery droplets that would consume anything in their path. The flaming rock had been awesome to behold, but liquid fire could seep into the smallest of crevasses and destroy just as effectively. She breathed deep and reveled in the power at her behest, caressing it to build it to even greater heights...

An impact from behind suddenly sent her sprawling.

Vivien lay there on the stones, the sharpest ones biting into the flesh of her distended abdomen. Anger flared within, heightening her senses to prepare her for the battle she knew was upon her. She swung her gaze to the man standing not far away, his chest rising and falling with his breaths, his curling hair laying in thick tangles down his back and around his broad shoulders. His eyes bore an expression of determination that she'd seen countless times. *No, the Wolf will not win this time.*

She rose into a crouch, gathering all her fury and might, concentrating it, focusing it. The Wolf seemed to sense it, and he leapt before she could cast. More swiftly than she'd ever seen him move before, he barreled into her, thick arms pinning hers to her sides, vice-like hands sliding around her wrists to subdue her. She lashed out with her feet, but heavily muscled thighs protected his vulnerable bits, and his toes danced out of the path of her heels. She twisted and writhed within his steely grip, and within moments sweat slicked her skin. She grinned at this newfound advantage, slipping out of his grasp time and time again, tiring him, wearing him down until finally he wouldn't be able to hold her any longer. Weariness threatened, but she somehow managed to thrust it aside, desperation fueling her. She could not let him keep her, could not let him beat her.

She needed this victory. She needed to feel strong, if even just this one time in her life.

But then he caught her. The Wolf snared her within a grip she couldn't escape, one leg wrapped around hers, his arms cushioning her as they both fell to the hard ground. Helpless she lay there in his arms, breaking the silence with a low growl that emanated deep within her throat. It surprised even her with the depth and tone of it, loud and menacing like some kind of animal, an animal she'd encountered only once before in all her life. She tried for a moment to place it, but then her senses were suddenly overwhelmed.

It started with his smell. The mild musk of his sweat consumed her mind, battering at the stranglehold of vengeance she'd tried so hard to embrace. She resisted, pressing all her weight against him, hoping... praying she could release his grip, her face pressed against the hard contours of his chest. In a gesture of futility, she put her teeth to him, biting into the skin around his nipple. He grunted and his entire body tensed, her ribs aching with the increased pressure. The salty taste of him hit her tongue and memories of intimate moments flooded her conscious, followed by the heady taste of his blood.

The Wolf groaned, not a sound of pleasure, but of pain, and he spoke. "Dear gods, Vivien, please..."

The sound of his voice heightened her other senses and her eyes swam into focus. Releasing his flesh, she looked up. The cut of his jaw was more prominent that it should be, his beard longer, the dark chestnut threads interspersed with silver. His neck shone with tiny beads of sweat, and his pulse could be seen at the most vulnerable part of his throat. His scent surrounded her, and the residual taste of his blood and sweat on her lips was intoxicating. But the feel of him... the feel of him surmounted everything else.

His arms around her, the hairs of his chest beneath her palms, his breath against her forehead, his legs entwined with hers...

A pressure deep within her pelvis she hadn't realized was there entered her consciousness. Arousal was swift and intense, shadowing all else. Images suddenly flashed through her mind, images of a dream she'd had many months ago. She was in a cave filled with luminescent moss. It lit the place so much that she could see as though the late day sun shone. The Wolf was there, in every magnificent detail, and the experience they shared suddenly didn't seem like just a dream anymore.

Her eyes widened with the shock of reality, her heart pounding a staccato rhythm against her ribs. All this time and she'd thought... she'd thought...

Why has he never spoken of this?

Again, anger surged through her. But this time it wasn't towards the murderous Liath and their fell city. It was towards the Wolf.

A strangled cry tore from between her lips as she abruptly bore everything she had against her captor. All her strength, all her desperation, all the hurt she'd endured through the years. She ripped herself free of his grip, and rising in one sinuous motion, she turned on her heel and began to run.

It was like her feet had wings, and she was grateful for the speed she possessed without knowing how she'd obtained it. She sprinted through the trees, away from the Liath city and into the unknown. Behind her she heard the Wolf. He didn't bother calling her name, knowing she wouldn't respond, and saved his energy instead on simply following in her wake until he ultimately caught her.

She knew he would. And strangely, it was no longer a matter of winning or losing. It was something different, something more primal. Something that pushed deep within the core of her femininity.

Without wanting to, she wanted him. At that moment, she wanted the Wolf like she'd never wanted any man in her life.

The angry part of her hated it. The puny part of her feared it. The rest of her simply wanted the hunger satiated.

The rational bits that remained with her shouted, *What has happened to you Vivien?*

She ran without tiring for longer than she thought she would, stumbling only when she reached the bank of a large lake that stretched further than her eyes could see into more forest. Sensing the Wolf behind her, her breath hitched in her throat in anticipation. He wanted her as much as she wanted him, and that knowledge made this waking nightmare of alien desires more bearable. Yet, the anger still burned, brighter than any ordinary fire, and she didn't wish to be caught. At least, not *easily*. She did not want to be taken, she needed to be earned.

Vivien waded into the lake, the cool waters slowly rising up, up, up her legs until finally it reached the juncture of her thighs. She gave an internal sigh as it lapped at her femininity, the water licking her like a gentle tongue, caressing her, relieving her need for such a sensation, yet building the arousal within. It washed away all the pain, all the indignity, all the self-recrimination. Her breasts rose and fell with the force of her breaths, and for a brief moment, she wondered where Dari'sii had gone.

But then the Wolf was there, and the wyrm was thrust from her mind. He hesitated for a moment, the water lapping at his feet, a myriad of emotions passing over a face he usually kept stoic during battle: sadness, a tinge of fear, and fierce determination. Coupled with those were love, devotion, and no small amount of pure, unadulterated lust. He stepped into the lake, his eyes boring into hers beneath thick brows that darkened his stare. Any other day and he would have appeared intimidating.

As he approached, Vivien stepped back deeper into the waters. She was a good swimmer, having honed her skill within the waters of the Fyresmee River beside her good friend, Mikarvan. They had played for hours, and she'd ultimately learned to out swim him. She knew the Wolf was also a good swimmer. But she felt she had a good chance, and after, she would go back to the Liath city and lay it to waste.

The Wolf watched as she slowly submerged her torso and chest deep into the lake. A part of her expected him to say something, but the greater part realized he was beyond words. He lowered himself into the water, crouching, and she knew he was coming for her...

The Wolf's head disappeared beneath water as she dove beneath the surface. Powerful strokes pulled her deeper, deeper, farther, farther, until her hands found the bottom. She held her breath, and the urge for a new breath was so much less than it ever had been before. She planted her feet within the silt substrate, and when she saw him appear from out of the darkness, her heart stuttered. Instincts from somewhere foreign rose her skin to gooseflesh as she understood he was not just pursuing her, but hunting her. *Oh gods....*

The moment he came into range, she lashed out. The pull of the water made her much slower, but her foot connected to his jaw, her second strike in close pursuit. It was caught in one of his hands, but she swiftly pulled back before he could get a good grip. She swam a circle around him, kicking up silt from the lake bottom. It made it more difficult to see, but she managed to grab onto his long hair and jerk his head back. She raked her nails along his throat, her fingertips feeling the scar that marred his flesh there, a scar given to him by the sharp edge of her husband's knife.

Before his hands could close on her, she kicked out of his reach and swam away from him, hard and fast. Within moments she crested the surface, took a deep breath, and plunged back down into the murky depths. She streaked past him on his way up, maneuvering out of his reach, twisting to the side and darting away. He was much slower than she in these waters, his bulk hindering him in ways it could not her, and she reveled in her advantage.

Vivien swam upriver, back towards the city, cresting the surface occasionally to get a breath. In truth, she thought she'd left him behind somewhere despite her body's thrum in response to his proximity. Schools of silvery fish parted to make way for her passage, just as much her physical form as the cocoon of heat that emanated from her.

But she'd underestimated him.

The Wolf came at her seemingly from out of nowhere, tackling her as she took another breath at the surface. He bore into her, taking her back beneath the water with his arms around her waist. She struggled against his weight, raking her nails over his arms and drawing blood. Yet he never relinquished his grip, taking her back towards the shore with powerful thrusts of his legs.

No! No, no, no! My advantage is here in the water. Back on land...

Vivien increased her efforts. She kicked and writhed, beat her hands along his chest and arms. He took her blows, somehow keeping his face away from her pummeling. His hair was an easy target, so she grabbed onto it, pulling hard. The Wolf took her wrist, squeezing it until she wanted to cry out, and he tore it out of his hair, trying to pin her arm behind her back. She savagely twisted, almost opened her mouth to scream when a pain blossomed in her side along her distended abdomen. The Wolf sensed something wrong, relaxing his grip, and she took advantage and kicked him hard in the gut.

The breath whooshed out of his mouth, emerging as a fleet of bubbles. Anger flashed in his eyes as he was forced to go to the surface for air, leaving her free to flee once more. But she was also out of air, her lungs screaming for sustenance. She crested the surface with such force, her hair whipped back when she raised her head, water spraying to land on the Wolf as he panted for breath. And when they both caught the air they needed, they glared at one another.

The Wolf's eyes shifted from grey to crimson and back again. Vivien slowly began to back away, the anger-filled tension rising swiftly. It was filled with lust and desire, each of them adding to it in spades. She stumbled on a rock at the bottom of the lake. The Wolf's eyes flashed...

Vivien turned to try and run, but within an instant he was upon her.

Her first instinct was to struggle, to get away. But the Wolf had another idea.

He thrust his hand into her hair, his fingers tangling in the damp tresses. She'd done the same to him, so she wasn't all that surprised. He pulled so hard her head snapped back. It hurt, and as she opened her mouth to cry out, his lips settled over hers.

Tendrils of fire swept through her, enveloping her, consuming her. She closed her eyes and for that moment, the rest of the world fell away and all she could feel was his lips against hers, his hand splayed over her swollen belly, his throbbing erection pressed against her side.

Vivien pulled away, hissing between her teeth. *No, I don't want to submit to him. I can't submit. Please, someone save me from myself!* Tears sprang past her eyelids. *Dear gods, please...* She opened her eyes. He was staring down at her, his gaze filled with the emotions he showed before, but for the first time she noticed that his eyes glowed. Not the red of anger, but *blue*.

She didn't have time to consider it as his mouth closed over hers again. Thoughts of escaping, from somehow struggling out of his grip, eluded her, and she wrapped her arms round his neck, bringing him closer. Passion surged through her in a vortex, taking all of her anger, all of her pain, all of her fear, and siphoning it into this moment, this action. She crushed her lips against his, her teeth cutting into his lower lip. He flinched but never let her go, releasing his hold on her hair and wrapping his arms around her waist. The metallic zing of his blood hitting her tongue made her inhale sharply, and it was then his teeth closed on her lip.

His bite was deliberate, her gasp muffled beneath his mouth. The Wolf breathed deeply at the taste of her blood, and he drew her lip into his mouth, sucking at it with abandon. His tongue worked over the wound he'd left and it stung, but the passion only heightened. Their lips only threatened to break apart when he bent to lift her up into is arms. The water poured off of her in rivulets as he carried her the remaining steps to the lakeshore. He then fell with her onto the silt, his arms behind her acting as a cushion.

Then his hands were everywhere, running over her arms and legs, pausing at her chest and backside. His lips made a course down her neck and chest to her breasts. He sucked hard at her nipples, making her groan. Since before she'd realized she was pregnant, they had been tender, and the pain of his ministrations sent shivers of pleasure shooting down to her groin. The sound only increased his fervor, exciting her to a level she never knew existed, and she bucked her hips up against his chest.

The foreplay had been their wild chase. Now, the Wolf made as though to put her into position, and she took the cue and rose onto her hands and knees, turning so that her backside pressed against his thigh. It came instinctively, the untamed thing within her deemed it natural. The Wolf's hands never left her body, but he hesitated for a moment before growling and pushing her back down onto the ground. "No."

Vivien flushed with shock and embarrassment, the thing within her rising up in anger. *What is this? He doesn't want me after all? I suppose I don't have to want him either...*

The Wolf moved to place his hands on her bent knees just as she lashed out, striking him full on the chest just over his scar. He fell back, but managed to grab her just in time. She landed uncomfortably on top of him in a sprawl of arms and legs. Anger scrambled about within her, clawing to be free. She raked her fingernails over his back and sides, leaving trails of raised skin that would soon bleed, and her feet grappled for purchase beneath her so that she could...

The smack-down was hard, harder than she'd ever been struck before except in battle. The blow across her shoulders stunned her for a moment, giving him time to flip her over onto her back. She made her own growl this time, low in her throat, one she'd never made before until she'd left Rithalion to go on her fool's mission. His eyes were filled with unbridled lust and determination, yet, she could see the worry that lurked there too, wary and guarded. His lips descended again, his hands clasping hers, raising them up so they rested alongside her head. His kiss was fevered, almost desperate, reigniting the passion that had been quelled when he'd rejected her. Confusion reigned for a moment. *Why did he say no when he shows me now that he wants me?* But then she was caught up again in the moment, anger shoved aside in lieu of ardor. The Wolf pulled his lips from hers and pushed her legs apart with his knee. His breathing hitched in his throat, and then became ragged as he pressed his pelvis into hers. His engorged sex lay between them over her thigh and, in a rush, she remembered how big he was.

She barely had time to take a breath before he plunged into her.

Vivien opened her mouth in a silent cry, tilting her head back to look upward. She lay there as her body adjusted to his girth, the initial pain giving way to mild discomfort. She panted beneath him, no longer resisting, trills of pleasure burrowing deep into her groin to nest there. And then he began to thrust. He was forceful, nothing like the lover she remembered from the moss-illuminated cave. The muscles rippled in his arms, across his chest, and over his sides trailing tiny rivers of blood mixed with sweat, as he bore into her over and over again. Long curling hair hung along both sides of his handsome face, and his lips were parted with the force of his breathing. Pleasure curled deep within the pit of her belly, growing, growing, growing. She clutched at the hands restraining hers, wishing she could reach up and touch him.

And then the world exploded. She thought she heard herself cry out as her vision darkened for a moment, the force of her climax making her toes curl into the silt substrate. She thrashed beneath him like some wild animal struggling to be free, her heart thundering against her ribs so loud she could hear it. Moments later, the entire forest could certainly hear his voice, and his body shuddered as he stilled over her, his eyes boring into her as though he could see into her very soul.

He hovered there for a moment, his breath coming in great gasps, sweat trickling down the sides of his face to drip onto her cheeks and lips. He didn't withdraw, and she could feel the length of him still buried deep inside. Moving slowly, not taking his eyes off of hers, he released her hands, placing his on each of her bent knees. He pushed up and her feet rose from the ground, until her knees were only a foot away from her shoulders. Then he began to move inside her again, slow at first, then faster and faster. The sensation was beyond her realm of experience, and the upward climb began anew. She could feel herself stretching, straining to accommodate him. The discomfort made her gasp, but still she climbed. Large, warm hands swept over her calves and thighs, over her hips and under her backside. He thrust deeper, deeper, and little sounds from her accompanied each one. Her hands freed, she reached out and grasped his forearms, her heightening sensation causing her fingers to tighten. Discomfort shifted to mild pain, but she rode that wave, going higher, higher, higher, her fingernails digging into his arms like claws.

Then she screamed. The force of her climax rivaled only the one that had come before. It made all her pain disappear, traveling from her groin both upward and downward to touch every part of her body all at once. The Wolf's voice echoed hers as he gave one final thrust, going deeper than she'd ever imagined any man could go. He remained there, his body pushing his seed within her recesses, only the briefest of moments before he was descending between her legs, his chest pressed against her breasts, as his lips claimed hers. He kissed her with a ferocity she'd experienced only during brief moments this day, and the coiled thing within her rose to meet him. Vivien wrapped her arms around his neck, pulling him closer. They twined their legs around one another, leaving no room to guess where one began and the other ended. They rolled about on the silt, their sweaty bodies soon covered with grime. Their lips never parted as they grappled to make themselves into a single being instead of two.

Finally, they just lay there, arms and legs tangled together, their faces so close, they breathed gusts of air that washed over their noses and lips. Under the autumn hues of a late afternoon sky, a strange contentment stole over Vivien. Drakkon wasn't there, had never even entered her mind since she'd killed him in cold blood a few hours before. Feelings of love trickled through her mind, quickly followed by hope. The Wolf lay within her arms, where he belonged, and she supposed she belonged in his as well. Feelings of affirmation swept over her as she closed her eyes, and she slept in the security of Ravn's embrace.

Like she'd always dreamed of.

Chapter Twenty-Six
Awakened Beasts

Ravn awoke to find himself surrounded by darkness tinged with the first rays of the approaching dawn. Vivien was nowhere to be seen, and scent indicted she'd left hours ago, at least two. He sprang to his feet, wincing when he felt the weakness in his body, and again when he remembered how he'd taken her the evening before. He'd let the beast within get control, and for that he'd pay the consequences.

He always did.

Ravn moved in the direction Vivien had gone, smelling her scent on the leaves of every tree, bush, or shrub she'd touched. And if he didn't have those markers, he had the ground. He moved swiftly, and before he realized it, he was entering the remains of the Liath city. Panic surged through him, thoughts of the day before suffusing his mind, and he wondered if he had the strength to counter her again. She'd been strong, more so than any mortal, and even now he couldn't understand it.

He jogged on, passing homes that had been deserted in the night, and when he passed those that had been destroyed by Vivien's firepower, smoke continued to rise into the still, morning air. Huge boulders lay strewn about, as though thrown there by the gods themselves, and if not struck by one of those, the roofs of the homes still standing bore holes from the fiery rain. Every once in a while, he'd pass the charred remains of those who had lost their lives to the attack: men, women, and children alike. Vivien's firepower had made no differentiation.

Ravn glanced around, taking in the desolation. *Why has she returned here? There is nothing left.*

He eventually found himself at the remains of the temple where they had been kept prisoner. Smoke still billowed out from the opening Vivien had created, and it was through there that he walked. Her scent was everywhere, up this stairwell and down another, across that hall, and the ones adjacent to it. Ravn spun in place, just wondering where in the world to go next.

It was then he heard her. Following the sound of her voice, he walked down the closest corridor until it opened up into a large chamber. For the most part, it had remained untouched by fire except for the smoke, which permeated the place in a thick cloud. Ravn stopped when he saw her. She was still nude despite the fact she could have easily found a robe to cover herself. It made sense, for he didn't want anything Liath-made to touch his skin either. Her hair had been pulled back and hastily braided, her face and arms still smudged with dirt and grime. A satchel hung from her shoulder, the strap crossing over her chest to rest at the opposite hip. It looked heavy, and he wondered what was inside it. Beside her was the white/gold wyrm he remembered from the day before. The creature opened its mouth and hissed, its teeth like slender daggers.

Vivien turned to look at him, her expression impassive, green eyes regarding him intently. "Why did you come?"

He frowned. "Why did you leave?"

Her expression saddened. "I came to free the others like her, but they are all gone."

Ravn looked again at the wyrm, then back to Vivien. A feeling of pride washed through him, followed by love and devotion to someone who was thoughtful of those who needed someone to stand up for them when they couldn't do it themselves. He slowly approached. The wyrm hissed again, but she did not deter him. When he stood before her, he brushed his fingertips over her face. "Of course, I came. You know I always do."

She gave him a smile that never reached her eyes.

"Maybe they went back to the place where they came from."

She nodded thoughtfully. "I hope so."

Ravn and Vivien walked back through the deserted temple, finding not a single soul but the ones who'd passed during the conflagration. Once they were outside, they then made their way through the abandoned city. Vivien was quiet as she viewed the carnage, her lips set in a grim line. She stumbled a time or two, and he could sense the fatigue weighing heavily on her. He wasn't surprised; after all the magic she'd cast the day before, as well as the chase that had ensued, it was taking its toll.

"Allow me to carry your bag. It looks heavy."

She stopped and looked up at him. Again, her expression was unreadable, but much to his surprise, she slipped it from over her shoulders and handed it over.

"What's in here?" he asked.

She hesitated. "Books."

He nodded and they continued on. He tried wrapping an arm around her back in an effort to support her, but she moved out of his reach. He could feel the familiar gulf widening between them again, stretching wider than it had ever had before, and he felt bereft. What they had shared last night hadn't been tender and romantic, but it had been filled with all the love he had within him. Hadn't she felt it too?

But there was more. Anger surged through him. *What had the Liath done to her?*

From the corner of his eye he saw Vivien flinch away. *How can she feel that? Am I really emoting that much?* The anger rose. *And why is she flinching? She knows I would never hurt her.*

The Wolf swung around, grabbing her arm. "Vivien, what did they do to you? Tell me!"

She recoiled, tugging savagely at her arm, her eyes wide with desperation to be out of his grip. Her voice shook, yet she remained calm. "Let me go Ravn. You're hurting me."

"You know I'd never hurt you! I'm not them. I've seen the ink on your back. Now tell me what else they did!"

She squeezed her eyes shut, her voice rising. "Stop! Let me go!"

He increased his grip, his voice rising to a hoarse shout. "Tell me!"

"NO! You already know what they did! Now let... me... go!" She pulled back so hard that her wrist popped. She screamed and he instantly released her, looking at his hand as though it was an alien part of him. "Never touch me again! Never!"

With a strangled sob she spun on her heel and started to run, when suddenly they both heard a masculine voice ahead. "Wolf? Vivien?"

Vivien stumbled to a halt, her chest rising and falling as she took deep breaths of air. The Lord of Swords and Truth stepped into view from an alleyway up ahead, his hands held up, palms faced outward in a show of peace. Ravn just stared for a moment, wondering if he was in a dream; he'd had so many during his imprisonment.

"We received word that you and Vivien had been captured by the Liath. We've been on the road for weeks, looking for you." Xadrian stepped forward, first glancing at Vivien's bare, distended belly, then looking back and forth from her to him. "Our scouts brought us here."

Vivien just stood there, continued breathing great gulps of air. Ravn could sense her indecision, the struggle of her mind to process what was real and what was not. There was a shout from somewhere behind Xadrian. He pitched his voice back without taking his eyes off them. "Over here! They are over here!"

First Torialvah rushed into view, followed by the Grand Magister and the rest of their retinue. Ravn watched their eyes widen in shock at the sight of them: unclothed, dirty and bruised... not to mention Vivien's very pregnant state. Surely, they looked as bad as they had been treated at the hands of the Liath. But then Ravn returned his focus to Vivien. She was staring at her husband, then at her father, then back at her husband. He could sense her disbelief before she spoke it. "No, you can't be here."

The Magister moved to step closer but Xadrian was wise enough to put out a hand to warn him back. "Jash'ari, we have come for you. We have come to bring you home." Jor'aiden's voice broke. "You are safe now."

Vivien just stood there, unblinking, her breathing coming faster. "You can't be here. I don't want you here."

Xadrian put his hands up again in a gesture of supplication. "Vivien, we..."

Torialvah strode forward, an expression of irritation on his face. "Stop this now. We have come to take you home."

Xadrian winced as the Magister's hand snaked out to take Tor by the arm, restraining him. Vivien's eyes were wide as she stared at her husband, her breaths coming fast and hard. And then it was abruptly over as she crumpled into a heap onto the ground.

"Vivien!" Ravn was at her side in a heartbeat, and Xadrian a beat later. Ravn put her head in his lap, felt for the telltale pulse in her neck before releasing the breath he'd been holding. Xadrian did the same thing, nodding his head in relief just as Torialvah and the Magister reached them. But Tor didn't stop to see to his fallen wife. He lunged for Ravn.

Tor's hand closed around his throat, icy cold and hard as steel like his namesake. The other man growled like some feral animal from the wilds, his face so close their noses touched. "Get your hands...off of...my wife." Anger made his words broken, anger so strong it made his entire body shake with the strength of it. Despite what he'd been through the past several weeks, a shock of energy swept through Ravn, and in the blink of an eye, he'd grabbed Tor's wrist and dislodged the hand from around his throat.

His voice was deep and gravelly, "I believe you should watch yourself, Lord. You don't know who you're dealing with."

"Likewise." With that, Tor swung, his fist connecting solidly with Ravn's jaw. The hit was packed with power, more than Ravn imagined would come from the lithe frame of the master blacksmith. In one fluid motion he rose, Tor with him. They stood over Vivien's unconscious form, seething with barely suppressed rage. Ravn clenched his fists, vividly aware of her at his feet, unable to get out of the way when things got uglier. Torialvah seemed not to really care, one of his booted feet dangerously close to an out-flung hand, the other stepping on locks of hair that had escaped her braid. And it was then he remembered the words of his friend, the man who had taken him into his home and made him a part of his family: *"If you strike the Lord of Ice and Steel, he will not forgive, and he will fight you, and perhaps he will lose, and she will never forgive you for murdering him. The hardest thing for a man of action to do is nothing."*

Ravn clenched his fists again, looked beyond Tor to see the Lord of Swords standing there beside the Grand Magister, his friend's expression pinched with strain. It took all his strength to step away from Vivien. He felt as though he was abandoning her, leaving her to an evil that he could not save her from. A feeling of helplessness welled within him, and for the briefest of moments he resented Xadrian's words, despite the truth he knew they carried. He could not lose Vivien that way. He refused to lose her to the man he had learned to despise above virtually all others.

Ravn took another step back, then another, until he finally felt safe enough to turn around. He stepped around the man standing behind him, so wrapped up in his thoughts, he almost missed who it was. Mikarvan stopped him with a hand on his shoulder, with just enough pressure to make him take notice without inciting residual aggression. "Wolf."

Ravn turned to Vivien's most trusted comrade. The expression in the young man's eyes was haunted, and fear for his friend lurked in their depths. But his voice was determined when he said, "I will take care of her for you."

Surprise coursed through Ravn, for he'd never experienced a show of compassion from Mika in the past. In a show of solidarity, Ravn placed a hand on the man's shoulder and nodded. "I thank you."

Mika nodded in return and moved towards Vivien as Ravn continued to walk away. Only once in his life had he felt so completely and utterly powerless, and he knew it wouldn't be the last.

Chapter Twenty-Seven
The Price of Freedom

"we don't know where the surviving Liath went. Right now, we have all of our scouts out there trying to determine where they might have gone."

Vivien glanced about the chamber, her breath hitching in her throat. These people, they felt so alien to her, including the ones sitting to her right and left: her father and her husband. The man speaking was the head councilman, a man they called Blue Moon Rising. At his sides were eight others, one of whom was her brother. Somehow Fire Hunter had escaped the ill-fated battle with the Liath, as had Evey, Gregor, and Katriona.

They were the *only* survivors.

A councilwoman they called Mystic River spoke next. "I am sure many of them are heading to tribes that house family members. So, they may not all be going to the same places."

Blue Moon Rising nodded. "Granted. That's why we sent scouts in all four directions. We will see what they have to say when they return to us."

"Well, the next important question is what happened to the city of Zormoth. It looked like all the stars of heaven fell upon it; you can see the remnants of burned rock all over the place," said Black Fox.

"Yes, and a massive conflagration," added Silver Heron. Many of the dead had been burned to a crisp."

Vivien's heart pounded against her ribs. She didn't want to tell them she had been the one to destroy the city, but she didn't see as she had a choice. Ravn had seen what she had done, as well several Liath survivors. If Isbandarian scouts decided to take any into custody, they would certainly tell the tale. It would be best if she told them herself as opposed to finding out later from someone else and punishing her for hiding important information about the enemy.

"What natural phenomena could possibly cause something like that?" asked Black Fox.

"Not anything I have ever heard of," said Fire Hunter. "I'm betting that it wasn't natural."

Hushed whispers filled the chamber and Vivien squirmed in her seat. She looked around the room, glancing from face to face, yet none of them even looked her way. None except the Wolf. He regarded her intently, his eyes never leaving her face.

Vivien startled at the sound of her father's voice beside her. "It took an astounding amount of power to cast spells of that magnitude. It would have taken a dragon mage that had both a fire and an earth dragon bound to him, and years' worth of study under his belt." She blinked at this proclamation. Her father was generally right about all things magic, but in this he was wrong. She'd had no wyrms bound to her at all, and she'd managed to cast the spells with only a few hours' worth of clandestine memorization.

"Indeed," said Blue Moon Rising. "They had a powerful priest at their disposal. However, it couldn't have been Drath Drakkon. He was found in his chamber in the temple with his heart ripped from his chest."

More whispering fluttered around the chamber and the Wolf's eyes had become piercing.

Blue Moon Rising continued. "Even more intriguing is that his heart was nowhere to be found."

Black Fox frowned. "What do you mean? It wasn't with the body?"

Silver Heron shook her head. "No, and they searched the chamber for it. It appeared as though someone had burned a hole into his chest to remove it, for the edges of the wound were seared black." She stared at the ceiling, wishing the mental images away. "There was a significant amount of blood that had dripped onto the bed and gobbets of heart left behind, though what that suggests I simply don't know."

Blue Moon Rising curled his upper lip. "The savages may have eaten it."

The Wolf continued to stare at her, his gaze boring into her soul.

He knew.

He knew she'd been the one to eat the dread priest's heart. The whispering had risen to a low murmuring and she'd broken out into a cold sweat. The child within gave her a kick and she tore her eyes away from his gaze.

Blue Moon Rising sounded the gavel. "Quiet now. Quiet everyone. This is not a social gathering." The room slid once more into silence and the man continued. "So, with Drath Drakkon indisposed, we are left wondering who could have cast that caliber of spells, killing so many in so short a time. It seemed to start inside the temple and then progressed outside to the rest of the city."

The Grand Magister spoke again. "Well, we have two among us who might be able to cast some light onto this mystery." He turned to Vivien, his mouth turned up into a gentle smile. "My dear, do you feel well enough to speak to the Council about your escape and what you saw?"

Even though she knew she would be expected to speak at some point, she didn't think it would be so soon. She hadn't spoken to anyone about her escape, not even Ravn, and the thought made her feel queasy. She looked past the lump of her belly down to her lap, where her hands lay. She hid their shaking by pulling her robe more closely around her. *Where is all my courage now, all that bravery I had mustered in the Liath temple? Is it lying somewhere in the streets of Zormoth, dead with all the people I murdered in cold blood?*

Finally she looked back up at her father, took in his cool calm, the kindness in his eyes, the laugh lines around his mouth and at the corners of his eyes. Oh, how disappointed he would be when he knew what she'd done. She didn't want to tell him, but she'd gotten a request from the leader of her people and she could not refuse. She gave a small nod. "I..."

A heavy hand came down on her shoulder on the side Tor sat. "Come now Vivien, tell us how you escaped the Liath. You've barely uttered a word since we found you." To all outward appearances, the tone of his voice was lighthearted. Yet, she heard the underlying note of irritation, as well as the command to speak now while she was being asked nicely by these important people.

The Grand Magister cast Torialvah a quick look of disapproval as he put an arm over her shoulders, brushing aside the heavier hand of her husband. "You don't have to speak if you are not yet ready. We still have a bit of time to spare for you."

Vivien heard the sincerity in his voice, wished she could take him up on his offer, but she needed to get this over and done with. She opened her mouth to speak, intending to start with Drakkon. She knew she should, knew that she needed to, but the words simply wouldn't come. The image of his face in her mind, the feel of his hands over her naked flesh, the pain... She closed her mouth, opened it again, closed it. She felt like he must have felt when he died, gasping for breath while he bled out of the hole in the center of his chest.

She ended up skipping him entirely, went instead to her grand finale. Her voice sounded small in the vaulted council chamber, much too small for a decorated warmage. Yet, it could be heard in every corner of the room. "I was the one who destroyed the Liath city."

Her breathing sounded loud in the silent chamber and the Grand Magister's arm slowly tightened about her shoulders. She waited, waited, waited, for someone, anyone, to say something. Her father turned towards her, his eyes haunted. "Vivien, we know that is not true. You couldn't possibly have done such a thing." He rose from his chair and turned back to the Council. "I'm sorry, it appears my daughter is unwell. Please excu–"

Vivien pitched her voice over his deeper one. "No! I did it. The Wolf can attest to it."

Everyone's eyes swung towards Ravn, and when Vivien looked at him this time, his gaze was one of utmost solemnity. He closed his eyes, almost as though he was burdened to speak the words that needed to be said. Finally, he nodded, his voice low when he spoke, "Vivien is telling you no falsehood. She burned the city."

The council chamber erupted into a cacophony of sound as people began to talk all at once. The Wolf opened his eyes and Vivien was awash in his pained gaze. Around the room people looked at her with expressions of anger, fear, and even hate. Her brother stood there, his expression one of intense worry, and she couldn't help being struck by it. The gavel sounded once, twice, then three times before the noise began to subside. Blue Moon Rising's voice shouted above all, a loud booming voice that squelched any remaining conversation or protests. "Quiet! Silence now or you will be thrown out of this chamber and never be allowed to return!"

Instantly the chatter stopped, no one daring to test the head councilman. His somber gaze took in the room to finally rest on Vivien, his blue eyes almost as piercing as the Wolf's could be. "Lady Vivien Valdera, you have made a strong statement here today. Do you understand the ramifications of that statement?"

She swallowed past the lump in her throat as she nodded. "Yes, Lord. I do."

"You are stating to the Council that you have learned the use of dragon magic. You know that means you have renounced your fae magic and your good standing with your people. You then used your newfound unlawful magic to destroy an entire city without regard to innocent lives."

Vivien just stared at the councilman. He only had part of her story: she hadn't intended to give up her fae magic, hadn't intended to renounce her people, hadn't intended to get captured or to learn dragon magic. Those things had simply just happened. Indeed, she had intended to reduce Zormoth to ashes, but the anger she'd felt, the humiliation– she hadn't been all there in mind or spirit. It was tragic, what she had done, and she knew she needed to pay the consequence. Tears threatened to gather at the corners of her eyes; she knew what that consequence was.

Dear gods, I don't want to die.

"Pardon my saying so, but the Liath are hardly innocent. And my sister had been ravaged by them for six weeks before she wreaked her havoc. Upon her behalf, I ask you to think of her mental state at the time, and for your mercy."

Vivien blinked as she turned to look at her brother. Never in all her years had he ever spoken for her, never had he shown her even an iota of kindness. But here he was, standing before his own people, his council brothers, asking for leniency. The threatening tears gathered and fell, her heart aching. For the first time, she felt accepted by another member of her family besides her father, and despite the extenuating circumstances that brought it about, it felt sweeter than any wine she'd ever tasted.

Blue Moon Rising regarded him somberly. "Fire Hunter, are you certain you wish to do this? You know it will place your status at risk, especially since it has been determined that this woman is a dragon mage. She has broken one of the most important laws of our people. Please think again before you make this request."

Anlon barely hesitated. "I have thought all I need to about it, and I wish to proceed with my request. My sister may have broken the law, but she does not deserve the penalty for causing the deaths of elvin lives she never took, nor Liath lives she did. She was under extreme duress at the time of this transgression and deserves leniency."

Blue Moon Rising nodded. "Fine. It will be marked that you stand in her favor, and the rest of us will be given the customary period of five days to ponder this. We will then cast our votes for or against your request."

Anlon gave a nod. "Thank you."

Vivien half expected the room to burst into some kind of sound, but there was none except for the deep sigh given by her father.

"While we deliberate, the lady will be bound and taken to the prison. This council session is..."

The Grand Magister stood and put up a staying hand. "No, my daughter shall not be placed into one of your dark, iron bound pits. She is pregnant and has been put through enough already. I will not have my grandchild placed at risk for the sake of brutish punishment. There must be another place."

Murmurs of agreement coursed through the chamber, causing Blue Moon Rising's initial frown of disapproval to shift into one of consideration. Children were a boon to all, and to place one at risk was a grave crime considering so many were lost during gestation. The fact that Vivien's child was still growing strong was an excellent sign, one only a fool would want to compromise.

"How about the old College of Magic?" asked Mystic River. "It's been abandoned for decades now, and she will be out of the way. It will keep her off of the ground and out of the elements, keep her safe while we determine what should be done with her."

Nods of approval were seen all around the room and the gavel was sounded. "It is agreed that Lady Valdera be kept in the old college for the duration of our deliberation. She shall not leave the premises under any circumstances but for one of life or death. This council session is adjourned."

Chapter Twenty-Eight
Closing Doors

They walked her through the dilapidated building. The corridors held an almost creepy feel, lined with floor braziers that had only recently been given the flames needed to see where they were going. The guards gave her surreptitious glances as they walked, almost as though they expected her to turn into a dragon at any moment and fly away, wreaking havoc in her wake. She supposed she couldn't blame them; dragon mages were wont to do such things. It had been told by the fae mages for several centuries, and not easy to discount.

They didn't walk far. Within moments she was inside a room that had been hastily prepared for habitation. Sherika turned up her nose at the place, her whiskers twitching. The feline had barely left Vivien's side since she and the Wolf had been recovered by the scouting party, and Vivien was comforted by that fact. That Sherika had obeyed her during the battle was profound, even more so that the tir-reath had led Evey, Anlon, Gregor, and Katriona to safety. Vivien owed her friend everything for that, and she wished she could express her gratitude with more than mere words and simple edible gifts.

The guards gave her one last look before closing the door behind them, leaving her alone to look around the windowless room. There were wall sconces, only half of which had fires for light, a bed that had been prepared with fresh linens, musty rugs over the floors, an empty desk, and a chest within which she could place whatever belongings remained to her. Her sword, refurbished by the Wolf, was gone, as well as all her clothing. All she had was what was on her back: an oversized tunic, a pair of mismatched trousers, and some boots that had obviously been borrowed from someone whose feet were a bit bigger than hers. Vivien sat on the bed as Sherika completed her investigation, and when the feline was finished, lay down on the floor with her glossy black side pressed against Vivien's right leg.

Her lower lip began to tremble then, followed by her chin. Vivien thrust her fingers into the thick fur around Sherika's neck and curled them into a fist. Sherika just gave a loud purr. It couldn't bathe most comfortable sensation, but her friend didn't care. All that mattered was that Vivien was there at her side once more. Vivien tightened her grip and the purring increased, offering a vibrating backdrop against which the tears began to fall.

How did I end up here in this place? Of course, she knew. She had somehow learned the use of dragon magic and used it against innocents. *But how did that happen? What evil did I do to warrant such a misfortune? But was it really so unfortunate? Had it not freed both myself and the Wolf from the clutches of the Liath?*

The image of Drath Drakkon emerged in her mind, resplendent in all his crimson glory. His dark hair fell down to the center of his back and over one shoulder. Sharp blue eyes regarded her with barely suppressed lust, his lips pulled up into a cruel smile. It suddenly became difficult to breathe, and the purring stopped. Sherika stood from her place, a low growl coming from deep in her throat as she stared at the doorway.

Vivien gasped as Torialvah opened the door. Icy blue eyes bore into her as he closed it behind him and swept into the chamber. Her husband regarded her with mild disdain where she sat, her hand still resting on Sherika's shoulders, and she pressed her lips together in the hopes of keeping her emotion at bay.

At first, he was quiet, just staring at her for a moment. His expression shifted from mere disapproval to open disgust, and his gaze became colder than she'd ever seen it before. "Didn't I tell you so?"

She swallowed past the painful lump in her throat and just stared at him.

"Didn't I tell you not to go? That you weren't needed for this mission?"

Vivien started to shake her head, slowly, and then with more deliberation. "I...I needed to..."

"No, you didn't."

His tone brooked no argument and she shut her mouth. Tor walked further into the room, his pace one of calm deliberation. She wanted to tell him that it was important work, that she'd been necessary to the mission to gather support from the other Elvish cities, but she already knew he didn't believe that.

"And now here you are," Tor continued, stopping to look all around, his tone uncharacteristically nonchalant, "locked up in an old musty college. None of this would have happened if you'd simply obeyed me. Instead, you lied to me about your pregnancy and went traipsing off to satisfy some whimsy for childish adventure."

Vivien swallowed heavily. It was interesting that he brought that up now, for she hadn't used the word 'adventure' in so many years. It was something she'd said to him a couple times when they were first married, a desire to see the world and find adventure. She'd only been sharing a handful of dreams, things she'd used to share with Mika... and Ravn. She'd wanted to connect with her new husband, find something they could occasionally talk about that didn't involve business or politics. It had been a dismal failure.

"I... I didn't lie."

He cocked his head. "Come now Vivien. Can you honestly say you didn't know you were pregnant when you left Rithalion?"

She regarded him intently, taking in his demeanor. She didn't sense any of the rancor or anger she'd expected him to display. Instead...

"The Master Healer, Mikarvan, told us you knew about it. You chose not to say anything of it to me. That is lying by omission, and you know it."

Vivien averted her gaze, not wanting Tor to see the flash of anger she felt. How dare Mika say anything? Hadn't she told him to keep it to himself? She took a deep breath. Oh yes, she'd made a threat...

"But none of that matters anymore." Tor strode forward, closing the distance between them as she rose unsteadily to her feet. Sherika moved to position herself between them and Vivien had to give a mental *hush* to keep the tir-reath from giving an auditory growl. He gave the animal the briefest of glances, shaking his head with a grimace of derision before finally stopping a mere foot away. "Because of your poor decisions, you are no longer allowed to practice magic. You are no longer a war hero, and you have given up your place in society. You no longer have rights to our child, and when he is born, I will take him from you."

Vivien felt the blood drain from her face. *No. No, he wouldn't do that. He couldn't possibly take an infant from the mother who birthed him.* But looking into Tor's face, into his icy cold eyes, she knew he would.

He curved his lips into a smile of triumph. "But don't worry. Even though you are unfit to be a mother, I have decided to keep you as my wife."

Vivien swayed backward as though she'd been slapped. Only by sheer force of will did she keep herself from falling back onto the bed behind her. A moment later it felt as though a heavy weight was settling onto her like a sack of stones.

"It doesn't matter what those filthy priests did to you," he continued. "I will keep you in spite of that, and you will continue to bear children for Rithalion. MY children. Their magic will be strong, and they will be the future of my people." He paused to regard her intently, his eyes boring into her like glacial daggers. "What did they call you? Oh, yes...vessel. That is exactly what you will be, a vessel."

She felt them then, hot tears falling down her face. She hated it, hated showing how weak she was in front of him. He hated it too, had told her more than once over the years. Somehow, she had broken free of her bondage with the Liath to walk right back into it again, this time with her own people, a people that Tor had referred to as HIS people. Perhaps she had never really belonged with them. A feeling of helplessness engulfed her. This must be how many of those human women had felt when they came to Rithalion and discovered that all they were useful for was breeding stock, vessels that would carry the next generation of elves. She no longer had the right to demand anything more.

Vivien looked up at her husband. He just stood there, tall and imposing. He looked more relaxed than she imagined he should be, for he'd always been so angry before when she did things he didn't approve of. This time something was different. Something... something...

And then she knew what it was. He had won. Torialvah had finally won, and there was nothing more to anger about.

Tor shook his head at her display of emotion, a smirk turning up the corner of his mouth. "You are pathetic Vivien, just like I always thought you were." With that he turned abruptly and departed, closing the door with a *thud* behind him.

She sank onto the bed, staring at that door for a long time. It was strange, the finality of that sound, like it wasn't just a door closing. It was like a chapter of her life had somehow ended.

Darkness had fallen on the city as the Wolf hesitantly walked through the archway of what he assumed to be some kind of flowering plant and into the tavern, still unsure of Elvish places in general in any city, but especially this one. At first, he had felt more at ease in Isbandar. It was a riot of life, coaxed out of the living world and built of living things like the forest where he had lived for a century. Trees were tamed by some magic, and had been shaped into buildings that wrapped the occupants in warm living wood. Only the Council Hall and college were made of stone, and the city set to put him at ease for a bit.

It was a place of quiet seclusion, punctuated by soft music played by humble musicians, but this was far more of an indoor garden than a drinking establishment. As elsewhere in Isbandar, the flora had been employed to a whole other level. Great ferns divided the seating places, and thickly grown bushes held out the wind, while woven branch roofs kept out the rain. The firepit was large, and there was layered landscaping that ramped in circles from that to the outside, darkest, ring. All the tables were full, and young low elves and humans were serving the clientele discreetly from the bottles and mugs brought from a pile of boulders at one end of the tavern, piled to make a shelter of sorts with the cracks in the rocks filled in with ivy and mosses. The effect of the whole was far more obvious than a section of stone walls or wood benches set into a wild place. Here, nature was tamed into an art and wound up being far more artificial for it.

Around the darkest periphery of the room there came raised glasses and howls from shadows that were obviously the La'athai. Immediately, other patrons turned upon the dark corners with nasty looks, all of them nearer the center in the light of the fire. They then turned to see the human standing in the entrance and their looks became even more hostile. The Wolf walked past them on the ornate stone paths around the circle, uncaring of the elves and their feelings toward him.

Katriona and Gregor waved to him from one booth, and he made his way there because he knew he should. La'athai popped up from their seats as he passed each nook, but he continued onward. Seven of the La'athai were packed into the little space made to be like a camp in the wilderness. Bronze tables with pointed feet were sunk into the soil and a few drinks of all kinds were spread across them. The soldiers all stood out of respect, but he waved them to sitting almost as their rumps left their logs and spun metal chairs.

The Wolf saw the quiet ferocity of his mood take over the nook and the soldiers he did not know as well immediately found interest in their drinks. Katriona looked stricken about the eyes behind her warrior's mask, but forthright Gregor cut to the heart of it. "How fairs our Jewel?"

The Wolf winced, and he felt the familiar pressure that told him his eyes were glowing softly. Katriona gave Gregor an unfriendly squint, and may have cuffed him if they were in private. The Wolf tried to let it go, sighed, and spoke with words dripping the oil of bitter herbs, "I have not been allowed to see her. I circle the College of Magic every day, over and over, but see nothing but the guards meant to defend this brave city from the terrible wrath of a pregnant woman and her small tir-reath."

A girl stopped by and asked his pleasure, if a little distantly. He ordered a blackberry-infused, fermented honey drink. As she left, his shoulders slumped a little and he gained a startling realization of how badly he was doing without his enchantress. He tried to buoy himself to the surface of his sadness with a deep breath. He felt no better.

Katriona reached out a hand to lay on his shoulder, but it was Gregor who spoke again. "Do you really think they will execute her?"

The Wolf felt as if punched by a giant in the chest and recoiled. Katriona struck Gregor, who yelped, then rubbed at his head as if to scrub away the pain with the palm of his hand. He had enough sense, then, to pitch his voice low, "I only mean that it shouldn't happen. It won't happen. Not while the La'athai are here. We won't let it happen, Knight Protector."

Katriona looked ready to slap him again across the back of his head, but a flash from the Wolf's eyes stopped her.

"Do you mean it?" The entire nook held its breath. "Do you know what you are saying, and do you mean it?"

Gregor froze in place like a hare in the shadow of an eagle, but he nodded. The Wolf looked around to nodding heads on all sides. Katriona reached out a comforting hand and touched his, then nodded. "We know. And we will be there for you, and her."

She leaned back when the serving girl came back with a goblet for the Wolf. His eyes were still glowing, and she skittered away without further question or comment. Ravn accepted the glass and drained it, then looked again from face to face with something akin to hope. These were her soldiers, and they would stand with her against an entire city if needed. Finally, he did not feel so alone. He set the goblet and a coin from his pouch on the table and stood.

"She needs to know we are with her."

The rest all stood, Gregor fumbling slightly. "Knight Protector, there is no way to get word to her."

The Wolf reached out. Gregor flinched a bit, but Ravn placed his hand behind the man's neck and pulled him forward to touch their foreheads gently. "Never accept that a thing cannot be done. And call me An'drath, I have protected nothing worthy of a title yet."

He spun from the nook as some elves, obviously well in their cups, stood from their nook on a lower level and faced him. One spoke, "Keep your voices down; we cannot hear ourselves."

Gregor rankled, but it was Katriona who snapped. "Go back to your wine. Your sneers and iciness speak plainly how you feel about your cousins from Rithalion. Your lack of hospitality in this city is what deafens you to nobler blood."

The elf shot back, "This mongrel thing disturbs me. This, and his dragon woman."

The curmudgeon abruptly recoiled, for the Wolf's eyes suddenly glowed like bloody suns. They lit half the barroom with his rage. The music stuttered to an end, and all gaped at the barbarian who turned to cast a glance at Katriona. "She must know she is not alone."

Then he left, at first at a walk, but exited the tavern at a loping run none dared impede. All the while, plans came to his mind, only to be examined and disregarded. The streets were dark, and the smaller, half wild tir-reath indigenous of the city hissed and spat at him, but caused him no delay. He did not end his run until he came to the home where he and Xadrian were quartered. Like the bar, it was open and airy, though far more enclosed from the elements, with the feel of being more art than nature. He rocketed through the gardens and slowed as he came through the door. The owners of the home, local nobles that treated him as a dangerous animal, were mercifully absent. He raced around the central pool to his door and opened it. There, amidst the carved wooden beds and furniture, Xadrian read quietly dressed in a robe.

He came alert in a moment, shifting to be near where Arisil hung in its sheath on his bedpost. "Trouble?"

"None you have no knowledge of before now," The Wolf tossed back. He threw open his trunk and rummaged through the few possessions. Inside there were no books, no trinkets, no keepsakes. He had lived over a century without any but the barest things, and he had not changed to be so Elvish in the last year. Yet, there were his knife, his armor, his Elvish clothes like the ones he wore now, as well as the shirt and tartan Vivien had procured for him in Elyrion– all recovered by a rescue team that had found the site where they had been ambushed by the Liath. The men had brought back what they could, and some of those things had been a few of his belongings. In the corner was a small leather bag of gold he had barely opened. Some of it was from the Rithalion Council, and some from Xadrian, but he'd had no cause to spend it. Normally the things he wanted could never be bought. Now, he pounced upon it. He took up his knife and carefully cut a strip from his green and black plaid tartan, thinking of the tir-reath, Sherika, the entire time. It was these two items he held as he went to leave the room.

Xadrian shut the book, pages slapping, and he frowned. "Whatever are you doing?"

The Wolf paused for only the briefest moment. "She must know she is not alone."

And he ran off into the night.

Captain Ashar looked on as Lorimath Agul looked out over the encampment. It had grown twofold over the past few days as survivors from Zormoth trickled in. Men, women, and children of all ages had joined the N'gali Tribe, and Lorimath was obviously not much bothered by this fact. The more people he had beneath his banner, the higher the warlord's status rose.

Not much more than three weeks ago, Lorimath had received word that Drath Drakkon had a Vessel within his grasp, the first in over two centuries. Somehow the half breed elf had survived the beginning stages of pregnancy, a first for any Vessel, and was swollen with child. Many doubted Drakkon's claim, but when word came that his priests supported his assertion, the man's status rose exponentially. Within days, the tribes were on the move towards the city of Zormoth, and all of them would be gathered in one place for the first time in history since the Dragon War.

Then, several days ago, the priests rose into a tizzy. Led by High Priest Dagnyar, they went to Lorimath and told him that they sensed a great shift. It told that someone was using a great amount of dragon energy, someone powerful. Three days later they found the first refugees from Zormoth. They told the story of a Vessel who wielded the power of dragon magic, and that she had destroyed the city with rains of fire.

Travel towards the city instantly ceased and Ashar headed the reconnaissance party of fifty sent ahead. The fae elvin scouts they encountered were overwhelmed and brought back to the main encampment. Over half of them Lorimath killed, and the others he kept as prisoners. Lorimath's methods were the most brutal of any man Ashar had ever met, except perhaps for the, now famed, Drath Drakkon. He wondered if the fact that they were blood brothers had any bearing on that fact.

"Warlord!" A warrior came rushing up to them. "Warlord, the M'dagi Tribe is approaching."

Lorimath nodded and turned to Ashar. "Captain, sound the horn. Bartolo, gather the high priests so that we may greet our brethren from the west."

The runner gave a brief bow and dashed off to do Lorimath's bidding. The warlord grinned as Ashar placed the dragon's horn to his lips. The deep sound of it reached from one end of the encampment to the other, alerting the people to the arrival of a potential threat. The warriors would be on alert as they treated with the other tribe, and with their increased forces, they would certainly best them in any fight. But Lorimath seemed unconcerned, his step light as they made their way through the sea of tents to the perimeter where the M'dagi were expected to appear.

"This will be a good day, my son."

Ashar turned to the warlord. In truth he had never been entirely certain of his parentage. Whether Lorimath was truly his father, or an uncle, or a more distant cousin, it didn't matter. He was second to the leader of the N'gali, and one day would inherit responsibility for his people. "Why is that Warlord?"

Lorimath gave him a smug grin. "Because this day I will make history."

Ashar waited patiently for him to continue. Lorimath had always been one for dramatic pauses.

"The M'dagi are going to be the first to join us in our cause."

"And what cause is that?"

"Why, to reclaim the Vessel, that's what. Together we can take her from the fae elves."

"How do you know they have her?"

"I learned it from one of the survivors today. He'd taken the risk of hanging around Zormoth after the attack and saw them take Umesh with them back to their weakling city of Isbandar."

Ashar nodded. Lorimath was a powerful warlord, and had a lot of clout with the leaders of the other tribes. He just might be able to do as he claimed, especially if it was under the banner of retaking the Vessel.

"Once we have the M'dagi with us, the other tribes will follow suit. I will be the one to accomplish what my brash brother could not."

"Why do you use that word, Warlord?"

Lorimath narrowed his eyes for a moment. "I have heard the stories the survivors tell, that he took the Vessel for himself. Knowing him, I can imagine what he did to her."

Ashar nodded again and watched as the warlord's eyes brightened again.

"Time is of the essence. We must act swiftly so that she does not give birth before we have a chance to get her back. We will destroy the people of Isbandar, and once we have the Vessel, we will use her to keep the other tribes in league with us. I can see a reunification on the horizon!"

Ashar nodded yet again, thoughtful. The warlord's goals were lofty. It would be a difficult path, but they were also attainable. He just couldn't help thinking, *At what cost?*

Chapter Twenty-Nine
Ring of Truth

despair. it's like a dark mouth that sucks one in, deeper and deeper, until all semblance of feeling is gone. It's a dark place, darker than any other, devoid of hope. The passage of time becomes muddled, and after a while, it doesn't matter, and the absence of light gives the shadows power until all that is left is...

Nothing.

Vivien barely looked up when the door opened to admit one of the guards. Why they wouldn't just leave her alone was a mystery. They brought her plates of food that they would leave on the table nearest the door. She didn't care for any of it, no matter how tempting the smell might be. Who wanted to eat when one's own people wished to imprison her? The very people she'd been told would be there to protect her just as she'd been trained to protect them? Who wanted to eat when one's husband wished to take away the only thing that mattered anymore?

She rubbed her hand over her distended belly and she was awarded with a *thump, thump.* Her breathing became raspy as familiar tears again sprang to her eyes. She was losing him... losing him...

Movement at the door brought her attention back to the guard who continued to stand there. His face showed more concern than the others, almost like he actually cared about her. He set the fresh plate down and picked up the old one from earlier that morning, untouched like all the others since she'd come to the old college. He looked like he was about to say something, but finally turned away, his eyes downcast, his head shaking. He opened the door wide to admit Sherika before quitting the room and closing it gently behind him.

Vivien gave a ghost of a smile. Sherika, her best friend, her staunchest ally. Everyone else had abandoned her: the Wolf, her father, her mentor, her cousin. Everyone except Sherika. The tall feline stood on her hind legs and sniffed the plate of food on the table, giving a yowl of entreaty as she glanced back at Vivien. She ignored the plea, instead patting the blankets beside her on the bed. Sherika instantly came, hopped up beside her, and curled against her side like she did every day. Vivien gave a deep sigh, luxuriating in the warmth, for she had become much colder as the days passed.

How many days has it been? It was only supposed to be five, but it felt like an eternity.

She stroked her friend's black fur, curving her fingers into the thick mass of it around her neck. Sherika began to rumble, a deep purr from the very depths of her chest. It was the sound that always told Vivien that Sherika was content... happy. Her fingers felt something unfamiliar nestled within the fur and they probed about until they wrapped around a cord.

Vivien sat up in the bed, bringing the cord from Sherika's mane. It was a deep green, easily hidden within the fur. She traced it to a knot that she was able to pick apart with her fingernails, and once it was loose, she slipped the cord away from the cat's neck. She was surprised when she felt something fall onto the bed beside her. She patted around for it until her hand wrapped around something warm and metallic. She opened her palm, and there, lying in the center, was a ring.

She gasped. It was beautiful. Intricately carved white gold twisted about in knots, defined by tiny crystalline gems, circling around to the centerpiece– an exquisite red ruby. She twisted it about this way and that, watching the red gem catch the light coming from the wall torches, making it gleam like fire. Even more stunning was that it was fashioned in the shape of a heart.

"Fyr'kaii."

She whispered the word without realizing it at first, the name the people of Zormoth had given her when Drakkon presented her to them as their Umesh.

The word made her heart beat a staccato rhythm. *Fyr'kaii. Fyr'kaii.* Strangely, it didn't bother her like it did then, and it seemed, somehow, fitting. With this ring, even more so, with its fiery red heart. Without thinking she slipped it onto her finger, the second to the last one. It fit perfectly, like it was fashioned just for her. She looked up from the ring and at Sherika, the cat staring at her through knowing golden eyes.

"Where did you get this my friend?"

Sherika just blinked, and for a moment it looked like her friend was smiling. Vivien picked up the cord again and realized it wasn't really a cord at all, but a strip of cloth. Slowly she unfurled the tightly wound fabric, until finally she saw a familiar pattern.

It was a deep green plaid, the same as Ravn's family tartan.

Vivien settled back down beside Sherika, clutching the strip of cloth. Then she just lay there, looking at the ring. The Wolf hadn't forsaken her, after all.

Mikarvan looked up from his book at the sound of the door swinging open. He narrowed his eyes at the Isbandarian guard standing before him, and was about to educate him on proper entry etiquette when the man spoke.

"I am here on behalf of Lady Valdera."

Mikarvan closed the book and stood. He hated that his friend was being kept imprisoned in the college without access to the outside world, and lamented not having the political or social clout to offer aid. A surge of barely suppressed anger swept through him, and the guard, taking in the abrupt shift in demeanor, swallowed nervously.

Mika's tone was stoic. "You have my attention."

The guard rallied his words. "She hasn't eaten since the day she was taken there, and on top of how she was treated with the Liath, she is thin and losing strength. You are the first person I have come to about this, even above the master healers of my own people, because I have heard you know her better than most. My hope is that you can help her."

Mikarvan stared at the guard, mentally praising him for this decision. "Tell me more."

"She is pale, and her eyes lackluster. She lays in bed all day, getting up only to use the pot. Today I saw nothing inside it. I fear for her and the unborn child she carries."

Mikarvan walked over to his travel sack and began to pull out some of the things he thought he'd need. "Go on."

"I believe that she has lost the will to live."

Mika sharply turned towards the guard, who looked like he might give in to the desire to cower beneath his sizzling glare. He then turned back to gathering his supplies, and within moments, was ready. "Take me to the Grand Magister."

With a look of relief, the guard gave a half bow. "This way Master."

Mikarvan followed the guard through the house within which he had been given shelter since arriving in Isbandar, and out the front door. Waiting there was a large gray tir-reath with soot black points. "Manas can carry us both for a distance." The guard mounted the tir-reath and held out a hand. "Please mount behind me." He took in Mika's hesitation and continued, "This way we will get there faster."

Mikarvan raised his hood, took the proffered hand, and mounted behind the guard, barely managing to grab the man around the waist before the tir-reath took off at a run.

Isbandar was a beautiful city, comprised of the living trees within which it was housed. The trees made up every aspect, from the grandest of buildings, all the way to the paths upon which people walked to get from place to place. It didn't just remain on the ground, but continued upward into the sprawling canopy, sustaining more people than Rithalion could even dream of. Mika took in the grandeur of the place as they ran, the natural beauty that surrounded every aspect of this place. He felt it would be a beautiful place to live...

If only the people there weren't so terribly harsh.

It wasn't long before they reached another home, one much the same as the one from which they had come. This was Fire Hunter's home, the Grand Magister's son, and Vivien's half-brother. He swiftly dismounted the tir-reath, stopping to take a moment to thank the beast for his service. The guard looked surprised, mayhap not accustomed to such respect, and bowed from his seat. "I hope you can help Master."

Mikarvan put a staying hand on the feline's withers. "Wait, are you not coming in with me?"

The guard shifted uncomfortably. "I don't believe it is my place. I..."

Mikarvan frowned. "You say you want me to help, but your help is needed as well. Please join me at my side. You are my only eye witness as to the condition of my friend. I don't even know your name."

The guard was thoughtful and Mikarvan could see the consequences of his actions going through his head.

"I will try my best to see that you are not punished for aiding a fellow elf in need. Please."

The guard nodded. "My name is Tanager."

Mikarvan just stood there for a moment, struck. This man had the same name as the bird that Vivien loved so much, the one whose likeness he'd fashioned out of wood so that he would carry a part of him into battle with her. He held out his hand. "It is good to meet you, Tanager."

The guard took the hand and slid down from the tir-reath's back. He turned to his companion, and holding Manas' face in his hands, whispered a command into his ear. The big cat then settled down on his haunches. "He will wait for us out here."

Mika nodded, and together the men knocked at the door. Several moments passed before a woman answered it and Mikarvan just stared at the vision before him.

Untamed crimson hair framed a small face, delicate in all its perfection, and it was accented by cerulean blue eyes that reminded him of a clear summer sky. "What can I do for you... uh... Master Healer?"

Mikarvan blinked and barely managed to rally an answer as Tanager looked at him with a confused expression. "We are here to see the Grand Magister please."

"Certainly, come in." The woman opened the door wide and the men walked in. She talked as she closed it behind them. "It's so good to see some people from Rithalion, the men and women who know my grandfather so well. He speaks so highly of all who came to the aid of Vivien. He simply can't stop. You must be Master Healer Mikarvan."

Mikarvan found himself surprised. He hadn't expected anyone to speak of him, much less the Grand Magister. "Why, yes, I am he."

She gestured cordially. "Please come this way. He is in the solar speaking with my father."

Mikarvan just watched her as she led them through the corridor of branches, leaves sprouting here and there to accent the place. She sported a simple dress, short and tight fitting as was worn by all women who lived in Isbandar. Yet, it was easy to see it was one made for a noble by the flared shoulder design. Her long hair fell in rivulets down her back, curling at the ends where they swept just past the center.

"Father, the Grand Magister has visitors." Mikarvan snapped back to attention as he realized they stood at the entry to another room. The woman stood to the side to allow them inside. "I will return with refreshments for our visitors soon."

Mika strode into the room, Tanager at his heels. Fire Hunter stood from his seat, as did the Magister. He lowered his hood and got right to the point. "I am here on behalf of Vivien."

Alarm spread across the Magister's face. "What is it? Is she in labor?"

Mikarvan shook his head. "Not that I am aware. However, it seems she has become unwell during her incarceration."

The Magister's expression shifted into an angry scowl. "It's no wonder! She being trapped inside that musty old sinkhole with no one allowed to see her but for–"

The Magister snapped his mouth shut before saying any more, his expression thunderous.

"I wish to go see the Council of Isbandar to get that lifted. I need your help as well as the word of this guard, Tanager," Mikarvan indicated to the man behind him, "who came to tell me about Vivien."

Tanager gave a half bow.

The Magister was instantly at the man's side. "Thank you so much for bringing this to our attention. You have done a noble thing."

Tanager nodded. "It is my honor to do what I believe is right. Lady Valdera is not an animal. She is a person. She is a person who has fought for her people. She deserves better."

The Magister's eyes watered with unshed tears, his shoulders slumped with the weight that rested upon them. "It has taken a simple guard, a man who does not know her as I do, to remind me of that. Thank you." He put out his hand.

Tanager took it. "You are welcome."

"Vivien. Vivien?" The sound of her name penetrated the darkness of her dreams. "Vivien, wake up." A gentle hand rubbed her shoulder.

Muffled voices conversed back and forth. "How is it that no one but one man cared to mention that she hadn't eaten for four days? Does no one in this city care about the plight of their fellow elves anymore?" said one.

"Is it not the same in Rithalion?" said another.

"I... I suppose it is."

"I, for one, don't blame her for any of this. Who would want to live locked up in such a sunless place?"

"But she should think of the child!"

"That's difficult to do when you feel there's nothing left worth living for. And gods only know what that bastard said to her when he...What's this?"

"It appears to be a ring. A very expensive one."

"The gem is exquisite!"

"Indeed, it is. I wonder where she could have gotten it?"

Vivien stirred, realizing that this conversation was not a dream, but instead, rooted very much in reality.

"She awakes!"

Upon opening her eyes, she saw Mikarvan hovering over her, his blue eyes clouded with concern. He gave a smile that didn't quite touch them, then leaned down to kiss her brow. "You sleep deeply my dear."

"H... how is it that you are here? W... where were you all these days?" Her voice rose as she came more into wakefulness. "Why did you leave me here alone?"

Mikarvan glanced behind him for a moment before putting a finger to his lips. "Shhh, hush. No one deliberately left you. We had to fight the Council of Isbandar in order to get in here to see you."

"Why did it take so long? I was so alone."

"Shhh, I know. I know. But we are here now."

"We?"

Mikarvan stood aside to reveal the people standing behind him: the Grand Magister, Fire Hunter, and Starling. Their faces pierced the gloom within her soul, sending in a ray of golden light.

Evey stepped forward, her hands behind her back. "We have something for you, something you can keep with you to bolster your spirits in this place."

Vivien struggled to sit up, and Mikarvan put his hands behind her back to help. Her body felt sore and weak. The child within gave a perfunctory kick. "What is it?"

A wide smile creased Evey's beautiful face, and as she stepped closer, she brought something out from behind her back. The polished wood glinted in the torchlight and the light in Vivien's soul grew. "My good luck tanager!"

The small bird carving was placed into her hand. "This... this is wonderful! H... how did you find it?"

"A rescue team found it at the ambush site. They saw it and recognized it as something that belonged to you. They brought it back along with whatever else they could find," said her brother.

Her gaze guiltily looked at all who stood there. "And the dead? They were brought back too?"

Fire Hunter hesitated before speaking. "What was left of them, yes."

Darkness pressed in upon her soul, quenching the newfound light and she looked down. "I couldn't protect them. I failed them." Her voice sounded monotone even though the agony in her heart was anything but.

The Magister made a small sound as Fire Hunter walked towards the bed to stand over her, his face alight with conviction. "No, I saw you. You DIED for our people!"

She stared at him, her chest squeezing tighter and tighter. "Then why am I lying here right now? If I died, why am I lying here brother?"

He sat beside her and picked up her hand with the tanager. His was much bigger, much warmer. She'd never felt her hand encased within his before, and she decided that it felt nice. "I don't know. I don't know how you survived that wound, but you did. But as far as I am concerned, you died for us, and you will always be a hero, no matter what other people say."

She took a deep breath, her throat closing with emotion. After all these years and he was fighting for her, fighting HERSELF for her. It was like something from out of one of her silly childhood dreams. She'd always wanted Anlon to love her.

The light broadened again, and the light lit up the darkest places in her soul. Her father came to stand behind Anlon and he gazed at her through eyes filled with love and devotion. She raised her other hand to reach for him, and with it came a strip of cloth with a ring dangling from it. The heart shaped ruby glinted and shone brighter than anything in the room, entering her soul and shattering what remained of the darkness that pervaded.

"Vivien, where did you get that?" Evey's voice was filled with awe.

She smiled, a secret smile, and decided to keep her knowledge to herself. "Sherika brought it to me."

Chapter Thirty
Continuing Mission

The wolf walked tamely into the Isbandarian council room. Rithalion had a chamber that was a testament to the talent and passion of the carvers of stone, but this was like a forgotten glade, a massive tree in the center rocketing toward a sky held barely at bay by gigantic panels of glass intertwined in the many branches that made up the walls. Trunks of molded trees had been made into benches and tables, and the gallery was raked on every side by level upon level of spiraling trees turned every which way by some elfin artisan in times long forgotten. The beauty was lost upon him, for he knew its purpose. Here elves sat in judgment of others of their kind, and often did so badly. The last time he had been here, the leaders of this city had spoken about putting Vivien to death. Not an hour ago, he had received praise for finally dressing like an elfin dignitary. In reality, the shirt of plate and mail, bracers, greaves, and weapons were for a whole other purpose. He mentally inventoried the dagger in his boot, the sword at his side, and the steel axe slung over one shoulder. He had come to hear the verdict, but he had no intention of letting these vain and fickle people take away the one bright light in his life.

To his side he heard a shift and glanced over. It was the Lord of Swords, dressed in full plate and mail, carrying the long blade Arisil at his side. Head shaved, scarred, and weathered, the old general was frowning as was his habit. The Wolf got the feeling Xadrian was frowning at him, however, guessing his intentions. The Lord had always been kind to him, and the Wolf wondered, when the moment came to fight, if the leader of the armies of Rithalion would fight for, or against, him. He turned back to the quickly filling chamber. It mattered not. He would never let them take Vivien's life while he yet breathed.

The Grand Magister of Rithalion entered the chamber and took up his solemn place by the molded tree table for the accused. The old elf nodded serenely to Xadrian and lowered his hood, then his eyes twitched to the Wolf and his whole demeanor shuddered. Blame, nameless but powerful, passed between them by eye contact. The Wolf took a deep breath and let go. Jor'aiden believed him a monster, and a monster he may be, but if the only thing human left in him was his love, then he would be guided by it like the only star in his personal sky. He would follow it wherever it led.

Next came Torialvah. Impeccable as always, cold and dark, he swept into the judgment hall as if it were some kind of grand soiree that was lucky to be graced with his presence. Sharp steps carried him to the table next to the Grand Magister. He looked to all the finely regaled elves in attendance, but he only seemed to focus when he glanced at Ravn. He gave a secret smile then, one that spoke clearly, *I've won and you never had any hope.*

The Wolf felt pressure behind his eyes and heard his heart in his ears.

Guards carrying iron tipped spears entered the chamber and surrounded the table where the Grand Magister and Tor stood. The Wolf had expected, like last time, for Vivien to be led back to the chamber, but she was nowhere to be seen. The Wolf tensed, and the hard hand of The Lord of Swords and Truth instantly clapped upon his bicep. The Wolf blinked at him, and realized the only reason he had not vaulted the woven wood banister and raced across the floor to her side, wherever she stood, was that hand.

The Lord spoke quietly, in excellent Lairdstongue, "You are my brother, and by what you do, so will I be judged. I stand with you, but we will stand together."

The Wolf gaped at him. The Lord had obviously learned his language at some point over the last year, but he had not imagined any elf would bother to learn his tongue for him except Vivien. Added to this was the idea that if he committed any violence here, it wasn't just he himself that would face the penalty, but Xadrian too. Hot shame burned his face. "I will not let her die, Xadrian."

The ancient general, the one man in the room who could face the Wolf in a fair fight, nodded gravely. "When my children died, she was as a daughter to me, brother. I will not let her go as easily as you would imagine."

The Wolf frowned, digesting this as a deep drum beat began to fill the room. It was gentle but insistent, full of power and solemnity. The Elders had arrived. The nine of them filed in, taking up positions around the grand oak that grew impossibly high from the center of the room. They intoned a prayer, then moved before the nine chairs of judgment to one side of the trunk facing the table where the Grand Magister stood. Without gavel or call, the chamber became silent and the nine sat reverently.

The Wolf pitched his voice low to the Lord of Swords, "Where is she?"

"Shhh," was the terse reply.

Blue Moon Rising waited for three heartbeats and stood again, walking before the rest and facing the table for the accused though she was not in evidence.

His voice was grave, but also clothed in a shred of doubt as it filled the chamber. "All in attendance will see that Lady Valdera is not here today." A murmur took flight through the crowd at this, silenced by one stern glare. "This is a practice unprecedented since the days of the Dragon Wars, but is done for much the same reason. The decision was reached that she is so absolutely dangerous she cannot be brought to appear before the court."

The Wolf shook his head to deny what he had heard. Even as a boy his father had told him the importance of seeing the person when he stood in judgment. Only by looking someone in the eye could one properly weigh the needs of law against mercy. Without that balance, awful things were sure in the offing. He looked to Xadrian in shock, but the general was stoic. Tor was unflustered, but the Grand Magister appeared to have been slapped. The elder mage's hands twitched and tiny fae flitted about his head and only winked out as he struggled to control his rampant emotions.

Dragon Vessel

Blue Moon Rising frowned at Jor'aiden but continued. "She will be informed of the court's decision once it has been pronounced."

Fire Hunter, Vivien's half-brother and one of the Elders, had the tight features that betrayed turmoil beneath the calm. He stood with power, but cool and devoid of passion, and spoke. "I must protest again as Vivien has not shown herself an enemy of the elvin people in any way–"

Blue Moon Rising spun upon him, wrath escaping him in a loud hiss. "We will not be having this conversation again! You are grotesquely out of order!" The silence after this rebuke rang. Fire Hunter sat, uncowed, and the head of the Council took several deep breaths before addressing the assembly again. "This is easily the most divisive ruling this court has ever had to bring to bear. Lady Vivien Valdera is a decorated hero, who at the same time has murdered dozens, if not hundreds, of women and children. Yet these were the Liath who she was held, and doubtlessly tortured, by."

The Wolf looked about the gallery and could smell discontent, hot and angry. The people of Isbandar were deeply divided about Vivien, and as he ticked through the favored courses of action of each faction, the resentment deepened. "This does not forgive the learning or use of dragon magic, and such carries a penalty of death. The court must acknowledge that it was not used in a hostile manner against the fae elves, but the law leaves no leniency in this instance but one.

"No death penalty has ever been levied by the court against a pregnant female carrying Elvish blood." He paused, letting that sink in to the crowd. He only began speaking again when whispers dared race among those gathered. "It is clear she cannot be freed, lest she be a danger to everyone in the city, for normalizing her tainted heresy will surely infect others. She cannot be killed, for the innocent life that grows within her. Finally, she cannot be exiled, for that same innocent life would doubtlessly be jeopardized."

The audience erupted. The force of the combined anger hit the Wolf like the smell of blood, and he felt his heart growl in response. Blue Moon Rising continued to shout at the gallery, but it became clear he was as much in control of the storm as a leaf in a tornado. Several of the council members left their seats to help calm the gallery, but the others, including Fire Hunter, approached the Grand Magister and Torialvah.

The Wolf did not hesitate, nor blink. He vaulted the living banister of wood before his section of the gallery and began marching toward the center and the table for the accused. Only after a half dozen steps did he realize that he had not been stopped and glanced back for Xadrian, who walked in lockstep only a pace behind. The old general nodded to the barbarian and squeezed his bicep. Even amid the tumult, the Wolf could hear Silver Heron's strong voice carrying, "With all other avenues blocked to us, we shall keep Lady Valdera imprisoned at the college until her child is born, and then we shall revisit the issue of exile or death."

233

Jor'aiden was flabbergasted and wiped a sheen of sweat from his forehead as he mumbled to himself. Mystic River placed a comforting hand on his arm to draw his eyes to her. "What we have is time. Time to learn from Vivien what were the circumstances of her learning dragon magic. What led to her destroying Zormoth, and how those events unfolded." Jor'aiden steadied a bit and nodded wordlessly.

Tor pursed his lips, his tone unaffected by worry or grief. "What circumstances would mitigate her eventual exile or death?"

Fire Hunter shook his head sadly. "We do not know. Vivien must confide to the court, and it must be soon. She must confide in..." he glanced from the Magister to the Wolf, "someone."

The Wolf finally saw a purpose for himself, and set his shoulders as if ready to charge a bear. "I will go."

Fire Hunter held out a hand and Xadrian stopped the Wolf by grasping his arm. Vivien's brother looked almost stricken to speak the next. "We face unrest here. We have men out searching for you who have not yet returned and have not received orders that you are safe. The Liath are on the move, and they doubtlessly will want revenge for the destruction of one of their few permanent settlements."

Xadrian shook his head once. "So, what are you saying?"

"Isbandar will not be able to aid Rithalion in your struggle, not until this is settled. The mission must continue. You must go to Sharderia and gain more support in your struggle against the Iron Coast, and you must travel now before the snows close the travel routes. Without the Knight Mage, you must all go and lend your voice to the Knight Protector." He nodded to the Wolf. "You must succeed."

The Magister and the Wolf spoke in unison, "I am staying," and then cast hostile glares at one another.

Xadrian nodded at them, ever the military man. He stepped close, out of earshot of anyone other than those he intended for his words, and looked Ravn in the eye. "I imagine Vivien will still be unable to have visitors outside of family and the master healer. Go to her Wolf. Now. Then meet me tonight where we sleep. I will marshal the La'athai."

The Wolf needed no more encouragement and he turned to go. His sharp ears picked Jor'aiden's voice out from the ruckus. "Why do you think you can get him to go to continue the envoy?"

He also heard Xadrian's answer, "I have sent him to the one person who can."

And it was at that moment his resolve hardened. He would not be anyone's pawn. He would not go to another city to entreat aid. Nothing would sway him from that decision.

She did not make trouble. She never made trouble. Considering the wards that were everywhere to shut down the college, and her docile nature, they had removed the guard from the door for all the good it did her. Vivien had fought the madness of solitude by shuffling from room to room, for her cell had no windows, no balcony, and no way to get to see the outside. At many times she had Sherika, and that helped, but the big cat often had to roam free under the sky. Vivien urged her friend out from behind stone walls and chose to suffer in her solitude. Even exploring was of little use. Apparently, her very presence was seen as some kind of magical contagion, a view she began to believe, as she left her not-a-jail-cell and walked through the abandoned college.

The Dragon Wars had been devastating for all sides. It had fractured the kingdom into barely connected city-states. All had given up dragon magic, but Isbandar had all but given up on magic as a whole. All the full-blood elves had stopped using their true names so that they could be safe from the name magic that could find them anywhere and strike them dead. Yet Isbandar had used the names without restraint and more besides. During the war, the Isbandarian fae elves had turned from the seleighe, forces of light and life, and embraced the unseleighe, destruction and harm, to fight the dragons. It was these choices that had left the few surviving mages of this city tainted in the eyes of their people. Some of the wizards had simply wandered away to live with the nightmares and memories of war alone in the wild. Others had gone to reside among the humans, who would see them and not judge them as impure. New generations were born, and if they had the talent for spellcraft, they explored it limply and alone, or not at all.

A century passed, and eventually novices had gathered around those that knew and burned to pass on their knowledge. The mages of Isbandar had returned to the old ways of master and pupil so that entire classes of mages could be corrupted ever again. This city produced only healing mages of any quality or quantity, and all others struggled in silence or left for other cities. The ways of the college were abandoned. And so this place was alone and forgotten, like her. The war had left wounds of loss and fear that went to the bone, and Vivien wondered if that many centuries gone conflict would claim her as well, or if she would simply be caged to rot away like this place.

The halls were clothed in cobwebs, carpets and tapestries turning to dust where they hung. Dirt blown in on the wings of errant breezes had fallen, and it muted sculptures, obscured signs, and built forgotten hills in the corners. The only things that remained as fresh as ever were the enchantments placed to lock doors and bar entry to anything of interest or power. As she approached, portals of all kinds alit with little, glittering fae with eyes that stared at her angrily. As she got closer, tiny burning brands, or sharp pieces of living lightning, seeping pools of darkness, or buzzing venomous figures appeared to hiss and screech at her unwelcome presence.

She continued down the hall to another stair where she passed onto a whole different floor, descending in hopes of finding a balcony and sky. She approached one where the crystal panes exposed the cold autumn outside and she hurried to reach it, her heavy belly tying her to the earth and tiring her quickly. But as she neared, brown swirls turned into tiny owl-faced men with six feathery wings. She slowed as they stared at her ominously. She came to a stop a dozen paces away and felt a deep hole in her chest where her joy once lay. Desperately, Vivien reached for the air spirits, hoping to contact them, to sway them, to feel them dance along her mind and soul like they had since she was a child.

She reached up a hand and, it was there, a faint, ever so faint, tremble in the aether to speak to the fae. The owl figures all spread their wings like an array of shields and raised taloned hands. They screeched at her without words but in a language that needed no translation. *Go Away.*

That place in her chest where she had always felt the love of the faerie was nothing more than a yawning pit that resounded hollowly. Her hand fell and she slunk back to the staircase to walk, walk, walk, until she found another exit. She approached timidly, waiting for some old friend of life or light to appear and turn her away, but nothing ever came. She threw herself at the unguarded door, and walked out onto a balcony to breathe fresh, crisp air as if she had never tasted it before.

The city was carved out of the forest itself. Everything was festive and clad in autumn regalia, yet it paled to grays in her mind under the pallid, cloudy sky. The massive trees lashed together in time long forgotten and spliced to create a roiling, labyrinth of a city. The walls, the college, and streets were the only stone in the winding, almost frantic, landscape. She caught glimpses of elves and human kin going about their lives, laughing or creating, building or selling, and she felt that emptiness inside of her again. She wished to be with them, among them. They were not of her home, but these were still her people. Or at least they had been. Now, despite her long years of sacrifice and suffering, she had been deemed–

Drakkon, huffing and puffing on top of her. An invader. Unwanted. Needing her in pain to be whole.

She staggered against the rail, and wrapped a protective hand underneath her distended belly. Waves of despair crashed over her and tears leaked from her eyes as she murmured sweet nothings to the one being in the whole of the world who did not reject her, did not judge her.

Balls of burning rock hurled from the heavens down upon the screaming faces of her victims.

With a groan she sank to her knees and gulped heaving sobs. Tor had been right, and their son, his most worthy son, would be taught to despise her in due time. No child could understand being violated by a people twisted and evil. He would understand screaming women and dead children. There would be no one there to speak for her. She would be reduced to a thing, a trophy to be looked at like a dangerous beast in a cage, a breeding mare to be used to bring new wizards into being. Every night. By the only man who would ever want to touch her and would do so coldly, harshly, without thought to how it might feel. He would mount her because it was a duty, *his* duty, and he would go about his responsibilities in Rithalion and leave her in a dungeon. He would accept the knowing looks and sad pats on the back for being so *brave,* so *noble* for the cause of elvin kind by keeping her locked up and pregnant–

And for keeping her away from her children.

She wept silently, and neither the sky nor the city, nor even the elves, cared. She searched about inside her mind for the stones to cast a curse at the one person she had...

Say it once more. Say my name.

She couldn't see through the tears, her whole body shaking. She didn't deserve him, for she had told him to go away, had tried to murder him in a fit of rage. Guilt swirled within her and blotted out every vestige of light inside of her, leaving her in a damned mire of her own worthlessness.

His voice was there again, in her mind. *Say it once more. Say my name.*

Her lips parted, her breath hitched in her chest, but she struggled to get out the words, saying them aloud in response to what seemed like a distant memory. "Ravn. Ravn, Laird of Blacach."

"My enchantress, my Elvish Jewel."

She wiped her eyes and the memory dissipated like the dream it felt it was. She looked through the thick pillars of the balcony banister like they were bars on a cage, her heart crying out in agony. It was then she thought she saw someone. She wiped her eyes again... then again. But the figure refused to be dispelled.

It was him.

She didn't know if he had seen her at the balcony from the street, been called by some friendly ghost, or her need whispered by a bird showing mercy for her tears. Whatever the reason, he had seen her, and Ravn heaved himself up, up, up the outside of the nearest building. His clothes were once clean and courtly, but had already been dirtied and torn by his uncivilized climb. Muscles, still recovering from the long torture at the hands of the Liath, had to be near their limit, yet he pushed himself harder. He was already sweating, his shirt sticking to lean muscle as he pulled himself up branch by branch or wedging hands inside cracks where mighty trees had been lashed together until they had become one. He continued to climb, glancing at her desperately, but focused upon nothing so much as getting higher, higher. Separated by a wide avenue and several stories, she could still hear him straining, hear his breath whooshing like a bellows. He did not flag, did not waver. His indomitable spirit pushed him on, his unflagging will, his...

He topped the branches of the roof and was still yet two stories below her. There he stood panting, at the edge of certain death, and reached out to her. His heavily calloused hand was an offering, a promise, a declaration that touched the hole that had been drilled into her and acted like fresh water running over bloody wounds. Her breathing had become erratic like the panic of combat. She thought about rushing down to find a balcony closer, but dared not leave his sight, dared not be turned away by more needling fae.

She wiped away at tears and smiled sadly. Again, he reached for her, seemingly impossibly far away. She tilted her head and raised a hand, hesitated. Ravn reached out again, grabbing branches behind him to lean out over the street like a madman, never able to come close to bridging the distance, but straining nevertheless.

She could feel his want, his need of her, but she recoiled. She was soiled, damaged. In all the world, this intense, crazy man needed her, but she quite simply was unworthy of his powerful love. Yet he reached for her once more, and she lifted a hand to reach back.

He nodded to her. His lips moved. *I love you.*

She nodded and said in words too weak to be heard, "I love you, too."

He acted as if punched, curling into himself and nearly collapsing from the roof. She felt a warmth envelop her, like a pair of arms embracing her. Thoughts swirled dangerously into hope, but she shook it off. When he looked up she again smiled as if remembering a dead loved one. "Go rest. You are not yet restored."

She read his lips. *Wherever I am, I am with you.*

Shame swept through her, remembering what she had been to Drakkon, and her shoulders drooped. "You shouldn't be. You deserve someone better."

There is no one better. I belong to you. I am your Wolf.

Vivien ached inside and felt more tears rising. "No, you should belong to you."

His face was blank as he backed away from the edge. A tightness she had not noticed in her chest suddenly released. Maybe he now understood. He walked away from the edge, along the roof of the house of woven trees, head bowed in defeat. This was for the best, for maybe now he would let go. He lashed out once, twice, snapping off branches growing in front of him as if they were twigs. She winced, but maybe now he could live his life with someone worthy of his kindness, his strength.

Ravn turned back when he reached the far side, and his eyes were incandescent blue. Her breath hitched as she abruptly realized what was about to happen, but she was equally powerless to stop it.

Ravn's feet thudded against the roof, racing back to the near edge. They pounded like thunder as his face became a rictus of determination set with two blue lanterns. His arms pumped, his hair flew in the breeze, he moved like an animal during the last ten steps of a hunt as he raced ever closer–

Then he leapt.

The avenue was wide, the stone far below, and she stifled a shriek as he vaulted from the building across and fell far short of her balcony. He disappeared below her and she crushed her eyes shut, waiting, expecting, the sound of the bone-shattering fall to reach her ears.

She waited, and waited.

There was a slight *thud*, and the sound of hands on the carved stone railing reached her ears. She snapped open her eyes to find him, impossibly, there standing before her. Startled, she stepped back, disbelieving. How did he make that jump? Wincing from the strain he'd endured, he held out one hand, dirty and bloody from his climb up the treacherous surface of the college. Slowly, gingerly, she took it. It was like holding a stone that had sat near a fire. He trembled, and she remembered the sprawling stables at Castle Blacach, and how the massive horses that resided there would tremble the same way under her hands. The blood on his hand tingled on her skin. Gently, slowly, he pulled her close until their bodies touched. His eyes still glowed blue like the furnaces of love itself, and she felt clean where the light bathed her. He leaned in, just a little, and Vivien felt her walls break. She flung herself against him, still shocked how much he had shrunk during their captivity.

Their captivity.

Shame swept through her and her initial desire to kiss him was quelled. Instead, she simply held him, held him in an embrace so tight, no one could tear them apart. His familiar warmth, and the feel of his arms around her, soothed her soul, and she just breathed, breathed in the scent of him: fresh sweat mixed with the perfumed scent of the bath oils he must have used earlier that day.

Ravn, I love you so much. I wish I was a better person, the kind of person you deserve. She finally pulled away, and for the briefest moment, she imagined maybe she could have been that person once, a long time ago.

Ravn cupped her face in his hands. His eyes searched hers. "Did you find my gift?"

She blinked and shook her head, suddenly remembering. She took one of his hands and pulled him away from the balcony, back into the sanctuary of the college. Then she turned back to him. "Ravn, you're not supposed to be here. I'm not allowed visitors."

She watched him swallow a retort about rules and laws before finally settling with, "I needed to see you." He stepped close again, his breath moving the tendrils of hair escaped from her braid. "You should know by now that I can't live long without you in my presence."

She looked up at him and a curl of heat settled into her belly. It was the way he spoke the words, the look in his eyes when he said them, that made a stir deep within. It must have shown on her face, because suddenly his arms were around her again and he was kissing her.

She kissed him back, any words she might have uttered lost in a single moment of raw emotion. Shame and guilt were forgotten as that curl of heat erupted into a flame, engulfing her belly and loins. She twined her fingers into his thick hair, pulling him ever closer, and the inferno that constantly burned within him chased away the cold that shrouded her heart. Tears flowed from two sets of eyes, meeting at their pressed lips to add a bitter saltiness to their passion.

She spoke onto his lips. "I found your gift. When it seemed I had been forgotten by everyone, it showed me that you were still out there, waiting for me. It is perfect and I love it."

His reply was husky. "YOU are perfect, Vivien. The gift is merely a reflection." He hesitated briefly before continuing. "I am yours."

There was a rush, a surge inside of her as his words cascaded over her soul. Her insides ached, and she felt as if she had trekked through blistering cold only to find warmth and safety in his embrace. Then she felt her heart shrink away from the comfort, afraid of it, for she feared it could never last. She shook her head, mouth failing to find sounds as she stood there before this titanic creature that wanted her, and loved her so completely. But he deserved more, so much more, than she could ever give. Sadly, she caressed his bearded face and he nuzzled into her palm. "You... you belong to you Ravn."

His expression resigned, he said nothing, but pulled her to him and held her as if nothing in the world would make him let go. She had no idea how long they stood there, but she knew it was longer than they should. If anyone caught them, there would be grave consequences for them both. She wanted to tell him to go, but words failed her again before he said, "They want me to continue the mission."

She looked up. Surprise swept through her, for she'd thought the mission was certainly over. "They... What? They do?"

He gave a solemn nod. "I told them I wouldn't do it."

More surprise. "What? Why?"

"I need to be here with you."

She pulled away. "N... no. You need to go. It's important."

He frowned. "Not as important as you."

"Ravn, please, you must go."

He pressed his lips into a thin line, displeased. "I will not place this mission above you."

"My people need you!"

"Your people," he fought to keep his calm, "have placed you in a prison. Their 'needs' are nothing to me. You are everything."

"How can you say that? I tried to kill you!"

He shrugged, mouth quirking in a lopsided smirk though his eyes betrayed some hurt. "Maybe I just have that effect on elves."

She gave a heavy sigh, nonplussed. "How can you love me so much? Even after what I did to that city, to you?"

His expression became solemn again. "Of all people, I know what it is like to battle a rage that is all consuming."

She looked up at him, into his eyes, and saw the sincerity there. Somehow, he knew. He knew and he loved her still.

"Ravn, please go." He started to protest. "For me?"

The Wolf winced, then shut his mouth, nodding sadly. She marveled at the power she held over him, that he allowed it. He was untamed, uncivilized by Elvish standards. He only pretended for her, and she loved him for both his wildness, and his ability to harness it.

Despite the coming sadness she smiled a little for him. "I am fed and I am safe, so be at ease. Go now Ravn, and serve the people I love."

He nodded. "Only for you."

She thought to counter him, she thought to argue for her people were worthy of his love, but she knew there was no point. He'd made his decision about her people, and that would take more than a few minutes to change, more time than they had without the potential of them being caught. She motioned to him to go and he walked back out onto the balcony. He looked back one last time before swinging his legs over the side and climbing down the carved facade of the college. Despite the danger of being seen, she watched him go, far more carefully, down to the street below. He turned and waved, and she could see the heartache in this lonely gesture, which she returned. Doubts of every flavor swirled through her, but the little seed of warmth he had planted within her held fast against the stormy frost. Then she remembered him writhing in a halo of flame, a conflagration she had called into being to force him away. She recoiled from the banister and all but dove back into the college, her heart beating madly and sweat springing to her brow. She shook her head, but the denial of her memory only added to the admission of what she had tried to do. She had tried to kill him.

And at that moment, she had to understand why.

She looked down the dark hallway before her, abandoned and forgotten. This was an entire college of magic dedicated to the fae, much like the place where she had grown to womanhood, deep in study. Yet this place felt alien and hostile. Her feet moved on their own, carrying her past unwelcoming eyes of immortal spirits bound to every important door. She ignored them, cradling her belly in her hands, and moving to keep her mind focused and introspective. Events had been hurled at her for over a year, and at no time could she find the time to sit and ponder how her life had changed.

A year ago, she felt bound to Tor by chains of marriage that were unbreakable, but only a few days ago she and Ravn had lay together as a man and a woman. It was something more frantic, more ferocious than she had ever experienced before, and yet that was simply where their bodies had led them. But it didn't feel like her. Drakkon's heart, the destruction of the ruined city, trying to kill Ravn, making love to Ravn... She felt like these were events that happened to a different person. She had never dared reveal how her magic had failed her over and over in the months prior. She had felt broken, lost.

Then she had discovered dragon magic. It had come to her with such ease, it was like she'd been born to it. It had come as almost a relieved surge, the fulfillment of a deep seating longing for connection and power. But she had never admitted the loss, not even to her father. She drew deeply into herself and fought for calm. She hugged herself against the chill of the stone building, and the musky, sweaty smell of the Wolf was lifted to her nostrils.

He was still out there. He still loved her. He had neither forgotten nor forsaken her.

And with those thoughts, she found a moment of tranquility. She began to walk. The passages were no more friendly, no less dark and forbidding, but she didn't feel like she belonged as a sequestered relic in this place of sadness and oppression. She lost track of the dust and forgotten memories, ceased to see the threatening fae, and looked inward. She descended stairs from the upper levels to the ground floor and its grand entry halls, and still she saw nothing. She delved within herself, deeper and deeper, wondering where the crack had appeared in her soul that had cut her off from the fae. She could not imagine the sin that had damaged her so, but she kept looking, finding that, at every corner, she smelled Ravn with his unflagging love for her. The more she sought to shake visions of him, the more they pressed into her mind and the further she walked until she snapped from her reverie and realized she had passed the cut stone blocks of the upper college. Now the walls were smooth hewn from the bones of the world itself, dug deep beneath the reach of the sun.

Darkness painted the corridor, becoming hungrier and more consuming the further from the stairs it went. Here there was no light, but somehow, she could see without strain. The hall she had wandered into felt sadder than the others, stained with a deeper hue of melancholy. It was dry and cool, but not cold. The complete lack of spider webs left her with the impression that no living thing wanted to be there. Yet, no hostile eyes burned at her from any of the scratched doors or any of the barred windows.

Barred windows?

She left the center of the hall and touched one of the bars, pulling back her fingers as the iron stung her skin and turned it red.

Elves. Elves were kept here.

She looked down through the gloom and lifted her hand. The fae did not come, and it instantly became like a muscle cramping inside her mind. Without even a thought she shifted to the syllables of the name of the golden dragonling that had whispered to her when she had freed it from Drakkon. *Dari'sii.* Instantly a tongue of flame flickered from her burnt finger, flickering with defiance at the dark and lighting the two dozen cells and the terminating door at the very end. It was a door like any other in the hall, but this one smelled of blood and fear.

She shuffled toward it slowly, unsure of her steps and feeling the weight of oppression become crushing with every moment. Yet, still she moved forward until her fingers caressed the wood and she pushed against it.

Iron fittings groaned as they shed rust and dirt. The abandoned door creaked and shuddered as it edged open. Inside, the room was dominated by tables on every side, with shelves of books cataloged behind. In the center, stained and scarred, in places gouged and burnt, was a chair of iron and oak, with heavy chains holding manacles for the wrists and ankles. She gasped and covered her mouth as the unrelenting flame from her burnt finger illuminated it all unflinchingly. The purpose of this room would be clear to any who saw it, and she could not believe its presence in an Elvish city even as her eyes drank it in.

Torture was performed here.

No one in the city would ever admit to it being here. Most would have forcibly forgotten its existence, a deep wound in the ethical temple of each elf that was involved in this dreaded secret.

She went into the room and edged behind the inquisitor's tables, circling the torture chair as far as she could get. It was as if she could feel the tears worked into the surface of the restraints, and the force of phantom cries made her tremble. She turned away from the chair, unable to bear the grief it implied. Her eyes fell upon volume after volume of ancient metal fitted and leather-bound books. Hand shaking, she took one down, set it on the table, and opened to a random page.

...the summoning of the dragon Tar'fyrion was a strenuous exercise, but being a being of fire and molten humors, such an exercise can be made easier by gathering...

She turned to another page.

...smaller dragons were a simple matter of dominance of will by the summoner, but the more powerful the Dragon, the more costly the bargain that must be struck in order to maintain a relationship. Some are satisfied with riches, others with baubles, but others require oaths of servitude, blood sacrifices, or mortal slaves...

She turned to another page.

...according to the subject, the components necessary to summon the power of a dragon is contained within its name. By application of the name of the dragon in question, its power can be accessed to produce effects similar to fae magic, but only in the most basic and barbaric – though powerful – nature...

She stumbled backwards and fell into an inquisitor's chair, dropping the book to the table. It fell open on an infinitely complex and detailed drawing of a dragon in flight. There were drops of spattered blood, brown with age, across the black ink on the vellum page.

These were the confessions of dragon mages. Dozens of volumes of everything they knew extracted by knife and needle and iron.

She felt an instant revulsion, but deep inside there was an inner voice that spoke up, and it became louder and louder. *Inside one of these is why you are a dragon mage, and maybe, why you cannot contact the fae.*

She shut the cover. She stared at the book for a moment, feeling it a fateful, malignant thing. Then she opened it to the beginning, and she started to read.

Chapter Thirty-One
Baths of Ardor

Xadrian watched, and winced, as the Wolf made his way down the line of La'athai, his face like a storm cloud and his steps impatient. His personal armor from Rithalion was lost long ago, and he had purchased a simple chain shirt to make up the lack. He stubbornly had on his kilt, a common wood axe, and simple boots. He looked like a vagabond mercenary more than a commander of elvin troops. The looks of disapproval meant less to him than a light rain. The soldiers were still excited to see their commander, though they were somewhat forlorn to leave the other commander rotting in a prison, no matter the mission's original purpose.

The fae-blood tir-reath growled and hissed at him. The soldiers that held the large mounts kept them in position, but one of the big cats swatted at the barbarian without hitting him. The huge human, muscles miraculously recovering after a few weeks of food and the constant exertion he put them to, ignored the animals' spitting and hissing at his passage. Xadrian glanced at the Grand Magister, who kept his face stony, but he, too, had to notice that the reaction of the mounts was not lost on the few citizens of Isbandar that had turned up to see them off. Torialvah had come, but from his look of disdain, he would be disappointed to ever see them return.

The Council of Isbandar had come to make formal farewell, but while their arrival had been heralded, their departure was almost sullen under a cold, gray autumn sky. No banners, no fanfare, and the half of the La'athai left behind to be with the Grand Magister and Vivien looked as torn as those who were eager to go and yet wishing to stay. He saw a gangly low elf come forward from those that were staying to salute the Wolf, then recognized him as Gregor, one of the survivors of the ambush. The Commander paused to salute back and nod, then Xadrian saw the elf's lips move unmistakably, *I will protect her*. The Wolf's face broke slightly then he pulled Gregor up in a massive hug that left the man's feet dangling from the ground. Xadrian heard the words, "You are Captain, now. You are in charge," from the Wolf and suppressed an objection. Only after several breathless seconds did the barbarian put the elf down, nod again, and continue down the line. Gregor looked stunned, as well he should. The man was not ready for command, but Xadrian kept his peace. It was done.

A woman, one of the original guards that left with Vivien and the Wolf when they first started on their mission, came next and spoke something official to the hulking man, but Xadrian saw more. She stood close to the barbarian, close enough that he could smell her, Xadrian was sure. The Wolf nodded at her and she returned to the formation to fuss with her newly acquired tir-reath. Xadrian had lived many centuries, and could see the slight spring to her step, the purpose that had entered her just by talking to the human. He took a deep breath and filed that away for later.

Finally, the Wolf made it to the front of the line and to Xadrian. The Lord of Swords glanced to his mount, Fenella, who hunkered down quietly but with her hackles raised and ears flat. Satisfied, he turned back to the Wolf. He looked past the man, to the hopeful La'athai, the mournful La'athai, to the disapproving crowds, then back to the highlander whose eyes were strained and more than a little dead.

Xadrian cleared his throat. "Brother, say something to the troops?"

For a moment, it looked like the Wolf might ignore him, but then something lit inside of him. He turned and looked to the College of Magic. Then he inhaled, and it was like watching him be reborn. His voice was so loud, it was like it rattled the whole world.

"I LOVE YOU, MY ELVISH JEWEL. I LOVE YOU WITH EVERY PART OF ME. I GO NOW BECAUSE YOU NEED ME TO, BUT I WILL COME BACK. ACROSS A THOUSAND CONTINENTS, A THOUSAND MOUNTAIN RANGES, AND A THOUSAND SEAS, I WILL COME BACK FOR YOU. MY LOVE IS ETERNAL."

Then he kneeled, letting his words reverberate in the silence that followed. Elves looked from one to the other, because the only ears that could understand his human tongue were Xadrian, the hidden lady he spoke to in the college beyond, and The Grand Magister. The wizard looked shocked to his core. Xadrian looked to the La'athai, who shifted uncomfortably.

Xadrian put a soft hand on the Wolf's shoulder. "Say it so they all understand."

The big man trembled, inhaled again, and then he howled.

It was a long, haunted, mournful sound. It was life, and loss, and hope. It washed over all assembled, but before the sound died away, the La'athai in attendance took up the call. It grew as each voice was added, creating something Xadrian had seen only once before. It struck him to his core, made the hairs stand up on his arms. He could see that the same effect on the surrounding Isbandarians, their eyes wide with the wonder of it. Finally, the howls died from the air and empty silence returned. The Wolf hung his head low and turned to take his place at the head of the procession.

Then, suddenly, his head snapped around. There, at the edge of hearing, came an answering call, echoing from the College of Magic.

Xadrian saw the Wolf's eyes sparkle with tears, then his fire started up, lit by that mournful call. The Wolf hardened inside, gathered his lost strength and walked to the white reindeer that was his mount. He leapt into the seat and howled again, axe raised. Elves mounted hastily, knowing they would have to chase him if they didn't move fast enough, and they were not wrong. They then swiftly left the city that was not sad to see them go.

None left behind had any doubt that they would see the flying chestnut hair of the Wolf again. They would see him no matter what stood in his way.

After an hour of fast riding, the Wolf finally let up on the reins of his reindeer. The poor thing was frothing, and stumbled as the Wolf dismounted.

Xadrian gave a high-pitched whistle to signal a stop to the riders close behind and it was repeated to alert the entire cloud of tir-reath riders, many of whom could not see the action, to home in on the pause and gather in strength. As they did, Xadrian brought his mount next to the Wolf. Fenella hissed and Xadrian sent a quick burst of air through his teeth, causing the big cat to stay bottle-brushed, but quiet, as the Lord of Swords approached the brooding human.

Xadrian frowned. "Will killing that deer save her?"

The Wolf turned dark red eyes on the Lord of Swords, boiling with menace and unspoken threats meant for other elves. Xadrian took the silent rebukes and stood strong against the blast. He simply gestured at the reindeer, who wheezed as it recovered from the extended run. The Wolf's rage evaporated. It was as if he shrunk three sizes as his head lowered and his shoulders slumped. His voice was barely a plaintive whisper. "What if they execute her and I am not there to stop them?"

Xadrian had no doubt what he meant by 'stop them'. He took a deep breath. "She is pregnant, Brother. We have time. If we are swift, we will be back."

When the Wolf looked up, his eyes were a pale pink, weak and hopeless, "How can you know?"

Xadrian moved forward and placed a comforting hand on his shoulder. "We will make it back here. We will. Giants, dragons, and Liath have failed to stop you and your love. We will be back."

The Wolf's face crushed into a war of forlorn hope and desperate misery. He took Xadrian in a powerful hug and shuddered with fear. Xadrian returned the embrace, unsure and overpowered by the emotions, but desperately trying to be there for his friend. He was struck by how light his clothes were, and how much raw heat came from his skin. The Wolf finally let go, cramming all his doubt into some corner of his mind with visible effort. "What now?"

"Your mount is exhausted, and the cats need rest after that sprint. We will take an hour to rest here. After, the pack and I will run ahead some more. If you keep a steady pace, you will catch us after we make camp for the night. There is a danger that you will meet Liath alone, but I do not think you care for danger while the sands run through the hourglass. Be aware and avoid conflict. This will be the fastest way to reach Sharderia, and then Moirdem beyond."

The Wolf stared at the ground as Xadrian spoke, dark thoughts obviously swirling in his head. Then he looked back to the general, and his eyes were again blood red.

"Tell me everything you know about Sharderia."

Xadrian smiled. "Oh, they will understand us very well, my brother."

Mikarvan stopped when he saw the college through the trees, massive and imposing. He imagined that it must have looked even more so before it came to such disrepair. It had taken him most of the morning to get this far, and he was glad to finally be close. He figured it would have been easier to use one of the tir-reath that the nobles used for such trips, but he saw no harm in going on foot. It wasn't like he had anything else to take his time.

He began walking again, this time with a bit more jaunt to his step. He'd only taken a few steps when someone walked onto the path in front of him, stopping to fold her arms across her chest.

Mikarvan stopped again, his eyes taking in the sight of her. Evey, the one they called Starling, just glared at him through narrowed eyes. "So where are you off to this fine morning?"

Taken aback, he just stared at her for a moment, reading the obvious displeasure in her stance. "Well, I'm going to see Vivien, see how she's doing."

Evey raked him with her gaze, up and down, before responding. "Dressed like that?"

He stared at her like she might be a bit daft. "Well yes, these are my healing robes. They declare my station in society while I'm working."

She sniffed disdainfully. "They look terrible."

He self-consciously looked down at himself, taking in the mild staining here and there, especially around the hemline where it brushed against the ground every once in a while. "Yes, well, I am in a new place. I've been dragging myself through the underbrush much of the day. I suppose I'm bound to get a little dirty."

She raised an arched brow. "You could have asked about for a faster route here. You're obviously incompetent."

Shock coursed through him. "What?"

"Just look at you. If you can't ask for directions, much less manage to keep yourself looking respectable, you are not the person who should be looking after my cousin." She paused to let that sink in before continuing. "I should come with you to be sure you are caring for her properly."

Mikarvan just stared for a moment, transfixed. This was probably one of the most ridiculous things he'd heard since becoming a master healer, and to hear it spoken out the mouth of this woman...

"I... I'm sorry. You are not permitted to come. I am the only one given permission aside from the Grand Magister."

"Why is he allowed to see her and no one else?"

"Because he is her father, of course."

"Well, I am also a blood relation, so you should take me with you. She needs me."

Mikarvan gave a deep sigh. "I am certain she needs you, but I am simply not permitted to bring you with me. I'm sorry."

She narrowed her eyes further, the blue pools sparkling with anger. "You don't seem to understand. Here, I am of higher ranking than you, and as such, you are required to do my bidding. Take me in to see Vivien, or I will have you taken into custody."

"Fine, you may come with me. But when you meet the guards at the college entry, it won't be me keeping you out."

For the briefest moment, Evey's composure slipped and he saw the vulnerable young woman beneath. His heart instantly went out to her and his only thought was to make it right. "Listen, I understand your frustration, I really do. I know you want to see your cousin. I can tell that you love her and that you want the best for her. I feel the same way. Vivien and I grew up together in Rithalion, and she was my best friend for a long time. When we were young, we would swim together in the Fyresmee River. We would run along the banks and pretend we were on the grandest adventures. I swear, her wellbeing is at the center of my heart. You can trust me to take the best care of her."

Evey's composure snapped back into place and her eyes flashed. She pressed her lips into a thin line and glared at him with distrust. "Really, how great a friend are you?" She spread her arms wide to encompass the college sitting in the distance behind her. "How great a friend to allow her to wind up in a place like this with problems like these? Who do you think you are, walking into this city all high and mighty with your master's robes and your healing magic?" she spat. "You are nothing compared to the family who loves her and cherishes her most. Nothing!"

Through wide eyes, Mikarvan watched as Evey spun on her heel and stalked away among the trees from whence she had come. He just stood there for a while after she left, feelings of guilt washing through him in tidal waves. Maybe she was right. How could he have allowed her to fall into such horrible circumstances. After her son was delivered, Vivien's life would be forfeit. Who would be there to save her then?

Chapter Thirty-Two
The Grand Inquisitor

VIVIEN PORED OVER THE volume spread out before her. It, and many others like it, she had taken from their resting place in the torture chamber and into her bedroom, where she hid them within the darkest recesses beneath furniture and musty rugs. What every child was taught about the Dragon War barely scratched the surface of what was in those books. They taught her about the history of the dragon and fae mages: their decrees against one another, their ply for societal support, and their constant battle for power. The war had become personal, for no Elvish family had been left untouched. It was brother against sister, father against son, husband against wife. It was ruthless, and it tore the Elvish people apart better than any sharp blade against flesh. It corrupted people, made them into beings of suffering and pain. And it was this way the Inquisitors were made into being, men and women from both sides who would capture and torture their prisoners into giving their deepest secrets.

Vivien shuddered at the thought, and for the hundredth time her mind was taken back into that torture chamber. How many men and women had died there, made to lay their souls bare to the ones who had once been their own people? How many people had been damaged beyond repair and cast out of society to live somewhere in the wilds without a family? How did she not know before now how sordid her people's history was, no better than the humans they liked to believe were so uncivilized and barbaric?

She felt shame as she read the texts, but refused to stop. She believed that somehow, someway, they might be her salvation. She was beginning to place her faith in the people about whom they were written, people who had died centuries ago. Maybe, they might save her.

So, she read day in and day out. She went back to the balcony upon which she'd met the Wolf, but once seeing her there, her guards closed it off and had the wards reset. There was no light other than that offered by the glowing stones in sconces along the walls, and her spirits plummeted. It had been hard enough living with the Liath, without the sunshine to light her spirit, but somehow it was worse now, as it was her own people keeping her from it. It was beyond disheartening, and the melancholy weighed on her soul, slowly crushing it.

Mikarvan would come to see her every two days to check up on her. He was assiduous about his responsibility towards her, never missing a single visit. His gaze would take her in, not that of a man attracted to a woman, but that of a healer assessing his patient. She didn't say much, just luxuriated in the presence of someone there to chase away the shadows. He always went away with a curve of dismay to his brow. Something about her made him unhappy, but she could never bring herself to ask what it might be.

Sometimes she would take a break from her reading. She would set the books aside and just lay there with her hands over her belly. She would feel the movements of the child within and sometimes speak to him. He would move even more at the sound of her voice, twisting and turning and kicking.

"You are my boy. I will never let you go."

The words were a litany, and after a while she began to believe them. It was easier than it might have been, for Tor never came back to see her. Often, she wished that Ravn was there, and she would look at the ring he had given her. The ruby heart shone with some inner radiance, almost as though it pulsed with a life of its own. Sherika still spent most of her waking moments at her side, like she never wanted Vivien out of her sight. The big cat would sit on her feet as she read, and curl up beside her as she slept. Sometimes Vivien thought of her mother, what she might say to her at a time like this, holed up inside of an abandoned magic college and expecting her first child. What advice might she get about the labor and delivery? What wonderful, kind words might she have heard? What gestures of love would she have experienced? More than ever, Vivien missed the mother she had never really known, and she ached inside.

And then one day, Dari'sii returned. The white/gold dragonet just appeared in her room one day after being gone for so long, since the destruction of the Liath city. Alarm swept through Vivien, so strong and so fast, Sherika awoke from her place on the bed.

You can't be here! It is dangerous!

The wyrm simply slithered to Vivien's side, rose up until she was face to face with her, and flicked her forked tongue. Twin tendrils of smoke rose lazily from her slit nostrils, and her eyes glimmered with mirth.

Sherika slunk off the bed, her eyes riveted on the young dragon. She made not a single sound as she approached, not even a warning growl could be heard. Her whiskers twitched as she sniffed at Dari'sii's shimmering scales, and her lips pulled back into a grimace of mild distaste.

Dari'sii just looked on, remaining still as the big cat smelled her fill. And then Sherika rose onto her hind legs until their heads were even. She slowly brought her face closer, closer, until their muzzles touched briefly. She inhaled of the twisting smoke, looked deeply into golden serpentine eyes.

Vivien felt relieved when the cat's mind relaxed. Sherika lowered back to all fours and padded back to the bed, leaping onto it with effortless grace. Fae animals like the tir-reath and dragons of all kinds would often attack one another on sight, but not now. Vivien was left wondering what might have been communicated between the two, and then realized it didn't matter as long as there was acceptance. Sherika curled back into a knot atop the covers before closing her eyes to resume her nap.

Vivien turned back to the wyrm, reached out to caress the smooth scaled face. Dari'sii rested her jaw in her hand, placing all her trust in her as before. Vivien could feel the young dragon in her mind, snatches of emotion that told a story of why she'd remained away for so long: the intimidating Wolf, Liath priests looking to recapture the freed wyrms, and fae mages who would kill her on sight.

Then why have you come here? I am surrounded by fae magic!

The dragonet shook her head. It didn't matter, for she was bound to Vivien now.

No! I set you free!

The wyrm shook her head again. It didn't matter. She loved her and wouldn't let her be alone.

But I set you FREE.

It didn't matter. She wanted to be there, at this time, in this place.

But I want you to be happy.

Happiness was what one made it. And she was happy where she was.

Dari'sii lowered herself down to the height of Vivien's belly and rested her face there. She closed her eyes and remained there for quite some time. Then she coiled herself around Vivien in a gentle embrace. She would not be going anywhere; even if she could not be seen, she would be there, waiting, ready to be called upon should Vivien need it.

But why?

A series of images passed before Vivien's eyes: the Liath, random humans, Torialvah, members of the Isbandarian Council. Vivien realized Dari'sii knew things she would never have imagined. Complex things. It meant she'd been hanging around the college for quite some time without making herself known.

The wyrm had never truly left her side. She had been watched over all this time by a cat, a dragon, and a wolf.

Mikarvan stalked own the path leading from the Isbandarian College of Magic, Vivien's prison. Anger determined his strides, tempered by nothing but the love he had for the woman contained within those shadowed walls. Thoughts swirled about in his mind, dark thoughts that involved the torment of those who had placed her there. He could see her waning, her light snuffing out without access to the outside world. Without the sun to recharge her soul, how could she go on?

He faltered when a slender form materialized from out of the trees ahead. Her beauty rivaled Vivien's, blue eyes colored like a summer sky and hair like fire. He was much more attracted to her than he should be, and with this in mind, along with their last ill-fated meeting, he schooled his expression into one of calm. "Starling."

She didn't bother with formality. "You seem upset this morning, Master Healer." Her eyes flashed and her lips pressed into a thin line.

Irritation rippled through him and he proceeded past her. "I don't see how that is any of your concern."

A hand on his arm stopped him. "None of my concern?" He stopped and turned. This time, her gaze was filled with sorrow. "Vivien is like a sister to me. Of course, it is my concern."

He removed his arm from her reach, keeping his air of calm, and began to walk again. "I am on my way to see the Grand Magister. Please excuse me."

She stepped up beside him and matched his stride. "Then I shall come with you."

He clenched his jaw, just wanting her away from him. She was a thorn in his side, a particularly long one, but unable to remove her from the path short of manhandling her, he was forced to tolerate her presence.

Fortunately, they didn't have long to go before the older elf came into view up ahead, walking down the same path. Another rush of irritation surged through him, for he'd hoped to rid himself of his nuisance before meeting the Magister.

He gave a slight bow of his head in deference to his superior, and out of the corner of his eye, he saw Starling do the same. He was slightly mollified by this gesture, for it meant she wasn't so far off the tracks as he'd feared.

Jor'aiden was the first to speak. "How is she? How does Vivien fare?"

Mikarvan gave a deep breath. "She fares well enough, given her circumstances."

Starling frowned and the Magister nodded. She was about to open her mouth to speak, but the older man beat her to it. "Given the circumstances?"

Mikarvan nodded. "I believe that her health is still not as it should be."

Starling seemed to relax a bit in light of his words, while the Magister tensed. "What are you saying Master Healer?" he asked.

"She's trapped behind stone walls every moment of every day." Mikarvan frowned. "Of course, it affects her. And whatever affects her affects the baby she carries."

Jor'aiden's tension deepened, and he became thoughtful. "Yes, I can see what you are saying. You must notify the Council and get them to grant her more leniency."

Mika gave a forced smile. "That's what I need you for."

The Magister raised a silvered brow, then resumed his pensiveness. "It is possible that they will see me only as a father who wishes to see his daughter left without restraint. They may view you more favorably."

Mikarvan nodded. "I can understand that. However, I believe you may have more clout with the Council, and you have always been a man to uphold the law and what is right for your people."

Jor'aiden pursed his lips, his thoughts focused inward as he continued to speak. "The Council is very busy today, but my worry about Vivien makes me want to go to them without haste. I am tainted by my desire to see my daughter well as soon as possible."

"What activity consumes them to the point that no one else may offer grievance?"

"Scouting parties have returned, and one of them has brought Liath prisoners. They are being brought before the Council as we speak."

Mika nodded in understanding. Surely this was a good thing, and maybe they would learn more about what the Liath's motivations were for ambushing the mission. However, he was just as certain the Council would be willing to hear he and Jor'aiden out in regards to Vivien.

"One of them is an acolyte."

Mikarvan's eyes widened. This was a great thing. An acolyte to one of the Liath priests was a rare treasure. They could discover so much more. "I hope they get answers from him. I am pleased you still chose to meet with me in spite of these events."

The Magister gave a nod. "Rumor has it there is one surviving Inquisitor in Isbandar, he will get answers. Come, let's go back to the Council Hall together and assess the attitude there. It is possible that this could play into our favor." The older man glanced at Starling, his gaze assessing. She was his grand-daughter, but also still somewhat of an interloper in the conversation. It was obvious she recognized this as she squirmed under the weight of his stare.

"Eveleen, you may accompany us, as long as you promise to remain respectful."

"Of course, Magister, you have my promise. Thank you for your consideration."

Mika grinned to himself as they both fell into step just behind their elder. The Magister's kindness wasn't lost on him, nor was it to the young woman beside him. It was plain to see that the man felt for Evey, knew that it was her concern for Vivien that drove her to be the annoyance she presented herself to be. His respect for Jor'aiden increased, but his own irritation persisted. Her words to him a few days past had rankled him, and it would take a bit of humility on her part to make reparations for those.

It wasn't a long distance to the Council Hall. There were hordes of people there, all standing inside and around the place, hoping to get some glimpse of the Liath prisoners. The atmosphere was charged, and Mikarvan could feel it in the air, just waiting...waiting. The crowd parted before the Grand Magister. Even though he wasn't their leader, they knew him, knew him as the most powerful sorcerer of their time, and that alone earned him their reverence. Mikarvan and Evey walked freely in his wake, the eyes of hundreds staring at them, wondering what made them so special that they walked at the elder's side.

They waded through the masses, across the public hall until they reached the center of the building, where the main chamber resided. Once there, a set of heavy oak doors were opened by a pair of heavily armed guards to admit them, and abruptly, there was an air of quiet as the din from the outside was closed out.

All eyes but for a few remained upon the trial at hand as the Magister and his small retinue walked down the central aisle to the front, where they proceeded to take a seat. Before them, standing before the Council, was an Isbandarian general dressed all in white. Alongside him was a Liath acolyte, his once brightly-hued blue robes dirty from sustained travel and weeks without access to clean water for washing. He was young, as most acolytes were wont to be, his appearance relatively nondescript but for the tattoo that ran along his neck behind his right ear. The Liath were proficient with their tattooing techniques, and their designs exquisite. Mika could only imagine how painful they might be.

He frowned at this thought, his mind going to Vivien, but his attention was abruptly brought to the attention of the white clad general and his prisoner.

The general's voice carried throughout the congested room. It wasn't overly loud, or grating, but it carried like the scent of overly ripe wild berries on a mid-summer breeze, reaching every corner of the chamber. "Allow me to clarify before the Council and all in attendance. The city was besieged by fire from the skies, you say? Fiery rock, like falling stars, or an eruption?"

The acolyte's voice was much more subtle, untrained. "Like falling stars. At first, we thought it an act of nature, but then we saw her."

"Who did you see?"

He looked somewhat triumphant. "It was *her*, the harbinger of what we have believed for so long."

"Please, tell the Council who *she* is."

"She is Umesh, the Vessel. I told you this already," the acolyte snapped.

The general nodded almost absently, caught up in his thoughts, his questioning of the young man before him in order to show the assembly... something.

Mikarvan was thoughtful. *Umesh, Vessel... that is a word rarely used in society, not even to refer to the ships that the humans use upon the seas, or a canister for dispensing drink. It simply is not used. Except for...*

"Yes, this Vessel. Please describe it to the Council for me."

"Not an it. The Vessel is always a she."

The chamber had grown quiet, quieter than any he'd ever heard except for when the Wolf was sentenced back in Rithalion. The Magister, sensing his disquiet, glanced at him for the briefest moment before diverting his gaze back to the trial at hand.

The general merely nodded. Mika found himself scouring his mind for the man's name, a strange name, even for one of Isbandar. He remembered something just as the man spoke again. "Yes, of course. Tell us about her."

The acolyte's demeanor shifted as he went deep into his thoughts. For a moment it seemed somehow strange, that such a prisoner think so far outside himself and increase his vulnerability to his enemies. But then he looked again at the general standing before him, strong and imposing in spite of the silver of his hair, radiating power beyond measure...

Ahhh, yes, I know what this man is. Once, there had been a small cadre in every Elvish city, back before the Dragon War had split the elvin people asunder. After, some cities, like Rithalion, had done away with them, deeming their methods too dark and potentially destructive to the more serene lives they wished to pursue. So, this man wasn't just a general. He was an Inquisitor, one who had found his talent in drawing the truth out of any enemy captured. He was adept at his craft, teaching the minds of his enemies to bend to his will, to reveal their innermost secrets.

"She was beautiful, her hair the color of deep gold awash with the crimson blood of the people she would ultimately sacrifice to whatever dragon gods she held at her behest. Her belly was round, as she was gravid with the first child of its kind to live so long within its mother's womb post conception–"

"Yes, tell us more about that," the Inquisitor interrupted. "Tell us about the Vessels and their children."

The acolyte frowned. "Everyone knows the history. The women's bodies could not sustain the pregnancies and they all died.

"The Inquisitor nodded. "So, what makes you believe that, in fact, this young woman was such a Vessel?"

"Drath Drakkon and the other priests confirmed it."

The Inquisitor was thoughtful, seemed like he might pursue that line of questioning, before finally nodding again and going back to his original question. "Tell us more about her."

The younger man shrugged. "There's not much more to tell. Only... only that they fashioned a tattoo for her, one that spans most of her back."

Alarm surged through Mikarvan as the Inquisitor raised a silver brow, an expression of surprise flitting across his face. "Really? Tell us about it."

"It is a pair of wings... dragon wings. They were a gift."

Mikarvan's heart thundered in his chest, nearly drowning out the words that were spoken next.

"A gift? I hear that tattooing can be quite painful."

The acolyte nodded. "Indeed, it can. But for such a mark to be placed upon Umesh was an honor. It shows what she means to the Liath people."

"And what is that?"

"She is the mother of a new race, a herald for our new supremacy in the world, and we will do anything to have her back."

Silence rang throughout the chamber for several moments. Even the Inquisitor was quiet, having heard something he obviously hadn't heard before. Mika just sat there, stunned. He'd asked Vivien about the tattoo once, but she'd never deigned to answer, the expression of agony that crossed her face too much for him to bear asking her again. Suddenly the world was much more insane than he'd imagined, and his dearest friend was in the gravest danger.

The harsh sound of the gavel took him out of his thoughts. Blue Moon Rising rose from his seat, his voice solemn. "The Council will adjourn for today. We will meet back here at the same time, two days from now. Everyone is dismissed."

ROSS & ROSS

Low murmuring accompanied the exodus, only the Magister, Mikarvan, and Starling remaining in their seats. When the place was finally cleared, they finally rose to approach the weary Council.

Blue Moon Rising walked from behind the podium, fatigue written across his face. "Good afternoon, Grand Magister." His gaze briefly took in Mikarvan and Evey. "What is it that brings you to us?"

Mikarvan took that moment to step forward to stand beside the Magister, his gaze taking in the seven other elders who remained seated at the curved table before them. Blue Moon Rising turned to look at him, a smile creasing his weathered brow.

"Master Healer Mikarvan Menaghar. It is good to be in your company again. You know, when you first got here, I was struck by how much you resemble your father. I knew him before the war as a great friend and a most brilliant healer. I am not surprised you rose in the ranks so swiftly."

Mikarvan gave a slight bow. "Thank you, Lord. It heartens me to hear of him, for I never got to know him much before he passed."

Sadness passed over the councilman's face. "Yes, he was a great loss to our people." He smiled again, a sad smile that showed the magnitude of his bereavement. "The Lord of Eclipse and Integrity will always remain in our hearts."

Mika struggled to compose himself in the face of the emotion emanating from this man. Such praise was an honor, and while he enjoyed it, his sadness overtook that. The people of Isbandar placed great emphasis on their healers, and they were given status rarely heard of in Rithalion. More than once he'd considered coming to live here, the place where his father had come before meeting his mother, but too much held him in the place of his birth. His dearest friend came to his mind, and the reason for their visit became paramount.

"Lord, the reason for our visit is in regards to the lady being held within your old college. Vivien Valdera is not flourishing as she should."

The old councilman's face schooled into one of solemnity, and his gaze became piercing. "So, you are here on official healer business, it seems."

Mikarvan gave a nod. "Yes, Lord. Her health is paramount to myself and the Grand Magister, her father. She is soon expecting to deliver a child, one that may one day hold an influential place in Elvish society. I beseech the Council for leniency towards her as she has always served her people well and we do not know the torment she endured at the hands of the Liath before we finally found her." His voice became pleading. "Please, Lord. She needs her people now more than ever. Please let us serve her some mercy as she has served to protected us with her life so recently with the battle with the Iron Coast."

Blue Moon Rising's expression hardened, his gaze intensifying as he regarded Mikarvan. He swallowed convulsively beneath the stare, but maintained his position, his eyes never leaving the councilman's face.

258

The other man spoke, his voice quiet as it broke the prolonged silence. "Your fierce protector turned her back on her people when she embraced the magic of dragons, and as such, we are no longer obligated to her. However, we do value the child she carries. If the babe is untainted by dragon magic, he may one day walk in the footsteps of his grandsire." Blue Moon Rising's eyes shifted momentarily to the Magister before settling once again on Mikarvan. "I will grant this leniency you request, Master Healer, but only because I trust your capabilities based upon my respect for your father, and the purity of your heart for much the same reason."

Mikarvan let out the breath he didn't realize he'd been holding, and he unclenched his fists.

"The Lady Vivien is to be escorted by my guards at all times, and she may only go out once a day for the duration of a single hour, no more."

Mikarvan nodded. "Your wishes will be upheld, Lord."

Blue Moon Rising narrowed his eyes. "Do not make me regret honoring your request, Master Healer."

Mikarvan nodded just as a voice echoed from across the chamber. "I believe you have made a fine choice Grand Councilman, a fine choice indeed. The Lady Vivien needs fresh air just like any of us, I believe."

Mikarvan tensed, his hands once more closing into fists as the Inquisitor strode into view. The threat the man posed to Vivien tumbled through his mind, making his jaws clench and the periphery of his vision pulse with white light. And to see him here now, advocating Vivien's departure from the college–

Blue Moon Rising turned abruptly. "Inquisitor, I didn't realize you were awaiting me. I know your time is valuable, I apologize."

The Inquisitor raised his hands. "No need Grand Councilman. I have some moments to spare."

Mikarvan gave a sharp bow, the need to be out of the Inquisitor's presence dominating his actions. "I thank the Council for their leniency in this matter, and I shall leave you to your business." The Grand Magister shot him a pointed look as he turned on his heel without a response and swiftly left the hall. He registered the Magister saying something to the Council as well, but didn't bother listening to hear what it was. It wasn't until he was outside the building and walking towards the trees that he realized that neither the Magister nor Evey had followed him. It was just as well, for he preferred his own thoughts, and only his thoughts, at that moment. And those thoughts would dominate his mindspace for the duration of the day.

Chapter Thirty-Three
The City That Has Never Fallen

Eveleen waited in the trees outside the old college. She hadn't seen Mikarvan since their talk with the Council the day before, had even stopped by the chamber he'd been provided for the duration of their stay in Isbandar, only to find him not there. As far as she knew, Vivien had yet to step outside the college despite the verdict that she be granted allowance to do so, and the only reason she knew, was because she'd been creeping around it, waiting, hoping to finally see her good friend.

Evey narrowed her gaze upon the college, eying the dilapidated monstrosity that her elders had told her had once been a vision of surreal beauty. Thick, twisted tree trunks surrounded an interior of stone, the only thing of its kind in Isbandar, and possibly anywhere else in the elvin realms. It had once been a marvel, a work of art that had taken decades to create by the finest of architects. It was a good thing they had since passed, for if any one of them had to see the ruin of such former glory, it would be devastating.

Squaring her shoulders, Evey stepped from the trees and approached the building. Even with her limited capacity, she could feel the hum of the wards that protected it, magic that would keep the fiercest of enemies at bay. They had been quelled to allow the prisoner within access, and then released to keep her trapped behind the walls. There was no way for Vivien to get out, and no one could go in unless given express permission, and the guards stationed there had been tasked with the duty of doing just that.

Evey stepped up to the college, taking a deep breath before pulling on the cord outside of the thick, magic-infused doors. If she'd knocked, it was possible no one would hear her through the thickness, and the reason why the bell pull had been instated. She could barely hear the chime sounding within, and restlessly waited for someone to come to her summons.

A guard came, one with ornamental studded leather, with a sword at one hip and a circlet of enchanted oak leaves around his brow. He looked down at her with an air of someone who'd been vastly disturbed until he recognized her and gave a hasty half bow, his expression incredulous. "Lady Starling! What brings you here?"

She mustered all the courage she had, for this was one of the Council's guardsmen, an elite. They were treating Vivien's imprisonment with the utmost seriousness. "I am here to see the Lady Vivien."

The guard's brow creased into a frown. "No one is allowed passage but for the Master Healer, the Grand Magister, the Lord of Ice and Steel, or a member of the Council."

She returned the frown. "I have been given permission to enter. Let me pass."

"I have yet to receive word of this, and until then, you shall not pass."

Evey looked the guard down, and then up again, schooling her face into one of distaste. He was a half elf; she could tell by the shape of his ears and the roundness of his face. Such a thing really didn't matter to her, for Vivien was also a half-breed, and that fact never lowered Evey's respect for her dear friend. But that would not stop Evey from using it against the guardsman now. His breeding and profession placed him in lower standing than herself, and as such, he should show her the deference she was due.

"You show me disrespect, guardsman."

A flash of apprehension passed over the man's face before he could hide it, swiftly followed by a show of determination. "I am doing what I have been told, nothing more, nothing less," he said.

She lowered her voice to a hiss. "I suggest you do as I ask, lest I bring you before the Council for insubordination."

Again, she saw the apprehension, albeit for only the briefest moment. It told her that he was younger than many of the other elite, and it gave her hope that she just might win her way. "I will continue as I am until I receive proper word. In the meantime, I bid you leave the premises."

Evey stepped closer to the guard, placing a hand on the door. "I shall not leave until I am allowed entry."

The guard's expression turned stony. He pitched his voice over his shoulder and began to call out, "I have a problem at the main entry..."

His voice abruptly cut off as Mikarvan appeared beside him. The healer regarded her from weary eyes, his hair tousled and his robes wrinkled. "Let her in, Three Rivers."

The guard deepened the frown that already occupied his face. "I will not do so until I have orders from the Council."

Two more guards appeared behind Mikarvan, expressions stoic. For some reason, the Master Healer had put in his word for her, and at any other time, she may have felt grateful. Instead, Evey struggled to quell the nervousness that threatened to weaken her legs and cause her to shake.

"The Council is busy with much more important matters. But the lady has permission to enter, so let her pass."

"Permission from who?" Three Rivers growled.

Mikarvan struck the man with a piercing glare. "From me."

A chorus of guffaws emerged from the three guards. "And you think that we will accept your word as permission for her to enter? I think not," said Three Rivers.

Mikarvan turned to him and cocked his head. "I thought that we settled the matter of my word last night, guardsman. Shall I remind you?" The healer raised his hand and a small orb of golden light formed there.

Three Rivers' gaze shifted from Mikarvan to the orb, then back again. "The matter of other visitors was never mentioned," he said defensively.

Mikarvan nodded and put his hand down, the light winking out. "Indeed, we did not. But this lady must be included in that, as she is my apprentice."

Surprise flickered across the guards' faces that mirrored what she felt herself. But she dared not question it, not here, not now, when it was apparent that Mikarvan was playing on her side.

"There was never any mention of an apprentice."

Mikarvan shrugged. "I am mentioning it now. The Lady Vivien's care now necessitates another pair of hands, a woman's hands, as she is entering the last stages of her pregnancy." He turned to the two guards still standing behind him. "Unless one of you would like to take on the responsibility?"

Both men turned a soft shade of red as they realized what type of care that might entail, care that included lack of clothing for the patient being spoken about. Evey put a hand to her face, over the smile that twitched at the corners of her mouth. "N... no, Master Healer," said the closest of the two. "That won't be necessary. Bring your apprentice in."

Three Rivers shot the other guard a pointed scowl as he slowly removed himself from Evey's path. She wanted to offer a gloating grimace of victory, but chose against it as she entered the dark college. Immediately she felt a hand at her elbow, Mikarvan leading her deeper into the building and away from the prying eyes of the guards. She could feel his urgency, and it propelled her alongside him until they finally stopped at a grand staircase. He turned her around to face him and she instinctively took a step back.

"What's going on? What are you still doing here? You didn't return to your quarters yesterday."

He put a forefinger to his lips. "Shhh. I don't need them hearing us." He frowned. "And how do you know I wasn't there? Are you stalking me?" he whispered.

She folded her arms across her chest, her cheeks burning. "You can keep wishing that I was, Healer."

His brows pulled into an irritated frown. "I said be quiet! And since you can't, let's go upstairs."

She considered resisting as he took her elbow again and led her up the stairwell. She wasn't a child that needed someone holding onto her to keep her in line. Thing was, for some reason, she didn't really mind him having it there. His hand was warm, insistent but gentle.

At the top of the stairs they turned down the first corridor and into the nearest room. Once there he stopped again and turned her to face him. He pulled a folded piece of parchment out from the breast of his robes, took her hand, and placed it within. "Since you already know where my chamber is, you won't need me to tell you. But I need you to get all of the things on this list and bring them back to me here."

"What? Why?"

"Because I don't want to leave Vivien alone here."

She shook her head. "But you always have before."

"That was before the Inquisitor."

"You can..." She stopped speaking then, realization of what he was thinking dawning on her. She was less quick to begin speaking again, trying to keep calm for the sake of remembering the conversation later. "Why would the Inquisitor come to see Vivien?"

Mikarvan regarded her intently, his gaze assessing, like he was trying to decide how much he should tell her. "You heard the acolyte's testimony. It described Vivien."

She put her hands on her hips, the parchment crumpling in her hand. "That description fits a lot of women, Master Healer."

He shook his head. "Not the part about the tattoo."

She felt her eyes widen, followed by the wetness in her throat turning to ash.

He nodded. "Yes, she bears the described mark."

Evey shook her head. "No, that's impossible. She can't possibly be the carrier of some demon dragon child!"

Mikarvan put a palm over her lips. "Shhhh! Please, you have to be quieter!"

The look of genuine alarm on his face bade her pause, and she nodded her agreement before he removed his hand. "So, you think the Inquisitor will come here to question Vivien."

He answered her statement as though it were a question. "Without a doubt. And I want to be here when he does."

"Do you think you can stop him?"

His expression became pained. "No, but I can try. And if I don't stop him, I can at least be at her side."

She shook her head. "You think he would actually allow that?"

The look of pain intensified as he shook his head. "No."

She just nodded then, turning her thoughts inward. She supposed she'd do the same thing Mikarvan was, despite the uselessness of it. The Inquisitor would break Vivien down, make her relieve the atrocities she'd endured with the Liath, make her spell out every truth of her life, even at the expense of her mind. And if she wasn't easily forthcoming, he would use the tools he'd learned centuries ago, and he would use them to create a husk of a woman, someone too far gone to ever be herself again.

Evey began to shake, and her breath whistled past the gargantuan lump that had suddenly lodged in her throat. She wavered on her feet, and only Mikarvan's firm hand on her arms kept her steady. "Not now! Starling, not now. I need you to go and get the items I requested from my chamber."

She opened her eyes, not realizing she'd even closed them. The Healer stood close, his breath washing over her forehead like a warm breeze. "Please, I need you to do this. Go and get some of your own things. Then, you can stay here with Vivien too."

She blinked the tears from her eyes and nodded.

"Hurry!"

Evey nodded and rushed from the room.

Xadrian watched the Wolf as closely as he could during the few hours that he saw him each day and just before bedding down for the night. He rose as the barbarian did, well before dawn. They would exchange a few words, the Wolf would gobble some leftover meat from the evening stewpot, a ration of bread and some dried fruit, and then be on his way on the back of the tired reindeer. The main body of the expedition would move after breaking camp at dawn. They passed the Wolf sometime after the noon meal Xadrian was sure the barbarian ignored. Sometimes he was riding, but other days he walked his mount. While he walked, Xadrian could see the Wolf with a random rock or log, hefting it with arms that were quickly filling out, bouncing back from his terrible imprisonment by the Liath. The riders of the tir-reath would then continue until dusk, make camp, and let the big cats out to hunt. Only when it was late, once all the men and mounts had eaten, tents pitched, guards set, and fires lit, would the Wolf trod tiredly into camp. He then cared for his mount and ate hastily before falling asleep under the open sky.

At some point, it rained heavily for three days and the La'athai took bets as to if the Wolf would put up his tent. The bets grew, and in the end, they all lost. The Wolf threw the tent over his mount, shucked his armor so his skin steamed in the cooling air, and lay there facing where the stars would be. Then he was up before dawn by some inner knowledge of the sun's travels and into his sodden armor. He did not pause, did not complain, did not falter. Xadrian kept close eye on the human, but he exhibited nothing so much as iron determination and tight control. The Lord of Swords knew there would be no release for the thrumming tension in his soul but for the return to Isbandar, to see Vivien safe and free.

The terrain became hilly and broken. It was a stark landscape dressed in the fiery colors of a chilly autumn. The way ahead too often became a steep incline or a sheer drop off, with hidden caves and numerous streams. Xadrian had the La'athai backtrack several times a day. He knew that things must be the same for the Wolf, yet, every night, the barbarian came into camp without fail. The following days turned colder and everything but the Wolf was frosted from rain caught by the chill. Again, he stood, readied his mount, gathered his gear, and headed out. He did this each and every day for a full week's travel.

Then came the noon meeting on the tenth day. The La'athai caught up to the Wolf, who was leading the reindeer with a tether to his belt while pressing a sizable log over his head. Xadrian called a halt and motioned over the barbarian who discarded the impromptu weight. The Lord of Swords dismounted Fenella and tossed her a stern look to keep her from hissing as they spoke. "We will be there in a few hours. It is best you stay with us now."

The Wolf nodded solemnly, a flickering of red in his eyes the only sign of rebellion. "Liath?"

Xadrian chuckled "No, not this close to Sharderia. No Liath that want to live, anyway. But we are coming into owned lands, and a lone human may have trouble here, even if riding a fae mount. And there is, of course..."

The Wolf looked at him quizzically, but did not pick up on Xadrian's meaning. In ten days his once simply ragged hair had become wild and untamed, his beard back to a short cascade of frosted chestnut, and his muscles surging again with barely contained power. His simple mail shirt and axe showed signs of rust, and his kilt and jerkin had lost stitches and whole threads. Xadrian pursed his lips. "You do not cut a fine military figure, Brother. You may make our job harder simply by looking so poorly as a member of a delegation from a great city."

The Wolf frowned "I will do my best, nonetheless."

Xadrian put out a gentle hand and squeezed the Wolf's arm. "We have made good time despite weather and wearing. I hope this will take only a few days and we can be on our way again."

The Wolf said nothing, maybe joining in that hope, and maybe afraid to voice any desire lest he chase it away like a small bird. They ate hastily, but kept the tir-reath close. They were remounted as soon as they could be, and continued to Sharderia. They came across no travelers, nor did they see habitation, but all the travelers could feel eyes upon them. Finally, after a long day in the saddle, the woods parted to reveal their destination. Despite his normally stoic demeanor, the Wolf gasped.

It sat on a natural motte of stone, surveying a valley on all sides. The valley ahead was covered in low, thorny growth like a wide moat filled with teeth. In summer there would be high hedges of green hiding finger long thorns that could pierce leather like it was butter. Now they stood like the corpses of dark witches, linked shoulder to shoulder to form alleys under the eyes of doom. A delicate path wound through the thorns back and forth to place any invader at the mercy of the tiny wooden daggers or under the withering fire of archers over and over. But it was the rock face itself that made the Wolf pause. The wind and the rain of uncounted eons had cut Sharderia from the face of a steep rock face. Thick veins of softer rock had melted away, leaving a wide beehive of streets and caves, and he would wager, a wealth of catacombs beneath and within the rock face The whole of it had been honed and polished by innumerable elvin masters, working to make the outside impregnable while taking the removed stone from the inner reaches and building on top to provide towering fists that promised to see forever, and strike down any that came under their gaze from any one of a hundred ballista positions.

Xadrian rode next to the human and nodded in agreement to the wordless exclamation. "Behold. Sharderia- The City That Has Never Fallen."

The Wolf nodded knowingly, then urged his mount down into the killing fields.

There was no pomp and circumstance to their arrival, but they arrived all the same. The gates were closed as they approached, but a series of horn blasts, one from atop the wall, the others from further away, had the great oak barriers swinging open before the group had time to do more than slow.

The gates opened to allow the troupe to enter, and immediately shut again behind them. The city street seemed claustrophobic to all assembled aside from the Lord. With a timing that showed centuries of military precision, a tall elf was walking to the gate to meet them. As he approached, he removed an intricate helmet to expose sharp, hawk like features. His head was shaved, as Xadrian did himself, eschewing vanity for practicality. His clothes were tight fitting, with a shining breastplate, bracers and greaves, the intricate loops and whorls almost polished off from uncounted ministrations of leather and fine stone dust mixed with rendered animal fat. His sword was an effective tool, worn in a low-slung rig made to be snatched to the ready in but a moment.

Xadrian smiled at his approach and hoisted an open hand towards the ambassador. "Well met again, Jolu'zaahr."

Jolu'zaahr returned the gesture, then turned smartly to fall in line with the procession at the head to not slow their progress. "And to you, Lord of Swords and Truth. I had hoped the years were kind to you since the war."

Xadrian nodded. "And you. The messenger hawk arrived?"

"A week ago. We have been expecting you. The Council was notified when you were spotted late yesterday and should be convening as we speak." The Wolf started and their host noted it. "You seem surprised."

The Wolf shook his head, but said nothing.

Xadrian waited for the silence to start to become uncomfortable and then motioned to the walking elf and the human riding just past him. "Elf named Zaahr, of the honorable house Jolu, this is the Wolf. He is my friend and my brother."

It was Zaahr's turn to look incredulous. "Your brother?"

"He has earned it many times over, my friend."

Zaahr cast the Wolf an appraising look, but the human was quietly and seriously taking in every detail of the rock city around him and paid no mind. Zaahr judged the dirty clothes, rusted chain shirt and axe. Finally, Zaahr spoke again. "That is a serious gift to bequeath upon any other being, especially a human."

The Wolf focused on the soldier, turning his formidable presence loose for the first time. His eyes flickered red as he rumbled in Elvish, "I told him so, but he refuses to recant it."

There was a pause, then another, then Zaahr threw back his head to release a laugh as clear and crisp as a bell. "No. No he wouldn't. The Lord of Swords and Truth that I trained with would never make such a statement out of passion or mistake. You must be exceptional. I offer my honest and deep apology if I have given offense." Xadrian released a breath he did not remember holding, and The Wolf simply shook his head to dismiss the thought. "So, what do you think of Sharderia?"

Xadrian tried to relax, though he knew the Wolf's strong suit had never been conversation with any but Vivien. But the answers: "There are no humans, everyone has little hair, everyone is armed, and the city seems empty," were harmless enough.

Zaahr smiled wryly, "You ride into a city of warriors. We are not as driven by art or majesty as other cities. These together mean hair is kept short for battle, and only human soldiers often come to our doors. Few choose to stay before leaving to ply their new knowledge. Together, these are the reasons for your first observations."

They went just a little further. Xadrian, who had once studied there, tried to look at the tall, walled in streets abutted in natural rock with fresh eyes. There were many doors and courtyards carved for markets and travelers, but no homes. The walls were covered in carvings and ivy, leading a more open feel, but on first impression it must seem very crowded. He nodded that the streets were bare in comparison to Rithalion or Isbandar, with soldiers going about helmeted unless in deep conversation, others wearing studded headbands to take the place of helmets as they worked, and only the elderly or very young being bareheaded. And, of course, the Wolf was right. Everyone carried at least a long dagger meant not for cutting grain or meat, but obviously an implement of war.

The Wolf finally asked, "And the why is the city so empty?"

Zaahr smiled, "It is not. You just haven't seen it yet. Here are the dens where we keep the tir-reath."

The procession stopped to the wide entry of a cave dug into the side of the street. Zaahr called a guardsman on patrol to take the Wolf's reins and lead his mount to a stable a few blocks over. Another he tasked with staying to lead the La'athai to the barracks. Xadrian stood back with a secret smile seeking to peek out as Zaahr came back to find the Wolf giving orders for the men to see to their mounts. Zaahr was shocked to see Katriona listening to the Wolf and then passing on assignments to the elves. So shocked, in fact, Zaahr simply watched as elves saluted the human and even referred to him as Knight Protector.

Zaahr looked to Xadrian askance and said quietly, "What have you brought into my city, Xadrian?"

"Someone amazing, Galathe," he responded, using his friend's true name just as his friend had used his own. "He is my brother."

And Zaahr nodded solemnly as the Wolf walked over. Zaahr looked at the barbarian with new eyes. "Knight Protector of Rithalion, are you ready to see the Council?"

"Yes." The Wolf remembered himself and looked at his travel ragged self, then to Xadrian for disapproval. But Xadrian felt none.

Zaahr smiled. "The road dirt fits you, and your urgency. Let us get you there without delay."

Chapter Thirty-Four
Victories and Doubts

and then why is the city empty?" the Wolf had asked.

"It is not. You just haven't seen it yet," Zaahr had replied.

And he had not.

Xadrian had told him many things, that the Sharderians were finest elvin warriors that history had ever seen and that they used helmets the way those from Rithalion used hoods or hats. Their 'shield' names were used the way Rithalion used titles, or the way Isbandar used descriptive names to protect them from some maleficent magic. He knew the whole of the city was carved into the living rock, but he could not have imagined just what that had meant.

The surface was plain enough, certainly not more alien than the wicker and wood city of Isbandar, but once below the surface, it all changed. A lifetime ago, the Wolf had seen glowing crystals held in brass cages in the cave of the warlock who lived at the edge of Pergatium swamp. He had seen them again in the council chambers of each city he had been to. Perhaps they had been found in other elvin buildings he had not frequented, but here, now, they were everywhere and they glowed like full moons. The tunnels were not cramped, dirty things, but wide boulevards where elves went about their business like it was any other given day. The surface was cold and getting colder, but here it was a pleasant cool and never seemed to waver. The elves on the surface were armed with long knives or small hammers, even hatchets. Those beneath were armed for war with side swords. Every head was shorn short. All wore simple, rugged clothes that offered some protection with reinforced leather or drapes of chain and metal plates. Beside him on one side walked Xadrian, who looked as if he had seen it all before, but on his other side was Katriona. Even she looked off balance by this place and these people.

They came to the council chambers of Sharderia and he saw the same kind of pictures carved above the doorway, but they were far less delicate than the ones in Rithalion. He took them in, and realized now how it told the story of the creation of the elvin cities and eventually the Dragon War. Then they passed through. The Wolf steeled himself to feel the heavy oppression of politics settle in on him.

Once again, The City That Has Never Fallen surprised him. All of the council chambers he'd experienced before had been lofty halls of judgment and pomp. The ceiling here was domed, with light spread to every corner by beautiful chandeliers holding many glowing crystals. Otherwise, the room was brutally functional. A round table, heavy and thick, sat in the center of the room. Around the table there were beautiful, but square, and weighty chairs. Separated from these by a dozen strides were railings and then hundreds of the same kind of chair in flat rows from wall to wall. The seating was not ranked, nor on high in balconies. This was not a place for theater, but deliberation. Ideas ruled here, not position.

He was guided to one side of the circle with Xadrian and Katriona. Then those from the city, only a few dozen, were guided in along the aisles from each corner of the room. It was only scant minutes of standing before the Council came in.

Councils in other cities were as pale ghosts, almost alien due to centuries of age and wisdom, but also separation from hardship and strife. Here, not so. The councilmen and -women of Sharderia were of various ages, though it was hard to judge in elves. Yet, after so long living amongst them, the Wolf noted the oldest would have platinum hair, and carried a certain distance from energy or emotion. At least half of these nine did not. They filed in and did not wear full robes, but only open white vestments that exposed their clothes and weapons. It was only then that he realized he had not been disarmed for the first time walking into a new council chamber. Their helmets, too, were the simple leather headbands common amongst elvin folk not fully prepared to venture into danger. As they took their seats, they drew their swords, and in one case a mace, from their sides and lay them on the table in front of them pointed toward the center. Xadrian did the same, so the Wolf and Katriona followed suit. Then the headbands followed, and Xadrian and Katriona lowered their hoods. With no hood of his own, the Wolf felt slightly out of place and could not stop himself from shuffling slightly. Only then did the Council of Sharderia sit and bade them do the same. The Wolf took a deep breath, readying his patience against the hours of droning...

A woman dressed in a shimmering mail coat beneath the white vestments, spoke. "Your message was troubling, Lord of Swords and Truth."

Xadrian nodded. "Our need is great."

A man dressed in heavy black leathers, who smelled of coal fires and had soot worked into every pore of his huge, muscled hands frowned. "What kind of attack are you expecting?"

Xadrian shook his head. "Last time they brought war hounds, giants, and thirty thousand men. Next time they will come with everything, and we will be lost."

A delicate woman on the end, dressed simply, but with complicated braids of the deepest black shot with gray, looked to the Wolf. "Were you captured during the battle?"

Xadrian took a quick inhalation. Katriona bristled visibly but kept silent. The Wolf felt no reaction to the question, and simply shook his head.

"We know the Lord of Swords and Truth. We understand this is Katriona Dunlavvy, a soldier and captain of the guard who has chosen to accompany the La'athai, the Wolf Pack. Who are you?"

There was a definite pause, but the Wolf decided that simplicity was best. "I am the Wolf."

Every member of the Council was taken aback and looked to one another. Again, the raven and steel haired woman spoke. "You are a wolf of the Wolf Pack?"

Katriona answered, "He leads the Wolf Pack. When they marched to certain doom through Pergatium, he guided them to safety. When they found the dragon there, he fought it with hands and fists. Not only did he live, but he won. When they faced thirty thousand, he led the charge. When giants attacked, he faced them with steel and courage. When we came to warn you of the dangers–"

Xadrian warned, "Katriona–"

But she did not heed, "–and we were ambushed by Liath, he was captured–"

"Katriona–"

"–and fought his way free."

The Wolf felt a deep well of despair open up inside his chest. He swallowed, but it could not be filled. It was a sucking nothingness that promised only coldness and sorrow. He barely heard her say, "He is a leader of both humans elves and fights for us better than some of our own."

He lay a hand on hers and she fell silent, the room stinging with her words.

There was a quiet moment and then the councilwoman across the table stood. "Is this true?"

The Wolf shook his head. "No." Xadrian, Katriona, and the whole Council were agape. He felt something inside now, a certainty. It was the whisper of a forest fire coming hot and raging inside of him. He felt compelled to stand to face the cold elf on the other side of the table. "I am the Wolf. I lead the La'athai with Lady Vivien Valdera. I did none of this alone, for she and they were always with me."

The elf inclined her head. "You will be fighting in the coming battle?"

"With every drop of blood I possess."

"They call me Keil'asil, but that is not my name." She looked to the others on the Council, who all pondered carefully. Finally, she spoke again. "My true name is Abrigale Hilas."

There were murmurs from the audience. The Wolf nodded. "I am Ravn Blacach, and I fight for Rithalion and Vivien Valdera. I must return to the side of the woman I love, Councilwoman Abrigale Hilas. But before I can, I must find help to defend the people she is worn to protect. I cannot return until this is done. Will you help us?"

Abrigale looked through the Wolf, as if weighing the next words. "How many soldiers do you need, Ravn Blacach?"

The Wolf glanced to Xadrian. "I have gathered that the Lord of Swords and Truth has told you the situation is dire and he spoke truly. We need absolutely every soldier you can spare."

Abrigale looked to the other members of the Council and each nodded in turn. "The City That Has Never Fallen shall not turn our cousins in Rithalion away in their time of need. You shall have them, soldiers to the last one. They will march as soon as they are provisioned."

Ravn sat heavily in his seat, tension and hope and despair flooding out of him in a rush. His head was spinning, his pulse pounding. He nearly missed Xadrian's heartfelt thanks and Abrigale's next question.

"What will you do now?"

Ravn stood. "Sleep, for we must depart at first light."

The plainest dressed councilman looked troubled. "You will not rest?"

And just then a crushing wave of lonely loss washed over Ravn's soul. He blinked back tears and shook his head. "We must go to Moirdem for we are not finished with our quest."

They all looked to him with understanding. "We pray you find equal openness and wisdom in Moirdem."

Vivien remained still as Mikarvan ran his hands over her belly. Despite the comfort provided by the extra pillows that Evey had brought, she remained tense, every muscle prepared to leap from the bed and get her to safety should the need arise. She hated that she felt this way, for now it was her dearest friend who examined her with the gentlest of touches instead of Drath Drakkon. The Liath priest had been fascinated by it, touching her often in the darkness of the night. He would start this way, his clawed hands roving over her belly until they slid downward, where he would then enter her with his fingers, as though trying to reach up inside to touch the child resting within–

"Vivien?"

She snapped out of her reverie to find Mikarvan regarding her intently, his eyes dark with concern. "Vivien, are you in pain?"

"N...no. Why?"

His eyes locked on hers, he slowly reached out to pry one of her hands away from the blanket she had held in a white-knuckled grip. She instantly released it, shame flooding through her to reach her cheeks, where it settled to burn. He maneuvered her hand so that his fingers threaded through hers, his expression shifting to one of sadness. "You never used to fear me."

She took a deep quivering breath that lodged in her throat just beyond the lump that had formed there. She blinked back impending tears and struggled to clear it. Her voice came out as barely a whisper. "I'm sorry."

He gave a smile that didn't reach his eyes. "Don't be. I just wish you would talk to me, confide in me. Like you used to."

She lowered her gaze, considering. There was a part of her that wanted, needed, to confide in someone. Yet, the agony was still so fresh, and the fear...

Several moments passed, and when he realized she wasn't going to reply, Mika spoke again. "Vivien, I'd like to examine you internally. By my estimation, you are even months into this pregnancy, and because of your heritage, we don't know when you will deliver. I'd like to see how close you might be."

Her heart stuttered in her chest, a shroud of fear settling over her. *Examine me internally? What does that mean? It sounds like...*

"Half-breed women generally fall within a window of eleven to thirteen months gestation. In my mind, you can deliver at any time." He paused for a moment before continuing. "However, I must say, at this point I feel I might be a bit off on my original assessment. You seem to have grown quite a bit since the last time I measured you, and you could be further along than I thought."

Vivien looked up again and took in his concerned expression.

"It's definitely not your diet, for you still don't eat what I believe you should. You're not gaining weight all over, it's just in your belly. So, I know it's all the baby."

She stared at him, studied his expression to see what lay beneath the surface. And then she saw it. He wasn't just concerned for her or that he thought he was off on his assessment–

Her eyes widened. "You think something might be wrong with the baby."

It wasn't a question, but a statement spoken out of certainty from knowing him so long.

Mikarvan sighed and gave a solemn nod. "Yes, I do."

Vivien looked away from him again, took her hand out of his, and steeled herself. "Do what you feel you must."

His tone was quiet, plaintive in a pained way that made the lump come back in her throat. "I'm not going to hurt you."

She blinked her eyes free of the tears that threatened and sniffed them from her nose. "Just do it."

He rose from her side on the bed and moved to the end. "I need you to move down here."

Her body shook as she did as he bid, rising from her place to sit at the end where he indicated. Mika went back to retrieve one pillow, placed it in the middle of the bed, then gestured that she lay down. Her shaking increased as she complied, her heartbeat increasing in tempo. *I have been in battle before... BATTLE! Yet here I shake like a child about to be punished for raiding the pantry.*

"I need you to bend your legs... yes, just like that. Now I need you to spread them for me."

Her eyes widened in shock. She had never been in such a position before, not unless... Thoughts of Torialvah soared through her mind, forcing out the better ones of the Wolf. She was vulnerable, laying there under the scrutiny of this man. No longer her friend, but a Master Healer of Rithalion. It reminded her not only of sex, but the time she'd lost her first baby, the one that lay cold and dead in the ground where she had buried him.

Unbidden, tears streamed from her eyes, and she bit her lower lip to keep from moaning with the anguish her thoughts caused. She, too, felt cold and alone, lost within a past that gave her so much pain.

"Vivien."

She snapped open eyes she hadn't realized she'd shut, found that Mika stood beside her, his face just inches above hers. "Every woman goes through this when birth is near. I swear, I will not hurt you." He placed his hand on her forehead, sweeping it gently down over one cheek. "You can believe in me."

She swallowed convulsively and nodded, realizing she was sweating when he took his hand away and felt the coolness of the air over her skin. He positioned himself between her parted legs, looked at her as he placed his hands on her inner thighs. She jumped at his light touch, felt shame rush through her once again, and hated herself for her weakness.

"Vivien, I need you to relax. Start with your bottom and work your way up your legs." He smiled encouragingly. "You can do it."

She nodded and did as he bid, her muscles quivering as she worked to relax them, her legs naturally falling apart so that he could view her most intimate of places.

"I'm going to slide my hands down here, and I need you to stay relaxed. Can you do that for me?"

She nodded again, felt his warm hands slide gently over her flesh to that place she felt she never wanted to be touched. *But the Wolf touched me there, the day of our fight. And I'd let him make love to me—*

No. We hadn't made love. It was something else. Something angry. Something primal. Something I had to have.

"Now I'm going to enter you. It might ache a bit as I push deep inside, but as long as you stay relaxed, it won't hurt."

She nodded and felt his fingers enter. She gasped as he pushed them deep inside, arching her back with the intrusion. His expression was one of concentration as he felt around, then, once he was satisfied, he nodded and withdrew.

Vivien felt her body go limp as the healer closed her legs. Hot tears streamed down her temples to wet the pillow beneath her head, and she squeezed her eyes tightly shut. *It's over. It's over and I'm still here.*

"Vivien."

She opened her eyes and her friend stood over her, hand outstretched. "Let's get you comfortable again."

She nodded and she allowed him to help her back to the head of the bed. He positioned her pillows, covered her with the blankets, then settled down to lay beside her. He put an arm around her, just above her belly where it would be most comfortable.

"Your cervix is beginning to open. That means that your body is preparing for birth. However, it's not open enough to make me believe that birth is imminent. I would like to check you this way every week, so that we can keep up on it."

She nodded. "And the baby. Is he well?"

He hesitated only the briefest of moments. "I could sense nothing wrong while I was inside. I believe that he is just fine."

She gave a deep sigh of relief she didn't realize she felt. "Thank you."

He stroked a hand over her hair. "For what?"

"For being patient with me."

"For you, I have eons of patience." He chuckled then. "But only for you."

Mikarvan waited for Vivien's breathing to slow to that of someone sleeping before he slipped away from her side. He looked down at her where she lay, the mound of her belly protruding beneath the blankets. He'd lied to her when he told her nothing was wrong. Rather, everything he'd sensed the moment he entered her was greatly amiss.

He'd gone into her with fae magic in tow, a basic spell he used to get a vague idea of what may be going on inside a person he wished to treat for some ailment of which he was uncertain of the origination. Right away he'd felt resistance, and as he probed deeper, the magic had been snuffed out entirely.

As Mika stared down at his friend, a woman he'd loved as long as he could remember, he felt genuine fear. For in the truest sense, she was indeed a mage of dragons, and for all he knew, inhabited by one. Maybe, just maybe, she was the Vessel the Liath spoke about after all.

Chapter Thirty-Five
Fickle Justice

Evey walked past the guard into the college and rolled her eyes. It was the same guard every day, who annoyed her beyond reason. She didn't know his name, not because he'd never given it, but simply because she didn't care to bother listening when he spoke it.

"Lady Starling, let me help you with that!"

She rolled her eyes again. "No, no I can manage myself, thank you."

The man took hold of the bundle of clean clothes and plucked it from her arms. "I believe you, but I am here and can help. I mean, what better way to use these strong chest muscles than to help you, eh?"

He put the bundle under one arm while flexing his bicep with the other, grinning stupidly all the while. She just gave him a quelling glare and continued towards the staircase. She found his attention to her disturbing and wished he'd just leave her alone. She despised him and all the other guards in this gods' forsaken place, for, to her, they represented all that kept Vivien trapped there. Evey saw Mikarvan and her friend sitting at the dining table in the adjoining room and they waved when they saw her pass. The guard continued to babble as she made her way up the stairs, the bundle hitting her back a time or two because the fool followed so closely. Once in the corridor, she hastened her pace, only wanting to be free of him until the next time he accosted her. A few steps before she reached the door to her chamber, he rushed ahead and opened it for her, a flourishing gesture urging her inside. "There you go, my lady!"

She gave a small sigh, pointing down the hallway a bit further. "I'm going to Vivien's room for a bit."

"Oh! Yes, of course."

He then preceded her down the corridor, and once at the appropriate door, opened it once more with the same flourish. She stepped up beside him, about to ask him for her bundle, when she stopped cold in her tracks. There, in the middle of Vivien's room, were three men. They were dressed in dark leather tunics and trousers, and each had a kerchief covering the lower half of his face. They were armed, each with a knife at his belt and a sword already in hand.

Evey screamed as the guard abruptly threw the bundle into the room, hitting the middle man square in the chest before swiftly shutting the door and holding onto the handle with both hands. Strings of epithets could be heard beyond the barrier just before the handle began to quiver. The guard began to pull back on it, straining against the weight on the other side.

Shocked, she just stood there for a moment, taking in the ramifications of what was taking place. These men had come to kill Vivien.

"I– I need you to get my whistle."

Evey's attention was pulled back to the straining guard, the tendons in his neck bulging as he tried to keep hold of the door. One foot was propped against the wall, giving him the leverage he needed to keep it closed. "What?"

"Get my whistle! It's hanging from a cord around my neck."

She rushed up to the guard, feeling around his neck for the cord. His hair was pulled back, so it wasn't difficult to find, and she began to pull on it. Meanwhile, the men on the other side of the door were making headway, their greater strength causing the door to begin to crack open despite his bracing.

"Hurry!"

Evey pulled hard on the cord and the whistle popped out from beneath the guard's studded leather vest. He hissed between his teeth as the door cracked wider... wider. Fingers emerged first, then a hand. She grabbed hold of the whistle, placed it to her mouth and blew.

Suddenly they were stumbling back. The guard caught himself from falling, drew his blade as the three men emerged from the chamber. "Run Starling! Run!"

Evey turned to bolt down the hallway. She didn't know if the short-lived whistle blow had been heard, had to warn the others that they were in danger. She only got several steps before she felt a heavy weight from behind, a pair of arms wrapping around hers to keep her from lashing out.

"Oh no you don't. You're staying right here."

She screamed again, abruptly stepping back in the hopes of taking her captor off guard. But he was ready for that maneuver, dragging her back to pin her chest against the nearest wall. Her face pressed against the stone, she saw the guard and one of the other men, their swords ringing off of one another to echo throughout the corridor. The third man stood to the side, his voice rising over the sound of the fighting. "We don't want to hurt you! Just let us go and do what needs to be done! The longer that woman lives, the more in danger our people become! She is a scourge upon us all, and she may be the death of us if we wait any longer!"

Helplessness coursed through Evey, the weight of the man behind her making it hard to breathe, much less scream again for the help they so desperately needed. A twinge of worry tapped at her mind for the guard; she didn't like him, but that didn't mean she wanted him to die. To his benefit, he was very proficient with his use of the blade. The steel glinted in the light offered by the wall sconces as he wielded it deftly and with deadly precision.

But his opponent was better. First blood was drawn as the interloper's blade sliced into the guard's arm above his studded bracer.

"You can stop this now! Set down your blade and let us do our duty, not just by this city, but for all our people! We will cut the dragon mage down and keep our people safe from her treachery!"

A commotion down the hall alerted Evey to the presence of others before the weight off her back was lifted. She turned from the fight to see the other two guards, swords drawn, rushing towards them, the man who had been holding her against the wall drawing his own weapon to meet them. The third man, the one who had used nothing but words until that point, also drew his blade. He stepped towards the ongoing fight, up behind the first guard and, in an act of cowardice of the worst kind, sheathed his weapon into his unsuspecting back.

Evey slapped a hand over her mouth to keep from screaming yet a third time, her heart hammering in her chest. All the ill thoughts she'd had of the man such a short time before flitted through her mind and made her ashamed. The guard slid off the sword and onto is knees, his face a rictus of agony as he choked, blood burbling from his mouth to drip down his chin and onto the stone. The guard fell and the coward then turned, his gaze meeting hers. Time seemed to slow for a moment as he regarded her from eyes devoid of regret for what he'd done. All that shone there was the passion of his mission, and collateral damage was not a hindrance.

His voice rose over the sound of battle. "Kill them!"

Evey sprang into motion, darting down the hall, away from the coward towards the four combatants. The fighting brought her up short, and uncertainty rooted her there for a moment. Stay where she was and she'd die, try and maneuver around the fighting and she *might* die. She chanced a look behind her, but the coward had not moved from his place, simply stared at her. She heard a man cry out in front of her, and she thought it sounded like Three Rivers. A moment later there was another cry, and she turned to see that both of the guards were on the floor, their opponents prepared to strike them down.

It was then Evey saw her. Vivien stood several paces down the corridor on the other side of the men, Mikarvan just behind. Her eyes glowed a brilliant green, making her a vision of ethereal beauty that Evey had never encountered before. Vivien lifted one hand from her distended belly, looked as though she was reaching out towards the men–

And the corridor erupted into a cacophony of sizzling energy.

Veins of bright light spidered across the walls, concentrating at the doors, where they coalesced to form randomized webs. They crackled and hissed, the wards enchanted into them making them pulse as though they had a life of their own. What had always been a hum before was now a gyrating pulse of sound, the wards straining to do what they had been made for. The corridor was lit as though daylight had been captured there, and behind Vivien, Evey saw that help had finally arrived in the form of four other guardsmen who must have heard the whistle calls of the two guards still lying on the floor. They stared in awe at the spectacular vision before them, unmoving.

And then the screams started.

Evey's attention riveted to the attackers. Their swords glowed yellow-white as though in a forge, and had fused with the flesh of their hands, making it impossible for them to release the weapons. The interlopers howled in agony, their off hands trying in vain to pry their fingers from around the hilts. The cloying scent of burning skin filled the air, followed by the sickening sound of flesh peeling from bone as the swords finally dropped to the floor, the hilts surrounded by blackened crisp. The men scrambled at the daggers at their hips, the sheathes burning away until the glowing blades finally fell beside their longer counterparts.

Then, Vivien simply lowered her hand. The doors abruptly shifted back to dark, and all that remained was the flickering flames in the wall sconces.

The murmuring of the crowd enveloped Vivien as she walked through the wide corridor and into the public hall. There, people were gathered, so many people it was difficult just to walk. From them she sensed a myriad of things: awe, anger, resentment, pity. She struggled to shut them out, closed her eyes and allowed herself simply to be led by the hand at her elbow, a hand that belonged to a man whose fingers pressed hard into her skin, not out of anger or a desire to punish, but out of fear.

The Grand Magister led her through the public hall and into the main chamber of the Council Hall. There, more people had gathered. She opened her eyes and saw that every seat was taken, all by high elves that held the greatest status in Isbandar. In the center of the chamber sat the Council, the same elders she remembered from the last time she had been there. These were the ones who would now decide her fate... again.

A voice inside protested. *But they do not know! They weren't there!* The injustice of it stung. They could not possibly understand, yet they were comfortable sitting in judgment of her. Suddenly she felt closer to the Wolf. This must have been how he felt every time he was made to stand before the Council in Rithalion. The Magister led her to the appropriate seat, the one designated for those who were on trial. Directly behind it was seating for those who were in support of her. The only seats taken were those held by Mikarvan, Eveleen, and to her dismay, Torialvah. Her husband's face was set in unmoving stone, which she appreciated, though she was sure it was done for decorum and not for her benefit.

Blue Moon Rising rose from his place and stood before the pulpit. The gavel was struck only once in order for the murmuring of the crowd to cease, and the place was thrust into complete silence, everyone intent upon what was about to unfold.

"Lady Vivien Valdera, by the grace of this Council you were allowed to stay within the old College of Magic during your stay in our city. While there, you chose to break your word, and you used dragon magic."

He waited, then, letting the moment grow heavy and begin to fester. She felt guilt for the many mysteries she had divined from the interrogation notes she'd found, felt frustrated by her lifelong adoration of the fae that had abandoned her, felt so very alone, knowing the one champion that would never desert her was so far from this place.

Vivien lowered her eyes to the floor. When it became clear Blue Moon Rising was awaiting a response, she spoke. "Yes."

The mass intake of breath was more powerful and damning than any outraged invective could be.

His expression darkened, his eyes flashing with suppressed anger. "Your continued flouting of Elvish law is disgraceful, despicable, and deeply concerning. You leave us no choice, Valdera. We have been lenient, even merciful, but it is clear you have become too much of a danger to–"

Her father jerked, as though he barely managed to stop himself from leaping the table before them and rushing the councilman. He did stop himself, but his voice escaped with an equal amount of aggression. "This is outrageous! You cannot truly believe–"

Blue Moon Rising's face went from an angry frown to a furious rictus, "Grand Magister, you overstep your bounds! You are not in charge here. I am! Now be silent or I will have you thrown from the chamber!"

Jor'aiden shuddered, and visibly swallowed the rest of his words. Vivien could feel his emotions, rolling off him in waves: anger, helplessness, fear. And she knew his pain was all her fault. As he began to tremble, she felt something snap within her and she began to see everything as if watching from outside herself. It all seemed so distant, somewhat surreal. Every detail was captured, and everything became so important as she abandoned the storm raging inside her heart.

Blue Moon Rising sat and surveyed his perfect kingdom, having successfully cowed the great Grand Magister of Rithalion. Expressions of doubt and consternation dominated the faces of the other members of the Council. Ripples of emotion passed through the packed gallery, many of which mirrored those of her father.

The Grand Councilman began again, speaking with calm deliberation. "It is clear that Lady Valdera is a threat to this city and she will pay for her transgressions by–"

Jor'aiden bowed under the tone of finality, but Starling, like a yellow flash of sunshine, stood up from her seat behind them, "You cannot punish her! She was acting in defense! She SAVED people!"

Blue Moon Rising was silent for the briefest of moments, his face reddening. "SILENCE!" he exploded. "I will have silence! Guards, remove that woman!"

Vivien watched as the guards at hand did not move.

His baritone voice was like a slap across her face, resounding throughout the full chamber. "I said remove her!"

A guard from near the door hesitantly began to come forward when one of Vivien's jailors, from the group of guards closest to her, stood to bar the path, holding up a hand and shaking his head.

Blue Moon Rising's eyes looked like they might pop from his head. "YOU! Guard! Remove yourself AND that woman!"

The guard walked to stand at Vivien's side, removing his helmet. It was the one called Three Rivers and he spoke quietly, but certainly. "No. Grand Councilman, you are making a mistake. Lady Valdera did just as Starling has said."

More guards came from the hallway, but two more of Vivien's jailors stood at attention to block them. Another came forward to join the first that stood defiant of Blue Moon Rising and the rest of the Council. It was one of the men who had fallen before the interlopers at the college. He seemed to have healed well, but his face was tight with the strain of remaining upright for so long.

The Council was stunned. The gallery so quiet one could have heard the beating of a bird's wings. Blue Moon Rising finally broke the tableau with an angry snort. "What is the meaning of this?"

The first guard spoke, "I am Three Rivers."

Then the second, "I am Bronze Eagle. We were told to bring Lady Vivien Valdera for trial."

Blue Moon Rising was crimson, gesticulating wildly as he expostulated, "YES?!"

Murmuring broke out on all sides. Bronze Eagle looked to Evey, then back to the councilman. "There has not been a trial yet, but you are passing judgment." A dangerous silence descended on the room. "You may wish to punish her for what you think she did wrong, but know you are also punishing her for saving the lives of the men you posted at that college."

Blue Moon Rising was still crimson, but he began to laugh at the argument laid before him. "This is preposterous!"

Three Rivers snapped his spear butt onto the floor, making a deep wooden *thunk* like a gavel. "Do you even know who attacked us, Councilman? It was Crimson Bear!" The whole room gasped, "Crimson Bear, hero of the Battle of Thorn Ridge, Blademaster of Isbandar. He, his prized student, Winter Moon, and his son, Thunder Tree... each an expert of bladecraft that few of us could have matched. They were ready to murder us, and we were tasked to defend Lady Vivien Valdera. You may say that the Lady was already under the threat of death, but she did not use her magic to defend herself, but to defend US."

Blue Moon Rising's rage bounced off the walls like stones hurled by giants. "You speak without invitation by the Council and are relieved of duty!"

"You can dismiss my service, but not my words!" Three Rivers spat back. "And if this is justice, then I wonder what my duty is to, Councilman!"

Vivien could see it all. The men who had confined her to the college standing guard over her, the people on all sides in the galleries. Many were hostile. Some were confused. They began talking, sometimes yelling, at each other, until disorder ran rampant. The whole of the shaped, fictionally perfect glade of Isbandar, the council room itself, was a storm of discontent and noise that painted the walls so deeply it may never be removed. Tears began streaming down her face as she grieved for the peace of these people, her people, and its bitter ending.

Look at what I have done.

Then Anlon stood from his council seat. He banged the Book of Laws before him over and over. The percussion was deep and meaningful, but was unheard over the tumult of chaos and fear. Finally, he slammed the book onto the table and the symbol of justice worked into the metal of the binding popped off and went skittering out onto the floor. Her half-brother was breathing hard from lifting the weighty tome, but the chamber was finally coming under control.

Into the shredded silence, Blue Moon Rising's voice left a palpable frown. "We see how dragon magic has divided us as a people once again. It sets us against one another, and so we have no choice. Bring forth the Grand Inquisitor!"

Doors at the far end of the chamber were abruptly opened, and a white robed figure entered. From the moment of his entrance, silence spread amongst the older elves as if his sobering presence rippled from every step he took. Vivien saw him with dispassionate eyes and knew that he was old, very knowing, and extremely somber.

He came before the Council and every member sat a little straighter, a little more humble, and none looked him in the eye. By the time Blue Moon Rising spoke, the room held its breath without demands for silence.

"Inquisitor, you have served the people of Isbandar for centuries."

The white robed figure nodded, his voice holding the weight of centuries of duty and pain. "Yes."

"You have the skills to determine the truth from the accused, no matter where she has hidden them inside her mind?"

Again, one nod. "Yes."

Blue Moon Rising frowned as if passing judgment. "Ply your trade as you see fit in regards to Lady Valdera and report back to this Council."

"I shall begin preparation at first light." The figure spared one glance, and one glance only, at Vivien. His eyes were leaden, even regretful. Then he walked slowly from the chamber. Vivien spared a glance at her father. He was pale and his face was a sheen of sweat. He did not look back at her.

Blue Moon Rising stood again. His voice was raspy from screaming, his shoulders sagged, and his words held only a fraction of the command they held before. "You, disobedient guards, are dismissed from service to this Council and this city. Newly appointed guards will take Lady Valdera to the college. Twenty men will take the job of the seven original guardsmen, to ensure the safety of our city."

"Six." Bronze Eagle's voice interjected dispassionately. "There are only six of us left." Naked Feather died in the attack. Lady Valdera saved the rest of us from potential death as well."

Blue Moon Rising hesitated, his uncaring facade slipping for a moment to reveal the small bit of regret harbored within his heart before it was slid back into place, his demeanor hardening into stone. "There she will be held under guard until her true nature can be revealed. The Council has spoken! Clear the chamber."

The Grand Magister suddenly whirled upon Vivien and took her into his arms. He whispered vague apologies to her out of a constricted throat. Over his shoulder she could see her half-brother where he sat with the rest of the Council. Anlon's face was a mask of misery and grief. She marveled at it the same way one was in awe of a wolf at the kill, or a bird in flight. Everyone was trapped in one emotion or another as she was taken from the chamber and led through the streets back to the old, dilapidated College.

All she felt was a buzzing numbness. And at that moment, she truly hoped to not feel anything ever again.

Chapter Thirty-Six
Guarding the Jewel

GREGOR GIEL HAD SPENT much of his life aspiring to be a good man, then a good soldier, and even hoping for command one day. When command had arrived, it turned out that he may have needed a little more seasoning. Then again, since being a simple soldier, he had become La'athai and sometimes being a good La'athai meant something different than being a good soldier. The Pack fought like wolves, and today Isbandar was learning that. He held the scrap of cloth to his face, staunching the cut on his cheek given to him by the fist of a city guardsman.

The tavern was a shambles. The beautiful structure of woven reeds and thin trees had a few new holes. When the barkeep finally dared emerge from wherever she was hiding, he would tell her the place needed more windows. Failing that, he'd blame the city guard. Part of the trellis had been demolished, and that was definitely their fault. He looked from one La'athai to the next and saw grim nods and even carnivorous grins all around. A few missing teeth, a few broken bones, but they had given better than they had gotten. All eyes turned sour, however, as they looked across the tavern to where the city guards lay sprawled. The local healer was tending to them first. To be fair, they were worse off all in all, but it still felt unfair.

"You lead these... these?" The Captain of the City Guard had his upper lip curled and a massive frown, looked like someone invisible was following him around with a little turd held under his nose as he stepped over the battered wreckage of his men. Gregor felt a trill of fear, but looked back to the other La'athai and steeled himself the way he thought the Wolf would.

He lowered his voice as far as it would go. "These are La'athai, Captain."*I sound like an idiot*, and he coughed back into his normal speaking voice. "I would hope for at least a little respect from someone of your station."

The man sniffed his turd. "They will earn respect if they do not tear up my city. Perhaps a day in jail will cool them off?"

Suddenly, Gregor felt the fear fall away, and certainty thrummed through him. "I wouldn't do that, Captain."

The captain's grimace vanished. "Oh, and why not?" Perhaps the offending turd smell was gone, replaced with the perfume of him being able to pass judgment down any way he wanted.

Gregor felt his blood rise and his fists started to clench. "Because these are blooded soldiers who see themselves as standing guard over their commander, wrongly imprisoned. They take that job very seriously."

The captain rocked back as if struck and came very close to hiss at Gregor. "How dare you question the judgment of the Council of Isbandar!"

Gregor hissed back, "We were taught to dare by your men, who snickered about her imprisonment and said that she was better burned alive in the city square. Your men started this, so if you come in and jail mine for defending her right to a trial, thing will go very badly very quickly. They are becoming convinced that no ma er what the truth of the matter, she will be found guilty."

He let *and when at happens* hang in the air unsaid.

The captain jerke back again, then frowned to cover his retreat. "All my life, I have seen soldi rs at idle, and know that they soon become trouble. Find a way, La'athai. Kee them busy." He then turned without allowing comment to go to the other side of the tavern to see to his guardsmen.

Far from snubbed Gregor cheered inwardly. *I faced him down! I did it!* He reached over the bar nd picked a bottle of cider at random, tossed a coin from his pouch onto the ar to pay for it, and uncorked it with his teeth. He dismissed the idea of earching for a glass and took a swig. It tasted of apples and cinnamon, wood and earthy with a tart zing of summer. He heard a gasp, looked back toward e door to see the crimson hair and the mercurial blue eyes of Starling, Viv n's niece, as she entered the tavern and stopped to gape at the wreckage. He niled at her and lifted the bottle in salute as she picked her way through the prawled guards that were now getting a proper dressing down from the capt n. Apparently, he had learned they had *also* dared to question the judgmer of the Council of Isbandar and were getting another beating for it.

Starling came ose with concern written across her face. "What happened?"

Gregor smiled wi ely, taking another swig. "Well, as it turns out, we had a disagreement with so e of the local watchmen."

She looked at th group of La'athai, and then more closely at the city guardsmen. She squir ed. "Is that a bite mark on that man?"

If I find out who d that, I'll buy him a drink. "Well, discussions got a little tense."

Starling seemed have a dozen more questions but she shook them off. "Gregor, your Lady n eds you."

Gregor lowered t bottle to the nearest table, instantly forgotten. "What is it?"

She came close, pitching her voice down low. "The man at the council today, he is an Inquis or. He will soon be visiting her." Gregor shook his head. A young low elf of m stly human heritage, he had only heard of Inquisitors in passing, or what the y did, during his time in school many years ago. He wracked his mind, try ng to recall, but it simply didn't come to him. But by the tone of Starling's vo e, he could guess that it was nothing good for Lady Valdera. "Plus, there re more guardsmen with her now, but we are afraid with the college so empty that another assassin may get in–"

Gregor halted h r with an upraised hand, cursing himself. The whole reason so many of th m had come out drinking was to take the edge off the worries they had about her safety. He thought hard, wondering what, if anything, he could do What would he be allowed to do?

What would the Wolf do?

There was, of course the obvious answer.

"You have to come with me. I think I know what to do." Gregor turned to the La'athai, "Time to run, pack-of-mine. Leave your drinks, there will be more later if we are lucky."

Starling shrugged. "Where are we–?"

"Not here."

To a soul, the La'athai gathered themselves and begin to file out of the tavern. Gregor followed behind, making sure none stopped to taunt or kick the defeated guardsmen, and pausing himself only long enough to pass off the opened cider bottle to the captain. "Peace offering."

Once in the street, they formed into a cloud of soldiers and took off at a jog, Starling working hard to keep up after a few blocks. The streets were so different here, more of a tangled mass of oversized deer paths that ran between the woven homes of Isbandar, but they traversed them easily for all but Evey knew where they were going.

In minutes they had gone a fair distance, and came to a hill festooned with tall trees bearing thick branches. Tir-reath lay along those branches, resting and watching them with detached curiosity. An entrance into the hillside was well travelled, and the La'athai raced into it.

Evey paused, clearly nonplussed. "We are going inside there? It looks like some sort of animal's den."

Gregor took her by the arm and steered her along with the rest of the pack "Come on."

They entered the dark hole, the musky scent of so many large cats enveloping them immediately. Glowstones were lovingly embraced by ornate bronze wall sconces. The soft light illuminated chamber after chamber of alcoves large enough to lay down in. About half of them were filled with lounging felines. A caretaker smiled and waved as she fought with one of the big cats to remove some furs from the nooks where the tir-reath had been hoarding them. The La'athai waved back and moved onwards.

They passed the first sand pit latrine, a row of nooks all empty but for one that had four tir-reath sleeping in a pile, and even deeper into the den. They came to a final chamber of about thirty nooks and the tir-reath there bounded down to see their masters and mistresses.

Gregor spoke quickly. "Taz, Seth, grab your mounts and watch the hall." Both La'athai took their mounts and moved to obey.

Only then did he turn to Starling and level his eyes at her, hoping he hid his fear well. "Tell me everything."

That was why, in the middle of the afternoon, Gregor, Starling, and nine La'athai came to the gates of the college of magic. The council guards were very much equipped like the city guards, but they had more polish on their gear, nicer clothing and an air of superiority. The guards stood straighter, for the La'athai were equipped for battle and amply armed.

"What business do you have here?" one guard asked.

Gregor decided to give a winning smile. "Escorting the young healer to her assignment."

The guard frowned, but Starling slid past them with a slight smile on her lips and entered the college. The guard's frown became deeper. "We are not letting all of you inside."

Gregor made a dismissive wave. "Oh, we don't want in."

The other guard shook his head. "So, move along, then."

Gregor felt his smile move from friendly to feral. "No. I think we will wait here." Then he turned to the others. "I'll go with one other to make the first pair, next leaves in five minutes." Then he and Taz left at a moderate walk, starting the roving patrol around the building to guard the Lady inside. The walk was good for a moment as they relished the confusion of the council guards behind.

Taz shrugged. "That worked perfectly."

Gregor smiled, but remembered poor Rohan and his never-ending pessimism. He'd never forget his death at the hands of the Liath that ill-fated day, and Gregor missed him greatly. Then his eyes caught movement and he narrowed them to slits. "Who goes there?"

"So, you shiny, breast-plated tosspots finally..." The sardonic voice trailed off as the dark haired, dark eyed Gregor walked into view. The man shook his head. "You are not guards."

Gregor shrugged and stepped a little ahead and to the side, hiding Taz's body enough that she could put her hand on her sword without too much notice. He held up his hands to show they were empty. "We're in service to Lady Valdera, and we are worried about her safety here."

The man nodded. "You are right to be. The swordsmen and assassins she saved us from could have killed us all."

"You were there?"

"Seven of us were. One of us was slain. The rest of us spoke for her at the trial and were dismissed from service for it."

"Then why are you here?"

The man stiffened, emotion tightening his body as if waiting for attack. "She saved our lives. We know where to guard to make it harder for anyone to try to get in again. We have decided that is what we are going to do."

Gregor looked him over. "Unarmed?"

He smirked. "Do you have a spare sword?" Gregor shrugged, and he saw the idea blossom in the man and leap whole out of his mouth without consideration. "Or maybe a uniform?"

Gregor blinked hard. "You want to become La'athai?"

"If you are sworn to her service, I would be. I know all six of us would be."

"And you say you know where we have to watch?"

"No matter what, I'll tell you everything I know."

Gregor looked behind him to see the next pair of La'athai coming around the corner, walking too fast and coming too early. At the moment, it worked out in his favor. "Taz, head back to the Pack and enter the end of the rotation. Remind them to not get into it with the guards under any circumstances. I'm going with... uh?"

"Bronze Eagle is my shield name."

"I'm going with Bronze Eagle to find his companions and gain six new La'athai."

Taz shook her head. "Lieutenant, can you just... *adopt* someone into the La'athai?"

"I'm guessing An'drath will be happier than Valdera would be displeased." He slapped Bronze Eagle across the back. "Half my Pack are sleeping in the barracks for their shift in twelve hours. We can find you weapons and armor."

They started to walk briskly and Taz passed them at a jog headed back to the entrance to the college. Bronze Eagle jerked his chin at her. "Is she right? Can you really just make us La'athai?"

"You have the heart. And if someone makes me in charge of the ceremony, it will be a drinking contest, but I have one convenient rule that I follow at times like this one."

"And it is?"

"Nobody ever said I couldn't."

Chapter Thirty-Seven
Temptation

The envoy had departed as they had arrived: without fanfare and without delay. The sun had barely risen, and the trees had been assaulted all night by frost and were losing what brown, withered leaves clung to their skeletal branches. The tir-reath were not happy and had to be coaxed from their warm dens, but by the time that was done, the Wolf had departed the city gates astride the large, white reindeer and plunged back into the wilds.

Zaahr had seemed to want to make some apology when they had departed, and a look from The Lord of Swords and Truth had indicated wordlessly that The Wolf should be grateful. He still wore his kilt, but beneath it he had strapped thick leather plates. His arms and chest were likewise covered in vambracers, gauntlets, and paltrons. His chest was now wrapped in a thick leather vest with steel plates sewn between the layers. At his side was a new sword made of Elvish steel and a long dagger, though he still had the simple woodsman's axe on the back of the deer. He had a new thick cloak and the most comfortable rigid boots he had ever owned. It had not taken much to look grateful to Zaahr, but he kept to himself that he still felt a deep cold of loss inside.

They were all freshly provisioned, packs groaning with food and water. And though only one night off of the road, the animals and men were heartened by the night of warmth and comfort so that the next day travel did not feel quite so punishing. The absolute success of having fifteen thousand competent and trained soldiers coming to Rithalion lifted their spirits even further, even as the land felt the first fingers of cold winter claw autumn from the trees and sky. Of their number, the only one that did not walk lighter was the Wolf, and he knew it.

The image of Vivien living behind bars of iron came whenever his eyes were closed even a moment. The hardships were nothing, the cold was nothing, thirst was nothing. All that mattered was getting back to her side. He would awake each morning with the memory of her scent stolen from his nose. He had lived for a century wandering the wild places with no comforts to keep him warm, but now that he had found her, it was like coming in from the cold to a warm fire, only to have home snatched away. He was no longer inured to the solitude and loss. The first day, the Wolf found it went faster to lead his mount and jog ahead of it so it did not have to carry his impressive weight. Speed was needed, for the Liath had become a sharp bone in the soup.

Suddenly he was there, hung upside down, blood draining from a hundred tiny wounds into jars and bottles. Cruel faces swam into and out of focus. It wasn't when they stabbed him with needles or cut him with knives, but when they slapped him lightly like he was an old hound piddling on the floor. It was when they treated him like he was harmless, and he was impotent to stop them. He shrunk into himself and he shuddered.

He shook free of the visions of torture, suddenly angry with himself. His monstrous body had healed itself as it always did. And Vivien, kind Vivien, tender Vivien, had suffered so much more at the hands of the demon elves than he. He shoved the pain and doubts of his capture into a pit at the back of his mind and marched on, determined to make better time to Moirdem than the guessed fourteen days. Yet, as he walked through the cold, hibernating land, the sound of his boots crunching frost in the morning and slogging through wetness in the afternoon, the echoes of his own helpless screams came again from the pit where he had hidden them. Finally, he stumbled into camp a couple hours earlier than was his norm.

Katriona was there, golden haired and fit. She took the reins to his mount and helped him set down his saddle and packs by his tent. His legs wobbled as he settled down, and he made only slight protest as Katriona took his beast to be fed and watered. There was a fire built, and he relished the warmth. One of the other La'athai brought him a thick stew laden with meat and he nodded his thanks before gobbling it up and unbuckling his armor.

"You look tired, brother."

The Wolf had not heard Xadrian arrive, and shook his head. He had long since begun to feel safe amongst the La'athai, the least Elvish elves he had ever met. Still, it was a bad habit. "Walked the reindeer. Made better time. Travel two more hours tomorrow on the tir-reath. I can make it."

"Wolf..."

It was even the hint of protest that caused his eyes to flash red. "I am not killing the animal."

Xadrian's features tightened. "You are killing yourself."

The Wolf set down the vest on a blanket spread before his saddle, lay upon it with his head on the saddle, and dragged his cloak over himself as Katriona returned. "Didn't you hear, Lord? Dragons, giants, and Liath couldn't do it. Walking surely won't."

Then he shut his eyes and pretended to sleep.

He heard Katriona half whisper at some distance, "Will he harm himself pushing so hard?"

And Xadrian's reply, "He is driven. Tortured, even. Tomorrow we will ride for two more hours and then set camp."

"But..."

"You have your orders." And his tone brooked no argument.

It was then that the Wolf fell asleep.

His dreams were stark and frightening, with lighting the color of blood from no known source. He wandered the halls of the ziggurat where he had been imprisoned, searching for Vivien. He called for her, crashing through doors and even walls of dreamt stone, but all he found was maniacal laughter and the echoes of screams.

He woke up what felt like an instant, and yet a lifetime, later, but the sky was already lighting with false dawn against a lid of heavy clouds. He could see the breath of every sentry and early stirring soldier, and his own most of all. Steam rose from his shoulders as he gathered his gifted armor and weapons back onto his person and collected his gear. The cloak over his shoulders was wet from the moisture pregnant in the air, and chilled as it was ignored by the timid sun. He breathed in and could almost smell Vivien's light musk. He shook away the comfort and fetched his mount, then loaded her with saddle and packs. The tir-reath had traveled faster, but now that the weather was turning bitter, they huddled in unhappy piles with each other, too big to snuggle with their masters inside of the small, portable tents.

He finished tightening the last buckle as Katriona came from her tent. Askew and disheveled, she looked to her commander with lips pressed into a thin line. "Two hours more on the ride, then?"

The Wolf nodded.

She did not dissent, nor bargain. She nodded like a good soldier. "We will see you at camp."

The Wolf felt a shadow of a smile pull at one side of his face. "Thank you."

He led his mount off. First at a walk through the maze of tents, then as he passed the sentries, he returned salutes and broke into a jog. The Wolf ran through a hundred details in his mind over and over. How long would it take the Iron Coast to muster? How long would it take the elves to respond to calls of aid? How much food could be stored in that length of time? Would the Liath come into play, somehow? And the constant stream of worry drowned out the echoes in the pit.

He travelled until noon and then fed the reindeer from a sack of grain before eating his own leathery dried fruits and salty nuts while on his feet. They drank from a fast-moving stream and walked instead of resting.

They came into camp, man and deer, tired and worn. He fed and brushed the sweat from his mount, then went to the command fire and lay out his things. Katriona came to him with freshly fried skillet bread cooked with meat, potatoes, cheese, and nuts worked into the dough. He ate the crumbly golden disk greedily and nodded his thanks. He saw the look of concern on her face, but could not spare the energy to address it. He fell asleep in minutes.

He awoke to almost total darkness, but the state of the fire told him it was nearly dawn. He worked wearily, mechanically. He readied his mount, gathered his gear, loaded up and left before even Katriona was awake. He walked and jogged guided by his sense of direction without sun or stars. The short hiatus from the road in Sharderia had worn out, and the constant jog then walk pace was beginning to wear him down again. His mind disconnected from every moment, and he felt himself snap into place, unsure of how many miles had passed. He would curse himself and try to focus again, only to begin hearing the screams in the pit of his mind and fade off again.

Then, at the start of the afternoon, which looked more like twilight, the sky cracked open and the rain began to fall in thick sheets. Man and deer lowered their heads and pressed onward. Eating was difficult, and they had to drink from their stores of water for every creek was muddy and churned. Still they pressed onward. A little after the appointed time, the Wolf saw the struggling lights of the campfires from the top of the last hill he would crest that day.

He trudged into camp, the sentry giving a tired salute. Many of the elf-blood soldiers had doubled up in their small tents, using the spare canvas to rig coverings between the trees so that the tir-reath would be spared the worst of the rain. He unloaded his mount under the awning and carried his gear through to the sputtering command fire. The tents had been pitched on a slight incline, and the area around the uphill sections of the tents had been trenched almost a hand deep. It collected the water into a fast-moving channel around the sleepers, and left them dry. He continued to the fire where he looked at the sodden ground and felt a part of him give a resigned sigh.

"Come in!"

He could barely hear the words over the sound of the rain, but there was Katriona, with the flap to her tent open, gesturing. Without much thought, the Wolf bent double and entered.

Katriona, having supplied her own, had a slightly larger tent than others, but once the Wolf entered and brought along his gear, the space was filled to capacity. He went to his knees under the low ceiling and set down his saddle.

"Stop!"

He stopped, looked to each of the four walls with a hand going toward his long dagger. A musical trill halted him. It was Katriona's laugh. She giggled at him like a young girl, covering her mouth with one hand. "I just meant you are getting water everywhere."

The Wolf closed his eyes, and shoved the threatening screams back into the jail, and faked a smile while he took deep breaths and tried to let the knots go from his shoulders. When he opened his eyes, Katriona wore an expression of deep concern. She got to her knees. "Wait. Just wait, Knight Protector."

She was wearing only a white shift that came to mid-thigh, and now that it was dark, she seemed a shadow of a departed queen, The Wolf blinked twice but stood still as she came the knee-step or two toward him and began relieving him of packs and saddlebags, putting them in the corner but away from the canvas walls. Then she took his cloak and held it out of the tent to ring it out. Surprisingly, when she brought in the bundle, it shed a little water but was mostly dry. The process, however had sluiced water down her arms and legs, with a splash on her chest that turned the white shift transparent where it touched her skin. One pink nipple pressed, puckered, against the cold cloth, but she paid it no mind. He swallowed.

His leather must have been similarly treated, for the water had already beaded and slid off. The shirt was not so lucky, and while she wrung it out though the flap, it was still dripping wet. Still, she unbuckled the stays to his arms and chest, removing the pieces and placing them in an orderly mess. Then she reached to his sword belt.

"Kat–"

She shushed him as the belt came free and she plopped it, the sword, and the dagger in their sheaths, down on her cloth and leather pallet. Then she turned back. She took his belt in powerful hands meant to bend a bow and–

"Kat–"

"Shush."

–undid the fasten, taking the leather and kilt in one mass, exposing his manhood to her. Woken from cold slumber by her breast, it did not stand at attention, so much as hang heavy and full in anticipation. She wrung out the kilt as well, but where the linen shirt had dripped and came back damp, the heavy wool of the tartan gushed water and sluiced her front from neck to knees and came back still sodden. She focused on it, shrugging and laying it by the door behind her. Her front was cold and wet, the shift giving no protection to modesty. She looked him in the eyes, though, not a hint of flush or shame.

"Kat–"

"Boots," she said. He blinked at her. "Sit down and take off your boots. Remember, I don't do boots."

He felt like he had walked into a dream, too hot and too close to everything around him. He shuffled his bulk to sit and removed his boots, but long before that he heard the dove-wings sound of her removing her shift and letting it flutter into the far corner. The second boot came off as she rummaged in her own pack. He swallowed hard as he turned to find her sitting, gloriously cross-legged, with a dry rag and bottle in her hand.

Her body was lithe and taut. It had spent many human lifetimes in training and it had burned all traces of fat from her, but could not rob her of her femininity. Her breasts were pert and firm, with the small nipples of a woman who has never suckled a child. Her hips were gentle and filled with muscle. The line of her pubic hair was clean and the hair short, as if she'd trimmed it with sharp knives before taking to the ride from Isbandar. He lowered his eyes. She thrust the rag and bottle in front of them, her voice containing a slight grin.

"Oil up your sword, Knight Protector."

He looked into her face, which indeed had a carefree smirk upon it. She sat upon the pallet without a hint of shame, and offered him to do the same. He took a deep breath, reminding himself that these were elves, with different ways as he maneuvered his muscle beside her. She took the weapons belt from behind her and gave it to him, then pulled her hair back as he made it ring from the sheath.

He began to carefully go down the length with an oiled rag, chasing away the wetness and guarding against rust. It was a simple task, a common task, and he felt tension seep from his shoulders. He took a deep breath, working the oil into the intricate designs on the hilt.

"Who is Ravn Blacach?"

The Wolf felt the words like a cold crash against him. He froze. The admission had seemed proper in the council chamber, but hearing that name, here, from lips other than Vivien's, made his blood stop in its flow. He set the sword aside. "It is what I was."

She placed a light hand on his shoulder and moved it along scars gained from fighting a bear in Rithalion. "Who you were?"

He nodded.

Her fingers moved to another scar on his back, where an Elvish arrow had pierced him after he had saved the Lady of Moonlight and Love. "When?"

He lowered his head. "A long time ago."

She moved, cool and smooth against his skin as she proceeded to sit between his thighs. The cool air still puckered her nipples and he felt the silken texture of her hair along his shoulder. Her vulva pressed against his half erect penis and he felt it jump at the attention. There was a wetness there, a dampness that could not be explained by the heavy downpour of rain. Her muscular thighs were on either side of his hips, and her arms around his bull neck. But her face was still serene, her motions confident as she traced other scars and came to the massive Y that dominated his naked chest.

"When you got this?" He nodded wordlessly. He inhaled through his nose and he could smell her sex like a giddy perfume. He felt his eyes begin to pulse and he knew they glowed some color as his staff came to attention in a moment, looking to plunge into her. She smiled kindly. "You are a mighty warrior, Ravn Blacach."

"I am a monster. The Grand Magister says so."

"I don't see a monster. I see a man in pain. Always so strong, but always in pain."

Ravn breathed fast and shallow through his mouth, but he swore he could already taste her. Her smile took on an impish quality and she shifted, allowing his erection to pop up between them before she straddled it with her lower lips. He felt the wetness of her warm opening against the base of his shaft. His manhood was over-taught, like a water skin filled to bursting. It needed release, and it thrummed for the blonde mound that cradled it so gently with its welcoming heat.

She whispered in his ear, "I've hurt, too." She slid up the length of his shaft, pulling against his neck to leave a trail of her lubrication from his sack to the head peeking out of his foreskin. She hung there, tip of his spear against the aching entrance to her heaven, settling just enough to put the tip at the opening. "Let us be together and heal each other just a little."

He could hear his heartbeat. He was certain she could hear his heartbeat too. His blood pulsed and his head swam with urges to take her. He blinked. For a split second, he saw not Katriona, but Vivien straddling him there. In that moment, he nearly lost control and plunged into her to the hilt, pumping deeply for all his life was worth.

But it wasn't Vivien.

It was Katriona.

He whispered, at the edge of control, "Please..."

She whispered back, pulling herself close until her nipples pushed into his chest. "What?"

"I..."

She dragged her nipples back and forth. "Yes?"

"I..."

She let loose just enough to look him in the eyes. "Yes?"

They glowed. They were glowing blue. "I belong to HER."

She looked shocked, and almost settled upon his shaft. Then she backed away and sat again on the pallet between his thighs, his rock-hard erection still looking for her. She looked a little hurt, then confused. She did not ask who 'her' was, but threw her long golden hair from her face. "You... you know we are different? We are elves."

The Wolf shook his head, feeling it clear of the primordial lust. "I am not."

"Wolf, she is so confused. Her life is in constant upheaval. She's emotional and flighty and indecisive."

Ravn shook his head. "You do not know the woman I know. She is none of those things."

Katriona's brow furrowed, "I respect her and follow her into battle, but can you honestly tell me her life has not been chaotic?"

Ravn smiled into her green-flecked blue eyes. "What kind of man says he loves a woman if he does not mean he will be there in any uncertainty?"

"You are crazy." She looked downcast for a moment, then shockingly took his phallus in her hand, halting its deflation momentarily. "It is nice to know you find me attractive."

The Wolf felt himself blush as he gently took her fingers from him. "Yes."

"So, you are in love with Vivien Valdera."

"Without question and without hesitation."

She sighed and shrugged, scuttled back to lay on the pallet. "Well, the least you can do is warm my bed, Knight Protector. Sleeping next to you may be like sleeping next to a bonfire, but tonight it will be welcome."

Ravn thought to protest, then shrugged and lay down on his back. He slept without dreams for the first time in weeks, but woke to find her hand again wrapped around his morning erection. He gently disengaged her, dressed, and left to relieve himself. It was before dawn and the rain continued to assault the ground with a sense of malice. He had no time to delay or deviate. The rain had caused them to slog until they found the ancient trade route.

Raised by great magic in ancient times by the elves, it was like the road in Rithalion, made of huge hexagonal blocks. Once there, they would travel another seven days.

And he did not sleep in Katriona's tent again.

Chapter Thirty-Eight
Spare No Detail

he entered the chamber quietly. Books lay forgotten on shelves. A fire crackled behind a vented brass screen in the fireplace. The floor was covered with thick woven rugs. It had survived well despite centuries of neglect. He remembered studying in this very room in his youth. Before the war. Then, it had been a refuge, but now it had forgotten solitude that soaked in to every pore of every surface. He relished the silence, needed it. There was far too little silence in the world. He could feel her eyes upon him immediately, and he paused to smile and nod. People so often assumed his job was about screaming and violence. It was not. It was so often about serenity; no one would ever believe it.

The subject was a beautiful woman, though pregnancy and strain had robbed a great deal of the color from her cheeks. Once immaculate hair was slightly askew and her clothes were disheveled from being stored in a pack or pile on the floor instead of in a wardrobe. As prisons went, she had a wonderful accommodation. But it was still a prison, and she was clearly a creature that did not thrive in captivity. Even here, in a comfortable chair in the small sitting room in the college, she appeared cornered and hunted. She had spent many years of her life studying magic in rooms just like this one, yet it brought her no peace. He noted it and then let it slide from his mind.

All but two chairs had been removed, and all the tables, so it was starker than he would like. Yet it was needed in this case, as were the soldiers. The two guards behind her were alert, and their very presence made her wary. Wary people all had one thing in common, in his experience.

They all had something to hide.

He smiled again and she looked at him askance. He sat in the chair, adjusting his robes to smooth out any wrinkles and make sure the multitude of amulets, rings, bracelets and trinkets were hidden. Every Inquisitor before had left him one or two of these devices. She was a mage, and so he knew she could feel the power crackling inside of them. Each was designed to a singular purpose: to defend him from magical attack from dragon mages, their spells, and even dragons themselves. They were his armor against her.

She did not say anything, so he opened simply, "Good evening, Lady Valdera."

She nodded abruptly. "I expected you days ago."

He smiled slightly, a small kindness to her. "I imagine you did. You know who I am?"

"You are the Grand Inquisitor." Waves of apprehension came from her, an incoming tide of fear.

"That is correct. You know why I am here?"

"You are trying to find out if I am a dragon mage."

"Well, no. We already know you are a dragon mage." He paused just a heartbeat, expecting some kind of excuse or denial. When it did not come, he simply moved onward. "What I am here for is to determine how, when and why."

"I don't understand."

"You have already used dragon magic in defiance of Elvish law. That is not in doubt. But what we have is a celebrated and decorated Knight Mage of Rithalion who has broken one of our most sacred taboos. You understand the concern?"

She looked back and forth at the guards that stood at attention behind her. "What concern?"

"We will find our way there. What I need to ascertain to begin with is when exactly you began to study dragon magic and how long you have been a Liath," he said simply.

Color drained from her face, and her fingers rubbed against palms he was certain were already sweaty. "I am not a Liath."

The Grand Inquisitor leaned back into the chair, focusing his mind on presenting a relaxed facade. The more at ease he appeared, the more agitated the subject would be. "By the very definition, you are."

She leaned forward in her seat, body becoming rigid and causing the guards to become alert behind her. "That's not true!"

He nodded and adopted an understanding tone. "I need you to help me understand that."

Vivien slumped back in her seat, tears rimming her eyes, hands cradling her belly. "You can't understand."

Again, the grand Inquisitor smiled sadly. "We must try."

She shook her head, but she told him. He took no notes. But closed his eyes and committed every detail to his prodigious memory. He had trained for decades for this job as a young elf. Now all the lessons he had learned were about to be applied.

Sometimes she told vivid details, and others she simply related moments of time. Her tale was tragic, and fraught with peril and adversity. He made no comment, and instead let her meander from point to point, culminating with her capture by the Liath and her eventual escape. The candles burned low and the fire was dying late at night by the time she was done. She was weeping openly. He casually produced a handkerchief from a fold of his robes and gave it to her.

He stood slowly and nodded to her. "Thank you, Lady Valdera. I think that is enough for today."

She gasped around her tears, "Today? What more do you need to know?"

He spread his hands a bit, feigning powerlessness. "There are questions I have, but not today. We have not paused to take a meal and you should be allowed to rest."

He turned to go, but her next words stopped him. "How long have you been an Inquisitor?"

He considered dismissing her question, but he needed to keep her talking, and sometimes it required exposing oneself just a bit in order to make a subject strip themselves bare. "Since the Dragon War."

She looked taken aback. "How many Inquisitors are there?"

His eyebrows shot up. "In this city? I am the only one."

She looked as if she had been slapped. If she had been alabaster, and then wan, now she looked almost green but for the deep red circles under her eyes. "There is only you?"

The Grand Inquisitor nodded. "Only me, now. I was trained a very long time ago, and trained to the direst need. It has been a long, sad thing to know my purpose was born of the pain of my people, but it is my duty and I accept it."

Then he left. The guards, he knew, would take her back to her chamber. She would be fed and confined there. He went to a lower floor and opened a door with the wave of his hand. He entered his temporary abode and sat at the desk. It amused him earlier in the day to occupy the same chamber in his old age that he had while studying magic, but now he waved all memories away and opened a thin blank book, whispering to the fae hidden in the thin rod at his hand to start the end smoking with heat. He plied the red-hot point to the page, burning the words into the thick vellum. His script was tiny, but he filled page after page with notes of Lady Valdera's version of events. He worked far into the morning, then lay on the bed in a night shift and slept.

He awoke drenched in sweat, a scream almost to his lips.

He closed his eyes and pulled his emotions away from the images of blood. Few alive remembered the stained and gouged chair in the dungeon of the college. The Grand Inquisitor remembered. He could not forget. For scores of years, he had dreamed of the unending screams that haunted that place, the things that were done. But for scores more he had been an absolute expert in interrogation with no reason to interrogate. His very presence had been considered too horrific to ever be used on lesser criminals than the dragon mages. He had been unused like a warrior's sword long into retirement. He had been happy to leave his purpose aside to live in solitude. The nightmares had even decided to leave him alone. He ran a hand through hair white with age, not yet silver. It came away soaked.

He stood and walked hesitantly past the open book of notes to the window. With a simple wave of his hand the fae inside the opening peeled back the twisted lattice of branches and taking away the panes of glass held between them. He saw the new dawn coming over the forest to the east. Weeks ago, the sunrise had brought him hope, peace. Today it was like it had been so long ago; he saw the sun and feared what would come of the day. He closed his eyes and tried to control the nest of snakes angrily twisting in his stomach. He could give himself only a moment, for he had a day to get started upon, and his efforts were less than successful.

He motioned the [ ]e window back into place and turned back to the spartan students' room. He m[ ]de the bed with crisp edges and he removed his night shift. This he folded n[ ]atly and placed on the fresh bed. Out of the wardrobe he produced clean robes and calmed his mind and body, putting on every piece with ritual precision[ ]Finally came the defensive amulets, the rings, the bracelets, and bracers[ ]He had once commented to a senior that with such an array of defenses he [ ]ould be able to survive even a dragon's breath. The old elf, finally dying, ha[c] shot out a cold, dry hand and gripped his arm fiercely, saying, "*Let us hope s[ ].*"

The Grand Inquis[ ]or smoothed out all wrinkles from his vestments, picked up the book of notes [ ]n Valdera, and left. He did not meet Vivien in the halls, nor her healer, and it [ ]vas just as well. He nodded to the council guards as he exited the college an[c] walked the city streets toward the Council Hall. Most in the city had been hap[ ]y to leave him in peace, had been glad to forget his kind ever existed. Now the[ ] had been forcibly reminded of his presence. The eldest looked at him with fe[ ]r, or awe, or respect. Most of the others had never been told his kind existed, [ ]ad faces that were frightened, or surprised, or uncertain. He solemnly nodded [ ] them all, aware that in these robes he was no longer an elf, but a symbol, a p[ ]ition.

He entered the ch[ ]mbers unmolested, trying and failing to take a moment to marvel at the ma[ ]ive copse of trees that had been shepherded into the massive building. He [ ]ook another breath to steady himself, but found that any comfort he could gath[ ]r wandered lost and alone inside the hollow inside of his chest. He continued [ ]cross the elf-crafted glade of judgment and through a doorway into the wa[ ]ens beyond. He took the turns from memory, and soon stood at the door for [ ]ue Moon Rising.

The portal of brai[ ]ed branches was yanked open as he arrived. Fire Hunter was there, being all b[ ]t pushed out the door by Blue Moon Rising. The Grand Inquisitor instantly as[ ]essed the elves and determined neither had hardly slept, nor probably ate, or e[ ]en rested since the council session two days before.

Fire Hunter drew[ ]up short of bumping into the Inquisitor. He looked shocked and moved a[ ]ide, only able to mumble an apology before Blue Moon Rising ushered him in[ ]"And as you can see, I have an appointment. If you will excuse us." With that, [B]lue Moon Rising shut the door in Fire Hunter's face.

The elder statesn[ ]an sighed. The Grand Inquisitor saw him try to draw more energy from an [ ]mpty well inside, and wondered if, indeed, he truly had not slept at all. But w[ ]ere rest could not be had, the man seemed determined to make due with formal[ ]ty. He moved behind his desk and motioned for his guest to have a seat, but ins[ ]ad of sitting himself, he leaned forward, staring intently at the Grand Inquisito[ ]. "You spoke with her?"

The Inquisitor n[ ]dded calmly, "Of course, Councilman. Long into the night."

Blue Moon Risin[ ]'s face creased into a deep scowl. "Why did you not come to me sooner?"

The Grand Inquisitor felt a moment's irritation, then let it pass from him as if being washed away by a gentle rain. "Because our appointment was for this morning."

Blue Moon leaned even further forward and set his knuckles upon his desk. "You could have come. I told you this was urgent."

Immediately the Inquisitor slipped into his professional mind-space. It was a mask he had been taught to wear during an interrogation. Immediately, Blue Moon Rising's ire could not touch him. He saw him with new eyes, and easily found a way to push him off balance. "Councilman, I understand you came to Isbandar after living in Pergatium?"

Blue Moon Rising straightened as if he felt the prick of a dagger at his back. "What do you mean?"

The Grand Inquisitor took a deep breath, as if dealing with a recalcitrant adolescent. "You were not in Isbandar during the trials. The Interrogation is a delicate thing. It requires subtlety. Gentleness. It cannot be rushed."

The councilman frowned deeply. "I know of the interrogation room in the basement of the college. Take her there and get the truth from her."

Again, the Grand Inquisitor felt his ire rise, and had to exert control to stop from shaking phantom screams of pain from his ears. "You do not know how these things are done."

"Do not be coy."

"I am not being evasive in the least. The chair is in a dungeon, Councilman. The dungeon is for the guilty. It is not for those you hope are guilty."

"You have used it hundreds of times in the past!"

The Grand Inquisitor stood, and Blue Moon Rising's eyes went wide, as if seeing the elderly elf before him for the first time and sensing the hard interior beneath the civilized exterior. He spoke without anger, but with a voice of command that had stripped minds bare and exposed dark secrets. "And the dungeon, like delving into a soul, comes at great cost to both those who do the interrogation and those being questioned. It should not be done because of an old elf's fears."

Blue Moon Rising shook his head in obvious denial of the truth and spat back. "But for the good of society–"

The Inquisitor cut him off. "Society is not a thing. It is a concept."

"What?"

The Grand Inquisitor sat again, smoothing out his clothes, his voice, and his brow. "Society does not exist. It is what we call all the things too numerous to mention. It is a mother caring for her child. It is money, for which we pay others for work we cannot do on our own. It is normalcy so that we know we can walk the streets and not be murdered out of hand. It is laws that say that the guilty are punished and the innocent are not. It is all of these things and more, but it is, in the end, a concept. I will not destroy a life to uphold an idea, no matter the idea, knowing that the very act of destruction violates the idea itself.

Society depends on elves being elves, and I will not destroy this woman to mollify the fears of anyone. Even you."

The silence that followed was like the eye of a storm that left Blue Moon Rising panting, and the Grand Inquisitor serene.

The councilman's next words were bitter, heavily chewed before speaking. "So, what will you do?"

"I will do what needs to be done, when it needs to be done. Not before."

The Inquisitor noted Blue Moon Rising had a sheen of sweat on his forehead. He was back in control, if just. "What is your intent?"

The Grand Inquisitor nodded, as if the right question had finally been asked. "I have listened to her story. I have taken notes. I will now probe for details. I will find inconsistencies. I will find all the loose threads and pull, unraveling lies to bare the truth. Then I will know where to look should I have to Delve into her."

"And that can be done quickly?"

"As quickly as is safe for mother and child, but she spoke at length. Good liars keep stories short lest they leave threads that cannot be rewoven into their tapestry. Bad liars will bear many falsehoods that can be questioned and cannot be reconciled. If she is a Liath agent, I will know even before a Delving."

"Then go, now." The councilman turned away in silent dismissal.

The Grand Inquisitor stood and smoothed his robes again. He turned to leave but paused. He took off the mental harness of his profession and looked back. The man looked tired, so tired. Blue Moon Rising had never been a cruel man, nor a harsh leader. Yet...

"Councilman, I worry that your past has clouded your present."

Blue Moon Rising shot him a steely glance. "Which of us has no past?"

The Inquisitor nodded sadly. "And such a past. But I fear that you are not sleeping. It clouds judgment. You should rest before we speak again."

But pride, such pride, welled up in the councilman to create storm clouds on his face again. "Find me evidence of her betrayal, and I shall sleep."

The Inquisitor took steps to the door and lay a hand on the knob. He felt the words come from him, taught to him many centuries ago as he began to learn his profession. "Some betray everything they love for money. Some believe in their actions, citing conflicting duties and so they follow a harmful ideology. Others for ego, hoping to gain status or importance. Some are extorted, and fear repercussions if they do not do things to harm some in order to save themselves. But they are not the hardest to interrogate."

"And who is, then?"

Still facing the door, the Inquisitor sighed. "Those that betray what they believe through an act of conscience. They are the dangerous ones. They believe the actions, no matter how wrong, are correct because they believe them to be the right thing to do."

"And you believe this to be the case for the Valdera woman?"

Dragon Vessel

The Grand Inquisitor opened the door. "No, Grand Councilman. I am speaking of you."

And then he was through, leaving the councilman to sit, and think, and hopefully sleep. The Council Hall was still all but empty at this early hour in the morning, so he passed without incident, left trying to quash the memories of screaming Liath in that damnable chair beneath the college. He held the memories barely at bay, not noticing the comforting and beautiful wooden hallways, the ornate doors, the guards, or anyone on the street outside.

"Grand Inquisitor?"

He started slightly, then saw Fire Hunter approaching him on the street. The agitation from the meeting with Blue Moon was there, the nightmares were there, the screams of his past, and he could not help but pull on his professional face. "Peace unto you, Councilman Fire Hunter."

He was worried, sweaty hands moving erratically, and probably short on sleep as well. "Please, call me Anlon."

The Inquisitor had not known, and was almost shocked from his professional demeanor by the revelation of the man's true name on a city street so easily. "It is my sister, Vivien. Please, you must–"

"No." The word was flat, hard, and final.

Anlon looked slapped. His grey eyes were wide and glassy and his hands frozen in a state of almost begging. "What?"

"No." The Inquisitor took a deep breath. "No. I am sorry." Then he walked past the councilman on his way to the college.

That was the hardest thing, for loved ones of the accused would come and beg for mercy, for understanding, sometimes just information. Inquisitors gave nothing in return. They were not the instruments of justice, but of truth, and the truth would be had no matter what. He entered the college and gave fast instructions to the guards, then stopped by his quarters. Within the hour he re-entered the study he had chosen to use for interrogation, but it had changed.

Instead of friendly chairs by a mild fire, there was a heavy table and two rigid chairs set across from one another. Lady Valdera had obviously been sleeping and was bleary eyed and slightly worn around the edges. The Grand Inquisitor sat down across from her with a distant smile.

"Did you not hear enough last night?" she asked a bit peevishly.

"Indeed, I did. I just need you to tell me again."

She looked confused. "Which parts?"

From within his robes, he produced the book that contained every detail of her confession from the previous night. He opened it to the first page, making sure she saw the notes therein before pulling it closer to himself and producing his fae stylus. "All of it, please. From the beginning. Spare no detail."

And there it was. Her green eyes flashed, wondering if she had left out any detail. And what that would tell him, and what if she added it now? Or omitted it? He smiled at her in an innocent, comforting way that he knew chilled subjects.

"Please, from the beginning?"

Chapter Thirty-Nine
Cold Welcome

They had seen no elves, no humans, but Xadrian had known the way and brought the Wolf close at hand mere hours before they had reached the gate. For miles there had been naught but heavy forest and the strangely clean octagonal blocks of the ancient elvin road. Then, as the group of twenty-three came to the summit, the thick growth might as well have parted before them and exposed the colossal entry into Moirdem.

The Wolf looked along the wall from west to east, marveling at the same white stone that made up the old roads and separated from the forest by scant feet. Tall as three men on each other's shoulders, it was free of dirt or crack, nick, or abrasion. The wind whipped down the alley between with frigid fingers, as bitter as a wasteland as it clawed at his eyes. The arch around the entry was surrounded by the same kinds of pictures he had seen around the Council Halls of other cities, though much bigger, and far more of them. Xadrian gave a rare smile as he brought Fenella close, her hackles raised, and stared at the ornate surface. "The history of our people. In ancient times, elves lived in small societies, and were often wiped out by humans, monsters, or dark races that sought them harm. A great hero arose, Li'orteaus. He cobbled the elvin sanctuaries into a kingdom and ruled wisely for hundreds of years."

The Wolf saw the elves around him smile, as if at a story from their youth. Xadrian pointed to the next block. "Li'orteaus had nine children from nine wives. They each thought they were to be the next king or queen of the elvin lands. Li'orteaus knew that the kingdom would not survive such strife, so he placed each in charge of a territory, each with their own city." He pointed to the next panel. "Rithalion, Isbandar, Moirdem, and so on. They were each a kingdom in their own right, but we were supposed to be tied to one another. It was not to be."

The Wolf shook his head. "I have never met an elvin king."

Xadrian shrugged. "The royal families exist, but they do not rule anymore, and most pure blood elves have at least a drop of them in their heritage anyway. Now the Councils rule over the city-states."

"So that is why we meet with Councils and not royalty in these kingdoms?"

"Precisely."

"There are no scenes from the Dragon War," the barbarian noted, looking to the arch of pictures.

Xadrian's smile became sad. "This gate was ancient before that conflict, Brother. All this is history a millennium old."

The Wolf looked across the doors and parapet above, and saw what was missing. "No guards?" Among the pattern of swirls and carved leaves, he finally realized were vines carved across the doors, and there was a hand-print pressed into the stone.

Xadrian dismounted. "It is an old road, and an old gate, old even as elves judge these things. It was made only for those who knew to find it and could open it."He pressed his hand to the imprint, and the massed swirl of carved vines crawled to life, curling and slithering like giant snakes away from the center to open the far side of the hill, and the valley beyond.

The valley was stark, blazing colors of autumn swept away by the crusade of frosted nights. And yet it exuded health, a growing place that was only sleeping and waiting for spring to waken it to full bounty. It stretched on into clouds, and from the valley ridge above, the Wolf could see fallow fields, resting orchards, a mighty river that poured into a massive lake sparkling in the cold light, and settlements that freckled the valley leading all the way to the shining white beacon of Moirdem itself. It was tall and proud across the lake, veiled in the distance but still graceful and beautiful and protected by the wall that disappeared along the ridge in both directions.

The Wolf stood speechless.

Xadrian remounted Fenella, "Of all our cities, Moirdem escaped the war. This is how the elves used to live. This is the life we lost."

The Wolf nodded, unsure, as he led his reindeer through the gate and the rest of the group followed. "Why is there not a wall like this for Rithalion?"

Xadrian smiled sadly as he entered, the gate slithering closed behind him, "Moirdem's gates are labors of love, and took master magicians a lifetime to create. I don't know if there are wizards alive that can make them anymore."

The Wolf mounted up, and though the group of low elves appeared energized by being within striking distance of their last goal, they still moved like soldiers who had spent many nights and days wet and cold. As their mounts walked, the soldiers watched the world around them with wonder.

They passed massive clan houses of farmers and herders made of the same seamless white stone as the wall and the roads. Elves watched them curiously as they worked the fields in a strange fashion. They were leading reindeer into the rows of harvested plants. There the animals waited patiently as the elves hooked them to bronze plows and then patted them gently. Then each reindeer walked calmly but purposefully, turning the frosty dirt and unused vegetation back into the soil where it would wait for a new year of planting, but without needing to be followed by any hand at the plow. In a field of vines on trellises, raccoons raced to climb the green laden wooden walls to pick handfuls of frosted berries and bring them back to baskets where the elves would direct them as if they were farmhands. In an orchard of trees, owls snipped fruits just bruised by the cold and flew them to set them gently in bushel baskets in a similar fashion. The Wolf watched the peaceful routine of it all and wondered at it, seeing it but not quite understanding how.

Then he remembered Vivien and her affinity to the horses so long ago, and nodded to himself.

"Deep thoughts?"

The Wolf turned to Xadrian and shrugged. "The same thought. Her."

Xadrian frowned "Wolf, everyone here knows you and trusts you, but these people do not. Moirdem is sandwiched between the bulk of the elvin kingdoms and the wilds where no living races inhabit. They are proud, and wise in the old ways, but also sheltered."

The Wolf shook his head as if dislodging a fly. "Speak plainly, Xadrian."

"They will not be impressed with a human general leading elves into battle, but they will be afraid of something that looks human with eyes like candles." The Wolf sat straight in the saddle and frowned, nodding, "They will not accept you without knowing why your eyes glow, or turn red, and we will have no answers for them they will like. If we are to win their aid, you must be calm. Calm and quiet. You *must*."

The Wolf took a deep breath and nodded. "For Vivien's sake."

"For all our sake's, Brother."

And though they spoke no more of it, the Wolf continued to chew over these words, for it presented a startling problem. Should he lose his temper, or even lose his calm and become agitated his blood red eyes would reveal him to be more than human, and doom their mission. He thought of the responsibility he now held in hands hobbled by his legendary temper and his heart quailed.

The buildings became more common and more populated. Here and there were tradesmen, metalworkers, makers of fabric, and woodcraft. Then came the odd tavern, a massive tree marking the graveyard on a distant hill, and then homes. There was no welcome. In fact, other than the staring at the Wolf, there was little comment whatsoever. So, it was they progressed without much comment until they came to the ferry at the edge of the lake, and the ferryman told them they could not bring outside animals into the city. They backtracked to a den where they paid some coin to house and feed the tir-reath, then had to backtrack further to find a friendly farmer that agreed to house the Wolf's reindeer for just a few coins.

Only then could they pay the ferryman to take them to the ivory city of Moirdem.

The city was ethereal, magical, and foreign to the Wolf's eyes. It was a place of razor straight streets and tall walls festooned with windows. Tirinian were everywhere, these yet another breed both brightly colored and striped. Flying bridges connected it all above streets where beautiful elves walked without worry about their business. Even with the coming frost, they wore clothes meant for fashion more than practicality with impossible hairstyles that were brightly colored and assembled into fantastic shapes fueled by whimsy.

Every eye latched onto him, which he was used to, but he was not coming as a hero, or an object of lust, or caution. He felt like he was a lion being led on a leash down the city streets to the massive Council Hall, so far removed from home he could not be feared but only seen as a barbaric curiosity. He breathed deeply, constantly finding his center of being to live moment by moment. Night was falling as they approached the Council Hall. No one waited on the steps for them but the guards by the door, no parades were arranged, no banners flew. As they crossed the massive square before the towering Council Hall the guards in shiny, silvery plates with cloaks and sashes of sky blue and emerald green knocked on the doors behind them. By the time the small band of twenty-three had started up the wide staircase, the door had opened and a single elf came forth.

The Wolf had learned to tell old elves from those truly ancient. The ancient ones had ice white hair, and pale eyes with only hints of their former colors. They had a wispiness about them. Not in form and only barely in physique, but mostly in spirit. It was a calm state that spoke not of peace, but of finality, of a nearing end that would come in whatever way their species faded from life. Most of the council members he had met wore white robes, but this elf's were shimmering silver.

Xadrian immediately removed his hood, and the soldiers all removed their helmets. The Wolf saw surprise flicker across the face of their greeter. There was a half a heartbeat as Xadrian waited to be greeted, but then spoke as if nothing was amiss. "My shield name is The Lord of Swords and Truth. I am the General of the Armies of–"

As Xadrian spoke, the greeter filled his lungs as if to stave off complete frustration but held up a hand and interrupted, "I know, Xadrian Ilorra..." The assembled La'athai started at hearing his true name spoken so casually. "...and you will find no need for silly shield names in this city. We were informed of your arrival weeks ago, though you are here sooner than expected. I am Councilman Polithar Al'sangui and I welcome you to Moirdem." The Wolf snapped his eyes closed and breathed deeply, ignoring the tone that said they were decidedly not welcome. "Please collect your servants and come with me."

The man turned and so did not see Katriona start forward as if lunging into the conversation, only to be halted by the iron grip of Xadrian at her elbow. He shook his head once and then continued up the stairs with the La'athai in tow.

The Council Hall was by far the most elaborate they had ever visited. Glowing crystals were spun into silver chandeliers and wall sconces, twinkling like bright stars. Every surface was carved or painted or both. Marble had been plated in gold and depicted animals romping gaily through the forest, nude elves cavorting among them. The Wolf picked out predators and prey often frolicking together and stifled a pointless laugh. The game they would play in real life would be far more brutal and require quite a bit more red paint.

Four council members each had their own marble podium from which to address the assembly that would sit in luxuriously carved pews of dark stained oak. In the center of the hall, between the council members' positions there lay a large crystal-paneled silver case. It glowed slightly, little sparkles of golden essence winking into existence above it and fading out like burning embers. Yet podiums and pews were empty, as were the floor and halls, but for the silent guards in blue and green who watched their every move through cold eyes.

Councilman Al'sangui led them through the beautiful chamber at a brisk pace, then through a large archway flanked by guards. There was only a small hallway to another chamber. He motioned them inside. "You may stay here."

Xadrian's step stuttered, but he moved to the side. The Wolf was right behind him, and ignored Al'sangui sniffing the air loudly as he walked by. They were all wearing elvin armor at this point, but they had been on the road a long, long time. He moved to stand next to Xadrian and let the other La'athai file in. This room contained carvings of guilt and despair, odd angles making every elf form disturbing to look upon. There was a single simple table and chair and four pallets on the floor of each of the five cells made of bronze bars. A modest door in the corner announced its destination to the outside by the closed and latched view port at head height. The Wolf knew without opening the hand sized port would also have bars.

Xadrian's face was flushing though his countenance might as well be carved of stone. His voice was flat, as he turned to Al'sangui, "Councilman, there are not enough beds."

He chuckled, "You are early, and we had to make do with what we had. Your humans can stay here, we will take you and your second in command to other chambers." Al'sangui looked pointedly at Katriona, the only other full blood elf in the room.

The archer flipped stray blond hairs from her face and placed her hands on her hips. "I believe–"

"–We will stay with our men. Unsupervised soldiers can be rowdy." Xadrian fixed her with a piercing gaze and she closed her mouth, though not meekly.

Al'sangui's eyebrows shot up, "Really? Well that never happens here. Must be the *breeding* that *civilization* brings." He paused meaningfully. All motion in the room had stopped, but none spoke. "In any case, I shall leave you. Water will be brought for you to wash, and food will be provided."

And without further pleasantry, Al'sangui left the room, two armed guards outside in the hall the only clue he had ever been.

The Wolf turned and motioned for the La'athai to finally take off their heavy travel packs and find places to rest, but Katriona was not done as of yet. She paced, fuming for half a minute until words began hissing from her as if a kettle on a fire. "If *that* is a leader of these elves..."

"Katriona–" Xadrian began wearily.

"...then the only soldiers they have in this city..."

"Katriona–" Xadrian said in a warning tone. "...wet themselves at the sound of drawn steel," she plowed on.

"Katriona!" The Wolf pitched his voice low, but it still carried the menace of rolling thunder. There was a glint of red that blushed the walls for a second, so he turned from the door and took a deep breath to settle himself. When he opened his eyes he waved his hand before them, but there was no pressure, no glow. He breathed again.

Katriona stood with a frown of her own. "They put us in a jail."

Xadrian looked pointedly at her and then to the doorway where there stood guards loyal to the Council just outside. "And we will be grateful for the shelter. We come here as beggars."

Katriona sent a withering glance at the doorway and nodded grudgingly. "You are right, Lord of Swords and Truth."

Each cell had a hole into the cesspit below, so while there was no privacy, at least there were privies available. Water was brought by a close-mouthed guard in two buckets and another followed close after with deep saucers to pour it in and rags that were at least clean. Finally, the soldiers were able to wash themselves. The last pair were Katriona and the Wolf.

The Wolf poured the murky water down the privy hole and then they refilled the saucers and stripped down. Some of the soldiers had been modest, others had removed every shred of clothing on his back. The Wolf and Katriona were of the latter, wiping sodden rags across themselves to move frigid water into every crack and crevice to work out the dirt and foul odor that had taken residence there.

The Wolf kept his eyes and his mind on his work until Katriona hissed at him, "I can't believe they referred to these soldiers as human."

The Wolf paused, then continued cleaning without comment.

"And to put us in jail..."

Memories welled up, but he bit off a retort and took a deep breath to find his calm again. He nodded to her. "They have not taken our weapons, so they do not see us as an enemy. It is a test. Meet it head on with discipline."

She considered this and then smiled evilly at him. "You think so?" Then she turned, nude and quite unaffected by the fact, and walked out to meet one of the guards set just beyond the doorway. The Wolf heard, "We have washed but need more buckets of water, and soap if there is any to be had. It will do little good to wash our bodies and then put back on clothes still stinking of travel."

She came back in, swaying her hips more than was strictly needed.

Xadrian raised an eyebrow, imagining the effect her nudity would have on the guards. "Was that necessary?"

She shrugged, light breasts bobbing. "Why should they be more comfortable sleeping than I will?"

Xadrian sighed.

The La'athai had traveled with weight given to gear and food, so few had spare sets of clothes. Most had spare socks and breeches so all that had them, donned them. They settled down to dice or card games. Some of the mages pulled out thin books and read. When food was brought, they lined up dutifully and accepted it graciously. The thick vegetable stew was warm and inviting, and everyone gulped it down greedily.

A brazier was brought in by guards and lit, letting the smoldering charcoal warm the room. Most gathered what covers they had from the road and slept. Closer to the table, the two leaders and Katriona, as befitted her bloodline, spoke quietly on their makeshift beds.

"What do you think it all means?" Katriona asked, forever worrying at the bone of their cold welcome.

The Wolf shrugged.

Xadrian shook his head, voice near a whisper, "What it means is that help here is buried under a great avalanche of stone. We will have to dig deeply to uncover it."

The Wolf nodded and lay back. Though he pretended to sleep, he could only think of his love, so far away and in a prison of her own.

Chapter Forty
Churning Waters

VIVIEN STARED AT THE MAN across the table from her. His white robes were immaculately kept despite four days of almost nonstop questioning, his blue-eyed gaze was as alert as ever, and his braided white hair lay, unfrayed, over one shoulder. He regarded her like he always did, with cool dispassion, and she knew he had no care for her. She'd told her story, over and over, each time trying to find some detail she may have missed. And each time, she tried to tell it as though she'd never told it before. No one else knew her story as intimately as he did, and she hoped no one would. She'd lay her heart bare, her soul, the very essence of her, recounting her time spent over the past year with her husband, with her father, with the Wolf, and finally with the Liath.

And yet, it wasn't enough.

The child within kicked something deep inside and she grimaced. He'd been more active these past days, mayhap reacting to her heightened state of distress, or even more alarming, that he was preparing for birth. Several times a day she rose to pass water, and the guards would escort her to the bath chamber, only leaving her side so that she could have some modicum of privacy. The only other time was in the evenings when they escorted her to her bedchamber. She'd fall, exhausted, onto the bed and sleep until she was awakened in the morning by Mikarvan, who made her choke down whatever food he could get in her.

The rest of the day she didn't bother eating at all. There didn't seem to be enough space in her belly anymore, and the strain of the interrogation made her heave pathetically into the pitcher that Evey left in the chamber every morning, filled with water they could drink throughout the hours they spent together.

To his credit, the Inquisitor didn't eat either.

Vivien watched as he slowly closed his book, *her* book. By right it was hers, since within its pages were written every single thing she'd ever told him. That was her story written there, and she could only imagine it joining the others that resided in the torture room beneath the college. That didn't bother her as much as she thought it might, for in a way, she supposed it belonged there, part of a larger story that had been told by countless dragon mages that came before her.

Dragon mage. I am a dragon mage.

Somehow, that thought no longer bothered her like it once did. Dragon magic had saved her, after all. Her and her son.

"It seems we are finished for today, Lady Valdera."

She almost startled at the sound of his voice, not realizing that the chamber had been silent for several moments. Surprise flitted through her mind, for the questioning usually lasted longer into the day, and it was barely past the noon hour. She looked up at him as he rose from the table, an air of finality in his movements, an expre sion of resignation on his face. That also surprised her, for his face rarely spo e to her at all, shrouded by the impersonal mask that he slipped on every time he was in her presence.

"I will return tom, rrow morning. Please be well rested, for it will be a long day."

Vivien regarded h m impassively. What he could possibly ask her had been covered already, over and over again. But the air about him was so different this time, so...

She watched him walk from the chamber, a feeling of dread stealing over her. She just sat there unmoving, several moments longer until Evey found her there. "Vivien, come : id get up. You should get something to eat and rest."

Her friend's expr ssion was tinged with worry, the corner of her mouth pinched. Mikarvan w : there a moment later, helping her from the chair and up to her chamber. Onc there, he checked her like he had several days before, pushing his fingers de p inside, the pressure making her wince.

"The baby has m ved into position for delivery, head down. This is a good sign." Mikarvan gav her an encouraging smile. "Your cervix is ripening, preparing for birth."

She eyed him as ance, taking in his demeanor. Something didn't seem quite right.

"What aren't you lling me?"

Surprise swept a ross his face, and he hesitated for a moment before responding. "Nothing Everything appears to be progressing normally. I don't foresee you going in o labor anytime within the next several days, so rest easy."

She narrowed he eyes, regarding him intently. His explanation seemed good enough, but stil it felt like there was something he wasn't telling her. "I can tell there's someth ng else. I want you to tell me."

He looked at her ensively before finally making a decision. "Fine, I'll tell you. Torialvah has t en here a time or two, wanting to see you. I'd have thought he would hav known that you were with the Inquisitor, but he's more daft than I gave him c edit."

Vivien felt her m uth curve up at one corner, the rancor in Mika's tone lightening her mood bit. "Yes, well, I used to give him more credit as well. Fret not."

Mikarvan smiled en, bent over, and planted a kiss firmly on her forehead. "You look utterly ex austed. I want you to get some rest, and after, you are getting a decent mea " She was about to protest when he cut her off. "No excuses! I mean it thi time. Eat you must!"

With that said, h backed out of the chamber and closed the door. Sleep was upon her before s e could think of what he might make her eat.

Mikarvan walked briskly through the corridor, down the stairs, and to the study where the Inquisitor had made his accommodations during his stay at the college. It had been disturbing to learn that the man was always there, ever present to make Vivien's life a living hell whenever he chose, but Mika could do nothing about it. The Inquisitor outranked him, both in years and status, and his hands were tied.

His thoughts were filled with Vivien as he walked. Each day spent with the Inquisitor made her thinner, and her complexion paler. He could see her losing strength, strength she needed for her upcoming delivery. Of course, he'd lied when he told her about Torialvah. The man hadn't once bothered to come, not even to ask about her welfare. In his estimation, Torialvah was better off dead in a hole somewhere. But the excuse had been the only one that would come to his mind. He'd forgotten how astute she could be, especially when it came to him. But he had no way to tell her the true reason behind his worry. He'd felt the same sensation of wrongness when he examined her again, this time even more so than the last, and it scared him.

Mika reached the Inquisitors study. He rapped twice on the door, then twice again when he didn't instantly get a response.

"Enter."

Mikarvan didn't hesitate to open the door, walking into the study without a word of greeting. The elder looked up from his book where he sat at the desk, an unreadable expression on his face. "Yes?"

"I would like to know how much longer the Inquisition will last. The strain is becoming too much for her and she is becoming weaker every day. She needs her strength if she is to survive the birth."

He spoke formally, without tone inflection. "The Inquisition will take as long as it needs to, Master Healer."

Mikarvan frowned, his anger rising. This man seemed to have no care for Vivien at all, like she was a thing to be broken down to the point of surrender instead of a living, breathing person carrying a child. "Have you really no care? None at all? Imagine the people you would devastate if your methods cause complications for her during birth. You know how high mortality rates are!"

The Inquisitor scowled, the first emotion Mika seen the man give since he'd first moved into the college four days ago. "Indeed, I am aware. Now, if you will excuse me, I have a long day ahead of me tomorrow."

Mika just stared at him for a moment, disbelieving. How could a man be so cold? But then he remembered Torialvah, and he just shook his head. They belonged together to rot in some hell, and he hoped one day he'd get to watch, albeit from a distance. He strode briskly from the study, slamming the door behind him on his way out. Anger coursed through him like a wild river, but he knew he must tame it before he saw Vivien next. She needed him to be calm, cool, collected, and most importantly, there for her at the end of every day. And if it was within his power, he would save her, even if it took every last breath from his body.

He'd promised the Wolf that much.

The following morning, they were brought more water and larger tubs and a morning meal consisting of pan-fried tubers, boiled, shelled and spiced eggs, and hearty, dark bread. The Wolf had awoken long before it came, and immediately the pressure of time began to vice tightly around his head. He spent the minutes before the others were awake and food was brought settling himself and letting go of everything. Xadrian's lessons about letting go of the past and the future to only be in the moment he was living in had begun to make sense and bear fruit. Once the meal was delivered, again by guards and not servants, they had ample time to consume it before Councilman Al'sangui again appeared just outside the doorway.

Xadrian, eating at the table in the lone chair came to his feet and all the rest of the party followed suit.

Al'sangui smiled benevolently at the General and the group as a whole. "Ah, I see you have finished your morning repast. I hope it was to your satisfaction."

The Wolf heard the missing intent behind the honeyed words and closed his eyes, taking firm hold of his temper, so he only heard the exchange.

Xadrian, of course, spoke. "We thank you Councilman Al'sangui. The generosity of Moirdem and its Council is legendary and does not disappoint."

The councilman's voice dripped honey and cyanide. "I am glad for this. Well, your midday meal shall not disappoint, either. I shall check in on you after your final repast of the day." The Wolf heard a slight shuffle of his feet and believed he was leaving.

Xadrian's words hooked him, though. "Oh? We will not be seen by the Council today?"

"No."

"Has the timing of our audience perchance been discussed?"

This time there was genuine mirth in Al'sangui's voice. "The Council is very busy, you understand, and the consensus is that we will be able to see you on the day you were estimated to arrive." The Wolf could hear the tension in the room snap under sudden strain.

There was a definite pause, then Xadrian replied. "May my soldiers then explore the city?"

"I..." Al'sangui stuttered, "I cannot think of a reason why–"

Though clearly headed for –*that would be advisable*, Xadrian became cheerful and accepted the non-proffered consent. "Excellent, Councilman. It is not often any from Rimalion comes to Moirdem, and we are eager to see it all."

There was another definite pause, but when he spoke, Al'sangui's voice was one who had just bit into bread and found he had crunched his teeth into the corpses of weevils instead of toasted seeds. "Quite."

The Wolf heard the councilman depart, and opened his eyes to a mix of confused and smiling faces.

Xadrian faced them all sternly. Gone was the false joviality. Gone was any pretense of civility. He was a military commander. "Dress."

And with that word, everyone scrambled to obey. They forwent armor, but carried their weapons. So, wearing road-worn and slightly dirty armor padding, stained boots, and untidy hair they marched confidently past the guards at the door, who began to follow at a respectful distance out of the Council Hall.

In the square, Xadrian pulled Katriona close. "Take them. Visit the city. *Experience* everything. No fighting no matter what. Meet back here at noon."

She nodded with an impish gleam in her eye, and she gathered the bulk of the La'athai and headed west. Xadrian nodded to the Wolf and they headed east. The guards shadowing them looked from one to another and split off so that each stayed with a group.

Moirdem was already awake, with elves bustling about their day. The Wolf immediately regretted his almost petulant desire to pack clothes as close to his homeland styles as possible. He walked the streets in thick boots, a loose-fitting wool shirt, and a kilt. Those they saw on the streets were already bundled against the cold. He stood a head and a half taller than almost all elves, especially those with a pure lineage, and though he had no need of heavy clothes to stay warm, his attire made him stand out even more.

"Look taller." Xadrian murmured. The Wolf looked to him, knowing his face showed a heart full of confusion. Xadrian glanced at him and nodded. "Be the Wolf, Lord Blacach."

The Wolf blinked twice, then felt the words of his general and his friend sink in. He set his features into stone hard determination and stood taller.

It was as if a switch had been flipped. The street full of elves noticed him as if he had tossed off a cloak. People saw him and gazed with wide eyes as they scurried out of the way. Elves dressed in exquisite finery acted like children fleeing before an oncoming wagon as he took every measured step.

A young lady, pale skinned with the deepest black hair and eyes, fell just in front of them after seeing him and looking far too long. The Wolf darted forward and snatched her from her fall with hands that had battered metal into submission. Everyone stared as he lifted her from her fall as easily as one might a mouse and set her on her feet.

Her face flushed and she looked from the Wolf to the General. She nodded to the latter and addressed him. "Thank you."

The Wolf nodded back, and spoke in heavily accented Elvish, "You are welcome."

Then he brushed past her without another word. Xadrian walked beside him, unable to contain a smile. Across rooftops and in the streets, tirinian played. The two traveled a few more streets and the Wolf began to chafe at so many eyes upon him. "Xadrian, what are we doing?"

"You, Brother, are being human." He patted the larger man on the back. "And that is enough."

The Wolf looked behind him and saw the guard still following, but not too close. Too close was not needed, he could spot the Wolf across any crowd in this city. At least it gave them privacy to speak, "So I am being human?"

"Yes, my brother."

When no more explanation was forthcoming, the Wolf huffed. "Moirdem does not appear to want to help. Why do you think they will change their minds?"

The Lord of Swords and Truth made a tiny shrug. "They do not want to help. Luckily for us, they have no choice." The Wolf again passed him a confused look. "In ages past, there was one elvin kingdom. It fractured after the death of the King into independent city-states, but we agreed in principle to remain close, as if cousins. Then there came the Dragon War. Moirdem was all but untouched by that conflict, and it was devastating to the other elvin cities. Moirdem stood by and watched it all happen. This city was untouched out of all the elvin havens, some of which were destroyed."

"So why will they help now?"

"Because to salve their conscience after the War, Moirdem signed unbreakable pacts with the other cities, to come when called. They made oaths to gods and fae that, when they were truly needed, they would answer. Those pacts are here. They still bind this city and this Council to us. We will ask, and they must answer."

The Wolf felt the new information both calm him and give rise to new consternation. "So why are we here?"

Xadrian shook his head. "First, we must address the Council. We must be *allowed* to ask."

The Wolf smirked. "What if we kick down the doors and demand to ask?"

Xadrian shook his head again, "We kick down the first door and the council guards will surround us. They will kill us or eject us from Moirdem. In either case, we do not get to ask."

"But none of that explains what me being human here does."

Xadrian looked down for a moment, then back up, facing the hard truth head on. "The kingdom of the elves was carved out of the wild places away from the humans. We fought humans to survive. That has been more than three millennia ago, but Moirdem remembers. You and the La'athai here are a reminder that humans exist, and that we can reproduce. Nothing will make them want to see us faster than reminding their people of that fact."

"So just being here will make the Council see us more quickly?"

Xadrian nodded solemnly. "That is my plan."

The Wolf shook his head. "Fickle."

But he said no more against the idea as they made their way through the city streets. The whole group met back around noon and reentered the Council Hall to find thick slabs of bread with heavy glass jars of both sweet and savory preserves, honey, and butter laid out in the jail. The La'athai consumed them with gusto, smirking back and forth about the day's events so far. Xadrian and Katriona spoke quietly in a corner while the others ate, the two planning more adventures for the La'athai when Al'sangui appeared in the doorway to the jail.

The councilman's face was like ruddy thunder, hands clenched tightly as he hissed out the words, "General, if I might speak to you?"

Xadrian feigned surprise, shrugged off his talk with Katriona, and walked lightheartedly to the doorway. But rather than move into the hall, Al'sangui began his heated words immediately. "General you MUST control your..." he realized he was going to say something uncouth and reached for an alternative, "...SOLDIERS!"

Xadrian blinked at the man, sounding shocked. "Why, Councilman, whatever do you mean?"

"They were out and about town all morning!"

"Well, yes, we discussed not keeping the La'athai caged like animals for the duration of their stay."

"I have had complaints!"

"Oh? Well, what kind of complaints have you received?"

"Why were they armed, General?"

Xadrian smiled easily. "They are soldiers, Councilman. They have taken oaths to defend the elvin people. They can hardly do that with harsh language and fists full of bread."

Al'sangui looked shocked, then his anger doubled as he gestured wildly. "The tall blonde one went into a vendor's shop and *touched* everything."

Xadrian turned to the room, "Matthew?"

The soldier in question popped to his feet at attention. "Sir, I was shopping for my sister. I have never seen cloth that luxurious at home."

The General nodded, the man sat as if his strings had been cut, and he turned back to Al'sangui, "Shopping for cloth does not seem to be especially disruptive, Councilman."

Al'sangui's face became redder. "The small, dark one proposed to a woman he met on the street!"

Xadrian glanced at another La'athai and frowned a bit before turning back. "Councilman, love is a fickle thing."

The man clenched his jaw and shook visibly as he growled out words, "The big one groped young Lady Lo'thurinam in the street!"

Xadrian looked shocked. "The big one? Which one is that?"

Al'sangui stalked past the General, brushing aside soldiers until he stood just before the Wolf. The highland barbarian could see a flash of concern on Xadrian's face by the door as Al'sangui lifted his finger like a magic wand and poked at the Wolf's chest. "Him! He groped her!"

The Wolf stood very still. He breathed. He let it go.

He did, however reach down very slowly to grasp the councilman's finger as if the whole hand was proffered and squeezed with slightly more force than was necessary as he pumped it up and down. He spoke in heavily accented Elvish, and broke up his speech. "Pleased. Meeting you."

It was then that Al'sangui remembered that this was a barbarian. It was a good eighteen inches taller than he. Eighteen inches, *and* heavily muscled. The Wolf saw the realization hit the councilman because it played out all across his face. Al'sangui rescued his finger with difficulty and held it to his own chest as if it had come close to being severed in a set of teeth.

Xadrian had come up behind the man. "I was there, Councilman. I am sure the Wolf is sorry for any discomfort the Lady Lo'thurinam suffered, but she was about to take a nasty tumble. Barbarians of his tribe are taught to revere and protect women, and that is what he did. There was nothing inappropriate in his actions."

Al'sangui turned to the general, rubbing his finger fiercely as if to scour dirt and pain away. "Well I am sorry, but you have caused disruption in the city of Moirdem. Your privilege of travel from this room is revoked."

Xadrian honestly looked troubled. "But you know where that leads, Councilman. These soldiers will get... rowdy." Al'sangui had a turn to look shocked, but Xadrian continued speaking. "They can't really be blamed. You said it yourself. *Civilzation. Breeding.* But I will speak with the La'athai for our next six excursions into the city."

Al'sangui huffed and left, pushing through the crowd. The La'athai grinned as a whole but Xadrian made a 'be still' gesture. "Eat. Then we go stretch our legs more."

And they did, but this time instead of splitting into two groups they split into pairs. Eleven groups left the square with orders to not be rowdy or violent. The two guards picked Xadrian and the Wolf, and Katriona and Matthew. They were helpless to follow the others, who were sure to cause more consternation.

Again, the guard hung back, so the Wolf felt safe to ask, "Why don't they just kick us out if they don't want to see us?"

"The Pact is a magical thing. The Council cannot know if refusing to see us over some petty thing will violate it. What they can do is make us wait a week, then another, and another."

"What would happen if they did violate the Pact?"

Xadrian looked pale, like the name of a childhood nightmare had been named. "No one knows, but all the stories we have of those who violate Pacts are filled with horror. They have welcomed us in under the guise of civilization. We ate on their table, and that binds us by the laws of hospitality."

The Wolf was swamped by memories of the smell of a swamp, walking for weeks, a fall from a rock face, and such talk from the Warlock of Pergatium.

He stopped as a small child came forward and blocked their path. He was a thing of innocent brightness, golden hair and golden eyes just beginning to become almond shaped. He stared openly at the Wolf, who smiled at the tiny being. He knelt before the boy, who felt at the Wolf's round ears, then to his own, also round ears. He stood there, just feeling as something of a grin crept across his face. Gently, giant to child, the Wolf pressed his forehead to the boy's. "You are not alone."

The boy looked at him when he pulled away and nodded.

"Athandrus, come away from him! Athandrus!" The call was shrill and afraid, but the boy was not. Yet he left dutifully toward the voice of his mother. Barbarian and General continued onward.

"Xadrian, that boy was–?"

"Pure blooded? Oh yes. His ears have not started yet. Some do that later than others."

"But one is not born with them?"

The General shook his head. "No. None of us. At birth we look very human except in the rarest of cases."

"Strange. You start your lives looking like us, but all your people think it is such a bad thing to be human."

Xadrian flinched. "We do not all–"

The Wolf shook his head. "Even in Rithalion your pure bloods are Lords and Ladies, Grand This or That, Councilmen or Lords. Your soldiers are part human, your laborers, your farmers. In Moirdem it is worse, but it exists in every elvin city I have seen."

Xadrian pondered that in silence as they took the next turn, coming back to the Council Hall Square where the others waited for them. Finally, he stopped and gripped the Wolf's arm. "I am sorry, Brother."

The Wolf nodded. "Of all elves, only three have ever treated me like who I am and not my race, even once. One is you. The other is the Lady of Moonlight and Love."

Xadrian tightened his lips, knowing who the third had to be. "Thank you, Brother."

They met in the square, and then went to the jail where a strange squash, one that shredded into noodles when the pulp was eaten, was served with a creamy sauce and roasted green plants the size of a cow's eyeball. They had barely begun eating with their mess kits when Al'sangui appeared again at the doorway.

The room quieted and he addressed no one in particular, clearly unhappy about the announcement. "I will come tomorrow to collect you for a task. If you can complete it, I will believe your cause is dire and see you at your convenience. If you fail, you will leave this place and never return."

The room was quiet, expectant. Xadrian spoke. "Can we know what this test will be?"

The reply was fast, harsh. "No."

Xadrian took a deep breath. "We agree to your terms."

Chapter Forty-One
Avalanche from the Past

The grand inquisitor gestured to the cushioned chair beside the fire. "Please, have a seat, Lady Valdera."

Uncertainly, she walked to the chair, hesitated before seating herself. He could understand her reaction, for the environment was vastly different than it had been the four days prior. Where there had once been nothing but an oak table with hard, straight-backed chairs, there was now a merry fire in the hearth, two cushioned chairs, a plush sofa, and a rug beneath their feet to keep the chill away. He moved the other chair closer to hers, then sat down, his knees almost touching hers. She slightly recoiled, trepidation entering her gaze, and she licked her lips nervously.

Most of the night, the Inquisitor had prepared for the spells he would be casting this day. After, he fell into a fitful slumber. He'd awoken, again, in a cold sweat, the threads of the dreams that haunted his sleep sticking to him like a web. Once more, he questioned himself of what he was about to do, for, as far as he could tell, a woman innocent of the allegations made against her sat before him. She had not wavered from her story, not once in the four days he'd questioned her.

And in his experience, liars always wavered, at least a little. Always.

He chose to disregard her negative reaction, chose instead to focus on his words. Mikarvan's warning from the afternoon before had rattled him a bit, a stark reminder of what was at stake. He was about to Delve into the mind of a pregnant woman. He had no idea how that could affect the unborn, and that caused no small bit of anxiety. But he couldn't show the Master Healer that, nor could he waver now in front of his subject. He needed to retain his aura of cool indifference, do what he needed to do as swiftly as possible, then leave her mind.

"Lady Valdera, we are going to do something different today."

A frown creased her brow. "Yes, I can see that, Grand Inquisitor."

A smile threatened his cool demeanor. Even now, in the face of adversity, she had spirit. He could appreciate that, as it reminded him of himself. It showed determination and strength of character. It showed courage. This thought heartened him, for maybe she would come through this just fine after all.

"Lady Valdera, I believe you are innocent of the allegations against you."

Her eyes widened with incredulity. "You do? Then why are we here?"

He held out a staying hand and shook his head. "But my beliefs don't matter. This is not my decision to make. There are others who still doubt."

"But why? You are the Grand Inquisitor."

He held up his hand again. "I believe there are things that have happened to you, things we do not understand. This is where their disbelief arises."

She took a deep breath, then another, biting at her lower lip the way he'd noticed she would when she was nervous... or afraid.

"We have to convince them, make them believe beyond any shadow of doubt that you are as innocent as I believe you are. When I look into your mind, and see nothing there, I can prove it to them."

She swallowed heavily, her gaze darting up to meet his, a gaze filled with fear. "Please, don't do it. There must be another way."

He shook his head sadly. "I am afraid there is not."

"Grand Inquisitor, please." Tears slipped down her cheeks. "Please don't do it."

"The Delving will go easier if you surrender your mind to me, offer no resistance."

She began to sob openly. He allowed her the time to do so, knowing that it was her way of preparing herself for the inevitable. His heart ached, hating what he must do, but feeling duty bound to perform this task. But in the end, she would no longer be questioned by any of the law. She would be free.

She dried her tears on the handkerchief he'd provided, gathered all the strength she could muster, then sat still in the chair. Yet, he waited, waited for her to say the words.

"I am ready."

He offered a conciliatory smile, one he hoped might offer some bit of comfort. He then offered her his hand.

She just looked at it a moment, her fear battling with the newfound courage she'd dredged up from her heart. Finally, she took it. Her hand was small, and cold, within his, and he was glad that he'd asked for a blanket to be brought in with the rest of the furnishings. She followed where he led her to the sofa, and when he indicated she do so, she sat there.

"I need you to lie down. It will be a long day, and I do not wish you to overtire needlessly."

She nodded and complied. He positioned the pillow behind her head and an expression of surprise swept across her face when he brought the blanket up to cover her. He then went back to get the chair he'd been using, positioned it close to the sofa and sat down.

"I am going to put one hand on your forehead, the other on your chest over your heart." He motioned to the places as he mentioned them. Then he took her hand again, cocooned it within his own, larger hands, and spoke with conviction. "I will not hurt you, Vivien."

Her eyes looked up and into his. They were quite beautiful: blue, grey, brown and predominant green all in one small place, intermingling to give them a unique appearance he'd rarely seen. They searched his face, looking for the sincerity there, and when she found it, she nodded. "I believe you."

He smiled then, a smile he hadn't found in his heart to give to anyone in a long time. *Now I know why they follow her...* He placed one hand over her forehead and she closed her eyes. He placed the other hand over her chest, felt her heart beating just beneath it before closing his own. He began to speak the ritualistic words, words born of magic. Not fae magic; not dragon magic. The magic of the Inquisitors was something different, something wilder than either of those two things. He spiraled down, down, down, into Vivien's mind: into her thoughts, her desires, her most intimate memories. She offered no resistance, opened herself to him.

She trusted him, and the realization made him weep as he delved deeper, deeper, deeper...

At first, he floated. It was always like this, in the beginning. It was a subconscious memory, one the mind would never share with the conscious. It was one so far back, it was difficult to understand, but one he'd come to believe as something the mind experienced before birth had taken place. There were vague images, vague sensations around the body, and even more vague auditory stimulation that included a rhythmic swishing sound. He sped through this and other memories, memories that grew sharper and sharper over time. Vivien experienced them all with him, cruising from memory to memory, thought to thought. Infancy passed into early childhood. Images of the Grand Magister were predominant, accompanied by feelings of love, trust, and security. All the people she'd met, all the events she experienced... they were all there, waiting for him to tap. He saw no reason to do so until he came to one that garnered his interest, one that involved a plethora of emotion. Intrigued, he slowed down...

The carriage bumps over the uneven terrain, and in spite of the cushioned seat, I rub my bottom for at least the tenth time that morning. The discomfort would ordinarily be bothersome, but not today. I smile happily as I look out the open window. An endless array of trees passes by the carriage, verdant with rains from the spring season. The mountains are more beautiful than I'd imagined they would be, so different from my home in the gorge. The grass, the trees, the birds and other animals... even the air is different. It smells so... so *green*!

My thoughts turn inward as we continue. I was ecstatic when Father had invited me to accompany him on his journey to treat with the mountain folk. It was something not ordinarily done, for elves and humans rarely mingle, but Father explained it to me. "The humans, they are not like us. They have their strange hair, their strange clothes, and their even stranger habits and customs. The humans of the Iron Coast, they are bad people. They seek only to invade and defeat whoever they can for wealth and power. But those of the mountains are peaceful and have respect for the other races that live in this world with them. Would it not be profitable to form some kind of alliance with such people, to have solid bonds that will last for generations to come? Would it not be a boon to have such people at our side if the need for aid should ever arise?"

My eyes grew wide. "You mean like a war?"

ROSS €ROSS

Father nodded so berly. "Yes, like a war."

I shook my head. Why would people want a war?"

"There are many easons why people fight, but mostly for resources like trees for wood, iron ore for making weapons, and arable land for planting crops."

"But why fight w en we can all share?"

Father had regard d me intently from solemn blue eyes. "Some people can never share. They onl want to take what belongs to others and use it until it is all gone."

So, for three wee ss we traveled up, up, up into the mountains. Through gusting winds and pel ing rain, we continued without stop except for the nighttimes when everyone rested before starting again the next day. Patiently I waited, waited for th day Father would tell me that the wait would soon be over. That was this n orning when I awoke. And now I could hardly wait any longer. I snap out of ny thoughts to glance over at Isandra, the young woman sharing the carriage ith me. She'd made it clear on more than one occasion that she could wait. I frown. *Killjoy*. I return my gaze to the open window. It makes for much bette viewing.

It is then I hear it the blaring of horns in the distance. My heart leaps in my chest and skips a beat *We are here!*

It isn't long be ore the road curves. The horns sound louder, now accompanied by drun rolls. I fidget in my seat, wishing I was in the front with the driver so that I co ld see everything coming up. Isandra gives me a quelling look, but I refuse to b subdued. This is Father's mission, an important one, and he'd invited me! I am allowed to be excited. Out the window I begin to see a line of men standing at attention. They wear what appear to be skirts, all bearing a pattern of l es and squares I've never seen before, and helms. Each has a spear in his righ hand.

At last, the carria e rolls to a stop. The horns have become quiet, as well as the drums. Within m ments the door is opening and Penjayko, the driver, is standing there. "Com my ladies. We have arrived at Castle Blacach!" In spite of her words to the c ntrary the entire trip, Isandra can't wait and almost leaps out of the carriage. N sty thoughts surface in my mind, but only for an instant before Penjayko is ex ending his hand towards me and smiling. Unlike Isandra, I graciously take his hand and allow him to help me down. The scene that meets my eyes is like vas one from out of one of my storybooks from home.

It is a huge castle Built of stone and mortar, it is easily several stories high and sprawls behind t e retinue of people standing before it. Father is there, holding out his han in my direction. "And this is my young daughter, Jash'ari."

I step forward, s ddenly feeling very timid. Everyone's eyes are on me, including those of a y ung boy who seems to be my age. He wears dark green trousers, a white shir and a decorative sash patterned after the men's skirts. His hair is a dark che tnut, tied back behind his head, curling tendrils shaping his face. His eyes are storm-cloud gray, wide with wonderment. It is then I realize he may have never met elves before. I take Father's hand and hold it tight. He is my safe haven, my light. Without him, I would be lost. But looking into the eyes of the young human boy standing beside his own father, I see the same kind of light, and it's intriguing to me.

The man standing beside the boy bends at his waist before me and offers his hand. His hair is brown, as is the tightly trimmed beard that adorns his face, and a golden circlet made of branches and horns perches atop his head. "Welcome to Castle Blacach. My name is Liam, Laird of this land, and this is my wife, Aileen, and my son, Ravn." His warm, brown eyes fill with sincerity as he gestures to each in turn. "I hope you enjoy your stay with us."

The words he speaks are familiar, as they had been taught to me by Isandra for months before this trip, yet, the way they are spoken is very different. Liam has a lilt to his words, an accent I find pleasing. It makes him a bit difficult to understand, so I catch only part of what he says. But his meaning is quite clear: that the woman and boy at his side are his family, and that I am welcome in his home.

I take the proffered hand and bow the way Father has said I should. I slowly speak the words I've learned, hoping they sound right. "Thank you, Laird. I am pleased to be here."

The man beams, a smile that lights up his eyes and makes them sparkle. He gently draws me forward to stand before the boy. "Ravn has been in knots waiting to meet you, and I believe you will be great friends. He has so much to show you. Why don't you go with him and see the castle?" Liam glances up at Father. "That is, if the Grand Magister is comfortable with it."

Father gives a grin, the rare kind he reserves solely for me, and nods, speaking politely in the language of our hosts, "Run along now. Mind your host and remember what you have been taught."

My chest tightens with happiness, and following his lead, I reply in the same tongue, "I will, Father. Thank you!" I look at the boy Ravn, who continues to stare at me through wide eyes for a moment until he takes hold of himself. He gives a brief bow and then holds out his hand. "It would be my pleasure to show you my home Lady Jash'ari Magisteress. Please come."

Surprised at his misuse of my father's title, I struggle to keep the smile that threatens to take over my entire face, as well as the burble of laughter waiting to work its way up my throat. "Thank you, young Laird. It would be my pleasure as well." I release Laird Liam's hand and reach out...

Ravn's hand is warm and dry to the touch, not sticky with sweat like most boys. When his fingers curve around mine, it feels like they are just the right fit, bigger, but not too big. I feel a sense of comfort, like my hand belongs there.

Ravn looks at me, his eyes searching mine for a moment. *Does he somehow feel the same way?* But then he urges me along to follow him up the stairs and into the magnificent castle.

The Inquisitor left that memory, then flew to the next one that shined brightly to him.

I run. The grasses slap against my trousers and boots, but I don't let the long blades slow me down. My long hair flies behind, my chest rising and falling with the force of my breathing. I chance a look over my shoulder and Ravn is still there, his face red with determination, a sheen of sweat over his brow and down his neck. A trill of excitement sweeps through me and I increase my pace despite the gentle upward slope. Never have I felt so wild, never have I felt so *free*.

The days have been like something from some kind of dream born from the books I like to read at home back in Rithalion. Breakfast is served to Father and I every morning alongside the Laird, Lady, and their son. After, I explore the castle and all its many mysteries, visit the town and talk to all the people we see, and run the countryside alongside the young laird until my lungs are full to bursting with the greenest air I've ever tasted. I come back in the evenings, the hemlines of my trousers filthy with mud, and I hide them in my travel trunks with the hope Isandra will not find them for a while and take me to task. I have learned the language of the mountain people quickly. Inundated by it all day, and even into the evening, I know more than I thought I'd ever learn. And Ravn has been there to help me the whole time.

The castle looms ahead, majestic and serene upon its cliff-top perch. In front of it is the sprawling town that looks to it for protection, and behind is a steep escarpment that ends many, many feet below in a sea of jagged rock. I forge onward, pumping my arms to keep my momentum. The castle gets bigger and bigger until I can see the individual stones that make up the walls. Almost there. Almost there. And then my hand slaps the stone, so hard it causes my palm to smart. A moment later and Ravn is beside me, his own hand slapping the same stone.

"Whoop! I did it! I win!" I jump in place, then turn and embrace my friend. He returns the hug, but, out of breath, Ravn soon pulls me down to the ground. I easily comply, exhaustion winning over the thrill of my victory, my legs trembling from the exertion. We sit there for quite some time, backs against the cool stone, sides pressed against one another's in a show of camaraderie. Ravn is easily the best friend I've ever had, although, I suppose that isn't saying much since no one back home wants to be friends with the half-breed daughter of the Grand Magister of Rithalion.

About an hour later I walk beside Ravn on our way through the courtyard. He is a bit quieter than usual, his demeanor a bit standoffish. Maybe it is because we were up earlier than usual, forgoing breakfast to see the guards at practice. The captain, a man Ravn called Moray, has a kind smile and quick wit. He makes me laugh, joking with the men as he puts them through their rigorous paces. He is a master swordsman, better than any of the other men, and a good leader. He works twice as hard as any of his subordinates, and he is fiercely dedicated to their welfare and training. It is easy to see he wants them to be better men, not just because they will serve their laird, but because they will also be serving themselves.

I look at my companion, his usually smiling face creased with thoughtfulness. "Ravn, is something the matter?"

He stops to look at me, his expression one that depicts some kind of struggle. I frown and stopped alongside him. After a moment he offers a surly shrug. "Maybe."

I freeze. He seems... upset.

"Have I done something wrong?"

He is pensive for another moment as he considers this question. Then his shoulders slump. "No, you have done nothing wrong."

I just stand there and look at him, taking in his defeated expression. "Then tell me what it is. We are friends, remember?"

He hesitates a moment, then nods. "Well, it's just... you won the race. And... and if the boys in town knew, I would be..." His voice trailed off and I was left to try and decipher the rest of what he would say.

I nod, understanding blossoming. The boys at home are the same. They have to be best at everything, especially when it comes to the girls. "I... I'm sorry..."

His voice is gruff. "No, don't be. You won fair. You are faster than me. But... but I have to..."

I supply the words, "Accept it?"

He gives a gusty exhale. "Yes."

"Do not worry. No one has to know but you and me. It will be our secret." I offer a conciliatory smile.

He shakes his head. "No, when I accept it, I want to feel like everyone can know, and not feel bad about it."

I ponder this for a moment and nod. "I like that, Laird Ravn. I believe that you will be a great leader one day, just like Moray."

His eyes brighten. "Really?"

"Oh yes, you will be a wonderful laird."

"How do you know?"

I give a wide smile. "I just do."

Ravn chuckles. "Come on, let's go into the stables. Mother will be looking for me to start my chores and I'd rather be with you."

I giggle. I've done the same on more than one occasion, especially with Isandra. I take Ravn's hand and we easily slink into the stables without anyone seeing us. The scent of fresh hay hits my nostrils the moment we enter, along with the odor of too many animals crammed into one space for far too long.

The horses are new to me, for we don't have them in Rithalion. I love the varying colors: black, brown, white and every shade in between. The markings often tell them apart, white socks on one, a blaze down the forehead of another.

I love their personalities, for each one is so different. I speak quietly. "Why do they stay in here? The horses?"

"This place is their home. They have shelter from the elements, and security from predators," said Ravn.

I ponder this. "But what about their freedom? Do they not yearn for it?"

It is Ravn's turn to consider. "Yes, I believe they do. But they get to roam the countryside every afternoon. And many of them are exercised by the men every other morning. They like being brought back here in the night time. I think it is because they feel safe here, and they are fed grain that cannot be found in the gazing fields."

I nod, understanding most of what he'd said. "So, they are happy?"

"I believe they are, yes. My father takes great care of his animals. He says I must, as well."

I smile. "I am glad to hear this."

Ravn grins and leads me up the stairs and into the loft. Here, there is an abundance of hay, and it cushions us as we sit down. For a moment we just look at each other, silly smirks on our faces, knowing that we shouldn't be there due to chores that need done by one young laird. But after a while, Ravn's expression shifts. His eyes roam over my face, seemingly taking in every detail. He lifts a hand, slowly reaches out, and touches my hair.

"You are so pretty. I've never seen a girl like you before."

I sit still, not really knowing what to say.

"Your hair is so smooth, and shiny." He looks into my eyes. "Your eyes are so green. And your ears..."

My breath catches in my throat. Yes, that is a big difference between us. My ears are shaped much differently than his. Where his are nicely rounded at the top, mine are elongated and pointed. They aren't half as long as a pure-bred elf, but long enough.

"...I like the shape."

I blink. "You do?"

He nods emphatically. "Oh yes. They are nice."

"Th... thank you young Laird."

His gaze slides back to mine. "Why do you call me that?"

I frown. "Call you what?"

"Laird."

"Is that not your title?"

He shrugs. "I guess it could be, but I am not a laird yet."

"But you will be," I point out.

He nods. "But I'm not today."

"So, I shouldn't call you that?"

"I just... it feels so formal."

I regard him thoughtfully. "I suppose maybe you are right."

"Just call me Ravn."

I brighten. "Alright."

We both smile then, happy with our agreement. A thought abruptly comes to my mind and I chuckle.

Ravn cocks his head. "What?"

"Why do all the men here wear skirts?"

His gray eyes grow wide, sparkling with merriment. "Those aren't skirts! They are kilts!"

"Kilts?"

He nods. "Yes, and when my father deems me a man, I will get my own kilt!"

His eyes shine with pride and anticipation and I can't help feeling happy for him. "When do you think that will be?"

"His expression turns serious. "I don't know. For everyone it is different. I have heard some boys get theirs as early as twelve years old!"

"What must you do to get one? Is it hard? Is it..." I struggle to find the word. "...dangerous?"

He shakes his head. "No, all you have to do is prove that you are becoming a man, show that you are beginning to think like a man, act like a man."

I nod thoughtfully. "How old are you now?"

"This is my tenth summer." He regards me intently. "How old are you?"

"This is my fifteenth."

Surprised flits across his face. "That can't be. You are so.... so short. You look at least two years younger than me."

I shrug. "Maybe I am. Elves age much differently than humans."

He frowns. "What do you mean?"

"How old do you think my father is?"

He is thoughtful. "Maybe thirty summers?"

I laugh and the sound fills the entire loft. "He has seen well over three hundred."

His eyes widen. "How can that be?"

I laugh again. "It's just the way elves are. We live a long time."

"How long will you live?"

"I do not know. I am only half elvin, and every half elf is different."

"What does that mean? Half elf?"

"My father is a pure blood elf." I take a deep breath before continuing. "My mother was human."

Ravn regards me solemnly. "Was? You speak of your mother as though she is not here anymore."

I return his sympathetic gaze, my chest tightening in that all-too-familiar way. "Yes, she died after she..." I struggle again to find the lairds-tongue words I need. "...birthed me?"

Ravn is still. "She died after you were born?"

I nod. "Yes. She never fully recovered, and then she came down with a..." I thought again. "... sickness. A fever. I have no memories of her." I take a deep breath. "But my father says she was the love of his life."

Ravn is silent for a while, then gives me a sad smile. "Then she must have been something great."

"What?"

"Your mother. She must have been something great. For a man to have seen around three hundred years to pick her out and say she was his greatest love, that must mean she was special."

My chest tightens a bit more and I lay down on the hay. "I... I suppose you could be right."

Ravn follows suit, burrowing into the golden strands. "I know I'm right."

"How do you know?"

"He smiles. "I just do."

The tightening lessens a bit and I smile back. Then we just lay there on the hay, looking at each other's faces. I watch as Ravn's eyes finally drift closed, and, feeling tired myself, I allow myself the same luxury.

Sleep bleary eyes blink open when I hear a commotion below. A woman's voice, filled with fear, is prominent. "Where could they possibly be?"

A man's voice follows, consoling. "I don't know mi'lady. But we are doing all we can to find them. I have everyone searching the countryside, the town, and the castle."

As the shroud of sleep falls away, I wonder what, or who, they could possibly be looking for. I glance over at Ravn, and he, too, is wiping the residue of sleep from his eyes. He looks around, takes in our surroundings, and frowns. "How long have we been up here?" he whispers.

The creaking of the ladder leading up into the loft takes the answer from between my lips. My friend's question is wary, almost fearful...

A head of black hair, followed by broad shoulders emerges. Ravn's voice shakes as he speaks. "Moray?"

The man at arm's expression shifts from one of intense strain to shameless relief. "By the gods, Ravn! Is this where you've been all this time?"

"I'm so sorry sir! We must have fallen asleep."

Moray pitches his voice down below. "Mi'lady Aileen! I've found them both here in the barn!" He then turns back to them. "You have been missing for hours! The whole guard is out looking for you two!"

I watch Ravn's eyes widen as he realizes the gravity of his situation and his complexion pales.

The man gestures them forward. "Come now, it's getting late. Let's get you down from here."

We both slowly crawl forward. I can feel Ravn's tension; his body thrums with it. He has told me many things about his parents, and while they are very kind and loving, they can also mete out a vicious punishment if the crime warrants it. It puts me on edge and I wonder what my own father is thinking, and if he has been worried as well.

In silence Ravn climbs down the ladder as Moray goes on about their extensive search. I simply follow suit, a feeling of dread settling into my chest.

It is obvious many hours have passed, for the sun has almost set. Long shadows converge in the corners of the barn, broken only by the light cast by the lanterns that have been lit along the main walls. I crowd close to my friend once we are aground, and for a moment we just stand there. Without turning around, he grasps my hand in his and a feeling of security sweeps through me.

Then the lady of the castle comes rushing through the open doors. She stops and takes one look at Ravn, her face an impenetrable mask of suppressed emotion. But then it slips and tears are in her eyes as she closes the gap between she and her son. She grabs Ravn and pulls him close, wrapping her arms around him in a way that makes a lump form in the center of my chest. Tears fall on the top of his head, tears only a mother can shed, and my heart twists in agony. I wrench my gaze away from the reunion, glance around for my father. But he isn't there.

"Ravn, where have you been all this time? I've been sick with worry!"

"I've been here mother. We didn't mean to, but we fell asleep up in the loft. We didn't know how late it is. I'm sorry!"

Aileen smooths her hands over his face and hair. "It's alright. It's alright now. All that matters is that you are found and that you are safe. I love you so much. I could never stand to lose you."

She bends to kiss him then, one on each cheek, and when she is finished, Aileen looks to where I am standing. An unreadable expression crosses the woman's face as she approaches. I stand my ground, not knowing where to go if I were to flee. Aileen's eyes are stunning, colored the same storm cloud gray as Ravn's, and her hair is like golden honey. When Ravn's beautiful mother stands before me, all I can do is take a deep breath and look up, hoping that she will not punish me in Ravn's stead.

That thought is erased within a single moment as Aileen falls to her knees before me. Then, a heartbeat later, arms are circling me, pulling me close, closer, until I am pressed against warm softness.

I exhale in a contented sigh and allow myself to relax into the motherly embrace. Aileen's arms are strong, yet gentle... firm, yet giving. She is softer than any woman I have ever hugged before, and she smells of lavender and chamomile. I tentatively return the embrace, luxuriate in it, dream in it. I imagine this must be what my own mother's arms would have felt like if she wasn't dead and gone. Aileen doesn't say anything; she doesn't need to. All of her emotion is in the embrace. Feelings of love rush over me, and I feel safe, safe like I feel only in my father's arms.

The voice is husky, filled with some unspoken emotion. "I'm glad you are safe little princess."

I tighten my grip, and suddenly I feel like I never want to let go.

The Inquisitor moved on, his interest piqued. To see the Wolf as a boy, that was incredible. And he knew it was, indeed, the barbarian. He'd gleaned that from emotions surrounding the memory, not to mention the similarity. Despite his age, and the years of scarring, it was obvious that he and the boy were one and the same.

Until the Delving the Inquisitor hadn't known that Vivien had lost her mother as an infant. The feelings young Vivien had experienced with the Wolf's mother had touched him, and he realized he'd become invested in her story already, wanting to know more about the intriguing woman in his midst.

He cruised along again, at a slightly slower rate, wondering what else he might find. And when he found it, he slowed again.

Peals of laughter float through the air and I turn in the direction of the sound. It is Emma, of course. She is always laughing and giving her position away. I grin to myself. It makes my job that much easier, so I can't complain. I pelt off in her direction, dodging the trees and shrubbery that get in my way, leaping over fallen logs and bracken. I stop a few moments later, listening intently. This is where she and her sister are much better at this game than I; their hearing is much better.

I quiet my breathing, straining to hear. *Surely, she is here somewhere close. My hearing isn't that bad.* The sounds of the forest surround me: the winds moving through the leaves, the song of birds in the branches, the scampering of small animals in the litter over the ground. The bellowing of a bear in the near distance bids me pause, sets the hairs on my arms to rising. It doesn't sound happy.

My voice shakes as I shout, "Emma! Evey! We should go. There is a bear close by!"

Silence rings among the trees. Where once there had been birdsong above and skittering at my feet, there is now nothing but the winds. Even it sounds somehow subdued, as though waiting for something to happen.

"Emma? Come out, game's over. Evey?"

The bear bellows again, closer this time. It is angry; I can tell by the tone of its voice. This time it is followed by a shrill scream.

I spring into a run. My heart hammers against my chest as I fly over the landscape, somehow missing the pitfalls that would have gotten me any other time. I hear another scream, then another. *Oh gods, no. Not Evey too.* The next roar of the bear is so loud I stumble to my knees just as I reach the clearing.

The bear is there, hulking over a massive fallen tree, its width easily two of me lying side by side. He is tall, bigger than any I've ever seen, and his brown fur is dirty and matted. He lunges. Evey's next scream is anguished, and when I see the slender form of Emma fall at the monster's feet, I hear another scream. This time it is from me.

Oh, gods no! Please no!

Without thinking, I pick myself up and run towards the bear. The animal has his head lowered over Emma, and as I get closer, I hear the crunch of bone. Again, I scream, over and over, my heart crying out in sheer agony. My heart beats a staccato rhythm in my chest, and my body shakes with the force of my sobbing.

"Get away from her! Get away!"

The bear raises his head, entrails dangling from his maw, and looks at me. I keep screaming the same litany, but the bear just ignores me and returns to his meal. I bend down, pick up a heavy rock from the ground, and hurl it with all my strength.

The stone strikes the bear in the side with more force than I knew I possessed. His head snaps back up in a spray of bloody saliva, and he glares at me before emitting a massive roar. I stand stock still, fear making my heart skip a beat. And then he charges.

I stand frozen until I hear Evey scream, a mournful sound that sets me into a frantic run. Fear courses through me, giving my feet wings once more. I don't think I've ever run so fast, or so far, in so little time, but it doesn't matter. The bear is faster. I feel his hot breath at my back, reeking with the blood of my niece, just as I slide beneath a huge rotting trunk covered with eons of forest debris.

My breath comes in ragged gasps as the bear roars again, a frightening sound that seems to shake the ground I lie upon. I scoot as far back in my lair as I can, and I barely escape the enormous paw that claws at me from the entrance. He swipes again, and then a third time, before he ceases.

For a moment there is silence and everything is still. My throat is raw from the force of my screams, and my eyes feel swollen. My mind is filled with Emma lying there on the ground, her belly ripped open, blood soaking the pale blue sundress she'd decided to wear that morning. I wonder if the bear has gone back to find her body and I hope that Evey has–

I hear a scuffling sound at the entrance just as the bear's muzzle pokes through. I lurch back as he snuffles around, snorting when he catches my scent. He withdraws and I squeeze my eyes tightly shut, hoping he just goes away.

The scraping of claws above me makes me almost jump out of my skin. Chunks of moldy debris rain down on my head and I scream again despite the pain. I cower there, not knowing what to do, too afraid to crawl towards the entrance lest I get mauled by wickedly sharp claws. My heart beat drums in my ears, taking away all sound, and then a rush of air from overhead tells me that he has broken through.

I stare up at the bear and he is larger than I had ever imagined. He roars yet again, rancid breath and spittle washing over my face. His eyes are wild... crazy with some unfathomable anger that can't be quenched. His fur is filthy with neglect, a dark patch behind his elbow more than the rest. From the center of it is the broken shaft of an arrow. A stench hits my nose, a pervading scent of rot that would have made me gag at any other time but this one. Instead, all I feel is desperation, clawing through me like some wild thing yearning to be free.

And I think of fire.

The bear makes to lunge. I know in my heart it will make no difference, but I raise my hands in front of my face–

And suddenly the fire is there.

Hundreds of tiny, shimmering fireflies explode from my hands and into the bear's face. He rears back onto his hind legs and I watch in awe as they pelt him from every direction. The smell of burning fur permeates the air as he swipes at his head, swatting at the fireflies. But they keep returning, buzzing around him.

And it's then I realize they aren't fireflies at all. They are fire fae. And they are there to abet my escape.

I grasp at the jagged edges of the ancient log. They crumble beneath my hands as I seek the purchase I need, but finally I am on my feet again, running, running, running–

Until I smack into a warm, hard surface. Arms wrap around me as I begin to fall back, arms that pull me close. I bury my face into the familiar scent of my father's robes and sob uncontrollably, relief washing over me in waves. With Father there, nothing can harm me. I hear men shouting, hear the bear roar for the last time, and then a heavy thud.

But then there is a hand on my arm, ripping me from Father's grip, spinning me around. My older brother stands before me, his green eyes sparkling with disbelief, pain, fury, and everything in between. In the distance behind him stands his wife, agony etched on her face, and Evey, standing in the circle of her arms, her face red and wet with tears.

"Look what you have done! Because of you and your foolishness, my beloved Emmalyn is gone!" He takes my other arm in is other hand and shakes me until my head rocks back on my neck.

Father shouts, "Son, stand down!"

But my brother doesn't seem to hear, continues to shake me. "I've told you time and time again to never come so far into these woods. And now, because of you, she is gone! You are an imprudent, entitled brat who has no care for anyone but herself!"

"Anlon!"

"And I hope never to set eyes on you again! Ever!"

Father grabs hold of my brother's hands, ripping them free of my arms. I crumple into a heap onto the ground, stunned. He is right. This is my fault. I should have listened better. It didn't matter that we had all decided to break the rules. I was the leader. I am always the leader when we play. It's always been that way.

I hear Father and Anlon argue, but their words find no meaning. I just sit there and shake, guilt taking me in its iron grip and crushing my heart. It is my fault. My beautiful niece is dead, all because of me.

Shaking, the Inquisitor took his hands away from Vivien. She proceeded to curve around the mound of her belly and into a fetal position. Tears streaked down her face to wet the pillow beneath her head, and her lips trembled. She was pale, far too pale, and he knew that their time together was done for the day.

In silence he took himself from the room, stopping at the nearest guard. "Go get the Master Healer and bring him here," he said solemnly. The guard rushed to his task and the Inquisitor slowly walked to his room. More than ever, he felt his age, and guilt oozed from every pore. The memory he'd tapped had been one that had changed Lady Valdera's life forever, the one that had placed her into Rithalion's College of Mages as one of the youngest students to ever walk its halls. It had made her the excellent mage she was today, but it also haunted her, even now.

The Inquisitor entered his room, closed the door behind him before collapsing onto the bed. He then lay there in the darkness, remembering the long ago past.

Chapter Forty-Two
The Trials

Al'sangui met them in the morning just after their breakfast of porridge, the look of smug superiority boding ill for the group as a whole. "Come. Bring your things. If you fail you will not be back."

La'athai collected their gear in a rush, slapping armor on and throwing weapon belts over shoulders while carrying barely rolled bed mats in their arms. Al'sangui lead them out of the Council Hall, around the building to the rear. There they saw an empty alleyway and a set of buildings on one side with their backs facing the street, and the wall of the Council Hall on the other. Everything was made of the strange elvin stone without hinge or seam, but the Council Hall had a sizable balcony twenty-five feet into the air.

Al'sangui turned and faced them with heavily lidded eyes. "Does anyone possess grapnel or rope?" The group shook their heads. "Good. Your task is to get to that balcony, my office, before I get there."

And he turned to leave, the guards going with him.

Katriona looked upwards as they left and uttered a vile curse so egregious others flinched.

The La'athai exploded into voices.

"How long will it take him?"

"Ten minutes for the gelded bastard, I bet. Maybe less."

"A pyramid of people."

"With ten minutes? No time!"

"Make a rope of belts?"

"No grapnel."

"Tie it to a sword?"

"It'll bend if it doesn't cut through."

Xadrian's face was furious. "Think, people. Think!"

The Wolf looked up to the building with its blank face to this alley, then the width of the alley. "I have it."

Xadrian looked to him. "Brother?"

But the Barbarian was already moving, "Make loops out of your belts and link them. Now!"

And he ran at full speed out of the alley and then away from the college and back down the next street. As he had hoped, the front of the buildings here had windows. Better, one had a trellis of roses creeping up the front of the building. He vaulted the low wall into the front yard and to the trellis. Without pausing he attacked the wooden net, hauling himself up, pushing rung after rung. Roses scratched his hands and left blood seeping from dozens of wounds, but he could not stop, dared not stop. Up and up he went, hands in agony.

A voice called from behind as he crested the roof, but he ignored it. He made the short eight-foot jump from one house to another, sliding slightly on the unnaturally smooth surface. He looked over to the Council Hall, saw the grand windows to the empty office, and steeled himself. He backed up as far as he dared, sprinted forward with everything he had, and leapt into open air.

He heard a cheer beneath him as he flew over the La'athai like a bird. He landed on the wide banister and jumped down to the floor of the balcony. Then he turned and held out aching hands dripping with blood. "Belts!"

Xadrian frowned. "Brother?"

"Belts!"

Katriona snatched the chain of secured belts and threw them up. He caught the end, the other almost dragging the ground. "First! Hurry!"

Katriona got on one loop and he began reeling her up, hand by hand on the looped belts. His fists screamed in pain from the dozens of cuts and punctures, but still he pulled and pulled. Finally, her hands slapped onto the thick stone railing. He pulled her over the edge and then tossed the loops back down for another. Then he pulled the next soldier up, then the next. The wounds on his hands were trying to close, and given mere minutes they would heal like all his injuries, but he kept pulling up soldiers and splitting the fresh skin, leaving his hands to bleed in rivulets that rained down in remorseful tears to patter onto the street and the La'athai he hauled upwards. Next Xadrian came, and only five more left.

"Thank you, brother. This balcony is well cramped."

Katriona's voice held a certain dread. "Did he say on the balcony or in his office?"

The silence was thick with perceived failure. Xadrian barked, "He said both. Sure bet unless we get to his office, he will say we failed. Get us inside."

The Wolf continued to haul as he heard more commotion behind him. Another up.

Katriona cursed. "It's locked."

There was a crashing tinkle behind the Wolf but he dared not stop.

"General?"

"He said no grapnels, but no other rules were mentioned. Reach through and get us inside or smash the thing in."

A loop slipped from his hand but the elf held on. He continued to pull until another cane over the banister His hands were beginning to stiffen badly. He could only tell he held a loop of leather by looking. Another.

He looked at the last two La'athai below, and his hands were aching in the joints from the strain. "Both! On now!"

These elves had followed him into certain death; they did not hesitate to grab on. He wrapped his leg around one of the stone pillars of the banister and hauled, hearing leather creak in protest as he pulled, hand over hand, loop by loop. There was a name inside of him, a call toward heaven.

It was a name. It was Vivien.

He just kept pulling until the last, possible, second.

Dragon Vessel

Councilman Al'sangui opened the door to his office. He stared, open mouthed, at the crowd of soldiers buckling belts back around their midsections while they smiled wolfishly.

Xadrian walked smartly across the red carpet to the councilman and very pointedly did not salute, bow, or give any manner of greeting. "When can we meet the Council?"

Al'sangui shook his head. "Councilwoman Os'turil will meet you after your evening meal."

Xadrian nodded brusquely. "La'athai, back to our chamber."

And the men began to file past the councilman who examined the office left behind. "If she comes to the jail and you are not there she will leave, and you will fail."

Xadrian stepped in between passing soldiers, letting the Wolf pass behind him, carrying his red cloak. He stared into the eyes of the councilman, letting his resentment show for just a moment. "We will not fail."

Then he followed the Wolf into the hall, past the shocked guardsmen.

Al'sangui yelled after them, "Did you have to break my window?"

"Should it have been locked?" Xadrian tossed back.

The guardsmen caught up to them and lead them through the halls back to the jail. They waited outside as La'athai filed in, dropped their packs, and fell to the floor as the thrill of action and fear faded from their systems. The Wolf opened the cloak wrapping his hands, shrugging sheepishly at the bloodstains as he held it out to Xadrian, who took it and buried it in his pack. Then he turned back to the Wolf. "Your hands?"

The Barbarian held up his open hands, encrusted with old blood, but bearing nothing else but thin white scars from the ordeal. Xadrian nodded. "Good. Wash them now." He leaned on the lone table in the room and addressed them all. "Well, if we leave this place, we can be sure that the councilwoman will come while we are gone, so we cannot leave. Make use of the time. Sleep, talk softly, play cards. We must be here and we must rest. Now they are certain we won't be easily dissuaded. That means the next test will be worse. Be ready for anything."

The team did, and awaited the arrival of the next council member. The Wolf sat in meditation, seeing Vivien's enchanting green gaze every time he closed his eyes. He struggled to feel a part of her, but icy memories of so long alone in the wild whispered to him that he was, and always would be, alone.

Lunch came, a simple soup with not quite enough bread to go around. Katriona smiled wryly and told the men to dig into the rations in their packs. "Looks like the legendary generosity of Moirdem has run dry sooner than expected."

Xadrian frowned. "We are not offended enough to retreat from this place. They will try to offend more."

The hours dragged onward, and none of them dared leave. The Wolf simply sat in the corner, feeling Xadrian's worried eyes upon him. He knew

345

that the general thoug t the same of his impetuous actions. He had climbed the trellis, and had to hav left drops of blood all down the face of the building and the rail. There was a c hance that someone would notice, and they would send a healer to see to the v ounds of whoever had been hurt. No wounds would be found, of course. No to mention, if Al'sangui had seen his ripped and torn hands, or worse, witr ssed them healing, they would know he was not really human. None of the a'athai knew how the elves of Moirdem would react to his monstrous nature, nd they could not dare let them find out.

Dinner was serve I, simple bread and butter in clay crocks. The La'athai grumbled only a little and supplemented the fare again from their packs. They readied themselves to meet the councilwoman, but she did not come. After another hour, they ag in sat down and busied themselves. Katriona visited the Wolf in his corner and asked after his well-being, but the Wolf answered her only with head shakes and shrugs. She was a good friend, but he could not be close to her. He could not let himself fail Vivien, and he could not waver in his need for her, for he was sure she would not waver for him.

He let the worries wash away, and images of Vivien came as surely as the sunrise follows every moon in the sky. He felt his heart tremble, for he didn't just remember her eye s or her smile, but the pregnant heaviness of her breasts, and the passionate tightness of her love. He could smell her personal perfume and it filled him with a heady thrill like strong liquor. He could feel her press her lips to his in an al nost animal need and–

"I am Councilwor an Os'turil. Come with me."

The Wolf's eyes napped open and he saw at the doorway an old elf that wore the silver robes of this city's Council in a fashion that was particularly austere. She wore no bangles, rings, or earrings, no necklaces or decoration of any kind. Elves were scrambling to their feet to follow her, and the Wolf followed suit. Os'turil did not pause, or even slow as she walked away, truly not caring if any of th m kept up or not. They did manage to gather behind her as she took to the sta rs with a vigor that would have impressed a human one tenth her age. It was a pace that brooked no questions, and they asked none.

They exited on th fifth floor and into a wide open, almost cavernous room with bundles of glow ig stones on every wall and hanging in baskets from the ceiling. There were i assive fireplaces, fully stocked with wood and lit, all along the walls. The flickering fires cast sordid shadows and took him to another time. He had a moment of vertigo as he looked upon the rows upon rows of books, scroll, and tomes in bookshelves set in rows as far as the eye could see. He glanced up to where balconies were not, and still expected to see a massive dragon pee ing down at him with glowing eyes. It flashed before him for a second and he ha I to shake away the vision.

Os'turil was alrea ly speaking. "Hunt down a fae creature. You may use these books to learn v hat lives in the area. Find a wild one, capture it, return here and tame it. I wil be back before breakfast."

And then she left.

She was barely out of the room when the La'athai began chattering. Xadrian's voice cut through it all. "There is no time. Does anyone know of anything tamable that lives in this area?"

"Tir-reath?" said one.

Katriona shook her head. "Unlikely. Tir-reath for hundreds of miles around were captured and tamed thousands of years ago. You'd have to travel days to find one. Even then, wild tir-reath will kill you and eat you if they do not flee faster than you can follow."

The Wolf blinked. He saw the massed pile of dragon bones in the courtyard of Pergatium. He shook his head. He could hear his heart, feel it beating against his chest.

"A Dulkalur?"

"In one night? Without being eaten?" Katriona retorted.

The Wolf felt the pressure behind his eyes manifest. He heard Zah'rahm, the dragon chuckling right behind him. He spun to see only the glass-paned double doors to the outside. Still, he began to sweat.

"A giant?"

"Same with a giant, or a spinemonkey, or... anything, really."

"Let's get one of our own tir-reath..."

Xadrian cut in. "She said a wild one. Even without a saddle, the fur will show saddle wear. They will put a saddle on it and it will accept it because it has been trained to and we are lost. Even domesticated tir-reath take weeks to quit bucking the saddle."

The Wolf felt the heat of the fires, but like it was on the inside. His skin felt too tight, and he took steady, measured steps toward the nearest set of double doors. As he approached, he could see his eyes glowing red. He opened them, and stepped out into the icy blast of an early winter. It shocked him, and he felt the memories fade away.

"Let's get one of the farm animals, then–"

Katriona cut him off. "If they check for saddle behavior, they will check for local marks for who owns the damn thing."

"Wolf?" Xadrian called.

The Wolf waved him back to the conversation and took long breaths. He waved a hand in front of his face, the argument playing behind him in the library. He saw no reflection of light. He took deep breaths, letting the creeping dread fall away. Only after a few minutes he heard a soft sound nearby. He cocked his head and heard it again.

"*Tiktiktiktiktik,*"

The Wolf turned to see a bright red and orange striped tirinian looking at him like a lost hound, creeping closer, ever closer.

"*Tiktiktiktiktik,*"

The creatures found him in every city. The Wolf gasped as realization downed upon him.

"Xadrian!" The creature started, but only backed up a few steps.

ROSS €ROSS

The General all b t flew to his side, hand on his blade. He looked around. and saw nothing. "Wl t, Wolf?"

The Barbarian po ited at the creature as the rest of the La'athai came to see what was happening. A few cooed at the cute little thing, others shrugged and rolled their eyes. "Are these things considered fae creatures?"

"Yes. Tirinian are fae creatures, but just barely so."

"What's it matter" Katriona dismissed the little squirrel/cat with a wave, "Tirinian are not figh ing animals, or farming animals. You can't train them to do anything, especiall in one night."

The Wolf smiled at her. "Get me a chair."

The plan was form ed in minutes.

Councilwoman (s'turil returned before dawn. The La'athai mustered sleepily from the floo where they had brought their packs and laid out bedrolls to make sure they wei there to meet her.

The Wolf heard tl :ir exchange by the stairs.

"Did you tame a c eature?"

"Several," the Ge ieral replied.

The reply was as slapped from her mouth. "What?"

"Several, more t an one, Councilwoman." There was a definite pause. "Please follow me."

The Wolf saw he stoic face shatter into shock and denial when she saw him, sitting in one of he library chairs, every square inch of him carpeted with tirinian.

Tiktiktiktiktik.

Her face twisted a if chewing food rife with mold. "What is this?"

The General wav d dismissively. "You said a fae creature, but you did not say how closely to th fae it had to be linked. So, we gathered these and taught them this trick."

Os'turil's cheeks lushed a rosy hue and she shook slightly. "General, tirinian sit on guests I am impressed you have gotten them to tolerate the presence of that.... hin . Nonetheless, this is not evidence of training."

The General feign d surprise. "Oh, you haven't seen the trick yet."

He waved to the La'athai. They had tested the trick over and over, but everyone held their br ath anyway.

Three La'athai be an removing tirinian from the Wolf, setting them on the floor.

The Wolf was ca eful to speak in his native tongue. "Come, Red. Come, Blue. Come, Spots." .nd as each was taken from him, they would turn to leap back up, snuggle as close to him as they could, and started up their little hiccupping purr. The Wolf smiled absently, remembering Vivien trying to free him of a blanket of t inian in Elyrion, and having as little luck. It would not matter if the Wolf ca led to them or not, for they would seek his warmth and snuggle against him u itil he moved.

Tiktiktiktiktiktik iktiktiktik.

It was unlikely that Os'turil understood what he said, but the meaning was fairly clear. She spun upon Xadrian who already had accepted a book from the library she had given them access to. It was already open to the page on tirinian. It described them in flowing Elvish script as animals of very little fae influence in their makeup, but fae nonetheless. It also mentioned they were near impossible to train except by masters of the craft.

Either she knew what it said, or she guessed, for she shook even more, fists balled. She hissed her next words. "Go to the council chambers. Stand at attention. We will meet with you when we have prepared ourselves."

And she stalked off, leaving Xadrian frowning after her. The Wolf stood gingerly, and the tirinian poured off him in a riot of color. When he looked unlikely to sit back down, they hesitantly skittered out the doors to the outside, and down the face of the building in search of food, or rest, or a warm fire to sleep by. The La'athai smiled to one another and clapped each other on backs and arms, but Xadrian was still and thinking deep thoughts, looking to the archway where Councilwoman Os'turil had disappeared.

The Wolf approached as Katriona reached Xadrian. "What?"

Xadrian did not hear her, he only turned inward to himself before finally focusing on the rest of the world and shouting orders. "Wolf Pack! Eat from your packs! Eat and drink your fill, we will forget what food tastes like before we eat again, I wager. Void yourselves. Drop everything at the cells. Quickly and quietly. Move!"

And it was done just so. The La'athai were already eating and draining waterskins as they marched downstairs. They gobbled food as they dropped packs, weapons, and armor. They drank while excreting into the simple privies of the jail cells, then left, stuffed and sloshing with water, toward the Great Council Hall. Once inside, they saw guards along the walls, there to watch them perform the proscribed task.

And there, the La'athai formed up to attention.

Xadrian frowned at them like a mighty storm, saying, "Stand, and stand forever. The lives of your loved ones at home depend on this."

Then he, too, stood at attention.

And waited.

Chapter Forty-Three
Breaking Down

The inquisitor regarded Vivien as she entered the chamber. She was pale, more so than usual, and beneath her eyes was a dark shadow, likely caused from lack of sleep. Dread was indicative in every body movement as she made towards the sofa. Once there, she lay down and resumed the position she'd been in two days prior. She simply closed her eyes, and she waited.

The Inquisitor pushed away the guilt that suffused him. He was unaccustomed to such compliance from a subject, and he found that it messed with his mind. It was obvious she had suffered since last they had met, yet, here she lay before him, unarmed.

She is innocent, you fool. Why must you persist in this?

The Inquisitor quashed the rogue thought and seated himself before her. Taking her lead, he didn't offer greeting, merely placed his hands upon her chest and forehead and closed his own eyes...

With the clearest voice I can muster, I recite a summarization of what I had learned from the texts the apprentices had been given to read over the past several weeks. The master is patient, is always patient, no matter how silly the question or how much stammering is made during recitations such as these. It is something I can finally appreciate about the academy, something that is positive amid all the misery I experience daily.

When I finish the recitation, my ears are greeted with a few moments of silence. Sensing something amiss, I look around, notice the expressions of disgust on the faces of the other apprentices, the look of enthusiasm on the face of the master. My heart sinks. What have I done wrong this time?

"Miss Valdera, that was quite impressive. Your powers of memory retention are quite extraordinary. Has anyone ever told you that before?"

Feeling the color drain from my face, I sink back down into my seat. "I, um, I don't recall Master Hoylanchar," I lie. My father had told me that very same thing on many occassion, lauding me for learning the language of the Lairdlands so swiftly and effortlessly, my ability to remember names, dates, and events from history, and my uncanny affinity for mathematics. Regret washes over me, for I belatedly realize I need to tone that down here at the academy, where I am constantly being judged by the other apprentices.

"You are already prepared for testing. Please meet me in my office after lecture so that I can administer it to you. After, I will provide to you the next text in my lecture series and you can join the next class."

"Yes, Master," I reply in a small voice.

He gives me a wide smile as he proceeds with the next lesson, and once again I chance a glance around the room. The atmosphere has definitely become tense, and the expressions of disdain on the faces of my peers makes me shrink further down into my seat.

ROSS ₵ROSS

After lecture is called to a close, I am the first one out of the hall, making haste towards the appointment I have been given. But I am not fast enough. I am roughly shoved from behind and I fall to the floor, books and parchments sprawling over the smooth stones. Someone else kicks the books against the far wall, and other crushe the parchments beneath her boots.

"You have a great memory, Miss Valdera, so remember this," says a boy's voice from behind me as he pulls my hair.

Then, as quickly as they had come, they are gone.

I just lay there for a moment, letting the tears stream down my face. The other apprentices hate me, and I know it is because I am the half-breed daughter of the Grand Magister. At that moment I become angry, not at the other apprentices, but at my father. Why has he put me in such a lawless place? How he can he allow me to be treated this way? Certainly, he must have known that I would be castigated here?

My body aches as I pick myself up. I slowly collect my crumpled parchments and my trampled books, then turn towards the closest exit. I don't want to take the Master's test. I don't want to rise to the next class where I will be tormented even more by apprentices that will be older than the ones who taunt me now. I don't want to see the academy ever again. I walk out of the building and dump everything into the nearest bushes and begin to run. I don't stop until I am beyond the city outskirts.

I take off my boots and walk along the bank of the Fyresmee River. The beauty of the place makes the sadness within me swell and I allow the tears to come anew. I love the sound of the rushing waters, the songs of the sunset tanagers that fly from treetop to treetop, the wind in the branches high overhead. I pick up a fist-sized rock and throw it into the waters, listening to the splash it makes as it hits. I pick up another, and then another, throwing them as far as I can into the river. The repetitive action is somehow therapeutic and helps me think past the tumult in my mind. Maybe, just maybe, my father doesn't know what has been happening at the academy. Certainly, he knows many things, but how could he know this unless someone tells him? Thing is, I don't want to be the one to tell him. I actually don't want anyone to tell him. I don't want him to know how weak I am. I don't want him to be disappointed.

I reach down to pick up another rock when I hear a splash in the river, the same sound my rocks have been making as they hit the water. It is then I sense someone behind me. I quickly turn to find a boy standing several feet away. He wears the robes of a healer's acolyte, blond hair shining in the late-day sun. I just stare at him, for I hadn't realized I was no longer alone.

"How long have you been there?" I say.

His blue eyes twinkle and he grins. "Long enough to know that you don't throw very far."

I purse my lips. "Maybe not, but I bet I can outrun you any day."

He cocks his head. "Really? We will have to test that out sometime."

DRAGON VESSEL

I scoff. "Sometime? I don't even know you. You act like we will see each other again after today."

"We know each other now, so why wouldn't we?"

"We don't. I don't even know your name."

"I am Mikarvan."

I sniff. "My name is Viv..."

"I know who you are."

I purse my lips again. Of course, he knows who I am. Everyone knows who I am.

"So now that we know one another, we can see each other again and we can run," he says.

"Maybe."

His shoulders slump. "Why just maybe? I can teach you to throw farther!"

It is then I realize that he honestly wants to meet me again. I can't help wondering why, but I don't ask. "Alright, we can do that."

His eyes brighten again and he approaches to stand in front of me. He holds out his hand. "Here, let me show you." I put my rock into his hand. "See, you hold it like this," he demonstrates, "and then reach back and throw like this." The rock leaves his hand and it hits the river several feet past my best mark. He is definitely skilled.

"How do you know so much about rock throwing?"

He shrugs. "I come here a lot when I want to just think. I think and I throw rocks."

I grin at how silly that sounds. He smiles back. "What else do you do here?"

"I have adventures."

I regard him speculatively. "Adventures?"

"Yeah. Epic adventures. You want to be in one?"

"I don't know. Tell me about one."

"Alright. There's this one where I meet a dragon that wants me to help it save the Elvish nations from bad people."

I narrow my eyes. "That's blasphemy. No dragon would want to save fae elves."

He frowned. "Well, it's my adventure and this one does."

I put my hands on my hips. "Fine, what color is it?"

He grins. "It's all colors."

"What?"

"Yeah, it's a rainbow."

"No dragon is rainbow colored."

"Well this one is. I saw it with my own eyes."

I give a gusty sigh. "Fine."

"No really, I saw it. I saw it in a dream. That's how I came up with the idea."

I just nod and look at him askance. He's a strange boy, that is for sure.

333

"What? You're giving me a weird look. You want to still be my friend, right?"

"I didn't know we were friends."

He frowns again. "Of course, we are friends. I just told you about my adventure."

"Well, then you shouldn't be going around telling strangers about your adventures."

"You aren't a stranger anymore."

"But I was," I point out.

"Not really. I know that you are Vivien Valdera, the Grand Magister's daughter."

My shoulders slump, and the reason why I am at the river rushes back to my mind. "I wish he wasn't my father."

He gets quiet. Then, "You are blessed to have one."

I almost choke on my next words. "I... I'm sorry. I didn't know..."

"I know you didn't. That's why I'm not mad at you. But just know that you are blessed."

I think of my father and I nod. "You are right. I am. I should never have said that."

Mikarvan holds out his hand. "Come, I will show you my dragon. I think she will like you."

I blink in surprise. "You want to start the adventure today?"

He shrugs. "Why not?"

I hesitantly place my hand in his. "All right. But what will we fight with?"

"Oh, I have swords."

"How many?"

He smiles. "I have one for me and one for you."

I return the smile and follow him away from the beach. Two swords... it was like he'd been waiting for someone to join him on his epic quest. Just waiting. As we walk, the tree cover thickens until we are deep in the forest. He leads me just a bit farther until we reach a weathered old oak, and beside it a wide shrub. He reaches within and a moment later pulls out a wooden longsword.

I gasp as he places the weapon into my hand. It is perhaps the most beautiful one I've ever seen. "Who carved this?"

Mikarvan puffs out his chest. "I did."

"Really?"

He chuckles. "Yeah. You seem so surprised."

"Well, yes. These are really very good!"

He bows. "Why, thank you my lady!" He reaches into the bush and pulls out the second sword. "Now we are ready!"

I raise my sword with a wide grin. "Onward, my liege!"

"Your family is higher ranking than mine. You should be my liege."

I give him a cross look. "Are we on an adventure, or not?"

Dragon Vessel

The Inquisitor slowly moved forward, saw Vivien return home later than usual to a distraught Grand Magister. He watched as she embraced her father with a ferocity that he reciprocated in kind. The great love between them was palpable, even in fast motion, and the Inquisitor couldn't help but smile at the feelings that filtered through to him.

He continued to move through the memories, paying attention to those at the academy. Vivien received accolades at every level of advancement, and ultimately became respected by every apprentice that walked those halls. She never really had close friends there, and the only person she allowed to get truly close to her was Mikarvan. Him, and the young human, Ravn. The Inquisitor slowed for a memory when she saw the barbarian for the second time, about twelve years after the initial meeting. The young man was married, and the Laird of his castle. The friendship between the two only grew during her stay, and the Inquisitor could see the attraction between them plain as day.

The Inquisitor scoured the memories in Lady Valdera's mind. There must be something somewhere, something that gave him a clue as to what might happen later in her life, something that would show him that she'd been predisposed to dragon magic. But he found nothing.

It was at one particular memory that the Inquisitor stopped again, this one many years later. Vivien was riding a dappled reindeer in the northern forests. She was once again in the Lairdlands...

The scouts glance at me every once in a while as we near Castle Blacach, and my sense of unease rises. We have been on the road for over three weeks now, and as we've approached, the men have sent out patrols at the beginning and end of every day to make certain that the path is clear. Last night they had returned to tell me that we would reach the castle today, but to be forewarned, it is not as it used to be. I'd questioned them about it, but they'd only shaken their heads. "You will see," said Peyotyr.

I hold my breath as we near the bend I remember from over twenty years ago. The disquiet I feel has only risen throughout the morning, but now that we are here, excitement thrums through my veins. I wonder how Ravn has been all this time, what he looks like, and if he has any children. As we get closer, I can make out the highest tower, the one Ravn and I had stood upon the final night I was there when last I saw him. The one where he'd kissed me.

A feeling of warmth washes through me. I have never forgotten that kiss. Over the years I'd even dreamed about it, magical dreams. But they'd never come close to the actual experience.

We turn the bend, and my jaw drops in shock.

The castle I remember from my fondest memories is no more. Discolored walls overrun with ivy rise into the air. The cobbled lane leading up to the place is overgrown with weeds, and the courtyard the same. The stables, behind and to the right of the castle, are in disrepair, and look as though they have been unused for several years. A stab of worry impales me and won't be shaken. I don't know how Ravn could let this happen to his father's house. The inhabitants regard me and my retinue warily while one man walks over to greet us. He nods to the scouts and they give a nod in return. Peyotyr brings his reindeer close. "This is the man we encountered last night, my Lady."

I ride forward. I stop my reindeer a few feet in front of the man before I dismount and walk the rest of the way to stand before him. I speak in perfectly executed Lairdstongue, for I had brushed up on it before coming. "I am Vivien Valdera from the Elvish city of Rithalion. I am here to see the Laird of Blacach."

The man stares at me uncomfortably for a few moments before responding. "I am Armun. The Lady will return later today, but please make yourself comfortable while you wait."

I just stand there astounded. This is so different from what I remember from my youth, when my father and I had been graciously accepted into the castle with open arms. Of course, the people had been unaware of my arrival this time, but it had never occurred to me that they would not show the same hospitality.

Armun's discomfort had grown, and he was quick to speak again. "You look like you have been on the road a long time. Allow me to offer you refreshment, and if you wish it, fresh baths for everyone in accompaniment."

I nod. "That is very gracious of you. Thank you." I turn back towards my party and offer a translation to all who don't know the language. Everyone dismounts and the scouts take the reindeer and lead them towards the stables while the rest of the company looks on. In total there are thirty of us, all travel weary and tired. Peyotyr and one of my guards come to stand beside me. "This doesn't seem quite right, my Lady. I recall a different reception when last we were here," whispers Peyotyr.

I simply nod and follow Armun into the castle, the rest of my company behind. I wonder what happened to the place, but even more, *where is Ravn?*

For most of the rest of the day we wait. The castle staff provides a meager refreshment and a place to rest in the main hall. The best part was the hot bath that each of us were given, accompanied by mild soaps for our hair. After a while I walk around the periphery of the castle. The wind blows over the cliff, buffeting my hair, bringing with it the long-ago sound of children laughing. In my mind's eye I see a boy and a girl racing towards the wall where I stand. Closer and closer they come until first the girl and then the boy smack the stone beside me and fall to the ground in exhaustion.

A smile tugs at the corners of my mouth at the memory and I look down the cliff face at the rocky escarpment at my feet. It looks treacherous and I dread to think that anyone has fallen down there. I turn away from the cliff, about to return to the main hall, when a boy turns the corner. My eyes widen at the sight of him. Tousled chestnut curls reach his shoulders, and his eyes are colored blue-gray. He looks like none other than the boy I just imagined, the

Laird of Blacach in his younger years when I first met him. Surely this must be Ravn's son!

I give him a beaming smile. "Hello," I say in Lairdstongue. "My name is Vivien. Who might you be?"

He hesitates for a brief moment before speaking, as though wondering if he should be talking to me. "My name is Daffyd."

"You must be the young Laird who will someday inherit this castle."

He nods and I smile again. I knew it... I knew this was Ravn's boy!

"Where are you from?" he asks. "Are you really an elf?"

"Yes, I am. And I come from a place called Rithalion."

He nods. "Why are you here?"

"I'm here to see your father. I knew him when we were children."

He narrows his eyes and looks at me suspiciously. "My father isn't here right now."

"Yes, I know. I'm just waiting for him to return."

"And the other people inside?"

"I journeyed a long way. They are my guards and help keep me safe while I travel."

He nods again. "Well, I don't know when my father will be back. He's been gone a long time now."

I blink in surprise, not expecting that response. "Well, Armun says that he and your mother will return this evening."

The boy regards me with another suspicious look. "That's what Mother keeps saying, but he never comes." He cocks his head to the side. "You are an elf. How did you know my father when you were children?"

I am puzzled by his responses but I answer his question. "I came here for a visit, like I am now."

He shakes his head. "That's not possible. My father never lived here as a child. He lived in the city of Moxorith."

I frown. Either this boy isn't who I think he is, or he has been told falsehoods. I wrack my brain for where I've heard that name before, but by the time I figure it out, I hear the clattering of horses' hooves on the uneven cobbles of the courtyard. The boy turns and scampers away, almost as though he is afraid to be seen speaking with me. I make my way to the courtyard, mulling over what I have been told, and my belly clenches. The city of Moxorith is in the Iron Coast.

When I arrive, a woman and her retinue have dismounted, the horses being led away by two young stable hands. I recognize her right away; the waif-like figure, pale complexion, and mouse brown hair are the same as I remember. It is Ròs Blacach, Ravn's wife. I look at the three men, hoping to see that one of them is my friend, but all are strangers to me. I watch as Armun approaches her, talking in a low voice. She gives him a deep scowl and shouts, "You did what?"

"My Lady, I didn know what else to do! They traveled so far, and they are our guests..."

"You invited st ngers into my home without my permission!" she interrupts. "What if th y are cutthroats?"

"My Lady, they h ve been–"

"Yes, I know the 've been here before! But that doesn't mean I want them in my house!"

I stand there in s ock, listening to Ròs carry on. Ravn had told me about Ròs' flare for the dran atic the last time I'd visited, but never thought it was like this. The two enter t e castle and I rush to catch up, not knowing what she might say to my peop before I get there. I needn't have worried.

I walk in and catc her in the entry before she has entered the main hall.

Ròs stares at me, her light blue eyes widening with recognition. "I should have known it would e you," she says in a whispered voice.

I wonder at this tatement, but don't comment. "I am here to see your husband. Where migh he be?"

Ròs curls her up er lip into a smirk. "Wouldn't you like to know?" She gives a dramatic sigh. 'He isn't here."

I keep my voice evel even though all I want to do is scream at her. "I realize that. If you cou d just give me some direction, I can leave you in peace."

She wipes the smi e off her face. "All right. Follow me."

Ròs leads the w y through the castle, up the central staircase, down a hallway, and up anoth r staircase. I know where she's leading me before we get there. Together we wa k out onto the balcony. Maybe it is the state of disrepair, or maybe it's the pers n I am with, but somehow it doesn't seem as impressive as it did the first time I'd seen it. Ròs stops before the balustrade. I follow suit and we look out upon the landscape below us.

I break the silence "Why have you brought me here?"

Ròs turns to look at me. "You asked me to give you some direction as to his whereabouts. So h re we are."

I just look at her, onfused.

"You see, this is here he died."

The breath leaves ny lungs like I have been punched in the guts.

"With both his m tress and infant child, he leapt right from the spot where you are standing. I re ember it like it was yesterday, and even now I can hear the sound of his body itting the rocks below."

I can't breathe an I blink back the tears that threaten.

"Evening was ap roaching, and it was too dark to get them. But late that night the wolves cam and dragged them into the woods. The next morning, we sent out a hunting par y. They had been torn apart, their entrails eaten, their..."

"Stop!" I shout th word without meaning to. But I just needed her to stop, to stop spouting the l es that issued from between her lips. The Ravn I knew would never have don such a thing. Never.

Ròs just stands there, regarding me smugly. "Stop what? You wanted to know, so I told you."

I shake my head. I simply can't believe he is gone.

"I can see you don't want to believe me. But you can ask anyone here about his death, and they will tell you."

I swallow heavily, look down the escarpment I had contemplated less than an hour ago. No, he can't be gone. He just can't.

But somehow, I know he is. Ròs is simply too certain.

I look back up at Ròs and anger swells within me as I remember my conversation with Dafydd. "I've met your son. He has beautiful eyes."

She stares at me with a steely expression, her gaze calculating. "So, what will you do now Lady Valdera? Now that you have your answer?"

"We will be gone within the hour."

The Inquisitor mentally recoiled from the agony he felt in Vivien's mind, an agony that rivaled Emmalyn's death. He didn't linger and exited, lifting his hands from Vivien and sitting back into his chair. She wept silent tears that crept down her temples in rivulets and dampened the pillows beneath her. She didn't look at him, didn't speak, didn't even blink. She remained still on the sofa, not making a single sound. The Inquisitor rose, stood over her for a moment to see if she might at least acknowledge his presence.

Nothing.

Heart-heavy, he once again went to the guard to tell him to fetch the Master Healer before leaving the room. Slowly, albeit surely, he was breaking Lady Vivien Valdera, Mage Protector of Rithalion.

Chapter Forty-Four
The Last Trial

the wolf had spent a century more alone than in the company of any speaking being. He stood at attention with a certain ease, legs bent, and let his mind wander. It never went far. It always found Her.

The guards along the walls eventually changed, and no one came for those from Rithalion. After several more hours, in the early evening, the first La'athai fainted, but none dared move to help. No one from Moirdem came either. After several more hours the first La'athai voided himself in his kit, but did not break formation. Afterwards there was a roar of flatulence and excretion, liquid and solid, and the smell filled the Hall. The Wolf may have wet his kilt, but at least his solid waste fell free of him. None commented. None left. The one who had passed out woke, and stood again. They waited as the council guards swapped out every few hours.

Night came, and the only light left to them came from the glass dais in the center of the room near the podiums of the Council. It glowed with a steel-gray sheen, and the Wolf thought he saw slight shadows slithering along the aurora. He only watched it for a few hours before his thoughts drifted back to Vivien, his heart aching. He felt sleep come for him and he shook it off fiercely. She was locked in a cell somewhere, and the only way he got back to her was to stand here.

So, stand he did.

More fell, morning came. All were standing with the dawn, smelling of excrement and in puddles of urine. Still, they stood. They had eaten not at all since the morning of the day before, and were served nothing this day, nor given leave to take sustenance. Night arrived and more fell, exhausted. Katriona was among them. Still the rest stood still, though many wavered from time to time, feet numb, backs and legs aching. Still, they stood.

The crystal case still glowed, and it illuminated nothing so much as steely determination.

Morning came, and servants wheeled in a cart, set with freshly baked bread, crocks of preserves, and crystal pitchers of cool, clear water. It was wheeled in front of them, and then the servants left. They were given no leave to eat, so they did not, even though stomachs growled loud enough to echo in the chamber. Soon the bread stopped steaming and the smell faded. Some fell. More excreted. None lay down but for the inability to stand.

The guards always changed. Night came. Morning came. The Wolf kept standing. Xadrian, beside him, kept standing. He lost track of who else made it, and he dared not turn around. He stood at attention, and more time passed.

Guards along the wall abruptly snapped to alertness. An elvin woman came in, face in a fury. At her hip hung a longsword with a hilt made of leaping tirinian. She was wiry but light of build, yet her heavily muscled arms and hands said she could handle her blade with drilled expertise. She was dark skinned, as if kissed always by the sun, but far too homogenous. Her black hair was tied back in a complicated knot as tamed and uniform as the breeches, boots, and tunic she wore.

She looked to the La'athai. "How long have you been here?"

It took many moments for anyone to answer. They were wavering, hungry, and without sleep. Xadrian answered her, but he had to think long about it. "Three days. Three nights."

"But why?"

Xadrian swallowed dust into his dry throat. "We were told to wait at attention for the Council."

She looked stricken, "Please, go lay down. Sleep and eat. Rest. I will make sure the Council sees you tonight."

Several La'athai, at the edge of endurance, collapsed at those words. Xadrian, however, held up a hand to halt any from leaving their station, never stuttering from his own vigil. "We cannot. Our need is dire and this is the task given to us."

Her face became a rictus of outrage and she stormed from the hall shouting, "Father! Father! What have you done?"

They could hear words from far off spoken at great volume, the voices came closer, as well as steps on the white rock floors. The guards again went to attention.

Os'turil, Al'sangu, the warrior maiden, one dressed and colored like her sibling, and another two council members entered and faced the La'athai.

One of the councilmen they had not yet met shook his head as if speaking to a slow child. "Oj'le athain, it was necessary to prove..."

The warrior woman exploded. "Beasts in the fields are treated better than this! You could not have doubted their hearts, or their mission this much. You could only be taking joy from their suffering!"

The elder looked at her appraisingly, and a little hurt. "Joy? You think so?"

The other council member, a woman, with hair shorn short but in her silver robes, frowned. "That is inappropriate, Lady General. This was my task set before these people—"

Oj'lexathain spat the words at her, "Then you are a monster, Kaltheria!"

The Council blanched and the other soldier opened her mouth heatedly, only to stay silent as the elder councilman raised a single finger. "Monster, you say? Let us see." He motioned to the La'athai and continued to them, steps easy and untroubled. He passed to the back row of the standing soldiers, wrinkling his nose at the smell of offal. "You, soldier. I am Councilman Hadarion, and I ask, did you fail to stand at attention this whole time?"

"I failed many times, Councilman," the La'athai replied passed lips chapped and cracked for want of water.

Councilman Hadarion frowned. "And yet you stand here as if to fool us?"

"No, Councilman. We stand here because our will is to stand, even if our body fails us. To stand with those who persevere."

Hadarion blinked and inclined his head, a gesture repeated by the General and her sibling both. "Interesting. You, there, who are you?"

"We are from Rithalion," another La'athai answered, speech slightly slurred.

Hadarion smiled indulgently. "I mean to speak plainly, soldier. I mean the name of your unit?"

"We are the Wolves." At the sound of that word, those that were standing made straighter their posture.

Hadarion feigned surprise. "The Wolves? How dreadful. Why ever would you wish to be called Wolves?"

The soldier shrugged. "One of our commanders. He is the Wolf."

"Your commander is a wolf? Does he often bark orders?" Hadarion laughed at his own jibe, and the other council members followed suit.

The soldier wavered on his feet, missing the condescending tone. "No, Councilman. One of our commanders is called The Wolf."

"How *delightful*. And you. Are you proud to stand here?"

"We stand for the lives of those we love. Mothers, fathers, grandparents, siblings, and children. We will stand here as long as we have to. As long as we can." And the soldier collapsed. First to his knees, then on his haunches, before toppling over.

As the soldier spoke those words, the whole of the Council ceased to be merry. They shifted from foot to foot, and ceased looking at the La'athai. General Oj'lexathain of Moirdem looked admiringly at the formation, her counterpart confused. Hadarion took a deep breath and remembered the smell. He covered his face with his sleeve to block out some of the stink as he turned. "See? They are grateful to stand."

Katriona said in a rasp, "We are to stand at attention until we meet the Council."

Oj'lexathain's eyes became wide, catching his meaning. "You have succeeded, Wolves of Rithalion, for the Council is here. Rest."

There was a pause, then only three were left standing: Xadrian, Katriona, and the Wolf. Most passed out immediately.

Hadarion frowned at Oj'lexathain. "If you were not my daughter, I would–"

"Unless the next words out of your mouth are, 'make you stand at attention for three days and nights', I doubt I'd have reason to complain," she shot back. "What is the next test?"

Kaltheria tossed her head like a mare smelling a predator. "It is still mine. One of them will fight our champion."

Oj'lexathain hissed in air through her teeth. "I will not combat them."

Kaltheria shook her head. "Not you, insolent soldier. Lady General Ul'lessa will be my choice. They will face each other in combat using Elthari Sath'hara."

The other warrior woman started. Oj'lexathain folded her arms and looked to her. "Well, sister?"

Ul'lessa was softer, with shorter hair than her sibling, but she carried a matching blade. She looked to Xadrian, then to Katriona. "No."

Hadarion gaped at Ul'lessa. "What is this?"

Ul'lessa's features hardened. "No. Elthari Sath'hara is a holy thing, father. One does not defeat a foe that is already half dead unless life and death hang in the balance."

Hadarion gestured wildly. "What do you think this is?"

"I–"

"Well?"

"I–"

Hadarion walked to her, towering above and glowering at her, no longer her Councilman, but her father. "Tell me!"

She closed her eyes and took a deep breath. "Death is accepted by a soldier, Father. Dishonor is not."

Color drained from his face as he looked at her. Then he turned away.

Ul'lessa nodded to Xadrian. "We will have your soldiers helped to quarters where they may rest, wash, and eat until tomorrow morning. When they have recovered, I will face you in combat."

Xadrian could only nod.

As they were led out, La'athai waking one another, and in some cases carrying one another, the Wolf passed by and saw Oj'lexathain put a hand on Ul'lessa's shoulder. She shrugged it off. Hadarion looked at them both with eyes that burned.

The food was better than bread and water by a far cry, and they had not been taken to the jail, but to rooms on the upper floors. They washed the filth from themselves, and then slept. They ate and drank all day, and though they knew they had survived another test, the burning in their legs and feet reminded them of how badly they could be expected to be treated from here on.

With proper application of food and rest, the Wolf felt himself renewed, exertion having an even less permanent effect on him than wounds. He felt guilty, for even with a day of bed-rest, water, and soups, many of the La'athai were still aching and unsteady. Come dinner, however, they were brought down to the council chamber where Kaltheria, Os'turil, Al'sangui, Hadarion, and Ul'lessa waited patiently. The Council was in their robes, but the General was in a loose tunic and pants, the traditional kit of an elvin hand-to-hand fighter. General Oj'lexathain was conspicuously absent. The room had been cleaned, but the Wolf thought he caught a faint stink of offal still hanging in the air.

The Council was at their podiums and Hadarion made a motion to get on with it. Ul'lessa nodded to him and turned to the La'athai. "Welcome, cousins. The test set before you is single combat. Elthari Sath'hara. Who do you choose–?"

Xadrian was reaching to unbuckle his sword when Hadarion interrupted, "NO!" His denial reverberated in the hall. "No, the envoy from Rithalion says humans are a threat to them. Fight the human so that they may prove their need." He smiled slyly. "The big one. What is your name, boy?"

And for the first time in days, the Wolf felt his temper begin to simmer beneath his eyes. He shook his head to clear it and took a deep breath to center himself.

Xadrian spoke in his home tongue. "Your name."

"I am the Wolf."

Hadarion smiled and made to mock him, but something was trickling through his brain. He looked as if expectations were clashing behind his eyes, but he could not make the leap between the Wolf Pack, and the human here called the Wolf.

Ul'lessa nodded. "Wolf, you are my opponent. The first to seek mercy or lose consciousness will be the loser. Do you understand?"

He replied in Elvish. "Yes."

Xadrian was shaking his head, but accepted the Wolf's sword, rusty iron axe, and dagger. He hissed at the Barbarian in the tongue of the highlands, "You have had a few lessons, but she must be an expert. You cannot win."

The Wolf fixed him with deep, sad eyes. "The only way to get back to Vivien is through her?"

Xadrian nodded once and accepted the elvin armor off of him, piece by piece. Then the Wolf turned, and without a word, walked away from the La'athai. He took four steps forward and planted his feet apart. He nodded to General Ul'lessa. She left her spot by the podiums and came just out of arm's reach. She raised her hands in a show of respect. The Wolf returned it.

"You don't have to do this," she whispered.

"Yes. I do."

And then the fight was on.

Within seconds, the Wolf knew everything he needed to know about Ul'lessa and her knowledge of Elthari Sath'hara. He had faced men, and giants, and dragons. He had even faced the Lord of Swords and Truth. The last was a gifted warrior, but a master of the sword. Ul'lessa was a prodigy of fighting with her hands, and she was fast. She called upon her Elvishness easily, and landed five strikes in the first three seconds. The Wolf never saw them land. His thigh, ribs, gut, chest, and gut again simply blossomed into pain and he reeled back. He swung wildly and was certain he never came near her.

He found his footing and saw the much smaller woman was not winded, not concerned, simply calm in the moment as she kept a perfect fighting stance. He entered one himself, and without being told, they clashed once more. Again, too fast, she kicked his thigh, ribs, and neck, bouncing out of range as he tried to grapple her. He stumbled as she placed a perfect forward kick into his chin and stars erupted behind his eyes. He stumbled to his knees.

"Finish it!" Hadarion shouted.

"That is not who we are, Father!" Ul'lessa shouted back. The Wolf felt dark emotions begin to struggle, fueled by the pain of his beating and he ruthlessly quashed them. He looked at his opponent, and she was just waiting patiently. "Please, ask for mercy. I don't want to hurt you."

The Wolf stood, muscles tight and aching from bone-deep bruises, "I cannot."

She took up a fighting stance, as did he. The next moment, she shoved him, face first, into the hard rock floor, and he felt his neck creak and pop.

He heard her again. "Please."

The Wolf raised onto his hands and knees, shaking his head and damning the burning tension along his neck and spine. "I cannot."

She pursed her lips. "Then I have to end it."

And she leapt forward and struck him viciously in the juncture of his spine and head, behind the ear. Hands like anvils of bronze struck him, again, and again. Each time he took the blow, each time he saw the timing, and when she tried again, he shifted She missed his head, but did not strike the floor. Yet she was overextended and he got a hand on her ankle.

"No–" he said.

She twisted and spat like a cat dipped in hot honey, but he held on. He caught one, flailing hand and brought her whole body off of the floor. Then he slammed her to the ground. Her breath *whooshed* out of her and she wheezed and gasped. The Wolf knelt just out of reach and breathed, feeling his torn muscles repairing, his hurts fading. He took a breath and let it all go. She looked to him, confusion spreading across her face.

"Not," he gasped. "Not. Who. We. Are."

She nodded to him and stood shakily. They faced each other.

"I can give you no quarter."

"I ask none."

And she hit him, once, twice, a third blocked, then she tried to sweep his legs. His mighty tree trunk legs held, and he kicked out once, catching her in the rump and sending her sprawling. She tumbled to her feet, favoring one leg, but was back onto him. She hit him left, right, center, and all again. She hit his abdomen again, and again, and again.

All elves had a reserve, a place inside that they called upon in times of great need. It made them faster, stronger, deadly. Even a few the Liath could do it a little, though their discordant nature made it much less effective. The more elvin blood the fae elf had, the more they could call upon.

General Ul'lessa called upon it all.

She struck his body over and over, then crouched low under a blind counter-swing to rain strikes across his belly, his chest, then knee his groin and roll away. The Wolf collapsed to his knees.

"There! The human has failed!" Hadarion crowed.

"No!" cried Xadrian.

"No! He moves!" echoed Ul'lessa.

The Wolf was standing, breathing, centering himself. His whole midsection was a blaze of pain, and his body felt strangely detached. But he was standing.

He faced his opponent, who now breathed deeply with heaving shoulders. She came in for a flying leap and he met her with a fist in midair. She slithered around his strike and grappled his arm, her weight bearing him down to the ground as she wrapped herself around his arm and pinned her legs about his chest. She wrenched as they fell together, extending her entire body to break his right shoulder, his elbow, anything, as she strained against his preternatural muscle mass and snap the limb. The joints popped in protest, but held. He felt the hard floor strike his back but he was already moving, rolling over and slamming his arm into the ground twice. The arm never reached the floor, for Ul'lessa absorbed both blows and rolled away awkwardly.

He snatched at her leg and she kicked at him, but he landed one strike on her thigh before she kicked him off, breaking his thumb on his left hand. He growled low, and flexed the digit against the torrent of pain, then felt it set and begin to heal even as it swelled.

Ul'lessa's breathing was ragged, and her movements slowed. "Please ask."

The Wolf shook his head. "I still cannot."

She came in with an exhausted, clumsy strike and the Wolf took it in the chest, but trapped the wrist with the fingers of his broken hand, then placed the other hand on Ul'lessa's throat. He collapsed on top of her and trapped her legs. He squeezed just enough to feel the muscles start to give. Just enough to let her know there was more to come. He let up enough for her to breathe.

"Mercy," she cried. "Mercy."

The Wolf let go and lay on the floor, panting next to his opponent.

Hadarion howled in contempt. The La'athai cheered, several helping up their champion. The Wolf gently pushed them away and leaned over to offer a hand to Ul'lessa where she lay on the floor. She looked up at him.

"Not who we are."

She took his hand and stood unsteadily.

The Council was shocked, cowed, but for Hadarion. His face was a seething red cauldron of spite.

"You face my test last."

Xadrian sneered, "Will you not yet honor the pact with my people?"

Hadarion's eyebrows shot up. "Oh, you say there is a pact? Fine." He motioned to the crystal dais. "Bring it forth, and we shall honor it."

Xadrian set his face in a mask of determination and marched to the dais, which became brighter as he approached. He reached out a hand–

"No!" Ul'lessa shouted, causing Xadrian to recoil.

The crystal-paneled dais, containing all the pacts and wards, contracts and duties of Moirdem, gave birth to a being of steel and hate. It was there, then it was not, but in between those instants, it lashed out at Xadrian and missed him by the width of a hair.

The other council members shifted and looked away as Hadarion cackled, "Bring it to me, peasant beggar. Bring it to me now!" He laughed again. "Maybe your pet human should try!"

And in that moment, the Wolf felt something inside him snap.

Hadarion's laughter continued, but it did not concern the mountain man. The Council did not concern the mountain man. His iron axe concerned him. The Wolf swept it up from the floor and stalked to the dais.

He hit the crystal-paneled compartment on the top with the axe. It rang like a bell, but was left without the smallest blemish. Eyes that were far from mortal peered from the surface, eyes that burned with murder. He hit it again, but to no effect. He reached out his left hand and the steel fae lashed out at him. He yanked his hand back but did not escape the thing's razor-sharp claws. It drew a bone-deep cut across his heavily swollen palm and blood splashed along the top of the box, turning it into a ruby pane.

Xadrian was saying something. Hadarion was laughing hysterically. Ul'lessa was saying something. The Wolf heard none of it. He was remembering the door to the Council of Rithalion. He was remembering the fae that had been summoned to hold him, to bind him. Since he had visited the warlock the second time, he had healed his injuries. His whole life he had been warm even in winter. Every fae magic had failed...

...as soon as it had touched his blood.

He drew back the axe again, roaring to the heavens in defiance of all things elvin as he brought it down with all the might his working right hand could bring to bear. The fae was wavering, weak, and disappeared as he hit the bloody crystal pane, which shattered with a deafening shriek. A gust of wind whipped through the chamber, and the smell of burnt iron assaulted every nostril.

The room had frozen, even the guards unsure and turned into statues by indecision. Hadarion's face was caught in a mask of hideous laughter as Xadrian calmly walked to the case and began flipping through loose sheets of vellum. Katriona came from behind the Wolf and took off her cloak, wrapping his bloody hand tightly so none would notice the flow conspicuously slowing.

General Xadrian pulled one sheet free of the revered bundle, the top page now spattered with blood, and brought it to Hadarion's podium. The councilman looked at the piece of paper as if it were a living serpent hissing at him.

"Rithalion requests aid in our darkest hour as proscribed in the Pact our cities have made. Keep a thousand soldiers for your own defense, but we require your swordsmen, bowmen, riders, scouts, healers, and warmages. We require them all, and we need them now," said the Lord of Swords and Truth.

Ul'lessa nodded behind him. "I will get my sister and we will gather to march immediately."

Os'turil was weeping openly, Kaltheria shook with rage, and Al'sangui looked stricken.

"How?" the latter asked.

"Pacts were never made to be broken," Xadrian answered, defiantly. "We will take our leave. We must travel far to defend our home."

Chapter Forty-Five
Ice and Steel

The mournful tone of the violin fills the grand hall, swiftly followed by the harp, a myriad of flutes and pipes. I sit, alone, feeling out of place. I don't belong here with these other people even though I've met many of them before. Here there are no hoods, it was all to be informally formal. Noble elves and their unwed sons and daughters fill the place, everyone clad in their finest. Most of them are full blooded, and the only reason I am there is because I am the daughter of the Grand Magister. My status brings me on par with those of pure heritage even though I am only half, but my breeding potential sets me higher still. My ability with magic makes me a commodity.

I'd resisted of course, and for years my father had allowed me my freedom. I am nearly eighty-five years old, past the time when I could have taken a husband. I think a part of me had still somewhat hoped, waited even, for Ravn to come for me. It was impossible, I knew, for he was long dead for fifty years. But it is difficult to reason with the depths of one's heart.

I watch the lords and ladies dance to the music. The women are beautiful in their flowing gowns, each one a different hue. I look down at my own gown, velvet smooth, deep green with silver embroidery. The Lady of Moonlight and Love had given it to me as a gift, saying that it complimented the red highlights in my hair. I know I should get up from my place of refuge, for I'm certain my father is looking for me by now, but I sit for a while longer. Even though I know it is my duty to my people to marry and beget children for Rithalion, I do not wish to do so.

But Ravn did it. He married Ròs because it was his duty. He fulfilled his obligation to his people, and now I must do the same.

Not for the first time, I wish Mikarvan was here. My best friend would have made all this so much more bearable, but he had not been invited. He, also, was a half breed, and it is my duty to marry a man of pure heritage. My father and the other elders in my life had made that abundantly clear for so many years, I'd never contemplated marrying him.

Except maybe that one time...

I give a shuddering breath, but become still when a shadow looms over me. I look up into the smiling face of a young man. He wears a long tunic that matches my gown, and his pants and vest are light brown. "Lady Vivien, I am the Lord of Alder and Axe. I was hoping you wouldn't mind sharing the next dance with me."

He holds out his hand and I blink in surprise. I hadn't expected anyone to bother, for no one ever had before except for Mikarvan. Sensing my hesitation, he begins to lower it, but I swiftly place my hand within his. "Thank you. I would enjoy a dance. I think I've been sitting here much too long."

His smile widens as he wraps his hand around mine. "Yes, it has made us wonder, I must confess."

"Who is 'we'? And about what?"

He skipped to the second question. "You seemed so introspective. We wondered if perhaps you were waiting for someone. When no one appeared, I finally gathered the courage to approach."

Shame floods me. "I... I apologize. I didn't mean to..."

The lord places a finger to his lips. "Shhh. No apologies are needed. You weren't doing anything wrong. Besides, I won in the end because I was first to reach you."

He winks and I feel my face flush. "I just didn't expect that anyone would want to talk to me, much less dance."

He gives a slight frown. "Why not? You are the prettiest lady here."

A smile finally breaks across my face and I chuckle. "I won't dance with you if you lie to me, Lord Alder."

His eyes widen and sparkle teasingly. "Me lie? I would never, Lady Vivien."

"He leads me out onto the dance floor and we banter back and forth as we dance. After the song is over, another lord takes his place, followed by another, and then another. I can't believe I'm having so much fun, meeting some new people, seeing some others I've not met in a while. I begin to tire, and just as I'm about to step away from the dancing, another man approaches me. He is a bit older than some of the others, tall, with startling blue eyes and hair so dark it's almost black. His long tunic and pants are white, both decorated with black embroidery. He gives a half bow and offers his hand. "I am the Lord of Ice and Steel."

Despite my fatigue, I place my hand within his and offer the same bow. "My Lord, I am Viv..."

He smiles, a captivating smile that pulls at my insides. "I know who you are Lady Valdera."

I flush. "Of course, you do. How silly of me."

He leads me into the next dance, a slow haunting melody. He pulls me close and the blood thrums through my veins. His scent is intoxicating, a blend of perfumes I can't identify, and his steps are measured and concise. He is stunningly handsome, and his hand at my lower back rests there as though he's known me for years. He watches me intently as we dance, and unable to look away, I return his gaze.

At the end of the dance, he doesn't release me. Instead, he leads me into the next dance, and then the next. He doesn't speak, but regards me with an intensity I've never experienced before. Finally, he releases me and the corner of his mouth pulls up into a smile. "I'd like to accompany you for some refreshment."

I return the smile, smitten. "You are welcome to do so."

We spend the rest of the evening in one another's company. I notice that no one else approaches me, but I am content in the presence of the Lord of Steel.

Dragon Vessel

The next morning, I wake up when Moira barges into my room, excitement oozing from every pore of her being. She helps around the house, especially when my father and I aren't around to do much. With his position as Grand Magister, and my dedication to school, we don't have time to do the things that need to be done. We were lucky to find her, and she and her young son fit into our household perfectly. She's a good friend, and in many ways, like a sister to me.

"Vivien! You're not going to believe this, but this was just delivered!"

I wipe the sleep from my eyes. It had been a late night at the gala, and I am glad to have the day free from any obligations. But now Moira is standing here at the foot of my bed, holding out a small red velvet pouch. I quell my irritability and gather my wits. *A red pouch... that meant...*

I quickly pull back the covers and Moira moves to the side of my bed. "This is so exciting! Someone wishes not just to court you, but to marry you!"

I take the pouch from her hand. It has a gold braided drawstring, and I can feel something substantial within. *This is crazy.* The color for courting is blue. It gives two people time to get to know one another before a decision is made about a partnership. But this one is red, an intention for marriage. *Who would want to marry me?*

"What are you waiting for? Open it!"

I give a tremulous grin before I pull open the drawstring. I tip the pouch upside down, and a beautiful necklace pours out onto my waiting palm.

Moira gives a tiny gasp at the same time I do. I hold it up for us both to see. Sunlight coming in through the window makes the green gems inlaid into the piece sparkle.

"Who is it from?" Moira whispers.

I put my fingers into the bag and find a tiny roll of parchment nestled at the bottom. I pull it out and unroll it to find a message.

A set of jewels to match your eyes. I hope you enjoy them as much as I enjoy you.

Lord of Ice and Steel

I just stare at the message, dumbstruck.

"Well? Who is it from?"

"The Lord of Ice and Steel."

Moira's eyes grow round. "I hear he's been the most eligible match for decades. And he chose you! What an honor!"

I hold the necklace up again, just taking it in. I've never owned anything so exquisite. Certainly, my father would have obliged me had I articulated a desire for such things, but I never felt the need. Instead, my jewelry consists of very little: a matching necklace and bracelet set that belonged to my mother, the sword my father gave me many years ago after earning my first title, and the magus ring I'd earned from being top of my class for several years in a row. These are simple things that mean so much to me because of what they symbolize. *But this, this is...*

I think for a moment. This, I suppose, can be a symbol of the first day of the rest of my life.

Moira reaches out her hand. "Here, let me put it on you!"

"N... no. Wait, I think I'd like a bath first."

She smiles. "Of course, you do! I'll work on getting it ready."

I stare at the necklace after Moira is gone. I'm not ready to wear the necklace. I'm not sure I'm ready for the rest of my life to begin just yet.

Throughout the week, more pouches arrive. They are all blue velvet, each containing something the givers hope I will like. I can only choose one, and when I choose, I will send something back to the giver, something that I hope he will like. This is often difficult, for only brief amounts of time had been spent in one another's company. So, in most cases, there is research done by both parties, asking other people about what the person likes, what is their profession, and so on.

None of the lords gave anything like the emerald necklace. And they wouldn't, because the necklace was a thing that had been given in a red pouch with an intent of marriage. It is unusual to get a red pouch without first having received a blue pouch and spending a requisite amount of time together, but it was not unheard of.

I line the gifts up on the dining table, the messages from each lord above them. One lord gave a set of earrings inlaid with gems that are my favorite color, another gave a ring with runic designs all around it for my profession, and yet another gave a bangle with the image of a tir-reath, my favorite animal. The last was from the Lord of Alder and Axe. It is my favorite, for it incorporates all those things in a beautiful pendant that I can hang in my window. The light shines through the amethyst eyes of the tir-reath, and the runes around the image give it an exceptional glow.

My father comes up beside me and looks at each of the gifts. He then puts a hand on my shoulder and I turn to face him. "Have you thought about the proposal made by the Lord of Ice and Steel?"

I swallow back my nervousness and look down. "I have a little."

The Magister puts a finger beneath my chin and raises my head. "It is alright to feel a little afraid. This is a big decision in your life, followed by a great change."

I nod.

"The Lord of Steel's proposal is an exceptional one. He has a high standing in society, and his bloodline is good. Your children would have an excellent chance of having a propensity for magic."

I nod again.

"I know you like him. I saw how much time you spent with him at the gala."

ᵭʀᴀɢᴏɴ Ᵹᴇꜱꜱᴇʟ

"Yes, I like him very much. I... I just hate to have to choose." I indicate at the table. "Everyone put so much effort into these gifts."

My father nods. "They did."

"I hate that they will get nothing in return for their efforts."

The Magister sweeps his hand down my hair. "It is simply the way of things," he says gently.

"I feel I don't deserve to keep them."

"To return them would be a slap in the face. They are yours to keep. They were made for you."

"I wish I could at least thank the lords."

My father smiles. "Now that, my dear, you can do."

I give a tremulous smile. "Really?"

"I have never read a word in societal dictates that says you can't."

I smile wider. "All right! I'll do that!"

He holds up a forefinger. "But first you must respond to the Lord of Ice and Steel!"

Excitement ripples through my guts. "I already have some ideas on what I should get."

The Inquisitor moved forward briefly, pausing not much father into the future. It was a beautiful scene, and the music mesmerizing. It reminded him of a similar day in his own past, and he began to experience it with no small amount of nostalgia.

I walk among the trees. They tower over me like sentinels, witnesses to all who have walked here before me. Birds sing in branches that sway in the light breeze, complimenting one another to create the perfect melody for a perfect day. In front of me are four small girls carrying baskets of multihued flower petals that they throw onto the path, their giggling laughter making me smile to myself. My gown whispers about my feet as I move. I didn't choose it, for it is the traditional garb worn by all elvin women on this auspicious day– shimmering gold trimmed in black lace.

As I approach, I begin to hear the drum of the bodhrán, followed by the dulcet refrain of the harp, flutes and pipes. I stop at the bend in the path, wait for the right moment signaled by a chorus of the sweetest voices in Rithalion. Then I walk again, around the bend...

Both sides of the path are crowded with people. Most of them are family and friends, the rest the noble families of the city. At the end stands my betrothed, and surrounding him is the Council. My heart hammers against my ribs, but I continue with the cadence of the music. Before me stands my destiny, the man I will be bound to for the rest of my days. The Lord of Ice and Steel is resplendent in marital attire that matches my gown: shimmering metallic gold vest, shirt and trousers trimmed in black velvet, black knee-high boots, and a black silk sash about his lean waist.

I step to his side and we both turn to the Council. I don't see the gift I'd given him, a necklace I'd had fashioned of steel, blue diamonds, rubies, and onyx. I'd put much thought into it: the steel and blue diamonds were for his name, and the rubies and onyx were for his profession as a master weapon-smith. The emerald necklace he'd given to me is proudly displayed and is cool against my chest. A twinge of hurt suffuses me. *Why isn't he wearing it?*

The council elder begins to speak, but I hear very little of what he says. It is more a civil ceremony than anything else, detailing our duties to our people, and the choices we make affecting all who live in Rithalion. My mind keeps returning to the absentee gift. It also ponders on what will happen after the ceremony at the temple. The thought makes me both nervous and excited at the same time. I suppose if I knew him better, that nervousness might not be so prevalent, and not for the first time, I wonder if I've made the right choice.

The civil ceremony doesn't last long. The Lord and I are led to a pair of snow-white reindeer and we lead the marriage procession to the temple situated at the heart of the city. It is a round, domed building constructed with granite blocks that have a golden shimmer, streaked with veins of obsidian. I look at my betrothed as we ride, but he doesn't turn towards me, mayhap absorbed by his own thoughts. I wonder if he also wonders if he made the right choice.

We dismount the reindeer at the entrance, then walk inside. The central chamber is immense, and at the center is a raised dais upon which an elaborate alter rests. Surrounding it are statues that depict the likenesses of the gods. The Council presides over another ceremony, this one dedicated more to the gods and our duty to one another. Just like the last ceremony, I don't hear much, for my mind is consumed with what comes after, my nervousness making me sweat in the long, gossamer gown.

Finally, our clasped hands are bound together by a strip of silken cloth and the ceremony comes to a close. The crowd around us erupts into applause. I look up at the Lord of Ice and Steel and offer a tentative smile. He regards me intently, his pale eyes giving nothing of his emotion. My heart plummets a bit, for even just the smallest smile of reassurance would soothe my frayed nerves. He seems so distant, so detached.

The crowd leads us to the periphery of the chamber where there is a series of bedroom suites. The people line up on either side of the entry, and as we walk among them, they wish us well with words and gifts. The Council and the Grand Magister follow us to the entry. We walk through and my father closes the door behind us.

Silence reigns.

I look around the opulent room. An intricately carved canopied bed dominates the space before us, covered with pillows and blankets made of the softest silk. On the far side of it is a pool, steam rising from the surface of the heated water. Towels and an assortment of soaps lay beside it. On the other side is a small table upon which rests a spread of breads, fruits, and nuts and wines. Unlike any bedchamber I've seen before, there are no bureaus, desks, or

DRAGON VESSEL

chairs. The function of this room is made clear by the presence of only the bed to sit upon.

Overcome with a sense of dread, I dared not do it.

I don't look at the Lord of Ice and Steel as he makes his way around the room. It isn't long before he comes to stand before me. My heart races in my chest. Still, I do not look at him. I feel his hand envelop mine, the first gesture of camaraderie I've gotten all that day, and I swallow heavily. He pulls at my hand. "Come, let us share a glass of wine. It will help you relax."

I allow him to lead me over to the table where he pours two glasses. He hands one to me, waits for me to drink before he partakes of his own. The liquid is smooth as it goes down, leaving a warm trail down into my belly. It doesn't take long for the beverage to affect me as we talk about the mundane things about our lives: our work, our families, our pasts. We eat of the repast that has been left for us and he sits down on the bed. I follow suit and we fall back to lay there side by side. I find myself opening up more and more as my inhibitions flow away.

The Lord of Ice finally turns to me, strokes my arm and shoulder with one hand before leaning in to kiss me. His lips are warm and move deftly over mine in a gentle caress. My heart beats a staccato rhythm against my ribs as his hand moves from my arm to my back and down to my rear. He begins to unbutton my gown. For a moment I think about the nervousness I'd felt before, but somehow it is no longer there. Without further hesitation, I begin the process of disrobing him as he does the same with me, and when we are both naked, we rise and walk to the steaming pool.

The waters envelop us as we enter, rippling about our bodies as we move together in another passionate embrace. He presses his lips to mine and I reply in kind, opening my mouth to his seeking tongue. Ardor makes my belly clench in anticipation, and I can feel the length of his manhood pressing between at the junction of my thighs. I can feel his want of me with every kiss of his lips, every touch of his fingertips, every breath that washes over my heated skin.

We take pleasure in one another as we bathe, lathering up one another's skin and hair, the slick soap adding to the enjoyment. Then we rinse off, not bothering to towel dry on our way out, collapsing onto the bed in a tangle of wet arms and legs–

The Inquisitor stopped there, not willing to intrude upon the rest of this particular memory. It wasn't his business, and was pretty certain that he would find nothing there that would incriminate Lady Valdera. He moved forward again, briefly, and happened to notice something. He didn't stop, but slowed down a little to examine it. It told a lot about the so-called lord that Vivien had married, the way he'd thought about their union right from the start. Vivien had finally found the gift she'd had fashioned for him, a gift that was traditionally worn on a couple's wedding day. She'd come across it many weeks later, in a discarded pile of his things after she'd moved into his house. She'd picked it up and held it in her hands, weeping openly. She'd then tossed it back into the pile, never to be seen again

Chapter Forty-Six
Mournfully Innocent

Ashar looked up from the fire, listening to the massive, and growing, encampment come to a restless stop around him. He breathed out in relief, for the road from the north had been long and hard on his people. Often a solitary man, he had no time alone in weeks until now. Meat was caught on the move and brought to the caps to sizzle on spits. It brought him no joy or satisfaction, the day's exertions beating upon him like a blunt steel bar. Moving this many people required constant tending, shepherding, and browbeating. Ashar spoke with the voice of the warlord, yet many would try to topple him from his place of authority if they could— some to try to take his place, but others just to watch him fall. Everyone knew they were within striking distance of Isbandar, and focus was thankfully moving from petty squabbles and traveling disputes to reinforcing gear, sharpening blades, and filling bellies. He closed his eyes, but the footsteps he heard brought them immediately open again.

Lorimath entered the circle of tents and Ashar stood to show his respect.

"Please, son… sit."

The closer they came to their goal, the more Lorimath used the familiar, and often affectionate, title for him. Ashar had begun to suspect that Lorimath was using it to bind the captain to him, to lessen the chance of a quick knife thrust to change a commander into a warlord. Ashar was unhappy being commander to hundreds, unhappier with thousands, and yearned for his simple raiding parties of dozens, but Lorimath would never believe him. Yet, as leery as he rightly was of hidden threats from within, the warlord moved freely and without a customary guard. It added to the thought that he was divinely inspired, untouchable. Ashar remained standing.

"How goes the march?"

Ashar breathed deeply. Since the M'dagi had joined the N'gali, several more tribes had come from far and wide. Just like Lorimath had wanted, they rallied under one banner for the first time in history, all in the name of Umesh. "The N'gira tribe is slow, and late to camp again, but that was to be expected with their numbers and being unused to travel. Food is scarce, but manageable. We must have water soon. The prisoners–"

Lorimath answered as he always did. "There is water aplenty in Isbandar."

A horn sounded on the western side of the camp. It was a war horn. Lorimath and Ashar traded a look, for they had both expected this far sooner. They moved as one out of the circle of the warlord's innermost camp and moved to the western side where the knot of movement and noise told them they needed to be.

The ring of dragon elves deferentially parted before the tall, armored form of Lorimath. The warlord paused only a moment to whisper to one of the lieutenants, who ran off to do his bidding. Then they were at the center of the group where two scouts stood, bloodied, and stripped of everything. One had several arrow wounds that were red and angry from the iron tips that had cut his skin. The other had blood covering the entirety of one side of his face, the head wound deep and dark.

Ashar looked upon the pitiful sight of them being spat upon, stones hurled at them while they held the heads of their slain mounts. Should one of them drop their head, they would be kicked and beaten until they picked the body part back up, and both had dropped their treasure at least once by all appearances. They were wavering on their feet as Lorimath joined in the taunts, causing the crowd around to laugh uproariously. After a few minutes, he collected three thumb sized stones from the ground and rolled them in his hands.

"I am Lorimath, Warlord of this great host, and you live at my sufferance."

The fae elf that had many arrow wounds gulped. "Great Warlord, we–"

Lorimath hurled the rock as fast as he could at the speaker, who yelped when it struck his chest.

"Warlord–" he began again, cut off by Lorimath hurling another rock and striking his knee, dropping him to the ground.

"Wait!" he pleaded. "Wait, wait, wait!" He struggled slowly to his feet, holding the large tir-reath head in his hands warily "What do you want of us?"

Lorimath paused, as if to consider, and then nodded to himself. "I want to know why this one," He indicated the one with the head wound. "Does not speak."

The arrow elf looked to his companion, eyes wide, but the bloody elf said nothing. Ashar studied him. He was not in shock. He was not unafraid. The bloody elf was watching everything and giving up nothing. He was detached and yet present, letting the moments pass even as he accepted he could do nothing to change them. Ashar nodded to himself, approving.

"Clouds Dancing, he is asking about you." The arrow wound elf began to fray. "Say something. Damn it, say something! Milord he–"

Lorimath hurled the last stone at the arrow elf's head and struck with the sound of a melon being thumped. The elf fell backwards to the ground and dropped the head of his mount's corpse. Immediately, several dragon elves descended upon him and kicked him viciously. As it went on, Lorimath turned lazily to Clouds Dancing.

"So why do you not speak to me?"

Clouds Dancing did not look at his companion being beaten. "I am not here to entertain you."

Lorimath smiled mirthlessly. "I can think of very little you have left to do in your life."

The standing prisoner's eyes quailed ever so slightly as four more prisoners, all scouts captured by the host, were brought forward through the crowd. They, also, were bloodied and weak, beaten for many days as they walked with the corpse heads of their beloved tir-reath. "Then kill me and be done with it."

For all their differences, Ashar admired the hardened scout, admired his spirit, but he could not save him from what was coming next.

Lorimath drew his sword and the elf before him looked a little relieved. "So you won't speak with me, Clouds Dancing?"

The scout looked to his brethren for support and found none. They had all been broken. He set his jaw. "I will speak. We will all speak. All of Isbandar will speak as one to you when the time is right."

The dragon elves on all sides shouted at him, mocking him, and only subsided as Lorimath raised his steel sword.

"You will all speak to me as one?" Lorimath got a nod in return. "I like you, Clouds Dancing. Let me help you speak with your people. In fact, all of you can deliver a message for me." He lashed out to his side, cleanly decapitating one of the broken scouts. The warlord spun and caught the disembodied head before it had a chance to fall. Lorimath held the head out to Clouds Dancing by the hair, facing the silent scream toward the scout. "You can tell them we are coming."

The Inquisitor walked to the Council Hall, deep in thought. Just that morning he had left the College of Magic, packing his things and taking them back to his home where they belonged. The entire time he'd thought of his meeting with Blue Moon Rising, and the councilman's response to what he had discovered about young Vivien Valdera.

For most of the day yesterday, the two had stayed closed up in the room he had used for her Inquiry. It was a room he had chosen and fashioned himself, with nice furnishings and a happy fire in the hearth to keep them warm as he conducted his business with her. Certainly, it was different than any other Delving he had conducted before in the bowels of the College, but to him it had felt proper. The harsh measures he had used on dragon mages of the long ago past didn't seem to pertain to her, so he had cast them aside.

He was glad he did.

For he had found Lady Valdera innocent of the charges that had been made against her.

In the last session of Delving, he had focused more on the events leading up to her imprisonment in the college: her meeting the Wolf for the first time during that fateful ambush with the Lady of Moonlight and Love, her dealings with her husband, her near death experience with the Binding spell, her growing friendship with the Wolf, her part in preparing the La'athai for battle against the Iron Coast, her adversity in the swamps of Pergatium and the incident with the dragon, her trip over the falls after the battle, and her discovery that the Wolf was really Ravn Blacach, her discovery that she was still pregnant despite having lost her son, her mission to bring the elves of the other city states under Rithalion's aegis, her capture by the Liath...

That was where the Inquisitor focused the most. He watched as she somehow escaped what would have been a mortal wound for most men, watched as she was named Umesh of the Liath people, watched as she got raped over and over again, watched as she read over Drath Drakkon's spellbooks, watched as she befriended the wyrms he kept imprisoned there. The magic of the fae had begun leaving her much before all of that happened, and the way he saw it, Vivien had used what she had at her disposal in order to survive. That thing had been dragon magic, and she'd used it to kill Drakkon, free the Wolf, and escape the temple.

Vivien had not turned away from fae magic. For some reason, fae magic had turned away from her. And it was only after that did she begin to use dragon magic. And on several occasions, even after she'd used dragon magic, did he note that she'd tried to contact the fae.

To no avail.

The Inquisitor was certain Vivien was not a traitor. Rather, she was a victim of circumstance. She was a victim of trauma, and after that, her own people had imprisoned her and made her a victim yet again. Now, at that moment, she was sitting in the College of Magic, staring at the flames in the hearth. Just staring. For he had perpetuated the victimization cycle. He had entered her mind and made her relive all that she had endured in her life, breaking down all the details she would have been better off leaving forgotten in the recesses.

Shame flooded the Inquisitor as he entered the Council Hall and made his way to Blue Moon Rising's study. He wished he could take it all back, wished he would have listened to his instincts that she was not guilty as charged. A Delving had been unnecessary and damaging to her, not to mention, the unborn child she carried. What had made him this way, so willing to second guess himself? Was it because of peer pressure? Was it guilt over what he'd done in the past? Was it simpler than either of those things and that he was just too old to be doing this anymore?

The Inquisitor didn't know, and he wasn't sure he wanted to know, as he walked into the study without bothering to knock on the door...

Mikarvan watched Evey watching Vivien. It was a silent affair, for Vivien rarely spoke. She'd answer questions, but gave only the barest of responses, and she never perpetuated conversation. She spent her days just walking around the place, looking over her brother's maps or looking out the windows. Sometimes she had tears in her eyes, but more often than not, she had an unnerving expressionless stare that made one wonder if she was really there anymore.

The day after Vivien's last session with the Inquisitor, the Council declared that Vivien was free. The message arrived via one of the guards who then went to inform his comrades that their duty at the College was over and that they were to report back to the Council Hall. The College was a flurry of activity as everyone prepared to leave, and Mikarvan and Evey waited until everyone was gone before gathering Vivien to take her to Anlon's home, where she would stay for the remainder of their time in Isbandar.

Mikarvan wished the College good riddance as they left.

It had been over two weeks now since that last session, and Vivien was no better today than she had been then. And now, as he watched her from across the room, the sinking feeling that had been dogging him settled deeper into his mind. Vivien had been broken so far down, that she may never return. He blinked away the tears that threatened. He didn't want to believe it... refused to believe it. But he couldn't help that gnawing fear from taking root and growing within him. And while that fear grew, his hate did as well. He despised Isbandar, and as soon as she'd recovered from the birth of her child, Mikarvan would take her from this damned city and never return.

But even more than he hated Isbandar, he hated the Inquisitor. In those waking moments in the darkness before sleep stole over him, he'd think of all the ways he could hurt that wretched man. He'd come up with countless ways, all of which involved the skill he'd developed over the past century. Some of them made him smile.

Mikarvan blinked again. He hated that he hadn't kept his promise to the Wolf. The barbarian would be devastated when he saw Vivien again, and the thought made him cringe. But maybe, just maybe, the Wolf was what Vivien needed. If anyone could tear her free of this, it would be him. Armed with that knowledge, Mikarvan would speak about the Wolf to Vivien often. He never got a reply, but every once in a while, he imagined that he saw a flicker of something in those green eyes. It gave him the hope he needed to keep trying.

But that wasn't the only thing that Mikarvan tried. On several occasions he'd plied his skill, in different ways at different times. And it was at these times that he lost a lot of that hope. His fae healing magic simply wouldn't work. He'd tried to see what was wrong in her mind, and it was simply blocked to him, just like when he tried to discover what it was that was so unusual about her pregnancy. And more often than not, his magic was simply snuffed out, as though there was something there taking the energy away.

The only way he could rationalize it was that she was now a dragon mage. Because she used dragon magic, he was unable to use his skill. It didn't make sense to him, for he'd read about several instances in which fae magic had been used to heal their dragon magic-using counterparts. And once again, he was left with the thought he'd had once before...

What if there really was something inside Vivien, something the Liath had put there? The thought terrified him to his core. He didn't want to believe it, but there were so many signs that pointed in that direction. Mikarvan rose from his chair and left the room. Only time would tell, and in the meantime, all he could do was keep hoping.

Vivien's life swam be 'ore her eyes. Every moment from the time she'd first had consciousness. Every good thing, every bad thing, everything in between. All brought to the fore of her mind by the Inquisitor and his desire to find her guilty of some heinou crime. He'd fast forwarded through much of it, but that didn't matter. She'd 1 lived every good deed, every indignity, every reward, every injustice. It was as though it had happened all over again, and the painful moments dragged he down like a quagmire, sucking her deeper and deeper into some dark abyss rom which she didn't know how to escape. If she *wanted* to escape.

Vivien walked a ound the manse. She only knew she did so because she'd have brief moments o clarity and she'd see what was before her. Sometimes it was the scenery outs de a window, other times it was a tapestry or a map hanging on a wall. More often than not, it was the dull grey of the ceiling above her bed. But mostly, s ie was unaware of her wanderings. She spent most of her time locked inside he mind going over the events of her life, one by one until she felt she might go r isane.

And it had all bec me so clear.

It was interestin; to see her life through the lens of the adult she had become. The focus w s so much clearer. She saw her father, how he doted on her, put her above a else. It was easy to see why Anlon had hated her so much, for all he'd ev r wanted was what she always had. She saw all of her masters at the academ y, how in awe of her they had been, and the deference they had given her. N wonder the other apprentices had been so jealous of her, for all they'd ever wa ted was what she had. She saw the Lord of Swords and Truth. He'd always b en so hard on her during sword training, harsh almost. But now she could s e it was because of the potential he saw deep inside of her, that the harshnes she'd once seen was really the depth of the love he felt for her. She saw Tori lvah. Now she knew that he'd never truly loved her. And the reason she knew hat was because she'd seen true love firsthand. Not just from her father, the l ord of Swords, The Lady of Moonlight and Love, and Mikarvan. But becaus she'd experienced it from the Wolf.

The Wolf.

Her heart quailed it the thought of him. What Ròs had done quaked her to her very soul. Ròs ha l hated Ravn, had hated Vivien too. And looking back, she knew it was beca ise Ròs had known that Ravn loved her. Everyone had known. In her mind' e re, she could see the way Moray and the rest of the castle staff had smiled at he r, had treated her as someone special, more than just a visitor from the elvin realms. Ròs had hated that. How Ravn had survived his fall was still a mystery to her, but Vivien wasn't sure she would ever mention it. The last time she had rought up his past, he'd shared the worst story she'd ever heard.

DRAGON VESSEL

And then there was the boy, Dafydd. Ravn had a son. And if her guess was correct, he was the offspring of that ill-fated union between Ravn and Ròs just before she pushed him off of the balcony. He was certainly dead many years by now, but there was a good chance that Dafydd had fathered his own children.

Somewhere in the Lairdlands, Ravn still had a family...

Vivien put a hand to her belly and sadness engulfed her. She also had a family, albeit a fractured one. When she was at the College, her father had rarely come to visit her, and only now that she was in Anlon's home did she see him more regularly. And then, she could tell he didn't know what to say to her anymore. She could see the questions in his eyes, the judgment there. He didn't understand why it had been so easy for her to summon the unseleighe, or to take up the yoke of dragon magic. But he didn't bother to understand, for he'd never come to talk to her about it, almost like he was afraid of what he might hear. At least her brother was no longer her enemy. He had become a staunch ally and a good friend. Other than Mikarvan and Evey, he was the one who would sit down and talk to her every evening. The sound of his voice was soothing, and it gave her some hope that everything wasn't entirely wrong in the world.

Not even the Wolf Pack knew what to say anymore, and so they didn't speak at all.

She wondered where the Wolf was, and hoped that he would one day return to save her from herself.

Chapter Forty-Seven
Enemy at the Gates

The city slumbered and did not see him arrive. There were guards on the walls, of course, but they were meant for armies, not single elves. They had unwisely let the trees grow close to the wall, and that made it easy. The wizard enjoyed nature, loved the forest, but he would never let it endanger him. That was just common sense. Not so common for Isbandar, as it turned out. Yet, he would not complain. He just watched the pair of roving city guards pass, more proof they had no idea what was coming, and then walked up to the wall.

He felt the raw fae power emanating from the wall, trapped there by eldritch pacts. The creatures inside felt him to, smelled his power and hated him. It was simply bad luck for them that they were trapped in there and he was out here. Bad for them, good for him. He found one of the chains inside his mind that lead to the aether and a very powerful, very angry, dragon that lived there. He yanked it a little, channeling the fraction of the power there to send it surging into his body, and he leapt. Above, faint purple figures started to fade into existence, waiting to grab onto his spell and use it to rip him apart. He sailed upwards and let go of the power, let go of it all as his momentum carried him up until he simply stepped onto the top of the wall.

Without the spell, they could not feel him, could not see him, and the guardian fae winked out of existence as if they had never been. From there he found his way along the wall, following the walking guards too far back to see, and took the next set of stairs downward to the street and simply traveled down the boulevard as if he belonged. He knew once he was inside the wards, he could use dragon magic if he needed it, for as powerful as they were, the shields would protect from spells outside getting in and vice versa, but it could not span the gap from here to the aether wherein he drew his power. The goal, however, was not to use magic at all. He must be unnoticed. Being noticed would be fatal.

He passed the College of Magic, a once mighty institution forgotten and forlorn, and scoffed. It would have been a bastion of defenders if they had not been so cowardly and let it go to seed. They would fight with apprentices and masters as if it were millennia ago. Far less efficient, cohesive, or wise. Fear always made the stupid do predictably idiotic things. He stopped by a fountain outside of the building, a tree weeping water from willow branches, and splashed some on his face.

He looked into the water for a moment, slightly dismayed at the ratty appearance of his dark robes. He never thought about this in the swamp. He had old coins in his pouch. Enough for room and food, but not enough for new clothes. He moved on.

He could only hope no one would notice or care. In any case it was too late for a room or dinner tonight, a traveler this late would raise far too much suspicion. Suspicion was the enemy now. He had to find a dark corner and lay low until morning. He had to find Vivien Valdera and take care of her before it was too late. After centuries of waiting, it was almost over, but now events were moving faster and faster.

The dragon mage paused by a shop where hung a cage of glowstones. They turned the window into a mirror and he took down his hood to see his haunted and cynical eyes staring back at him, predicting certain failure. But he could not fail. Not now.

Esgrynn, the Warlock of Pergatium, pulled his hood back up and became another shadow in the streets.

Blue Moon Rising had always been good at waiting. It was a very elvin trait, and he took pride in this ability. Since the Valdera woman had been rescued, all that had changed. His inner sea of tranquility and order had been overturned by her every day since. The chair he sat in was a living thing of twisted vines holding thick branches to bear his weight in comfort. He rubbed the surface of his desk, a living tree bent to the service of his people that sprouted out of a cutting merged into the very floor of the living Council Hall. He closed his eyes and tried to lose himself in the living, breathing city that was his home. It rang hollow. Valdera continued to plague him. She was a danger to all the remaining elves of the world; he knew it! If only the Inquisitor could see that. If only he–

There was a knock, but only the briefest of them, and the door flew open without being given permission. He opened his mouth to scold the offender, but the face of the guard that stood there gave him pause, a chink in the armor that the low elf took to speak first.

"Councilman! A scout has returned!"

Blue Moon Rising was already on his feet and heading toward the door. "Just one?"

The city guard looked stricken, his color so drained he appeared green in the afternoon light. "Yes, sir."

Blue Moon Rising pushed past into the hallway, inwardly scandalized that the guard hesitated in giving way. "Is he coming to report?"

The guard's hand clenched and unclenched as he followed, and his voice shook. "He was on foot, and has been taken to the healers in the sanctum."

The councilman drew up short in the hallway. Scouts never went out alone. "Is he hurt? What happened to his tir-reath, his partner?"

The guard shuffled and removed his helmet, showing hair plastered to his face with cold sweat. "He..."

Blue Moon Rising gave him only three quick heartbeats before snapping, "Out with it, man!"

"He came on foot stripped of all armor and weapons. He wore chains that were embedded into his skin so he could not lay down his burdens." The guard stopped, trying to control himself from gagging.

Blue Moon Rising had no time for niceties. "Guard! Report!"

The rest came out in a rush. "He was pierced by the links of chain. Strung onto the chain, through the mouths and out the severed necks, were the heads of six scouts and their mounts."

Silence filled the space in the hall between them. Blue Moon Rising spoke, but he was swamped with dread. "This is monstrous. Who would do such a thing?"

"The Liath. The scout says they are less than a day's ride out."

Blue Moon Rising stood for what felt like days, unable to breathe. "What else?"

The guard seemed to deflate, "He says that *THEY* are coming."

Blue Moon Rising, leader of the Council of Isbandar, clasped his hands within the sleeves of his robes of state so that none could see them shake. He tried for a brave voice. "Ring the warning gong."

The gong had rung for hours, and everyone had come. Soldiers had rallied across the city. Old soldiers had reported for duty for the first time in hundreds of years. Mages, long eschewing the college to teach magic, had gathered everyone they had ever taught: master, journeyman, and apprentice. The Liath had come, and everyone who could fight– hunters, smiths, and even brawlers had come to defend the city walls. Perhaps too late, Isbandar was learning what it was to be all alone against an implacable foe. They were learning, to their peril.

Jor'aiden thought of his daughter, and his heart ached to be by her side. But his place was here, defending her and all the other daughters of the city. Little though that might do. Vivien had been listless and withdrawn since her interrogation sessions with the Inquisitor, and whatever hell she had endured at the hands of the Liath had obviously been compounded by those sessions. He was useless by her side and just as so here. He was the Grand Magister of Rithalion, but he was in Isbandar, and the father of a dragon mage. None looked to him for guidance, none leaned on him for support. His only touchstone, his son Anlon, had been whisked away. As councilman and the master cartographer of Isbandar, he was gathering his maps to fortify the city and plan for the defense. Jor'aiden knew it was right for him to do so, and it would save lives, but for now he wandered the battlements feeling as alone and as old as when he believed his daughter lost in the battle with the Iron Coast.

He climbed the woven wood stairs to the top of the walls, seeing the living structure had already been sung to by the local mages. Long, thick thorns the size of swords had sprouted to face the outside world with sharp teeth. Ancient fae had been awakened from their slumber and he felt their power thrumming through the wards that stood as magical walls against dragons and their kin. Without purpose he walked the top of the wall, passed by hurried young men half dressed in armor and often carrying buckets of seeds to grow into trees to seal breeches in the wall, or arrows to rain down upon the Liath, or sometimes simply themselves lost in thought of a horrible end that was likely to come.

He reached the city gates and looked out. The forest was light as hair on a newborn's head near the wall, but within half a bowshot became thick and impenetrable but for the white stripe of the elvin road that soon disappeared around the gentle turn. He watched it listlessly as preparations continued all around.

He saw a lone figure walk carelessly along the paved stone road. He watched it absently, noticing the way the female walked easily, without the crazed fear that plagued the top of the wall, or any within it. He tried to take comfort from the calm demeanor, but little voices deep within his heart screamed at him that something just was not right. She carried a sword, and was dressed in heavy leathers like a warrior, but her gear was ramshackle and seemed makeshift. He blinked as he watched her approach, unmarked by any others around. She was not challenged, and she did not stop. Jor'aiden's fears cried louder and louder as the figure came closer until he could not ignore them any longer.

He cried out, "Watch the road!"

And every elf within the sound of his voice halted and looked. It was only after his warning was given that he realized why he felt such unease, and it had everything to do with how at ease the figure walked. No one who knew the Liath were coming should be unafraid, unless–

She raised an off-hand, arm stripped of armor and ready to take to a shield that was, for now, missing. The arm was covered in a riot of multicolored tattoos.

"Hail the gate!" the figure called.

The elves of Isbandar looked to one another, confused. There were guards and soldiers, workers and laborers present, but no leaders. No one was in charge. Jor'aiden frowned and called back after many moments. "Hail the road."

"I have come from the only true elvin people, and act as herald of their arrival. We have demands which must be met, lest we rain fire and wrath upon your homes."

Nobody that heard those words dared breathe. Jor'aiden felt his insides burn at her claim to be from the only true elvin people. Something inside him whispered that he was the Grand Magister of Rithalion, and it gave him steel to slip into his voice of authority. "Go on, Herald."

"Give us our Vessel. We know she is here. Give us Umesh and we shall leave you in peace."

Jor'aiden bit his tongue but fae made of sky static and fire danced around him, for he knew they asked for his daughter.

The herald laughed mockingly. "Put away your pets, grandfather. She cannot mean so much to you people. She is one of us. She is ours. Bring her forth at dawn tomorrow or we shall come and take her."

The Grand Magister mentally ran through all of the pacts, covenants, and deals he had made with fae through the centuries. He considered a thousand ways to strike down the braggart, but he held himself in check. He was the Grand Magister of Rithalion, not Isbandar. He had no place attacking a herald to this city. He choked down his rage at her with effort.

"We have heard your message, Herald. It shall be delivered."

She smiled again and shrugged, her duty done. None on the wall moved as she turned smartly on her heel and skipped away carelessly. The act was strangely ominous in the silence that followed her departure.

Jor'aiden snapped clear of her spell first. He pointed to a guard and yelled, "You, there!"

The guard shook himself free, but his voice cracked, "Sir?"

"Did you hear her words?" The guard nodded. "Repeat them." And he did. The Grand Magister nodded grimly, afraid if the demands would be answered. "Go tell your masters. Do it now, young man."

The guard ran off, and the harried preparations took on a horrible, nightmarish speed. There was the sound of thousands of axes in the distance, and every elf shuddered.

The Liath had arrived.

Jor'aiden continued to watch the road from the wall as elves rushed about him on all sides. The cheerful herald disappeared, but there was soon movement aplenty. Trees quivered as axe strikes slowly whittled away at their lives. It was a dismal dirge of splitting wood that brought every elf to a stop as the first tree uttered a final splintering cry and fell with the sound of falling leaves. Then another, and another. Eventually, the elves of Isbandar went back to work as trees continued to be felled by an untold number of axes. Jor'aiden waited and waited, and soon the autumn curtain of a living forest was torn away to reveal some, then many, and within hours a mighty host of Liath. The dragon elves continued to clear forest with abandon, taking joy in the wholesale destruction of that which their brethren found peaceful and beautiful.

They cut down the forest right up to the city walls, casting sneering looks to those beyond as they pulled the felled trees back to their growing encampment. There, they were shorn into logs and stacked into palisades from which the dragon elves could sally for their attack. It took most of the day to accomplish. Yet, as Jor'aiden looked across the battlements and into the city, people were disorganized, harried, panicked. None had orders to attack the enemy, so none did. Guards tried to keep orderliness, but the elves had never considered being under siege. The common people would have scavenged for weapons and found most of the weapon smiths had been drafted to do work for the city. Those that had weapons would be selling them for food. That would turn everyone's thoughts to food, but if the Council was wise, they would have taken all they could of that as well. Those that had food were not selling or telling of their stockpile. Not that any of this would matter if the Liath got into the city.

Once the sun started to set, he was sure the Liath would keep to their word and not attack until the next day, and he left the wall. No leaders had ever arrived to take charge of the frightened population. He tried to walk with confidence, calmly, but as an outsider, his presence was barely noted as these elves tried to care for their own.

He arrived at Anlon's home, the modest walls of woven oaks secured from the rest of the city by La'athai outside, keeping guard with stern glances and sheathed weapons. Their leader, Gregor, nodded to him.

"Grand Magister, is it true?"

He could only be asking about one thing, so Jor'aiden nodded. "How is she?"

Gregor was not the kind of being the Lord of Swords and Truth was, and so his face showed his pain at the answer. "The same."

Jor'aiden nodded, and walked past him and into the house. She was there, in the front room, staring at one of Anlon's thousands of maps. But she did so without really seeing the leather surface. Her eyes were red from weeping, and a cup of spiced tea sat forgotten at her elbow, growing cold. One hand or the other never left her heavy pregnancy. Mikarvan and Evey sat with her. The latter looked up to him and tried to give a warm smile, the former sat slumped in a chair, snoring slightly. Jor'aiden made a 'be still' motion to Evey, which she heeded, but the motion drew Vivien's attention.

She looked at her father, flashed a half second smile lacking much sincerity, then she went back to the map as if it may show some new information. She said nothing, and Jor'aiden had no comforting news. He could only see the corrected copy of an ancient map depicting the heart of the old elvin kingdom, showing Isbandar, Sharderia and Moirdem.

The familiar ache, a thing that had always been with him since the loss of Vivien's mother, took hold of him. He closed his eyes to hide his tears and left for his room. He shook his head, for whatever the Inquisitor had done, it had taken the light from his little girl and his ire was never far from the surface because of it. Then he remembered his daughter longingly from before the battle with the Iron Coast, and how she had always been so happy.

He reached for the knob to his bedroom door and stopped.

No. That was not true, was it?

She had shown moments of happiness, but since her wedding to that feckless curmudgeon, there were always garlands of sadness draped around her until...

He slipped into the room and shut the door, butting his back to it, finally unable to stop the tears. He remembered the last time she was truly happy. He thought of the maps he studied, and the baby inside of her, and knew. The Wolf could always make her smile like nothing else in the world mattered.

Dragon Vessel

Night had fallen when Gregor came off of his shift guarding the outside of the house. Constant duty would be hard on any soldier, and he was exhausted. He waved silently to Michael, the only other one in the whole place not standing guard or asleep, but the mage barely waved back as he pored over his tomes, hoping to find some clue as to how they would survive a city that hated them, and the Liath, who hated everybody. Gregor left him to study and went to the dining room. All the furniture had been crammed into the kitchen to make room for the pallets arrayed all over the floor. He went to his and proceeded to strip off his armor and padding, unbuckled his sword, and took off his boots. Sniffing himself once, he did not so much decide to have a wash as was driven there by necessity.

He sulked slightly that the bowls laid out all had dirty water in them, and took one out to the rain barrel out back, dumped it on the ground and filled it. He returned to the hall where the bowls sat on a table and grabbed a washrag. He wet it and ran it over himself. He grumbled a bit about yet seeing the privileges of rank. He dunked his head into the icy water, and was annoyed at how long his hair was getting before he thought to search, half blind, for the driest towel to rub the dirt and wet from his head.

He lay down on the pallet, feeling every part of his body sag with coming rest. Then he cursed silently. He had forgotten. He shouldn't forget, couldn't forget. He sat up and pulled on his crusty, sweaty jerkin and padded, barefoot in his leggings, toward the stairs. Mikarvan snored softly in the front room where the shelves of maps and atlases were kept, the place where Vivien liked most to sit quietly. He felt a shudder run through him, for the look in her eyes on those days terrified him, shocked him to his core.

He paused before her door and knocked quietly, always secretly and shamefully hoping she would be asleep, that she would be silent, but tonight, as always, she responded with a quiet "Come." She said it as if she didn't feel she could stop anyone who decided to walk in against her wishes.

She, a small woman who had always felt so large in his heart, was suddenly shrunken. She was the heart and soul of the La'athai, and she looked disheveled and beaten. Her clothes were put on without care, her loosely curled hair left to tangle indiscriminately. She finished food dutifully but without enjoyment, and her eyes were sunken and hollow. It stabbed every La'athai to the core, for they all loved her. Gregor tried to keep the pity from his face, tried to keep the shock and draining faith from the outside world. He was certain he failed. The only grace of the moment was she did not stir from her bed, nor turn to look at him to see any of it.

He opened his mouth to speak, then closed it. Then opened it, then closed it. Nothing in the world seemed right, and nothing sounded positive or hopeful.

He swallowed heavily and took a deep breath, but his voice still came out timid. "Mage Protector?"

She was still as the grave, then stirred, peeking out of the covers she used to armor herself against the world. She looked to him with one, blurry eye. He stood there, soul quavering, as he saw the woman he had so much respect for looking so pale and sallow.

"Yes?" she finally asked in a half-whisper.

His mind finally found traction on familiar ground. It all came in a rush. "The La'athai continue to keep watch. The Liath have not entered the city, and none have come to make good on the demands of the dragon elves." He took a breath, the report given. She stared at him, and he found he was standing at attention in his filthy uniform without weapon or armor. A half-mad commander and a paper soldier caught in the middle of the night looking at one another. Every morning and every night he gave his report, and she did what she always did. She nodded and started to turn away.

"What are your orders, Mage Protector?" popped out of his mouth, to the surprise of them both

She stopped sinking back into the bed and turned again to look at him.

"Your orders, ma'am?"

She shook her head and began to sink back down.

"Your orders?" he asked, insistent and a little desperate.

Again, there were heavy moments between them before she laughed bitterly. "What would I possibly tell you?"

And if Gregor wasn't at attention before, he was in that second. "There is a city of people, half of whom want to kill us. There's an army of Liath that damn sure want to kill us, or worse. You are days from giving birth if your healer has his head on right, and you've got me in charge and I'm telling you I've run out of ideas. I need you Elhari Jashi. *We* need you. There are only twenty of us left and we need you."

She stared at him and shook her head. "You cannot know what you ask."

A fire began in him, and it sent bubbles of anger into his words. "You think you have it bad now? In a week you'll have something too small to cast a spell or swing a sword. It will need all of us to get out of here alive, and we are all it has got."

Her voice broke as she said, "Gregor, I relived every one of my failures."

He thought about it. He knew, *knew,* that her pet healer would be ushering him out of the room if he were awake. Starling would be scolding him icily for pushing too hard with someone so fragile. But she wasn't fragile at all. She had to remember that. He nodded. "I understand."

"You don't!" she snapped, springing out of bed to face him.

He thought to quail a little from her, but held his ground and frowned. "I do. And they are probably horrible memories, but those failures aren't real."

She sloughed off the clinging blankets and slapped them into the floor. "They happened!"

"Yes, they happened, but they didn't happen *again*." He took a deep breath, letting his mouth go on since it seemed to know what it was doing at the moment. "You saw them, and I understand that it hurt, but they did not happen again. You just saw them. And all of them, *all* of them, you lived through when they were actually happening. You lived and brought a bunch of soldiers and mages together into a fearsome fighting force that loves you and would die for you."

That thought seemed to scare her and she drew up short. "Die for me?"

"Well, to be honest, we would rather not, but we will. We'd rather live for you. Fight for you. That is what we pledged to do. We are keeping to our oaths." He nodded solemnly, but couldn't keep a wry grin from his face. "You took an oath to lead us, Jashi. I gave you as much time as I could, kept this up as long as I could, but we need you. We need you NOW."

She waffled, caught between deflating and coming up for air from the murky depths of her depression. "I can't."

"You are the only one that can." He pressed his lips into a thin line. "We need that woman I challenged to a sword fight all those months ago in the swamp. The one who could have torn me apart in an instant. The one who kept up with An'drath."

He saw that memory buoy her for a breath, then again, she tried to sink. "I don't believe I am that woman anymore."

He shook his head. "Doesn't matter."

She stared at him, aghast. "What?"

"It doesn't matter if you believe. In the end there is that woman: mage, duelist, and leader. And then there is the one that is afraid, alone, and hurt. Which does this one need?"

And she looked at him, down to his arm ending in the finger that pointed at her heavily distended belly beneath an ill-fitting night gown.

The silence between them was still vast, but now it had started to crackle with fire.

"It was so much," she whispered.

He nodded. "I believe you, but you have to know it didn't happen again. You just saw everything you have survived, and those things that have made you strong."

"Strong?"

"Strong enough to build an army. Strong enough to lead it. Strong enough to face death as the tip of the spear against iron men and dragon elves." He took a deep breath. "Strong enough to win the heart of the Wolf."

She gasped. "You..."

He shrugged sheepishly, the clown overtaking the soldier in him a little. "Blind men would see. He loves you and I know he is coming with the reserves we need. He comes for you, but we have to be alive when he gets here."

She shook her head, but her voice was stronger, finally in the present. "We will never get out of here. We don't have the men, the resources, or the weapons to fight drag ns."

Gregor sighed co ically. "Well I wasn't there, Mage Protector, but I heard that you escaped a cit of these lizard-humping degenerates by yourself. It was one of the main reaso s they put you in prison as I recall."

She looked at hi warily, almost angrily. "I don't know if I can do that again."

He shrugged. "I'l settle for destroying half of them. We can mop up the rest."

She frowned, but he liked it better than her cowering inside herself. "It's against the law, soldie ."

"Well, begging y ur pardon, ma'am, but I figure there has to be a council and a city for there to e a law."

She paused, looki g into the mirror of the vanity and sounding pitiful, but not as pitiful as befor . "You don't care what I am?"

"I know what yo are," he said with all seriousness. "We all know what you are. You are our h ro, our inspiration, and our leader."

He could see her hinking. She wanted to be upset, but she also wanted to laugh a little. "We ne 1 a city and a council for there to be a law? Who in their right mind left you in harge?"

Gregor shrugged gain. "The only man who could. The Wolf."

"And why did he o that?"

"Because he kne I would never leave your side, and that I would always need your help. Pleas help me."

She nodded at hin , her face wincing and her hand going to her belly, "This is your way of getting me get back on my feet?"

Gregor sighed he vily, tension rushing away from him and leaving him smiling. "My genius i so often unappreciated."

"Go to bed, soldi r," she said. And for the first time in weeks, it was an order. Gregor smiled and saluted, turned smartly, and then crept out into the hallway. As he shut t e door, he saw her facing the mirror on the vanity. She was quietly repeating o herself over and over, "It did not happen again. It did not happen again..."

He padded down he stairs, past the sleeping healer, and into the room of snoring soldiers.

He was asleep be ore his body came to a stop on the bedroll, but for the first time he truly fel that he had belonged in charge of the La'athai. He was just grateful the real c mmander was back.

Chapter Forty-Eight

The Vices Tighten

The cats and wolves were miserable, and there was no defense but to continue on. The cold and clouds had procreated to make mounds of thick, wet snow. Katriona woke to tir-reath howling at the carpet of it already on the ground, and the day got no better.

She dressed in several layers and buckled her armor on over top, but when she opened her chilly tent to the world, her face felt naked and exposed against the teeth of real cold. Her eyes immediately began to water.

The winter had been thought to have already arrived, but only now did they appreciate its terrible majesty. The wind was howling almost as loud as the forest cats, and it brought the pummeling test of frost to the tents of the poor travelers. The fires had long since died during the night from the constant pour of wet, and the guards could hardly be seen as they were half covered on the windward side from the clingy, white blanket. The Wolf had not left early, as was his custom, but instead he was as entrenched with the others as blinding snow hurtled at them from the sky to stick on them and rob them of all warmth. He looked half feral, long hair and beard sparkling with white flakes that melted upon him at the slightest touch, and his eyes were banked coals as he spoke with the Lord of Swords and Truth. Katriona immediately headed toward them.

Xadrian was frowning. "We have pushed ourselves hard, Wolf. This storm will have to end in a day or two, then we can make better time again, safer."

"Safe for us, but not for her." The barbarian shot back. "They mean to kill Vivien. I have done as she asked and now I will not stop until I am by her side."

Xadrian opened his mouth for a retort, but Katriona interrupted, "How close to Isbandar are we?"

The Lord of Swords did not look pleased by her interjection, but simply replied, "Five fast days on tir-reath on clear roads. In this?" He gave a shrug.

Katriona looked up and down the elf road, "The snow is less deep in the forest. Perhaps we could lose less time if we cut through instead of following the road?"

The Wolf looked at the General expectantly.

"We may, but the snow is treacherous there as well. There is also no path." The Wolf nodded. "I will give you one."

Xadrian shook his head. "It is not just a matter of having a trail blazer, but the drifts of snow will sap our strength. Your mount won't last half a day."

But the Wolf was already up and shouldering his gear. "I will forge the path through the drifts and I will leave the mount with the group."

"Wolf, this is insane!" Xadrian barked, face flushing.

The Wolf rounded on him, and though The Lord of Swords did not shy from him, Katriona found herself taking a step back from his glowing eyes. "Morcso than jailing a hero of your people for having the audacity to escape your most hated foe? Moreso than leaving her defenseless among those jailers?"

Xadrian huffed. "Very well. The chances of us being ambushed in this weather are slim. Still, stay close, and understand none of us has a perfect knowledge of the wilds here. We are going to be traveling by guesswork for most of this."

"I have lived a century in the wild places. Give me the direction you want, and I will lay the course."

Still frowning, Xadrian nodded, then turned to the camp and raised his voice. "Up! Up and about! Break camp. Cold breakfast and a cold march ahead. Fill your waterskins with snow and keep them close to your bodies. We leave in minutes. MOVE!"

And the camp scrambled to obey.

Soon they followed in the Wolf's footsteps into the wild places, always sure of where he had been for his mighty legs had cleared a path through the drifts of snow that sought to delay him. At the end of each day they found him, steaming in the cold from melted snow, exhausted.

The tired La'athai would clear the ground and build a dome by pulling over saplings and tying them down, strapping tents together to form walls, and leaving the smallest opening they could high above for a flue. Then they built a fire in the center, fed it with whatever they could find, and the rank-and-file took turns braving the cold to stand guard outside. The melting snow soaked them to the bone, and they shivered against the night. They slept in piles with the animals, but all fought for space near the Wolf, for he was warmest by far.

But he was always up by dawn, got a new direction from Xadrian, and was out of the tent before the others were awake. He moved all day, never complained, and never stopped.

Day after day, they followed him through snow that piled higher and higher.

Jor'aiden had awakened at dawn to go to the Council Hall, but it had been a madhouse. The Council had shut itself behind warded doors and had done gods knew what for the last day. He had waited all morning, then looked for a way to dismantle the wards but they were too old, forged by dozens of mages working in tandem, and he could not force entry even if he had been given a full day without molestation, and the guards were sure to stop him. So finally, he had stormed out of the Council Hall, past the hastily erected fortifications of that building, and out into the street.

The night before had intensified the air of malignant mania on the streets and the dangerous smell of burning wood was everywhere. Elves were closing off their naturally grown windows and doors with crude boards and sharpening whatever metal they had at hand, as if makeshift weapons and wood would stop what was about to happen. Yet, they toiled. People were still in search of food, but none that had it were sharing. Those that were able, were working. Those that summoned were divining pacts with the most powerful fae they dared. The temples were packed tightly with people praying, and soldiers collected weapons and prepared armor. In the midst of it all, Jor'aiden walked, useless and alone. Much of the time his mind returned to his poor daughter, and then he made haste to somewhere else chaotic to fill his thoughts.

He entered the main square by the city gate, and found it eerily calm though the smell of burning was strongest here. Everything that could be done to fortify here had been done first. Now there were just guards, soldiers, and drafted citizenry waiting in probably the only quiet place in the city for the inevitable. They only looked at him, too tired from a night spent in utter terror to stop him as he climbed the naturally woven branches that formed the stair to the living wall.

He trained his eyes to the distance, and saw the devastation that the Liath had wrought. They had not just cleared forest, they had denuded the landscape... all around the city unless he missed his guess. Hacked up corpses of trees lay strewn everywhere. At first glance, the way that the logs had been laid seemed haphazard. Jor'aiden was not a military man, but even he could see that they gave lanes of cover for advancing troops. He looked left and right, and saw the full bundles of arrows on the wall, patiently awaiting war. In that moment, he was certain that none had been fired on the Liath that had been in range and working in plain sight. In the distance, a crude wooden palisade had been erected, hiding the mass of numbers from sight. By the size of it there were tens of thousands of troops, at least.

Curiously, outside of the wooden walls, groups of Liath toiled over almost a hundred large metal distillers. They had teams feeding fires around the metal barrels fitted with long tubes that ran down out of the fire a good six feet, and others collecting some kind of liquid from the noses of the sealed vessels and taking it into the compound.

Beside him, a very young voice asked, "What are they doing?"

Jor'aiden glanced over and saw a young elvin girl, older than a child but not old enough to have children. Her fiery red hair had been shorn messily short, and her amber eyes never turned from the work the Liath were doing over a bowshot away. She had found raw leather and draped it over herself in protective layers, wrapping her limbs in the same and securing them with thick leather strips. Her shoes were simple, and much patched from years of use. Her belt was another messy affair, without fittings or even a ring. She had three knives slid into the leather without benefit of sheaths. One was an old but proper dagger, and though rusty, was long enough for her to use as a shortsword. The next one was a kitchen knife, and the last a small hunter's skinning knife stolen from only gods-knew-where. She had outfitted herself as best she could for war and now stared at her enemy without doubt or cowardice. He hoped there were thousands more like her in the city, getting ready.

Jor'aiden turned back to the distillers, eyes tearing slightly from the smoke floating toward the city. "They are distilling wood tar like humans."

The girl shook her head. "What for?"

"The Liath, like humans, rely more on alchemy than we do. If I remember correctly, wood tar can be used to seal wounds, or to preserve wood. I honestly can't imagine why they would need so much."

Her face crinkled in thought. "They built those contraptions?"

"The distillers?" Jor'aiden thought for a moment, happy for the distraction. "Dragon elves have no home, no cities to call their own. When they come to war, they carry everything they own. There must be a dozen tribes or more behind those walls, to have felled and moved this many trees. I imagine they brought them along because they are here and then put them to work, little one."

"I am not little, old man," she shot back.

Jor'aiden suppressed a smile, for he was very much reminded of another young girl who was something of a firebrand in her youth, though this one was more confident by far. "If you are not little, then I am not old." He looked at her with a hint of amusement. "You think that both of those are true, do you?"

She glowered at him in response. "You should be at home, should you not? Helping your family prepare for what is coming?"

She looked around at the sullen defenders that moped around the structure, some looking forlorn out over the denuded landscape, others down below looking inward in despair. "If they get past the wall they will surely get to my home. I might as well try to stop them here."

Jor'aiden shook his head. "Your mother–"

She frowned even more fiercely and snapped, "My father was a human and died years ago. My mother has never known much of what to do with me since. I am more wanted here, I assure you."

Jor'aiden blinked, his blood running cold at the matter-of-fact delivery of such pain. He closed his eyes and shook his head. "I am The Grand Magister of Rithalion. My son lives deep in the city, Fire Hunter the Cartographer. Take your family to his house and mention my name. They will protect you there."

"You think that once they take the gate that they will stop until they reach your son's home?

Jor'aiden closed his eyes again and lowered his head, for he had to be an honest man. "No."

She looked out onto the road and gestured with her chin, "Then I will help the city stop them here."

Jor'aiden followed her point and saw the Liath herald again, only half a bowshot away. She sauntered carelessly, eating an apple, weapons and *ad hoc* armor jangling slightly. He looked to the sky, and through the clouds of smoke saw it was, indeed, the time she was to arrive. She stopped a few dozen feet away and smiled. She called out around a mouthful of fruit, "Hail the gate!"

The words galvanized the guardians of all stripes, bringing them to the top of the wall where they watched with bated breath as the herald ate. He waited as minutes ticked by and growled as he came to understand that there still was nobody in charge, and no speaker for the city here. He fought past propriety and hurtled back, "Hail the road!"

"I am the herald of the True Elves and I have come to hear of your surrender." Fear, cold and electric, ran along every soul on the wall, but none answered. She picked out Jor'aiden. "You! You are the one I spoke with before. What is the reply?"

Jor'aiden tried to project calm as he looked left and right slowly, searching, hoping for anyone who could speak for the city. Finally, he decided there were none.

Then the red-haired girl with the knives spoke out. "There is no response, harridan!"

The herald's smile became fixed, eyes glassy. She dropped the uneaten portion of the apple to the road at her feet and gestured grandly. "We understand, wayward cousins. We shall give you one more day to consider. But also understand that this comes at a price; we will give you time, but not breathing room."

And with that, she pointed to the girl at Jor'aiden's side, stomped on the apple, grinned wolfishly, turned, and left.

Jor'aiden turned to the girl, who was far paler now than defiant. "What is your name?"

"Zi'anna."

"Well, Zi'anna, now you have seen evil first hand. More importantly, it has seen you and knows your face. Go to Fire Hunter's manse and stay there with my daughter. Please."

Zi'anna turned her head and saw the herald skip away. "I think your daughter should sharpen some knives and help on the wall."

And when she met the wizard's eyes again, she meant every word of it. Jor'aiden felt his shoulders sag. "I wish she were anywhere but here. She is about to give birth."

Zi'anna nodded. "Then we shall defend her and her child."

It was lunacy, romantic fantasy, but she was deadly serious. "Close your eyes," he said.

She did, without question, and he held a hand over them and lifted his other hand. He called upon deep reserves for an ancient, subtle name. It answered as a pair of ghostly eyes hanging just over the girl's head. It was not cold, or hot, it simply was. It was a watcher fae, and all it did was–

"Is there something behind me?"

Jor'aiden let the fae go and dropped his hands. "You can feel the fae? Have you ever been tested as a mage?"

She shrugged, face showing confusion. "Yes, once. But they said I didn't have enough of the talent for it. And Mother could not pay what was asked of the mage to apprentice me since we have no college here to–"

But Jor'aiden was looking at her makeshift weapons, her slapdash armor, and knew. "Silence."

"Silence?" Zi'anna blinked at him incredulously. "Who are you to–"

"I am the most powerful magician in Rithalion. I am now your master and you are my apprentice. And if you are going to fight in this battle, you will do it beside me so that if you die, at least I will die first so I don't have to see it happen."

She shook her head as if waking from a dream. "What?"

But above all things, the Grand Magister was a teacher, and despite the chaos all around, he remembered how to be a teacher. "Apprentice. You will be a great mage one day but for now you are an apprentice, and you will follow my instructions if you wish to remain so."

Zi'anna gulped, and thought hard. Mages were powerful, and power had its draw. They were often well off, and that had to be a draw as well. It took only a second before she nodded, her eyes brimming with tears.

"Good," he said. "That is settled. Now, repeat precisely what the herald said."

She tried, but it was only close.

"No. She said, 'We shall give you one more day to consider. But also understand that this comes at a price; we will give you time, but not breathing room.' Repeat it."

She did, solemnly.

"Good. First go to the Council Hall and demand an audience. You have a message from the Liath." She looked scared at the prospect, but he plowed on. "After delivering your message, gather your family–"

"It's just my mother and me."

"Don't interrupt. Get her and whatever you need and go to Fire Hunter's home." Zi'anna began to look suspicious. "Use my name, Jor'aiden. Then, when she is there, you eat then come back here."

Zi'anna nodded. "Where will you be?"

Out in the distance, the massive walls of the palisade split and five hulking catapults were being pushed and pulled by hundreds of Liath out into the cleared road before them. Jor'aiden snapped back to the moment and spoke breathlessly. "I will be here. Someone must be. Now, go."

She turned and started down the stair, coltish legs flashing, but then she stopped. "When will you teach me to summon a fae?"

Jor'aiden never stopped watching the catapults move ponderously into position. "It takes years of preparation and study to summon even the smallest fae. Given the circumstances, I may have you try tonight. Now stop delaying. Do as I have ordered."

And off she went. Jor'aiden stayed, and watched the Liath move the siege engines. They still wept sap and were obviously built from miles of rope and bundles of freshly cut trees. He saw them load the arms with wicker spheres woven of the branches of slain trees. He watched them pour the pitch they had made over the greenery and set it alight.

He was alone when he watched the Liath begin to launch the burning balls into the city.

He knew the whole of Isbandar was surrounded by wards to stop dragon kind and their magic. They were ancient, and mighty, but utterly useless against balls of burning twigs. One landed down the street and immediately extinguished. The men cheered a bit, but not the mage. They were not meant to burn the city down. The dragon elves were being true to their words. Because it was not meant to burn, but to vomit cloud after cloud of thick, choking smoke.

Ten thousand Liath were there, cheering as sphere after sphere was launched into the city. A dark haze soon blotted out the sky. Jor'aiden eschewed summoning a fae he may need later and simply covered his face with his sleeve. He watched more missiles were launched, and the Liath army just stood there and jeered.

They had been given time, but not leave to breathe.

A strange, bitter woman had been brought to her brother's home by a young girl bearing the name of Jor'aiden. The older elf's incessant complaints had driven Vivien to her room, her room where she could latch the door and be at peace while she steeled herself for what was to come.

Within the dark, candle-lit chamber, Vivien paced among a sea of stolen tomes. They were all spread around her, open to the pages she felt she needed most: spells. She had taken many of them from Zormoth, and secreted them from all others who never expected her to smuggle a forbidden collection of dragon magic into prison. The rest she'd taken from the College. Now she consumed them all. Many of them she had painstakingly catalogued in her own book that Anlon had generously given to her when she had come to live there.

Her heart ached at the thought of him out there, strategizing with the army's generals. She supposed it was his duty as Master Cartographer, the best in Isbandar, Elyrion, and Rithalion all together. His beautifully rendered maps adorned the halls of his home, maps that showed every city, town, and village from Isbandar to the Iron Coast.

Vivien stopped at her desk to gather her personal tome. In it she had written all that she felt of relevance, all interspersed among the dragon magic spells she had learned from the temple in Zormoth and the College of Magic in Isbandar. Once she finally made it home again, she would place it beside a similar tome she had of fae magic. Side by side, they would dominate her workspace, for they were her most precious possessions.

Except for one other.

Vivien reached for the ring that hung from a long cord around her neck. It, too, was precious, and it never left her person. Besides the long-lost sword he'd had refurbished for her, it was all she had of the Wolf.

She suddenly felt a cramping sensation, one that reminded her of her menses but much stronger, and she brought her hand down to her belly. She just stood there for a moment, holding her breath, Sherika and Dari'sii looking up from their places on the bed, regarding her intently from green and gold eyes. When the sensation finally passed, she breathed normally again and once more resumed her pacing. Those sensations had become more prevalent as of late, and she imagined it must be because of her impending delivery. She chose to ignore them, for she had bigger things to worry about.

Vivien walked over to the nearest tome, turning a couple pages to a spell that intrigued her. It was a Summoning concentrator, one she'd deliberated over for days, reading it over and over to get the words just right. It was an ancient spell, a mighty one, one that would help call the greatest of dragons. Of course, she would never use it but she somehow felt compelled to learn the words anyway. It was captivating and awe-inspiring; the words themselves sounding grandiose and powerful in a way she couldn't describe. It was something a mage would use in order to prepare for the coming of the dragon, detailing the terms of his arrival, how they would conduct their business, and how he would leave once that business was finished. She was tempted to scribe it into her own tome, but once the Liath had come, sending their great spheres of smoke over the city walls, she had discarded the idea.

Vivien sat before the tome, reading over the spell. A haze permeated the air, caused by the smoking orbs. She'd been tempted to try and help, but her advanced pregnancy kept her indoors, as much out of harm's way as possible. Duty to her people vied with duty to the child she carried, making her feel torn, but motherly obligation won out. She riffled through the pages to the end, to the last few to find them blank. It was as though the writer had intended to write more, but never got the chance. She turned the pages until she reached the last one, and once there, she stopped. There, in the center of the page was a single word.

Tsor'aya.

Vivien stared at the word, at the page surrounding the word. There was brown smudging, and what looked like the imprint of the side of a hand where it had touched the page as the word was being written. The word itself was colored the same brown, a brown that reminded her of old blood...

Tsor'aya. She whispered it in her mind and a chill went through her body. There was a power to it, a spine-tingling power that prickled at her scalp. And it was then she knew it wasn't just any word. It was a name.

She startled from her reverie when she heard a ruckus outside, another of many that the La'atha took care of from their post surrounding the house. The rift her very existence in the city created had caused a division among the people of Isbandar. Those who wanted to turn her over to the Liath had arrived at her brother's house in droves, keeping the La'athai busy well into the night. She was grateful her soldiers were there, for without them, she certainly would be either seriously maimed or dismembered, just to get her to the other side of the city walls.

She listened intently until the sounds of fighting were over, was about to start reading again, when she felt the cramping sensation again. It was a bit stronger than before, but she sat through it, rubbing at her belly. The child within was strangely quiet, unmoving, and she couldn't help wondering about him, hoping that he was well. She took a deep steadying breath, wrapping her robe more tightly around her. Winter had come early this year and it was cold. She glanced over at the bed, warm and inviting, considered climbing into it for that promised warmth and possible rest. It was late, well into the wee hours of the morning, and she was beyond tired. But then she shook her head against the idea. The incessant fighting would only keep her awake.

She rose and walked to the fire, tossing another log onto the low flames. They sprang to life and she hunkered before them for a bit, relishing the warmth that reminded her so much of the Wolf. Her heart ached at the thought of him and she wished he was there, holding her in his embrace, keeping the chill at bay. Long, deep breaths let her peel away her worries and just remember the comfort of him. She finally rose from the fire, glancing again at the bed to still see two sets of eyes watching her, alert and unblinking. Then another episode of cramping gripped her, making her stop in her tracks. A low moan escaped her throat as she stood there, waiting for it to pass.

Maybe I should lie down after all. maybe I just need to rest. Vivien didn't resist the impulse this time, walked over and climbed in. Tir-reath and dragonling situated themselves around her, offering what comfort they could. Another bout of fighting started again, this time with shouting of profanities, followed by the shriek of a tir-reath. A lonely tear slipped down her cheek and her throat burned. *My people hate me so much, my own people. How did I get to this place?* But she knew how she had gotten there. The fae had left her and dragon magic had taken root in the hole they had left behind. She'd watched it happen all over again as the Inquisitor flash forwarded through her mind, making her remember things better left forgotten.

And some things better *remembered*.

That brief flash had reminded her of the spells she'd learned in Zormoth, and it was these that went into her new tome first. They were spells she hadn't even used, but just simply remembered from poring over them so desperately, spells she prayed would one day give her freedom.

Vivien closed her eyes, wincing as another assault hit her abdomen. She curved around the bulge of it, trying to breathe through it instead of holding her breath. Somehow, it helped her endure it a bit better. After it was over, Sherika positioned herself close to her belly, the rumbling of her purr easing the tension in her muscles. Dari'sii coiled around her back and rested her wedge-shaped head on her hip, twin tendrils of smoke rising from her nostrils.

Against the odds, Zi'anna had summoned the smallest of fae. Mages said, only among others of their kind, that the first fae one summoned said everything one needed to know about an elf. Zi'anna's first fae were fae of light. They were beautiful, delicate things that flitted and winked out, leaving flashes of light that left blue spots on the eyes. Without the discipline of study, or knowing exactly how, the girl had summoned them, and Jor'aiden was very proud.

After her efforts, Zi'anna had slept soundly next to the wall on a bedroll made from strips of leather. Jor'aiden had slept not at all. Cold had descended like a cursed anvil, and the skies were turning threatening even without the constant clouds of smoke that besieged the city. His lungs and eyes constantly burned from it, though the lower caste elves seemed far less afflicted.

When Zi'anna awoke, and even before she'd shrugged off her leather cover, she asked, "What do I learn next?"

Jor'aiden smiled and her lessons began. They took a break at mid-morning to find food, and at last there was some to be had. Great cauldrons had been brought from the city center at someone unknown's orders. They had been filed with flour and milk, water, tubers and mushrooms to make a thick soup. Armed soldiers, guards, and draftees were serving themselves with barely contained zeal.

The armed guard near the cauldron put out a hand when he saw Zi'anna. "For those on the wall only. Move on."

The redhead bristled, but Jor'aiden was faster to reply. "Fool, this is my apprentice, and we are the only mages you have to help you on the wall unless I miss my guess. Feed her."

The guard looked them both over. He took note of Jor'aiden's robes, guessed at his station, and relented meekly. The girl had just filled a small bowl made of hard bread when she stopped and looked to her master.

"What?" he asked.

"They have stopped."

And they had. Since yesterday, hundreds upon hundreds of smoking tinder balls had been sent over the wall, but not now. The silence was almost unsettling. "Eat."

The girl ate her soup, followed by the bowl. Jor'aiden then offered her his own.

"You're not hungry?" she asked.

The Magister shook his head and she began to demolish the food. He smiled and wrapped his robes more closely to fend off the bitter cold. "Old men do not eat much," he lied. It would just taste to him of caustic smoke in any event.

After she was finished, they went straight back to the spot he had begun to think of as their home on the wall. There, he lost himself in teaching her what she needed to know. It would never be enough, but he imparted what he could. She managed to call and hold a feeble light fae in her thrall, the little thing dancing about her hands as she giggled. "Why is it not hot?"

"It is not fire, apprentice, nor heat, though you could call such things. It is just light. Happy and simple, light."

The fae flew under one of her arms and she put out a finger. It lit upon it like a butterfly, and Jor'aiden marveled at her control. He opened his mouth just as he heard the words, "Hail the Gate!"

Master and apprentice left what they were doing and sprinted up the stairs to the top of the wall, the light fae winking back to the aether.

"Well," said the herald on the road, "the old man who says not enough, and the brat who says too much."

Jor'aiden frowned. "Speak the words of your masters."

She chuckled in response. "Do you have a reply?"

Jor'aiden looked left and right, and saw none leaping to be the spokesman of the city. "No."

"Know this: we are not forever patient. This is your last warning. Give up the Vessel or reside forever in a cold grave. We march upon you tomorrow. We leave these messengers as reminder." As she turned away, the catapults started again.

The arms of the engines had been filled, not with one large thing, but with dozens of smaller things. They came as a cloud and made violet flashes as they passed overhead and into the city.

"What was that?" Zi'anna cried.

"It is the ward of Isbandar. They could not stop them, but they don't like—"

"Master!" the apprentice shrieked.

He dove beneath the protective lip of the wall as a flurry of fist sized rocks pelted the gate and flew above to enter the city with a bright, violet flash. No more came at head level, and one elf had been hit in the arm, which was messily broken. All fires on the wall summarily went out. Jor'aiden looked around, then rushed back down the ladder and back to the cooking pot. A single one of the rocks lay nearby, a hastily scrawled blue rune covering the surface. It glowed malignantly. The guard at hand was trying to relight the fire beneath the steaming, almost-gone soup, but his flint and steel wouldn't even make sparks.

More rocks flew overhead, aimed more deeply into the city.

Jor'aiden growled, "That is a dragon rune, imbued with power."

Zi'anna crouched down and reached toward the rock, "It isn't cold. How will this make us cold like a grave?"

Jor'aiden summoned the least powerful fire fae he could and pointed to the stone. It touched the rune and a belch of oily black smoke erased both from existence.

The flint sparked and the hot wood caught immediately.

"Oh, I think these things will make us cold all the same." He looked to his apprentice. "You remember her message?"

Zi'anna repeated it word-for-word.

"Good. Go deliver it, and be wary of the rocks from the sky."

And she went. Jor'aiden wrapped his robes more tightly about him, and wondered what a day and night without fire would do to Isbandar.

Chapter Forty-Nine
Birth of a Prodigy

"Vivien! Vivien, you have to wake up." She groggily opened her eyes to see Mikarvan standing over her, gently shaking her awake. Somehow, she'd fallen asleep despite the sounds from outside and the cramping in her belly.

"W...what time is it?" She looked around. She must have forgotten to latch the door. Dari'sii was nowhere to be seen, but the books were still spread out in the open. She sat stock still for a moment until Mikarvan responded.

"It's past midday."

She relaxed at his lack of reaction to the forbidden scrolls. To one only trained in the healing arts of the fae, the words to circumscribe dragon magic would mean as little to him as those for fae battle magic. Then the import of her words struck him. "I slept that long?"

"Yes, and it was good for you. I didn't want to awaken you until it was completely necessary."

She frowned at the solemn tone of his voice. "What has happened?"

"This morning the Liath issued an ultimatum."

"What kind of ultimatum?" she asked grimly.

Mikarvan pressed his lips into a thin line. "To either hand you over to them, or they will pillage, rape and murder until every soul in this city is either dead or enslaved."

The air whooshed out of her lungs as though she'd been kicked in the chest and she lay back on the pillows. "Do they have the forces to do it?" she whispered.

Mikarvan nodded gravely. "They are at least ten thousand strong."

"How do you know that? It's a forest out there!"

He shook his head. "Not anymore. They cut it down."

She widened her eyes in shock. The forest had been dense, a strong barrier against any who thought to easily ride up to Isbandar. It had been beautiful, and now it was gone, wasted by the toxic Liath.

Mikarvan put a comforting hand on her arm. "Vivien, we have to get you out of here. Now. People have heard what is coming for them if the city doesn't do what the Liath command."

She looked up at him, haunted. "No, I should hand myself over. There are too many lives here that would be lost because of me."

Mikarvan looked at her in shock, his jaw hanging open for a moment before he pulled himself together. "What? Are you daft, woman!"

She simply shook her head, a feeling of despair sweeping over her. "No, it is the right thing to do."

Anger flashed in his eyes. "So, you really think that the Liath will stop when they have you in their filthy clutches?" He tightened his grip on her arm. "Well, they won't! They will still come, and they will still try to raze this city to the ground."

She shook her head, her voice a monotone. "You are so certain?"

"I would bet my very life on it."

He took a deep breath, pulled her forward until her head rested against the wall of his chest. "I won't lose you again, Vivien." His voice was heavy with emotion, and she thought she may have heard it crack just the smallest bit at the end. She inhaled the scent of him, took it in and let it calm her tortured soul, let it wash away her fears.

"I trust you, Mika. I will come with you."

He tightened his arms around her briefly before letting her go. "Good, because I already packed a bag for you."

Vivien climbed out of the bed, stopping when she felt the chill in the air. She looked over to see that the fire was out, but that extra blankets had been piled over her on the bed. She saw the wood still by the hearth, untouched, and looked at Mikarvan. "It's terrible cold in here. Why did you not keep the fire going?"

His expression was grim. "I couldn't. The Liath mages put them out after they issued their demands. The entire city is without fire."

"How did they do that? The city is warded!"

"They cast ensorcelled rocks over the wall, spells that didn't activate until the rocks hit the ground. The only places unaffected by the magic were the College of Magic, the Council Hall, the prison, and any noble's house that might have its own wards."

Shock rolled over her for a moment until Mikarvan tugged on her arm. "Come, you need to hurry. The La'athai are waiting."

She did as he bid, quickly donning the clothing he had waiting for her: trousers, a chemise, and over-sized long tunic. He left for a moment and she looked at all the books spread around. She hastily shoved them back into her satchel and slid it under the bed, keeping only her personal tome of distilled knowledge for the pack she would take with her. He returned and wrapped an oversized winter cloak around her; if she were to guess it was one of Anlon's. Then, keeping her slippers in place, he shoved a pair of boots over her swollen feet.

They met Evey in the hallway as they exited the chamber. She was clothed in much the same way, heavily burdened with the bulk of Mikarvan's packs filled with healing supplies. He took half of the bags before taking Vivien's hand and leading her out the front door. She blinked at the snowy 'scape, fat flakes falling to join their comrades in a blanket that covered everything.

And there, standing in a line before her, were the La'athai.

They were dirty, tired, and battle-worn, their tir-reath sitting beside them. They all stood as tall as they could despite the numerous injuries they had sustained over the past two days. There were several moments of silence as she just stood there, proudly looking over the men and women that had defended her with their lives every second they had been in Isbandar. Every second they had been there, in the background, defending her honor, her integrity, and her person. Tears sprang to her eyes that she quickly dashed away with the back of her hand. She didn't want them to see her cry.

She slowly walked towards the line. Gregor stepped forward at her approach, removing his helm and kneeling before her, head down. "Elthari Jashi."

She remembered how good it felt to be called that name as she put her hand on the crown of his head. "Captain Gregor. Thank you for your service."

He looked up at her, his eyes twinkling, a grin across his lips. "Always for you Mi'lady."

She then walked down the row, greeting each kneeling warrior with their name and an expression of gratitude. And by the end, her heart soared. These were her people. She loved the Elvish nation, wanted to do her duty to them, but these La'athai, they were her people. And as they gathered their gear, hiding their armored persons and weaponry beneath oversized cloaks, she felt her heart open to this concept, felt it embrace it as truth. And for the first time in a long time, she felt she knew her place in the world, and she accepted it.

Vivien walked back over to Mikarvan, who must have noticed the change in her, for his smile was so genuine, it touched his eyes to make them sparkle. "Now I see why they love you so much."

She took his hand. "So, where are you taking me?"

"His eyes glinted mischievously. "To prison."

She laughed at his joke, but only when he didn't laugh with her did she begin to realize he might not be joshing her after all. "What?"

"It is the safest place. No one else will think to go there right now. The elites are already being evacuated to the college, so we can't go there."

She nodded, watched as a pair of the La'athai and their tir-reath left the group and made their way to the road.

"We all made a plan on how we should get to the prison," he continued. "First two pairs of La'athai spaced thirty minutes apart, followed by you, me and Evey, then the remaining three pairs follow after. It will be cold, so everyone will pile into two or three cells and the tir-reath can help keep us warm."Mikarvan smiled again. "Come on back inside. It's warmer in the house than it is out here. I only brought you out because I knew you'd want to see the Pack before we implemented the plan."

"You thought right. Thank you."

"You're welcome, Elthari Jashi."

Esgrynn watched the city disintegrate like a block of salt in the rain. People were fighting among themselves. Food, weapons, safety, none of them were being purchased cheaply and very little was being sold. For days he had slept in the streets, for there was nowhere else to go, but his fears of being rousted by the guardsmen were completely unfounded. Every guardsman was on the wall or near it, along with everyone who could even hold a weapon competently. His poor attire made all who saw him think he had nothing of value, which of course was not true, but fit his needs perfectly. When they saw he had nothing of value they avoided him, thinking he would be in need of something instead. No one had anything spare to parcel out, and so he became invisible.

The invisible could overhear many things. That is, if there were people to overhear. The smokers tossed over the walls had been a good thought by whoever was leading the dragon elves. They had all but shut down traffic in the streets and he had been forced to hide in an all but an abandoned flower garden until people were back out again. Then the cursed extinguishing stones had been tossed over the walls. So, while he could move around, he could not keep warm. When he had finally been forced by the cold to huddle with strangers near one of the few working fires, he had heard a flurry of gossip, and that had finally given him some leads to chase down as he hunted his prey.

His day from that moment had been spent chasing the ghost of Vivien Valdera. First, he learned she was in prison, but she was not. The guards had been stripped from the place, and other than some very hungry caged miscreants, it had been empty. Of course not, she had been *imprisoned*. But not at the prison, no. She was at the abandoned college of magic. Esgrynn had cursed, for he had passed that very place that first night in the city. He had circled back around, but no, Valdera was not there. The college was guarded, though, and hundreds of purebred elves, nobles all, were filing with family members into one of the few buildings in the city most assured of being able to withstand dragonfire. Dragon elf swords, however, would dig in just fine. *Fools.*

She had been set free weeks ago. This prospect meant she would be much easier to approach, but far harder to find. That was when he heard that she was staying with her half brother in a small manse to the west. It was there he headed next.

It was a quaint place, modest and unassuming, but he noticed three things immediately. The first was that there were ruts worn in the grass down to the mud all around the place, as if patrol had been made over and over and over. The second is there were no guards, and she was supposed to have a personal guard called the Wolf Pack, or somesuch. And the third was he felt no spark of magic in or on the place. Vivien may have been hiding her talent, dampening her magic footprint, but he was good at sniffing such things out and he didn't believe she was good enough to hide from him.

He knocked politely, and the door opened a crack. He huffed, "Well, Esgrynn, nobody's home."

"Hello?" replied a timid voice.

Esgrynn thought briefly about running to hide somewhere, but then he would get nowhere in his search for Valdera. So, dressed like a beggar, or more accurately a mad hermit, he strode in. The house was nice, but the details did not concern him. It had the smell of many unwashed bodies living in too confined a place for many, many days.

His eyes locked onto a tattered, used-up half elf. She lounged on a couch, as if the weight of her misery could not be held up by a chair alone. She was not old, but she had the same kind of faded soul that very old elves often did. She was spare, sparse, and had probably only summoned the urge to ask if anyone had been there out of habit than any real interest.

Esgrynn steeled himself. "I am looking for Vivien Valdera."

The half elf woman sneered. "Gone. Like my own child. Like all of them."

The conversation was already too banal for Esgrynn, and her presence made him, a man who lived in a swamp, feel dirty. He clenched his teeth. "Where did she go?"

She laughed, but mirthlessly, already turning over. "Prison."

"And her guard?"

"Those crazy bastards? They went with her."

"And you didn't go?"

Her reply was spoken to the back of the couch, and the tone was sullen. "I don't belong in prison."

Esgrynn shook his head and left without further comment or closing the door. One of the first places he had checked had been the prison. Now he was out of leads. He breathed deeply, trying to calm his rage and focus on what he knew. He knew Valdera was a competent battle mage, and so his next course of action would be to walk along the wall. Walk, and listen.

The walk to the prison was a bit slower than Vivien would have liked. The snow had continued to fall, making the road a muddy slush. All around, the trees were covered in white, giving an air of tranquility that was broken by the stragglers who headed toward the college. The cramping from the night before had started again as they waited for their turn to leave Anlon's house, slowly getting stronger and stronger as the minutes passed. From within the folds of her cloak, she clutched at her belly, squeezed her eyes shut from within the hood that shrouded her from the others. She didn't want Evey and Mikarvan to worry, and hoped it might recede again once they got to the prison and she was given a chance to lie down once more.

She stumbled with the next onslaught and a supporting hand at her elbow kept her from falling. "Vivien, are you alright?" asked Mikarvan.

When she didn't answer right away, he stepped in front of her and looked into her face. His brows creased with worry and she realized her expression had betrayed her. "What is it? What's wrong?"

And it was then she felt it, a popping sensation deep inside, followed by a warm trickle between her legs. Weakness suddenly turned her legs into jelly and she sagged against him, her breath coming in gasps. "Something's happening. I think the baby's waters broke."

His eyes flew wide in alarm and he pitched his voice up the road ahead. "Evey, hold!"

Within a moment she was there and Mikarvan was speaking before she could utter a word. "Take another one of my packs, the big one here."

"What's going on? Why is she so pale?"

"The waters have broken. The baby is coming."

Evey took the pack and Vivien gasped as Mikarvan lifted her into his arms. "Come, we need to hurry!"

Vivien wrapped her arms around his neck and allowed herself to be carried, each of Mikarvan's hurried steps jarring her body. She buried her face into his neck and moaned, the spasms in her belly worse than ever. She could feel it in her back and between her legs, making her crotch ache.

And then it was gone. It receded the way it had come, slowly and without fanfare.

By the time they reached the prison, she was in the middle of another contraction. Mikarvan set her on her feet, helped her along a long staircase leading down into the bowels beneath the forest. Through the pain she could feel it getting warmer as they walked, the cold from above unable to permeate the layers of soil and rock. She could feel the magic of the place, thrumming all around her, getting stronger and stronger. The wards prevented the dragon mages' magic from entering, and wall sconces had fires that allowed them to see as they moved ever deeper. When they reached the bottom, she was urged along a stone-lined corridor that led into a massive chamber. Gigantic root systems stretched down from the high ceiling, and around them were the prison cells, all lining the chamber along the periphery. Mikarvan led her past the largest root, quite possibly the largest she'd ever seen, and into the nearest cell. The La'athai that were already there, seeing that something was amiss, rushed over.

Mikarvan's tone was authoritative. "She needs something to lay on, something more than just a single pallet."

Two of the men went to their gear and each brought his bedroll. After the pallets were rolled out and laid onto the floor, one atop the other, Mikarvan helped her lay down. One full waterskin covered with an ermine fur was placed beneath her head, and another man brought his skin to her lips. She drank and settled down, the scent of unwashed bedding wafting into her nose. But she didn't care, just grateful the men were there and that, without thought, had given her all they had to bring them comfort during the night ahead.

And then she labored. The contractions were like waves, ebbing and flowing inside her. The waters would gush with each one, soaking the pallet beneath until Mikarvan asked another be brought. By then, all of the La'athai were there. They settled outside the cell, any one of them rushing to do Mikarvan's bidding when he declared it. Two remained near the surface, trying to keep apace of events that might be unfolding there.

Hours that felt like days passed. Over the night, tension rose, along with the ambient temperature. Vivien cried out with spasms that she could now feel throughout her entire torso and down her legs. Sherika stayed by her side, never leaving, her purring a constant comfort. It hurt when Mikarvan examined her, but she said nothing, simply let him do what he must. But each time, he reported that she was slowly, but surely, getting closer.

It was early morning when the La'athai guarding the prison entrance rushed to the cell. "Master Healer! Something is happening!"

Mikarvan rose from his place at her side, was about to usher them out to hear the news himself, when she spoke. "No, I want to hear what they have to say."

The two men pushed past Mikarvan and into the cell. Vivien saw a look of shock cross over the healer's face, yet he said nothing as the men approached closer. She couldn't help feeling a bit of surprise herself. These men still followed her, in spite of what had happened to her, in spite of the vulnerable position she was in now, they followed her. They had to know she had been raped whilst she was in the hands of the Liath priests, yet it meant nothing to them. She was in the throes of childbirth, unable to physically lead them into any battle, and that, also, meant nothing to them. This realization gave her strength, made her feel powerful in a way she couldn't describe.

"Commander, the Liath have summoned their dragons!"

Mikarvan's face paled and Vivien's heart sank.

"Even now, if you listen closely enough, you can hear them battering at the city wards. Isbandar is under siege!"

Silence filled the cell and the chamber without, everyone listening intently. And then they heard it, as though a massive explosion were going off from very far away. But even more, they could *feel* it, a tremoring of the ground all around them. The place remained silent until they heard it again, and then again...

Vivien felt the next contraction coming, spoke before she would not have the capacity. "Go back to your post. Report back to me if you see or hear anything new."

The men gave a smart bow before replying in unison. "Yes, Commander."

More time passed. She didn't know how long, for her world was filled with pain. Never before had she felt agony like this, like her entire body was being ripped apart. Evey became a constant at her side, holding her hand and talking her through the pain. Sherika remained on her other, a warm presence that made her believe that, somehow, she would live to see the next day. She missed Dari'sii, but knew that the prison wards kept her out. She still didn't know how the wyrm had managed to get into the college, but she supposed it didn't really matter.

The voice of the guard from earlier reverberated through the cell. "Commander, pandemonium has broken out! People are afraid and looking for shelter! They are coming here!"

For a moment she stopped breathing. Sweat covered her body, had soaked through the gown she wore and damped her hair. The expression on the La'athai's face as he saw her lying there shifted from one fear of that which was coming from the outside, to fear for her. Damn, she must look a sight.

"Go get Gregor," she panted.

Moments later the captain was there, worriedly taking her in.

"Gregor, tell the pack to arm themselves for battle. However, the people are not to be harmed. Do you understand?" Her tone brooked no argument and he gave a hasty bow before rushing out to do her bidding.

She slumped back onto the pile of furs that had been situated behind her, and when she looked at Mikarvan, worry creased his brow. But she knew it wasn't just about the danger that was about to arrive at their doorstep. "What is it?"

He cleared his throat anxiously. "The labor is taking longer than the usual. So I am a bit concerned."

"What do you need to do?"

He hesitated and she frowned, wondering at his trepidation. He was the Master Healer of Rithalion. He delivered children all the time, with very high success. It felt like something was wrong, that he was keeping something from her. She just couldn't imagine what.

"I am going to check you again, see what I can do to help."

She nodded as she felt the next contraction hit her, and she screamed.

Evey watched as Mikarvan worked, her hand shaking within Vivien's. Something was amiss, she could see it in his face as he concentrated, wincing a time or two as if struck. Finally, he withdrew his hand, slick with fresh blood, and shook his head with an expression she could only describe as dread. Vivien screamed again and sobbed in agony, clutching at Evey's hand as though she might take it from her arm. Sherika gave a high-pitched shriek, a sound the tir-reath made only when they were afraid or in danger. She pierced Mikarvan with her gaze, pressed her lips into a thin line.

"Do something for her! Do something!" She was surprised how much her pitch resembled Sherika's.

He leveled his eyes at her, and they were dark with emotion. "Go tell the men that four of them need to stand guard before this cell. Tell them they are not allowed to leave their post, no matter what happens."

Evey was about to protest, but he cut her off with a shout. "Do it now!"

Evey tore her hand from Vivien's grip, stood as though a fire were beneath her. She'd never heard Mikarvan speak to her that way before, not to her or to anyone. She rushed from the cell and into the main chamber, saw that the La'athai were equipped and ready. Gregor saw her and approached, a grim expression she'd never seen on him before etched on his face.

"Master Healer says that four men are to guard the cell. They are to remain there, no matter what."

Gregor just stood there for a moment, taking in her words, and his eyes became pained. He knew what the order meant– that every other La'athai in that chamber could die, and the four guarding Vivien's cell could do nothing to aid their comrades. He swallowed heavily and nodded. He knew that the order was necessary, but that didn't mean he had to like it.

She watched as he chose three of his comrades, and she wouldn't be surprised if they were the best he had. They positioned themselves before the cell and Gregor followed just as the first people arrived down the stairwell.

For a few moments she stood there, waiting... waiting... The La'athai acted as though they belonged there, herding the people away from Vivien's cell and further down the line of prison cells on the opposite side. The people kept coming, cold and damp from the snow, their faces filled with fear. First ten, then twenty. Before she knew it, there were over fifty people. It wasn't much longer before someone recognized them.

"Those men! They aren't from here! They are the ones that arrived here with Vivien Valdera!" someone shouted.

Eyes wide, Evey watched as the people looked around, took note of the La'athai keeping them on one side of the chamber, then across to where Gregor and the other chosen three stood guard.

"By the gods she's here! The Valdera witch is here! We've found her!"

Her heart beat a staccato rhythm as she watched the La'athai get into battle formation. More people came down the stairs, and having heard the man's declaration, stopped to stand at his side. "If we get her, we can end this! We can end the siege!"

Just then, Vivien screamed.

Everyone was still for a moment, wondering what was happening. Then a woman spoke up. "She's in labor! The witch is delivering her demon child!"

Evey stood there for just a half second longer in time to see the people rush towards the La'athai before turning and running back to the cell. She paused by Gregor, put her hand on his arm, just above his vambracer, and looked up at his face. All but his eyes were covered by his helm. "Please protect us."

He gave her a nod and she darted inside. She saw Vivien writhing on the sweat-soaked pallet, her teeth tightly clenched around another scream. Mikarvan was between her legs, a long tool before him that looked like spoon-shaped pair of tongs. "Evey, get me the other pail of water!"

She reached behind him, grabbed the pail and set it at his side. It was already steaming; he must have heated it while she was talking to Gregor. Fire fae twinkled in the air, then settled onto the tool. "What is that?"

He took a clean cloth, dipped it into the hot water, and wrapped it around his hand. "It's called a forceps, a tool to help deliver the child. He is coming, but he needs help."

The fae blinked out and Mikarvan picked up the heated forceps with his protected hand. He let it cool for a few minutes and Evey moved up to Vivien's head, grasping her hand and holding it tight. "I'm back now, love. I'm here."

Vivien attempted a smile that got lost in another agonized cry. Outside the cell, the sounds of an angry crowd could be heard, along with shouts from the La'athai. Evey looked up at Mikarvan and caught his gaze. "It's time," he said.

Vivien screamed as Mika carefully inserted the forceps. Evey squeezed her eyes tightly shut, hoping... praying this would soon be over. "I've got him. Alright Vivien, you need to push now, push with all you've got!"

Vivien's back rose off the furs as she pushed, tears streaming down her face in rivulets that dripped onto her gown. After several moments she slumped back. "Oh, gods please save me!"

"Vivien, you can't stop now! Push again!"

She dug her nails into Evey's hand as she surged up again, her face turning red with the effort. Evey hissed, felt the nails break the skin, and then the burn.

"You're doing good! He's coming! It's almost over now!"

Evey heard the crowd get louder, followed by the ring of steel against steel. Vivien slumped back again, exhaustion in her every breath.

"Only five seconds and then you need to push again for me! Come on, you can do it!"

Vivien lurched again, her nails digging deeper into Evey's hand. Silent tears sprang to her eyes but she held tight onto her Vivien, unwilling to let her go.

Mikarvan's voice got an excited edge. "He's almost here! I can see his hair, and it's the same color as yours! It's beautiful!"

This time Vivien smiled. It was wonderful to see, a radiant smile that touched every corner of the cell. It seemed to give her strength, and she continued to push...push...push.

And then she let out a moan and slumped back onto the furs, relaxing her death grip. Evey heard a slap, swiftly followed by a tiny wail. She looked at Mikarvan, saw him rubbing a towel over a small red form lying on the pallet near Vivien's feet. Then he swaddled it, rose, and brought it to Vivien's side.

His voice broke as he spoke. "Vivien, your son is here, and he is well!"

Vivien opened her eyes and turned towards Mikarvan. Evey huddled close to Vivien, not wanting to miss the first glimpse her dearest friend would have of the child she had labored so long to have.

And there it was again, that smile, the one that lit up rooms and made a Pack of men and women fall in love with her almost at first sight. Vivien reached for the tiny bundle, pulled aside the blanket to reveal the tiniest face Evey had ever seen. She watched the miracle occur where mother and child were linked at first touch. Vivien would now forever feel this boy, linked to him for all of her days.

Her voice was a whisper. "Alsander. Your name is Alsander."

DRAGON VESSEL

Evey jerked when she heard a familiar shout. It was Gregor. "There are too many! We can't keep them back without hurting them!"

She rose from Vivien's side and rushed to the entry. There, just beyond the four La'athai guarding the cell, were over a hundred people. The mob struck at the La'athai still standing, pushing ever closer. The fighting got closer...closer. Evey heard a cry from behind her, one from Vivien, as she delivered the afterbirth. Gregor drew his blade and the other three followed suit. His voice was fraught with desperation as he shouted to the crowd. "Get back now! Get back before people start getting hurt!"

A hand at her shoulder made Evey turn back. Her eyes opened wide to see Vivien standing there, the child cradled, naked, in her arms. "Let me by Evey."

Fear struck her through the heart, making her stutter. "N...no! You can't go out there! They will kill you!"

"Evey, step aside."

It was an imperial tone, one she'd heard only once before. It was back in the city of Elyrion when Vivien had seen Anlon for the first time in scores of years. It was a tone that told Evey there was not going to be a fight, at least not a long one, because Vivien would win. Evey looked back at Mikarvan, saw the same look of abject fear on his face that she felt in her heart...

...but she stepped aside.

And suddenly there was no one there between Vivien and the crowd. The people closest stopped first, their eyes riveted on mother and newborn. It spread, people stopping just to look at her, expressions of incredulity on their faces. Vivien stepped out of the cell, her gown stained with blood, feet bare. The La'athai moved to flank her, parting the crowd to allow her passage. She stepped slowly into the middle of the chamber, and once there, held the naked boy in the air before her.

He was perfect in every detail. Tiny feet and tiny hands with even tinier fingers and toes. His head was slightly misshapen from his journey to the outside world, his ears rounded at the tops, his eyes open. He let out a wail, a wail that sounded like every other elvin child before him.

The baby wailed in indignation, but Vivien continued to hold him out for every set of eyes to see. Not a soul uttered a sound.

And then something happened. First one, then two, then several golden fae appeared in the air around the baby. The crowd made a collective gasp that swept from the center back, everyone seeing something that had only been seen once before.

"The Grand Magister! The spirit of the Grand Magister is in this child!"

The people whispered excitedly, as the fae cavorted wildly about the baby before winking out. Vivien finally lowered her arms, brought the baby close. She swayed on her feet and Gregor put a steadying arm around her back. A woman stepped forward, her eyes bright with joy. "Please, may I touch him?"

Vivien hesitated but the briefest of moments before nodding. "Yes. Then you will see that he is real, and is just like you and I. He is elvin."

"What is his name?" she asked.

"Yes, tell us the baby's name!" said a man.

Vivien looked out over the crowd. These were not fighters. They were regular men and women with homes and families they feared would be destroyed by the Liatl. They had been frightened, but now hope shined in their eyes. Her gaze stopped at a familiar face, one she had become so accustomed to those last several days she'd spent at the old college. The Grand Inquisitor gave her a small smile as the crowd got more excited, everyone talking at once.

"May I touch him too?"

"Please tell us his name!"

Vivien returned his smile and cast it towards the people surrounding her, people that needed a ray of light in the darkness that threatened. "His name is Alsander Jor'aiden Valdera."

Chapter Fifty
The Dragons Come

day and night meant little for rest, anymore. The city was awake at all hours and it would be this way until the attack. Panic would simply not let them sleep. The air was warmer than it had been, but it was moist, and fog descended upon the city like a thick funeral shroud. Jor'aiden thought about his daughter, about her unborn child, and about the young girl beside him and wondered if any of them would live through what was coming.

He felt very alone, a feat since he had managed to destroy all the anti-fire runes throughout the immediate area, and so he had one of the few fires in the city burning right there. It had brought stragglers from all around, just to watch the fire and absorb some of the warmth. Guardsmen and soldiers, citizens and the lost, they all came and watched the fire with heavy eyes burdened with knowledge of what was to come. It would have been possible for the small crowd to gather wood and make their own fires, but it may have been that they needed the closeness with others as much as the light. The whole of the city had been cold and quiet through the dark hours, but dawn was coming and that meant the herald would come again.

Zi'anna moved restlessly against him and then settled down again to sleep. Jor'aiden could not help but smile at her. She was such a bright, innocent thing. He thought about his own daughter and ached inside. He wished her peace, and hoped for her survival, but it had become clear that there was little he could do for her in the madhouse that was Isbandar. Since they had released Vivien, the Council had issued no orders, made no proclamations. They were paralyzed with fear, and so then were the citizenry. The defenses were bolstered, but not with any logical thought. He was happy for her release, but the method had left her broken, a shell, and he could not reach her.

In truth, he struggled to find his connection to her. She had been gone so long, thought lost twice, and perhaps that was the truth of it. He had lost children in the Dragon War, and had felt the severed connection with his offspring that brought such terrible loss. It was something every elvin parent shared with their young from the moment they first touched, and his connection to Vivien had been lost so many months ago after the battle with the Iron Coast. Even before that. She had called the unseleighe. It was an unthinkable act for an upright, respectable mage. He had tried to keep close to his daughter, but she always seemed to be moving away from him. Ofttimes with... Him.

He breathed deeply and wished for a glass of something red, warm, and mulled. Though it might warm him, it would not chase away the vision of the Wolf and his undying love for his daughter. And as much as he hated it, more than he wanted steaming wine, he wished the barbarian was here. He knew their love was doomed, but he also knew Vivien would only leave this world after the Wolf had given his very last breath trying to prevent it.

Out beyond the wall, horns began to blow, and Zi'anna finally stirred.

"What is happening?"

Jor'aiden felt his heart sink but kept his face stony. He helped her up and then stood himself, "I imagine that the Liath are mobilizing. Yesterday was the final warning. In any case, we had best go and see."

Zi'anna bounced up the stairs but the Magister followed at a slower pace until he reached the walkway around the top of the wall. Before them, the thick curtains of swirling white currents revealed little. They traveled the short way to stand over the gate where a city guardsman, face tight with strain, looked out into the heavy mists. Muffled sounds of activity were all around and Jor'aiden looked behind him into the entry square of the city. Fighters were already flocking to the wall from the streets beyond, appearing out of the fog at the sound of horns. Some were armed and armored, others wore only warm clothing and carried knives or hammers from kitchens and workshops. They, too, thought they knew what was coming.

Jor'aiden looked into the murk, noting the shifting shadows white and dark in the gloom. The Grand Magister shook his head in frustration, then looked up and down the wall as far as he could before the elvin defenders became indistinct shapes. All of them were tense, rigid, holding their breaths. He looked to the short defensive towers on either side, and saw the ballistae were still unmanned.

Then uncounted voices beyond the walls made a sound. It was something like a grunt, and like a huh, ha, and haraugh, at the same time. It deep, bestial, a war drum made with voices.

Zi'anna crinkled her nose and looked at the crowds of others on the walls. "What are they doing?"

The old mage frowned, "They are preparing to attack. They are going to summon dragons."

The child looked up at him, eyes wide, and try as she might to stop it, she was started to tremble

"There can't be that many of them out there." someone said.

The mage and the apprentice looked at the guardsman who had spoken. He was breathing as if he had run many miles, and his eyes were glassy.

"They are dirty nomads, scattered tribes. There can't be that many of them." He repeated to no one as thousands of voices continued to turn grunts into a chant. "The huge encampment, fine. But we've never seen more than a few hundred at a time. It's a ploy, they just want to cause fear."

Jor'aiden searched his heart for something comforting, bolstering, uplifting to say. Zi'anna spoke first, "They are doing a good job."

Then the fog began to lift.

Out across the killing field of fallen logs, the Liath had assembled. They were dressed in a mishmash of steel armor, heavy furs, and raw leathers, carrying iron and steel weaponry. They fought with a hodgepodge of horn bows and hand weapons. Some were riding the horse-sized reptile beasts they cultivated from swamps in the north. Jor'aiden swept the line of the enemy with his eyes, quickly estimating over ten thousand battle ready troops. What was more disturbing than the great number of the enemy was their complete stillness.

Then there was a sound, like a mountain walking on broken bones, a wind flying on shattered wings. This last left the fog churning like an enraged waterfall, but then there was a sound like a forest fire screaming in pain. Huge gouts of fire exited the mouth of a large red dragon, and it chased away the fog like scattering insects before a vengeful palm. It exposed the host in its entirety, and a moan of desolation went up from the city. Five greater dragons, bodies the length of three or four adult men with necks and tails reaching even further, stood by their masters. They exuded a terrible majesty, a desolate beauty, and a hopeless kind of awe. One roared, and the other four tried to be louder. Every elf in the city could feel the sound reverberating in their chests. Another sound then washed over the wall from the enemy ranks. It was cheering. The Liath grunted their chants as more and more dragons came to the call of their priests. Many of these were the length of two men in the body, with long tails and wings beyond that. There were a dozen, and growing, number of smaller dragons, from those with the body the size of an elf to those the size of dogs.

"Those dragons are giants!" Zi'anna breathed.

"They get even bigger; let us hope none of these dragon mages are strong enough to call any." Jor'aiden looked down at Zi'anna, and for a moment he saw all the summers running through the grass, all the winters curled up by the fire sipping cider, her children by her side, and their children, and their children. He ran a gentle hand down her chopped red hair, "Apprentice, it would comfort me greatly to have you deeper in the city."

She looked up at him. "I am going to fight."

He nodded, and she gave a small smile just before the world erupted into violet. A high-pitched shriek assaulted them from all sides, a sound made physical by virtue of its size and strength. Jor'aiden opened his eyes and found he had pulled Zi'anna down beneath him, but the whole world was awash in bright purple light as if an amethyst sun had crashed down upon them. The searing bright light and the cacophony of sound went on and on until suddenly ceasing, but continuing to rattle their bones even in its absence. Jor'aiden glanced around. A few steps away, the guardsman, trembling as if with palsy, simply turned and ran right off of the walkway above the gate. He fell without ceremony or control, landing hard on the road below. The Magister glanced over the wall and saw, rather than heard, the Liath cheering.

He stood up, and saw the dragon looking back toward the others of its kind. While the rest were slowly coming to help, it stood alone for now. It appeared to be primping itself, proud of its efforts as ten thousand dragon elves cheered it on.

"What was that?" Zi'anna cried.

"A dragon breathed fire at us." Jor'aiden replied without much emotion.

"And we are alive?"

"The Guardian F_e of the wall protected us." The Magister saw all the defenders of the wall scattering for the stairs as if there was somewhere they could run.

Zi'anna took a shuldering breath. "What was that sound?"

"It was the guard ins. Dying." Jor'aiden grabbed her and pulled her down as the next blast hit. I seemed to go on forever, but when it ended, they again stood up. The wall wa as yet untouched.

"Master, what do we do?" Zi'anna cried.

The old man look ed left and right, seeing the wall clear of defenders and frowning. As he spoke, he lost more and more control of his temper. "The wards will hold, but not forever and we cannot defend the wall. There is no one in charge. The genera s of Isbandar are not here. The mages of Isbandar are not here. The Council is not here! There has never been anyone in charge!"

"MASTER! You are here!"

Jor'aiden turned to her. "I haven't fought Liath since the Dragon War. I am not a master of tactics I have no authority here, child!"

"But Master, you HAVE fought them before! More importantly, YOU are here! That is the only thing that matters right now. We need someone, anyone. Please!"

And the dragon, having come another two hundred feet closer, breathed fire again. Zi'anna du ked down, but though the purple shield of guardian fae screamed and died by the hundreds, the ward held, and Jor'aiden watched the blast hit. The heat was intense, and it melted snow in every direction for a dozen yards, but Jor'iden felt something snap as he faced the maelstrom of flame and was untouc ed.

He called upon wind spirit he had known for a very long time. He whispered to it harshly, angrily. A hazy slip of wind and clouds, it saw the mighty target and nodded. It reached for several bundles of arrows laying forgotten on the wall.

The dragon finished its exhalation and turned back to receive more accolades. That was when Jor'aiden's wind fae hurled the loosened bundles of arrows, breathing the n out faster than any bow could push. The shafts were hurled so fast they whistled in the air, fletchings hissing as they arced up and then down, stabbing with murderous intent at the fire dragon that stood within bowshot of the wall. The first arrow landed and the thing recoiled, and a few dozen more followed just after. Not even a tenth of them hit, but those that did caused the dragon to rat loudly and withdraw from the assault. The cheering petered off.

The dragon would only be hurt for minutes before its miraculous constitution healed itself completely. Yet, when Jor'aiden felt the wind fae, it was pleased with itself for hurting such a hated foe, he felt him summon his own mettle. He called upon it to push his words far across the whole of the city, out to the Dragons and their butchering Liath.

"You are unwise to have come. I am Grand Magister of Rithalion and I defend this wall. So, come and die, mongrels. You will find only a meal that will choke you if you manage to get your cracked teeth around it." He let his voice fade, and for a moment took heart from his own defiance. It was bluster, pure bravado only worthy of a much younger and far less wise elf. But it gave the enemy reason to pause. A few defenders heard him and trickled back into the square, and Jor'aiden pointed as if at a lacking student. "You! Go collect those that have fled and bring them back. You! Load and fire one ballista, and you take the other! You two, help crank and load!"

"I don't know how!" one plainly dressed elf carrying a simple wood axe replied.

An earth dragon beyond the wall coughed up a massive bolder, like blowing a bubble, into its mouth and hurled it. The rock the size of a wagon shattered into sand against the ward with a sound that would shame a thunder-strike. The shower of pebbles cascaded around the Magister, who did not flinch. It poured around him and he raised his voice to a hoarse shout.

"Learn, damn you!" The Magister bellowed. Then he turned to Zi'anna. "Get to the Council any way you can. Tell them we need soldiers. We need generals. We need defenders, now. And if you see anyone who can fight, send them here."

Zi'anna nodded and ran off.

Jor'aiden turned to face the wrath of the Liath, and gathered his determination to himself as a knight dons armor.

Grand Councilman Blue Moon Rising had bade him depart the Council Hall. The building was packed full of the lesser nobility, the council people and their families, as well as food, water, and soldiers. The Grand Inquisitor had been more than useless there. Even less useful than the Grand Councilman and his retinue. They gave no orders, and made no decisions. They were paralyzed with fear, and that had made them notice the Inquisitor again. His mission had been to find and secure Vivien Valdera, and not for her own safety. Blue Moon Rising saw her as both the reason for the attack, and the solution, eager to give her up or see her executed. The argument that had ensued had rocked the rafters of that once respected building. In the end, the Grand Inquisitor had departed, but not on the mission he had been given.

Finding her had been easy.

The Grand Inquisitor now held the small bundle, made sure the tiny boy nestled within remained warm despite the cold without. At his side was Master Healer Mikarvan, a good man who had done his job in the best way possible given the circumstances he'd been provided. Both mother and child lived, both were healthy, and as far as he could see, unharmed. The delivery had been described in detail by Eveleen as they prepared to leave the prison, a place that was rapidly filling with refugees from the city that needed a place of safety. For

Vivien and her Pack had more to offer. Despite the cold and the frightening aerial battle above the city, he took them to the one place in the city that was the most protected. His home.

From beneath his hood, the Inquisitor glanced at the young woman on the other side of Mikarvan, one of the strongest he'd ever met. In spite of the pain she must still be feeling, and the passing of blood from the delivery, Vivien walked without complaint. She'd handed over her precious bundle without hesitation when he'd offered to take the baby, and it told him she trusted him implicitly for some reason he could scarcely fathom. It made him feel good inside, like he had a purpose outside of the title he'd borne for the centuries after the Dragon Wars. It made him feel like he had someone who saw him as a man and not just a profession. He watched the La'athai as they did what she bade them, saw the adoration in their eyes. Now he understood why they were like that, why they fought for her no matter what the cost. The reason he knew was because he thought he might feel the same way.

Beneath a sky darkening with the coming night, the four elves and one tir-reath passed as quickly as possible, reverberations from the attack upon the city's shields casting a light show overhead and a trembling beneath their feet. No one they passed paid them any mind, everyone intent upon the safety of themselves and their families. The rest of the La'athai and their mounts walked around them, albeit at a distance to keep attention away. Luckily, his home wasn't far, and it wasn't long before they were walking up the steps and he was removing the magic lock from the front door.

Everyone filed in and he left the door ajar for the La'athai as he led Vivien to the nearest bedchamber. He brought a jar of glow stones and placed it at the bedside while Mikarvan helped her down onto the bed. The Inquisitor then handed her the bundle just as the child within began to cry. He left the chamber as the Master Healer began to help Vivien undress so she could nurse, and went back to the entry to urge the La'athai inside. The men expressed their gratitude as they entered, and he showed them to the other three rooms that comprised his home. What little food he had, he offered to the men, and making certain that Vivien was finished feeding the baby, took some to her, Eveleen, and Mikarvan. Vivien regarded him intently as she ate, and finally asked what was on her mind.

"Inquisitor, why have you brought us here?" She looked at the food he'd brought. "And you have given us all you have. Why are you doing this?"

He smiled. "My home is one of the most heavily warded buildings in this city, that is why. And you are my guest. I give you all I have because I can."

She simply nodded, tears in her eyes. He moved towards the bed, and seeing his intention, Mikarvan stood so the Inquisitor could sit beside Vivien. "I have seen your heart, Lady Valdera. I offer you shelter in my home because I believe in you. I believe you will do great things, and that you will do those things with the elvin people in your heart. I offer you food so that I may help give you the strength to do that."

Oragon Vessel

She began to cry then. He put an arm around her shoulders and she put her head on his chest. Tears came to his own eyes and he just held her there for several minutes until her crying ceased. She looked up at him. "Thank you for believing in me Inquisitor. It means more than you know."

"My name is Orisar Valhathan. I will stand by you as long as you have need of me."

The room was silent for a few moments, the importance of this moment not lost an anyone there. Vivien gave a deep breath, then exhaled, her body finally relaxing. "I would like that very much."

He tightened his grip around her shoulders, holding her close, and she once more rested her head on his chest. A sense of belonging swept over him, and he closed his weary eyes. For the first time in a very long time, he felt contentment.

Chapter Fifty-One
Icy Treachery

The screaming of dying fae went on all night. Jor'aiden sent orders around the wall from the front gate, and an ad hoc kind of messenger system had been set up with the younger volunteers. They ran missives along the wall, from the armories of the city, and to the defenders. The Liath were amassed with a much smaller force on the lesser, eastern gate as well. They were not really there to breach the wall as much as to plug up any route of escape from the city. There were few soldiers here now, mostly citizens, guardsmen, and desperate elves defending Isbandar. They shuffled arrows to where bowmen were getting low, as well as bolts for the ballistae studding the walls. During the night, the big dragons had learned that in order to do significant damage to the wall, they had to get within bowshot, and though they healed arrow wounds in minutes, they still felt pain. The enemy mages had pulled in the smaller dragons en masse, creating a swirling cloud of targets for the bowmen, and give cover for the large dragons even while weakening the ward themselves. Thirteen of the smaller dragons had been felled to missile fire, shot over and over and over until not even their healing ability could save them. Yet there were dozens more besides battering the ward. Ever since the wounding of the first dragon, they had taken to the air, hurling vengeful elemental blasts upon the shields. It was like a nightmarish thunderstorm, sky lighting up with thunder or fire. During this time, the Magister was not silent.

He had sent wind fae into the sky. All but invisible in their native element, they pulled the air from beneath dragon wings, forcing them to crash into the ward where violet guardians ripped them limb from limb. That had worked five times, and two others had been smashed into the earth hard enough they never moved again, but there were so many slowly chewing away at the violet dome that kept the enemy from Isbandar.

Liath had moved forward into the killing field. Their dragon-horn bows did not have the range of the fae longbows, but the logs they had felled were barriers behind which now they could hide. Elves shot at elves from behind cover, and from on the wall. They died without comment or pause.

It was late when a break in the action came, dragons circling the city high above. Zi'anna tiredly plucked at his sleeve. "Master?"

He turned, leaning on the rough surface of the naturally grown wall to see several dozen robed elves leading many hundred armored soldiers, walking in lockstep, down the main road to the gate. A councilman in white, hooded robes lead them.

Jor'aiden felt his flagging strength surge again and he used a wind fae to slow his jump from the walkway to the street far below. He walked to meet the leader, but felt bitterness overtake his gratitude. "This is it? Where are the rest of the soldiers? The Mages?"

"This was three-quarters of all I could convince to follow me, the rest are at the east gate, father."

And the councilman removed his hood, to expose the face of Anlon Fire-Hunter to Jor'aiden.

The Grand Magister did not so much hug the Master Cartographer as collapse into him. After almost a minute, they broke their embrace. "Your sister?"

The youngest of the council shook his head, "There are rumors. Many say she had her child, a boy, and suckles him in secret. The Grand Inquisitor has disappeared, and Blue Moon Rising is convinced she has corrupted him and he follows her. I have not seen, nor heard, from her."

Jor'aiden staggered a bit at the news: of his new grandson, of his daughter's continued life in a city that despised her, and of a Grand Inquisitor of the fae elves following a dragon mage. He barely heard his son snapping out orders, "Relieve the men on the wall. Captain? Take a dozen men and make some fallback positions for when we must retreat. We need to make the bastards pay for every street they take. Magister? Get your mages spread out. Send the healers along the wall to give aid, but keep them on the ground. We do not have many, and losing one to a loose arrow will be bitter."

Jor'aiden found himself as the soldiers moved to obey. "You sound like a general."

Despite the danger all around, Anlon chuckled. "What I wouldn't give for the Lord of Swords and Truth right now. I bet he could hold this whole city with a dozen cranky cooks wielding kitchen knives."

Jor'aiden laughed "Yes, well he could." Then he shook his head sobering quickly. "I wish he was here."

"Get your hands off me! I was defending this wall while you were hiding under the council beds!"

Anlon looked up to see Zi'anna had been watching all the proceedings and now a soldier of Isbandar was attempting to shoo her from the battlements. "And who is this?"

Jor'aiden called above, "She speaks the truth, young man. She is my apprentice. She stays here with me."

Anlon's eyes flew wide. "It's been scores since you took an apprentice."

The Magister shrugged. "It was time."

Then another swarm of arrows came over the wall. The returned shafts were sent by seasoned and trained troops, eliciting cries and screams from those beyond.

"Father, you can barely stand. Get your apprentice and yourself somewhere to sleep."

Jor'aiden reached out and felt the ward, so much weaker than this morning. And he looked down to the spot where the frightened guardsman had fallen, to be carried off for care and never returned. He nodded, putting way foolishness and pride. "Zi'anna, attend your master. We will find rest."

But they did not go far– to Zi'anna's hovel, in fact. They slept like the dead, on simple beds, in the ramshackle hut, but not for long. The sounds of battle were everywhere until they weren't.

Jor'aiden came instantly awake, for he knew the ward had been breached.

Of all the people in this city, only one he knew had stood up for it without fail. Only one had shown true courage. Only one deserved to stand with him at this moment. Zi'anna's eyes snapped open with a start when he shook her.

"It is time."

She had been at the prison. Had been. He had discounted the words of that nattering old crone, but she had spoken the truth. Esgrynn ground his teeth in frustration and sat in the bottom level of the prison and just listened. All the people could talk about was the baby, her baby, the one that summoned fae as an infant. Those that doubted Vivien Valdera were being mocked to one extent or another, those that believed in her were vindicated. Yet none, not a single worthless sheep in the herd, knew where she had gone. She, twenty soldiers, an equal number of tir-reath, and a newborn, had simply disappeared into the streets.

He stood and crossed to the stairs leading out of the prison, the close press of bodies making sure that he would brush against a dozen strangers in his path. With the full heat of his anger beating in his brain for release, he hoped that one of them would take offense. None did.

Again, he was on the street. They had all but emptied as the attack had become more immediate. Off in the distance, he heard the battle horns of the Liath sound, and Esgrynn cursed lewdly, loudly, and viciously.

He had run out of time to find her and do what needed to be done.

A knock at the door roused her. She hadn't realized she'd drifted off to sleep after the last feeding she'd given the baby in the wee hours of the morning. In his place in the large cushioned chair near the bed, Orisar must have done the same, for his voice sounded drowsy when he spoke, "Enter."

Gregor opened the door and nodded to both of them in turn. "There is a man here to see you, Commander."

She noted the expression on Gregor's face and gleaned the identity of their visitor. She glanced around the room, saw the light of day shining through the curtained window. "Where are Mika and Evey?"

"They left the house earlier this morning to give aid wherever they can."

Sometime in the night, Gregor had come to tell them that the wards had come down. It had been strange to not hear the constant barrage overhead anymore, replaced by an almost eerie quiet. They all had known what was happening at that very moment, that the city walls were being breached and that soon the Liath would be inside the city.

Sensing her unease, Sherika gave a low growl from the foot of the bed, and the Inquisitor rose from his chair, instantly on alert. Vivien followed suit, gently laying the baby down on the bed so as not to wake him. She smoothed her hands over her rumpled clothing and took a deep breath. "Let him in."

Gregor returned to the room moments later with a disheveled Torialvah. It was strange to not see the well-manicured Lord of Ice and Steel that she was most familiar with. He was a perfect example of how the rest of the city population also looked: underfed, un-bathed, and mentality focused solely on survival. He stood there for a moment, taking in the room before settling his gaze on her. "Vivien, it is good to see that both you and our son are well."

She nodded.

He glanced at the Inquisitor, then at Gregor, who still stood at the door. "I would like to speak with you privately."

A surge of nervous tension swept through her. She knew why he was there. It wasn't for her at all. It was for her son. But she calmed her mind with the reality that the La'athi were right there in the house. There was very little that Tor could do to her, or Alsander. She nodded to both men and they silently left the room, closing the door behind them. She was certain they would stand outside it, listen for any sound that might indicate a struggle, and she grinned inwardly.

"What do you want, Torialvah?"

He splayed his hands, palms up. "Just to see with my own eyes that you and the child are faring well."

"You have seen that we are, yet you are still here and have requested a private audience."

He nodded. "Yes you are right. I am still here. I would like to hold my son."

Her belly clenched spasmodically, memories of their last conversation marching through her mind. She didn't want him anywhere near her baby. "He is sleeping."

He gave a small smile, the kind that used to melt away her anger and frustration. "I can see that. Please, let me hold him."

She hesitated. She didn't want him to touch the baby, yet, she didn't want to cause trouble where there might be none, wanted to keep peace in a city filled with war. She scooped the baby out of the bed, careful not to jostle him, and handed him to his father.

The look on Torialvah's face was like none she had ever seen before, a mixture of wonderment and delight that took away the harsh lines and coldness. Before her suddenly stood a man… a man who had found love for the very first time. Once, she had thought he loved her, but now she knew he had never come close.

"He is so beautiful," he breathed.

She said nothing, just stood there and watched. Once, this may have caused her pain, but no more. Courtesy of the Inquisitor, she had sifted through all of her memories of Torialvah and found none that gave her any inclination to believe he would have been a good husband or father. She was glad her eyes were open, that she could truly see the man standing before her now.

And he was found lacking.

He finally looked back up at her, his gaze the epitome of seriousness. "Vivien, I want to see him live a long time."

She was taken aback. "Indeed, so do I."

He cradled the baby close to his chest. "I am afraid that may not happen."

She swallowed heavily. She had borne the same thought, even before the baby was born.

"Vivien, you know the wards have been breached. Greater fae have been summoned to combat the dragons and there is fighting in the streets."

"Yes, I know all that."

"It won't be long before the fighting reaches us here."

She was silent and they stood there, regarding one another intently.

"You know you can stop the fighting."

She drew her brows into a frown. "What?"

He nodded. "You can. You can stop it. You can stop the death and destruction that has already begun to break down this city."

Fear sliced through her like a dagger and she began to tremble.

"You can stop the Liath from ultimately making it here. You can save countless lives, including that of our son."

"You think I should go to them," she whispered.

In a few footsteps he closed the distance between them and put his palm against her face. "It is the only way to stop them. The only reason they are here is because of you."

She blinked away the tears that leapt to her eyes. She remembered what Mikarvan had said when she'd proposed giving herself to the Liath several days ago. "What if the Liath still continue to take the city?"

"I don't see why they would. They would lose so many of their people. Certainly, the lives of their warriors matter to them." Tor shifted his hand to her shoulder. "Listen, I know why you didn't want to give yourself to the Liath before. You had your son to consider. You didn't want him in their clutches. But he will be safe now, safe while you do what you know in your heart needs to be done." His voice became pleading. "Vivien, please..."

As she stood there, her gaze pinned to a patch of wall beyond Tor's shoulder, a moment of clarity swept over her. Torialvah had never begged her for a thing in his life, and he wasn't about to start now. Not even the life of his son would stoop him that low. No, Torialvah wasn't begging her, he was manipulating her into getting herself killed. Not at all for the sake of the Elvish people, but for himself and the uncontested ownership he would have over their son. Not only that, but there would be no one to show the world what a worthless degenerate the Lord of Ice and Steel really was.

However, there was the more pressing issue of the Liath army. Gregor had been on the city wall. He'd told her their numbers and she knew that the forces of Isbandar could not keep them occupied for long. In that moment, she made her decision. She would fight for her people. There was no question of it, for she knew it was what he'd been trained for, what she'd been born for.

Vivien swung her eyes back to Torialvah. Something of her thoughts must have lingered there, for he blinked a couple of times before finally settling on his imagination playing tricks on him. "You are right. They are the reason I am here. My people are counting on me to make the right decision for them."

Vivien turned and made her way across the room to her travel pack and supplies. Tor stood silently by as she donned her winter clothing. She had no weapons, and it felt strange not to be arming herself for the battle she knew was ahead. All she had was Ravn's ring and Mikarvan's tanager. These she would take with her. She'd hate to lose them to the Liath, but she hated even more to be parted from them. Besides, they would have to kill her to get them.

She finally turned back to her husband and held out her arms. "I would like to hold my son one last time."

Torialvah maintained an expression of solemnity, but she didn't miss the gleam of victory in his ice blue eyes as he handed her the child. She held Alsander close, smiled to herself, and walked towards the door. She heard Tor begin to voice opposition as she opened it. Just as she knew they would be, both the Inquisitor and Gregor stood on the other side.

Gregor frowned the moment he saw her attire. "Commander, it is not safe beyond these walls."

Without a reply she continued to walk through the house and into the main living room where many of the La'athai spent their time when not outside patrolling the perimeter of the Inquisitor's home. Gregor and Orisar followed, along with, what she imagined, was a disgruntled Torialvah. When she entered, the Wolf Pack came to attention and stood, awaiting whatever orders they might receive.

Vivien spoke in a clear, concise tone that brooked no argument. "I am leaving with my husband to try and stop the Liath threat. I do not want you to follow." She then turned to Gregor, who stood behind her with a frown of dismay. Not caring what it might look like to the rest, she stepped close and placed a hand at the back of his neck to pull his head close to hers. She whispered in his ear words only he could hear, words that made him become still. When she pulled away, his face bore an unreadable expression, one never seen before on the captain of the La'athai. She then placed the baby into his arms.

Torialvah moved forward. "My son will stay with me."

Vivien shook her head. "No, he will stay with my pack. They know how he will be cared for."

Tor's tone became icy. "I am his father. I will decide how he will be cared for, and by whom."

DRAGON VESSEL

Her tone was one of determination. "I think not. I am his mother, and I say he stays with my Pack."

Torialvah became thoughtful, then pulled his lips into a sneer. "Fine, have it your way. This issue will be dealt with soon enough."

Vivien just gave a small smile. "Indeed." She gave one last look at Gregor before turning and leaving the room, Tor at her side. None of the pack moved to stop her, but a voice behind her halted her before she reached the front entry.

"Lady Valdera, I wish to go with you."

She turned back to the Inquisitor, her brows creased into a frown. His expression was one of determination. He knew that she knew what he was going into, knew she would resist. He was ready to plead his case, ready to fight with her if need be. She obliged him. "No, they will kill you."

"Maybe. But you need someone to go with you."

Her frown deepened. "I went alone before when I was abducted. I can go again."

He shook his head. "But you don't have to. I am offering to be there at your side."

"No, they will kill you," she repeated.

"Not right away."

She gave a deep sigh. "Why would you sacrifice your life like this? Our people need you!"

He stepped up to her, pushing aside Tor to take both her hands in his. "I have done many things in my life, many terrible things all for the sake of our people." He looked down at their clasped hands. "Over the years I have come to regret some of those things." He was quiet for a few moments before finally looking back up at her. "I am an old man, Vivien. There have been times in my life when I turned away from the hard path, a path that may have brought me the reward my heart desires. Now, my opportunities are limited, and I no longer wish to waste them.

"Yesterday I pledged myself to you. To me, that is a promise to stand by your side no matter how difficult the path. I want to do this not just for you, but for me as well. I want to feel that I have done something right in my life, something I can be proud of. But it's more than that even." His gaze became intense. "I want to be the man you believe me to be, the man I see reflected in your eyes when you look upon me."

Vivien regarded him intently, saw the sincerity in his eyes. A feeling of sadness swept over her. This man had lived his life for his people, so much that he had forgotten to live his life for himself as well. It struck her hard, so hard she felt it like a fist to her gut. She wanted to think about it, wished she could, but now it was her time to make the sacrifice that he had made over and over again in his life. She thrust it aside, shuttled it to the back of her mind to ruminate upon one day... if she had the chance.

Vivien wanted to stand there and refuse his request, refuse his aid to stand by her side. She hated that she didn't have the determination he did. She nodded. "All right, bu we are leaving now."

The Inquisitor ges ured towards himself, clad in all his winter attire. "I am ready."

Chapter Fifty-Two
Summon the Fae

The greater dragons had led the assault for day and night and day. They had been enough, and the ward had fallen. Master and apprentice were both somewhat confused as they returned to the gate. The entry square to the city had been transformed by ladders, furniture, wagons, barrels, and other items taken from wherever they had lay and stacking them in nailed together piles to limit Liath movement on the streets and provide cover. Zi'anna smiled to see the preparations, but Jor'aiden was chilled. It showed that the elves expected the Liath to get inside. The pair had to weave past them, Jor'aiden noting the clay bottles wrapped in oil-soaked rags nestled on the side away from the outer wall.

"Father!"

Jor'aiden found his son had been joined by four times as many troops while he had been asleep and they had manned the wall waiting for this very moment. Zi'anna in tow, the Magister hitched up his robes and climbed the stairs like a much younger elf. His boy awkwardly carried a plain sword. Anlon had always been far more an artisan than a warrior, but the soldiers around him saw his councilman robes and obeyed him without question.

"Everyone to the wall! Bowmen to the wall! Mages to the wall!" Fire Hunter turned. "Well, here we are, Father."

"Are you ready?"

"Mystic River defected from the Council as well and sent us more troops. She's on the other gate."

Jor'aiden frowned. "But are you ready?"

A hooded mage, already attended by a dozen air fae, nodded to the Grand Magister and answered. "We are as ready as we can be." Seeing the confusion on Jor'aiden's face, he continued. "I am Ipsar, apparently the Magister of Isbandar."

Jor'aiden saw the smoke clear. The greater dragons had been pulled back well out of the way of any fighting. Meanwhile, the Liath assembled in lines to march into the city. He spared the mage beside him a glance, "Apparently?"

"We haven't had one in over two centuries." Ipsar shook his head, "Ancestors, fae, and gods forgive us, but we never wanted one. Too much power, too much influence for one elf to hold."

Jor'aiden nodded, knowing of Isbandar's need to shun even fae conjurers.

"I promoted him." Anlon said absently. "Seemed like we needed one. What are they doing with their dragons?"

The greater dragons had been pounding the ward all night. They were exhausted, heads held low, and many were bristled with arrows and bloody wounds that were slow to close. Many of the smaller serpents disappeared with the sound of a thunderclap back into to the aether. Only several handfuls remained. Ipsar frowned. "What are they doing? Are they giving up?"

"You are not old enough to remember the Dragon War. Look!" Jor'aiden pointed, The Liath were parting ways for five elves in intricate robes of different colors to move to the front of the army. "Some were allowed to go home by their masters, others were only brought to our realm and paid whatever was due in order to take down the ward. They also left once their pact was ended. But those big ones—"

Zi'anna's voice was disturbingly small, and pitifully hopeful. "So, they won't have their dragons?"

Jor'aiden watched the five dragon mages make intricate signs in the air, his voice heavy. "No, little one. There will be dragons."

The greater dragons trumpeted to the sky a clarion call for death. Five times it happened, and each time it was a sound so loud it could be heard in the soul. Jor'aiden looked along the wall and all the defenders were crouched behind the wooden palisade, so he peeked above. The Magister's stomach churned.

"Son?" Jor'aiden said, numb.

The others looked but said nothing.

"Son." Jor'aiden grasped for his son's arm, but dared not take his eye from the display beyond the walls.

"They are coming in. Right now, they are coming," Anlon whispered.

"Son!" Finally, he tore his eyes away from the damnable beasts and spun his boy to look at him "Move your men!"

Anlon looked into his father's eyes, and then his pupils shrunk to pinpricks as he finally understood. "Off the wall! All of you off the wall! To the streets!"

Jor'aiden pulled his apprentice into his arms and leapt. Air fae gently placed them on the ground and then they ran. Anlon and Ipsar had their clot of men from the wall and down the stairs in seconds. Stragglers were left behind, gawking at the oppressive horror of the terrifying glory of each of the five, massive beasts. In more heartbeats, it was too late to escape. With almost careless power, the great dragons, out of reach of the ballistae, unleashed streams of elemental destruction on the gates. Without the wards, the wooden structure shattered into airborne splinters and smoke.

Jor'aiden and then Zi'anna peeked around the corner as the accumulated fire and thunder blast hit, and watched the section of living wall that had stood as a gate to Isbandar for hundreds of years be churned into a gaping hole. They ducked back as burning detritus flew by, bathing the area in the smell of charred wood. Before the debris had time to settle, Ipsar was swearing viciously. He sent one of his airy followers to flit into the hole in the wall, blowing smoke away The biggest dragons were already turning away, and withdrawing further, but all the rest of the winged serpents were marshaling with the army. Horns blared deeply, darkly from beyond the wall.

Ipsar, shuddered. "They are coming."

Anlon sounded stunned even over the ringing in Jor'aiden's ears. "But not the big ones?"

Dragon Vessel

Jor'aiden shook his head. "The big ones are more valuable than their weight in gold. If we kill one, they won't be able to summon it for thousands of years, making the true name of the thing worthless. They'll keep them in reserve to pound areas of resistance. The first wave will be their butchers and the lesser mages with the smaller dragons."

"What do we do now?"

Jor'aiden looked to the shattered ballistae towers, to the road filled with Liath that were coming, to the dragons that galloped on the ground to avoid arrow fire from deeper in the city. He gritted his teeth. "We fight. Here. Now."

Anlon shouted without hesitation. "Archers to the walls! Make them bleed! Mages to ready, summon and loose!"

It was whispered that the Liath were bred without any caution, that children showing fear fresh from the mother's womb were bashed to death with rocks. Some said that death was preferred to losing one's Elvishness, the connection to all things. Jor'aiden thought wryly that it was far easier to be brave when horse sized dragons galloped at the fore of the army. A few bold serpents took to the sky, and clouds of arrows launched forth seeking them out. The fae mages sent sprites of the air onto the wall, clearing smoke from the archers' field of view and lending their arrows both speed and accuracy. The dragons smart enough to be on the ground roared and began to rake the wall with blasts of fire, lightning, and scouring, sharp stone.

"What now?" Ipsar was breathing fast, too fast.

Jor'aiden felt himself become detached, almost weightless. His emotions continued to scrabble at the walls of his soul, but somewhere else, somewhere far away. Instead of heeding them, he just let them be where they were, and sought strength deep within himself. "Do you know any of the Deep Pacts? Any of the old names?"

Ipsar shook his head.

"Then direct your mages and let me be."

The Grand Magister of Rithalion bolted across the street and into an inn where the door had been removed to be made into a barricade. It was empty of people, so he tried to block out the sound of war outside and breathe deeply.

"Master?"

Jor'aiden hissed, "Hush, now."

The dragon elves were confident, because they knew old names of dragons. Colossal dragons summoned through ancient names. Fae elves knew names too, and while they ordinarily never spoke them, they did teach them for days like today. Jor'aiden knew four, but one name had been used in the Dragon War, and the fae could no longer respond to it. One was haughty and proud, demanding the service of thousands to worship him like a God. But there were two others he knew and one was brash, and arrogant, but it had one trait...

Jor'aiden began his chants, his gestures. He heard the dragons roar no further than the wall, but he kept the gossamer threads of the summoning alive, chanting each part of the name longer than any other he knew.

"Grospaxil'thanix. '

Several moments passed.

"Grospaxil'thanix

Then, WHY HAVE YOU CALLED ME?

Zi'anna heard it, and her head swiveled madly to try to find where it came from.

Jor'aiden huffed in air but dropped to one knee. "Your Lordship, mighty war-emperor of fae, Commander of the Rock and Growing Things, your admirers desperately plead for your aid."

IT HAS BEEN CENTURIES SINCE ANY HAVE CALLED ME. YOUR PETTY TROUBLES ARE NONE OF MY CONCERN.

The apprentice heard the distant, angry tone to the voice and also dropped to one knee without being told. As terrifying as the voice was, this was one of the Great Old Fae. It was no spell summoned drone to be cast at an enemy, nor a soldier fae to be summoned to fight alongside elves in battle. This was a force of nature, and it could destroy him at a whim. Jor'aiden took a deep, centering breath.

Outside the dragons crashed through the rubble of the gate, butchers scrabbling behind as arrows appeared to come from every nook, crook, window, and shadow in the city. Dragons roared. Liath screamed their battle cry.

He drew on all the writings about Grospaxil'thanix, of his grand power, but also his character. He tried again. "But, Your Grace, you live for righteous battle, for the adoration of your people...?"

Grospaxil'thanix, still present only in spirit, chuckled and it rattled the ground, YOU OFFER GLORY, BUT I HAVE SEEN A THOUSAND BATTLES, AND A THOUSAND KINGDOMS FALL BEFORE ME. WHAT COULD YOU USE TO TEMPT ME FROM MY REST, LITTLE MAGE?

Outside, deaths were sounding, some defiant, some pitiful.

Jor'aiden tried one last time, "Your Grace, there are dragons."

There was a pause.

"Many, many dragons."

Again, a pause.

THEN I SHALL FIGHT.

The ground shook, leaves fell from trees, buildings quaked, men fell, dragons stumbled. Then all went silent. Master and apprentice ran to the doorway unsteadily, unable to resist seeing.

Grospaxil'thanix arrived like an eruption from the ground, tossing dragons and Liath alike as if they were no more than dried leaves. It emerged from the grave of the gate like the very voice of retribution, bigger than two homes, towering over all. Its body was massive and rounded, covered in thick skin made of loam and moss-covered plates. The head was a curved, armored cone, with two tiny eyes and nose slits protected deep in bone hollows. His jaws had teeth that looked like extensions of his bone head plates, wide and sharp, promising shearing power that could swallow two men whole. Grospaxil'thanix was not sleek, but within seconds arrows began flying at him, dragons began attacking him, and all the bluster of the Liath army was simply turned to the side, showing he was powerful. One small dragon, the length of two elves in the body, lunged at the mighty legs of the elder fae. Its teeth sunk in, but only soft loam trickled from the wound, and Grospaxil'thanix kicked out the other leg almost casually, sending it sprawling into a nearby building from which it did not move again. The remaining dragons took to the air, and began spitting a rain of destruction down upon the armored plates of Grospaxil'thanix's back. For all the world, it appeared to only make him dirty for he did not even pause in his gargantuan gate.

Yet, more were coming. Still more were coming.

Lesser fae mages called what spirits they could as attackers split around the destroyed gate and began pouring over the walls. The going was much slower, and the defenders had time to rush to meet trouble with bared steel.

The attack into the breach viciously blunted, Jor'aiden ducked back into the abandoned inn and knelt to the floor. Zi'anna watched in mute horror at the scene on the streets as the Magister began gathering his strength. Grospaxil'thanix was prideful, bloodthirsty, and vain. The last name he knew was none of those things, but it was a name he had, and the last chance he had to summon aid. He began sending his tendrils of call out, little bits of his energy pulled from his soul and woven into a mighty summoning. This elder needed to be sought, to be coaxed, and he did it as carefully as a thief prying jewels from a crown while it was still being worn by a warrior king.

"Yari'montasylva..."

He felt the tendrils shudder with the word. He had to block out the battle, the city, the whole world to hear them jitter towards his goal.

"Yari'montasylva..."

He was delving deeper, deeper into the aether. It was a world of energy and emotion, a place that existed before all others and would exist long after. The colors blinding, the sounds deafening. Light and shadow, fire and ice, water and sky were not separate things, but a wondrous 'scape that had driven lesser mages insane.

"Yari'montasylva..."

He did not speak; he did not have to. The elder fae took it from his soul. He heard Zi'anna scream back in the real world, but he had to block it out. He had to be serene as Yari'montasylva poured over his soul and read every part of it with fingers that could peel layers of steel from the edge of a sword.

I WILL COME.

And with a snap that produced a migraine, he was back in his own mind, in his body, in the inn.

A Liath warrior stood over Zi'anna who lay sprawled on her back. He held two iron swords but was flailing at the three painfully bright fae circling around his head. The mindless things poked at his eyes, causing him to howl with agony. Yet in moments he would realize they were no real threat, and slaughter the girl.

It was his apprentice, but he only saw his daughter.

Jor'aiden felt wall inside himself crackle and break, and the surge of pure rage and fear exited his mouth as dark, hurtful things that began reacting to his unspoken call. The warrior then noticed him.

It was a wordless cry he made as he flung out his arm in a blue robed sleeve.

They came in a torrent from his call, gathering from all the dark places in the gaps of branches and plants that made up the walls and roof and very floors of the inn. They were made of pincers and blades, of rot and darkness. The unseleighe came to him as if he had been doing it his whole life, once the barriers of discipline and mores were lifted from his mind. The wave of fae hit the warrior from every direction, eroding the warrior and removing whole swaths of hair, skin, armor, eyes, nose, and fingers. The raider fell to the ground, blood pouring from half a dozen exposed arteries.

Only once it was done, once the fae were gone, could he hear Zi'anna screaming.

He looked to the body, to his hands, to the body. Those were the dark fae, unseemly, forbidden. He was the Grand Magister, above reproach. Hands. Body–

Zi'anna.

The sounds of battle finally imprinted on his mind, reminding him of the danger right outside even as exhaustion crashed over him. He staggered to the young girl and grabbed her hand to haul her to her feet. She latched onto him with both arms and tugged at him as if never to let go. He glanced at the doorway and, seeing it clear, patted at her head while making soothing sounds. Suddenly he understood his daughter, her summoning of the unseleighe, her use of dragon magic.

He understood, and accepted her.

Then there was a sound. Like two waves meeting in a thunderclap. It was followed by a strange wail. Part moan, part shrill whistle, part song. It was everywhere.

Zi'anna wiped tears from her face. "What is that?"

Jor'aiden smiled, grimly. "Reinforcements. Now, come. The gate is breached and there is fighting everywhere." She let go, but regretfully. "You did very well with that creature. You have good instincts, and no one can teach those. You have the makings of a great battle mage."

"Is that what you are?"

He smiled again, trying to push back at the exhaustion and the regret he felt thinking about his daughter. "No, but my daughter is. And she is the best mage I know. Now draw your dagger." She drew the hunk of rust spotted steel and wiped her eyes while studiously avoiding looking at the corpse in the room. "Keep your eyes moving, notice everything."

His steps were heavy as Jor'aiden and Zi'anna moved to the door to the inn.

Dragon Vessel

Outside they could see half of the main gate. There, Liath poured around the legs of Grospaxil'thanix as it lashed about with heavy feet and vomited razor-sharp shards down upon elf and dragon alike. Across its back, dozens of smaller dragons gnawed, but it did not seem to notice.

Yari'montasylva floated above. She was massive, easily fifty feet across. Her body was flat, and diamond shaped, with massive wings that extended out as seamless extensions of her body. She flapped them lazily as she flew, almost serenely, but from her bottom extended a forest of hundred-foot-long, ribbon-like tentacles covered in powerful suckers. Inside each sucker was a vicious fang, and the tentacles began harvesting Liath and dragons below.

In the streets, elves had made shield walls and were fighting the spurts of Liath that escaped the ground bound elder fae. Several of the barricades were already ablaze, denying the enemy their cover when the fae elves retreated. Down their own street towards the gate was clear, but in the other direction a group of Liath were bashing upon a shield wall of Isbandar defenders. Jor'aiden started to formulate a plan, but then seven elves, obviously civilians with scavenged weapons and armor, came from an alley between the inn and the fighting and mercilessly hacked at the Liath before anyone was aware of their presence.

Jor'aiden and Zi'anna bolted past the civilians hungrily scavenging the dead Liath and two of their own fallen, and were admitted past the shields thanks to the royal blue robes of a Magister, and a shouted order from Anlon.

Jor'aiden stumbled past the line of soldiers and collapsed on the curb. He was so tired from the second summoning that his bones ached, but soldiers scurried on all sides of him as more raiders appeared at the end of the street. The shield wall parted and the scavenging militia ducked into safety behind their ranks. Jor'aiden heard his son shouting again and had to get Zi'anna's help levering to his feet.

"Take ten soldiers to the corner of the main thoroughfare and Oakenshott Street. You take charge of ten citizens, wait down the road at Carahill. When the soldiers engage in battle, bring them in from behind. And you, seven bowmen should be safe at the artists' building on Arias Street."

The Liath met the shield wall just ten yards away. Steel and iron clashed. Anlon turned to the citizen group. "Do it again. Circle around the alleyway and hit them. Now back to you. Get to the top of the tall building and unleash ten arrows at the enemy apiece, then withdraw to Tomlin Place. Stand on the lip of the tall fountain and shoot the raiders past them." Jor'aiden watched in wonder as his son, Master Cartographer for the city, moved his men from place to place like pieces on a board. Not just holding key points, but blocking others and reinforcing where maximum damage could be inflicted on the invaders. Perhaps the Master of Swords and Truth was not here, but Anlon Fire-Hunter was, and he was making the enemy bleed for every step. He noticed the Grand Magister and pointed at the elder fae in the sky, "Father, that was you?"

Jor'aiden nodded tiredly.

"The fae at the gate has slowed their advance, and many of the larger dragons are fighting the one in the air. You gave us a chance."

He could not see Grospaxil'thanix at the gate, but he could hear the fae bellowing. Yari'monta sylva in the air was surrounded by dozens of dragons of every size, but– "She did not draw any of the largest."

Anlon shook his head. "No, they are still in reserve. But we have slowed their invasion into the city, and that means a lot. I can only hope the rest of the battles are going as well."

Jor'aiden looked to his apprentice, who held her dagger at the ready and watched the battle just yards away. "We've seen no mages, yet."

"No, they won't send them past the fae at the gate, and only small pulses of raiders can get through. We can handle the smaller groups so far."

The Militia hit the Liath from behind again, losing another man in the clash and screams. They began scavenging equipment the moment the dragon elves were dispatched.

"Then let us hope Grospaxil'thanix can endure." Jor'aiden shook his head as citizens without weapons came forward to also claim arms and armor from the dead.

The Magister had allowed himself to forget that elves killed elves, and he hated it as much now as ever. He tried to gather his strength to himself, tried again, but ultimately, he felt used up and hollow from the summoning. Anlon put a hand to his shoulder. "Father, rest. We will truly need you soon."

Jor'aiden nodded, moved down the street and entered a house also stripped of the door. He barely saw the place, but he saw the ornate couch in the corner and move to it where he first sat, then lay.

Zi'anna stood next to him, then spoke quietly, "Rest, Master, I will watch over you."

He smiled, not sure he could regain his strength as the sound of battle was rejoined outside.

Suddenly he started awake. There was a titanic roar, as much indignation as pain. Then it ended with a crash and a cheer.

Jor'aiden started to move, and Zi'anna was there. "Master, it's been only a few hours."

He felt markedly better, but even if he hadn't, he would be needed.

He took Zi'anna by the hand and rushed to the second, then the third floor. Out the window, saw it happen. Grospaxil'thanix had killed thousands, held the gate all but alone, and slowed the enemy advance. Finally, the dragon priests had sent forth one of the huge, ancient dragons into the fray. It came from the sky, breathing gouts of fire that could engulf entire homes across the elder earth fae. Grospaxil'thanix bucked under the heat of it, and then trumpeted a gargling, gravelly blast of sharp rock in return. The golden hued dragon screamed in pain as its wings and joints began to bleed form the assault. Then it flew deeper into the city as Grospaxil'thanix coughed boulder after boulder at the gold, turning ponderously and giving chase, leaving the way behind him unguarded.

Dragon Vessel

The Liath cheered and began to rush the gate.

Jor'aiden no longer felt bone weary, but still had to shake himself to readiness, "Now is when the real battle starts, apprentice. Steel yourself."

They exited the building and saw Anlon was already looking toward him. Jor'aiden nodded grimly. Anlon began shouting more orders. Down the street, raiders were coming. Without being ordered, archers on rooftops opened up in a deadly hail.

Jor'aiden summoned fae of the growing things on every side, and vines whipped up from walls on both sides of the street and reached out to snag at running raiders, slowing them down and making them easy targets. He felt even this little thing drain him. He would have to husband his strength where he could but he could not ration it all. The battle was now being fully joined, and he was needed.

Chapter Fifty-Three
The Sacrifice

Torialvah opened the door and the three stepped out. The sound of distant fighting carried on the wind, a wind that heralded the onset of rain. They walked towards the city gates, towards the sound of the fighting, and had barely made it a block or two before it started to come down. It was heavy, and within moments all were soaked through their layers and they were shivering. People stood in the streets, waiting, waiting for the enemy to come. These were not fighters, rather, the common folk: merchants, farmers, bakers, clothiers, butchers, smiths, furriers and apothecarists. They held swords and shields that had been handed down for generations in their families, most likely from a relative who had once been a soldier. Some had simple wood cutting axes and long knives. Others had any blunt weapon they could find. Most of them were men, for the women and children had been sent to the prison and the College of Magic.

And although they didn't walk alongside them, there was a host of men who followed at a distance behind and alongside. Vivien recognized them for what they were: the people in the city who wanted to see her turned over to the Liath, the people with whom her husband had found the easiest alliance.

It wasn't much longer before they reached the fighting. It was easy to tell the sides apart, for the Liath wore crude leather and furs while the Isbandarians wore worked leather and more finely made winter vests and trousers. Torialvah stopped short, roughly pulling her to his side. Of the Liath there were many, and they slowly pushed the Isbandarians back. They didn't stop, pausing only to hack and slash at the injured as they continued forward to the heart of the city.

Orisar shook his head slowly. "It is as I had feared."

Vivien sensed Torialvah's hesitation. The Liath were brutal, stopping for nothing and no one. The three of them could find themselves with swords in their hearts before even a single word could be uttered about her surrender.

Tor swung her around to face him. "See those Liath?" He pointed at the large group before them. "Use your magic. Kill them."

She frowned. "I thought we were handing me over to them?"

Tor gave her a malignant grin. "We need to find someone of rank to stop the battle. Or do you shy away from helping mere fae elves?"

She gave him a hardened glare. She supposed he was right. They were a scourge upon this city and the lives of her people. She glanced to Orisar, who nodded in sad understanding. Before she realized what she was doing, she spoke the words to her spell and the magic was there, filling her, feeding her starving soul. Then she stepped out into the open.

No one paid her any heed as she threw her first flaming missile, or the second, or the third. She struck them down, one right after the other, Liath from the front periphery. Her aim didn't need to be that accurate, for if she missed her target, there was another right beside him to catch it. The men screamed as the missiles struck, huge darkened holes where they had entered smoldering from the fire still burning within. It wasn't until she threw the fourth that she garnered any attention at all, and that being from the opposing side, the Isbandarians wondering who had come to their aid. And when they saw her standing there, recognizing her, they seemed to gather strength, pushing back harder against their foes.

She threw a fifth and a sixth. Finally, the arrogant Liath were forced to take note. Their leader stepped out from among the fighting, sword bloodied from those he had slain. He was dressed the same, if even more simply. He was more weatherworn and leathery, but the differences in him went deeper. She could tell he was a leader, for he bore an air of significance and serenity in battle that none of the other men possessed. It was an air of power, not over magic, but over men. He looked her over, knew what he saw: a small woman garbed for winter, hair streaming around her face from the winds, hands holding orbs of fire. To any of the other Liath, she may have been just another Isbandarian woman. They may have looked past the flaming hands, simply considered her a threat, and attacked.

Not this man.

He lifted the small horn hanging around his neck, and without taking his eyes from hers, blew on it once.

Vivien's heart hammered against her ribs as the Liath ceased their efforts and pulled back. The Isbandarians allowed them to do so, grateful for the reprieve. They looked at her expectantly, hopefully, praying that she might deliver them from their reality of near certain death. The Inquisitor stood by her side. She didn't know how he got there, only that he was there. He took that moment to take her arm, a bastion of strength against the fear that tumbled about in her guts. Tor arrived at her other side moments later, his hand positioning itself possessively about her upper arm. She cringed inwardly, hating his touch even though it was through several layers of cloth.

The Liath leader slowly approached, sword still drawn. She was tempted, very tempted, to throw the last two missiles at him. However, she refrained. It would only end in more bloodshed and the Isbandarian men who looked upon her as their salvation would certainly perish. The flames lessened, and by the time the leader stood before her, they were gone.

He was dark haired, with eyes so pale they were nearly colorless. His voice was deep. "Who are you?"

She swallowed, was about to answer, but never got the chance. "She is the one you call 'Vessel'," said Tor. "I am here to give her to you, an act of good faith that you will cease all military efforts upon this city and leave us."

The leader was thoughtful. "So, your leader does not know that you are handing her over to us?"

Torialvah stood a bit straighter, as though he'd done the right thing by acting against the men and women who ruled this place, and shook his head. "No, the Council is unaware."

Dragon Vessel

The leader laughed then, a full-throated laugh that echoed throughout the, now still, street. "That makes this transaction that much sweeter." Vivien heard the malice in that laugh, the cruelty. They would not be getting through this unscathed. "Prove to me that she is who you say she is."

Torialvah raised a dark brow. "The magic doesn't convince you?"

The leader drew his own brows into a sour frown. "No."

Vivien's breaths stilled as Tor nodded. He then turned to give her a pointed look, a small smile turning up one corner of his mouth. "You heard the man. Take off your clothes."

She just stood there for a moment, shocked. All her bravado was gone, only to be replaced by fear. It curled about within her belly, twisting, turning, making her feel sick. Orisar's hand tightened at her arm, echoing her sentiment. He didn't like this turn of events.

Vivien took one deep breath. Then another. She disengaged from the Inquisitor and stepped forward. Looking the leader of the Liath in the eye, she began to disrobe, opening her top and letting it fall down her back, exposing her breasts to the cruel wind. Not a man uttered a word... not a single one. Both sides looked at her as though she were some kind of messiah, someone who could somehow save them from their lives.

The leader looked upon her, a hunger in his eyes. It wasn't for the warm hole she could offer his manhood, rather the reward he might receive by being the one to bring his people the thing that they all fought for. "Turn around," he instructed." Her belly was still distended from her recent birth, making her appear to still be pregnant, and the tattooed wings on her back sealed her fate, showing him that she was the woman who had been taken by Drath Drakkon. He nodded, then looked at Orisar.

Torialvah's smile widened. "Yes, I provide a bonus. This is the Grand Inquisitor of Isbandar."

The leader's expression hardened and he gestured above his shoulder. Another man appeared from the mass of Liath soldiers to stand beside him. His gaze remained locked with Vivien's. "You have the power to destroy us all, yet you choose not to do so."

She nodded. "My hope is that you will cease your attack upon this city."

"So, this is the condition of your surrender?"

She nodded once.

"You will remain docile within our keeping as long as we obey this condition?"

She nodded again.

He gestured at the man beside him. "Lieutenant, take them."

The Lieutenant called another man to his side. That man took the Inquisitor while the Lieutenant waited for Vivien to cover herself. She did so slowly, hoping, praying, someone would do something to save her. It had begun to snow and a tear dripped onto the freshly fallen whiteness at her feet. *Wolf, I wish you were here. I wish you were here.*

The captain looked at Torialvah. "You have brought us the prize we have asked for. You have done this against the wishes of your leaders."

Torialvah nodded. "I felt it was in the best interests of Isbandar, as well as the other elves residing within the free cities."

The captain nodded thoughtfully. "But who are you to question the authority of those who have been elected to oversee the wellbeing over those they have been chosen to protect?"

Torialvah just stood there for a moment, not knowing how to respond. Vivien completed dressing herself, pulling the winter tunic over her head and settling it about her still-rounded waist, her attention riveted upon the two men. "I am not from this city, so they were not elected by me."

The captain nodded. "But, when you enter another city, are you not bound to obey the dictates of the leaders that rule there?"

Torialvah gave a sharp nod, face twisted to show his disdain for the question. "If they are worthy. These are not."

"I agree." The other man smiled and stepped closer, turning his sword this way and that, the sun shining off the blood-crusted blade. "I thank you for bringing Umesh to us. She is a prize we have fought hard for, one we would not have ceased fighting for."

Tor nodded. "Thank you. My mission was to help you get what you wanted so that my people could get what they wanted in return." He blinked pointedly at the commander. "So, now the fighting stops?"

The captain nodded as well, bridging the distance between them. "Soon enough."

"No!" Torialvah snapped, his temper letting loose. He took Vivien by the elbow and pulled her close, owning her one, last time. "The deal is not struck if you cannot finish it. The fighting stops now. Do it, or take me to someone who can."

Vivien looked at Torialvah, how he stood, and the eyes of the captain flickering down to the hand she could not see. She knew her husband's hand was on his dagger, one honed to a razor's edge. The one he had once used to cut the Wolf's throat.

The captain backed away, the warriors around him following suit. Tor smiled as the captain then said simply, "Follow closely."

They walked as a knot though the broken streets of Isbandar. People were dying on all sides, and screams fought against the sounds of dragons and fae warring in ways both large and small. Vivien struggled inside with so much devastation, yearned to toss off her husband and her promise in order to fight for the people she heard suffering all around. Still, she remained quiet.

Then, by one of the massive fountains in the center of the city, she saw it. Liath of all types and ranks parted before the captain and let him pass to their destination— a colossal war-horn made of the skull of some huge beast. Intricately carved, garishly painted, the captain blew into one horn curved low across the face. The sound resonated in the hollow horn and then in the clay

DRAGON VESSEL

plugged skull to exit the other, broken horn as a low, brutish sound that spread across the city.

The captain regarded Tor through flinty eyes. "You have what you have bargained for." The master blacksmith made a retort, but it was lost in the words that came from the other side of the square.

"Ashar!" A contingent of mounted Liath led by a man upon a black horse clad in black leather and black furs came into view. The speaker's face broke into a wide grin as Liath skittered out of his way so he could cross without pause. The captain waited until they stood before him before giving a brief bow. "Ah, son! You would only signal for one reason, I am sure. You have not disappointed me, have you?"

"My Lord Lorimath, I have brought to you that which you seek. I have brought you Umesh."

Lorimath regarded Vivien appraisingly. "How do you know it is she?"

"She is pregnant, and she bears the mark Drakkon placed upon her. I saw it with my own eyes."

Lorimath shifted his gaze to the captain. "You have done well, Ashar."

"But that is not all." He pulled Orisar to his other side. "This man claims to be the Grand Inquisitor of Isbandar."

Lorimath straightened in his seat, his gaze hardening. He dismounted and walked over to them, his demeanor ominous. He stopped before Vivien, looking her up and down, then moved to Orisar. "Grand Inquisitor, how did you get yourself in this situation, eh?" He then turned back to Ashar. "You have brought me a boon, Captain, and for that you shall be rewarded. Come, let us take them to the priests."

"Wait!" Torialvah pushed forward and many Liath reached for weapons or tightened grips on those already at hand. "The fighting has stopped? You will withdraw?"

Vivien sensed something terribly amiss, but she could only gasp and cry in her mind. *Tor, no!*

The Warlord frowned dangerously and looked to Ashar. "Who is this?"

Orisar looked on in horror. "Lord, you–"

The Liath guard holding the Inquisitor cuffed him to silence. Tor took no notice of the warning tone as he pressed on. "You will withdraw your forces?"

Ashar began to reply, but Torialvah raised a hand to silence him and answered. "I am the Lord of Ice and Steel of Rithalion. I am the one who has delivered your Umesh, and I am the one with whom you are bargaining."

Vivien wasn't sure, but she thought she saw annoyance fade into amusement in Ashar's eyes. "It is true, Warlord. This one defied his Council and gave Umesh up without a declaration. He is not from this city and they do not even know he is here surrendering."

Lorimath considered, lips pursed, looking Tor up and down. Tor stood proudly. Orisar watched the unfolding tableau and shook his head.

Lorimath then smiled. "Get your people to surrender as we demanded."

Tor's face registered bewilderment. "You heard your commander. These are not my people. I am of Rithalion–"

The Warlord grinned. "Then what does it matter if we stop fighting?"

Ashar motioned to Vivien. "Umesh says she will come quietly if we halt the attack."

Lorimath looked at her and Ashar, his face the picture of annoyance. "Umesh, you will come quietly if we stop our attack on the Isbandarians?"

Her heart beating a staccato rhythm, she nodded. Orisar made to object and was cuffed again, harder.

Lorimath frowned. "As you wish. But ask me for no more boons." He looked to Ashar. "Take her to the priests and seize the traitor."

Tor looked for who they meant to imprison when four hands grappled him and held him tight. Liath soldiers leered at him as one took his beautiful dagger and tested the edge curiously. "What are you doing? Let go of me you filthy–"

Lorimath looked almost bored as he remounted his horse. "You have what you bargained for. We have ceased fighting unless attacked, but nothing was said of withdrawal. We will hold positions until we commune with the priests." He looked pointedly at Vivien. "On this you swore to come quietly."

Sweat began to bead upon Tor's brow. "Then unhand me and let me go!"

Lorimath looked theatrically surprised. "But why? You are a man devoid of honor, and for that, you deserve nothing but death. You have renounced the laws of your people, renounced the wishes of those who have been elected to lead you to a greater place. By your own admission, you are not protected by, nor part of, Isbandar. For that, you are a disgrace and are not afforded the protections extended to them by Umesh."

For the first time, Tor's face registered fear. "Vivien! Kill them!"

She started as though dealt a physical blow. He was crazy, thinking that she could just do such a thing out of the whimsy of someone else, especially surrounded as they were. She would be struck down within moments.

Lorimath smiled widely, his tone like that of a cat who had cornered his mouse. "Oh, she can't remember? She swore not to, just as you bargained for."

Vivien heard the words spill out of her. Despite his abuse, despite his neglect, despite everything, this was her husband. "Please don't kill him."

Lorimath looked to her darkly. "I said no more boons." He rolled his eyes. "But this last one I will grant, to show I am merciful." He looked to those soldiers holding Torialvah. "Strip him and chain him to the war horn. Make certain his dishonor can be seen by everyone who walks by. We will release him only after all is settled."

As the men began to drag him toward the horn, Torialvah turned his head, maniacal ice blue eyes settling upon her. "You planned this, didn't you?" he screamed. "I shun you! I cast you out of my house and my life. You are no longer my wife. You are nothing to me. Nothing!"

Shock rooted her to the spot. How in the world she could have planned such a thing as this was beyond her. Torialvah fought the Liath warriors as they pulled him back, back, back until he stumbled and fell. Vivien quaked as one of the men drew the dagger he had used to mark the Wolf. She wanted to look away, but for the life of her, she couldn't even blink her eyes lest she miss something. The soldier knelt before the man who had once been her husband, and as the others held him in place, began to carve a word onto his forehead.

Amidst Torialvah's screams, the Warlord and his commanders looked on until the soldier was finished. The Liath then divested Tor of his clothing, and lashed him to the war horn. Only then did she see what they had carved. There, upon his forehead was a single word.

Traitor.

Vivien felt another hand join the one already at her arm as she turned away from him, closing her eyes tightly shut against the maelstrom of emotions that seemed to hit her all at once. The captain sounded his horn again, this time three blows in succession. The hand pulled at her arm, gently at first, then with more insistence. Finally, she began to walk. Behind her followed the Captain and the Liath who followed him. Ahead Lorimath tossed back, "Make sure to put them in iron. Oaths go only so far."

"Gregor, what do we do?" Taz exclaimed.

But Gregor just watched, in shock. After all this, after everything, it was over. She was walking into the arms of the Liath, and doing it willingly, because of some silver-tongued bastard. Gregor truly hoped someone shoved a sword into him, and soon. The infant Alsander in his arms made a noise and snuggled into his swaddling clothes, reminding him of a further complication to his day. He looked to the other La'athai, all of whom shared his looks of shock and dismay.

"She gave us an order" he said breathlessly.

"Yes, but she is going to die!" Taz pressed.

"She gave an order," he repeated, then looked down at the innocent, unprotected bundle in his arms. "Mikarvan was called to work on the wounded. Where are they taking the wounded?"

Taz pursed her lips. "I don't know any more than you do, but he would."

Gregor followed her nod and saw a soldier with a messily wrapped head wound leading two civilians in makeshift armor and weapons, one with an arrow in the arm and one with a mangled hand, down the street.

Gregor shouted out, starting the baby to crying, "Ho, there! Where are the healers?"

The two others looked at him listlessly, but the soldier looked angry with the world as he snapped back, "In the square at the College of Magic."

Gregor waved his thanks, then turned back to the men. "Everyone, mount up! College of Magic!" Then he realized that of the six former guardsmen who had entered their ranks, only three had tir-reath, and they were far more pets than mounts. "You three, double up with your packmates. Come on people! Vivien said protect her son, and that is what I mean to do."

The La'athai ran to gather the big cats but for Gregor and Taz, "What do we do about the Jewel?"

Gregor rolled her question around in his head, finding no solution. "Well, she is the commander. She gave an order and we have to obey, but the first priority is to get this kid to safety."

The La'athai were assembling, hurriedly fitting cats with riding harnesses. One soldier handed over Gregor's own mount, Portia. She snuggled him for a moment and then stood eager for the harness.

Taz frowned at him. "And what about our new members, they really don't have–"

"One thing at a time!" Gregor snapped back, making Alsander begin to wail again. They cinched their harnesses tightly and leapt aboard the big cats. Within a few streets, the newborn had settled back down to sleep, and Gregor was thankful. Ten minutes later, they were at the College of Magic. Bedrolls, blankets, tables, and chairs had been heisted from homes all around, and they were packed with the wounded. Precious few healers traveled currents between them all, doing what they could. Healing fae were everywhere, summoned by the healers who looked threadbare and worn for the effort.

"Mikarvan! MIKARVAN!" Gregor shouted.

Several healers pointed to one in particular, but before he could move more than dismounting his tir-reath, Evey approached. "Gregor, you cannot interrupt him. I don't know what Vivien wants, but–"

Gregor hefted the newborn. "Jashi surrendered a half an hour ago to the Liath. She left us in charge of her newborn. We need someone to take care of the child while we figure out how to commit mutiny, save her life, and avoid being executed for it."

All color drained from her face. "And you are going to leave him–"

"–Alsander."

She rolled her eyes. " –Alsander, here?"

He shrugged. "Safer than fighting through Liath with him in tow. And if the Liath break through this far, the twenty-six of us will not be able to stop them."

Evey struggled visibly with whirling thoughts, but she was at heart a relation to the Grand Magister of Rithalion, and she steeled herself like only they could. "Give me the child, but I don't know how well I can defend him."

Gregor had an inspiration as he gently handed over the precious bundle. He looked at Taz. "Get me the new guys."

They came over in seconds. "You six, defend the child to your last breath. You three! Never mind your names, you have tir-reath. If this place is overrun, take Alsander and get out of the city any way you can on cat back. Get him to Rithalion."

A brand new La'athai blanched. "How do I–"

DRAGON VESSEL

Gregor took his jerkin in his balled fist and drew him close. "Be. A. Wolf," and then let go. "I'm sure there's armor and weapons around from those who don't need them anymore. Arm and shield yourselves of anything you are missing, and don't let this kid out of your sight."

Everyone nodded understanding. He turned to Evey. "Be safe."

"As safe as we can be."

He turned smartly and went back to Portia. Taz followed closely. "We are still under orders to not interfere. There is no one here who can countermand her order–"

Then the answer dawned on him and he turned and pressed his lips to Taz's. When they parted, she slapped him. He laughed maniacally. "Get the tirreath! Mount up!"

La'athai scrambled to obey as Taz shook her head at him. "Have you gone insane?"

"Yes! Mount up anyway."

Taz did. "She gave an order, and we have to find someone of higher rank to countermand it."

"Who can possibly do that? Who would do that?"

"Her father is on the wall somewhere, and as far as I'm concerned, he outranks the Jewel."

Gregor addressed them all, giving the La'athai areas of responsibility. "We know our Jewel needs us. We know she said to stay behind. Our only chance is to find The Grand Magister on the wall. We spread out in pairs. We find him. Whoever finds him first, howl like her life depends on it and we will meet there." He looked to the four guardsmen only recently entered into Vivien's service. "Time for all of us to be wolves." All the La'athai howled as one and Gregor realized he was the biggest child of idiot, for in this moment he was having the best time of his life. "WOLF PACK, GO FORTH AND HUNT!"

And the La'athai spun themselves in different directions and took off as if launched from a catapult.

They were several streets away when Taz and he slowed down, circling a knot of fighting rather than obeying instincts that said dive in and wreak havoc. They stopped at the next street and saw it was clear. Taz took the moment to huff. "Go forth and hunt? You really just make this up as you go along, don't you?"

Gregor shrugged, smiling at her behind his helm. "I'm glad somebody noticed."

"Oh, I've noticed all along."

They dashed down another street, then saw soldiers of Isbandar destroying a small clot of tired Liath. "I'm surprised we are still alive, is all."

Gregor shrugged. "Day isn't over yet."

Chapter Fifty-Four
The Fragility of Captivity

Shackled in iron that had already burned away the top layer of skin at her wrists, Vivien walked towards the city gates with her captors. Fighting throughout the city had stopped, the Liath standing in concentrated groups, waiting for their next orders. Beside them were dragons, small dragons a man long from the tip of their snouts to the base of their tails. The place was in shambles: buildings burning, goods lying about in the streets alongside the dead and dying. In the shadows were the fae, waiting for the fighting to begin anew. She looked up at the city walls as they approached, saw the smoking hole that was once the gate. She hoped her father was safe, for she knew he'd been spending most of his time there.

They walked through the hole and beyond where once there had been a thriving forest. Now it was nothing but a wasted battlefield. Lifeless Liath lay scattered about, hit by the city's ballistae that had left deep scores in the ground. The living Liath gave their brethren not even a glance as they passed, and she wondered at the lack of care. In the distance there was a city of tents surrounded by a log wall, and it was that they approached.

Vivien fell into step beside Orisar as they were taken into the heavily guarded encampment. Some of those guards fell into place alongside them as they walked through the makeshift gates, drawing their weapons as they began to pass through. It was easy to see the division of the people. The Liath tribes had come together in order to pursue a like purpose, but those tribes did not necessarily trust one another or really care to be in the presence of the others. The retinue, which had grown to be almost one hundred and fifty strong, wound through the encampment, garnering the attention of those who were there, men and women who were not on the front lines of the attack upon the city. These were most likely the smiths, the cooks, the carpenters, the hunters, the healers, and all the others who made a vast encampment such as this thrive.

They wound throughout the bivouac and Vivien was amazed at the size of it. The number of soldiers that it housed, most of which were currently in the city, was astounding. And this didn't even have any of their families. She was certain there was another, maybe much larger, encampment not more than a day's ride away. These people were nomadic, and where the men went, their women and children went with them.

They got to the heart of the encampment. Vivien could tell, because here the tents were larger, more luxurious. These housed the Liath leaders: generals, strategists, priests, and anyone else who held any position of authority due to their use of magic or military status. She and Orisar were taken into the largest tent, and waiting there was a half circle of five priests surrounded by approximately fifty of lesser status.

Vivien stopped at the sight of them. They wore the same robes as those worn in Zormoth, reminding her with vivid clarity about her time spent at their hands, especially those of Drath Drakkon. She was nudged from behind once, twice, then more insistently until she was shoved forward so hard, she fell to her knees.

Lorimath walked ahead to stand between her and the priests. He raised his hands skyward. "You are gathered here to witness the return of Umesh!"

Shouts of joy erupted throughout the tent. Vivien lowered her head, slowly picked herself up from the ground, and waited for the adulation to pass. The captain was given the accolade he so obviously deserved, and Lorimath given the same for being the man under whose leadership it had all taken place. No mention was made that she had been surrendered to them, or that the man who surrendered her had been publically chained, naked, in the cold with knife wounds in his face.

She was hauled into the center of the room. Even through the layers of clothing, Lorimath's hand was bruisingly tight around her arm. They removed her shackles and she was commanded to divest herself of her clothing once again. When she stood naked before them, she saw many of them looked upon her only with unadulterated lust. These were the ones who touched her first, moving their hands over her belly, her breasts, and ultimately, between her legs. She hardened her heart as she suffered the indignity, but Orisar looked away, shame turning his cheeks a shade of red.

One of the men hardly touched her at all, an older man with silver hair, one of the five highest ranking. He simply put a hand on her belly and nodded. She didn't know what he was nodding about, for there was no child in there anymore. None of these priests had realized that, and in her eyes, it made them all the charlatans she always thought they were. "She is a threat. She must be Bound."

Vivien stiffened. She knew what he was saying. Memories of the last time she'd been Bound by magic swept through her mind, along with the accompanying fear. She recoiled from the priest, stepped back, back, back until she hit the warm, hard wall of a man's chest. Hands griped her upper arms, unyielding hands, and she took a deep breath. She took a moment to get hold of herself, and then spoke. "I have come here of my own free will. You have no need to Bind me."

Lorimath regarded her keenly as he placed the shackles back around her blood-encrusted wrists. "My priest says you are a threat."

She nodded. "I understand. But we have an agreement, made before you and the captain."

The priests turned to Ashar, whose only outward sign of nervousness was his slight shift from foot to foot. "Indeed, she said that the only condition of her surrender was that we cease our attack upon the city," he said.

Lorimath made a gesture for silence to the captain as he turned back to her. "You are dangerous and will be Bound. We cannot accept the word of a captive that she will not visit harm upon us."

Lorimath turned dismissively and started to walk towards the tent flap.

Dragon Vessel

Anger surged through Vivien, and she muttered the words of a spell beneath her breath, much too fast for anyone to stop her. The priests moved towards her as the guard holding her arms hissed and abruptly let her go, his palms red from the heat coming from her body. "You can try," she replied.

Lorimath stopped and looked back. The guard gave an apologetic shrug, cradling his burned hands. The priests had all stopped, and they regarded her warily.

"The way I see it, you can't Bind me, at least, not at great cost." She gestured towards the priests. "They can try to do it, but I will fight them. The only way they will be able to stop me is to kill me." She gave him a smile and he pulled his thick, dark brows into a frown. "I don't see how that will help your cause, as the child I carry is the reason why you are here in the first place." At that moment, the shackles fell from around her wrists to land upon the ground, the only thing breaking the silence that reigned.

He wanted to seize her; she could see the desire written across his face. But he dared do no such thing. He knew she was right, and he hated that. "Keep her here, heavily guarded," he spat. He then disappeared through the tent.

Ashar approached her as the priests filed out of the tent to follow their leader. He picked up the manacles, now a twisted lump of metal. He looked at her wrists, which had already begun to heal from the wounds the iron had imposed upon them, and she saw the awe flit across his face before he schooled his expression once more into one of nonchalance. "You may have cornered him for now, but I would not rest easy if I were you. Lorimath's wrath can be a formidable thing."

She regarded him intently, staring into his colorless eyes. "Why are you telling me this?"

Ashar smiled. "Because I like you, *Fyr'kaii*."

She frowned. "Why?"

"You have a warrior spirit. That is hard to find in many women anymore." With that, he turned and left.

Vivien just stood there a moment, and then, seeing her clothes still lying on the ground and feeling the cold, she donned them once more. Orisar stood against the wall of the tent, his head lowered. She wished he'd never come, for he was much too old for this, and given the chance, the Liath would certainly kill him. He was one of their most hated enemies.

She couldn't help thinking they would use him against her...

It wasn't long before a priest re-entered the tent, one of the higher-ranking five. At his side was a dragon three times her size, his shimmering scales a deep brown, accented by red at his muzzle, legs, neck ridges, and tail. He was not free as she imagined he should be, instead, had a gossamer rope looped around his sinuous neck. It was a Binding spell just like the one they wished to place upon her.

The priest muttered a few words of a spell with which she was unfamiliar, then made an overhead gesture that took in the tent surrounding them. He then turned to her. "My dragon will guard you. If you try to escape, your companion's life is forfeit." He glanced at Orisar.

"I will fight for him," she said.

The priest shrugged. "Maybe, if you are quick enough." With that, the man left.

Vivien just stood here, thinking. This dragon was there to make sure she didn't leave. *Why are these people so concerned I'll break my vow? Unless...* She swallowed heavily. Unless they had no intention of stopping their siege against the city. At this point, the Liath had to take it, even for just the resources it would provide an army of this size. It was that, or starve at the beginning of winter on their way to wherever they made their homes.

Vivien trembled at this harsh reality, remembered Mikarvan's words to her not so long ago. The Liath never had any intention of not finishing what they had begun once they arrived at Isbandar. They didn't have the resources not to.

She slumped to the ground beside Orisar, realized she was more a fool than she'd ever thought. The dragon settled himself several feet away, far enough to give him the space he desired, yet close enough to burn the Inquisitor to a crisp within a moment's notice if he chose. His emerald eyes regarded her steadily, with an air of nonchalance, one of neutrality.

Fatigue battered at her, but she refused to sleep. The Warlord could return any time, and she had to be ready. The dragon continued to watch her with unblinking eyes, and she couldn't help wondering about him.

Vivien closed her eyes. She thought of her connection with Dari'sii, and the ability the wyrms had to speak with her when she released them from their chains in Zormoth. She reached out with her mind towards the dragon lying several feet away, wondering if she had the same ability and if he'd hear her. She asked him a simple question, simple for any dragon mage, but one she didn't really have the full answer to.

Dragon? How are you here?

His head snapped up, twin tendrils of smoke rising from his nostrils as he regarded her. Then he narrowed his eyes. *Who are you, and why can you speak to me?*

She shrugged. *Can't all of the priests speak with you?*

No, not all.

She was thoughtful. This was not like the conversations she had with Dari'sii, which consisted more of feelings and desires. She wondered if it was because this dragon was much older. He would have had time to master language, unlike the younglings with which she had connections before.

Yes, they are much too young to speak your tongue.

She was surprised and he chuckled. *I can still pick up on your feelings, only, I also have the mastery of your tongue.* His demeanor suddenly shifted, and his gaze became piercing *You have not answered my question. Who are you, and why can you speak with me?*

My name is Vivien, and I speak with you simply because I can.

Dragon Vessel

More smoke rose from the dragon's nostrils as he contemplated her response. She was aware when he finally accepted it as an answer; she could feel it within the link they shared.

You also have yet to answer my question. How are you here? She decided to ask another one as well. *Why are you bound with chains?*

The dragon just sat there for a few moments, pondering her questions and the response he should give. If she concentrated enough, she could feel the shadows of emotions he kept deep inside: anger, sadness, and strangely, longing.

I am here because I was Summoned. I am chained because I did not come of my own free will.

Shock swept through Vivien, followed by even more questions, more than she thought she had the right to ask. The dragon regarded her inquisitively, like she was a creature he'd never met before. She did not ask the questions, but he decided to answer them anyways. *Once our names are known, we can be Summoned. Sometimes we provide them as a show of trust, other times as a reward for doing a great deed. Every once in a while, it is whispered upon the winds and we no longer have a choice. Your priests Summon us with their magic. They call us by our names, and no matter how big or how small, powerful or weak, we must come. Then, once we are here, we are Bound. We no longer have the ability to return to the place where we are from, and we are forced to serve the one who called us. That is the way of things.* The dragon snorted. *You would do the same.*

Vivien considered his words, then shook her head. *No, I would not.*

The dragon chuckled and shifted his position, crossing his forelegs before him. *I do not believe you.*

She shrugged. *My word is my honor. I am sorry you don't believe.*

He cocked his head again. *Prove it to me.*

Vivien considered this request. She was loathe to do what he asked, for it would imperil her friend. She wanted the dragon to believe her, but did the benefit outweigh the risk? She regarded the dragon. His eyes had become piercing again, as though he could see her very soul. She knew he could divine her thoughts, so now he knew about Dari'sii. The realization made her afraid, and she wondered if she had done the wrong thing by speaking to the dragon in the first place.

Bring her here.

Vivien shook her head. *No, it is dangerous.*

The dragon narrowed his eyes again, this time until they were slits. She could feel his distrust of her, that he was suspicious of her. *Why do you care so much?*

Vivien became suddenly still. *Because I love her.*

The dragon rose from his place and approached, his demeanor menacing. *Prove it!*

She also rose from her place as Orisar's whispered voice penetrated the silence. "Vivien, what is happening?"

She was about to respond when she suddenly realized she no longer had a choice. Dari'sii had taken it upon herself to come, and she was there, in the tent, hiding in the shadows. Vivien's heart leapt at her friend's courage, but it shrank beneath the fear she felt. If the priests knew Dari'sii was there, they would find a way to imprison her, with or without knowing her name.

The dragon's anger died away, replaced by a slew of emotions that Vivien didn't have a chance to pick apart before he spoke again. *Where is she? I would meet this spirit who has won the heart of an Elvish mage.*

Dari'sii slithered into view. She was more beautiful than ever, her white/gold hide almost glowing in the near-darkness provided by the walls of the tent. She came to Vivien's side, then rose to her full height and coiled herself lovingly around Vivien's body, her wedge-shaped head just above Vivien's shoulder.

The dragon got closer, close enough that he could sniff at both Vivien and Dari'sii. Vivien sensed his apprehension, his suspicion. *She has not been ensorcelled. You would have smelled it right away.*

He looked up and into her eyes, so close that the tip of his muzzle almost touched her nose. *How do you know?*

She gave a shrug. *I just do.*

The dragon snorted. *You are like something I've never met before.*

She frowned. *What do you mean?*

The dragon turned away then, a melancholy taking over him. Vivien watched as he returned to his place and lay down once more, returning to his vigil. She felt his acceptance; no longer did he doubt her. But she also sensed a great sadness. She wanted to help him, wished she could...

How can you get free of your captor? Is there not a way?

The dragon's voice was colored with bitterness. *There is no way, unless the mage chooses to let me go. I have been on this plane a very long time now, decades if not longer.* He lay his head on his forelegs. *There is no hope for me.*

Vivien's tone was plaintive. *There must be a way.*

Only the death of my captor will free me.

Dari'sii unwound herself from Vivien, disappearing back into the shadows, and ultimately leaving the tent. Vivien considered the dragon's words, and it all fit together. That was why Dari'sii never left when she'd freed her of her collar. She was still bound to Drakkon, bound to this plane. Only his death freed her, and she had the choice to return where she belonged. But that didn't explain the other wyrms that Drakkon had imprisoned. They had not left when Drakkon died, rather, they had waited...

It hit her then, what had happened. The wyrms had been free to go, yet they had stayed. Vivien had thought that they were still bound by the collars around their necks, but in actuality, they had stayed for her. *They had stayed to reward her for a great deed.*

Dragon Vessel

As far as Vivien knew, she was the only one who now knew their names. Shaken by this revelation, Vivien looked at the gossamer rope that bound this dragon. She once more rose from her spot beside Orisar, this time approaching the beast. His head rose from his forelegs, and he watched as she knelt beside him, allowed her to touch him as she ran her hands over the rope. Just as she'd thought, it was a spell, a complex weaving of words and runes that made up the rope. Certainly, if it would be woven it could be undone.

Vivien pored over the rope, picked apart the various strands and studied them. She delved into her mind, thinking of all the spells she had learned since her capture by Drakkon. She began to see how each strand may have been developed, elements taken from different spells to create the complex matrix before her.

She took what she knew of counter-spells, and the rope began to unravel. Orisar's voice broke the silence. "Vivien, what are you doing?"

It was only then that she realized the dragon was standing over her prone form where she worked on the rope. She imagined what it must look like, and she grinned to herself. The dragon's eyes shone with interest, yet, he had not found it within him to actually hope that he might be freed.

It was the dragon who alerted her first to someone's approach. His voice in her mind alerted her, quickly followed by Orisar's frantic gesturing to return to her place beside him. Vivien just made it back into place before the tent flap was flung aside. Lorimath entered, followed by the captain and one of his priests. By his demeanor she could tell he was still angry, yet his expression was calm. He took a chair and sat down before her and Orisar. "I have heard stories about you Lady Valdera, and I have a hard time believing most of them."

She made no reply, kept her face expressionless.

"What happened to the city of Zormoth?"

She felt it coil within her, a familiar sensation she hadn't felt in a while. It curled up in her gut, waiting, waiting. She flicked her gaze to the priest, then to the captain before returning to Lorimath. She wondered if she should tell him the truth just before speaking, her voice a monotone. "I destroyed it."

Lorimath's expression remained neutral. "With whose help?"

The coils tightened. "I did it alone."

Irritation flashed in his eyes. "I don't believe you. No one has that much power."

It swiftly rose within her, the thing deep inside, and Vivien rose from her place. The captain put his hand on the hilt of his sword, and the priest adjusted his stance, ready. Her gaze captured Lorimath's and held it. "First, I burned a hole into Drakkon's chest. I dug out his heart and ate it. I remember the blood pouring down my chin, down my neck and onto my breasts. I was naked, for he liked to keep me that way. It was easier to rape me if I didn't have clothing getting in the way."

Lorimath's eyes widened as she took a step towards him. "Did you like seeing me naked, Warlord?"

He made no reply, just stared at her.

She took another step. "I then incinerated every priest in the temple. I can still smell their flesh burning in my nostrils." She lifted her head and drew in a deep breath, taking in the air. She could smell their fear, and the thing inside her rejoiced.

"When I left the temple, I rained fire down upon the city, burning everything I could see and more. I can still hear the screams of the people as they tried to escape."

The men all stared at her. The captain's knuckles were white on the hand holding the sword hilt, and the priest had called the dragon to his side.

Lorimath was the first to recover. He rose, and salvaging what dignity he had left, made himself walk three steps towards her, to at least match the ones she'd made towards him. "The man with the you, the one they call Wolf–"

Vivien rose her voice over his. "Stopped me from destroying the city completely." She bridged the gap between herself and Lorimath, heard the hiss of steel as the captain drew his blade, felt the dragon's breath at her back, waiting. She cocked her head and looked up at the Warlord. He was tall for an elf, his hair long and thick down to his shoulders. It was dark, just like Drakkon's had been. He looked down at her, brown eyes searching her face... searching.

"How is it that you are carrying a dragon child?"

She knew this question would come eventually. She didn't have an answer for it, never did. More interesting, she was no longer pregnant, and still these people insisted she was carrying some kind of abomination. She considered coming up with some crazy answer, something they might believe other than the "I don't know what you are talking about" she'd provided before. Maybe they would stop asking...

In a bold move, Vivien stepped closer, so close they were almost touching, her gaze never leaving his. "One day I was swimming in a pool outside the bounds of Rithalion, alone. It was a place I'd never been before, surrounding by walls of rock. I found a tunnel beneath the water and swam into it. When I emerged on the other side there was a small cave." She thought fast, saying the first things that came to her mind. "Tired, and uncertain I could swim my way back, I got out of the water. It was dark, and the only way I could see was because of the glowing moss on the walls. I walked, going down tunnels where the moss grew. I don't know how much time passed: hours, days, weeks... but after a while I emerged into a massive cavern. And in the center of it was a magnificent red dragon."

Lorimath was enthralled, his eyes shining. Vivien smiled to herself, enjoying her little story. "I stumbled inside, weak and tired from my long journey through the tunnels. The dragon eyed me hungrily, his golden eyes blazing like twin suns. He approached me ever so slowly, and I could feel his excitement growing with each step. And then he was there, standing over me. I went to my knees and he enveloped me in darkness. I couldn't see or hear, but I could smell him, and I could feel him all around and inside of me."

Lorimath's eyes had become wide, and they shone with excitement, lust emanating from him in waves. She lowered her voice. "I had never climaxed so strongly or so completely."

Silence reigned throughout the tent. The men stared at her as though she was some kind of mythical beast read about only in the oldest of tomes or told about in stories to the youngest of boys and girls. Lorimath's voice was slightly ragged when he finally spoke. "Who else knows this?"

"No one, Warlord. You are the only one I have ever told."

An expression of triumph suffused his features and he gave her a toothy smile filled with the promise of a reward, one she was certain would come to her in the middle of the night and involving very little clothing and a great deal of humping. "Good girl."

He then turned away, gesturing to his men as he swept back out of the tent the way he'd come in. Again, there was silence, and when Vivien turned to look at Orisar, his shoulders were shaking with laughter. He shook his head in mock shame and she shrugged, giving him a lopsided grin. "What? He deserved it."

He instantly became solemn. "Vivien, this is serious. The atrocities he could visit upon you–"

She frowned. "He can try," she interjected.

"These people are dangerous. They have magic you can't comprehend as of yet, magic that can bind you to them, make you a slave to them for the rest of your life."

Her frown deepened. "Fae magic can do that too."

He nodded and sighed with resignation. "Yes."

Contrition washed over her. "I'm sorry. I know you are worried." She sat down beside him, suddenly tired. It wasn't that long ago that she had delivered her son. Her body had healed swiftly: the pain had ceased, as had the bleeding. But fatigue pressed upon her, and sadness for want of her child in her arms. Her breasts had begun to ache, and they had developed an overly tight feeling, as though too full. As she thought about it, she felt an unfamiliar sensation from the center of the breasts that moved towards the nipples. She put her palms against them, easing the burning she felt, and she noticed a slight dampness where the nipples pressed against the fabric of her clothes. She swallowed past the lump in her throat; Alsander must be hungry, and she wasn't there to feed him.

She felt a comforting hand at her arm, looked up into Orisar's kind face. He didn't say anything; he didn't need to. She put her head on his shoulder, and overwhelmed by fatigue, relaxed enough that she began to drift.

Chapter Fifty-five
Confluence of Circumstances

Esgrynn heard. The whole city was shouting it.

He ground his teeth until they hurt. *All of his work for nothing. NOTHING!* She had given herself up to the dragon elves, who would then most assuredly kill her. Maybe not today, or tomorrow, but all his visions would cease to come to pass. He had to find her. There was only one thing certain; he was currently in a hostile city and she was not. He tried to strangle his anger and only succeeded in making it more vicious. Fighting was slowing down in the streets, but he could not cross over the battle lines from where the fae elves controlled to lines held by dragon elves. So, he had to move around the main boulevards.

He avoided scattered knots of fighting, though there were few. The defenders were exhausted, and the appearance of the elder fae had been a firebreak to the enemy entering the city. The massive fae presence at the gate had been gone for a while now, but the fae that had floated through the sky had retreated, battered and leaking streams of white sand, to perch on the College of Magic and just wait. He drew a wide path around the monstrosity and began heading toward the section of wall along the front of the city. The Liath would definitely take Vivien to the encampment they had built.

So that is where he had to go: Over the wall, and toward Vivien Valdera.

It took hours to circle around to the wall facing away from the main thrust of invasion, but once there it was all but deserted. Just one, slack jawed human local watched him listlessly as he paused for a moment and vaulted the edge, calling on the power of an air dragon in his thrall to slow him before he hit the ground and broke something. It was still cold, and he slogged through short drifts of snow.

Then, deep horns blasted out across the whole city. He knew that sound; the battle had begun again.

It took many minutes before he cleared the arc of the wall and could see the primitive fortress in the distance, five massive dragons lounging outside. While they wouldn't see him as a friend, they would know what he was and think he belonged there. Dragons were infamous for caring little about the trivialities of lesser beings. Other than the hacked stumps of trees and piles of logs that would have acted as shields from incoming arrows, there was little remaining cover after the dragon elves had been at it, so he stayed near the wall to avoid the notice of any archers. He walked at a brisk pace without worry that some bumbling city guard would try to gut him, or some fumbling fae mage would sense what he was and try to duel him, or some gargantuan fae would try to eat him. Any of which could have happened if he were inside the city. He congratulated himself on being clever.

Then a small group of dragon elves raised up from a particularly close stack of logs and jogged toward him. He frowned. *Complications.* Two had bows with nocked arrows, two had iron swords. One had a finely-made steel sword decorated with birds obviously scavenged from some fallen foe.

I know that sword...

The one with steel would be the leader. They were not being cut down by arrow fire, so Esgrynn pursed his lips and waited impatiently as they drew close. Then the leader made a big, showy gesture and an earth dragon the size of a large dog erupted from the ground and slithered sullenly behind him. It looked like a trod-upon salamander with wings. At last, they came within comfortable speaking distance.

"Halt!"

Esgrynn rolled his eyes. "No, I don't think so."

That draw them up short. It may have been his certainty, or his disdain. Whatever the reason, his refusal set them back, despite the fact that he had already halted. He didn't recognize their tribal markings, or any designs on their equipment, but the fact that they were outside the city while all the pillage and rape was inside spoke volumes.

The leader puffed himself up. "Yes, you will."

Esgrynn shook his head. "No. Not because one of my lessers tells me."

Again, a pause.

Esgrynn watched the mageling pump himself up. "Who are you?"

Over the centuries, Esgrynn had perfected his sneer. "None of your business, whelp."

"Whelp? What if I have my men shoot you right here?" The youthful dragon mage snarled back, a lap dog puppy growling at a wolf.

All it did was irritate Esgrynn further. He drew a small knife from an inner pocket of his sleeve and held it up. With barked command, liquid trails of electricity began oozing from the dragon runes he himself had inscribed, condensing along the blade and leaping to the ground in long, yellow threads.

"If you think you can," was all he said.

Then, over the sounds of battle within the walls there came a howl. It was close to the real sound, but it was obviously created by an elvin mouth only a few streets into the city. The roving guards started to hear it. Then it was repeated, over and over, sometimes close and sometimes far away.

Every Liath had heard tell of the man beast that fought for the fae elves. The huge, wolf-like thing that could not be killed, and trepidation showed on their faces. The dragon mageling opened his mouth as one howl faded from hearing, but then a new voice, powerful and strong, answered the wolf-call from out past the city in the woods that remained. Twenty or so elves, mounted on tir-reath, and a mountain of a man on a reindeer, burst from the woods at a full run. One of the elves, aboard a big, long haired tir-reath, wore familiar armor. It meant that Esgrynn might yet survive this. The huge human raised an axe in one hand and howled again. There was a visceral quality to it that reached into the soul. Esgrynn had no doubt who that was, and it meant that he might not after all.

Dragon Vessel

"What is that?" asked one of the archers while the whole group turned to face them.

Trouble, thought Esgrynn, but he had one thing to deal with before facing that particular part of his past coming at him at full speed. He waited, just for a second, then hissed, "Don't be fools! Shoot them!"

The dragon elves heard the authority in his voice and asked no questions, nor turned to face him. The two archers unleashed arrows– one caught on an incoming warrior's shield and another missed completely. The two swordsmen moved ahead of the archers and raised their own shields while the mage hung back and began working on a spell. Esgrynn saw his opportunity and moved.

The dragonling barely squawked a warning when his dagger entered the back of the mage. There was a sizzling pop as flesh was converted to charcoal and steam instantly. The dragonling, now free, sank back into the aether with nothing tying it to this realm. Esgrynn was still moving, drawing the knife across the throat of one archer with another pop and hiss of steaming blood and then lunging to put it in the face of the other. Next Esgrynn pounced on the warrior to the left and set his deadly weapon into his arm. The captured lightning turned a whole section of the arm into a burnt husk. The man dropped his iron sword and fell to the ground screaming. With so many dragons roaring, weapons clashing, and elves screaming just inside the city, the few seconds of his massacre had gone unnoticed until now.

The lone warrior turned to him, weapon raised as his companion went pale and slumped unconscious on the ground.

"Wait, you are with us!"

Esgrynn looked at the long, rust flecked sword, then at the tiny knife he had labored so hard to create. *Sacrifices must be made.* He shrugged. "No, I'm not."

He took a step back and, as the warrior raised his shield to defend his torso, sank the knife, blade first, in the soil at his enemy's feet, covering his ears in the steel's split second of travel.

The knife, charged with the powers of the sky, touched the earth and erupted into a pillar of lightning that punched a hole in the clouds. Esgrynn cursed bitterly as his ears still rang despite the protection of his palms, still dazzled though he had closed his eyes. *Nothing ever, ever, ever goes according to plan.* His hearing and vision cleared just as the fae elves reached him. *And more delays, MORE delays.* He barely spared a glance at the dead swordsman at his feet, half of his body untouched, the flesh and equipment on the other half burnt or melted by the death of his knife.

The group slowed as they approached him. All were cautiously aggressive and a few had fae in attendance. He had displayed powers of a dragon mage in front of them, yet they were held off from attacking by a vehement "YOU!" That came from the human barbarian.

Esgrynn smiled. His constant visions had played this moment out over and over, with many iterations, but he had not guessed it would come to pass now.

He reached up and lowered the hood of his tattered robe, and the elf in the aged battle armor echoed, "YOU?"

Esgrynn smiled. "Hello, Brother. How is my sister?" There were several moments of shock as the whole group tried to come to terms with this new information. Esgrynn however, could only spare them a few breaths. "I understand, you're confused. There is no time." Another howl went up inside, all the voices in chorus closer now. "Your men need you inside the city. The city gate is in the hands of the dragon elves and if you try to get in that way you will be cut to ribbons. I can help." *And, of course, I can't have you following me.*

The Wolf frowned. "But—"

Esgrynn snapped, "You always do this, every time I see it! But- but- but- I am here offering to help you." He motioned to the corpses still steaming in the cold. "I am obviously not in league with your enemy. You are in a hurry. I can help, and all you do it question me!"

The Wolf bristled, but Xadrian made a motion. "This is Shaladrea's brother. He has helped me before and I trust him."

And that settled that, much faster than in all but one of his visions, which had not ended well for him. He remembered a select something from another vision. He reached down and picked up the bird-festooned sword from the turf. He held it out, hilt first, to the human. "And this, I think, means something to you, and you will need it." The Wolf's eyes went wide as he accepted the sword from the hermit. He said nothing, but went very quiet. "Now, allow me."

Esgrynn tapped into the power of a pair of earth dragons in his thrall. With the raw energy he grabbed onto the ground and whispered their names to it. To the La'athai, the ground spontaneously trembled, it shook, and then massive mounds of earth pushed up from the dirt to form wide ramps from the outside of the city to the tops of the city walls. Theatrically he raised his arms as if pulling the earth with his bare hands, straining against some imaginary weight.

The Wolf recovered from the shock at seeing the Tanager Sword in his hands. "But wait, who are you? Why are you here? What are you doing?"

Again, a howl came from the city within, eliciting from deeper inside, and carrying a sense of a question.

Esgrynn feigned great effort. "Would love to talk, but your soldiers are waiting inside and I can't hold this forever."

Xadrian hunched down along the back of his long-legged cat. "La'athai, over the wall!" and kicked his mount into a loping run up the dirt embankment to the top. The others filed behind at speed, with only the Wolf left behind.

His eyes bore into Esgrynn, full of disturbing promises. "I know you, Warlock. I know your help comes at great cost."

Esgrynn managed to make his arms shake as if with fatigue. "Great help comes at great cost, but it is not as if you can turn down the aid right now, is it?"

The Wolf shook his head like a horse dislodging a biting fly and frowned. He then followed the rest up to the top of the city wall.

Esgrynn dropped his pantomime of effort and reversed his spell, pushing the soil back to the ground and making sure he would not easily be followed. Another howl rang out, and it was answered from above.

"Well, at least I can continue undisturbed, now."

Shrugging off the loss of his favorite storm knife, he continued his way to the dragon elf encampment.

Vivien jerked awake to the sound of a horn sounding in the distance, followed by the answering roar of over a dozen dragons. Her heart beating rapidly in her chest, she waited, wondering what that meant. Orisar was tense beside her, probably thinking the same thing. It wasn't long before she heard the attack begin anew. She chafed beneath the bonds she had imposed upon herself, hated herself for her stupidity. She could be getting ready to fight right now, helping her father on what remained of the front wall, but instead she sat in Lorimath's tent, doing nothing. *The Liath are not upholding their end of the bargain. I deserve to be free.* Vivien looked at the dragon that still watched her not far away. *He deserves to be free.*

Vivien rose from her place, once more approaching the dragon. He raised his head, watching her suspiciously. She stopped before reaching him, hunkered down in front of him. *What if I told you that I can set you free of the spell that Binds you?*

The dragon snorted a puff of smoke. *I wouldn't believe you.*

Let me see it again and I will try.

The dragon regarded her intently. *Why would you do that for me? I am here to kill your friend if you try and do anything stupid.*

Because all things deserve freedom. She cocked her head. *Is this stupid? Will you kill him if I help you?*

He didn't give her a reply, but she knew when he acquiesced; she could sense it through the link they shared. She crawled over to him, and once more worked at the spell-woven rope around his neck. She didn't know how long she worked, only that her muscles became tired from sitting in the same place for so long. And then, with a sudden fizzle and a pop, the spell was broken.

The dragon reared up from his place, unfurling his massive wings. Tables and chairs overturned and the tip of one wing tore through the side of the tent, causing it to collapse. He then screamed in defiance, so loud she slapped her hands over her ears. But his voice was in her mind, speaking over his roar. *He knows his spell is broken and he is coming!*

Alarm swept through Vivien. This was something she hadn't taken into account, and she berated herself for her thoughtlessness. Of course, the dragon's master would know that his spell had been unwound. She heard a rumbling sound, followed by a trembling of the ground. This was a very powerful priest, one she knew she couldn't possibly match. She looked over at Orisar, fear for him making her heart lurch in her chest, and indecision rooted her to the spot.

Then the dragon was there before her, lowering his head to look her in the eyes. His breath was hot against her face, and his eyes gleamed a pale gold. *Do not worry, my friend. He is mine now.* He then put his face alongside hers, as though to tell her a secret. His voice was a low hiss. *Slag'nassiossss.*

With that sibilant word, her fear was wiped away, and in its place came strength. He had given her his name, and his power was mighty.

The ground abruptly bucked and Vivien stumbled forward. The dragon shrieked again, rising to full height. A deep crack rent the dirt floor of the tent, right under her feet, and she fell to her knees. The priest burst through the entry, another spell already at his disposal. Sharp spires of rock thrust up from the ground, one just barely missing the dragon as he rose and tore through the roof. Orisar scrambled to her side, helping her up just as the tent collapsed around them.

They staggered beneath the weight of the canvas, felt something long and heavy fall to the ground beside them. Vivien sought to control her rapidly beating heart, to focus beneath the stifling fabric. "Hold your breath."

As far away from Orisar as she could reach, she clutched at the canvas, the acrid smell of burning filling her nostrils. She allowed the fire to burn only long enough to put a sizable hole in it before snuffing it out. She pulled at Orisar, who coughed on the smoke as they climbed out from beneath it, and stopped just as the airborne dragon exacted his wrath.

A gout of sand flew from his open maw, blasting the priest. The force of it stripped the man bare of his robes, then his skin, scouring him bare until all that remained was a skeleton. It happened so fast, that the bones didn't crumple until after it was done, landing in a haphazard pile of sand where a man had stood only seconds before.

The dragon winged in place, looking around and taking in the men that had come running when the priest began casting his spells. They all stood there, stock still, hoping the dragon would stop there. The men scattered when the dragon swept towards them, the deadly sand stripping them bare just as it had the priest. Some of them ran past Vivien and Orisar, sheer terror on their faces. Vivien took her friend's trembling hand, calmly leading him past the dragon as they walked out of the bivouac the way they had come in.

Once the largest dragons on the field had entered the fray, the elder fae had been beset, unable to quell the raiders on the ground. One dragon attacked the huge, blue flying fae. The second struck and leaped out of danger near the other side of the city while a gargantuan fae gave chase, following from street to street, destroying buildings in its haste. The third was destroying whole swaths of town with fury and doom when it wasn't testing the ward on the College of Magic or the Council Hall and creating bright purple flashes when it struck.

Liath had come in stages, like the progression of a disease. First had been footmen, then mounted charges on the terrifying dracoari the adepts rode into battle, all had been repulsed until now. The footmen came in waves that pounded the defenders back street to street, door to door until now they were trapped in a square facing a section of city wall. Jor'aiden and lesser mages were summoning fae as fast as they could, the soldiers of Isbandar were holding the streets connecting to the square, and some La'athai had reinforced them at some point, but they were being beaten back by the sheer number of Liath. They were retreating on three sides to a center with no escape.

All seemed lost.

The Wolf tried to breathe, but if he sucked in cool air, he exhaled smoke. On the wide parapet, the La'athai from the envoy all watched in horror.

Xadrian frowned. "We can make a difference here, but we need room to maneuver with the tir-reath."

But the Wolf was already off of his reindeer, sword in one hand, woodsman's axe in the other.

"Brother!"

The Wolf felt it all, the pressure behind his eyes, the heat, the feel of his knuckles popping where they tightened on his weapons. He barely paused. "If the La'athai are here, SHE is here. I will give you room."

And as he said it, his whole world became bloody and red. He howled at the top of his lungs, not slinking into battle, but charging down the stairs with eyes glowing like bright red coals in the coming dusk. The crowd of Liath looked up, and one leapt up onto the stairs leading to the top of the wall. Another followed suit, but the Wolf's first strike with the sword batted his enemy's weapon away and the he hacked the axe deeply into the man's body, nearly severing an arm at the shoulder with the first strike. He kicked the body of the first into the second, stepped on the neck of that soldier with a hideous crackle. He faced a dozen Liath, but as he hit the ground with bloody weapons, he planted his feet wide and roared like a demon into their faces.

For all their talk of courage, they all smelled of fear and backed up three steps into the line of men behind them. Deep inside, Ravn felt a moment of trepidation as swords and spears and axes came up against him. Then there was an answering wolf call inside the circle of defenders in the square. He thought only one thing.

Vivien.

He lunged forward as if possessed.

Blood flew in all directions as if thrown by a demented painter. Everywhere he saw enemies and everywhere his steel and iron struck. Layers of leather parted like cheesecloth before him, and exposed mortal parts to air and sky. He lashed out on all sides and the Liath gave way, or died. Errant strikes were turned aside by his fae elf armor, giving him no pause as he continued to take step after step over enemy corpses until he found someone of rank and mettle who stood up to him.

Other Liath scrambled over themselves to get out of the way as the villain smiled menacingly. The leader was obviously a woman of note. Her armor and helmet were of hardened steel, her long-bladed spear intricately carved with dragons and wyrms colored in dark enamel. The raiders pulled back to give them space as she twirled the haft in her hand.

"Have you ever faced a woman warrior, barbarian?" She waited a half a heartbeat and then thrust forward with the spear.

The Wolf batted the bladed haft away and leapt forward, bringing the iron axe down upon her head. The blade caught on her helmet, and what it didn't cut, it crushed. He left the axe where it lodged and drew the steel sword from her sheath as her corpse fell.

"Yes," he growled.

But then the circle around him began shrinking. The rank-and-file Liath had finally realized their numbers, and were closing in on him, step by cautious step. He shook his head and smiled wolfishly. "You have given me what I needed."

They stopped at once, mesmerized by the angry pulsing of his eyes. One finally asked, "What?"

"Room."

And, indeed, they had pulled away from where he had entered on the street and been pushed back by his ferocity. It had provided a relief of pressure from those attacking the line of fae elves at one end of that square. More importantly, it had left a void at the base of the stairs, and it was from there that the mounted La'athai came in a torrent, Xadrian at the lead. Faced away from the incoming cats and wolves, the Wolf struck ahead, piercing an elf through the heart. Another battered at him with a shield, and he kicked him down and severed a foot with a disdainful cut. A third came from behind, wielding a massive mattock, but an arrow from above pierced him in the chest. The Wolf glanced above and the two Wolf Pack fae battle mages were sending spells down from above, protected from vengeful spears and arrows by two soldier La'athai. All the rest had left behind their arrows and Katriona was playing her bow like a harp, sending arrow after arrow down into the Liath ranks, with no thought toward conservation.

In mere minutes the La'athai had acted like a knife in the guts of the Liath attack, relieving the western flank of the square. The Liath tried to rally and surge forward again, but then broke upon the cats, the general, and the rage of the human that refused to die.

Finally, the enemy started to retreat.

"Pull back! Pull back!"

Dragon Vessel

Xadrian's call was not a welcome one, but falling back meant seeing Vivien. He turned and retreated back, forming up with the La'athai who made a fist of a formation and hit the Liath still clawing at the line of Isbandar soldiers protecting this street to the last defended square. They struck mercilessly and savagely, and once the enemy were dead, they gained entrance to the plaza. Tired soldiers from that street marched to the other two streets to bolster numbers where the fighting was still going on. The Wolf knew vaguely that the elves could feel the deaths of those close to them, and every face was wan and drawn with grief. Casualties were mounting in the city, and it showed of every Isbandarian.

The wounded were everywhere, laid out and helpless. Some civilians were helping the living into a rich home next to the wall, but there was really no safety anywhere.

The Wolf watched Xadrian meet with Vivien's half-brother and her father, but she was nowhere to be seen. With a stomach grinding painfully as if in the fist of a giant, he began scanning the faces of the wounded and the dead. He glanced at Xadrian, and saw Gregor and a few other La'athai were speaking to the group of noblemen. They looked back at him, faces, grim.

Random babbling fears reached out of the pit in the back of his head, whispering awful, unthinkable things to him. He felt the century of living alone come back to him as a comfortable mantle, settling down upon him as the only way to keep the terrors at bay. He stalked to them like an animal. Jor'aiden looked at him dangerously, and Gregor quailed a little, but as he steeled himself and he opened his mouth, Xadrian stepped in front of the subordinate and held up a hand to stop the barbarian.

"She surrendered herself to the Liath. She is in their encampment."

And suddenly he stopped feeling... anything. The sounds of battle went away. His limbs went numb and his right hand slackened, dropping the stolen sword to the ground with a clatter he did not hear. Only the sword in his left hand, covered in tanagers, remained in his fist. Xadrian said something, but he looked away. He staggered, and the world spun. He saw the three streets, blocked off by Isbandarian soldiers and civilians, nearly swamped by Liath gnashing with iron weapons. Above the city, far away, a gigantic fae trailed streams of white sand as it burned and bled. The blue dragon breathed a bolt of lightning at the fae, but in return for the fresh scorch-mark, it found itself entangled in the fae's tentacles. It roared in agony, but the Wolf's world was still in silence.

The five or so of the La'athai that had stayed behind were coming from the battle lines to join the twenty he had brought at the center of the square. They were staring at him. But there was someone missing. Someone not here. He finally heard something. His heart. It was beating faster. Faster.

Vivien is not here.

He felt the pressure. He did not breathe. He did not let go. He sucked in air into the furnace of his rage.

And he roared.

The sound rattled windows and stole momentum from the attackers, but it gave no release. It was not a sound meant to release, it was a sound meant as a promise of what was to come. He did not realize he had moved to the central street. He had no memory of shouldering soldiers aside. All that mattered was getting to the Liath, and once there, he butchered like a demon. He could see the bloody red glow of his eyes touching everything in front of him. He blocked a strike and reached out his free hand to crush the screaming face of the Liath in front of him. He sent out a kick and felt a ribcage crackle beneath his boot like matchsticks, sending the enemy into five others and tumbling them all to the ground. He moved into the space and slung his sword like a death warrant. Limbs flew free of bodies and screams barely registered to his mind. All he heard was his heart, and her voice. Her cries of pain.

And the sounds made him even more savage.

He yanked a hammer out of the hands of an attacker, and with a three-pound mass of metal he began clearing a path like a farmer reaping grain. He heard shouting. Maybe shouting for him, but he didn't understand what was being said. All he knew was in the crush of attackers, he was a burning coal in dry tinder. The Liath that saw him broke and ran, or were broken before his rage.

He ripped a shield from the arm of one Liath and threw it sidearm like a discus. It flew into the forehead of another, crushing it as the first Liath caught the edge of the tanager sword in the jaw, removing it from his face. Three attacked him at once, spears seeking vulnerability. He dropped the sword and caught two, but one pierced his leg at the seam of his Elvish armor. He felt the pain as a hot mixture of alcohol on a bonfire and as he went down on one knee, all three Liath pushed in. He twisted the shafts in his hands, snapping the heads free. The two spearmen tumbled forward and he stabbed first one and then the other in the face with their own spearpoints held like daggers. Liath were fleeing on all sides as he dropped one and pulled the spear out of his own flesh even as the soldier continued to lean in with all his might. The Liath finally let go and turned to run, but the barbarian stood and reversed the spear, hurling it through his retreating back before sending a broken spearpoint into another raider and then retrieving his sword.

But he wobbled as he stood, the deep puncture in his thigh leaking bright red streams of blood. He went back down to one knee, legs weak, breathing hard.

The Liath ceased to flee, and watched him as if he were an angry, wounded bear. He removed his helmet, and let it fall to the street with a clatter. His eyes did not glow so bright, his thigh itched horribly as the wound struggled to close. His strength was returning, but it would not be in time. He heaved himself to his feet and motioned at the ragged line of Liath that filled the street.

"Come. Now. I must kill you all to find her, and so you must come closer."

Dragon Vessel

They looked from one to another. One came forward, followed by another. Then more. They kept their weapons up as they came foot by foot. In his rage he must have killed at least fifty. He had pushed them forty feet back from the entrance to the plaza, but now it was the end. All he knew was that he could not stop moving forward. None of them were willing to let wounded prey escape.

They came closer.

The first drew back his sword as he came close enough to strike. The Wolf raised his sword to defend himself.

All around the Wolf erupted into roars and hisses.

Liath screamed as twenty La'athai, mounted on the same number of tir-reath, blew past him on each side, crashing into the enemy with claw, steel, and fury. The raider in front of him went down with jaws at his throat, and screams erupted from the demoralized invaders. The Wolf slumped to the street as the enemy was shoved backwards and felt his wound close and his strength finally returning. In seconds, forty of the attackers were dead and the whole knot of Liath were in a rout, running back up the street as arrows whizzed down upon them from Katriona's bow and fae harassed and murdered them. The La'athai pulled back to surround their commander as he stood.

Xadrian clapped the Wolf on the shoulder. "You are the maddest human I have ever met."

The Wolf looked back to where the long section of street. It was strewn with Liath and parts of Liath all the way to where the line of soldiers were being thinned out to reinforce the other streets. "Well, they have relief, at least."

"Your bleeding has stopped."

Without looking, the Wolf nodded and glanced back toward the center of town where the Liath were still fleeing. He flexed the leg, "Still stiff."

"One day you'll have to tell me how you do that."

The Wolf shrugged, tucked the tanager sword into his belt and found a hammer large enough to be used in two hands lying discarded on the street and tested it with a swing. "Ask Jor'aiden."

Before Xadrian could reply, they heard the horns. Deep and powerful, they reached into the chest and rattled the soul. It was followed by a massive roar louder and more terrifying than the horns. All the tir-reath began to howl, hunkered low with ears pinned back.

Xadrian and Wolf breathed the same word in different languages, "Dragon."

Then it appeared around the bend in the road three blocks away where the Liath had retreated. The body was the length of four elves, and it galloped without using its wing to take flight. It was an orange-yellow that faded to red along the belly, scales glistening like oiled metal in the low light of coming dusk. Just behind came the tide of Liath, emboldened by their new champion.

The Wolf hefted his hammers. "La'athai! To the square!"

ROSS &ROSS

At his order the Wolf Pack gave the slightest indication to their mounts and the tir-reath bolted for the square, carrying their hapless riders along. Only Xadrian remained. He held out his hand to his brother.

"Come! Fenella will carry us both!"

In response, the Wolf switched the hammer to his off hand and drew the Tanager sword, pressing the grip into Xadrian's hand. "Get this to her. Tell her she was always my only thought."

Xadrian looked at the sword in shock and spat. "Wolf, you cannot defeat a dragon!"

The Barbarian picked up the hammer. "You think there is safety in the square? Get to Jor'aiden. He may be able to stop it. I will buy you time." He kicked Fenella's flank and that was all she needed to sprint toward the square, taking Xadrian with her despite any commands to the contrary.

The Wolf did not watch him go. He instead turned to the dragon that was barreling down upon him, shaking the ground. It angled toward him, looking to turn him into paste beneath its clawed feet.

The Wolf raised the hammer, feeling peace come over him. It was the end. Finally, the end. And if he could fight well, if he could wound this thing, Xadrian and the Pack would find Vivien and save her.

IF.

The thing was closer, barreling down like a mountain of lava. He could feel the heat and the ground trembled through his boots. Then it was there over top of him, moving fast as a horse at full gallop.

He raised the weapon higher and took a deep breath. He let go of loss, of certainty, of fear, of IF. He let it all go and exhaled thick steam into the cold air. Then he dodged to the side, putting his whole weight behind a two-handed strike.

The creature may have had scales that could not be pierced but for the strongest strike, but the eight-pound head of the hammer connected solidly with the left front knee. The bones cracked and shifted, and the thing roared a yelp as it tumbled and slid into someone's wooden home, collapsing the front and half burying the beast. Yet by the time the Wolf had regained his balance, the dragon was already shaking off broken branches that made the timber and walls of the home. It caught sight of him and its eyes glowed red. It curled the right leg, flopping uselessly at the joint, close to its body.

The Wolf charged the beast as it opened its mouth. He measured the steps with his mind, and realized he was too far away. He dove to the side as the beast breathed a line of hot death. It hit the home behind him as he rolled away from the path of destruction. The blast went on and on, an expression of pain as much as rage. Once it ended, the dragon closed its maw and saw the Wolf had regained his feet and his weapon, then charged the mouth of fire. The mouth closed as the hammer came from the side, smashing at where the jaw met the skull.

Dragon Vessel

The dragon squawked in a deafening tone and swiped at the Wolf with its good front talon. His breastplate went flying and left behind a bare chest covered only by two deep gashes and the ruined remnants of the padding beneath. The dragon then took to the air, leaping backwards onto the destroyed building, perching on the edge of the roof that groaned dangerously under the weight.

The Liath, having finally caught up to the charging dragon, stood a mere thirty feet from where the Wolf struggled upright. At the fore were four people of some obvious import. Two priests and two warriors leading the less than eager horde. The elder of the two priests looked disgusted.

He shouted, "Stop struggling with that insect and kill him!" The Wolf looked from the priest, to the dragon, then back to the priest. He heard the dragon inhale.

Straining every tendon, his chest screaming in agony, he hurled the hammer at the elder priest.

Then, as the dragon spouted fire, the light of the sun, the sky, the whole world, was suddenly stolen. Flame coated the dragon because of the broken jaw, but it paid no heed, because fire dragons would never burn. The hammer hit the priest and buried itself into his chest to the haft.

Fire hit the Wolf, and the whole world went dark.

Chapter Fifty-Six
The Bargain

Esgrynn saw the brown dragon rise from the encampment and rise into the air. It circled lazily once, scouring the ground below with blasts of high-pressure sand. Esgrynn felt his stomach fall away, but as he raised his hands to enslave or banish the beast, it faded into nothing with a deep boom. It had returned to the aether that was its natural home.

He pursed his lips, fearing that he was late again. His heart thudding like the footfalls a herd of a hundred giant beasts, he sprinted toward the narrow gap in the huge wooden palisade. The gate was built to slow down and compress an enemy advance. It was placed where there was a gap in the outer wall, with an inner wall of logs and outer wall to make an enemy come in, and turn left or right, and then have to turn again before assaulting the encampment. The sounds of the distant city were muffled even more as he entered the killing field, just as Vivien and a robed elf entered from the camp side.

For just a moment, they all stopped and stared at one another.

Vivien reacted first, shouting, "Dragon–!"

"–mage," Esgrynn interrupted, raising his hands before him. "Yes. Both of us. I am Esgrynn, and I am here to take you to safety."

She frowned, "I don't–"

"–know me or trust me. Yes, I know," Esgrynn finished, desperately trying to tame his temper at having to do this again. "But I am newly arrived. I do not dress like your enemies." He raised his face inside the hood. "And I bear no tribal markings. See?"

Her face twisted. "So who–?"

"Vivien, you must trust me, because I am the only way you will make it out of this place alive."

She looked to her companion, who shook his head slightly.

"How–?"

"I studied to become a dragon mage, but I was born a seer. I have dreamed of you since I could dream, about this day most of all. It is how I knew how to find you, and how I know what you are going to ask." He looked pointedly at the older, robed elf. "But you were never there."

She frowned. "What if I do as you ask?"

Relief washed over him. "Then you will live. A new future is coming, and I have sacrificed most of my life to making it happen in ways large and small. You must come with me if it has any chance to happen."

"Why?"

Esgrynn fought the urge to rub his eyes in frustration. "You are incredibly powerful, but untamed. I have to take you from this place or you will die before you learn to harness your new magic."

Her face reflected awe, confusion, doubt. "I don't know why I have this magic, or how I lost touch with the fae."

Esgrynn started at the honestly new question coming from her, for he had never heard it in his dreams. He knew he had her. "I know." She set him with a piercing gaze. "I do. Come with me, and I will teach you what you need to know."

A building topped over in the distance, a massive moan of thousand-year-old wood murdered by force or fire.

She looked through Esgrynn and whispered. "My baby."

And Esgrynn knew he had lost.

She and her companion rushed past him and looked down the road, past the stumps of felled trees, to the smoking ruin of Isbandar.

He shook his head. "There is nothing… nothing you can do."

Vivien felt her legs lose their strength and she leaned heavily on Orisar.

In the distance, immense dragons flew over innumerable smaller members of their kind in a concerted attack to turn Isbandar to rubble. They were huge, larger than any she had ever seen before, colored shades of burnt umber, bright crimson, and blued steel. They winged in circles over the city, rays from the setting sun highlighting their most prominent colors of gold, red, and blue. The blue dragon tussled with an elder fae in the skies. The mighty winged beast slung its tail at the dragon, but only succeeded in chasing it and hindering the attacks. The umber dragon popped above the buildings and lashed out with fire, diving back down beneath boulders hurled at it from some kind of gigantic thing Vivien could barely see. She could only imagine it was a fae, for its call was alien and predatory, and its footsteps rattled the earth as it crashed through building after building chasing its tormentor. Above it all, a huge red circled. It would circle the Guild Hall, lighting up the wards a brilliant purple as it battered its way in, only to be distracted and make a pass along the streets, laying down sheets of flame to the sound of distant screams.

"No!" cried Vivien, her voice drowned out by the cry of souls lost in the blast. She stumbled to her knees, Orisar at her side. He shuddered, his arms around her shoulders and he moaned into her ear, an agonized sound that reflected what her heart felt at that moment. A sense of desperation welled up within her and her mind raced, thinking...thinking...thinking of what she could possibly do to stop what was happening.

The tension through her body became as taught as musical strings and the ruby dragon pulled up and away from the city. Dark smoke rose from the devastation. The dragon circled again, looking for the next place he would strike. The city was bleeding. Her people were dying. Somewhere in there were Mikarvan, Anlon, Evey, the La'athai, her father– Her heart skipped a beat.

And her SON.

DRAGON VESSEL

She felt it again, rising from her belly. It was an ancient wrath that was consuming and potent. She had fought it to submission in recent weeks, but now she tapped into it, drew from the strange certainty to find strength to stand.

"Vivien?" Orisar whispered

"Don't be a fool," the one called Esgrynn huffed.

The fury she forged into determination. Her heart thumped in her chest so loudly she could hear it in her ears as her eyes followed the distant dragons.

Tsor'aya.

The name came, unbidden, in the form of a whisper she could barely hear, and her breath hitched in her throat. The words to the Summoning spell came to her mind, the one she had memorized by wrote, the one she never thought she'd use. She remembered the words that had come before it, words written by someone who had printed a name on the last page of their book, a name written in blood.

Summoning a greater dragon is not an endeavor to be taken lightly. Rather, it should be done only in one's darkest hour. One should keep in mind that the price of such a Summons can be very high, one that may never be repaid within a single lifetime.

Tsor'aya

Vivien closed her eyes tightly shut, felt the tears squeeze from between her lids and slide down her cheeks.

Tsor'aya.

She began the incantation, speaking it aloud for the air to hear. The words came easily to her lips, as though she had spoken it before. And power like she had never known before stirred within her breast.

The men were speaking over top of one another, pleading or scolding her.

"Vivien! Vivien, what are you doing? Stop!"

"I can sense the power in the name you are calling Valdera! Not that name, you are not ready!"

She heard the voices as though they came from far away, voices that seemed like they spoke to someone else. Desperate voices filled with fear.

"Vivien, you can't do this! It's too powerful! It will kill you!"

It was easy to sweep them away, the power surrounding her slowly drowning them out until she heard nothing but the words in her mind, words she spoke without hesitation, words she spoke from deep within her very soul. Only vaguely did she feel the winds, chill winds that swept against her face, whipping her hair out into a fan behind her. She held her arms away from her body, hands up, raising them until they were above her head as though in supplication to the gods.

And then the incantation was over, and she spoke the name into the air. "Tsor'aya!"

For a brief moment there was stillness, like the calm before a storm. Her heart pounded against her ribs, and her breath was fast and hard. She heard the breathing of the two men at her side. They spoke no words now, only waited for what was to come.

Suddenly the world was plunged into darkness. It was as though all the light had been sucked away and concentrated into a place above where she stood. It happened fast, within the space of perhaps two or three seconds. But for Vivien, it felt longer, like she was seeing in slow motion.

It started out as a pinprick that got bigger, and bigger, and bigger. The light was painful to behold, so bright it felt like it could burn one's eyes. All of a sudden it was there, a dragon so massive it outsized the dragons that had just been called to attack the city. Then the light returned to what it had been before, dispersing throughout the 'scape.

Vivien watched as the dragon winged towards them. It would be easiest to say it was white, but that wasn't entirely the truth. It was a rainbow. The scales shone with every color from the spectrum, all muted with an opalescent gloss. There were muted shades of red, blue, green and yellow, all shifting as it moved beneath the rays of the sunlight. The dragon landed several yards away, the impact creating ruts in a shrubby terrain filled with the stumps of the trees that had once grown with such majesty, and walked the rest of the way to stand above Vivien and her comrades. She could feel the apprehension emanating from the men, the fear. Yet, they remained at her side.

The dragon narrowed its eyes and lowered its head until it was level with Vivien. The voice that entered her mind was feminine, yet deep, resonating throughout her skull with the power of a thousand stars. *YOU DARED TO CALL ME?*

Horrified, Vivien just stood there, every thought stolen from her mind with those five words. If she'd been full, she'd surely have urinated herself as she fled the magnificent beast, hoping beyond hope, praying beyond prayers that the thing wouldn't make chase. Instead, she stood her ground, her body trembling, and struggled to control the fear that had insinuated itself into every pore of her being.

The colorless eyes narrowed further, and the mouth opened just enough to display wickedly sharp rows of teeth. *"Answer me now, puny elfling! I have no patience for those such as you. Only the greatest of your kind have dared call me before, and you are nothing compared to them. With your untamed power, how did you manage to call me, and WHY?"*

With all the strength she could muster, Vivien swallowed back the fear, pushed it away from herself and bound it with metaphysical chain and lock, turning the key to keep it there. *"My need is as great as the mages that have called upon you before."*

The dragon reared her head up at this statement and she laughed. Vivien threw her hands over her ears at the resulting roar that shook the very air around them, winced at the pain that came from both within and without. Her two companions fell to their knees in abject fear, cowering before the beast she had called from gods only knew where. She wanted to do the same, but by some monumental force of will, she remained upright.

The dragon looked down upon her then, thick smoke rising from her nostrils. Through the connection they shared, Vivien could sense the surprise the dragon felt, mingled with curiosity. *You have piqued my interest little elfling, however, my patience is thin. You had best show me this NEED quickly, lest I break this paltry Binding of yours and you make your way into my belly.*

Vivien's mind raced. She didn't have much time. She'd read about these dragons in the tomes she'd collected, dragons that, once bored, would swallow the mages who'd called them whole. Her fear pressed against the chains that bound it, straining the links and threatening to overwhelm her like it had done Orisar and Esgrynn. She knew how to show the dragon, but the thought petrified her to her core.

The best way to show a dragon anything was to touch it, let it into one's mind so it could truly SEE.

Sweat damping her brow, Vivien took one step, then another. She approached the dragon slowly, raised her hand to show her intention. The dragon lowered her head again, meeting Vivien halfway. The eyes were no longer colorless, instead shimmering blue. They reminded her of the Wolf, and how his eyes would do the same when moved away from anger and into his resting state. For a moment she felt the love she had for him, let it suffuse her with the strength she needed to close the remaining distance. Then, ever so lightly, she touched the dragon's muzzle, right in front of those terrible rows of teeth.

The connection between them flared to life.

Tsor'aya was suddenly there, not just in her mind, but everywhere. Vivien could feel heat, heat like she'd experienced only with the Wolf or on the warmest of summer days, and she could hear a thunderous beating. It took her a moment to realize that it was the dragon's heart. Once again, she was reminded of the Wolf, and her fear ceased its pressure against the bonds that held it. She closed her eyes and concentrated, determined to show this dragon what she needed her so much for.

It only took a few moments, and when she was done, she slid her hand from Tsor'aya's muzzle and let it fall to her side.

Vivien opened her eyes to the intense stare of the dragon, a gaze so piercing it was as though she could see into her soul. This time, when the dragon spoke, her voice was not quite so loud in her mind. *Your need IS great, little one. However, it does not outrank the needs of other mages I have aided in the past. They, too, had loved ones whose lives were at stake.* The dragon cocked her head. *But tell me, why should I help you? What do you have to offer me in return?*

Vivien's heart stuttered in her chest. She'd forgotten this part. Well, not entirely forgotten; she'd known it would come up. She'd hoped that she would have come up with something she could possibly offer, something befitting a creature of this magnificence. Instead, all she could think of was one thing.

And it scared her so much, she now found she couldn't say it.

The dragon waited patiently for a moment before her eyes narrowed once more, turning a shade of purple. The voice this time was low, laced with menace. *You expected to bring me here and offer me nothing in return?*

Vivien shook her head, the fear once more battering against the chains. *No! No, I... I'm just afraid that what I have to offer might not be enough.*

Tsor'aya regarded her intently, her eyes shifting back to blue. *You won't' know until you tell me little one.*

Vivien regarded the dragon back, took in the beautiful wedge shape of her head, the long sinuous neck with a mane of spines running down the length, the opalescent scales that shifted color in the waning light of the sun. She'd noticed that the derogatory 'elfling' had been replaced by 'little one', and hoped that it meant that, whatever she'd shown the dragon in her mind had garnered some level of respect.

Vivien took a deep breath, gathered her courage, and spoke again. *All I have to offer you is myself.*

The dragon's eyes swirled with a cacophony of color, each one blending into the next until she saw black, the presence of all colors at once. It frightened her a bit, not knowing what it meant, hoping that she had not angered the dragon beyond any type of reasoning. Black was such an ominous thing, all dark and filled with unknowns.

Finally, the dragon replied. *Of all of the mages that have called upon me through the centuries, none has ever offered me what you have.* Tsor'aya once more raised her head, looking down upon her. *I accept your offer, little one.*

Vivien trembled, her heart sinking in her chest. She lowered her head, for, in return for the lives of those in the city of Isbandar, she had just sold her own life, her soul.

Tsor'aya continued. *In return for the service you ask of me, I accept the gift you offer in return. You will be mine until the end of your days.*

Vivien looked back up at the dragon, tears in her eyes, and nodded.

I command that you stay here, in this world, that you go with the mage bowed here before me so that he may train you to harness your power. Of all the mages I have ever met, you are one of the likes I have never experienced. In you, I see change, I see a better world for all of dragonkind. Right now, that world is fraught with peril, and we are Summoned to this plane against our will. Our young are brought here to serve the wicked, and before they have a chance at life, they are snuffed out as though they had never been.

Vivien's eyes widened at what the dragon was saying. She could continue stay here, continue to live her life, be a mother to her son, be with the Wolf again. She may not have a place with the fae elves again, but she never had that anymore anyways. And she could learn to use dragon magic! *That is all? That is all you ask of me?*

Dragon Vessel

The dragon's tone became solemn. *The task I have given you is a big one, one that will take your lifetime, maybe more, to complete. You have a nation of elves that practice their magic as they have been for centuries, and it is up to you to change that.* The dragon's next words where a whisper in her mind. *In you I see hope for a better future, a future of better lives for our children.*

Vivien's thoughts shifted to Dari'sii and the other wyrms that had been imprisoned in the Liath temple, and understanding washed over her.

Do you accept the terms of our bargain?

How could she possibly do it? How could she possibly change the way an entire race of people practiced their magic? She had to try. Not just for the sake of a bargain, but for the sake of all dragonkind.

Vivien nodded. Without realizing it she spoke aloud, the import of the words taking over. "I accept your terms."

Goosebumps rose over Vivien's body as felt the unseen shackles of her oath wrap themselves around her. She could see Tsor'aya responding to it as well, her eyes closing briefly and reopening with a brilliant shade of green.

Let us go now, little one. Time is of the essence.

Shock coursed through her. "Us?"

Indeed, you are to come with me.

"But, I... I can't fly."

Tsor'aya chuckled, then said something that sent a jolt of surprise through her. *You can if you are on my back.* The statement seemed to surprise the dragon just as much; Vivien could sense it through the link.

Vivien nodded and walked towards Tsor'aya, who had begun to crouch low to the ground.

A hand grabbed her arm. "Vivien, what are you doing?"

She turned to see both Orisar and Esgrynn standing directly behind her, frowns of concern written across both of their faces.

"I'm going to fight."

Orisar began to disrobe as Esgrynn spoke. "You can't do this! It's dangerous! I mean, look!" He indicated her person with a sweep of his hand. "You can barely stand!"

It was only then that she noticed it: the swaying of her body to stay upright, the trembling of her hands, the lack of focus of her eyes. She was exhausted. The power it had taken to Summon the dragon was taking its toll. She shook her head, replied in a determined tone. "I need to do this. She needs me." She indicated to the dragon crouched behind them, waiting.

Esgrynn's tone was pleading. "Vivien, please!"

I can help, little one. Come close.

She turned from Esgrynn, walked past a half-naked Orisar, and up to the dragon. Tsor'aya brought her head close, then pressed against Vivien. Instantly she felt it, an out-pouring of energy from the dragon and into her. It was like nothing she'd felt before, an influx of so much energy at once making her feel strong, powerful.

Within the space of only a few moments, it was done. Fatigue no longer weighed upon her like a sodden winter cloak, and no longer did she sway on her feet. She could see clearly and she was alert to all that was going on around her. She saw Orisar fumbling with his clothing and now had enough presence of mind to question him. "Inquisitor, what are you doing?"

Orisar gathered up the small pile of things he had removed from his person and quickly made his way over to her. "You must put these on before you go."

Vivien shook her head. "Why?

Orisar shook his head. "They will protect you." He grabbed her hand and shoved a ring over her middle finger. When it proved too loose, he put it around her thumb. He then placed a bracer over her forearm, tightening it so that it fit snugly, followed by a tightly woven chain around her neck. "Hurry, take off your coat."

Vivien obliged, caught up in the frenzy of his mission. He helped her put on a light sleeveless vest with a broach pinned near the collar, then strapped a belt around her waist that sheathed a long dagger. "Orisar."

He continued as though he didn't hear, putting another ring on her other hand.

"Orisar!"

At last, he looked at her.

"I can't take all those things. If they here are protecting me, then..."

He put his forefinger to his lips. "Shhh. I know what I am doing." He reached out to her ear and she felt a stinging at the top as he closed something over it. Then he gestured towards the dragon. "Mount up."

She reached out and grabbed his arm. "Inquisitor, no! I will not have you lost to our people!"

He gave her a smile then, a sad smile that tugged at her heart, and he put his hand over hers. "Once, a long time ago, our people called me a hero. I suppose, in many ways, I was. But today, I am no longer that person. Today, that person is you." He repeated the words she had just spoken back to her. "I will not have you lost to our people! They need you. I am here with you, right now, for a purpose." He gestured to the things he had placed upon her person. "This is my purpose, to equip you for what lies ahead." He moved his hand to her face, cupping it gently. "Please let me do my job."

A lump formed in Vivien's throat as she nodded. She turned away from him and towards the waiting Tsor'aya, stepped upon the proffered foreleg and swung herself up between the spines where the neck met the shoulders. Without hesitation, despite any fear he may have felt, Orisar followed, standing on the dragon's foreleg. He tugged off Vivien's boot, placed an anklet just above her foot, then slid the boot back into place.

A sudden thought entered her mind. She dug around inside her pocket and withdrew Ravn's ring and Mika's tanager. The carved bird she placed within a small pocket of the vest, and the ring she held out to Orisar. "Please put this on the chain?" She indicated to the one he'd placed around her neck.

ĐRAGON VESSEL

Orisar nodded, unclasping the chain and putting the ring on it before re-clasping it. Then he just stood there for a moment, looking up at her, his eyes shining. He offered another smile, then stepped down.

Tsor'aya stood from her crouch and Vivien instinctively grabbed onto the spines in front of her. Behind her, resting tightly against her backside, were the next set, holding her firmly into place. Her heartbeat quickened as the dragon surged forward. She felt a tension between her legs, a coiling of muscle, and then another surge.

Upward.

Her chest bottomed out and she squeezed her eyes tightly shut. The wind rushed past her body, through the stands of loose hair that framed her face, and she struggled just to breathe. She heard a chuckle through the link, realized that Tsor'aya was laughing at her, and felt a rush of indignation. The chuckling intensified. *Don't be so cross with me little one. You must remember, that this is a first for me as well.*

Vivien instantly relaxed. Tsor'aya was right. This was a first for them both.

They soared towards the burning city, towards the red dragon that besieged it. It opened its mouth wide, going in for another pass...

Tsor'aya tensed, and for the briefest moment, there was that silence that comes before a great storm.

And then she ROARED.

It was louder than anything Vivien had ever heard in her entire life, reaching deep into her soul and making it quail. The only thing that kept her seated were the rows of spines in front of and behind her. But, somehow, she kept her focus, saw the gout of flame stop abruptly just as it left the red's maw. He looked up into the sky, hesitated as though wondering if he'd heard that battle cry correctly.

Sensing his indecision, Tsor'aya trumpeted again.

This time there was no question. She was coming, and she was coming fast.

Vivien hung on tight as Tsor'aya narrowed the distance. *Seven, six, five...*

The red shifted direction away from the city and winged towards them. *Four, three, two...*

Vivien saw death reflected in the red's eyes.

One...

Tsor'aya reared up at the same time as the red. Vivien held her breath. The impact of two dragon bodies almost toppled her from her seat. They screeched and clawed at one another, making deep gouges in one another's hides. Then they separated before their wings could foul. She breathed again as the dragons circled one another, each one assessing the foe, each one calculating their next move. The red was old, battle scars marring the shiny crimson hide, wings torn in places that had been unable to heal together. The neck spines were dark, almost black, as was the muzzle and the outline of the wings. Vivien had the distinct impression it was a male. She didn't know why, for there was no external indicator that she could see.

Then he attacked. Tsor'aya dove, trying to get out of the way of the great gout of flame, and as it enveloped her, Vivien screamed.

It was hot, so terribly hot. The flames licked at her skin, her clothes, her hair. It took away her breath, dried up the moisture from her eyes, nose and mouth. And just as she felt she wouldn't be able to tolerate it any longer, the flame was gone, falling away with the last of her clothing. She took deep ragged breaths, the scent of charred fabric filling her nostrils. In her mind she could sense a deep concern from Tsor'aya, and pain. The dragon hissed in anger, and then let loose her own weapon.

An intense beam of light shot forth from her mouth, striking the other dragon squarely in the side. He roared in pain before dodging out of the way, coming at her with claws extended. Tsor'aya pivoted, just barely getting out of the way before twisting about and whipping her tail over his vulnerable haunches.

Vivien held on for dear life, her knuckles white as she gripped the spines in front of her. She knew she should be dead, her blackened body lying somewhere in the city below them. Instead, cold air swept over her naked flesh, naked all but for the vest that Orisar had bid her wear. Around her arm was the bracer, and resting over her foot, the anklet. She still wore the belt at her waist, complete with dagger, and the rings. A hand to her ear indicated that the cuff was still there too. Then she remembered THE ring...

Vivien's hand shot to the place on her chest where she knew it should be. The comforting feel of it resting there salved her frayed nerves, and she took a deep inhale. *The Wolf is with me. He is still here with me.*

With new resolve, Vivien focused on the aerial battle she'd somehow found herself a part of. She wanted to help, needed to find some way she could help Tsor'aya get an upper hand. She remembered what she'd read about dragons from the lore books she'd collected. They were immune from attacks from their own kind, so fire would not help her here. She needed something else, something new that she'd never cast before.

The dragons met again, the impact once more jarring her from position. This time she fell sideways, barely hanging onto the spines to keep herself aboard. The edges of dragon's scales, roughly the size of her hand, dug into her inner thighs as she sought purchase, and she hissed as one of them cut deep.

Vivien righted herself just as a dark red claw raked Tsor'aya's side, right where she'd been just a moment before. Thick, steaming blood oozed from the wounds, dripping down the opalescent side in rivulets. Tsor'aya lashed out, her teeth sinking into the offending claw, and pulled. HARD. Off kilter, the red shrieked. Vivien began her short incantation just before he opened his maw, and by the time the flames erupted, she cast her spell.

A great gust of wind buffeted the red, the flames sweeping back to engulf his face. Through the link, Vivien could sense Tsor'aya's appreciation as she took advantage of the diversion and breathed. Again, the intense beam of light struck the red, this time full in the face. He shrieked in agony as it burned away his flesh and eyes, leaving the skull exposed.

Then he dropped.

Tsor'aya let go and in the darkness of early evening, they watched as the red began to plummet towards the burning city. After a moment he righted himself, but blinded, he no longer knew where to fly. Tsor'aya struck him again with her breath of sunlight, this time targeting his wings. Hole ridden and torn, he fell once more, his massive wings curving around his body, enveloping him like a bat might as it settles in for sleep. Even from their altitude, they heard him hit the ground, right in the middle of war-torn Isbandar.

"Vivien!" Orisar screamed. "Look out!"

The gold struck them from behind, settling over the opalescent back, leaving deep rents in the shining hide. Through the spell that Esgrynn had cast, Orisar could see it all, including the wounds the opal already sported, and the priest that sat upon the gold's back. And so, when Vivien fell, he gave another scream.

"No!" The Inquisitor slumped to his knees, tears streaming down his face. She was so small in the vastness of the sky, and the sprawling, burning city below. He couldn't believe it was over so quickly, had been convinced that, somehow, she would make it through. How silly he had been, so filled with stupid hope that, before she had come into his life, he had lost. He heard Esgrynn behind him, the dragon mage uttering more of his arcane mumblings, and wondered what magic could possibly save her now.

A great gust of wind swept by, the force of it making both men topple to the ground. Esgrynn quickly righted himself, muttered a string of epithets in a tongue Orisar couldn't understand, hands outstretched as he focused in the distance. Vivien's descent began to slow, first a little, then much more, giving her mount the chance to break free of the gold. The opal dropped and swept beneath her, Vivien's body hitting the fleshy part of one wing before she disappeared from his sight.

Orisar dared breathe a sigh of relief and he heard Esgrynn do the same. *Who is this man? And why does he have such a vested interest in Vivien?* He didn't have the time to ask as the dragons positioned themselves for the next attack.

Chapter Fifty-Seven
The Flight for Freedom

The dragon priest atop the gold brought her around for another pass as Tsor'aya banked gently to let Vivien slide precariously to her back and grapple upon the spines.

"Thank you," she gasped as she settled herself.

It was your dragon mage friend from the road. It is temporary in any event. This one has an experienced mage riding him, she paused to bank suddenly to avoid a wind carrying white hot pellets of burning fire on one side, then dove to avoid a hailstorm of burning liquid from the other. *The dragon is younger and smaller than I, but faster, and no fool.*

Vivien glanced back, and saw the opal's tail was mere feet from being snapped by the gold.

"They're right on us!"

Thank you. Tsor'aya pulled up short, coming to a stop in midair and falling to the street below. They crashed onto the slate roof of a house, pieces flying everywhere from under her massive claws. One the size of her palm hit Vivien in the chest and fell to her lap. She paid it no mind, for she could hear Tsor'aya's lungs going like a bellows as the faster gold sped by and began to circle wide around.

Vivien watched them circle gently, languidly, like predators sure for a kill. She shivered from the cold kissing her fire reddened skin, mixed with the certainty of impending doom. "What do we do now?"

We must fight, little one. And, trailing blood that steamed like molten red glass, Tsor'aya launched herself into the air. The dragons circled.

"Why does she fight us?"

You speak as if she has a choice. She is either a hired hand, paid for with an unbreakable bond to her true name, or she is a slave. Either way, she will fight to the death. With the mage riding her, she has no chance to dither or retreat. If he were gone, she wouldn't even be here.

Like knights on horseback, they charged one another.

"Why are we doing this?" Vivien shrieked.

Because she can't do this while flying into me. And Tsor'aya opened her mouth and breathed light that could kill.

The first two blasts missed, the gold spinning in air and dropping down, but the last connected with her rear leg at the joint, severing it completely. The dragon wailed in pain, but the dragon priest on its back looked giddy as he made fearsome gestures when they passed underneath Tsor'aya and Vivien.

Pain. Flame licked up as if they had plunged belly first into a campfire. The mage summoned gouts of fire that enveloped them both. Tsor'aya was becoming sluggish, obviously hurt. Vivien was again unharmed by the magic, though she saw the anklet sizzle into ash and fall off, dozens of precious gems falling free and snapping into powder in the slipstream.

"Tsor'aya? Tsor'aya!?"

I fear I will not complete our bargain, little one.

The opal dragon was still airborne, but she was slowing and even her mental voice was quiet, far away. The gold and its rider had already turned around and were flying toward them at breakneck speed, even with the dragon cradling one blackened limb.

Most of Vivien's dragon magic was based in fire, useless against the gold, and probably the mage, too. Drakkon's texts were all about fire, with barely a smattering of earth or wind magic, though she had access to the little dragons to supply her with the energy. She had spent decades learning fae battle magic, but it was all useless to her now. She had a thousand ways to summon fae that would no longer come to her, to meld their abilities to create new effects. Now, she couldn't do more than move a man-sized hurricane wind. She could make mud, or turn rock to sand, but couldn't even summon a stone from the ground below.

Then she looked to her lap where the flat piece of slat rattled trapped between her naked groin and the spines of Tsor'aya.

She snatched at it. "Charge him again!"

What?

"Charge them both!"

And from somewhere, the opal gathered the will to put on a burst of speed as they made a sharp turn.

Vivien felt the slate in her hands, memorizing the flat sides, the harsh edges and points. "At the last second, break right. Then come around behind them."

Tsor'aya did not reply, but simply charged.

The gold roared in indignant fury. The priest atop it was already preparing a spell. Tsor'aya was worryingly silent. Vivien simply felt the rock in her hands. Then just before they met, the other dragon went low, and Tsor'aya went right. The priest's upward blast of fire missed completely, and Vivien hurled the rock, side on, at the ground.

The dragons spun in midair, hunched to leave their riders at the apex of their sinewy poses.

The priest massaged his throat and his voice came out like the sound of thunder across the city. "Surrender, Umesh. Surrender and be mine. We shall stop this battle, and we shall rule, not as master and slave, but as king and queen of the Liath nation in this city. Your child is the first of his kind, and he will be–" He finally noticed Vivien gesticulating frantically. "Come now, you have nothing but simple spells at your behest, and we are masters. You are only a talented novice with your fire. Come to me and I will train you gently to lead our people into a new era of..."

But Vivien wasn't listening. Fire was useless, but stone was not. She did not know how to take one stone and make it thousands. She didn't know how to make them explode. But she had hurled the slate downward so it could fall hundreds upon hundreds of feet. And she knew how to summon the winds.

Instead of the stone hitting the pavement below, it was carried on hurricane force winds no wider than an elf, up, up, up, racing so fast it began to whistle along the edges as it spun. Up, and around, guided by winds that could knock a man over.

"Come, Umesh, fulfill your destiny with me."

She felt the growl come from the deepest parts of her. "I'll see you in the hells first."

But he did not hear. He only heard the whistling for a split second before the humble piece of roofing slate cleft his skull in two like the missed strike of a headsman's axe. The gold instantly vanished back to the aether in a sliding shadow of smoke, leaving the body to plummet down to the streets below.

Somewhere, a deep horn was sounding, the call to retreat for the Liath. The lungs that pushed the air were mighty, and continued blast after blast.

You might be meant for this, after all, little–

And that was when the blue hit them from behind and to the side.

Though spared being crushed to death immediately, Vivien felt agony as claws opened Tsor'aya from back to belly. Two talons caught Vivien glancingly on the left, opening her from calf to hip. Blood splashed down her side and she screamed with her mount. The blue bit viciously at Tsor'aya's throat, again and again.

Then Tsor'aya lunged forward and clasped the attacker's mouth with hers.

She breathed.

Light shone out of the cracks in their lips, and the smell of burning was everywhere. The eyes stopped glowing red, then blackened, and finally turned white. The light of Tsor'aya's devastating breath burst from the blue's eyes, exploding out of the back of the blue's skull. Then the corpse let go and fell away.

Dragonfire enveloped the human in a shower that would reduce him to ash. That same instant, Elder Dragon Priest Gynsol, Sethian's master, was killed instantly by the hammer strike. Immediately, the old yellow dragon stopped scouring the street with fire, looked to the corpse of the priest that had summoned him, and fled the pain of its healing injuries back into the aether, bargain fulfilled now that one of them was dead.

The light had returned to the world, and it was again near dusk, but try as he might, he could not imagine any of their number who was likely to know the name of a light dragon, let alone one that powerful.

Lorimath cursed floridly. "Sethian?"

The younger dragon priest shook his head "I cannot summon that one back; my master kept his name from me."

Lorimath grunted. "Useless thing, in any event. Couldn't even kill a human easily."

Which was a thought playing in Sethian's head as well, but with more questions than disdain. He shuffled aside thoughts about how spread out their forces were. He silenced the criticism of having the large red dragon burning a city they would have to occupy for the winter. He pushed aside the ire at having to come out at the front of the army with Lorimath the Warlord simply to be at his beck-and-call. Instead, he focused on the Barbarian, a man who had turned back three hundred raiders. He had been described as having glowing eyes and a roar like that of a dragon, and while he had looked mortal enough, he had done the impossible. He had faced a dragon on his own and injured it. His strength must have been...

Lorimath was speaking again. "Oh ho! Another champion comes."

Down the street came a man riding a huge, long-haired cat. He was outfitted in armor of an ancient family, but he rode and dismounted like a soldier. He unclipped his long cape from his shoulders, looked quizzically at the corpse, and then flipped it at the blackened pile of the barbarian in the road before laying it over the body. He bowed his head as if to pray for a moment.

Lorimath sneered. "Don't bother, you'll be joining him soon."

The soldier finished his prayer before standing and addressing the dragon elf. "Are you the one who has caused my people such pain?"

"I am Lorimath Agul, Warlord of this army. And yes, I am."

"Then you are the one I am here to kill," he replied, continuing to come forward, now only a dozen paces off.

Lorimath drew his sword of fine, Elvish steel. "You don't think all of my men will stop you?"

"I am the Lord of Swords and Truth, and I think they are already too late to stop me."

And then, in a blur, he moved.

Lorimath barely had time to parry and grunt, the newcomer's blade leaving a deep wound in the warlord's own. "I'll have your pretty sword!"

Both swordsmen called upon their Elvishness, their connection to all things, to move like lightning. Swords sang as they battered together. Sethian had never seen one of his people able to summon so much of his Elvishness, so completely. Two raiders moved to intervene, but Captain Ashar grabbed one by the arm to stop him. The other, past Sethian, continued onward and suddenly had his head snicked off by a blade he never saw coming.

Above, the screeching of dragons fighting rained down upon them, bright flashes of red and white creating a hellish display against the gray clouds.

The two warriors parted.

"You have killed many today," gasped the Lord of Swords.

Lorimath sneered. "What of it? We take what we want and earn it all through the deaths of others."

"I only mention it because your sword is notched," came the calm reply. And it was, the smoothness of the blade now a broken-toothed smile.

They leapt at one another again, but a heavy over-handed strike severed Lorimath's abused steel in two, then pass less than a hair's width in front of his face. The Warlord did not pause, but lashed out with a foot, catching the Lord of Swords in the chest and sending him sprawling. Lorimath pounced, scooped up the Lord's sword and rushed to meet him. The Lord of Swords looked back, started, and dove out of the way of the incoming blade. He got to his feet, a small smile on his face as he drew a second sword, shorter and finer, covered with birds. He did not engage with it, but instead moved left, left, back, back, back, avoiding Lorimath's swings with his own, ancient weapon. Now Lorimath stood within inches of the draped cape, facing the Lord of Swords and Truth.

Sethian finally saw what the Lord of Swords had: two glowing spots at one end of the cloth. He gasped, wondering what it meant as Lorimath laughed cruelly.

"So here you are, ready to die by this dirty human."

The Lord of Swords shook his head slightly. "I have learned never to underestimate that human."

"This one?" and he jabbed the cloak, the very tip of the sword coming out bloody.

"Yes," the Lord of Swords said as a blackened hand came out of the shroud and clamped onto Lorimath's left ankle, "that human."

The impossibly strong hand yanked the foot from under Lorimath and he went down. He made to jab the sword but the cape was thrown into his face. Sethian gasped again, mind reeling.

The creature, it was no human no matter how it looked, yanked the foot and whipped the leg like a rope attached to a pole. The sound of snapping bones was only occluded by Lorimath's screams. The creature's clothes were all burned away, the armor plates having fallen off under the punishment of dragonfire, the padding, breeches, and boots turned to ash. But the man that stood before them was black with soot, naked as the day he had been born, and leaking steaming blood from a puncture in his bicep. Not a hair on him had been touched by the fire. And his eyes... his eyes glowed like those of an enraged dragon.

Lorimath made to stab again, but the barbarian shook the leg, a jumble of bones at this point, and the sword fell from nerveless fingers.

Sethian looked back and forth, and every Liath face showed shock and fear. Captain Ashar next to him shook it off first and drew his sword, stepping forward purposefully. Sethian took three swift steps and took his arm. "Captain, do you see this?" Ashar looked at him as if he had lost his mind. "LOOK, damn you! Look at it. Do you know what that is?"

The creature picked up Lorimath and held him by the collars of his leather armor as if he weighed nothing. "Where is she?!"

The captain shook his head and glanced at the priest. "I don't know, but it isn't human."

Sethian leaned in close and hissed, "THAT is the vessel! It is Umesh. The REAL Umesh!"

The Wolf's eyes glowed and his voice held a dangerous and primal reverberation as he yelled, "TELL YOUR MEN TO SURRENDER!"

It was the voice of a dragon.

Ashar's eyes went wide, his mouth hung open. "It's male!"

"I can see that," Sethian snapped. "But look at the eyes! Listen to it roar! That woman they have is NOT Umesh. This creature IS. I think this is the creature Drath Drakkon was using to make those potions to rejuvenate the body. It all finally fits."

Lorimath spit into the creature's face. The creature slammed the Warlord into the wall of a standing building. Then again, and again, and again. Even the Lord of Swords blanched at the violence.

"What do we do?" whispered Ashar.

"It is Umesh. You can fight it and win, and we lose the Vessel for all time. Or we can stand down and win a new future for our people."

No one counted how many times it took, but eventually, the human-looking thing did not drop anything that resembled humanity to the street. Lorimath, the Proud and Vain had been reduced to bloody pulp.

Ashar glanced back toward the terrified raiders. "They won't believe us."

"Then we don't tell them. Say the Vessel told us to find this one," Sethian snapped quietly. Then the captain frowned and took the dozen steps to stand before the towering giant of a man.

The creature looked at the edge of sanity. "WHERE IS SHE?"

Ashar stood silent for a few heartbeats, then motioned back toward the center of the city.

The Lord of Swords brought the Vessel the cape turned shroud to wrap about himself, and gave him the steel, bird-covered sword, having collected his own from the street. Roars rolled like thunder from far above and flashes of light illuminated serpentine bodies winging near the clouds. "What is that?"

Sethian looked up and shook his head. "I am sure I do not know."

The creature wiped sweat from his face, leaving pale streaks in the soot, and a strangely savage smile. "It's her. It has to be her."

And his eyes shifted from red to blue. He howled down the street.

The creature fixed his glowing, dragon eyes on Ashar. "Do you surrender?"

Ashar nodded, sweat beading his brow. "We do."

Umesh frowned, blood leaking from his arm steaming in the cold air. "How do we stop the battle?"

"All of the battle?" The creature glowered at him, eyes turning red as tir-reath mounted soldiers came down the street behind him at a sprint. "Blow the war horn. It is in the city main square."

DRAGON VESSEL

"Halt the attack on the square. Gather your men and march them there. Now."

Chapter Fifty-Eight
Sacrifice and Destiny

Vivien closed her eyes tightly shut as they swiftly descended. Through their link, she could sense the all-consuming pain that Tsor'aya was in, felt the ebbing of her life force. She supposed she could sense the same about herself. Blood continued to flow freely from the gaping wound on her leg, and she felt a chill deep inside that had nothing to do with her lack of clothing. She struggled to hold on to the neck spines in front of her, feeling weaker and weaker with each moment that passed.

This wound was worse than the one to her chest, the one she'd gotten in the ambush. Somehow, miraculously, it had healed. She wasn't so sure she could recover from this one.

Vivien forced her eyes back open, saw the city approaching, the buildings getting bigger and bigger. Tsor'aya tried drawing out her wings, hoping to slow them down, but the one that had been mangled simply refused to unfurl. And then they were at the top of the tallest treetop structures, barely managing to miss them. Tsor'aya's one outstretched wing struck one, leaving a deep gouge in the thick trunk that supported it. The tops of the trees scraped against the dragon's belly and Vivien heard the thick branches snapping beneath the weight.

Lower, lower, lower. The branches began to claw at all sides until they were free of the canopy. Once below it, the structures on the ground loomed. Tsor'aya gave a massive shudder and, without any other warning, dropped.

Vivien was thrust forward as the dragon struck the ground, and pressed against the spines in front of her, managed to keep her seat as Tsor'aya slid along the ground for several feet before finally coming to a stop along the path that led to the College of Magic.

For several moments they both just lay there, unmoving, until Vivien's strength finally gave out and she toppled from her place astride the dragon's back. Her fall was cushioned by the fleshy part of the mangled wing; the slick, hot blood from the myriad wounds heating her chilled flesh. Her own wound throbbed, making her cry out in anguish.

Then she just lay there, bathed in blood, not having the strength to move. She shut her eyes and let her mind drift. Despite the terrifying past hour, her thoughts were of good things: memories of Sherika, the La'athai, her father, the Wolf, and finally her son.

Little One?

The sound of the dragon's voice in her mind made her jerk into wakefulness.

Little One, you must stay awake.

Vivien opened her eyes to see the dragon had moved her head to lay beside her atop the wing. The image was a bit hazy, with a halo of light around it. And at that moment she was struck by the beauty of the beast, a beauty that she knew deep in her heart would soon be gone from the world for a very long time. Tears sprang to her eyes and she smiled. *But I am so very tired. I wish to rest, if even just a little while.*

Twin tendrils of smoke rose from Tsor'aya's nostrils. *No, you mustn't allow sleep to claim you, lest you never awaken again.*

Vivien struggled then, tried to keep the encroaching darkness at bay. She could now see it for what it truly was. Death was coming for her. *I...I don't know how much longer I can do it.*

The dragon gave a mental nod. *Then I shall help you. Even now I am giving you what strength I have left. Otherwise, you would already be gone.*

Vivien furrowed her brows, realized that was the halo of light she saw surrounding the dragon. Confusion reigned. *But why? Why would you do this for me?*

The dragon gave a weak chuckle. *My life is over. I don't have enough strength to save this body. But even more, I need you to live. I need you to fulfill our bargain.*

Despite the fogginess in her mind, Vivien knew what the dragon was asking. She knew how the bargains worked. If one or the other of them were to die, the other was no longer Bound. They were free. But Tsor'aya, in exchange for saving her life, was asking her to remain true to the deal they had struck.

It didn't take but a heartbeat for Vivien to respond.

You have my promise. I will uphold our bargain, my friend.

Vivien suddenly found herself awash with emotion. Not her emotion, but emotion from Tsor'aya. It was respect, gratitude, camaraderie, and much to her surprise, an inkling of love. But it was more than just emotion, it was an influx of all the strength that the dragon had left to give.

Vivien took a deep breath, felt the power surge through her like a wild river. It reached every part of her: every nook, every cranny, from the top of her head to the tips of her toes. It took away all of her fatigue and all of her pain. She rose up on her elbow, saw the wound down her leg, slowly healing, bit by bit.

And through their link, she felt the dragon beginning to fade.

"No! Wait!" Vivien shouted the words aloud without meaning to. *Please, don't go just yet.*

Her voice was soft, gentle. It came as though from far away. *Shhh. Hush, Little One. My time has come. But there is one thing that I would tell you.*

Vivien leaned closer to the dragon, placed her cheek atop the smooth muzzle.

There was a great sigh, as though a gentle wind swept through the link. And within it were these words, *You...are...with child.*

Vivien's breath hitched in her throat, felt shock sweep over her as she sensed the dragon's passing. Tears streamed down her cheeks and dripped onto the beautiful face cradled in her arms. She waited, and waited. She waited for Tsor'aya's body to disappear back into the aether from whence it had come.

But it didn't. The dragon just lay there, motionless in death.

A great horn blast sounded in the distance as Vivien shook her head. "No. No, no, no. Tsor'aya, you can't be gone forever."

But deep in her soul, Vivien knew that she was. The magnificent light dragon could never be Summoned again.

The College of Magic, as expected, was still standing. Torches were lit all around it, lighting the hubbub of activity outside as the wounded were taken in. Vivien quickened her step, for it meant that Mikarvan would be there, and possibly even Evey. Her son was paramount in her mind, and she hoped that they would know his whereabouts.

The thing was, she was still naked.

Vivien stopped just before she came into view. Despite the darkness, she could see the still-healing wound on her leg. She still marveled at this ability even though she'd had it for so many weeks now. She imagined she could see almost as well, if not better, than Sherika. She wondered what Mika would say about the leg, for it still looked pretty bad. Even more, he would ask about the fact that she was covered in blood, and that she had no clothing but for the vest that had remained unharmed by the dragonfire.

Vivien stepped out into the light. At first, she wasn't noticed, but it didn't take long before the first few people began to gawp at her. One young man took action, shouting as he ran into the building, "Master Healer! Master Healer Mikarvan, come quickly!"

Vivien was almost to the door when Mikarvan arrived, rushing out after the man only to stop short when he saw her. His eyes widened, and before she could utter a word, she was in his arms. "Oh gods, Vivien!" With an arm around her back, he swept the other behind her knees and easily picked her up. "Miro, get me a basin of fresh water and some bandages!"

He quickly carried her into the college, set her down on a makeshift pallet in the nearest, most private room he came to. He instantly began running his hands over her, checking her for the wounds that had caused so much blood loss. "Mika... Mika, it's not mine."

He looked up at her, his blue eyes looking deep into hers to see the truth reflected there. "Then whose is it?"

"It's a long story, one I'm certain you don't have time for right now. Just get me some clothes?"

He frowned. "Vivien, this wound on your leg is horrendous. It needs–"

"Where is Alsander?" she interrupted.

Mika just stared at her for a moment. Then, "He is with Evey." He gave a small smile. "Right here in this building. Let me get them for you."

Mikarvan rose from before Vivien just as the door swung open. Evey rushed into the room, a pouch hanging from one shoulder that crossed over her chest. "Vivien! Oh, Vivien, I am so happy to see you!"

Vivien jumped up from the pallet and the two women swept each other into a fierce embrace. From the pouch came a startled cry and Vivien peeked inside. Nestled within was her son.

Tears instantly sprung to Vivien's eyes and she put a hand to her trembling lips. "Dear gods, I thought I'd never see him again," she whispered.

Evey unslung the pouch and placed it into Vivien's arms, then embraced her again, this time with a bit more care. "I was afraid of the same." Evey looked at her, her gaze solemn. "He hasn't eaten since you left."

Vivien nodded. "I'll do it now–"

"Not until you have that bloody grime washed from you," said Mikarvan, washbasin and towel in hand. "He could fall ill."

Vivien noticed Miro leaving the room as Mikarvan approached her. She handed the baby back to Evey, allowed Mikarvan to run the steaming water over her face, hands, arms, and chest. The water was dark red when he was finished. He then toweled her off. Vivien settled onto the pallet and Evey placed the baby back into her arms. It felt so good to have him there, so good that her tears flowed yet again. He immediately suckled at her breast, so vigorously she gasped with the pain it caused. Every settled at her side, her head on Vivien's shoulder, while Mikarvan reluctantly went back to tending the wounded.

Vivien continued to cry silent tears that seemed to have no end. The joy of having Alsander in her arms once more after the dragon battle and death of Tsor'aya, and the reality that she was in a safe haven while others were still outside the college walls, dying at the hands of the Liath, was overwhelming.

It wasn't long before the baby was in satiated sleep. Vivien wrapped him back up into the blanket pouch, standing to place it across her chest and over her shoulder. Evey regarded her through wide eyes. "Where are your clothes?"

Vivien just sniffed and gave a wry chuckle. "It's a long story. You should go back to helping the wounded. I promise I will stay here."

"Let me quickly try and find you something first. I am sure that there is someone who could give you the use of their cloak, or maybe even–"

Vivien nodded. "All right."

Evey smiled, opened the door, and almost collided with the man standing just outside it. Vivien felt her eyes widen, and her jaw slackened with shock. Standing there at the entry was the Wolf.

He was covered it soot and garbed only in a cloak, twisted and knotted around his waist, high on one side and dragging the floor on the other. He carried a sword in his hand but he was bare footed like a beggar. A wound wept fresh blood down his arm to join the gore that coated his hands and spattered over his scars. Despite his appearance, he was beautiful to her, the one person she wished to see above all others but for the tiny boy in her arms.

Dragon Vessel

Her heart stuttered in her chest, then picked up in pace as though life had suddenly returned to her after a long and lonely sleep. He was finally here, standing before her, and all she wanted was to have him hold her in his arms.

The Wolf looked at her... just looked at her.

She was all but naked, wearing only a sling pouch over one shoulder that hung across her chest and down to just above her shrunken belly. He imagined the child lay within, the child she must have borne in his absence, the child of another man. Her hair was windblown and wild, her legs awash with dried dragon's blood. But she stood strong. Her green eyes were red and raw from crying, and they were filled with something... something new.

He could not have loved her more.

He heard his heart in his ears, could feel it banging against the walls of his chest, but he breathed and breathed, trying to control himself. His torso was at tumult of emotion, but he took yet another breath. But all was well, for after many weeks, he felt he could finally taste air again. His arms ached to hold her, his lips tingled for want of her touch, but he only gave a solemn nod.

"You are alive," she said, all but a whisper stolen from her in that moment.

With great gravitas, the Wolf kneeled before her and presented to her the long-lost Tanager blade.

"I lived for you, as I have for longer than I can remember."

Vivien didn't hesitate. She rushed to him, brushing the sword aside and crushing his face to her breasts with her only free arm. He felt her heart against his face and the yawning rift within him was suddenly filled. She was a battered, worn, tired thing, but she pressed against him and he felt her skin like a cool wind that washed away his fears. He slowly stood and they embraced as equals. He held her gently, careful of the precious bundle between them. His arms encircled her like the walls of a castle, protecting her from the world outside and creating a place for the three of them for just a moment. He closed his eyes and inhaled. The scent of her invigorated him. It was as intoxicating as ever.

The baby in her arms made a tiny grunt, and he looked down into the pouch. He couldn't help but grin. "He is beautiful, Jashi," he breathed. "Your son is wonderful and will grow up strong and noble like his mother. I would die before any harm could reach him."

She gave a small smile. Her eyes searched his face, as though looking for something. When she found it, her smile widened and he pressed his lips to hers. A shock swept through him, none like ever before. It was like it was the first time he'd ever tasted her. He pressed harder, then remembered himself and started to pull back. But she resisted. She tangled her fingers in his mane of unkempt, chestnut curls and pulled him close again. They drank from one another, refreshing themselves from the bright spring of their love. Only after time lost all meaning did they stop. She didn't back away, but instead lay her head against his chest.

He inhaled deeply, reveling in the scent of her. His voice was husky. "I went as you asked and we have secured the men you need for Rithalion. I returned with the La'athai, Katriona, and the Lord of Swords."

She looked into his eyes, her green pools shimmering with emotion. "I am so pleased at your safe return." She shook her head. "I feared I would never hear your heart again. You are important beyond words to me, and I am thankful you are here."

It was as if some great weight lifted from his shoulders. He felt tears coming and blinked furiously at them. "Of course, I returned to you. I am yours."

Then he felt his limbs thrum with tension, knowing he had said the wrong thing.

But she did not react as he expected, only gently lay her ear to his chest again and pulled him closer around his waist. "You are." His insides grew, expanded, as if he were inflated and light. His head swam. Then she spoke again, tenderly taking the sword from his hand. "Torialvah cast me from his house. When we are home, I shall approach the Council myself. I shall break all ties to him. And then I will be yours."

Ravn held Vivien close, and cried into her hair.

Finally, after so long, after so many trials and tribulations, he was happy.

Chapter Fifty-Nine
Gathering an Army

The wolf looked at her as though she'd gone crazy. "What?"

"I want us to bring the Liath with us to Rithalion. It is the only way I can think of fulfilling my debt."

Vivien had told Ravn everything that had happened since his departure, elaborating on the relationship she'd shared with the greater dragon, Tsor'aya. He'd listened intently, his expression one of incredulity, his brows knitted with concern as she described the bargain, and even more when she talked about the aerial battle.

"Vivien... What... No. We can't do that. They are Liath. They are killers. They murdered my family and wouldn't hesitate to do the same to yours."

"Ravn–"

"We should leave them here to rot, and maybe the Sharderians will pick them off one by one as their army comes through here."

Likewise, Ravn had told her about the mission he had completed. Her interest especially piqued when he described the testing he and the La'athai had endured with the Moirdemese.

Vivien frowned. "As I recall, you were the one who stopped me from murdering their families."

He shook his head. "Not warriors, not priests. Just the women and children. I knew that you would regret it."

"Ravn..." She put a hand on his chest. "I DO regret it. I regret that the Elvish people are divided, that they are still fighting after all these hundreds of years. All for what? Two different ways of casting magic. These people have done monstrous things, granted. But they are still PEOPLE. Once upon a time there was an old dragon, a powerful one. For centuries she watched as her kind was abused by the very people who rely on them for their magic. Even she was able to see a better way, a better life for both dragons and elves."

He gave a deep sigh, clenching his fists at his sides.

"Ravn, I BELIEVE in this." Her tone was imploring. "Please, I need you."

He looked down at her. "Why?"

"Why what?"

"Why do you need me?"

Vivien became silent, wondering if she should speak the words that came to her mind.

Ravn waited, his gaze telling her that he expected a response.

She lowered her eyes from his, uncertain. Fear rattled about in the back of her mind. How much could she tell this man? She'd once told Torialvah everything that came to her mind, all of the things that made her vulnerable. She found that she was afraid to do that again with someone else, and it hurt her to even contemplate doing it.

"Vivien?"

She looked back up at him, blinking away the tears that threatened. "Yes?"
His tone was gentle. "Why do you need me?"

She closed her eyes and steeled herself. "Because... because you are my mate in life. I need you to stand beside me."

Ravn was quiet for a moment, introspective. Then, "All right. I trust you."
Vivien blinked. "What?"

He nodded and put his hand on her cheek. "I trust you. I believe in you, that you are doing the right thing." He gave a small smile. "I love you. And you, also, are my mate. You always have been."

He stepped close, leaned down and kissed her tenderly. She closed her eyes again, allowing the tension to leave her body. Again, he had proven to her that he was not her former husband, that he was entirely different.

"So, how do you propose we do this?" he asked.

"We must tell them." She pursed her lips. "I just need to figure out exactly what to say. Why would they want to follow me?"

Ravn regarded her intently. "Because it's YOU. To them, you are a messiah. If you tell them you need them, they will come." He held out his hands. "But there are thousands of them out there. How will we reach everyone?"

Vivien smiled, remembering the battle with the blue dragon and his rider. "You will see."

Vivien stood on top of what remained of the Isbandarian wall. At her right stood the Wolf, and on her left was Orisar, the Grand Magister, Anlon and Esgrynn. Spread upon the plain below was the Liath army. It had been three days since the fighting stopped, and during that time both sides had tended their wounded and taken care of their dead. The citizens of Isbandar were discussing the monumental task of rebuilding, and much to his surprise, Anlon had been asked to help lead the efforts. As a master cartographer, his knowledge was invaluable, and his ability to keep his head during the siege had been noticed by many. Those council members who had hidden were quickly deposed, and those that had braved terror with the people were in control.

At some point Torialvah had been freed from his prison, but he had disappeared.

Now leaderless, the Liath were experiencing a bit of internal fighting, the warlords jockeying to fill the position that Lorimath Agul had left behind upon his death. It could be viewed from the city walls, and as Vivien surveyed the army, she could see how the tribes had begun to place more and more distance between each other.

Many people wondered why they were all still camped outside Isbandar, but Vivien knew.

The Vessel.

Dragon Vessel

The Liath had rallied under the cause of the Vessel, and none were yet willing to simply leave it behind. And it was this knowledge that gave her power.

Vivien wasn't certain how many wyrms were imprisoned in the Liath camp, nor what elements they beckoned, but she cast her spell, hoping it would work. Much to her relief, the winds came and she spoke into them. They carried her words out to the masses below. "Greetings, dragon people. I am Vivien Valdera, Umesh of Rithalion."

Instantly she had their attention, every man, woman and child looking up where she stood upon the wall.

"You came in search of me, bargained for me, and then fought for me. The war here is at a standstill, no longer one worth fighting. But there is another one that looms!"

The Liath just stood there, riveted.

"It is a war that reached Rithalion more than seven months ago, a war that still threatens. It is a war that won't just affect Rithalion, but all Elvish cities. It is one that doesn't just affect me and the fae elves, but dragon elves as well! My request is that you follow me, fight for me once again. Fight for elvin freedom from the humans of the Iron Coast!"

The sound that met Vivien's ears was awe inspiring. Never had she heard so many voices rising together all at once. The Liath raised their fists and released a battle cry that seemed it would reach the very heavens.

Vivien waited for it to subside before continuing. "You are a part of me, and I am a part of you. Come follow me to Rithalion, for I need you there at my side. Together we can defeat this threat and have our lands remain in peace!"

Once again, the Liath raised their voices, the warriors pumping their fists into the air above their heads. Vivien turned to Ravn and he smiled in encouragement.

"I invite your leaders to enter the city of Isbandar so that we may speak about our journey together. Gather at the gate at high noon tomorrow and I will be there to lead you within." With that, Vivien took Ravn's hand and stepped down from the wall, a chorus of cheers in her wake. Her companions were silent as they made their way down, and once on the ground, Vivien turned to meet their stares.

For she had not discussed her plan with any of them but Ravn.

"We should reconvene this evening to discuss what we should say to the Liath leaders. The new Council might wish to attend as well," she said. Not waiting for a reply, she turned and left, Ravn at her side.

"The Liath are wild and untamed," said Ravn as they walked. We should have them moving soon, or they will be at each other again. And this city as well. Talk if you must, but do it quickly."

Vivien nodded. "I imagine we should plan to be back on the road within two or three days."

Ravn nodded his approval. "Then we will have to work fast."

"Indeed."

The two navigated the city streets back to Orisar's home. It was unscathed by the attack, and the most convenient place for them to lodge since Anlon's home housed both he and Evey, Mikarvan, the Grand Magister, and Zi'anna and her mother. Once inside, they removed their cloaks and boots, By the time they were done, Alsander had been brought to her by Lorelei, a good friend of Anlon's that he trusted implicitly.

Lorelei smiled as she handed the baby over. "He has just awakened Lady Vivien."

Vivien took her son and smiled back. "Thank you for watching over him for me."

"It's my pleasure, my lady."

Ravn followed Vivien into the bedchamber they shared, and once there she shut the door to close out the world. She unlaced the top of her gown and allowed it to slip from her shoulders. Her breasts were taut with milk and uncomfortable, closing on painful. Vivien caught him watching and felt a moment of self-consciousness. "What is it?"

He raised his eyes to hers. "So little of my life has been filled with beauty, I cannot take you in enough," he whispered.

Vivien felt her cheeks flush, not just with the praise, but the desire she saw reflected in the blue depths of his gaze. "Why thank you my Lord Blacach." She seated herself on the bed and as Ravn situated himself beside her, she placed the baby to her breast. Alsander took the nipple greedily, and she squelched the groan that threatened. The nipples were sore from the feedings, and she prayed for the day the pain would cease. As she laid back on the pillows, the other breast began to seep and she pressed the bed sheet against it to staunch the flow.

After a moment, Ravn took her hand and removed it.

She looked at him questioningly. "Ravn, it feels like he is not eating enough. I am producing enough for two of him. My breasts are full to bursting."

His eyes holding hers, he scooted down beside her and put his mouth over her breast.

Vivien gasped and held her breath as the warm wetness enveloped the nipple. It didn't hurt; he suckled gently, his tongue lazily circling the areola, swiping over the nipple, and then repeating again. The sensation sent little shocks up her spine and down into her pelvis. He remained there until she had to switch Alsander to that breast, upon which time Ravn sat up beside her again and put his arm around her shoulders. As expected, Alsander was sated and did not feed as much as he just held the nipple, breathing in and out of his perfect, tiny nose. But her breasts were empty enough for now, the worst of the pressure released.

Vivien sighed in relief. "Thank you, that is better."

ᴅʀᴀɢᴏɴ ᴠᴇssᴇʟ

They lay there for a while and Vivien's thoughts turned inwards, in particular, what the dragon had said before she died. Because Tsor'aya had no reason to lie, Vivien believed her. Somehow, she was still pregnant and the reality of that fact shook her to her core. How it had happened was beyond her, and why the child hadn't come when Alsander was born boggled her mind. In truth, she didn't even know when the child was conceived, but imagined it must have been before she left Rithalion. Certainly, Torialvah had taken her enough times for–

Ravn sweeping a fingertip down the baby's soft cheek. "It tastes good, you know."

Vivien shook herself free from that train of thought. "What does?"

"Your milk. It is sweet."

Vivien felt herself flush again. "Well, I suppose that is good to know."

He chuckled at her discomfiture. "I've always wanted to do that."

Knowing what he was referring to, she found herself blushing a third time as she carefully lay the sleeping Alsander beside her on the bed. "I am glad I can fulfill your fantasies, my lord."

His twinkling eyes suddenly became serious. "You are more than a fantasy. You are my reality, and I am so glad. You are everything I have ever dreamed of, and more. You make me happy."

Vivien furrowed her brow, thinking about his words. She remembered all the times she'd made him quite the opposite. Ravn reached up and rubbed the place between her eyebrows with the pad of his thumb. "You don't believe me?"

Deciding honesty was the best course, she shook her head.

"Well, then I'll have to prove it to you." He put his hand on her belly and leaned in to kiss her.

Vivien pushed at his wide shoulders. "I'm being serious. I've seen how unhappy I make you."

He took her hands into his much larger ones. "So am I. Those were but moments, nothing compared to the joy I feel when I'm with you, have always felt since we were children together" He leaned in again, and this time she let him press his lips to hers. It was a gentle kiss, a loving caress, one that she wanted to continue. But the baby lay sleeping and she did not wish to wake him. Somehow divining her thoughts, Ravn rose from the bed and took Alsander in his arms. Vivien took the pile of blankets and lay them on the floor and he placed the baby on top, covering him with the corner of the topmost one. Ravn then gathered her into his arms, and pressed his lips to hers once more.

It was a searing kiss, filled with all the passion he felt deep inside. She returned it in kind, grabbing onto his vest and gripping it in her fists, never wanting to let him go. He lifted her up into his arms, carried her to the bed, and lay her down there, following her down to lay beside her.

ROSS & ROSS

And it was there they stayed for the remainder of the day, resting in each other's arms.

Epilogue

The **Rotten Bitch** *was insane, that took no wit to see. She had killed the Laird, his woman, and his son to boot. Poor little sapling.*

Moray had to sneak into the field of rocks beneath the balcony his laird had built for that faithless, perfidious whore. He had to steal in like a thief, lungs heaving against the extra weight he carried from heavy meals and tankards of mead. While she luxuriated with her bastard, son-of-a-whore lover from the Iron Coast, he came and collected the body of his laird's mistress. He tried to be quiet, but it seemed no one above cared to check on the corpses strewn across the jagged rocks. At least not yet. He dragged her away stealthily, her slight frame broken and bloody almost beyond recognition. He took her first because he knew it was what Ravn would have demanded of his man-at-arms and oldest, most loyal, servant. He dug a deep grave to protect her from scavengers, but by the time he had it ready, he cursed himself. He was old, and spots swirled before his eyes from the effort. His legs shook as he pulled himself out of the grave. To his dismay, most of the night was gone.

Shame burned his cheeks as he knew what he had to do. Instead of digging three proper graves, he hoisted her body into the one as gently as he could. He then went back and brought the small bundle of torn flesh and broken bones that had been her firstborn son and lowered him into the same hole. A grave for the three of them, he reasoned, so that they could spend all eternity embracing one another. Only then did he return for his laird, hoping the young master understood.

He ached, but he pushed himself up the treacherous slope. His master's family was most assuredly cursed, but the laird's shade did not need to wander the land for lack of a resting place. He reached Ravn's body and grabbed him beneath the arms. Though wasted from hunger and long journey, he was still a fit man, and Moray had to heave him out of the rocks with great effort. He winced as he reached flat ground and his undependable old hands let go. The laird unceremoniously fell upon his back and lay with closed eyes pointed to the sky. Moray tumbled backwards and landed on his rump, jagged bolts of pain slicing up and down his spine and hips.

And then, staring at his liege lord laying all bloody and still, the dam broke inside of him and he truly wept. The boy, too young, had lost his parents. Yet, he had ruled wisely and kindly, with mercy and understanding for his people. He had been born to rule and govern well, he had. And if any dare say he was flawed, they could only point to a heart that was too full of forgiveness, of love.

Especially for the diseased harridan that had murdered him.

Moray thumped his meaty fist, knuckles the size of walnuts, into the turf once, twice, and again. He had *warned* the boy, but ever trusting and headstrong, he had run into the arms of that witch without his master-at-arms. And died. Because Moray had not been there to defend him. Just as he had failed his first liege and his wife, Ravn's parents, when the Liath attacked. Moray knew he was a failure, and would now die old and forgotten... as a useless, broken man.

He looked back to the corpse before him, and croaked out, "Forgive me."

But the dead could not forgive.

Moray took a shuddering breath and wiped at his eyes. The sun was coming up, and the laird had to be buried before she knew where or else she would surely desecrate his body for her amusement. Moray reached toward the corpse–

And stopped, hand outstretched.

The sword... the ornate, broken, elvin sword. The sword that pierced bag, dragon heart, and Ravn's mortal chest. The sword was *moving*. In the complete stillness of the morning, stirred only by a light breeze, the sword moved slightly. *Thub-thub, thub-thub, thub-thub.*

The broken sword showed a heart still beating. Against all odds, in the face of all lost hope, the heart of Ravn Blacach was beating, and moving the sword that whitch had used to strike him down.

He was struck by indecision for several breaths, but the coming light made the decision easier. He again took up the body of his fallen laird and proceeded down-slope. He carried him into the woods where he covered the grave of his woman and child hurriedly. Then he took his thick, mountain knife and cut down young trees and stripped them of branches so he could lash them together into a travois. It was nearly midmorning and none had come to disturb them. His limbs had been given new life, and his aching bones new purpose. He knew what he must do.

He had no food stores, no water. He dared not return for anything. He had a mountain knife, a space, and his naked, wounded Laird on the primitive sledge. He dared let no living person see them, for the heinous bitch would soon be hunting them. He would spend weeks pulling his liege lord across broken terrain. He would dribble water into his mouth, and cover him in pine boughs, feeding him tiny bits of whatever he could scavenge from nature as he walked mile upon mile upon mile. Once or twice he would check the angry, red wound made by the sword, but it never turned green and black. It always bled, but Moray came to believe that the trickle of dark blood from the heart in the satchel was running down the blade and mixing with the laird's own. It was the heart, his master had said, of a dragon. He only knew the boy was alive, and had to remain so.

Laird Blacach had said one other thing. The warlock of Pergatium had helped him hunt the dragon, and thus knew him. Moray had only one direction. He would bring his laird to the warlock and get magic to help the nobleman.

He would save Ravn's life or die in the attempt.

About the Authors

Tracy Renee Ross (aka. Chowdhury) was born in the small town of Tunkhannock Pennsylvania in 1975 and moved to Cincinnati Ohio when she was twelve years old. Growing up, she was an avid reader, especially of fantasy and science fiction, and she loved to write. She attended college at Miami University in Oxford, Ohio and studied her other passion, Biology. She graduated in 2002 and worked in cancer research for several years. During that time she picked up her love for writing again, and in 2005, her first book, *Shadow Over Shandahar- Child of Prophecy*, was put into print. With the help of her co-author, Ted Crim, the sequel, *Warrior of Destiny*, was published two years later.

Tracy currently lives in Liberty Township, Ohio. She is married with eight children, four cats, and a turtle She does various home renovation work, and in her 'spare' time she continues to write and promote her books. In 2011 the Shandahar novels were picked up by a small press, and the original duology was re-mastered and separated

ROSS &ROSS

into smaller volumes to make a series. More books have followed, as well as several short stories, and she is currently working on the final installments of the series. More information about the books can be found on her website at www.worldofshandahar.com, and she can be found on Facebook and Twitter.

James Daniel Ross first discovered a love of writing during his high school education at The School for the Creative and Performing Arts in Cincinnati, Ohio. In those early days, in addition to this passion, he was an actor, computer tech support operator, infotainment tour guide, armed self defense retailer, automotive petrol attendant, youth entertainment stock replacement specialist, mass market Italian chef, low priority courier, monthly printed media retailer, automotive industry miscellaneous task facilitator, and ditch digger!

James began his writing career in simple, web-based vanity press projects, but his affinity for the written word soon landed him a job writing for Misguided Games. After a slow-down in the gaming industry made jobs scarce, he began work on his first novel, *The Radiation Angels: The Chimerium Gambit*. Soon after came the sequel, *The Key to Damocles*, followed by other novels in the sci-fi/fantasy genre: *Snow and Steel, The Last Dragoon, The Whispering of Dragons, The Echoes of Those Before*, and many novellas and short stories. He shares a Dream Realm Award with the other authors in the anthology, *Breach the Hull*, and two EPPIE awards with those appearing in *Bad-Ass Faeries* 2 and 3.

James' books can be found on Amazon.com and at many retailers across the country. James himself can be found on Facebook. Most people are begging him to go back to ditch digging.

Øther Books to Enjoy

In a world beset by nightmares, another is coming. Two of the mightiest nations in the world are clashing in a war that will shake the Great Veddan River Valley to its core. The fae elves and the bronze dwarves look upon one another as foreign and alien, their conflict fueled by dark powers and bigotry. Pride and misunderstandings foil peace at every turn, and two star-crossed lovers shall suffer as their people descend into bloodshed.

Shandahar is a cur ed world. People will live and die. Wars will be fought, kingdoms built, discoveries made. For centuries, history will proceed apace... and then everything will come to a grinding halt and start all over again.

Shandahar is a wor d brimming with darkness, filled with no promise of a future but one. A prophecy. Spoken by the renowned seer, Johannan Chardelis, there is a divination that tells the coming of someone who can stop the curse. The snag? They have failed four times already.

Enter a world swirling with mystical realms and bloody battles, with enchanted forests and crowded cities where things are not always as they seem. Enter the World of Shandahar.

Picture a hero.

I bet he's tall, muscular, and chiseled... forthright and chaste with bright, shiny armor... takes on all challengers face-to-face... lots and lots of honor?

Yeah. I am not that guy. I am the antithesis of all of those things.

In this world, with so much gold at stake, with the most powerful people in the kingdom taking notice...

That shiny hero? Yeah, he dies.

I am the guy that can get the job done.

I am Fox Crow.

THE TROMBADOUR'S INN

Tales from the
Hapless Centoryan
2nd edition

Collected by
J. R. Chowdhury

Found within these pages is a wonderful assortment of tales and adventures from some of the most memorable people in the world of Shandahar! Come and meet Sirion as a young lycan hunter, Thane before he became corrupted by the greatest of evils, Sorn as a young rogue tempted by love, and Dartanyen before he meets up with the Wildrunners! You will meet some new people too, and experience the depth and richness Shandahar truly has to offer!

Seth and Kaila: writing partners, friends, lovers. Their relationship is a rocky one, and an argument sends Kai out into the night in tears.

A terrible accident leaves Seth suddenly facing the worst days of his life. Deep within the embrace of a coma, Kai struggles for her life, her mind trapped within the world she and Seth have created. And as the days pass, she continues to weaken.

The only thing keeping Seth from insanity is their book manuscript, and as the love of his life slips closer to death, he is desperate to finish what they started together. As their darkest hour approaches, Seth finally realizes what might save Kaila's life, and it is a race against the clock before she is lost forever.

Visit the website at
www.winterwolfpublications.com
for

Breaking News
Forthcoming Releases
Links to Author Sites
WinterWolf Events